Star of the Unborn

OTHER WORKS BY FRANZ WERFEL

NOVELS:

The Song of Bernadette

Embezzled Heaven

Class Reunion

The Forty Days of Musa Dagh

Hearken unto the Voice

The Pascarella Family

The Pure in Heart

Twilight of a World (Eight Long Stories and Short Novels)

Verdi: A Novel of the Opera

PLAYS:

Embezzled Heaven

Jacobowsky and the Colonel

The Eternal Road

FRANZ WERFEL

STAR
of the
UNBORN

TRANSLATED BY GUSTAVE O. ARLT

NEW YORK · 1946

THE VIKING PRESS

THIS BOOK BELONGS
TO ALMA

Contents

vii

CONTENTS

Part One: THE FIRST DAY

IRONGRAY TURF

The First Chapter

WHEREIN THE AUTHOR APPEARS TO BE PRO-LOGIZING, BUT THE READER SOON DIS-COVERS THAT HE IS APOLOGIZING.

THIS IS A First Chapter simply because it seemed inappropriate to begin this opuscule with a Second Chapter. The only factors that stood in the way of placing the words "Chapter Two" on the first page of this novel were the publisher's sense of propriety, the reading public's well-known propensity for the discovery of monstrous typographical errors, and, finally, the author's mania for originality, since he feared that some colleague in the gaily flippant era of romanticism must certainly have begun one of his rank works with a Second Chapter. For these reasons we begin with Chapter One, no matter how superfluous this chapter may be for the progress of the action, or, more accurately, of the exploration.

Since we are dealing with a kind of travelogue I feel the obligation to introduce the hero or, more modestly, the central figure of the occurrences here set forth. This particular literary form has the unfortunate weakness that the eye that sees, the ear that hears, the spirit that comprehends, the voice that narrates, the "I" that is involved in many adventures, constitutes the central point about which, in the most literal sense, everything revolves. This central point, candidly designated as F.W., is, unfortunately, I myself. Purely from an innate aversion to getting into difficulties, I should have preferred not to be I-myself in these pages. Still it was not only the most natural, but the only way, and I was regrettably unable to invent any "he" that could adequately have borne the burden of the "I" for me. And so the "I" of this story is not a deceptive, novelistic, assumed, fictitious "I" any more than the story itself is the mere offspring of speculative imagination. It happened to me, as I must confess, quite against my will. Without the slightest preparation or premonition, contrary to all my habits and instincts, I was sent out one night as an explorer. What I experienced, I really experienced. I am quite prepared to embark upon a frank discussion of this little word "really" with any philosophically minded reader and I am confident that I will win the argument in every instance.

As I inscribe this record I am still living, and living again. In the precise space between the words "still" and "again" lies the world of my voyage of discovery and exploration which I began as an ignorant, even recalcitrant, tourist, in order to complete it as a keen observer with a few new and definite ideas in my pocket. It would indubitably be a great mistake on the part of the reader to close the book in disgust at this point. Little mysteries such as "still" and "again" are the obscurities and riddles of a First Chapter which Chapter Two will soon resolve.

In order to obviate any grave misunderstandings, let me say at the outset that I am by no means a master dreamer. I do not dream more vividly than other people. When morning breaks I have usually forgotten my dreams. Now and then, to be sure, the gray dawn deposits a few strange tableaux and scenes on my counterpane as flotsam of the night. There is, for example, a dog that discourses in rational words. A radiant bride, whom I have never seen, clad in a trailing bridal veil, stands with open arms at my bedside. A bearded man in overalls who is called the Worker operates fountains that do not run water but strange beams of light. Again I see with indescribable clarity aged men who, instead of dying, become smaller and smaller until they are finally imbedded in the earth as tiny anthropomorphic turnips. Such pictures and scenes—as far as the memory does not eject them—are stubborn, self-willed germs that sprout and grow in the soil of fancy during the day whether you like it or not. Rarely, and yet once or twice in a lifetime, it happens that these autonomous visions, independent as they are of the inventive will, join into logical chains and epic sequences in a single night or even in several successive nights. Whenever that happens, a person would be a dull oaf indeed if he were not thrilled by the meaningful games that his soul plays behind his back, as if it were not a narrow, restricted ego but a boundless, infinite universe.

There are only two ways of becoming a historian of the future: scientific deduction and divination or fortune-telling. But scientific deduction would disqualify itself for cognition of the future by the process of scientific deduction. For science must always be careful not to make a fool of itself. Science would scarcely go further than a computation of probabilities.

Divination and fortune-telling, on the other hand, have the inestimable advantage of looking back upon a long and venerable practice which, according to incontrovertible tradition, has produced remarkably successful results. In order to be genuine, the prophetic forms of cognition must know only how to wear the veil of parable and to cast the shadow of mystery.

Stern eyes have been looking at me for some time. They are becoming ever sterner and now they even address me: "You are a man of fairly mature years. You certainly don't have enough time left to take superfluous trips. How much longer will you waste your diminishing working day? Don't you know what's going on in the world today? Weren't you yourself a persecuted victim? Aren't you still? Don't you hear the roar of the bombers, the clatter of heavy machine guns that envelop the globe, a Nessus garment woven of explosions? Worse than this noise, don't you hear the death rattle of the mortally wounded in a thousand places and at every hour? And worse than this death rattle, don't you hear the cry of torment and the dying gasp of the millions who are first ravished, then tortured, and finally massacred? Isn't it your responsibility to keep your eyes and ears focused on this monstrous reality that outfancies the maddest

visions of a pain demon and is, at the same time, as final as a
mathematical process? What higher duty have you than to catch
the cry of torment and the gasp of the tortured and to preserve
them in the graven word, at least for the brief span in which the
experience and expression of one generation remain intelligible
to the next?"

I can do nothing, oh, stern eyes, but lower my own before you.
I confess and acknowledge: my time is short and I am wasting
it unscrupulously. I have not forgotten that I, too, am persecuted.
Nor have I become too deaf to hear the roar of the bombers, the
clatter of heavy machine guns, the death rattle of the mortally
wounded, the cry of torment and the dying gasp of the ravished,
the tortured, the massacred. The monstrous reality, the mad
visions of a pain demon, constrict my throat by day and night,
where I walk and stand, on the street and in my room, at work
and at play. Of course I am neglecting my duty. But this reality
does not leave me even enough breath for an echoing groan to
the cry of torment.

In mitigation of my guilt I can only reply with an unexpected
banality. I had already purchased a huge stack of fine, smooth
paper. I had already sat down and on the uppermost sheet of
the stack—enough for at least two volumes—I had carefully
inscribed in beautiful Spencerian characters the words "Chapter
One." It was to be the beginning of the story that, God willing,
I shall one day dedicate to the ravished, the tortured, the massacred. But unfortunately the pen was no good. It is so hard
nowadays to get the right kind of pen. Even the best fountain
pens are stiff and hard and stubborn and too pointed and they
simply won't respond. It is a good thing that the reading public
knows very little about an author's workshop. A real author is a
man who writes with the most responsive, most sensitive hand,
not one who pounds inanimate keys. But just such a man requires
certain inspiring desk equipment. Above all he needs a good pen,
soft and flexible, capable of the most delicate, the most timid, serif
and of the blackest, boldest downstroke. Such a pen delineates
the structure of a sentence on the paper like a master drawing.

A good pen—and I am not facetious—is half the thought. So I went out to find a good pen. But I found only a tolerable one. The hunt occupied several days. On the night of the last of these days, however, this event befell me which I shall call "My Commission on a Voyage of Exploration." The material I brought home in spirit from this voyage was extensive, more extensive even than is indicated by a tome as voluminous as this threatens to become.

I had to make my choice. Before me lay the white sheet bearing the words "Chapter One" in large, round letters, and nothing else. These imperious words seemed to make the just demand that the story of our monstrous present should follow them in serried ranks. But I shuddered at the task: will not this monstrous reality become more real from day to day, and most real and true, perhaps, when it no longer exists? But the reality of my travel experience is spun of other stuff. It is likely to dissolve at the first crow of the cock or at the honk of a horn, and even the best memory offers no guarantee that it will not escape suddenly beyond recall. Therefore I must hurry.

And under the words "Chapter One" that are still waiting for the story of our monstrous reality, I decided to sketch the foregoing paragraphs. It is a superstitious trick. I have not forfeited anything. I have not given up my original task. The "Chapter One" that was to have borne an incomparable load, still stands empty. For this, I repeat in conclusion, with the full agreement of my readers, is not a First Chapter. Instead, Chapter Two assumes the function of Chapter One.

The Second Chapter

WHEREIN I MEET MY FRIEND B.H. WHO CALLS MY ATTENTION TO THE FACT THAT I AM INVISIBLE.

"WHAT! YOU'RE NOT dead, B.H.?" I asked my best and oldest friend and shook his hand, delighted to see him again. A weight fell from my heart at this meeting after so many years. In the course of the great flight from the Nazis he had been driven from place to place, finally to land in India, in the far northern part, at the Tibetan border, somewhere in the vicinity of Darjeeling, and the war had broken all communication between us. Who knows, perhaps I should have tried after all to write him a letter or to make inquiries through the Red Cross, to see whether I could help him. Although I had no evidence of it, I was convinced that he had perished.

B.H. smiled, and at the same time his large head with its black hair and fine, dark eyes trembled a little, in fact it almost shook. It had been a habit of his long ago when we were schoolmates whenever he succeeded in making a particularly devastating remark.

"I'm not dead," B.H. said with a twinkle. "As you see, I'm quite alive and in full possession of my faculties. It's you who are dead, F.W., and you've been dead far, far longer than you can remember."

"How can I be dead, B.H.?" I asked, offended by his frank-

8

ness which seemed to me in bad taste, although I had been guilty of the same indiscretion just a moment earlier.

B.H. looked at me long and earnestly before he made up his mind to ask, "Can you see me, F.W.?"

"Of course I can see you. How do you manage at fifty to look like twenty-five? No, even that's an exaggeration. You look exactly as you did the day we graduated."

"According to the present method of computing ages, I am a hundred and seven years old," he replied straight to the point. "But how about you, F.W.?" he insisted. "Can you see yourself?"

I looked down along my body. I could not see myself. A sudden shock galvanized me. I was invisible. To be invisible to others is depressing enough. But to be invisible to myself! I tried to collect my scattered thoughts and emotions. First of all, I noticed with surprise that I was feeling well, uncommonly well in fact, certainly much better than a while ago (when was that— a while ago?) when I presumably stepped out of a gate at a considerable distance from this spot and somehow lost my way on a strange road where I suddenly met my old friend B.H. Incidentally, I'm not at all certain that I am right in using the word "road." It was obviously leveled ground that extended evenly in all directions to the horizon without any sign of interruption on the right or left by embankments or roadside ditches. Under my feet was short, dry turf that expedited progress remarkably well and made walking a novel pleasure. The turf consisted of well-tended grass. But this grass had lost even the slightest tinge of green, the last trace of chlorophyll. It grew out of the ground in shades varying from white to irongray, like the hair on the skull of an aging though still robust man. The phrase "under my feet" was not a stylistic error, as one or another of my readers at once suspected. Although I was invisible to others and even to myself, I really possessed hands and feet and, in fact, the entire body to which I had so long been accustomed. While I was invisible, I was certainly not incorporeal. To be sure, when I felt along my sides with my good old hands, I felt nothing but space. But within this void I could feel my heart beating more regularly and calmly than ever; my lungs expanded and contracted; I could see, hear, smell, and taste. My youthful well-being seemed to arise from the fact that these sensory functions did not, as formerly, have to operate through a ponderous material body that was already worn out in spots. To use a banal and only half-suitable analogy, I felt as light and mobile as a fat man hopes to feel after a conscientiously rigorous reducing treatment. Was B.H. right, and was it really the rigorous, the eminently successful, reducing treatment of death that I had undergone with such splendid results? I did not doubt the possibility for a moment. And yet, though I don't know why, I experienced a sense of shame at this instant. I was ashamed not only on my own account, but also on B.H.'s. It was a shame similar to that of being naked, a nakedness, moreover, beyond all conception and imagination. In order to extricate myself and, perhaps, B.H., too, from this embarrassment, I muttered, "What a lot of nonsense we dream at times!"

B.H. shook his head with a touch of irony. "They used to hand out very silly theories about such matters," he commented.

"You aren't speaking about Freud's interpretation of dreams, are you, B.H.?"

He looked at me with an effort at concentration, as though he failed to understand me. "Who? Freud? Fraud? What's that? How do you expect me to remember names from the beginnings of mankind?" he asked a little disdainfully.

"The beginnings of mankind?" I echoed, and I clearly felt that a tinge of offended emotion colored the voice which rang from my invisible mouth and from my equally invisible inwards. "The beginnings of mankind? Were those the beginnings of mankind, my dear B.H., when we read Shakespeare and Goethe together, when we argued about Dostoevski and Nietzsche, about Pascal and Kierkegaard, in the parkways of the Belvedere? Don't you remember? It was just recently, it was yesterday, maybe it was only this morning, because you look like a college student right now. And then we entered the army in the First World War, you

and I, and later on we used to write letters to each other, and
we met again from time to time, for the spiritual friendship of
early youth is a strong bond for men's hearts. And you were B.H.
and I was F.W., and then the Nazis came, and I saw you once
more on the shore of our beloved Mediterranean. You were on
your way to India. What a sad parting it was for me! I felt that
we would never see each other again, for the Second World War
was already waiting just outside the park gate of the loveliest
French summer. We both had dreadful experiences, you in a
camp at the edge of Tibet and I on my flight from Europe. I
was afraid you had died in India. But maybe the Tibetan monks
taught you how to go on living forever in spite of everything!
I, on the other hand, am living in California at present. Still, it
may be that I am buried in California, for you have convinced
me of my fearful invisibility. And all of it is so terribly real and
recent! I don't understand your irony about the 'beginnings of
mankind'——"

"Our two situations, my dear F.W.," he interrupted me gently,
"are radically different. You have preserved all these memories
of the beginnings of mankind so vividly because you haven't had
a turn in the meantime——"

"Haven't had a turn?" I snapped at him. "What do you mean
by this infantile expression? You seem to have preserved a pretty
good memory of our high-school jargon. Have a turn? Do you
mean being called on by the teacher?"

"Quite right, F.W.," he nodded with a certain degree of pride.
"And it happens to be my turn just now, that is to say, I am
living."

I decided to keep quiet, although I had a hard time doing it.
By virtue of my invisibility, or rather my transparent, intangible,
and imponderable corporeality, my thoughts swirled in violent
rapids, and I understood and recognized many things in a novel
and penetrating manner. My spirit functioned in the nature of a
highly polyphonic orchestral score. A number of cognitions, like a
musical fugue, developed in harmonious confusion, and yet they
formed a meaningful entity of which I became fully aware. So,

I thought, B.H.'s sojourn in Tibet had a definite influence on him after all. Without a doubt he embraced the most orthodox form of the doctrine of reincarnation, in fact, reincarnation itself. That's what he meant by "having a turn." Should I for that reason turn away from B.H. and drop him like a hot potato? Does the doctrine or the practice of reincarnation contradict my own belief in immortality? No, I decided without hesitation. In the first place, my belief in immortality was no longer a belief at all but a well-authenticated phenomenon. I myself furnished the incontrovertible proof in my present invisible and yet animate state. According to the plain, unvarnished testimony of my best friend, I was long deceased and probably buried in Forest Lawn, if that fashionable resting place had not been abandoned generations ago and turned over to some oil syndicate for exploitation. Yet here I was, in passably good shape, and I felt and reasoned with increased acuteness. Thank God, Descartes' "Cogito, ergo sum" applied to me after death! What a moral victory over the "Sum, ergo cogito" of my materialistic opponents, those stupid literary hacks! But about this matter of reincarnation—wasn't it only yesterday afternoon that I had experienced a sudden enlightenment? The place, to be sure, where this spiritual flash of inspiration struck me wasn't particularly conducive to philosophy—a drugstore on Wilshire Boulevard. I forgot to finish my coffee. Just how was that? Just how did that go?

Every ego, I had reasoned, is immortal, but not every ego is a complete ego. Just as in the material world, for example, in the world of roses, an individual blossom must be repeated down to the last detail from time to time, just so it must be in the world of men, in physical, intellectual, and spiritual aspects. The variety of forms in nature is limited, and the same is true of the variety of forms in humanity. There is only a limited number of souls, of definite egos, much smaller than the number of names which these egos bear in the course of their permutations. Every ego, like a more or less successful book, appears successively in various editions, and each time under a new title. When God counts the souls on the Day of Judgment, as the Good Book says, he will not count three hundred and seventy quintillion souls, more or less, but only somewhere between seven hundred thousand and seventy billion, the fewer the better. At the end of time every ego will be a big bouquet of incarnations, a sort of dust-covered nomadic tribe that roved through the desert of eons. . . . Still it was most surprising that the B.H. of the present should be the spitting image of the B.H. of the beginnings of mankind! I felt a touch of vertigo and quickly interrupted this stream of thought. For a long time I stared intently at B.H. without realizing that my concentration could mean nothing to him. All right, old man, I thought; go right ahead with your drivel. I won't say another word. The whole business makes me tired.

B.H. stepped closer to me. Not the slightest reproach lay in his smile. "We've been invited, F.W.," he said and made a futile attempt to slap me on a shoulder which, of course, was non-existent for him.

"Invited?" I asked in a worried tone. But then I heard my own resigned sigh. "Do whatever you please. I suppose I'll have to agree to everything."

These words of mine sounded rather pitiful. But they produced the same sort of relief that a bewildered tourist feels when he puts the details of his day's activities into the hands of an experienced and trusted guide.

The Third Chapter

AFTER THIS CONVERSATION, which seemed very short to me, I began to scan the surrounding terrain with my invisible but seeing eye. Strangely, but without a doubt, B.H. and I, two confirmed city dwellers, had met out in the open country. It was the openest, flattest country that I had ever seen, and besides it seemed to be entirely uninhabited. As far as the eye reached there was not the slightest indication of a settlement, whether city or village. No structure of any sort rose from the smooth plain, no filling station near or far, no water tank, not even a single one of the big billboards that ordinarily grace or disgrace the loneliest desert roads. Yet, in spite of the limitless and unsubdivided solitude, I could not rid myself of the feeling of standing in a road. The dense, miraculously close-cropped iron-gray turf that completely covered the ground could be only the result of human planting and care. The entire region, from horizon to horizon, seemed to be a highway; a highway covered, not with asphalt, but with this mourning-colored carpet for promenaders; a highway without the slightest hint of traffic and yet somehow reminiscent of incalculable traffic, of a time when thousands of lines of flashing vehicles raced in straight, unbroken procession in both directions. Only gradually I became aware that the flatness and solitude were not as uninterrupted as I had first suspected. At great intervals my eye, as it slowly became

14

accustomed to the utter strangeness of this world, began to discern occasional groups of trees, or rather clumps of trees, for they were planted so close that no breaks or gaps were visible, and they gave an unnatural effect of compactness. These trees— and it took some time before I recognized them as trees—were all alike and quite low. Their rigid crowns were composed of leathery, almost black foliage, from which gleamed great waxy blossoms whose yellowish-white hue was tinged with hints of various colors. I had never seen similar plants. It occurred to me at once that if these clumps of trees concealed some form of life under their canopy, it must be a very delicate and woebegone life.

The sky was cloudless and in its deep blue solitude resembled the gray earth over which it arched. The time of day was presumably not far advanced, for the orb of the sun, somewhat larger and redder than in my memory, was just past its zenith and cast dazzling rays which produced a temperature that I can only call cold heat or hot cold. Although I definitely felt the need of dark glasses, I was becoming increasingly chilly in spite of my invisible state.

I looked questioningly, perhaps even impatiently, at B.H. He at once divined my thoughts. His manner of guessing my train of thought made me very uncomfortable. Was that the result of his Tibetan training, I asked myself, or was it the achievement of a human race that was far beyond its early stages? To the embarrassing feeling of nakedness caused by my invisibility was now added the timid shame that I was not quite able to conceal my thoughts, wishes, plans, my consent, dissent, my doubts, and my criticisms.

"Our appointment," he said without awaiting my question, "is taking place in California."

"What are you talking about, B.H.," I rejoined, unable to repress a trace of rising annoyance. "I know California. That's where I used to live. Perhaps I'm still living there, in spite of your curious theory concerning me and my death. Besides I don't remember having made an appointment with you. If you had told me that we were standing in the Middle West, back there where the endless prairies used to be, I might have believed you at once. But I know California pretty well. It is appropriately called a paradise, although certain snobs have been known to make disparaging remarks about this lovely spot and there are even some who claim to prefer the flat Florida landscape to the diversified west coast. These snobs slanderously call California a desert covered with artificial luxuriance, whose rouged roses, bougainvilleas, poinsettias, and other flowers have no fragrance, whose fruits and vegetables have no savor, whose inhabitants are good-looking but somehow Lemurian. That may be connected with the fact that long before the beginnings of mankind as we knew them, California was a part of the submerged continent of Lemuria. That may have influenced the character of the Californians. The Lemurians seem to have been a shadowy, trifling race, whited sepulchers, in a word, actors, who deceived the world with gay and false pretenses with nothing true and tested behind them. There is a contemporary expression for this Lemurian characteristic, the word 'phony.' And so the snobs of today—I mean our own today or yesterday—turn up their noses at California, chiefly because a certain famous city in that state produces films, those fantastic, photographic tales that have become the vogue of their time although, or perhaps just because, they are Lemurian. But maybe you and your contemporary humanity have completely forgotten what a film is."

B.H. shook his head slowly and gave me a frank look. "No, we really don't know anything about that."

"Never mind, B.H.," I resumed, slightly astonished at my own excited eloquence. "This California is largely a mountainous country. Toward the east rise the snow-covered Sierras on whose peaks perhaps no human foot has ever trod. But in the west too, where the Pacific Ocean gnaws at the shore, there are mountains and hills everywhere, even though they may be only sand dunes of weathered, decomposed granite. Between them are broad valleys planted with fabulous orchards—oranges, lemons, grapefruit. They blossom the year around with a fragrance that beggars description. And in April even the deserts bloom, pink and violet with their countless cacti. Wherever you turn the mountains tower in the blue distance. But here——"

"You forget," B.H. interrupted me, "that you have skipped several lengthy geologic periods." (It sounded like skipping a recitation at school.) "Meanwhile most of the elevations of the earth's surface have been leveled off, partly by the regular geological development of the planet, partly by the purposeful will of its inhabitants, and partly by that grandiose, decisive event about which I will say nothing at present, lest I frighten you too much. At any rate, there are no more mountains except outside the cultural zone."

Of course there was nothing to be said to that. Only to be grumbling, I muttered, "It's all so monotonous. I wish there were a city here."

"We are in a city," said my friend good-naturedly and chuckled over the point he had made, before adding after a while, "We are in a city, if you mean by that a connected settlement. Everything you see is city. California is the name of a city. After a few hundred miles it merges with cities that have other names, although the boundaries between these cities are of abstract, purely spiritual character, for the entire inhabited globe is a single city."

"All right, all right, call it a city," I said, tired rather than acquiescent, "although I get homesick when I think of the towers and gates of our medieval city back home, its stronghold, the Hradschin, its Gothic and baroque palaces. . . . What? And you say I've been invited here? Didn't you tell me a while ago that I had been invited here, or did I only dream it?"

His voice became quite solemn. "You have been more than invited. You have been summoned."

Without a doubt my invisibility came to the aid of my intelligence and my quick comprehension. I understood him at once. I had been "summoned." Whom does one "summon"? The spirits of the dead! Without any particular feeling of uncanniness I was such a spirit. And who "summons" us? Spiritualists, such as, for the most part, sweater-knitting old ladies, pensioned peacetime generals, retired officials, and their ilk. Everyone knows these simpletons that sit around a bouncing table.

"So it's come to that," I exclaimed angrily. "The same old nonsense that we used to laugh at away back in the beginnings of mankind! You summon the spirits of the dead! Plato, Napoleon, Jack the Ripper, and Madame Pompadour? It's beyond belief! And I, I can't help myself, and I have to be a materialization, although even that is an exaggeration, for I'm not even an ectoplasmic phenomenon, but just plain invisible. I exist only as a state of consciousness!"

B.H. remained calm and serious. "We have long ago rejected many things that would seem to you even more beyond belief if you knew about them; but we have preserved and developed a few things that you despised in your day."

"In my day? Wasn't it your day too, B.H.?"

"Certainly, F.W., among other days it was my day too."

"And why did you have *me* summoned, me of all people?"

After a protracted silence he asked me in return, "Didn't you have to think of me a great deal in the last few days, F.W.?"

"In any case, you seem to be solely responsible for getting me into the embarrassing situation of being here."

"No, there was general approval of your name," he quickly dissented. At his words a thrill of conceit ran through me, from my invisible pate to my invisible toes. Think of it! After fifty, sixty, perhaps a hundred thousand years, they still knew my name. Mountains had been leveled, oceans had dried up, the gravitation of the sun seemed to be failing, presumably the earth had moved farther from the sun and that was the reason for these glaring but feeble rays under which even a ghost like me felt chilly. Perhaps the days, too, had become longer, and human life with them. (Didn't B.H. say he was a hundred and seven years old?) And in spite of all these changes beyond measure and beyond concept, they still knew my name, the name of a man whose sole unmerited merit was the fact that between endless periods of dullness and laziness he had used a few phrenetic hours to fill a number of blank pages with words, rhymed and unrhymed. B.H., of course, guessed my presumptuous thoughts without delay.

"No, no, old man, that isn't it." He laughed almost maliciously. "People have hardly any appreciation for things like that now. I simply drew your name out of the alphabet; back in the dark days of the beginnings of mankind we would have said 'by chance.' All the members of the household liked your name and we agreed unanimously that F.W. should be our wedding guest and should cast a glance from his primitive time into our own advanced time. And through him we want to feel a breath of the invigorating air of that primitive era of which we know so little. That's all there is to it! That's why we summoned you."

"So now I'm not only a wedding guest but also a Darwinian ape," I murmured to myself. Quick as a flash I surveyed my unusual situation. I had died at least sixty to a hundred thousand years ago, at any rate an astronomical eon. I had not spent the interim between my death and the present moment in a state of complete unconsciousness. The life I had lived had produced such strong aftereffects in me that the well-nigh interminable interval had seemed no longer and no more significant than a short night. In this short night, to be sure, a number of things had evidently befallen me that had not yet made themselves entirely clear. My friend B.H., meanwhile, trained by Tibetan monks, had experienced one or more reincarnations, smart fellow that he was. And at this very time he was participating in an advanced era of humanity, in which a person of one hundred and seven years looked like an undergraduate of 1910. He it was who, thanks to the technically highly developed spiritualism of these times, had had me summoned into life, even though not genuine life (up to now I was not sufficiently swept away by my travel experiences to have any doubts about its genuineness). What was the difference? I should be less sensitive and less choleric. Moreover, my invisible state, though not comparable with true life, spared me the perils, risks, and intellectual dimouts of an existence identical with itself. I could let my curiosity rove freely. Such an opportunity would knock only once. These were my thoughts.

Aloud I exclaimed, "What are we waiting for, B.H.? We're not going to this wedding on foot, are we?"

"Certainly," he nodded. "We're going on foot; it's only four hundred miles from here."

My ears must have deceived me. I rotated on my own invisible axis and peered in all directions. "Where's your car? Where's the nearest parking lot? I assume that nowadays every infant owns a power perambulator, and while mother performs her household duties she guides it through the heaviest traffic with complete safety by short wave. We had almost reached that point even back in my time."

"By 'car' do you mean something that rolls on wheels?" asked the reincarnated B.H., strain of thinking and slight disgust about his youthful mouth.

I strove to keep my composure. "Listen to me, B.H. You claim we are in the middle of a city, that is, a connected settlement. But what kind of city is this that rivals the Pontine desolation of a primitive landscape that has either not yet been discovered or has already been abandoned? Don't you remember from your various reincarnations what a modern metropolis is, or at least, what it was? Have you forgotten the tens of thousands of sleek, smoothly gliding vehicles that were dammed up like a mill-stream by the red stoplights, to be released like a dazzling mill-race by the green lights? And have you forgotten the slowly rolling lava of greedy crowds before the plate glass of huge show windows that continually goaded the jaded sensuality to ful-fillably unfulfillable desire? And at night the circling, flashing figures in neon lights over our heads? What am I talking about? I feel as though I had been cast away in the most reactionary void, why, upon my word, in an extinct world of the most in-comprehensible retrogression! Is it possible that technology, at whose early cradle we stood and from which we expected an infinitely beneficent future, has been utterly wasted and lost in a span of sixty to a hundred thousand years?"

My old friend smiled tolerantly at my words. "It took much less than that span," he said, "to eliminate what you call technology, a concept that is completely lost today, although it was during this very span that the overwhelming event occurred which alone would have sufficed to extinguish the historical memory of mankind. This memory, however, was not entirely extinguished but only slightly blurred with regard to the times before the event. The fact that we still number our years from the birth of Christ just as in the beginnings of mankind may serve as evidence for my statement. But technology, if I remember correctly, was a primitive abomination composed of mass murder, gasoline stench, electric high tension, splitting of atoms, useless, slow haste, and a mania for enervating comfort. We couldn't stand it today without becoming seriously ill. Who, for example, could seat himself in one of those clumsy, wheeled vehicles—a few of them have been preserved as curios—without exposing himself to a nervous breakdown?"

He stopped and looked at me hesitantly. I noticed for the first time now that B.H. was wearing an old field uniform of the First World War and wrapped puttees. When I took a second, good look, however, I became aware that it was only an imitation, made out of some infinitely fine, silvergray, filmy material, the like of which I had never seen before.

"I don't want to offend you, F.W.," he continued. "Men have always strained and stretched their strength to the limits set by their age. Of course we too make use of technical aids, if you please. Only our technology is silent and modest, not physical and chemical, but Mental. Take a look at this instrument, for instance, that every contemporary carries with him. It spares our interior organs all adventures on rolling wheels, for you know our entrails were never intended to alter their normal position. It even spares us the adventure of primitive rocket voyages through the air, a form of travel that had such ill effects on the oxygen economy of human hearts and lungs that certain generations never managed to live beyond fifty years of age. All the generations that hurried back and forth through the air in order to buy and sell, had to accept as a natural law an early death by heart failure. Fortunately mankind has conquered such physical failings, I don't know how many tens of thousands of years ago! The historians don't agree about the exact date when the material form of traveling was replaced by the Mathematical-Mental manner. But there's not the slightest doubt that this date is lost in grayest antiquity——"

"Mathematical-Mental manner of traveling?" I repeated in confusion.

"This thing," he consoled me, "is based upon a fundamentally simple insight into the relativity of all moving points in the cosmos with reference to each other. It's as simple as all great things, and you can almost picture the honest, anonymous craftsman with smooth white hair who, in mythical days of yore, figured out the theory of relativity. In short, when we travel we do not move toward our objective, but we move our objective toward us."

As he made this explanation he held a thing under my nose that was larger than a watch and smaller than a desk barometer, in other words, about the size of a pocket compass. Since I had been staring at B.H.'s chewed fingernails, I did not at once become aware of the fact that I had seen instruments like this one long ago. It seemed to be a puzzle toy, such as I had owned in my childhood, in which certain little colored balls had to be maneuvered with skill and patience into certain small holes provided for them.

"I don't know anything about mathematics," I said evasively as I regarded the little toy with astonishment and with unspeakably sad emotions.

"Mathematics is only an auxiliary means," B.H. comforted me. "It is a tautological operation that equates one symbol against another in order to discover an unknown result by means of such equation. It's perfectly simple to climb around on the ladder of equations, as you'll see for yourself in a moment."

With his blunt index finger he pointed at the glass-covered dial of the puzzle. "Do you see the two concentric circles of little holes? The outer one belongs to the realm of mathematics. The pale blue globules go in there. Here! As long as you're invisible you can probably read this fine print without glasses."

And, sure enough, I read without glasses and without trouble: "Galactic Time"—"Planetary Time"—"Continental Time"—"Local Time"—"Galactic Space"—"Planetary Space"—"Continental Space"—"Local Space"—"Exact Declination of the Light Ray"——

"Well, here we are," said B.H. with childlike pleasure in his superior accomplishment, as he balanced and shook the pale blue globules into the holes with the above designations. The skill with which he managed the puzzle was quite beyond my comprehension.

"I don't understand anything about it," I blurted out, "and, what's more, I don't care to understand anything about it."

Undisturbed by my resistance he continued his instruction, following the inner circle of the instrument with his fingernail. "Now, take a look at this. Much more important than the mathematical-astronomical circle is the Mental circle. Pardon me, you might perhaps misunderstand the concept 'Mental.' It does not mean a mere activity of the intellect; we designate as Mental every impulse of the soul, every emotion that is washed clean and therefore spiritualized by the light of consciousness— Why don't you pay attention? Are you tired of listening to me? —Here, read along with me the designations over the little holes into which I will now roll the light green globules:

"'Direction of the Will'—'Urgency for Change'—'Certainty Regarding Objective'—'Probable Period of Impatience'—'Probable Period of Patience'——"

"Stop, B.H.," I interrupted him, seriously confused now. "I have been invited or 'summoned'—which is much worse—by utter strangers. I don't know who or what sort of people they are, what their names are, or how they live. I don't know their language, their habits and customs, their era, which is separated from mine, the beginnings of mankind, by eons that I can't even count in years. You've made your way through a number of reincarnations and have acquired a savoir vivre that lets you get along in any company. Have you any idea how I feel, a person by nature timid and embarrassed, who even back in the year 1930 never entered a strange living room without beads of sweat on his forehead? How am I to act? How am I to behave? The only aid to my nerves is the fact that I am invisible. You can't expose me to the friction of such a meeting after an eternity of solitary confinement!"

"Don't worry," he smiled cheerfully. "Your timidity, your embarrassment, stem from a cannibalistic civilization, a civilization erected upon pagan taboos, where high and low, great and small, rich and poor, beautiful and ugly, were separated from each other by yawning chasms! I promise you, you will meet the friendliest, the handsomest, the most tactful people at this wedding party, and in just a few minutes. You see, there's just the last light green globule left to get into the last little hole marked 'Keenly Directed Desire.'"

"Please have some consideration, B.H.," I begged, "before it's too late. You simply can't let me plump into this world without any information or instructions! Maybe it would be best to call the whole thing off. Please, please, help me! Maybe you could let me disappear. You know, I'm proud. I don't want to make a fool of myself."

No matter how painful this confession may be for the author of a travel-book, at this moment my conceit, my pride, and my fear were greater than my curiosity and journalistic inquisitiveness. But B.H. paid no attention to me; he was having a little trouble getting the final globule into the final little hole and moving our objective toward us.

"Don't be nervous," he said without looking up. "You won't feel a thing. By tonight you'll have your own instrument." And he took hold of my arm with his free hand, so that we formed a single unit.

When the last globule finally dropped into the hole marked "Keenly Directed Desire" there was a pleasant little snap, not one-tenth as distinct as the tiny electric shock that one got on

clear winter days in New York when one shook hands. I now
expected the distant horizon to rush silently but rapidly toward
our stationary spot. Nothing of the sort happened. You had to be
a keen observer to notice presently that the number, position,
and arrangement of the big clumps of trees in the desolate plain
about us had changed without any transition. One of these thick
groves now was situated not more than fifteen feet from us. The
waxy blossoms with their vague hints of color gleamed wanly
from the black leathery foliage. We had reached our destination
or, to be more exact, our destination had reached us. We began
to move our feet, B.H., his visible ones, I, my invisible ones. It
was strangely pleasant to walk on the gray nap of this carpet
of sod with which the entire aging globe seemed to be covered.

Suddenly I could no longer restrain myself. I stopped and
shouted at B.H., "I won't walk another step until you tell me
what you mean by the 'grandiose, overwhelming event' with
which you don't want to frighten me!"

The Fourth Chapter

WHEREIN I ACQUIRE INFORMATION, ENTER
THE HOUSE OF THE WEDDING PARTY, AND
MAKE MY APPEARANCE IN THE CIRCLE THAT
SUMMONED ME.

"IT WAS A perfectly ordinary day," B.H. began, "a weekday—"
He broke off and frowned out across the marvelously kept
lawn that miraculously covered the smooth earth from horizon
to horizon.

I felt that it cost my friend a tremendous effort to speak about
the "Event." In order to make it easier for him I continually
interposed questions. For example: "And you happened to be
living again on this ordinary day, didn't you, B.H.?"

"That's a question I can't always answer accurately, F.W.," he
answered sternly. "Remember this: at times my personal experiences become confused with general historical knowledge in
my consciousness. The Event, however, really is my own experience, although at the same time it is the greatest general impression that the human race has ever had. You know that great
impressions and severe wounds become perceptible only gradually, and that memory frequently tries to eject the recollection
of the instant of the trauma. At any rate, it was just a day like
any other——"

"Forgive me, B.H.," I interrupted again, "could you possibly
fix the date of this ordinary weekday a bit more definitely?"

"Well, if you insist on a date," he shrugged. "It was an ex-

26

tremely cloudy Friday. Furthermore, as every child knows, it
was a thirteenth of November——"

"I have serious doubts that there could be a cloudy weekday
nowadays, not to mention a genuine gray November Friday," I
said, sniffing the strangely dry air and looking up to the naked,
unbroken blue of the sky.

"A very good observation, F.W.," my friend approved. "Clouds
are a great rarity and highly appreciated by Mental man——"

"But you can't have a really genuine thirteenth of November
without a metropolis," I insisted stubbornly.

"For heaven's sake, you're standing right in the middle of a
metropolis," B.H. explained with some annoyance.

"But I assume," I gibed, "that your metropolis on that thirteenth of November presented a somewhat different appearance."

"That goes without saying," my reincarnated friend countered
my mild sarcasm. "Of course it looked different, and a hundred
years earlier and a hundred years later it looked different again.
I've come a long way, you know, my friend. On that particular
thirteenth of November houses were still—or perhaps again—
built *above* the ground. The Mentelobole, to be sure, had not
yet been devised. We did not move our objectives toward us, but
we moved toward them, with enormous and highly unsalubrious
speed. You would have approved completely of that metropolis.
We had to go through labyrinthine passages to get out into the
street. Sidewalks and roadways were still archaically separate
from each other. The traffic was terrific. Gyroplanes flew over-
head. Their speed made them as invisible as you are now, F.W.
Down below, men, women, and children crowded around huge
show windows behind which brilliant revues and musical
comedies were performed day and night by great artists. I even
recollect the good old milkman whose little cart was drawn by a
big dog hung with sleigh bells. It really was a pretty backward
period."

"And it was raining," I tried to steer B.H. back to his subject.

"No, it wasn't raining," he said dreamily. "It wasn't even driz-
zling. It was only very dark. Afterward the newspapers claimed

that an atmosphere of doom had prevailed before the Event. Neither I nor any of my friends had noticed anything at all. Of course, I mustn't forget to mention that even the nature-blind metropolis noticed the terrible excitement of the birds."

"And when did the birds begin to get excited?"

"It was said to have started shortly after midnight. By a rare chance I spent the night before the thirteenth at home. Millions and millions of birds invaded the metropolis of which I am speaking. Don't ask me what its name was. I simply don't remember it any more. But you can ask me about the birds if you want. There were all varieties that were then in existence: from condors, vultures, hawks, cormorants, down to swallows, wrens, and sparrows. Those are all the names of birds that I can recall. Flat roofs, roof gardens, spires and towers, balustrades, antennas, metal frames for the reception of cosmic rays, trans-shadow-disintegrator installations—everything was black, pitch-black, with large and small birds, and there was a squawking and wailing and twittering that beggars description. It was a single, sharp, jagged cry of anguish that vibrated beneath the low-hanging clouds——"

"And you call that a perfectly ordinary day," I said, shaking my head.

"So it was," nodded B.H. "A perfectly ordinary weekday, a Friday, and a thirteenth of November. The first newspaper extras reported this matter of the birds as early as two o'clock in the morning; so did the various agencies that transmitted ether waves. The Uranograph—you'll find out presently what that is—hadn't been devised at that time. We were just in the middle of a highly rationalistic era, and people had a more unquestioning faith in science than at any time in your experience. The learned institutes began to look into the matter without delay. By four o'clock in the morning they had examined, analyzed, and explained the phenomenon. They reported that it was connected with some sort of electromagnetic disturbance that led to the formation of recurrent chain lightning in the lower strata of the atmosphere——"

"It looks less and less like an ordinary day to me, old man," I interjected, and I could feel my invisible shoulders shrug.

"Believe me, F.W., with the exception of the bird cries, it was the most commonplace Friday imaginable. And how long does it take a self-respecting metropolis to get used to the most intense squawking and to go back about its business? Two or three hours. At eleven-thirty the world had become accustomed to it and the headlines in the noon editions of the papers dealt with the marital troubles of a world-famed ventriloquist."

"And at eleven fifty-five?" I asked.

"I had just begun to lather my face," B.H. replied thoughtfully. "It was the hour when civilized working people of that generation got up. You know, one of the most definite facts that I learned in the course of many reincarnations is this: the more advanced mankind is, the later they get up."

"And at twelve-twenty?" I persisted.

"At twelve forty-four," he said and took a long, deep breath, "at twelve forty-four I left my comfortable living quarters in order to keep an appointment for luncheon. Incidentally, there isn't a speck of truth in the report that some joker of a historian circulated to the effect that we lived in very convenient parlor-bed-and-bath-coffins in those days, that sealed themselves up mechanically after our demise and lowered themselves automatically into the ground. That's a pack of lies. Our living quarters may have been pretty small but they were as comfortable as an elastic glove. The times when men had to battle for a place in the sun and even more for a place in the shade were long past——"

"It's at least twelve-fifty now, B.H.," I urged him impatiently, for I had the feeling that he was trying to dodge the issue. "You stepped out of your living quarters six minutes ago. I'm afraid you'll be late for lunch."

"In fact, I'll never get to this lunch at all, F.W." He smiled pensively. "I will just manage to reach the city park right around the corner. You know I always preferred to travel on shanks' mare. So I had made up my mind to stroll leisurely over to my friends who had invited me. Of course, I didn't get very far——"

"Because the Event took place meanwhile?" I prodded him. He looked through me with a strangely disturbed expression. The recollection still seemed to confuse him.

"How can one," he asked the vacant space that I occupied, "how can one casually say of an event that takes no time, or practically no time, at all, that it 'took place'?"

"Practically no time is as good as any other time," I declared. "You mean to say that the Event lasted only a fraction of a second, B.H.? Perhaps you could express that fraction in numbers."

"You bet I can," he replied and quickly wrote a whole series of zeros in the air with an emphatic "one" at the end.

"I don't know anything about it," I pondered, "but it seems to me that such an infinitesimal fraction could scarcely be perceived by the senses——"

"'Scarcely be perceived by the senses,'" he repeated almost derisively. "I assure you we all thought the Event lasted an eternity. While it took place time stood still. Behind the thick, heavy wall of clouds of that thirteenth of November there suddenly flamed the empyrean, the heaven of fire which the ancients believed lay above all other heavens. How can I describe the indescribable? There was nothing—no city, no houses, no park, no boulevard, no trees, no I, no you—nothing—nothing but light, light compared to which all known light is murky dusk."

"I have always feared," I murmured, deeply moved, "that the sun might have a heart attack or a fit of insanity some time."

"Call it what you will," he said. "On that Friday, the thirteenth of November, the sun threatened to stampede. It's really not anything new; other stars have been known to explode without warning, that is, to grow to a million times their former size. I don't know whether we learned about Nova formation when we were in school together or whether that was a much later discovery. But the great thing about our sun is that, at the same time it stampeded, it restrained itself and remained its own master. In consequence, the result was not annihilation but the great

Event known as 'Transparency.' It can scarcely be called a physical occurrence. And yet, we experienced the Day of Judgment."

"It must have been terrible," I muttered mechanically, "terrible!"

"Terrible!" he exclaimed. "It was glorious, unspeakably glorious. If the brevity of the instant had been longer by one zero less, everything would have been over forever. If any creature on earth had had a lighted match in his hand during the Transparency, the atmosphere would have ignited and puffed out into space in a banner of flame. Why? Because the oxygen content of the air was trebled for several seconds before and after the Transparency. But fortunately there were no more matches on earth at that time, and no open fires, not even streams of lava. There are still scientists today who claim that the increase of the oxygen content in the atmosphere was responsible for the divine rapture, the ineffable ecstasy that filled me and all other living beings in that fraction of time."

"How can I imagine," I marveled, "that any sort of sensation can develop in such a fraction of time, B.H.?"

"You can imagine that instant, F.W., to have been like the climactic intensification of a never conceived symphonic movement—My God, that's all nonsense, you can't imagine it at all. But try to imagine that until now you have lived only as a figure in a picture and suddenly you step from the canvas, living and three-dimensional. Or, imagine that what you have regarded as life until now was only a spasm, a crippling, stunting contraction of all muscles, and all at once you are freed from this spasm and are whole and straight. That's about how we felt during the Transparency. You slept through a great deal, F.W."

"I didn't ask to be wakened," I replied, illogically nettled.

"Do you really feel so uncomfortable in your cloak of invisibility?" he asked, and I noticed that I had offended him.

"As I think over your clear account, B.H.," I resumed, "it was not so much a matter of an astronomical event that unfailingly led to destruction, as an infinitesimally brief hesitation on the part of the sun between continued shining and flaming self-annihilation; an instant of balance, so to speak, on the edge of a knife that found expression in the light phenomenon which you or the scientists call 'Transparency.' Outside of that, however, it seems to have passed without any perceptible effect——"

"It did have effects," he interrupted; "the Transparency was not a mere spectacle——"

"But no physical or chemical effects," I interposed, "except for the momentary increase of the atmospheric oxygen."

"You're wrong," said B.H., "the Event had a considerable number of physical effects. The fact that a few hundred thousand people died during the Transparency is of no particular consequence. But look up at the sky, F.W., and you'll see some of the effects, or to be more exact, you'll not see them."

Obediently I looked up at the radiant sky. It appeared much emptier, much quieter, than during my lifetime. Suddenly I felt a brief, curious shock. "Where are the birds?" I asked.

"The class of birds is gone since that Friday, the thirteenth of November," he replied with a sort of dragging solemnity, and then he added, "Their fright and their rapture were too great. They did not survive the Event."

B.H. had nothing further to say. He walked toward the dark clump of trees that stood a few steps away. After a quick, distrustful look at the sun I followed him.

❁ ❁ ❁ ❁
❁ ❁ ❁
❁

NOW THAT I SHOULD REALLY TURN my flying pen loose on the actual description of my travels in the Mental or Astromental time and world, I feel retarded, and, worse than that, I retard my fretting, and by this time, perhaps fuming, reader with me.

I am conscientiously searching my memory and yet I can't be quite certain how much advance information about this time and world B.H. revealed to me before we entered the house of the wedding party. Now—I mean right now as I write, when a few days and nights have elapsed since my return home—it seems to me that my friend was prevailed upon to give me a few scanty details before he made a slight bow in front of a tree-shaded garden gate and softly said, "We are here" into the void beyond, whereupon the gate opened.

But perhaps I am wrong; perhaps my reincarnated friend, who had so eloquently described the Transparency, or Sun-Catastrophe, kept me in the dark before he introduced me to his friends. B.H. was certainly not as eager to be of service to me as Vergil was to Dante, to make a very presumptuous comparison. In spite of our friendship a sort of suppressed rivalry existed between us. Like every true cicerone, B.H. wanted to see me, the tourist, in a constant dither of astonishment. And I, like every tourist, stubbornly resisted his efforts and preferred—frequently against my own will—to appear indifferent and blasé. The result was that B.H. was often offended and withheld his instruction from me. So I learned a good many unexpected facts without any explanation, through penetration and osmosis, I can't think of any better words. By the simple fact of my presence in it, this unknown world and time permeated me with a surprisingly rapid understanding of its peculiarities and immeasurable changes. This alone accounts for the fact that a very brief sojourn, measured in hours, furnished me enough material to render this circumstantial report. Yet this report represents only a selection from the abundance of things I saw, experienced, and knew, recorded as nearly as possible in chronological order, partly because I doubt the reliability of my memory and partly because I am afraid to tire my reader with too many novelties.

B.H. had managed to conjure up before my mind's eye such a glorious picture of the stupendous celestial phenomenon of the Transparency that it suddenly seemed to me, as I shyly looked up at the sun, that I had experienced it myself, that I had been there in body and spirit, although it had actually taken place several decamillennia before my visit, during the deepest depth of my sleep of death. It had been a reliable instinct that prompted me to insist upon being initiated into this phenomenon before passing over the threshold of the nuptial house. The increased importance of a wedding, the tying of the conjugal knot, was somehow connected with the sublime Transparency. Since our sun had suffered its "attack," that infinitesimal instant between shining permanence and explosive annihilation, which could so easily have reconverted our entire planetary system into most rarefied original matter, since that moment of moments a number of transformations had taken place in our poor, dear earth that were not less important than the disappearance of the birds. Although the moment of moments had been so brief that B.H. had hardly been able to write enough zeros in the air to define its brevity, it had been sufficient to produce a slight increase of the distance between the terrestrial globe and the sun. It was a totally insignificant increase that lengthened the earth's orbit, and with it the year, by an hour or two. Still this tiny expansion was reflected in the history of nature and of mankind, as was also the slightly retarded axial rotation of the earth which increased the twenty-four hours of the day to a similarly tiny degree by a handful of seconds. Untutored layman that I am, I merely report these changes without being able to describe, confirm, or justify them astronomically or physically. It will be up to the scientists to test the facts I brought home with me.

But the most skeptical scientist will not exclude the probability that even insignificant cosmic, astronomical changes are bound to have biological consequences. And I can't avoid blurting out in quite unseemly fashion the most important of these consequences as they affected the crowning work of creation. This was a very considerable increase in the span of human life. Whether this was due solely to the lengthening and slowing of the planetary rhythm or whether an ingenious reduction of the perils and malignities to which the flesh used to be heir was a contributing factor, this too is a question that I will have to put upon the shoulders of the scientists.

A certain shy embarrassment forces me to protract the moment of respite at the garden gate of the Astromental era. Once we have entered, it will be my difficult task to deal with an overpowering copiousness of grandiose progress that has nothing whatever in common with technical improvements and laborsaving devices, which we, in the beginnings of mankind, identified almost exclusively with the word "progress." This naïve and straightforward word encompasses a gross illusion, a fact with which even the less intelligent have now become familiar. The beelike industry of the changing generations leaves behind many a honey-drop of experience in the combs, which neither sun and earth catastrophes nor mankind's partial loss of memory can completely waste. Every clock that strikes the hours is a savings bank in which the accumulating seconds do not melt away entirely without interest. For living and suffering humanity time itself stores up a certain capital that, to be sure, can be cashed only at great intervals in the form of a tiny annuity, as though by the last will of a farsighted, penurious testator. Thus every generation is a tiny bit richer than its predecessor, even though only by the frustrations of the latter. This microscopic plus-value of increasing age is the only progress of mankind.

I do not disavow this thesis, even though I listened to an entirely contrary dogma from the lips of the Grand Bishop on the second day of my visit. The truth remains the same. The points of view are different. The age of the people into whose midst I was about to step—for the reader's peace of mind we were already inside the garden gate—could be extended without any trouble to the two hundredth year. It was customary for most people, however, to "go into retirement" some twenty or thirty years earlier, although old age entailed no inconveniences except perhaps a certain amount of boredom and surfeit. In this respect, however, I am prematurely approaching the second, if not the most important, experience of my visit, and it would be more than awkward from the point of view of the reporter as well as of the novelist to divulge this experience together with the meaning of the hypocritical word "Wintergarden" before the twenty-second chapter in the third part of this chronicle.

The general extension and retardation of life had brought with them a number of other peculiarities, some of which I guessed and with some of which B.H. acquainted me (at least so it seems to me now) before we came in contact with the people who had invited or rather "summoned" me to their wedding feast. It certainly did not require much acumen to perceive the impoverishment of life's diversity and profuseness, the remarkable curtailment of its variety, and the abatement of its passions. One glance out at the smooth desolation of the countryside was sufficient. So far we hadn't met a single human being. The conclusion I drew from this fact, confirmed by my friend, was correct. The former total of billions of contemporaneously living individuals had shrunk, or had been reduced, to the absolute minimum necessary for the preservation of the species. The next link in the logical chain followed inevitably: with such sparse population of the leveled globe, with communication simplified in the extreme by the travel-puzzle, national and linguistic differences could no longer exist. Humanity had been united since time immemorial.

On the one hand, B.H. was anxious to keep me in a state of astonishment. On the other hand, however, he didn't want me to make a fool of myself by appearing to my new contemporaries as a complete ignoramus. For this reason he expounded to me, somewhat rudely, the meaning of a wedding in the Mental world, and why it was a great social honor to be invited to this festival.

The area in which the change produced by the Transparency was most clearly reflected was, of course, that of reproduction: copulation, procreation, conception, pregnancy; in short, the entire process of propagation. It was not true, B.H. admitted, that all women were capable of becoming pregnant only once in their lives. That applied only to the most aristocratic and refined class among them. Like the wonderful trees in the fairy tale, they could bear fruit only once. On the other hand, the general refinement of nature was evidenced by the fact that the period of gestation had increased from nine months to almost twelve.

Even though monopedia, the one-child system, was the rule, exceptions, B.H. declared with grave mien, were more frequent

than the rule. Unfortunately I could not discover the percentage
of families that raised two or three children. The mania for
statistics that had been typical of my own age seemed to have
disappeared completely in the Mental era. But one thing was
quite clear from the intimations of my reincarnated friend. Anyone who came of a "prolific" family, that is, one that had as many
as two scions, could not be said to be of "good family." The prolific families thus formed the "lower class of society," although
the term "lower class" sounded absurd in a world that had
neither economic nor social distinctions, as B.H. maintained in
the same breath. At any rate, he did not conceal the fact that the
monopedic patriciate did not mingle with the "proliferous"
bourgeoisie.

It hadn't taken me long to figure out the tremendous significance of matrimony in this era. It had been raised almost to a
level of sacramental holiness, as it had in the Catholic Church,
one of the two institutions from the beginnings of mankind that
I was to meet in this world. (The second will be divulged at the
proper time.) As for the union of man and woman, there was
much less free erotic choice than in the liberal era of my earlier
life. Again there was a meeting of extremes, for the Mental
people of this most remote future had the same customs in this
respect as the superstitious peasants of most remote antiquity.
At a very tender age the male child had his bride assigned to
him. The choice was, to a large extent, preordained by certain
external characteristics and inner qualities of the children. Among
the external characteristics I include the indications that were
manifested by the stars. In the eons that had passed, man's relations to the cosmos of the stars had radically changed. I really
have to hold myself in check to avoid speaking at this early date
of the most overwhelming of my travel experiences that resulted
from the new relation of Astromental men to the cosmos of the
stars. They understood more fully than we could ever imagine
the relation of every point in the cosmos to every other point in
the cosmos, and the extent to which all mundane things depend
upon this unbroken tissue of interrelations. The word "horo-

scope" is much too crude; it sounds far too much like mechanical, amateur fortune-telling even to suggest the sidereal subtleties and finenesses that were invoked to protect the maturing spouses physically, mentally, and morally. On this basis their place of residence was regulated, their instruction, their play, their recreation, even their sleep. The youth and the young girl were permitted to meet only three times, at specific turning-points in their lives, before the betrothal. These three meetings were tests to ascertain whether perhaps a secret perversity, a hidden antipathy, an unexpected aversion, threatened to destroy the carefully planned alliance. Such cases of incompatibility occurred occasionally, but the agreement was then broken at once and the world had something to gossip about. It was better that they had something to gossip about now than later; which means that even in the Astromental world there were such things as love tragedies, adultery, and divorce, only they caused incomparably deeper suffering than in our world. But if everything went well, it was only necessary to await the thirty-third birthday of the bridegroom, when he reached the legally prescribed age of maturity. The hour for the wedding had come. This hour was, of course, preceded by months of preparation. These consisted of instruction, contemplation, self-examination, in short of psychic-moral exercises, to which the prospective spouses were separately subjected in order to make them tractable for the sacrifice of personality without which true wedlock is inconceivable. When these exercises had been finished to the satisfaction of examiner and examinee, the festival proper began, a true festival in every sense, that lasted for three days, the greater part of which was celebrated in the bridal house, the smaller part in public. The ceremony itself took place at noon of the third day.

Mention of this schedule is essential, since it forms the framework of my short but profitable sojourn in a future of which I never even dreamed. It is for the sake of this schedule that I am compelled to interrupt so near the source the hitherto scanty flow of my narrative. But I pledge here and now that, unlike other traveling pedants, I shall not hamper the unconfined fancy of my readers by means of maps, sketches, or any other sort of illustration.

* * * * *
* * *
*

"THIS IS THE FIRST DAY OF THE NUPTIAL FEAST of Io-Do and Io-La," said B.H., carefully closing the gate behind him. "Too bad you missed the forenoon." With these words he began to move ahead slowly.

I continued to stand firmly on my invisible but solid legs. A little stubbornly I asked, "What business have I at the nuptials of the distinguished couple Io-Do and Io-La?"

"But you're a special feature in their honor, F.W.," my friend replied without turning around. "Don't you understand?"

I understood. The apparition of a creature from darkest antiquity was B.H.'s wedding gift to the young couple on the first day of the festivity. In former days they used to make presents of apes, parrots, dwarfs, and court jesters. Today they gave "summoned spirits." Why not? Of course, it was still a question what they would do with an invisible ghost. Despite my state I had hot shivers.

I was about to make a cutting remark when B.H. said softly, his back still turned to me, "And I hope you understand that I wanted chiefly to give you a special present."

His voice sounded warm and sincere. He had indeed given me a gift that embraced all other gifts within it, namely life and consciousness. Torn between gratitude and annoyance, I fixed my eye on the scene about me. The garden through which I followed my friend was a real garden, although only by courtesy. It consisted of actual hedges, bushes, shrubs, beds, and a fountain, surrounded by gray sod; and all that was overshadowed by dense treetops with leathery black foliage that were characteristic of the flat country all around, which B.H. claimed to be a metropolis, so far I couldn't tell why. The beds, shrubs, and hedges in the garden didn't show a speck of green, and they were covered in modest abundance with flowers that were utterly strange to me. There were five or six varieties at most. The majority of them resembled very large anemones with very faint tints, pink, yellowish, heliotrope, and iridescent mother-of-pearl. Only one shrub blossom, that appeared to correspond to our rose, showed a decided, strong, dull color—rust-red. But it too had an artificial aspect with its thick, motionless petals, as though manufactured by a wax-chandler. I had to think of a luxury shop in Paris, near the Gare St. Lazare, whose show windows, filled with a wealth of such artificial flowers, magically captivated the eye. But the difference was that in those show windows art was trying to appear natural while here, in these bushes and beds, nature was apparently making a valiant attempt to look as artificial and unreal as possible.

In its entirety this medium-sized garden with all its pale-tinted plants and with its black leafy roof of strange, somber trees gave me the impression of shrinking from light and fearing the sun. This was all the more remarkable since I had the definite sensation that the sun had lost some of its radiant heat but had, at the same time, gained in penetrating brilliance and dazzling glare. Later experiences justified my suspicions: this fear of the sun, this shrinking from its radiation, was a natural protective instinct as well as a conviction among these Astromental people. Now I noticed a lot of large, I might almost say enormous, pale-winged butterflies and light green dragonflies that hovered with vibrant wings over the plants. As they soared, they produced a pleasing chirping sound, almost a melodious twittering.

"The butterflies are singing," said B.H. with a radiant smile. "They are our songbirds. It's April——"

"You're a renegade, B.H.," I blurted out. Although I said nothing further, I felt as though he had sold his parents because he appeared so perfectly at home in this strange world without birds and green grass. But I was carried back to the days before I had

fallen asleep to waken without warning on the gray-haired sod
of this remote future about which I am writing in the past tense.
I saw the garden of my little house, with the graceful stone basin
that was always kept filled with water for the birds. Golden
orioles and blackbirds and blue nuthatches darted in from all
directions, drank and bathed and darted away again. And all that
went through my mind and filled me with sadness. Then I looked
up at the blue, dead, empty sky of this day and contemplated the
cheerless, strange garden about me, and wondered how any sort
of plants could thrive in such a shadowy existence, even though
they were only wax and candy blossoms that didn't move. Of
course, B.H. divined my thoughts at once.

"The gardening is done by a central agency," he explained.
"The Worker does all that."

"The Worker? What's that?" I asked, unable to conceal my
startled surprise.

"He is also called the Bearded One or the Sleepless One," B.H.
replied. "But patience, old man, you'll see him."

But the thing I didn't see was "the house." B.H. had not deceived me. We were really standing in the middle of a city. But,
because of the previously mentioned fear of the sun, the houses
of this city were not built above, but deep down under, the
ground. Each garden crowned with leathery black foliage was
therefore a roof garden. Each individual clump of trees designated a dwelling. Nothing could be more diametrically opposed
to the scientific architecture of concrete, steel, and glass, the
industrialized architecture of my day in the beginnings of mankind that loved to drag screaming light and glaring noise into
the nerveless dwelling cubes, than this building practice which
fashioned a protective home for hypersensitive humans in the
bosom of the earth. The only thing visible above the surface was
a moderately tall, round superstructure of translucent material
that resembled a gun turret or observation tower of a battleship.
We entered this tower through a doorless aperture, whereupon the
platform on which we stood immediately began to sink. At the
same instant—and nobody can blame me for it—I had violent

palpitations of the heart. For that reason I was very glad when, upon our arrival down below, B.H. asked me to wait because he had to announce my arrival.

When I was finally in the reception room—I can't say whether I had been called or fetched—I was quite calm again and brimming with the impartial attentiveness and brazen curiosity of a genuine explorer, although I really didn't become quite aware of this purpose of my nocturnal mission until after my return home. Of course, my task wasn't as easy as one might suppose. I could not, for example, comply with the explorer's obvious obligation to keep stenographic notes in a little memorandum book, namely because of the peculiar light that pervaded this medium-sized and well-proportioned room. This light, or rather this illumination, was neither faint nor gloomy; it was, quite on the contrary, of a comfortable, mild brightness, but by some admixture that was new to me it succeeded not only in illuminating but also in softening the outlines of all objects, in making them pleasantly indistinct and attractively remote. If the word "aristocratic" can be used of any sort of illumination, then this was the most aristocratic illumination imaginable. I have purposely used the word "aristocratic" instead of "esthetic," because the illumination lent tact and charm to all objects. Fairly warm, with a yellowish, mellow tinge, it reminded me of the Welsbach gaslight of my childhood and of the serene family circle. Bathed in this domestic illumination, about ten or eleven persons stood about a strangely high, moderately large table that made me think of some creature caught unawares and playing 'possum. The people smiled with great satisfaction in my direction. They were not holding hands, nor had the room been darkened as the practice of a long dead era prescribed. Such hocus-pocus seemed to have become passé ages ago. Outside the homely circle of light, exactly halfway between these persons and me, stood the reincarnated B.H. Although his face was in the shadow, he somehow reminded me of an interlocutor, or a performer, or a barker in a freak-show, who had just said something particularly striking. With one hand B.H. pointed at me (voilà), with the other, at the company. From now on this was his symbolic gesture. The people who stood there looking at me attentively, candidly, and expectantly, wore no clothing except the delicate lace tissue that the strange light without a source cast over them. Or in simpler words, they were naked.

I, on the other hand, was no longer naked, let alone nakeder than naked, invisible. On the contrary, I was extremely visible, to my own discomfort. And to cap the climax I was wearing— horrible idea—I was wearing my dress suit with a stiff, badly dented shirt-front, wilted stand-up collar, and dejected white tie. I had probably been buried in this ceremonial costume more than a hundred thousand years ago, and even then this tailcoat had been—well, I won't exaggerate, but it had been nearly twenty years old. Next to its shabby lapel dangled the only medal that I had received in my life; it had been awarded by an art-loving but feeble government that was booted out of existence just three weeks after the rash bestowal of the decoration. What a curious exchange of roles! I, who had been summoned here as a ghostly body, as an ectoplasmic apparition, felt like the fat headwaiter of a second-rate restaurant in the company of radiant spirits. But they received me with wide, satisfied eyes, for my superannuated dress suit no doubt looked to them like a fantastic costume from the masquerade wardrobe of human antiquity, far more fantastic certainly than a knight in full armor and plumed crest would have appeared to me in my day.

Anyone who has ever entered a circle of people of a very strange race knows how painfully difficult it is to tell them apart and to find differences in their faces. Generally he tries to find differentiating characteristics in their physical build and in their dress. I could do neither. The persons about the table appeared to be of uniform build, of graceful, I might almost say dainty, figures, men and women alike. Their harmonious medium size refuted the customary concept of the gigantic, strong-willed race of the future, a notion that I too had in my time. And their dress was of as little help to me as their build. Even though these people wore the peculiar illumination like a light, loose housedress about their bodies, still it served to efface rather than to emphasize any differences. From the very start I felt that the nakedness of these figures had nothing in common with the nakedness or seminakedness that used to parade on the beaches in our days of bathing beauties. That really wasn't nakedness at all, but undressedness, unclothing of what was ordinarily clothed. This nakedness, however, was genuine nakedness; it was not at odds with itself, it could be regarded as the traditional costume at home, it did not have the hidden desire to attract attention and to arouse lust; it was innocent. If I were an ardent sectarian I could perhaps speak of the regained paradisiac nakedness. The old-ivory color of these Mental bodies, with no hint of cream and roses, of itself revealed and disseminated a sensuous coolness that is hard to describe.

The beauty of the delicately formed and fine-featured persons in the room did not, however, have the entrancing quality that we describe by the term "radiant beauty," the inescapable force that attracts the breathless beholder and makes him thirst as it refreshes him. No one here was radiantly beautiful; they were sternly beautiful or mildly beautiful or transparently beautiful. But since they were all beautiful my eyes had no standard of comparison, the basis of all rank, and so they speedily became accustomed to all this unaccustomed beauty. Added to this was eternal youth, or rather agelessness, one of the great accomplishments of recent eons. At first I took each of the couples present for the bridal couple, Io-Do and Io-La. But very soon I was informed that tradition and custom, ritual and secret hygiene, prevented the bridal couple from mingling freely with the wedding guests present in the house. They lay on couches in their separate apartments, near each other and yet distant from each other, indulging in contemplation, reverie, and introspection. The men and women whom I had taken for the betrothed couple were the parents and grandparents of the Bride and those of the Bridegroom. The grandparents did not appear older by a single wrinkle than the parents, and I never saw anything more youthfully vigorous than the cheerful parents. If any difference in ages

was apparent, it was only in the depth of the eye sockets. To
observe that, however, required a more intimate acquaintance
with this present which, as I write these words, has again become
most remote future. But stop! Inexpert reporter that I am, in the
analysis of my own impressions I almost forgot to mention an
important external circumstance. There was a difference, and a
very striking one at that. The people assembled here, these graceful individuals, wore wigs. Within the hectomillennium that had
elapsed, nature had apparently ordained the disappearance of
human hair. This trivial biological mutation, as anyone will admit,
is not even remotely comparable to the abyss that yawns between
the Neanderthal caveman and, let's say, Dante Gabriel Rossetti.
(The former also had to lose the wool from his pelt before he
developed into the latter.) The coevalists before whom I had just
materialized—please get this—had no hair either on their bodies
or their faces. What a saving of time and energy for the men who
didn't even need a Mental razor! As for hair on top of the head,
of course, if I want to be quite honest, I can't say whether they
had any or not; and I'm trying hard to be quite honest. I simply
couldn't find out. The wigs prevented me. But even these wigs
did not consist of hair. Hair was regarded as contemptible, as
atavistically disgusting. It didn't take me long to discover that,
and I was terribly embarrassed because I had no head-covering
of any kind. The wigs were actually only stylized headdresses
made of faintly luminous material in gold and silver. They were
reminiscent of the formal headdresses of Greek tragedians or of
the surrealist waves of daring show-window dummies of an
era which, from my present vantagepoint, was not much later.
The matter of the wigs, as I found out a little later, was regulated
by law. Up to the age of one hundred and twenty, people were
permitted to wear golden wigs. After that silver was in order.
But the ladies were still feminine enough to play a clever game
of back and forth between silver and gold when advancing age,
from hundred and twenty on, made it necessary.

Well, there I stood in my shabby burial suit, on my breast the
medal of a snug little two-by-four country that had gone to the

dogs while I was still living. My outward form had gone through
various stages of solidification from its original state of invisibility,
so that it was no longer ectoplasm or a ghostly body. Both
spiritually and physically I had become so completely "I-myself"
that, to be honest about it, I was perspiring with excitement.
I recognized myself when I listened to myself or touched my face
with my fingers. My tongue again came in contact with the gold
tooth in the left upper corner. I noticed that B.H. was making
embarrassed faces. Timidly—how could I help it?—I approached
this company that was so far ahead of me in cultural development and good manners; the time had come for me to "appear"
in compliance with their wish, a near troglodyte in dilapidated
condition, that is, fat, sweating, and in a boiled shirt. They all
smiled with pleasure at the sound of my old schoolmate's voice,
which carried a note of triumph under its ceremonious hoarse-
ness.

"I have the honor, ladies and gentlemen, to present our
esteemed guest, F.W., from the beginnings of mankind."

At these words the oldest man in the assembly turned to me
and bowed. The superlative doesn't mean a thing; he could as
easily have been the youngest. During the social conversation
that followed I learned that he was the so-called "Spokesman."
In smaller households, B.H. informed me later, the "Spokesman"
and the "House Sage" were one person. In this important house,
however, there was, in addition to the Spokesman and the House
Sage, even a third individual, who was called the "Permanent
Guest"! These male officials were drawn from the reserve of
bachelors which had been accumulated as a result of the strict
marriage regulations. The bachelors "lived along," and in this
manner a social problem was smoothly solved.

"We welcome you to our unassuming present day, Seigneur,"
the Spokesman greeted me. He let the baroque vocable "Seigneur" melt on his tongue. It seemed that they had agreed to call
me "Seigneur," not only to honor me but also to use this form of
address as a familiar bridge to my own era, a form of address
that was calculated to flatter me. The good fellow imagined at a

distance of a hundred thousand years that the people in the beginnings of mankind, from the Neanderthal man, let's say, through Nebuchadnezzar, to Mussolini, had scattered "Seigneurs" all over the place. He was puffed up with the pride of a philologist who has finally found an opportunity to use an extremely dead language, like Sumerian, perhaps, in practical dialogue with an ancient Sumerian.

As it turned out, I had no reason at all to poke fun at the handsome patriarch and Spokesman, for in the next moment I committed a horrible faux pas. I stepped up to this patriarch and extended my hand with an obscure mutter of acknowledgment of his greeting. But it happened that the custom of handshaking had been in disuse for eons, a fact of which B.H. should have apprised me at the time of our meeting when I tried to shake his hand. Worse than that, all physical contact was taboo in this highly sensitive era, just as hair was taboo. And so there was a little pause of startled confusion, as though the frivolously summoned primitive man in his uncouth manner had begun his visit on a discordant note, like the shriek of a slate-pencil on a slate. For a tenth of a second everyone squeezed his eyes shut. But a moment later they all tried to cover up my faux pas and make me forget it. Especially the ladies smiled encouragingly in the strange light that blurred their lovely faces and figures. One of the ladies addressed me, and her question was the same embarrassed question they used to ask back in the old days.

"Is this your first trip to California?"

"No, Madame," I replied truthfully, perspiring profusely with the psychic exertion. "Some time ago I lived here for a few years."

"How interesting! As a cowboy or as a goldhunter?" she queried archly and at the same time indifferently, parading her prehistoric knowledge with a slight note of vanity.

"No, Madame," I said. "Neither as a cowboy nor as a goldhunter; not even in the movies, but simply as a refugee."

I ransacked the pockets of my dress suit for a handkerchief and finally found one that wasn't clean because I had forgotten to send it to the laundry. I wadded up the handkerchief in my hand so they wouldn't see it too plainly and began to wipe my forehead in mortification. At the same time I was annoyed that a lady who had the privilege of seeing such a strange apparition should be far less excited than the apparition itself. She resumed the conversation with the indifferent blandness and adroitness of a conversing grand duchess or a debutante.

"Do you find our California changed, Seigneur?"

"To some extent," I lisped. "But I don't want to express an opinion too soon."

In the course of this insignificant interlude I became sharply aware that it was the most earnest endeavor of these people to avoid all embarrassment, all conflicts, all exertions, all arguments, all decisions, all serious troubles. This human race, in contrast to that of our time, had, in the course of countless generations, created an order, a mode of life, in which all resistance to the beautiful, the pleasing, the agreeable, the flattering seemed to have been broken. They did not feel the desolation all around and up above outside their house and their homely light. They knew nothing of green trees and green grass. Their grass was irongray. But so far I had no idea how much they worried about their gracious convention of an agreeable and comfortable life, which they had not bought cheaply but at the cost of great renunciation, as the recipe of all culture requires.

In search of help I looked around for B.H.

A double door opened.

The Fifth Chapter

WHEREIN I PARTAKE OF A FESTIVE MEAL,
AM ADDRESSED BY A DOG, AND INNOCENTLY
BROACH A DELICATE SUBJECT.

WE WALKED THROUGH a double door into an adjoining chamber suffused with a somewhat brighter light, in very much the same manner as any gathering of guests used to do back in the days of antiquity when dinner was announced. To my astonishment the room with the big center table was not the dining room but this one here, completely bare of a table and even of seating accommodations, served that purpose. In the middle of the room, surrounded by a low, circular railing, a reddishly lustrous piece of sculpture projected from a shallow cavity. It was an abstract work of art representing no recognizable form of life. It could perhaps best be described as a twin crystal inclined at a sweetly sentimental angle, in such a manner that the larger crystal rose above the smaller one as a mother above the child in her lap. And the more I looked at it, the more I became convinced that the abstract work of art represented the Madonna and Child, a theme for which a hundred thousand years are as a day. As I concentrated on the piece of sculpture it actually seemed to become ever clearer, more distinct, more beautiful in its form. It obviously possessed the quality of transforming, transfiguring, and intensifying the impression it produced upon the observer in the course of his observation.

49

I resolved at once to pay no attention to this work of art and on no account to become involved in a discussion of art. For, in the first place, it was much too soon for this subject at the present stage of my voyage of discovery. In the second place, I was surrounded by far too much genuine life to devote my interest to reflected life. And in the third place, I was vain enough to believe that I would not learn much of anything new in the realm of art. Moreover, I had no memorandum book other than my feeble memory, upon which I did not wish to inscribe too many details. I was quite willing to devote my entire attention to the people about me. As we had entered this new room with its clearer and more revealing light, these delicately formed, naked persons had been handed soft, light-colored, filmy materials, which they now draped gracefully about their bodies, almost in the manner of certain Greek and Roman statues.

B.H. had somehow managed to maneuver his way to my side. In sharp, hasty whispers he commented that no greater honor could be bestowed upon a guest than an invitation to a formal meal. Eating, he said, as far as it was only a matter of food and its enjoyment, was regarded as a completely private activity. In fact, eating was considered as private a pursuit as its opposite. Banquets, meals at which guests were entertained, were rarely arranged oftener than twelve times per year, and then only for some sacramental or ceremonial purpose, a holiday or baptism, a wedding or departure (for the first time I noticed that instead of the simple word "death" B.H. used the stilted euphemism "departure"). The custom of the religious sacrificial meal, I thought to myself, seems not only to have maintained itself but actually appears to be more vital than in my time, the time before my death, and I thought the word "death" literally as though out of defiance.

B.H. kept looking at me with an uneasy expression in his soft, dark eyes that I remembered so well from our long-past schooldays. I realized that he was not playing an easy role. He was an outsider himself, a state to which his sensitive spirit seemed to have condemned him as long as I had known him. His very appearance and costume, field uniform and wrapped puttees, proved that he did not belong in the current era. On the other hand, however, he was the medium, the mediator between this current era and the infinitely remote time before my death. It was he who had given these pleasant people the unusual enjoyment of communing with a departed spirit from the distant past, and not only in ghostly form, but in perfectly good shape, complete with dress suit and medal. As an agent who represented two parties at the same time, he obviously felt responsible for both. He showed signs of nervousness whenever I opened my mouth or made the slightest move since he expected me at any moment to make a social blunder. I really could not blame him for his anxiety, for his future might well depend on the success of this undertaking. If my appearance aroused satisfaction, approval, sympathy, not to say cordiality; if I inspired my hosts with the pleasant feeling that they, in their modernity, had far outstripped the ancient world from which their visitor had dropped in, then his position as an outsider would be materially improved. After the successful completion of this visit he could probably live in hopes of a somewhat warmer attitude and eventually complete acceptance on the part of his contemporaries. With a shade of dissatisfaction I observed that my Tibetan-trained, reincarnated friend treated the group about us with a trifle too much humility and obsequiousness and thus willfully accentuated their superiority over our common former age. This, however, was only one side of his nervous zeal, for he was no less anxious to impress me, the partner of his youth, the companion of countless drinking bouts and heated debates into the early dawn, with the superior qualities of a world into which he had willy-nilly enticed, summoned, and introduced me out of the sleep of death. I was well acquainted with this trait of his character. In many a conversation back in our days his eyes used to beg me to serve his gods, to accept and acknowledge the worth of a dogma, a book, a picture, an author, a composition, that he held high. And so poor B.H. was torn between the interests of the beginning and the end of an eon, the poles of a hundred thousand years.

Io-Rasa, the mother of the Bride, now invited the guests to dinner with a graceful, somewhat formalized gesture. I cannot say how I became aware of the names of the persons present. The connecting links of my experiences sometimes become a little blurred. I did as all the others. We stood in a circle about the piece of sculpture. Festive meals were consumed in a standing position. In this fact too, a thoughtful historian might discern a logical development. The ancient peoples, including the Greeks and Romans, had stretched out on divans in order to do full justice to their epicurean feasts. We, a scant sixteen or seventeen hundred years later, were accustomed to spend a good hour sitting on chairs, preferably with comfortable backs, while dinner was being served. These people stood up. But since they were endowed with a delicate albeit well-made physique, they would simply have collapsed at one of our normal social meals long before the hour was up. For that reason everything had to move along briskly in order not to overtax the fragile limbs of these youngest—and at the same time, most aged—members of the human family. The ancient deadly sin of gluttony had already begun to die out in my day of lettuce-eating reducing fanatics. To recline while eating, then to sit, and finally to stand—those are the stages in the climactic rise of man.

So we stood in a circle about the abstract work of art which appeared to serve the purpose of edifying the eyes and the soul while the body consumed food. (In a moment, however, it will become apparent that my thinking was quite obsolete if I imagined that only the body consumed food, while the eyes and soul, in contrast, required an esthetic stimulus. A definite seating arrangement—if I may use the old-fashioned word in the absence of both table and seats—was observed. It was, moreover, the traditional arrangement. The place of honor at the right of the lady of the house and mother of the Bride, Io-Rasa, was assigned to me, the exotic guest. At my right hand stood a lady of indestructible youthful beauty who was called "the Ancestress" and who was treated with marked respect by the entire assembly. She was the great-grandmother of Io-Fagòr, the lord of the manor and father of the Bride, and she was close to the limits of her life. The long span of life made it possible for five, and even six, generations to live and flourish contemporaneously. For the student of the Bible, who has in mind the tables of genealogy back to the Deluge, this fact will be neither disturbing nor annoying. The reduced population and the longer span of life here and now bore a definite relationship to each other that can easily be checked against the Old Testament. Only one person in the assembly about this nonexistent table was older than the Ancestress at my right: that was the Spokesman, the liveliest and most eloquent man in the company. These bachelors, who actually led a parasitic existence, earned their bed and board by wit, encyclopedic information, ability as raconteurs and entertainers, and by cavalierly ceremonious courtesy. They would have reminded any historian, on the one hand, of the Sycophants of Athens, on the other, of the abbés of the slightly later eighteenth century, all of whom were nothing more than outsiders and parasites of society. But, God knows, I was no historian nor any other kind of highbrow, and I regretted the many hundreds of recitation periods that I had skipped in order to saunter through the ancient streets of our city or to drink beer and play billiards in quaint little saloons. On my tongue burned a thousand questions that I wanted to whisper into B.H.'s ear. But he stood at the opposite side of the circle and was concealed from me by the abstract work of art. I regarded it as worse than inconsiderate to place a spirit summoned from the past between two charming ladies of the present instead of putting his mentor or Vergil helpfully at his side.

Gradually I became accustomed to the phenomenon of longevity. But how these human bodies remained youthful and unchanged even on the threshold of extreme old age is still a mystery to me. The breasts of the Ancestress at my side were as small and firm as those of any young girl. Was this the result of a new and unknown dispensation of nature, unimagined in earlier eras, or of a rigid diet practiced from early youth, or merely of an unspeakably cunning art of cosmetics? I must confess that this agelessness did not please me at all; on the contrary, it frightened me, it oppressed me, it seemed as uncanny as secret sin, the product of monstrous, highly cultivated wantonness, of sternly methodical egotism, that sacrificed genuine, compact life to an unending sham existence. The rosy flesh of the Ancestress exhaled a wonderfully delicate fragrance. Yet I avoided looking at her. I turned and twisted in search of help, trying desperately to catch B.H.'s eye.

I did not succeed, for Io-Rasa, the lady of the house, handed me a goblet of heavy crystal. The meal had begun. It consisted of six courses, each served in a crystal goblet of a different color and shape, the interior of which was not much larger than an egg-cup. It is apparent, therefore, that the meal consisted of a series of beverages, three of them very hot and three ice-cold. The hot ones were pale pink, terra cotta, and bouillon-brown; the ice-cold ones were pistachio-green, saffron-yellow, and creamy white. This liquid menu relieved me of the anxious embarrassment which had plagued me for some time, namely that I would have to manipulate a set of strange eating utensils. But I faithfully watched the mouths of my neighbors. They took tiny, testing sips from the edges of their cups, very pensively, very dreamily, and in silence. And so I supped the proffered liquid in like manner.

With a little imagination I could have deduced even before the meal that the human race had long lost its taste for solid food. The mere thought of feeding on dead flesh must have been more revolting to my new friends than the thought to me of devouring a human steak well seasoned with Worcestershire sauce. Their disgust seemed not, however, to be confined to meat alone, but also to vegetable food, to the consumption of every created variety, including even artificially produced types such as cakes, cookies, tarts, and all other bakery goods. To what extent this radical change in the history of nutrition was induced by the necessity of saving wear and tear on the teeth, I could not ascertain. I was aware, however, that the coefficient of deterioration in the highly advanced stages of nature imperiled first the hair and next the teeth. Nevertheless, the teeth that I saw glistened with enamel. So the dinner guests ate nothing but three salty-soupy and two fruity-clear courses, followed in conclusion by a milky-thickish liquid, and all that in the smallest portions imaginable. I confess that it seemed to me at first a rather unintelligible sort of eating, no, of drinking, no, of sipping or nibbling.

A while ago I used the old-fashioned and affected little word "sup," possibly to express my doubts that the proffered nutritive liquids, consumed practically a drop at a time, could actually sustain a man, even though he were only a portly ghost like me. Soon, however, I was to change my mind. All food that we eat has a twofold significance. In the first place, it provides an experience for our sense of taste; and, in the second place, it satisfies the body's demand for calories. The taste experience is concerned only with the substance of the food; the satisfaction of hunger, however, is concerned with the matter of the same food. There is undoubtedly a philosophical distinction between substance and matter; for matter is nothing but matter, while substance is matter raised to the power of an intrinsic idea. For example, water is matter, the sea is substance. Long ago—I am speaking of the time before my long-forgotten death—the matter served at our tables far exceeded the substance, that is, we had to consume a large quantity of meat in order to enjoy fully the taste experience of a roast loin of venison. This ratio had been miraculously reversed in the course of time. Here a maximum of substance was served us in a minimum of matter. And since we have already mentioned the sea, I must now say that the second course, the reddish terra-cotta soup, served in a heavy crystal, was the sea itself. It is true, indeed, that even back in my time I had tasted many a morsel, swallowed many a drop of the sea, or of the intrinsic idea of the sea. What, after all, are a dozen Whitestable oysters, washed down with the right Chablis, if not the substance of the sea? Or, even more properly limited, are they not the intrinsic idea of the North Sea? Or what of the claws of a Helgoland lobster with their impertinently elusive

sweetness that only manifests itself completely in the aftertaste?
Or the cheap Portuguèses, Oursins, Moules, Violettes, that are
offered for sale all day long on the street corners of southern
French coastal towns? These common, ordinary Portuguèses,
with their fragrance of seaweed and algae, are they not the
personification of the Mediterranean Sea? And what of a Bisque
d'Hommard at Prunier's in Paris? And a bouillabaisse in a fishing
village between Marseilles and Toulon? And a Grancevola, a
sea-spider, in a Venetian tavern, served with a little vinegar and
oil and pepper? It is not only the sea, the Mediterranean Sea, it is
an even more limited substance, the Adriatic. And still, in those
few drops of terra-cotta liquid I enjoyed all these things together
and simultaneously and, what is more, in an imponderable and
entirely indescribable manner. Each of the six courses thus
became a spiritual incorporation, a perceptive insensuation of
significant substances by virtue of their taste. We took a tiny sip,
two or three drops. These drops dissolved on the tongue and
diffused their pleasant warmth or chill, as the case might be,
through the entire organism, down to the tips of the fingers and
toes. Now, moreover, it became clear to me why we stood at the
meal, namely to afford the pleasurable sensation an easier opportunity to communicate itself to the most remote nerve endings.
Simultaneously with the physical pleasure, however, the most
agreeable series of concepts and images flooded the imagination,
so that presently, like all the other participants, I lingered, meditated, dreamed over every single drop of this Mental meal. Back
in my time only the most musical persons had experienced a
similar insensuation at, let us say, an orchestral performance of
Debussy's "La Mer."

In the pauses between courses, probably according to custom,
the Spokesman, the House Sage, and the Permanent Guest
delivered lengthy harangues directed, no doubt, at me, since I
could frequently distinguish the word "Seigneur." But I understood practically nothing that was said. My strange intellectual
capacity to understand and even to speak the language of this
period at the first attempt failed me from time to time and then

my replies were a jumble of German, French, English, Italian, and Spanish, and my forehead was wet with perspiration. At such moments B.H. became ashamed of me and peered out from behind the abstract work of art, prompting me with frantic gestures. But the others always understood me, or at least they pretended to do so, probably because of their fear of the inappropriate and unpleasant. But this understanding was limited, to be sure, as we shall soon see.

In the interval after the third course, merely to make conversation, I turned to Io-Rasa, the lovely mother of the Bride, at my left.

"The fare in your house is delectable. Frankly, I must say, I have never eaten so well in all my life. Of course, it is my first meal in my present, surprising existence, for I'll not even speak of my former life. You have an excellent cuisine, Madame."

B.H.'s head darted out desperately from behind its cover. I had committed a second unpardonable faux pas. How could one speak of food in this most esthetic of all worlds as though one were lounging around in a beer joint reeking of warmed-up goulash! I was frightfully startled. But the lady gave no sign of resentment. A charming smile ran over her lovely features softened by the diffused light, as in the most amiable manner she discharged her social duty of instructing me, the greenhorn, with gentle unobtrusiveness.

"We have no cuisine of our own, Seigneur. The recipes, that have been in the possession of our family for hundreds of years and that cannot be transferred to any other family without a notarial seal, are centrally prepared."

Aha, there it was again, that intriguing word "centrally" I thought, and raised my voice to ask, "Is it perhaps the Worker, Madame, who at the same time acts as caterer?"

"What do you know about the Worker, Seigneur?" asked Io-Rasa with some astonishment. "You are very well informed."

"Not sufficiently, Madame, not sufficiently by far," I rejoined. "But I suspect something very great and I know that he is the only one to wear a full beard."

"That's not all," she said, "and it's not quite exact either. There are a few other persons who wear the full beard."

All conversation about us ceased. Even without B.H.'s reproving glance I should have known that it was not good taste to direct several questions in succession to a lady. But my curiosity and the interest that the concept of "the Worker" aroused in me were too strong.

"Is the Worker only a man or is he also an object?" I asked, and I was ashamed of the question that reminded me of some silly parlor game.

But before Io-Rasa, the mother of the Bride, could answer my unseemly question, we were interrupted by a little incident that attracted the attention of the company. A dog ran into the room. It was a real honest-to-goodness dog, a dog with four paws, tan hide, big, hairy, hanging ears, and a longish muzzle. Slim, medium-sized, and extraordinarily vivacious as he was, I could not determine his breed. But he seemed to be a more concentrated epitome of dogdom than all the dogs of my time that had so often been the products of exaggerated inbreeding. I have used the word "dog." But what had become of the dog in a hundred thousand years of ever more intimate contact with man and human care? His physical form, hide, muzzle, ears, paws, had remained entirely doggish. But through the mournful and beast-bound foundation of this doggishness there leered, whined, sniffed, fawned, a sort of human likeness, or rather of humanishness. It was obvious in every approaching or receding bound, in the hesitation or decision of his motions, but most of all in his attentive, his calculating, his greedily appraising look. I could scarcely believe my eyes. I believed my ears even less when the dog began to speak. It was a barking, but a hundred times more modulated than the barking I knew. And out of it there developed quite naturally a vocabulary that may have been limited but was adequate for the expression of the dog's thought processes.

"Why, the dog is speaking," I blurted.

Everybody looked at me in surprise. So far I had felt equal to my adventure, in spite of my stiff-bosomed shirt and white tie.

Now my fine-featured friends seemed to think: "What's gotten into him? The dog is speaking! Didn't dogs always speak? Can there have been a time when they didn't speak?" Oh, you idiot, I said to myself, of course dogs have always spoken. The fact that they now speak a refined language lies in the law of evolution and isn't astonishing at all. When will my nerves finally become calm enough so that I won't constantly lay myself wide open?

Meanwhile the animal jumped up alternately on Io-Fagòr and Io-Rasa. With exuberant dog stammering he fawned on his master and mistress, babbling his words with the crafty and venal ingenuousness of a child motion-picture star. It was really funny; this morally corrupt animal spoke in an affected jargon. He barked in a sort of long drawn-out, bantering accent.

"Howdy, Mammy, howdy, Pappy, so there you are. Where've you been? How's about something for Sur? Today's the first wedding dinner, so there must be something for Sur. Some of the green stuff, please, the pistachio-green stuff. Io-La sent Sur upstairs. Who all is here? How's about letting Sur chase the ball around the fountain? Pretty please! What a life, what a life! You know Sur has to have his run. Haha, hmhm!"

Suddenly the dog sensed that things weren't exactly as they should be. He interrupted his baby talk and his pretentious barking (he was a good, round fifty-two years old, they told me). He began to quiver from head to foot, laid his ears back, pinched his tail between his legs, and, looking at me in horror, he uttered a long, singing whine. Well, I thought, at last you are noticing something. Your good old ancestors were less finished actors and speakers than you, but their primitive instinct would have spotted a ghost at once, a mile away at least, no matter whether it appeared in a boiled shirt or in the negligee of a grave shroud.

In whining tones the dog panted, "Mammy, Pappy, what's all this, what're you doing to Sur again? That fellow isn't s'posed to exist at all! That fellow doesn't exist! He doesn't b'long here with us. Let me out!"

In spite of his articulate words genuine animal terror now engulfed his shrewd humanishness. But I, dismayed at my situation and disgusted with the toadying manner as well as with the cowardice of the dog, grumbled to myself, "Nobody needs to be scared of me, and besides I'm not really dead at all. I'm breathing and eating, as you can see, my dear dog."

The master of the house, Io-Fagòr, even more embarrassed than I, made a quick end to the interlude. "Get out of here, Sur! Don't whine at our guest! Out into the garden, you fool, and be sure to get back on time."

Sur vanished without another word. No matter how human his conduct, his name was only Sur. The prepositive Io, which means I and thus implies immortality, was not accorded to him in spite of progress and pampering.

"Pray, forgive Sur's bad manners," Io-Fagòr turned to me. "After all, there are limits to the educability of dogs, even of intellectually and morally superior specimens. But certain ones of our democrats will not admit that. They are bitter because there are differences between the rights of men and of dogs. I need mention only the famous publication entitled 'The Accident of Being Born a Dog and the Obligation of Human Society to Make Amends to the Creature So Afflicted.'"

"That is certainly going too far," I managed to begin. And then a social accident happened to me that brought me, and as a result also B.H., into the most embarrassing situation. I was on the point of confessing to the master of the house in unvarnished terms my definite impression and honest opinion regarding the dog Sur.

"Your dog, my dear sir, is a thoroughly disreputable character." But suddenly I was no longer capable of speaking the language of this age in which I was unexpectedly a visitor. While only a brief moment earlier I had been conversing with these charming ladies and gentlemen of advanced age in their own idiom as unself-consciously as though it had been my mother tongue, now I suddenly could not force a single syllable of this idiom through my lips nor could I comprehend a syllable of it.

It was a horrifying feeling of impotence, of which I still retain a physical memory. My heart beat in my throat, and I thought I would suffocate.

"Votre chien," I stammered in French, "a un très mauvais caractère." The man looked at me, nonplused and uncomprehending. No one replied. I tried it in Italian: "Questo cane a un multo brutto caráttere."

The general embarrassment grew. Mechanically I muttered the sentence in a few other languages that I had picked up in the course of my long exile. It must have sounded like a Berlitz school: "Dieser Hund hat einen ganz schlechten Charakter—Ten pies ma bardzo marny charakter."

I was aware that Io-Rasa and Io-Fagòr were trying to help me over the situation with cheerful words. It sounded like Aztecan or Zapotecan: "Titl bitja, tapotla clan, potoltuk quel queme misesopono."

Well, now I was in a fix. It was nothing but saccharine twittering. If you look at a language merely from the outside, as at the front of a house, you have no idea of the inhabitants. Nor is there any difference, in the matter of language, between astronomical advancement or primordial primitivity.

"For heaven's sake, help me, B.H.," I groaned.

The face of my friend, who now emerged almost menacingly from behind the piece of sculpture, was very pale. He pressed his hand against his temple as though to emphasize the headache that I, his disgrace personified, had caused him through my conduct.

"Calm down, F.W.," he whispered sharply, "and use a little psychology, if you please. In the Monolingual language of this age offensive things that one importunately regards as truthful and candid cannot be publicly uttered."

Then it seemed as if my ears and throat suddenly opened again. Unexpectedly and unself-consciously I again became master of the current language, and with a polite bow I turned to the master of the house, Io-Fagòr.

"Your dog is very handsome and very intelligent," I said. It

came out smooth as oil, and the lie did not occasion me the
slightest pang of remorse, nor did I feel the least need of expressing what I really thought. Moreover, I recognized with an
inspired flash that in this day and age it was not at all necessary
to express one's thoughts, since up to a certain point everyone
knew them anyhow. To my word of praise I added the following question, "What breed is your dog Sur? I couldn't quite make
it out."

A new wave of astonishment went around. The Permanent
Guest asked uncertainly, "What do you mean by 'what breed,'
Seigneur? Isn't a dog a dog? There is only one kind of dog."

At this very point in the conversation I began to distinguish
the individual faces. Out of the pale background of general
beauty and youthfulness there emerged, visible to my eye for the
first time, characteristic traits and distinctions. The Permanent
Guest, for example, had a long nose and deeper hollows in his
cheeks than the others. Furthermore his forehead almost disappeared under the silver headdress of iridescent material. He
reminded me of the bust of a baroque prince of the Hapsburg or
Bourbon line with a powdered wig. I became so engrossed in
my study of the faces that I forgot to answer. B.H. therefore
threw in a remark in order to keep the conversation from lagging
and in order to help me out.

"My friend F.W.," he said, "was familiar with several breeds
and varieties of dogs in his day."

And with that he gave me an encouraging wink, inviting me to
dilate entertainingly upon this harmless topic that could hardly
get anyone into trouble.

But since I felt that I was being made unpleasantly conspicuous by B.H.'s encouragement, I remained silent and devoted
myself to a further differentiating contemplation of the faces.
Then the House Sage insinuated himself into the conversation;
his face was somewhat plumper than the others, with a trace of
a double chin. He impressed me as a vain and somewhat effemi-
nate individual who was dominated by the Spokesman and as a
superfluous figure of secondary importance in the household.

"In the folkloristic section of our Sephirodrome," he began rapidly, as though apprehensive that he might not be permitted to finish his sentence without interruption, "there are several dissertations that deal with a myth concerning five or six different varieties of dogs, each of which is said to have served a different purpose; one for the killing of animals, another for the guiding of the blind, a third for the guarding of little children, a fourth for the pursuit of criminals, and a fifth for the performance of certain magic rites connected with the goddess Hecate."

He was quite right to be apprehensive about his sentence, for the Spokesman cut him off with a curt gesture. But now I intervened.

"It would be a mistake to regard the subject of these dissertations in the Sephirodrome as a myth. You see, I have the audacity to use the word 'Sephirodrome' without even knowing what it means. No, that story about the breeds of dogs is by no means a myth but historical reality." And I began to enumerate: "Greyhounds and St. Bernards and chows and little Pekingese and wolf hounds and mastiffs and Dobermanns and terriers——" B.H. indicated by a gesture that it was enough. But now the Spokesman bowed in my direction.

"To you, Seigneur," he said, "who were reared in a colorful, magic world teeming with a variety of creatures, our modern world must seem woefully impoverished."

"Not impoverished," I replied with equal politeness, for I knew by this time that every word one spoke had to be agreeable. "Not impoverished, merely simplified. Does not life's ascent progress from the egoless, crawling throng to the unique personality; from the infinitely repetitive stereotype to the rarity; from antlike socialism to serene isolation? In this regard, ladies and gentlemen, your world seems to have risen far above ours, even though it may have lost its colorfulness and variety under your glaring and eternally cloudless skies. Is it not characteristic of all creative activity to produce at the outset in unbridled abundance? And at its zenith to practice critical selectivity and to incline toward genteel simplicity and almost holy sterility?

In my day we called that progression toward the classical and monumental."

B.H.'s eye caught me up short. My philosophy of culture seemed to have overstepped the bounds again. The words "holy sterility" stood out like an ink blot on a nice, clean birthday letter.

"My friend has always inclined toward generalities," said B.H. with a conciliatory smile in all directions. "That has been his failing as long as I've known him."

The master of the household, Io-Fagòr, however, lowered his head. My ability to distinguish faces had now developed to the extent that I was quite aware that this man was not only the most eminent but also the most consequential in the company. His face seemed to me paler and more masculine than those of the others. (The smoothness of the skin and the absence of all signs of shaving on the men's faces had at first impressed me unfavorably.) In his deep voice Io-Fagòr commented on my words.

"I understand Seigneur very well. He is quite right to praise our attainments. We could be well content with the conditions under our glaring and eternally cloudless skies, if only nature could be persuaded to grant these conditions a conservative permanence. But nature always has secret designs. And as far as man is concerned, our best families are not all equal to their task. Our lazy domestic life, our inactive, contemplative calm, our freedom from all compulsion, our cheerful, idle play— all these gifts that God has given us after the toil and trouble of well-nigh endless dark ages and that we may enjoy without pangs of conscience, all these things are no longer regarded as pleasures by our children."

And, turning with a deep bow to the Ancestress whose archaically stylized silver tresses curled about her flawless neck, he concluded, "Your generation, great-grandmother, reached the absolute pinnacle, for it knew no doubts."

The Ancestress smiled, her white teeth flashing and her eyes bright though they lay deep in their sockets. I don't know why

I suddenly experienced a slight shock at the sight of this beautiful face. I may have suspected the unbounded cynicism which the words of the Ancestress revealed or perhaps concealed. "Yes, what we've had, we've had."

My recent words seemed to have distressed the lord of the manor. It was up to me to correct my mistake. "Little as I have seen of your world with my own eyes," I began, "still I have a very fair idea of the tremendous strides you have made in the direction of a well-regulated existence. You have succeeded in trebling the span of human life and, what's infinitely more important, you have succeeded in eliminating the ugly deterioration of old age. You have, as far as I can see, realized a dream that is as old as mankind itself. The fountain of youth of the oldest myths and legends has become a reality. All of you, like the gods of Greece, are eternally young and eternally beautiful. I mention these gods particularly because it gives me a homely feeling to hear you mingle Greek words with your speech. But perhaps you don't know anything about the origin of these words. Moreover, you have solved the one problem that seemed the most hopeless in my day. Work is no longer a curse borne by a world of slaves for the advantage of a few profiteering politicians. And along with this curse you have also abolished the curse of technology that robbed slaves and profiteers alike of their souls by inundating them with mass-products, mass-pleasures, mass-art, mass-futility, and mass-murder. Everything in your world runs so incredibly smoothly. A delectable banquet, consisting of the most concentrated substances, the attar of roses of nutritive enjoyment, so to speak, is prepared centrally but on the basis of highly personalized recipes handed down by centuries of patrician generations. You travel by the Mental manner, moving your destination toward you by means of a toy, a procedure that does not involve the slightest cost and consumes no steam, no oil, no electricity or any other sort of power. You have unified the globe. There are no more races and nations, but only a single human family. There are no more languages either, but only a single language, the Monolingua, which is no artificial Esperanto but an organic, euphonious speech, and I must ask your indulgence for the harsh accent with which my primitive tongue is afflicted. Furthermore, there is no longer any distinction between city and country, the distinction between the scenically beautiful wilderness where the untutored peasant or mountaineer eked out a frugal existence and the overcrowded city, the wicked and infectious megalopolis where the proletarianized millions had neither space nor time. Fulfilling the social destiny of mankind, you have transformed the earth into a universal city, a Panopolis—forgive an old humanist for a classical pun—Pan and Panis, universal city and bread city. The necessities of life are delivered to your houses in the lightest, the most refined, the most enjoyable form, and all that without any pipes or hydraulic installations, the mere thought of which would spoil one's appetite. I confess that in my day and age I never dreamed that all this could ever be attained."

The meal seemed to be at an end. I had sipped the sweet, ice-cold, creamy decoction too fast, and I was beginning to feel a little high in a curious manner that accentuated my ego and made me talk too much and without any timidity. I presume I didn't make too good an impression. Throughout my speech Io-Fagòr kept his head lowered; I noted casually that his headdress was still of gold. He did not seem to agree with me. For that reason, perhaps, the Spokesman now tried to change the subject.

"Seigneur," he said, "you have just paid some very agreeable compliments to our present day, and the satisfaction of a kind and intelligent guest always pleases the hosts. We do not wish to tax the strength of our kind and intelligent guest too greatly, especially since he has come from far away to remain with us, we trust, for a good long time. But perhaps, Seigneur, you would favor us with a little causerie, a few well-chosen remarks, a few reminiscences of the life you left some eras ago, of the things that seem to you memorably different from our present life."

"Oh, but that would lead too far afield, Monsieur," I replied apprehensively.

"You need not speak in generalities in your few well-chosen

remarks, Seigneur," the Spokesman encouraged me. "Just speak in personal, purely personal terms."

The words "personal, purely personal" rang hypnotically in my ears. I vaguely felt a reclining chair with hard upholstery being pushed under me, and I dropped into it with relaxed muscles. The gentlemen and ladies formed an intimate circle about me. With astonishment I saw the vague outlines of the iridescent headdresses of gold and silver, the chastely blurred flesh color of the naked bodies under the diaphanous veils. My eyes sought out B.H. He smiled and seemed to be quite satisfied with me. Then I closed my eyes. At once the present time of a strange world of the future vanished and gave way to the past of a homely world of the present, a world which had, so to speak, stopped like a clock at the moment of my death. About the former, the present world of the future, I had just managed to wax flatteringly eloquent; to make a few well-chosen remarks, a little causerie, as the Spokesman called it, about the latter, the past world of the present, was far more difficult. I probably disappointed the cool, volatile spirit of the Spokesman who knew how to wrap up every problem in a few well-chosen remarks, since speaking was his household chore. I did not succeed in producing any striking aphorisms or noteworthy adages, but only vague circumlocutions, parables, and examples. After all, I was only a primitive man.

"I am now imagining, Messieurs-Dames," I began without opening my eyes, "that I am just twelve years old. It is the middle of July, the school year is over, last Saturday the report cards were distributed, and we have gone out to the country, the whole family, parents and children. . . . Ten weeks of vacation lie before me—an eternity of laziness, of curiosity, of physical pleasure and spiritual happiness: swimming in the lake, sailing, wild games with other boys, croquet tournaments, drives, outings, mountain climbing, picnics, unusual meals in quaint inns, garden parties, fireworks, rest on broad mountain meadows, sleep in forest clearings fragrant with cyclamen and spicy with the pine needles of

countless dead autumns. . . . Oh, how many adventures I feel
await me! Adventures. . . . It is still the fifteenth of July. . . .
Ladies and gentlemen, why does the twelve-year-old, staring out
of a dormer-window at the eternal, shadowy mountains, suddenly realize that one day it will not be the fifteenth of July but
the fifteenth of September and that all the adventures of happiness and freedom that now lie before him will then lie behind?
And how was it that at the very instant this thought came to him
it had really happened and the fifteenth of September was
actually there? . . . Do you understand me . . . do you understand me . . . ?"

I did not know whether they understood me. No answer broke
the darkness before my eyes. I tried to explain by means of
another example. "Back in our world we had a wonderful institution called opera. You've probably never heard anything about
it . . . opera. . . . Please help me out, B.H."

"Sympaian," B.H. translated.

"Sympaian," a few voices repeated in chorus, indicating that
the matter was not entirely strange.

"Sympaian or opera, it makes no difference," I heard myself
say from behind black veils. "I was more than an enthusiast; I
was a fanatic about the opera. The tenor has finished his aria.
In a moment the expansive melody of Amneris will follow, 'Quale
insolita givia,' and then the breathless 'Forse l'arcano amore
scoprì che m'arde in core.' And finally, balanced on the swaying
and shifting prop of a syncopated soft flourish of a single French
horn and a little, pianopianissimo roll of the kettledrum, there
blooms forth the intoxicating, the deliriant trio, crowned by the
sadly proud, vaulting notes of the soprano, 'Ah! no, sulla mia
patria non geme il cor.' All that I know, measure by measure; all
that I await, I look forward to it with longing; all that I want to
drink in once more and perpetuate in my soul. But at the
moment when the melody is about to unfold, the anguishing
thought takes hold of me that in an instant it will be over and
gone; and in my heart it is already gone, even before the accom-

paniment of the orchestra has begun. . . . Do you understand me . . . do you understand me . . . ?"

Continued silence. I still did not open my eyes.

"My time, Messieurs-Dames, was very short, measured by yours. It resembled in some respects the traditional melodies of our ancestors, whose beginnings enclosed their ends and whose endings enclosed their beginnings; while their notes still vibrated, they had already expired, for we carried them as sweet memories in our hearts, 'O terra addio, addio valle di pianti.' Time burned from both ends toward the middle, and the middle was my exposed and unprotected ego. At thirty years I looked forward to the fortieth, at forty to the fiftieth year—I, the most thoughtless, the most unprincipled sinner of my acquaintance. I always thought back or ahead, my watch never showed the present. And when it was all over, it had scarcely begun, and yet it had been going on forever. Do you understand me?"

I opened my eyes. The lovely Ancestress was approaching me. I tried to jump up. With her alabaster hand that looked cold as ice, she motioned me to remain seated.

"I understand, Seigneur," she said in her cynically vibrant contralto voice, "I understand that you clung passionately to life back in the beginnings of mankind."

And I, for my person, replied truthfully: "I often clung passionately to life, Madame, and as often passionately wished myself out of it. I assume that even today you know what it means to waken in the dawn to the sudden realization of the loss of a loved one, of a mother, a child . . . to waken as a condemned prisoner . . . to waken in a trench at four o'clock in the morning before the attack. We were always imperiled, always menaced by the loss and by the final fate of our own ego and of those nearest to us."

The "final fate" was a euphemism. I had already reached the point where I could not possibly have used the bare word "death."

Then the Permanent Guest, he of the characteristic baroque head, spoke: "Well, things have certainly changed in our time, for we set out on our final journey voluntarily and on foot."

I stood up and bowed. "Not I, sir, but you, have given the explanation. You are right. The difference lies wholly in the spontaneity and predetermination of the final eliminating crisis. Our nerves were terrorized day and night by the expectation of the unexpected. Every breath of our life was imperiled. Meanwhile mankind has performed its greatest act: you have tamed time, Messieurs-Dames. You are imperiled neither from without nor from within."

"We are imperiled," said Io-Fagòr after a significant pause. Understanding glances passed from one to the other. The ivory tint of their faces seemed to have become a shade bluer.

"We are imperiled, Seigneur," the father of the Bride continued, "more cruelly and more horribly than you ever were."

"Do not overestimate the contrast between the generations," I sought to calm him, mindful of the words he had spoken a while ago about the young people of the period. "At times the natural antagonism of children toward their parents becomes more acute. That is not a serious menace but a form of natural development. Back in my day we had a philosopher by the name of Hegel, whose works were very hard to read. Nevertheless, his theory of historical dialectics became a commonplace. A thesis produces an antithesis; the pendulum must swing from one extreme to the other, just to keep things moving."

"It is not a matter of antagonism between children and parents at all," rejoined Io-Fagòr, shaking his golden head.

"Could it be that you are threatened by a calamity of nature?" I insisted, prompted by inordinate curiosity. "Surely you possess the means to protect yourselves against glaciation or inundation."

"Certainly we possess those means," nodded the House Sage, "but the calamity that we fear is of an entirely different character."

I tried to catch B.H.'s eye. He avoided me.

"Doesn't he know anything about it?" asked the master of the household.

"No, not yet," replied B.H.

* * * * *
* * *
*

THE MEAL WAS ENDED. The circle about the abstract but disturbingly expressive work of art had broken up in obedience to a smile and a slight nod of the hostess, Io-Rasa. The fine-featured and well-formed men and women divided into two distinctly separate groups. It reminded me of the English custom, and I had the casual notion that many tens of thousands of years ago the world must have been unified and dominated by the Anglo-Saxons and that this puritanical after-dinner habit had been preserved from that time to the most remote future. Moreover it occurred to me that it was a prudish and almost hypocritical custom that had lost its cogent meaning in view of the absent, or at least restrained, emotions of the sexes.

Doors opened noiselessly and revealed three or four adjoining rooms, each of which was suffused with warm, variously colored light. This polychromatic illumination actually seemed to have replaced the dressmaker's art in the new world; for, as the handsome figures of my new associates moved gracefully from one chamber to another, they appeared to be clothed in costumes of new designs and colors, depending upon the source of light. At this point I must inject a personal comment into my account. My astigmatic eyes had condemned me to wear glasses during my whole life. After my decease, however, these seemed to have been taken from me. As a result my features perhaps looked a bit more attractive, but I was constantly embarrassed, and my task was made much more difficult since I saw everything only in blurred contours and sometimes only in vague outlines. There is a simple moral to be drawn from this circumstance: "Don't take the spectacles from the noses of your dear departed, for you never can tell. . . ." In this respect the Egyptians and other ancient peoples were much more prudent. They equipped their dead with a complete and well-selected outfit which put to shame even that of a wealthy bride. I would have been satisfied with a spare shirt, two collars, two handkerchiefs, and, most of all, my glasses.

Just as there had been no visible leftovers from the meal, so I was also unaware of any digestive aftereffects. I felt neither satiation nor unappeased appetite, nothing but a slight, cheerful warmth. Of course, I hadn't stuffed myself full of matter as I used to do in my good days (though stuffing had its points, too); I had only consumed substance, or perhaps only the idea of substance, from a tiny hollow of heavy crystal. I must direct the reader's attention to the fact—which probably did not escape him anyhow—that neither the preparation nor the serving of this meal required any domestic help, nor did I see any. Each little goblet of soup or beverage was passed to me by the hand of Io-Rasa in person. How it got there, and how the remaining goblets got into the hands of the other guests, is more than I can say. Blame it on my deplorable astigmatism. It occurred to me more than once that the next time a deceased person is sent out to make a report of this kind, an individual without any physical defects should be selected.

The thing that surprised me most was the fact that I did not feel the slightest craving for tobacco or alcohol. I neither groped in my pocket for a package of cigarettes nor did I look around for a glass of cognac. Could a hundred thousand years of abstinence have sufficed to wean me from these vices? But even if the weaning period had been too short, my ingrained craving could not have been satisfied. For the people in the new world I was visiting neither smoked nor drank. Along with all passions mankind seemed to have conquered its desire for stimulating poisons, the residue of Dionysiac self-destruction of which we were so foolishly proud in our youth that we vied in nightly excesses. How I used to despise the virtuous youths who couldn't stand much drink and who crawled into bed at eleven o'clock!

And how I admired the heroic figures who staggered from night-club to nightclub until early dawn with ruddy faces and bleary eyes! Incidentally we were not the only ones who revered the drinker and drinking: our near contemporary Plato—only some two thousand years before us—endowed his intellectual hero Socrates at the age of seventy with the ability to drink all comers under the table and still sneak out into the dawn with a fair show of sobriety. Well, Plato and we were wrong, and these people here were right. Their eternal youth proved it. Or were they really right?

At the first opportunity I made my way to B.H. and, in whispers, demanded information. "You see?" I grumbled. "Everybody is surprised that I don't know anything about the most important things. They simply can't understand why you leave me in ignorance. Don't be so reserved—or so jealous."

He looked furtively around and then led me into one of the smallest of the adjoining rooms, where we could expect to be undisturbed. But before we reached this surprisingly dark little chamber, I was addressed and drawn into polite conversation by several of the gentlemen. It was the emptiest conversation imaginable. I suppose a materialized spirit can't expect any other treatment. At the same time I must confess that everyone ignored my unusual circumstances in the most tactful manner, and no one gave any indication either by word or sign that I didn't belong here but had merely been summoned from the fantastic diversity of the primitive wilderness to the great simplicity of genuine culture. With unalloyed courtesy they put me at my ease and kept me from feeling too inferior.

Finally B.H. and I sat in the amber darkness of the little room that seemed expressly intended for private conversations. I, in my old dress coat, and he, in the copied uniform of a lieutenant in the First World War, formed an island, a fossil remain of the twentieth century, in an immeasurably advanced period. That is almost more than a metaphor, for the two of us from the most remote past were lodged in the amber of the present like two extinct insects. A deep calm was about us, for in this day and age no one ever raised his voice; no rough guttural, no cackling laughter, no shrill confusion, disturbed the peace. Even the most animated conversation of a large company seemed to take place behind vocal veils. Why, incidentally, my reincarnated friend wore wrapped puttees and an old military blouse, was something that I forgot to ask although I repeatedly made up my mind to do so. I must confess I felt indescribably relaxed, even exhausted, as I sat there alone with my old friend B.H. No one who has not experienced it—and who but I have?—can conceive the strain on body and soul of a sojourn in an era as remote and alien as this.

"Well, now, what is this thing that I don't know and that you are keeping from me?" I asked, and at the same time suppressed a spasmodic yawn of exhaustion.

"The Jungle," B.H. replied laconically and obscurely.

"The Jungle? What do you mean by——"

"Probably something different than you would mean," he interrupted me, and an expression of utter loathing came over his features. "I mean swinish hubbub. I mean deafening noise of merry-go-rounds and calliopes. And besides that they keep roosters and clucking hens."

"Why in the devil shouldn't they keep roosters and clucking hens?"

"Well, I suppose I'll have to translate it for you. What would you have thought, back in your day, of a farm where they raised vultures or murderous condors as domestic animals?"

After a little more fencing I finally learned the following:

Up to a few generations ago the entire planet, with the exception of some dead or uninhabitable spots and of the oceans that had shrunk considerably in size, had been subject to the prevailing morality; moreover, it had been completely covered with the gray, elastic carpet of sod that I had noticed on my arrival in this era. For some time, however, this picture had undergone changes. Chiefly "at the outskirts" of civilization something had broken out that was described to me in obscure terms filled with loathing, such as "Jungle" or "swinish hubbub." At first I couldn't get a clear idea of what was meant, but presently I understood that this mysterious affair was not only a matter of vegetative abnormality but that it also involved a human aberration. The vegetative irregularity appeared, however, to have been the cause and incentive for the later unfortunate developments. In a manner that human science could neither explain nor prevent, swamps had formed at various places on the earth's surface, and these had soon changed into a blossoming wilderness, into emerald-green oases, with mountainlike elevations, fragrant valleys, lakes, brooks, rivers, and tall trees. In spite of themselves, the eyes of observers were attracted to these dangerous islands which loomed blue on the horizon.

"And what next?" I asked in surprise, when everything was clear up to this point. "You act as if these charming variations in your dull prairies were as loathsome as smallpox and leprosy."

"They are smallpox and leprosy," B.H. reproved me. "Don't you know that the very worst thing in this world is backsliding and that the Jungle is a temptation to backslide?"

In abrupt, hasty words I learned that these islands were constantly on the increase and that one of these Jungles existed even here in the vicinity of California; that abominable flora and fauna had come into being—or rather, had come back into being—there; and finally, horrible to contemplate, that a new race of men had sprung up, conceived and born of deserters and delinquents who had been unable to resist the temptation to backslide. Apelike creatures had developed there, dwarfs or giants, varying from the noble norm that mankind had attained; savages, that littered their young like cats and carried them about as long; in short, a swinish hubbub.

"It ought to be a simple matter for your government to clean up these Rousseauist retreats from culture." I shrugged. "Don't you have the necessary death-rays to erase these Jungles in a jiffy, along with the roosters and clucking hens?"

He made a horrified gesture and stared at me with a pale face. "What are you saying? Don't you know that we are incapable of —of eliminating any living creature?"

At the last moment he had succeeded in avoiding the word "killing."

At this point we were interrupted. The Spokesman, the entertaining and considerate abbé of the household, stood in the doorway of the little parlor, and his silver headdress trembled a little as he apologetically invited us into the drawing room. There Io-Rasa, the lovely mother of the Bride, advanced toward us. I was annoyed because, in the first place, I should have liked to stay in our amber shelter a little longer and, in the second place, my curiosity had been sufficiently aroused so that I wanted to know more at once. Next to the Worker, the Jungle worried me most. I hoped that my sojourn in this world would be long enough so that I could at least get a look at this Jungle, where man, with the kind assistance of nature, had once again managed to cast off the burden of his good manners. Since I had never been particularly attracted to well-bred people, I anticipated that the Jungle would not inspire me with sufficient loathing. The charming mother of the Bride dispelled my absent-mindedness with a smile.

"Our children," she whispered, "are very anxious to speak with you, Seigneur. After all, the children are the most important people on these wedding-days, and your gracious appearance, for which we can't thank you enough, is intended as a gift for Io-Do and Io-La."

The lady pointed to a small and obviously timid man in a silver headdress. He was Io-Solip, the father of the Bridegroom.

"My dear in-law here," Io-Rasa went on, "will have the rare honor of conducting you first to his son, Io-Do. You will find him not only a charming young man but also an antiquarian and a diligent student of history."

B.H. and I followed the slender and timid Io-Solip, who walked ahead of us with a protective gesture as though he wanted to guard me against slipping on the unfamiliar terrain. Later I learned that the Grand Bishop had just announced his impending visit. Since the families concerned were very prominent, the prelate himself was to officiate at the wedding two

days later. The lady of the house had cleverly removed me from
the reception rooms. For the Church, now as in the past and at
all times, rejected every form of occult activity as a desecration
of true mystic endeavor and as illicit tampering with the forbidden. Since this activity, however, had recently spread alarmingly
over the entire globe and had, moreover, become so highly developed as to produce amazing results—as, for example, myself—
the Church, according to its age-old custom, winked at the practice without receding an inch from its position. It would, however, have been asking too much of a Grand Bishop to expect
him to exchange social amenities with an occult phenomenon,
with a poor soul in a boiled shirt and white tie, who should
have been elsewhere, presumably in purgatory, and who probably had only a short leave of absence from there.

The Sixth Chapter

WHEREIN I AM RECEIVED BY THE BRIDE-
GROOM, AM INTERROGATED CONCERNING
THE LIFE OF ANTIQUE WARRIORS AND
SOLDIERS, AND AM SHOWN THE MONU-
MENT OF THE LAST WAR OF THE PLANET.

As WE FOLLOWED the gentle and attentive father of the
Bridegroom, cherubic little Io-Solip, through a high,
vaulted corridor bathed in the dim glow of the invisible
moon, I distinctly heard the unmistakable ivory click and the
rolling of billiard balls.

"What is that, what is that?" I asked, standing still.

"What does it sound like?" B.H. reproved me as he impatiently
tugged at my sleeve.

Really and truly, in the anteroom adjoining the Bridegroom's
bedchamber stood a billiard table on four solid, short, thick
shanks, and covered with green felt, just like in the good old
days. I don't know why I was so deeply moved at the sight of
this object, which even back in the time of my youth had always
impressed me as something archaic, something inherited from
our ancestors. Ever so many valuable instruments of our civilization had vanished between the time of my last and first breath.
I saw, for example, not a single piano or any other musical
instrument, not even a mechanical one, no gramophone, no radio.
The billiard table alone, after a tiresome infancy in dingy pool-
rooms, chilly country houses, and damp resort hotels, had de-

78

veloped an almost phenomenal longevity. Here it stood, and it seemed to me that B.H. and I must be personally acquainted with it. But I didn't dare open my mouth.

The Bridegroom, Io-Do, appeared to have retired from the billiard table to his bedroom when he heard our approaching steps, for it was inappropriate for a young man in the days before his wedding to interrupt the period of contemplation and preparation by banal activities or games. The illumination of the room was again different from that in the reception rooms and the agreeable twilight in the corridor. (The more personal and the more intimate the purpose of a room, the deeper it lay buried in the bowels of the earth, quite the reverse of the custom of a period that located its bedrooms on the upper floors. The more private these people wished to be, the farther they withdrew.) In my days some psychiatrists and hyperingenious artists had dreamed of using various mixtures or color harmonies of artificial light in conjunction with musical sounds to affect the sensibilities of an overrefined or neurotic audience. Here these snobbish dreams had become sensible reality. Again because of their dread of the sun, my new contemporaries lived only by artificial light in their houses. Their estrangement from nature was complete. At the same time, however, I must repeat, it was necessary. The shrinking of the oceans and the resulting reduction of cloud formation was, as we know, responsible for an eternally vacant blue sky. The arid atmosphere offered scarcely any resistance to the ultraviolet rays of the sun. An entire day spent outdoors would have overtaxed the strength of a Goliath. What could be more agreeable, therefore, than a house in the bowels of the earth! It was more splendid, more important, more welcome, than four sheltering walls during a snowstorm in the old days. And equally satisfying and splendid and welcome was the artificial light, manipulated with the greatest ingenuity by human imagination. It reflected all nuances that nature seemed to have forgotten long ago, from the wind-whipped pallor of a March morning to the druidic moonlight of a silvery June night; from the lilac snow-whiteness of an undulating ski-course to the gold-saturated deep green of the forest. And the constantly renewed air, which I have so far forgotten to mention, was equally good —air as thin as that of mountain peaks and as loaded with iodine and salt as that of the stormy sea. It was an ideal sort of domestic existence. Like a chambered nautilus, the house protectively sealed off its dwellers against the cosmos. At the same time, it magically reproduced all moods of the cosmos in its narrow interior.

Father Io-Solip had opened the door. We followed him into his son's apartment. Io-Do, the Bridegroom, reclined properly on a low, square contraption which we might have described as a couch back in my time. He wore no wig, as I have wrongly designated the headdresses of my new contemporaries, but a sort of golden helmet. Furthermore, he was not naked, but enveloped in opaque, ·black, veil-like material. Black was the festive color for men, just as it had been in our day. B.H. looked at me. Without a doubt he was trying to gauge the impression that this handsome young man was making on me. In the few hours I had now spent in this new world I had not only learned to differentiate between human faces, but I had also developed a very sharp instinct for the interpretation of features. I could have given B.H. a concise answer in a few words: "A spoiled son of the wealthy class."

Of course, the word "wealthy" would have been nonsense. Where everyone had everything, no one was wealthy. Some time later I learned the first principle of legal philosophy concerning property rights. It established complete parity between the concept of the body as loaned property and the dwelling to which every human couple was definitely entitled. But actual practice went even farther than legal theory. It provided that dwellings should, if possible, be handed down from one generation of a family to the next, just as physical characteristics of parents are transmitted to children. Whenever a wedding took place, the young couple took over the house of the bride's parents on the following day. For the latter another house was generally made ready some time previously. With five or six generations living simultaneously, one of the many houses belonging to the clan in either the male or female line had ordinarily been vacated in the the meantime. There were usually more vacant houses than young couples who were unable to marry because the parents of the bride had no house into which they could move. Moreover, the local communities took care to maintain a proper ratio between population and available houses by appropriate planning and construction. Of course, this was a matter of simple arithmetic, since people showed almost no inclination to move about and to change their place of residence. And why should they, when it was possible to travel from one end of the world to the other by merely jiggling a few colored globules into the proper little holes of a toy? And besides there was no incentive to travel, since one end of the world was exactly like the other: everywhere the same prairie, the same irongray carpet of sod, the same groves of trees in whose black, leathery foliage waxlike or candylike blossoms gleamed, reminiscent of oversized, diseased magnolias. The multifariousness of life—with the exception, of course, of the Jungle and the swinish hubbub—lay below rather than above ground, in the deep and spacious caverns that were called houses without being houses in our sense, but which preserved the character expressed by the ancient writer Ibsen as "Homesteads for Humans." For this reason it was one of the greatest pleasures of the new occupants to transform the residence completely according to their own taste, to rearrange the interior from top to bottom, as soon as the former owners had left the threshold, along with their staff of Spokesman, House Sage, and Permanent Guest.

By means of osmosis and penetration I had learned a great deal by this time. I felt much less dependent upon my Vergil. From moment to moment I became more convinced that the life of this day represented the realization of the dreams of communism, but on a strictly aristocratic basis. At the same time it was apparent that the fulfillment of this dream had not taken place recently, but presumably countless generations ago. It occurred to me that my communistic friends back in the beginnings of mankind would hardly have approved of this sort of communistic world: a world without red flags, without marching masses, without perspiring gymnasts, without hoarse, croaking demagogues, without myopic atheists, pan-economists, material- ists, positivists, pragmatists, worshipers of technology and science; a world without tail-wagging intellectuals, who are even more stupid than they pretend to be, and who, out of genuine envy and by order of the moguls, pretend to be even more stupid than they really are. This, on the contrary, was a world of the most aristocratic individualism—for every family lived, so to speak, in its own castle—a touch-me-not world, a world of strict privacy, of good breeding and good living, a world that was tactful and natural even in intercourse with prehistoric ghosts, as I could testify.

And yet my impression of Fiancé Io-Do remained the same: a spoiled son of the wealthy class. He had the same delicately formed body as all his contemporaries and still he seemed some- how bloated. The corners of his mouth were turned slightly downward and there was an insufficient line of demarcation between his cheeks and throat.

"Seigneur has come to see you, son," his father, dear little Io-Solip, announced.

"I have been waiting for Seigneur a long time," Bridegroom Io-Do replied.

Including myself—in spite of my somewhat dubious existence —there were now five men in Io-Do's spacious bedchamber. I shall disclose presently who the fifth man was. An embarrassed silence hung over the group. I looked around for a place to sit down and waited for the Bridegroom or his father to invite me to be seated. No matter whether I was clothed in my portly, material body or in my unsubstantial, ghostly body, I felt very tired. My limbs in the shabby dress suit felt battered and bruised. But no one invited me to have a chair and to exchange my pain- ful, erect stance for a comfortably collapsed sitting position. B.H. had not informed me, among other things, that sitting, planting the full weight of the body on the comfortably supported buttocks, was an attitude that was assumed only in rare instances, as, for example, at table-tilting. My newly acquired contemporaries regarded sitting about as we (by "we" I mean the reader and myself after my return) regarded the squatting position of South Sea savages, as an animal-like and almost obscene posture. Nowadays people sat down only for very definite purposes. The basic positions of the present age were standing and lying. Only the unbroken line, whether vertical or horizontal, was considered dignified. We, in our primitive time, were still too close to the sacred act of erection that changed man into a perpendicular biped, and we sometimes had to relax by exchanging the unbroken line for the broken (sitting) line. At this particular moment I simply yearned for the comfort of the broken line. But it did me no good, for no one invited me to sit, and I could not just drop on the Bridegroom's couch.

As for the fifth man in our group, he was a Mutarian. He was a frail little man who wore neither a silver nor a gold headdress but frankly exposed his polished bald pate. Furthermore, unlike the other people in this house, he was neither naked nor draped in filmy materials, but was enveloped in a coarse, brown garment that we could at once have designated as a cowl if the hood and the knotted rope about the waist had not been lacking. I bowed deeply to this little man whom I took to be some sort of a clerical person, and it turned out that I was not entirely mistaken. The little man stared at me with large, strangely light eyes that did not reflect my image.

"He is a Mutarian," B.H. explained loudly and began to go into details as though the person under discussion were not in the room with us. "The Mutarians are more than a religious order or brotherhood such as you may have known back in your lifetime. They are bound not only by the three basic vows of Chastity, Poverty, and Obedience, but in addition by the three biological vows of Blindness, Deafness, and Muteness; that is, they are literally, and not only figuratively, blind, deaf, and dumb. In compensation they have so developed their inner senses of sight and sound that nothing remains concealed from them and

they perceive all sights and sounds by means of their acute
inner senses much more sharply and clearly than their mere
physical senses would permit. I won't say too much about it,"
B.H. concluded his explanations, "but unless I am mistaken,
Brother Mutarian Io-Fra sees us all here without seeing us and
hears our words without hearing them. In fact he sees and hears
so damn much that he sometimes scares me out of my wits. Am
I right, Io-Fra?"

The blind and deaf-mute Io-Fra smiled all over his strangely
smooth face in token of the fact that he had seen and heard
everything, in fact much more than could be seen and heard
with normal eyes and ears. The rosy smoothness of his features
reminded me of the delicate new skin that forms over first and
second degree burns. Io-Solip, the father of the Bridegroom, the
most affable and good-natured person I had met so far on my
exploration, could not refrain from contributing his share in
praise of the Mutarian.

"They can find anything, these Mutarian Brothers, Seigneur,"
he said. "You can hide a ball of yarn or a bottle of smelling salts
anywhere you please, and the Mutarian will walk straight up to
it and pull it out of the most secret panel. Shall we try it?"

"I wouldn't want to trouble the Reverend Brother," I said in
alarm. "I assume he has other duties in this house besides looking
for balls of yarn and smelling salts."

"The Mutarians," said B.H. with the evident purpose of putting an end to this awkward conversation about a fifth person
who was blind and deaf and who, for that very reason, could see
and hear more clearly than others, "the Mutarians have made it
their duty to offer their services and their abilities to brides and
bridegrooms during the period of the wedding holidays. That
explains everything!"

Certainly that explained everything. But it didn't explain why
Io-Do chose this particular moment to become impatient, in
fact, angry. "Nobody pays the slightest attention to me!" he
shouted at dear little Io-Solip, who was plainly startled. "You
bore Seigneur with all sorts of trite commonplaces and you don't

give him a chance to get interested in any of the important things here in my room. After all, I am the Bridegroom. Seigneur might evaporate at any moment and then I'd be left holding the bag. Why do you suppose I prepared all these historical questions for him? And besides Seigneur hasn't noticed a thing yet."

With a gesture of offended languor Io-Do raised his arm and pointed at the opposite wall of the room. The absence of windows in this era had never struck me so much as at this instant. In the definitely orange-colored light of the chamber—I soon learned that it was in imitation of the color of the planet Mars, or John the Baptist—the right-hand wall of the room turned out to be the display space of a museum. I looked in wonder but could not make out the significance of the rusty and dilapidated curios that hung there in great numbers. They were mostly thin tubes and pipettes, made of metals that were strange to me, some of them transparent as glass, others translucent as soapstone. Remnants of electric wire wrapped about the lower ends of these pea-shooters indicated their origin in an era of electricity probably not far from my own.

"There are a few very valuable excavated objects among them, some from periods before the Sun-Catastrophe," Io-Solip declared with paternal pride. As he spoke these words I discovered among all these uninteresting pipes that meant nothing to me, a primitive bow with a quiver for arrows and the wreckage of a strictly up-to-date sub-machine gun of the Second World War.

"Gentlemen," I exclaimed, "why, those are weapons. Two of them I know very well, a bow and arrow and a machine gun of the latest model—the latest model, of course, from a point of view that I held some thousand centuries ago. It is a practical automatic weapon without a tripod."

"Seigneur recognized the most important pieces in my collection at the first glance, the bow and the powder-gun," Io-Do commented with a show of respect.

"That's no trick, Monsieur," I replied modestly. "For these are the only weapons here with which I have firsthand acquaintance.

The rest of them, if they are weapons at all, are entirely un-familiar to me."

"The other objects that you see here, Seigneur," the Bride-groom expatiated eagerly, "are found much more frequently when excavations for new houses are made. They, too, date back to primitive times, but to later eras than the bow and arrow or the powder-gun. The scholars call them 'trans-shadow-disintegrators.' If you look more closely you can easily distin-guish the clumsy trans-shadow-disintegrators of primitive wars from the more advanced, slender ones of the Last War."

Although I could not exactly distinguish the pea-shooters from each other, I stepped closer, feigning a polite interest. The Bride-groom indeed seemed to be a great bellologist, a student of the science of war. His slightly bloated face glowed with the agita-tion of his monomania. Undoubtedly the younger generation was no longer as dispassionate as their elders. The Bride's father, Io-Fagòr, had been quite right in his complaint.

"The longest and thinnest of the trans-shadow-disintegrators," Bridegroom Io-Do continued with growing zeal, "were directed against cities that were built high up over the surface of the earth. Did you ever know any cities like that, Seigneur?"

"I never knew any other kind," I answered truthfully.

"The skyscrapers in these cities were a thousand to two thou-sand stories high," Io-Do went on enthusiastically. "Is that right, Seigneur?"

"In my time they only managed to get up about a hundred stories," I explained modestly. "The Empire State Building was the highest one I knew. Still, the skyline of New York was fairly respectable, especially for people coming from Europe, which had cities like Paris and Vienna that were splendid but never went in for tall buildings. It is not unlikely, however, Monsieur, that later history may have seen buildings that extended up into the stratosphere. I don't know."

"Well, that proves it," the war-mad Bridegroom interrupted, drawing rash conclusions with youthful indiscreetness, "that proves that mankind is indebted to the trans-shadow-disintegrator

alone for the boon of living no longer high up over the surface in the terror of the atmosphere, pitilessly exposed to the
rays of the sun and stars, but in the homely lap of the lithosphere.
The trans-shadow-disintegrators, you know, cleaned up that skyline of yours in a hurry, in fact, in a matter of seconds. And to
think that there are still people who deny the contribution of
former wars to the progress of the race, as, for instance, the
Official Guide of our Era or even my own father."

Poor modest Io-Solip looked dismayed. "I don't venture to have
an opinion of my own, son," he said. "I'm no historian and antiquarian. What do I know of that bloody myth that people used
to call war? All I think is that we, the people of today, are not
numerous enough for these ancient trans-shadow-disintegrators
on your wall."

Bridegroom Io-Do turned his young face eagerly toward me.
My ability to distinguish youth from age within this general
framework of youthfulness had meanwhile increased.

"May I assume, Seigneur," Io-Do asked, "that you took part
in the Trojan War?"

"Not in person, I regret to say," I rejoined, "although we
studied about this war in school until we were sick and tired of
it. Unfortunately the historians were never able to agree whether
this war really took place or whether it was the product of a
poet's imagination."

"But certainly you participated in other wars," the young man
insisted, "in which, as in the Trojan War, a part of the warriors
coalesced with animals that were called horses . . . ?"

"Oh, yes, cavalry still existed in my time, although it was becoming more and more motorized."

"And what was at stake in the Trojan War?"

"The worthiest object imaginable: the most beautiful woman
in the world."

"And in what war did you take part, Seigneur?"

"In the so-called First World War, from 1914 to 1918, Monsieur le Fiancé."

"Was that much later, Seigneur?"

"Yes and no. If you look at it from here, no."

"And for what reason was the First World War fought, Seigneur? What was it about?"

As I formulated my answer I was uncomfortably aware that I was not doing justice to the Second World War. But Lord, that was all so long ago and I was too tired to draw fine distinctions for this strange audience merely for the sake of my conscience.

"Well, now that you ask this question, my dear Monsieur, it's not so easy to say why the two World Wars that took place in my lifetime were really fought. It was all mixed up with a murky hogwash about unemployment and ersatz-religions. You know, the more fraudulent a religion, the more fanatically its adherents strike out in all directions. My former contemporaries had firmly made up their minds that they didn't want to have any souls or any personalities; they wanted to be egoless atoms in a material macrocomplex. One group adhered to a macrocomplex called 'Nation,' and made a fetish of the accident of birth in a specific country and among a specific people. A second group adhered to a macrocomplex called 'Class,' and made a fetish of the fact that they had been born poor and lowly and wanted no longer to be poor and lowly. These two macrocomplexes were, however, easily interchangeable for their adherents, since practically everybody was poor and at the same time was a member of a nation. And so most people of both groups didn't have the slightest idea why they had to kill each other. They really did it out of fear. But they were less afraid of each other than of their own leaders, and these leaders, again, were so afraid of the people whom they led or misled that they forced them to kill each other."

"I don't like your definition of war at all, Seigneur," said the Bridegroom stubbornly and, parading his learning, he added, "We have learned that wars between armed opponents were valiantly fought only when all human legal remedies had failed on account of the absence of a universal court of law. The wars of antiquity were, therefore, divine judgments, as our scholars have proved beyond a shadow of doubt. Bellum internecinum, that is, a war of extermination, was regarded as unfair and was forbidden; likewise bellum punitivum, or punitive war. It was also not permitted to employ percursores, assassins, or venevici, poisoners, against your opponent, and perduellio, that is, subornation of treason, was generally abominated."

After this little lecture Io-Do looked at me triumphantly from under his gold helmet. I had no way of knowing how far this baroque, chivalrous concept of warfare differed from his real views. I applauded silently in order to indicate the extent of my admiration.

"Your knowledge of the chivalrous rules of warfare is astonishing, Monsieur," I said. "You make me quite ashamed of myself, for I never knew all these expressions, or else I forgot them long ago. And yet, theory is one thing, practice another! Just take a look at the trans-shadow-disintegrators on your own wall. They were used exclusively for bella internecina, that is, wars of extermination."

The Bridegroom was about to make a rancorous remark but his father interrupted him. "You should not contradict Seigneur, son," said timid Io-Solip. "He saw it with his own eyes. He was there. Your knowledge comes from the Sephirodrome, from lectures, and from collectors' catalogues."

"Certainly, Seigneur was there," Io-Do pouted. "And so I should like to request most respectfully that he, as an eyewitness and combatant, tell us something of the First World War. Isn't that what it was called?"

I was startled out of my wits, for I found myself again in the same situation as a while ago when the Spokesman asked me for "a little causerie," "a few well-chosen remarks" about the differences between the old days and now. I looked for help to my friend B.H., who stood next to me in his simulated weather-beaten uniform of a lieutenant of the First World War. He grew pale and shrank back. But I did not hesitate to say, "Haven't we a man among us who rose to officer's rank in the First World War? He is much better fitted to furnish the information that

Monsieur Io-Do desires in the pursuit of his curious hobby of
ancient military history than I, who was a very mediocre soldier
and just barely managed to get my sergeant's stripes."

"Stop, F.W.," B.H. exclaimed and imploringly held his hand
over my mouth. "I never imagined that you would treat me so
unkindly, so unfairly. All right, it's true, I am reincarnated. But
I am much more than that. I am a contemporary of these gentlemen, a contemporary in every respect. I decline, I refuse, I
protest violently against permitting my contemporary self to be
brought into any relation with the apish affairs and stinking
barbarisms of antiquity. And you should be the last to do that,
F.W."

"But my dear old friend," I interrupted meekly and contritely,
"why do you walk around here in this fieldgray outfit instead of
dressing like your esteemed contemporaries?"

B.H. nervously pulled the faded military cap down over his
forehead.

"I am wearing this disagreeable disguise solely on your account," he said softly, "so that you might feel more at home and
not fall ill from a feeling of strangeness."

So that's it, I thought, he's a good fellow after all. He didn't
want to frighten me at our first meeting. But perhaps I wouldn't
even have recognized him if he had appeared before me in the
blurred nakedness or in the affected drapery of his contemporaries. At any rate, he recognized me at once, even when I was
still invisible. That proved that he was a better friend than I.
I suddenly realized that I had indeed acted unfairly by putting
the burden of our common antiquity upon him. All the thoughts
and aspirations of the reincarnated B.H. must have been directed
toward becoming a full-fledged member of the present epoch
and of its human society. To be sure, no reincarnated person
could ever completely belong to any particular time. Suddenly
I gained a still deeper insight into the problem. B.H. was typical
of the highest spiritual individual. But what is the spiritual individual if not one who has gone through several reincarnations?
The spiritual individual can therefore never be completely at

home in any age, and if he wants to adjust himself at least to some extent, he is forced to simulate membership in the society of his time. I tried quickly to make amends for my mistake and to attract the general attention away from B.H. So I closed my eyes and sighed in acquiescence.

"How can I, in just a few words, give you any impression of what we experienced in World War One or Two? Shall I describe the feelings of a relatively free young man who is unceremoniously jammed into a barracks with hundreds of others in order to be drilled, that is, to be subjected to a process of hardening and brutalization that fits him to be a soldier? How could I make highly developed people like you, who take no solid food and do not even expose your bodies to fresh air—how could I make you understand the condition of men living by day and night for months on end in trenches, dugouts, and foxholes filled with water and muck, their lives endangered day in and day out by divebombers, mortars, heavy artillery, field artillery, tank artillery, ships' batteries, machine guns of every kind, and God knows what else, until they pray for a severe wound just to be delivered from this horrible exposure? And worse than that, how could you gentlemen, who are so refined that a slight physical contact, as for instance a good old-fashioned handshake, plunges you into disgusted confusion, how could you ever get an adequate concept of what it means when a boy, maddened by rum, benzedrine, and party fanaticism, crawls out of his foxhole, gun in hand, and stumbles over muddy clods, shell holes, land-mines, and barbed wire, over black, bloated corpses stinking to high heaven, on toward the enemy, filled with a breathless, insane lust to twist his bayonet in that enemy's guts even when he has thrown up both arms and is screaming for mercy?"

At this point, in my attempt to avoid the relating of specific war anecdotes by uttering the above generalities, I was interrupted by Io-Do's clear voice. He lay stretched out straight on his couch, tightly wrapped in his black veil, and his face under the golden helmet shone with a dreamily attentive ecstasy that I could not understand.

"And how does it feel, Seigneur," he asked slowly, "when your own cold steel enters the enemy's body and a crimson fountain of blood gushes at you?"

I was shocked at the question and at the sensuously poetic tone in which it was uttered. But before I could gather my wits I heard someone groan softly. It appeared that delicate little Io-Solip had already become nauseated in the course of my recital, and now his son's question had finished him. He was ghastly pale, reached for his heart, and gagged a little. At once Io-Fra, the Mutarian, who had seen and heard everything without seeing or hearing anything, stepped toward the father of the Bridegroom and blew his breath on him, whereupon the latter quickly recovered from his blood-nausea.

"Our parents are very nervous, Seigneur," Io-Do chided the older generation. But Io-Solip apologized to me in deep confusion. "It will not happen again, Seigneur."

Suddenly Io-Do jumped to his feet and exclaimed, "And now we will show Seigneur the Monument of the Last War of the Planet."

To my disgrace as explorer and travelogue writer, I must confess that at this moment I was overcome by well-earned exhaustion. In spite of my dress suit and medal I was on the point of dropping where I stood. The news that I was to be taken sightseeing at this moment, no matter though it were something as important as the Monument of the Last War, simply filled me with terror. But I remained silent and made no mention of my fatigue—by no means from curiosity or from an explorer's impulse, but from pure cowardice and perhaps even from a sort of vanity. Could the materialization of a human who had lived a round hundred millennia ago fold up so disgracefully and ask for consideration of his body which, in spite of its completeness, was, after all, only an apparition? An apparition either had to dissolve or stand firm. There was no third course. Since I had not learned how to dissolve, I resolved to stand fast and to give no indication of physical weakness. But for the next few minutes all words and movements fell on my ear as though from a great distance and as though I were lying on the bottom of a stream.

Bridegroom Io-Do appeared to be very excited at the prospect of taking his antediluvian guest to see the Monument of the Last War. In a brusque voice he ordered the deaf, dumb, and blind little fellow in the cowl who served him in these days: "Io-Fra! My spare Mentelobole has somehow been mislaid. Find it, please, and make it snappy!"

The Mutarian, from whose inner sight and hearing nothing remained concealed, slipped silently from the room. Mentelobole —that sounded like some kind of toothpaste back in the twentieth century. But I was at once informed that it referred to the Mental traveling instrument that I had already seen. A moment later Io-Do handed me the Mentelobole which the Mutarian's inner sight had quickly discovered in its insidious hiding-place. I was quite embarrassed. Would I succeed in getting the little globules into the right holes in the puzzle? Now a minor quarrel arose between the Bridegroom and his father.

"How often do I have to tell you, son," Papa Io-Solip timidly ventured to criticize, "that you should not travel in a room or in any enclosed place."

"I'll travel anywhere I please, Papa. I'm a grown man and day after tomorrow I'm to be married."

"God willing, yes, son. But traveling in a room damages the house. And day after tomorrow it will be your house. So you are damaging your own house that the community provides for you and that you are to occupy for the next one hundred and fifty years."

The allusion to his own property seemed to change the son's mind. "Very well, then. Let's ride up," he said brusquely.

The room gently floated upward. Every room of the house could be separately elevated. How it was done, I don't know. Trained engineers will have to explain it. But just before we stepped out of the room to the upper platform of the house that resembled the observation tower of a warship, I noticed another object in the collection of weapons with which I was familiar but which had so far escaped me. It was a good, solid, single-action Colt revolver, a regular old-fashioned persuader from the last century, by which, of course, I mean the nineteenth.

* * * * *
* * *
*

I LOOKED AROUND DESPERATELY FOR B.H. and, having found him, whispered to him to tell me quickly upon what to concentrate my thoughts as I awkwardly and nervously tried to maneuver the last light green globule into the last little hole, marked "Keenly Directed Desire." He winked at me and whispered back, "Just think of an enormous, concave platter."

It really was an enormous, concave platter that extended under our feet in the next instant. But this expression is incorrect, since the change of place in traveling occurred without the slightest lapse of time; I should therefore say, "in the same instant." It was the largest place I had ever seen, obviously a public square, extending to the distant, perfectly circular horizon, which had been raised in such fashion as to form the rim of a concave platter. This rim was adorned with shadowy, theatrical architectural suggestions, as for example towers and turrets, gable ends, spires, battlements, and Gothic tracery. All of it was rather low, toyish, and artificial, as though to simulate silhouettes at infinite distances. The orb of the sun was declining in the west. The firmament was light green, the exact color of the Mental globules in the travel puzzle. Deep lapis lazuli shadows moved across it in rhythmic undulations. The sunset served to accentuate the two-dimensional character of the toy architecture on the horizon, which was only intended to differentiate by means of divers ornaments above ground the official edifices located far below.

"Where are we?" I asked B.H., and it seemed to me that not my skin but my heart was covered with goose-pimples.

"We are in the Geodrome," said B.H., "or, if you prefer, in the central plaza."

"Why, of course, Geodrome," I replied, as though I had known this designation all my life. I was no longer willing at this stage to act the part of an utter greenhorn.

I looked down at my brittle patent-leather shoes, whose appearance had not improved since the last time they had been squeezed onto my feet. The new pair that I had recently bought and that had to be among my effects somewhere, had sensibly and maliciously been kept with the heirlooms instead of being given to me. But before I could manage to become sufficiently annoyed at the stinginess of my esteemed heirs, I perceived to my great astonishment that I was wearing a pair of very narrow ice skates on the soles of my cracked shoes. I could not remember when and where they had been strapped on. But without skates, which all the rest of the party seemed to be wearing, locomotion in the tremendous Geodrome—the central plaza of California, or of the continent, or perhaps of the entire globe, how should I know?—would have been extremely difficult and wearisome, if not impossible. For the floor of this central plaza consisted of an icy substance, smooth as a mirror, that covered the entire surface of the circular, concave platter which, according to my estimate, was at least twenty miles in diameter. A foot-tour across its expanse or along the shadowy architecture around its circumference would probably have consumed days and would have required physical endurance which the delicately built and easily fatigued humans of the present did not possess. Moreover, the use of the Mentelobole was impossible for perfectly plausible reasons. For the Geodrome was an objective. Only objectives in their entirety could be moved toward the user by means of the Mentelobole. The travel-puzzle did not function within the confines of an objective, even an objective as large as the central plaza. In order to facilitate locomotion of the human body within the confines of a large objective without reviving prehistoric wheels and brakes, the metal-winged shoes of Mercury had been adopted, which not only afforded speedy progress but also the

pleasurable sensation of physical movement. Through contact
with the sharp runners of the skates the glassy floor became
elastic and promoted motion (even better than the irongray
sod), especially on the downgrade toward the lowest point of
the platter, toward which we were moving now. My fatigue of a
few minutes ago had totally vanished. With indescribable rapture I enjoyed the wind-blown speed of our glide. The gold-
helmeted Bridegroom whizzed along at the head of our group,
which had been joined by the ever-curious bachelors of the
household, the Spokesman, the House Sage, and the Permanent
Guest. I noted that their skates were strapped to fairly high
buskins, which were apparently always worn outside the house.
The Bridegroom alone was draped in black. The others had
wrapped their naked bodies in veils of various pastel shades.
B.H. in his fieldgray uniform and I in my dress suit brought up
the rear. And as I sped along I could not repress a childish shout
of joy, a sound quite inappropriate for an apparition of my age
who had been drawn fortuitously from the alphabet and summoned here. And yet the shout was justified, for it was perfectly
delightful to skim rapidly over the surface of this altered and
improved earth after such a long absence. B.H., who was responsible for my presence, seemed to understand my feelings and
smiled indulgently at my shout of joy.

My weak eyes were probably to blame for the fact that I
suddenly and unexpectedly found myself in the midst of a huge
throng that moved about a great circle fenced off in the middle
of the central plaza. My heart began to beat even faster than it
had done a few hours ago while I was standing in a dark corridor waiting for the signal that was to summon me into a pleasantly lighted room to appear before my new friends. I had by
now become accustomed to the bridal family; the ladies and
gentlemen of the household did not fill me with greater fear and
shyness than I had always experienced in the presence of strangers whom I had been required to visit. At this moment I was
petrified at the thought of losing sight of dear pompous Io-Solip,
of the Spokesman, the House Sage, the Permanent Guest, even

the Bridegroom, not to mention B.H., the little company of those who belonged to the household where I felt relatively at home. For it must be confessed that I trembled in my dress suit at sight of this crowd, of these hundreds of strangers, among whom I moved with the feeling that my resurrected physique could scarcely muster the strength to bear the compact presence of people who were actually separated from me by millennia in time and light years in space. I beg the indulgent reader to consider this point well, lest he despise me for my shaking knees and chattering teeth in the presence of this throng of humans of an unspeakably distant future. My mental discomfort—I should like to call it "historical discomfort"—was so intense that I could not even distinguish the individuals about me. Again I proved unworthy of my calling as a reporter of the future, for I can record my own jittering and chattering but not the objective picture of the crowd—unless I want to take recourse to pure fancy. This throng was a rhythmic entity, a swirling, a dancing, a spinning, a pirouetting, and a moving tapestry, embroidered with twittering, euphonious voices of silver, dull gold, light blue, pale green. . . . But imagine my discomfort when the crowd suddenly receded and I, shuffling on my skates, found myself standing with B.H. in a reverently cleared space. Of course, it was the Spokesman who hadn't been able to keep his mouth shut for, after all, it was his job to keep it open. From him the bystanders had learned the character of the apparition that had dropped into their highly developed and civilized world. The news spread like wildfire—to use a figure of speech that really belongs back in the beginnings of mankind. As for me, I was bathed in perspiration, for everyone stared at me with eyes distended with curiosity. All I could think of was to hold on to B.H.'s arm in a frenzy of distress.

"They are friendly people," my reincarnated friend soothed me. "They won't bother you. Pay no attention to them. Just smile all over the place, and be sure to show your teeth."

He supported me with a friendly arm and together we glided to the circular fence which had suddenly been cleared of people.

Bridegroom Io-Do, Father Io-Solip, and the three bachelors joined us; the multitude followed at a respectful, curious distance. In keeping with B.H.'s advice I turned and gave the shadowy human wall a forced, theatrical smile that left a bad taste in my mouth, remembering to bare my teeth briefly. I was unspeakably ashamed of this politician's grin. But it seemed to be effective, for a soft muttering of approval came back from the throng. I had long ago learned the lesson that the only way to get along in this new era was to be agreeable at all times and in all places. This toadying really didn't mean a thing. It was mere unfounded and undesigning amiability, good manners, friendly behavior; at the same time it was an unconscious apology for many dark ages in which men had bared their teeth only to snarl at an enemy, and for many other, later, but equally dark ages in which photogenic people had bared their teeth in order to sell themselves to the public.

I held on to the wrought-iron railing with both hands and looked down into an enormous, circular excavation which gave the impression of an old, long abandoned mine whose surface structure had remained intact while the lower shafts and galleries had collapsed or been drowned out. The impression of a mine was heightened by the fact that the sidewalls of the fairly shallow excavation were seamed with glistening mineral lodes and studded with glittering crystal geodes. In spite of my weak eyes I seemed to distinguish amethysts, topazes, and rock crystals. But today, after my return, I have the feeling that I saw not only semiprecious gems but also fabulous rubies and sapphires gleaming in the twilight. But that would have meant nothing, for the people of this age neither venerated gold, which had lost its importance as an index of value, nor did they make the slightest distinction between a lustrous glass bauble and a genuine jewel. In this respect they had reverted to the primitive and naïve state of naked South Sea islanders who prefer the cheapest glass trinket to real gems.

"This is the Monument of the Last War," said someone near me, and I craned my neck to see something in the broad excavation within or below the railing that might resemble an equestrian statue or a group of heroically muscle-bound figures à la Rodin. But I discovered nothing of the sort. Finally my unfortunately naked eye settled upon a spherical, rusty framework, about six feet in diameter. At first I could not make the slightest sense out of this sphere consisting of warped metal bands. Then it suddenly dawned on me that it must be an ancient celestial globe, manufactured long after my death but still in darkest antiquity. As my eyes became more and more accustomed to the ruddy twilight in the excavation, which now seemed to me to resemble not so much a mine as the basin of a great pond from which the water had been drained, I perceived that the dilapidated and warped celestial globe surmounted a gigantic pedestal made of skulls, similar to but larger than the so-called cairns which are found in the valleys of the Styrian and Carinthian Alps. My understanding of the psychology of the present had by now become so keen that I clearly felt the mythical horror that the sight of this foundation of skulls must have provoked in the hearts of these contemporaries who had deleted the word "death" from their vocabulary.

My dreamy contemplation was interrupted by the sharp voice of the Bridegroom which rang through the deep silence that prevailed in spite of the great throng behind my back.

"Where is the Official Guide?" he shouted. "He's not on the job although he was called up in plenty of time to prepare for Seigneur's arrival."

I wonder who called him up, I thought. It was only a few moments ago that Io-Do had the notion to make this excursion.

Père Io-Solip tried to calm him in a whispering voice. "You may be a bridegroom, son, and you may have the right to raise your voice as often and as loudly as you wish. But I still wouldn't parade my lack of self-control in front of the whole world."

"If the Official Guide doesn't get here this instant," growled Io-Do, "I shall personally waken the Global Major-Domo. I have the right to do it. A man gets to be a bridegroom only once in a lifetime."

"There comes the Official Guide now." Io-Solip sighed with relief; he certainly had a hard time with his spoiled boy.

As though he had actually crawled out of the bowels of the earth, a man suddenly appeared on the scaffold-like structure that rose from the floor of the mine or from the pond-basin and projected a few feet above the surface of the surrounding Geodrome. There isn't much to say about this man except that he looked like all the rest of them—beardless, ageless, and without wrinkles; just like the Mutarian at home, however, he wore no headdress on his smooth, round skull. For this reason I have classified the Official Guide among the high state officers. Meanwhile, the thousands who filled the middle of the central plaza crowded a little closer to the railing although only a small number of them could hope to see anything; for the monuments of this age, like the dwellings, were below the surface of the earth. The Official Guide cleared his throat for a long time but he had no microphone in front of him to amplify his voice. The only relatively technical instrument that I had seen so far in this Mental era was the travel-puzzle, the Mentelobole. Nevertheless, the voice of the Official Guide boomed out with such force and carrying power as if the air waves were set into increased vibration by some unknown trick.

"Esteemed Ios of both sexes!" He began his lecture with the chronic raucousness of all guides. "You have assembled in the Geodrome today in large numbers to examine the oldest of all monuments that remote antiquity has left here on earth; a monument whose meaning need not be discovered by scholars; a monument, documented throughout the ages by history and literature, that has occupied this very spot since the continuity of human memory began. As Official Guide of the Era it is my honor and privilege to welcome all those present, in particular, however, the dear little children who have been brought for the first time to see the Monument of the Last War for their education and edification. . . ."

The man on the platform which projected above the surface of the earth in the manner of a scaffold over an excavation made a short, shrewd pause for effect. Then he continued in a somewhat softer tone, and his oratorically fluent raucousness was more reminiscent of a politician than of a guide.

"Over and beyond that, esteemed Ios, I have the rare honor today of acting as the Official Guide for Foreigners—to use my full title and in the true sense of the word—and not only as an interpreter of monuments for the inquisitive and curious and for evening strollers. For there is a genuine foreigner in our midst thanks to the kind offices of the Io-Fagòr and Io-Solip families, next-of-kin to a bride and groom, respectively, who are celebrating their three great days at this time. We are deeply indebted to these highly respected families, whose unremitting efforts, ably assisted by a family friend who wishes to remain anonymous, have made it possible for us to salute a guest from the beginnings of the human race, a guest whose authenticity is proved by his white-skinned body and his stiff, coarse costume, as you can all see for yourselves. I salute Seigneur, with the wish that he may feel at home in our midst."

I didn't feel at all at home. It was one of those moments when one looks around for the nearest mousehole. The crowd applauded and whistled a little, about as a crowd might have done back in my day in greeting a third-rate celebrity of whom they knew practically nothing. Although it was obvious that I was not a success, I smiled my thanks in all directions and skinned my teeth. The Official Guide, who was suddenly holding a pointer twice as long as a fishing pole in his hand, pointed it at me.

"I take the liberty of calling attention to the fact," he said, "that Seigneur is paradoxically by far the oldest and by far the youngest among us. As a worthy member of primitive humanity he is of such incredible infancy—a baby in the history of evolution, so to speak—that everyone, and particularly the ladies, might be tempted to lay either curious or maternal hands on him. As a welcome visitor in our present day, on the other hand, he has survived two world epochs in complete physical vigor—two epochs so remote from each other that we recoil in awe before his incredibly advanced age. Isn't it so?"

A murmur of approval ran through the crowd. These people were living in a Mental era and therefore showed a more intelligent appreciation of clever paradoxes and antitheses than those of a period of journalistic reverence for facts. Despite my extreme old age and my extreme youthfulness, however, I felt exactly as I did just before I had fallen asleep, in other words, about fifty years old. I heaved a sigh of relief when the fishing pole in the hand of the Official Guide veered away from me and pointed at the dilapidated celestial globe.

"At that time, Seigneur and esteemed friends," he finally began his official discourse, "at that time when the metal workers pounded out the framework of this primitive replica of the celestial sphere from the metal then so widely used, humanity had already survived the worst. For the Last War was not waged like the Next to the Last War with hopeless fiendishness by all against all. No, it was waged by ten thousand selected men against another selected ten thousand. The two armies of ten thousand annihilated each other, down to the last man, in the space of three and three-tenths minutes. This proved that the warlike settlement of disputes could no longer really settle anything and could therefore no longer be regarded as up-to-date. At the expiration of the three and three-tenths minutes of destruction a few fanatical voices were raised, to be sure, who wished to incite the two parties against each other for the purpose of complete extermination. But strangely, creditably, and unexpectedly, the voice of reason prevailed for once. People recalled the horrors of the Next to the Last War which had devastated and depopulated the planet for many generations, which had made cave-dwellers of the survivors, had robbed them of science and technology, and, according to some historians, had even deprived them of the power of speech. The low stage of intellectual development of mankind at the time of the Next to the Last War is amply attested by their clumsy weapons. We are all familiar with the trans-shadow-disintegrators

that are found in inexhaustible numbers. The children in the Park
of the Worker play with these trans-shadow-disintegrators which
fortunately no longer expose the universe within the microcosm
by smashing the nuclei of the unicles——"

"I beg your pardon," interjected Fiancé Io-Do in defense of
his own collection of weapons.

The eyes of the Official Guide sought me out before he continued his interesting lecture. Naturally I am reproducing it here
in my own words and not in his; thus it loses a great deal of its
smooth coldness and its utter disinterestedness. To him, the
Official Guide for Foreigners of the Era, war and the horrors of
war were matters of greater indifference and unreality than the
long forgotten death rattle of shackled prisoners under the lead
roofs of the dungeons of the Venetian Doges to a Cook's guide
of our day.

"The era that immediately preceded the Next to the Last War,"
the speaker continued, "no longer resembled the beginnings of
mankind, an estimable eyewitness of which we have the pleasure
of entertaining in our midst today. Seigneur could probably
give us far more accurate information than the most learned
scholar concerning the life of primitive man, at a time when
every ten square miles sheltered a different tribe with a different
language, different habits and customs; when they lived under
tents or low, thatched roofs or, worst of all, in anthills of boxlike
skyscrapers. . . ."

I pressed B.H.'s hand desperately. "For heaven's sake," I
whispered, "I won't say a word. I simply won't do it."

B.H., evidently annoyed by my behavior, made a negative
sign to the Official Guide, who nodded indulgently and continued
his discourse without interruption.

"At the time of the Next to the Last War our globe was already
septilingual. There were only seven different languages, seven
different peoples, seven different realms, just as there are seven
colors. Some of these realms, peoples, and languages occupied
islands; the others were confined to the continents. The inhabitants of the islands were wealthier, more peaceable, more

intellectual, and less imaginative. The inhabitants of the continents were poorer in material things; they did not follow the dictates of universal logic but lived according to vague emotions and dreams that filled their hearts. They were dissatisfied with their mode of life, these continentals, and for that reason they were given too much to fancies and dreams, and usually morbid dreams. But all their fancies and dreams were filled with unbridled envy of the islanders, who lived easier lives. The envious peoples, incited by prophets and other demagogues, united in a coalition which finally, as a result of insidious and dishonest policies, declared the Next to the Last War on earth. This war, as I have already indicated, led to the almost complete annihilation of both power coalitions, so that the wretched remnants of the human race had to start all over again and required several hundreds of years to create a new, timorous civilization. This new civilization, however, when it had reached its zenith, was more advanced than the preceding one, for it was ambiglossal. There were only two languages, two nations, two realms. This dual system seemed, for a time, to be successful, and the political theoreticians were beginning to gloat that it furnished the indestructible basis for eternal peace, especially in view of the fact that both sides adopted a law famous to the present day, entitled 'The Principle of Reciprocal Intervention.'"

Delighted at this formula which could easily have averted the Second World War of my own era, I exclaimed, "Hear, hear! That's a first-class law!" Thereupon the Bridegroom, the Spokesman, the House Sage, the Permanent Guest, and a few others turned toward me with amazement and without comprehension, while my reincarnated friend pretended that he hadn't heard anything. The Official Guide, however, paid no attention at all to my parliamentary expression of agreement.

"It was an illusion," he said with the baritone vibration of a clever actor who lets his well-rehearsed speech reach an emotional climax only to die away in a cadence of futility. "The Two-Nation-System did not bring salvation to mankind, and many, many more eons passed and many changes took place in the constellations before man finally succeeded in eliminating the terrors connected with the natural conclusion of his life and before he attained that mild freedom and dignity which made war and the concept of physical hostility an absurd nightmare that modern man regards as a tissue of lies of eccentric historians rather than as a hellishly real torment to which his own race was subject millennia ago. Yes, if it were not for the trans-shadow-disintegrators and for the other weapons upon which our houses are, in a sense, built——"

"Hear, hear!" exclaimed the Bridegroom in a satisfied voice.

"And this monument of hammered metal, erected upon the twenty thousand well-preserved human skulls of the Last War. . . ."

At the words "human skulls" many children began to cry and wail. Their mothers tried to quiet them by soft words or by singing lullabies. A sorrowful buzzing ran through the crowd. The great throng retreated shyly from the fenced space about the monument as though no one had the courage to bear the sight of human skulls. Again someone—and this time it had been the Official Guide of the Era—had avoided the word "death." But what did he mean by the "mild freedom and dignity" that man had given to "the natural conclusion of his life"? Again and again I was confronted with the well-guarded secret of the present world, and this mystery made a deeper and deeper impression on me. But I quickly had to turn my attention back to the lecture, a few sentences of which I had already missed.

"And so," the hoarse eloquence struck my ear, "it was not the natural friction of economic necessity, as in the primitive stages of history, that led to this war, nor a difference in the manner of divine worship; it was nothing but purely absurd vanity. All of us—and particularly the pupils of the elementary Pedeuterion, to whom I dedicate a special word of welcome—know from our study of history that the two nations existing on earth at the time of the Last War of the Planet called themselves the Blues and the Reds. Now the Blues as well as the Reds, in the course of their history, had accumulated a vast number of illustrious names of great men and women in all fields of human endeavor, as for example, Divine Science, Cosmic Wisdom, Chronosophy, Starroving, Marveling, Foreignfeeling, Poetry, Science of Matter, Science of Perception, Music, Plastography, Pictography, Physical Agility, and Play, although the latter, that is the value of aimless play, was not understood in its entirety until just before our own time. So there were Blue and Red geniuses in abundance. They were called immortal and their names were surrounded with great pomp and circumstance, as a surrogate for the excitement of politics which, even at that time, had begun to pall. Then one day a Blue or Red astronomer made the suggestion to change the names of the stars, which had not been altered since time immemorial, to those of the greatest Divine Scientists, Cosmic Sages, Chronosophers, Starrovers, Marvelers, Foreignfeelers, Poets, Scholars, Pictographers, Singers, Dancers, Ball Players, Billiard Players, and so forth. The other nation replied without delay that they were delighted with the idea of studding the firmament with the names of Blue and Red geniuses. An illustrious world congress was convened and sat in sessions for several years. In the first few years there was perfect agreement among the delegates. At first the great geniuses of antiquity that had been preserved in history were transferred to the stars, and there was a goodly number of them; then followed the names of Red and Blue leaders in all fields. Unfortunately, however, there were infinitely more celestial stars than human stars, and in the process of renaming the denizens of the night skies with names now long forgotten, the congress was forced to resort to celebrities of third, fourth, and fifth grade. At that point an infernal demon blinked his eyes, and on account of some nonentity of a ball player or cabaret singer—the historians have never been able to establish which—the great quarrel broke out. The Blues —or it may have been the Reds—left the convention hall in high dudgeon and amid loud protests. A pinprick had been sufficient to arouse the slumbering national hatred and to disrupt the highly touted Two-Nation-System. At any rate, however, the stars in the sky were the cause of the Last War, as the duel of the twice ten thousand is called, the stars in the sky . . . definite progress . . . the stars . . . stars. . . ."

The words of the Official Guide of the Era died away in my ear. I could no longer understand them. It had become night and I raised my eyes to the night sky. I thought of a lovely summer night when I had similarly raised my eyes and thrown back my head until it was almost horizontal. It was near our house in the foothills of the Alps. The milky way arched over my head at that time too, but the moonlight was so strong that the fluttering veil of stars seemed a mere breath. And now I was dead. And as if that were not enough, here I was in the strangest of all worlds, a curio on exhibition. And how the sky had changed! There was as little similarity between it and the meager sky of that long past night as there is between a meadow rank with flowers in July and a meadow in March after the last snow has melted. I am no astronomer nor any other kind of stargazer; but the number of stars seemed to have increased tenfold since my lifetime. Was it only the drier, clearer atmosphere of the earth that revealed more millions of stars than ever before? Had new stars in countless numbers sprung into being? Or was it merely that the good old moon was gone?

Suddenly I felt a well-nigh dreadful sorrow rising in my throat, an ineffable grief, such as I had never felt before. I felt hot tears running down my cold cheeks—for it had become chilly by this time. I was much too sad to reach for my bedraggled handkerchief. I clenched my teeth and leaned my face against B.H.'s shoulder.

"What's the matter with you, F.W.?" he asked in a worried tone.

"I'm so sorry about the moon, B.H.," I stammered.

The Seventh Chapter

WHEREIN I READ THE LATEST NEWS IN THE "EVENING STARS," AM NAMED REFEREE IN THE MOST IMPORTANT DEBATE OF ALL TIMES, GAIN REMARKABLE DISTINCTION IN THIS CAPACITY, AND AM, IN CONSEQUENCE, PERMITTED TO PAY MY RESPECTS TO THE SLUMBERING GLOBAL MAJOR-DOMO, OTHERWISE KNOWN AS THE GEOARCHON OR WORLD-PRESIDENT.

THIS HORRIBLE GRIEF, this heart-rending sentimentality, these cosmic blues that drove briny drops into my eyes and gurgling meemies into my throat, were fortunately unfounded. I had suffered for the moon without any reason. Good old Luna had not disappeared from the heavens during my absence, had not been swallowed by eternal night, had not exploded into a million meteors as an aftermath of the sun's heart attack. On the contrary, she had remained intact and unchanged with all her four quarters. It did not require B.H.'s reassuring words to convince me, for at this moment the familiar disc rose over the elevated edge of the broad platter, throwing the distant toy architecture towers, turrets, gables, cupolas, and battlements on the eastern horizon into black silhouettes.

But I scarcely had an opportunity to feel elated over the existence of the moon, for, horrible to relate, a wild astronomical phenomenon suddenly began to take place in the night sky.

We have learned that the night sky of this era swarmed with at least ten times as many stars as a starry southern August night on a mountain top or on the high seas in the twentieth century. My earlier comparison with a flower-covered meadow in summer is fairly apt. The individual stars, in so far as they could be distinguished in these star-clusters, star-bunches, and star-veils, were many, many magnitudes brighter and larger than at that time, and the black space between and behind them seemed to have receded. In view of this profusion of heavenly bodies astronomy must have become a science whose inventory alone exceeded human powers. In my day, when the naked eye distinguished a scant three thousand stars, the universe had been compared to an exploding shell whose fragments, the stars, are scattered in all directions. In this theory the scientists, as so often, were laboring under an illusion. The dense population of the night sky of today by comparison with the past should have suggested the truth to me at once: *The universe breathes.* During the inhalation the stars are drawn together; during the exhalation they are scattered out into space. I was not to learn this great truth, however, until much later from the mouth of the High Floater.

Artificial illumination of the Geodrome, the central plaza, would have been completely unnecessary, even disturbing and annoying. We were bathed in light, totally different from sunlight and much weaker, but nevertheless light. It was a rich, bluish light that outlined people and objects as fully as sunlight but deprived them of color. Since the great secret of the spectro-analytic illusion lies in color, and since color rather than form belongs to the realm of Maya, I can designate this extravagant starlight as a spiritual light, more spiritual, at least, than that of the sun. So we stood, bathed in night-brightness.

And then the following incredible thing happened. As though four apocalyptic powers armed with invisible shovels, rakes, or brooms, were shoveling, raking, and sweeping the stars away in all directions, a small cleared space suddenly appeared in the middle of the firmament and grew and grew into a great black rectangle, a blackboard whose dimensions were measured in light years and at whose edges glittering star gravel was heaped high.

"What's that, what's that?" I stammered and pressed my left hand against the bosom of my badly crumpled boiled shirt.

B.H. seized my right hand and squeezed it peremptorily. "Relax, F.W., and keep quiet. It's nothing but an optical maneuver, of course."

"They shouldn't use the stars for optical maneuvers," I said with a bitter tongue and dry throat, and my knees quivered.

"Our relation to the stars is different from yours, my friend," he replied with a smile and held on to my hand just to be on the safe side, "since it has been definitely determined that our planet is really and truly the center of the universe and that there is, therefore, only one inhabited planet and only one human race, namely ours."

"What's that, B.H.?" I managed to say. "Has that really and truly been established beyond a shadow of a doubt? So the geocentric hypothesis has been more than victorious? I always knew in my heart that it would be victorious. For without it the faith in a spiritual destiny of this world is hard to maintain. I'm so happy, B.H., so strangely happy."

At these words I felt tears in my eyes again, but this time not from cosmic blues because the moon was gone but from a sense of deep, contented pride. My reincarnated friend looked at me in astonishment.

"Did you really wish that so much, F.W.?" he asked. "It seems to me that this fact increases our responsibility beyond words."

I had no reply to this justifiably worried moral comment. For at this moment the heaps of star gravel along the edges of the pitch-black, vacant rectangle began to stir, and individual, mischievous starlets began to skip and hop on the blackboard. In the next instant they had formed into a file of luminous characters, a headline of light, and I read without the least edification: "TODAY'S EVENING STARS."

And underneath in type of smaller size: "The Third Day of

the Fourth Earth-Month of the Seven Hundred and Forty-Second Sun-Week of the Zero Point Zero Zero Third Evolution in the Eleventh Cosmic Capital Year of Virgo."

And next to that in tiny type and enclosed in parentheses, a number in six digits that I could not make out, followed by the words "Post Christum Incarnatum."

"That's going too far," I said and recalled immediately that I had used this same phrase once before in the course of my adventure. An explorer is supposed to observe, keep his mouth shut, avoid interjections, and refrain from criticism. Of course, it was only after my return that I realized fully that I had been on a voyage of exploration. At this moment, however, the newspaper printed in starry type offended my taste. In a few minutes, perhaps, the signs of the zodiac would parade in the form of advertisements for beauty cream and laxatives! The cosmic impertinence of man had grown to absurd proportions.

"Marvelous!" I scoffed. "Now journalism and the advertising business even make use of the stars. That goes beyond my wildest dreams. The only saving grace is the fact that your newspaper appears in a single copy; at least no political-party mogul or advertising tycoon can clean up millions on the deal."

"There aren't any millions," said B.H., turning up his nose, "if you're talking about the rusty, corroded coins that we still find occasionally in the earth's crust. Since time immemorial everybody has had everything he wanted and even more. Everyone could satisfy his most morbid greed. But owing to the very fact that everyone knows that he can have anything, human greed has quite disappeared. On the contrary, it is regarded as a sign of good breeding to want less than one needs. Ostentatious wealth and the desire to outshine others would be regarded as a humiliating infirmity like sweaty feet or bad breath. I think I told you, didn't I, that we don't buy or sell any more?"

"You mean that there isn't the slightest possibility that I could buy anything that someone else owns, something that's unique and that can't be duplicated?"

"I'll be quite frank with you, F.W.," my reincarnated friend said with a smile. "Sometimes we play at buying and selling."

"I understand; just like roulette or baccarat or poker."

"At play everything is permissible," B.H. declared. "Play is a revival of the irresponsible time dimension of childhood."

"Quite right," our abbé, the Spokesman, broke into the conversation. "Play is a revival of the well-nigh eternal time dimension of childhood. That applies, however, only to genuine play, play that babbles along, so to speak, without rhyme or reason; such play is nothing but a dreamy surrender of body and soul to the elemental forces that surround us. Play for profit or competitive play has nothing to do with genuine play."

"And yet I like buying and selling better than any other game," said Bridegroom Io-Do stubbornly and added, "I would trade ten trans-shadow-disintegrators any time for a powder-gun in reasonably good condition."

"I don't know what our marriageable young people are coming to," the Spokesman disapproved, and shook his head so violently that he had to straighten his silver headdress which was slipping down over one ear. Suddenly, however, he pointed at the sky with his outstretched arm. "But what do you expect of our young people when even Cosmic Sages and Life Sages engage in contests?"

On the celestial blackboard new star headlines had appeared: "Greatest Controversy of All Times. . . . Match between Professor Io-Sum and Professor Io-Clap Continues. . . . Can Existence of God Be Adequately Proven? . . . Standing of Contestants to Date: Professor Io-Clap Leads by a Score of Seventeen to Fifteen."

I shall have to make a confession to the reader: the word "Professor" did not actually appear on the firmament, but instead something that looked like and approximated the Greek word "Sophistes." I don't remember much about the Monolingua except its strange chirping and twittering phonology that I compared to Aztecan a while ago; but I recall that it contained a lot of Greek derivatives and loan-words which were used to designate institutions of the time. The Greek language, and to a lesser extent also Latin and Hebrew, had survived through the decamillennia as the language of scholars and theologians, just as (and perhaps through the medium of) the Christian Catholic Church and one other primeval institution that will appear at the proper time in my narrative had. So it was not the word "Professor" that appeared, but something like "Sophistes Io-Sum" and "Sophistes Io-Clap." But since the word "sophist" has a derogatory connotation in our language, I have decided, in the impudent manner of translators, to render it with our noncommittal word "professor."

"What do you think of that?" B.H. looked at me inquiringly.

"It is certainly the greatest controversial question of all times," I replied politely, "but also the oldest; that is implicit in the formulation. I'd like to bet any amount—oh, pardon me, betting is taboo—that I won't read anything new on the subject."

B.H. was properly offended on behalf of his contemporaries. He turned to face me. "Isn't it proof of very considerable intellectual progress that people all around the globe are being entertained today by this match instead of, as in your time, by a baseball game, a radidiocy, or a strip-tease act?"

"Strip-tease acts are pretty superfluous now," I answered dryly.

My friend failed to hear this sarcastic reply, for, along with everyone else, he was again gazing at the heavenly bulletin board where the starry type had begun to move once more. Raised to cosmic dimensions, it resembled the running titles of the silent film or the flashing and fading neon advertisements on the boulevards of the great cities in our ancient time.

"Seventeen Points for Professor Io-Clap. . . . Fifteen Points for Professor Io-Sum. . . . Professor Io-Sum's Move Next. . . . In a tireless day's work of a full twenty minutes he has condensed his thought into sixty-four words. . . . Attention. . . . Stand by. . . . Professor Io-Sum's sixty-four words follow."

The celestial slate turned black for half a minute, even considerably blacker than before. Then the starlets began to hop about busily in order to proclaim Sophistes Io-Sum's doctrine concerning the greatest controversial question of all times, which I transmit as follows:

"Human language, even our Monolingua, is only the creation of a creature. The creation of a creature proves only the existence of the creature but not of the Creator. Creation, however, and man in particular, is the language of the Creator. Throughout this language the Creator proves his essential quality, Infinite Goodness, for, in spite of everything, every creature prefers Being to Not Being."

Good for you, you're a smooth old boy, Sophistes and Professor Io-Sum; you turned that out pretty cleverly on the lathe of the Monolingua in your tireless day's work of twenty minutes; what zeal, what industry, for the delicate constitution of the modern thinker, I chuckled to myself. It's a good, solid aphorism, a little more literary than professorial, and certainly not inspired by humble faith. The thought juggles sixty-four words and wraps them up in a cloud of haze fitting for such subjects. But if I take a good look at the thought itself, then I recognize it as one of my oldest acquaintances, or at least as something that very closely resembles an old acquaintance. In reality it isn't one thought at all, but two, very cunningly mixed. Creation is the language of the Creator. I wasn't more than nineteen years old when I timidly put things like that down on paper. Such ideas all come from the prologue to the fourth Gospel: "In the beginning was the Word, and the Word was with God," and so forth. The second thought is really the important one: God proves Himself in His goodness in the fact that we, His creatures, prefer existence to nonexistence, in spite of everything. So you also have the words "in spite of everything" in your vocabulary, esteemed Ios of both sexes? Eternal youth or agelessness, longevity to the point of satiation and even of boredom, security and freedom from care in every aspect of existence, no war, no work, all material goods produced by a first-rate Worker with a beard—blond, I suppose—and delivered right into your houses. The chief aim in life is play, babbling child's play at that, relaxed surrender to the cosmic forces, while a bit of gambling or playing for stakes is illicit friction and against the rules. And at the end, since I assume that even this Mental life must come to an end, I suspect a perfectly miraculous trick, the most interesting detail by far of my present visit and I am looking forward to my initiation into it. Yet even here I find the words "in spite of everything" and perhaps they do not differ materially from the glorious "in spite of everything" from which the slaves and martyrs of Rome built the Christian Church. Who knows, who knows? At any rate, I'm curious for Sophistes Io-Clap's counter-move.

A dusky murmur rustled about me like the sound of distant surf and interrupted my meditation. The crowd of humans in the central plaza had meanwhile increased at least fivefold. Presumably tens of thousands assembled every night in the giant bowl of this agora to promenade in the bluish, black and white, crystalline starlight, read the "Evening Stars," and exchange opinions about the various Mental matches. Hundreds of groups moved about, describing graceful curves on their skates. The figures in their iridescent draperies formed an intricate pattern. Gold and silver headdresses quivered and glistened restlessly. From the circular railing around the pond-basin that held the sunken Monument of the Last War a reddish, martial glow emanated. The Official Guide of the Era had long ago withdrawn to the interior of the earth. The heavenly blackboard, upon which Professor Io-Sum's hypothesis had been reproduced several times in succession stared down again in pristine blackness. I was touched by the fact that the deep concern of all these people around me was not occasioned by the election of some county official of a political party, nor by a strike in an industrial plant, nor by a stock market crash, but by the greatest controversial question of all times, the proof of the existence of God, concerning which, I heard, secret bets were being made.

Bridegroom Io-Do turned toward me with a regretful shrug. "I am very sorry, Seigneur, you're not in luck. Today, on the third day of the week, they always have the dullest program."

I asked him what sort of program would be provided to-morrow, for example. He replied that there would be a "Riddle-Soirée" tomorrow, but there was no time for an explanation of this word, since the black rectangle was again blossoming with starry type. It was now Professor Io-Clap's turn to strike a counterblow.

"Fifteen Points for Professor Io-Sum. . . . Seventeen Points for Professor Io-Clap. . . . The last round of the contest is under way. . . . Io-Clap, the great improviser, is now preparing his reply to Io-Sum's new argument. . . . He will successfully complete his tremendous mental exertion in four and four-tenths minutes. . . . He still has two and two-tenths minutes to go. . . . We are about to witness the conclusion of the world's champion-ship match over the greatest controversial question of all times. . . . Keep your eye on the sky. . . . The committee has already come to an agreement whether the decision is to be made by a general vote or by the verdict of an umpire. . . . Keep your eye on the sky. . . . Three and five-tenths minutes of work have now elapsed."

"That's what I call a very fine job of Americanized journalism and artificial suspense," I whispered in B.H.'s ear.

My friend looked all around and then whispered back, "But don't forget that the object of the suspense isn't a horse race but the proof of the existence of God."

"Two things haven't changed, B.H.," I shrugged. "Man and his intellectual limits."

Again the dusky murmur ran through the crowd, for the stars were writing and writing:

"Four and two-tenths minutes. . . . Professor Io-Clap is still performing mental labor. . . . Four and four-tenths minutes. . . . The work is finished. . . . Keep your eye on the sky. . . . Professor Io-Clap has condensed his opinion into one hundred and fifty words. . . . The last round is about to be concluded. . . . Professor Io-Clap's one hundred and fifty words follow."

Again the slate turned black, much, much blacker than ever before. The subscribers to the "Evening Stars" stood in breathless silence and even my heart under its boiled shirt beat faster. Amid the general tension the starlets began to reassemble and record Io-Clap's thought.

"My opponent maintains that the will of the Being to Be and not Not to Be affords conclusive proof that this created Being emanated from an uncreated Being. But I ask Sophistes Io-Sum: Can an affirmation carry its own negation within itself? Can Being grasp the idea of Not Being? Can Life, in so far as it does not belong to its opposite, have the power even to want this opposite? Three times: No! The instinct of self-preservation, the incontrovertible will of Being to Be, is not a mutable quality, but a subsistent principle, in fact the essential nature of Being itself, from which it cannot be divorced. The will of Being to Be is therefore irrefutably immanent and signifies nothing but itself. It is a fallacy not permitted by the rules of logic to deduce from this will to Be a transcendental, conscious, personal, and benevolent origin of Being."

Holy mackerel, this time it really was professorial. Give me my dreamy Sophistes Io-Sum every time, with his sensitive heart and his illogical fallacies. Io-Clap, on the other hand, and his style are simply re-editions of our involved Messrs. Hegel to Heidegger. In Io-Clap's diction the Monolingua sounds almost like German. Moreover, Io-Clap manifests the real skulduggery of a German professor who was always ready to bring his professional jargon to the assistance of "the will to Be," no matter whether that will was named Fredericus or William II, or—or— what was that fellow's name?

Once more the starry script appeared in the sky: "Can Life, in so far as it does not belong to its opposite, have the power even to want this opposite?"

Why shouldn't it have the power to want it? That's where we have him, that cunning sophist. He knows very well that Life can sometimes passionately want its opposite. (I noticed, by the way, that even here the word "death" was replaced by the euphemism "opposite.") Perhaps even today there were occasional cases of suicide or of terrible diseases. To provide for these cases the professor protects himself by smuggling in the subordinate clause about Life that "belongs to its opposite." Wonderful, wonderful! I know all these tricks. And strangely enough, at this particular moment I felt a satisfied patriotism for my own era, the beginnings of mankind, and had a cunning sense of contentment that philosophy and metaphysics apparently had not made the slightest progress since Heraclitus, Plato, Aristotle, Thomas Aquinas, Descartes, Kant, Schopenhauer, and Bergson. On the contrary, any change that had taken place was in the nature of a retrogression, for debates of this sort, which we had conducted in dark corners of obscure cafés, were obviously regarded as titanic intellectual efforts in this day and age.

"Don't you think, Seigneur, that Sophistes Io-Clap formulates his point in a highly intelligent manner?" the Spokesman inquired, and his face under the structure of silver curls resembled that of Voltaire, a strangely youthful and handsome Voltaire, to be sure, and not the well-known satirical ape.

"Impeccably intelligent," I replied courteously. "I'm only surprised that after so many intellectual shipwrecks throughout the millennia people still make the same mistakes. In the beginnings of mankind we were well aware that the greatest controversial question of all times could never be decided by intellectual means alone, although the Roman Church regarded the existence of God as a fact susceptible to the insight of human intelligence."

But before the Spokesman and the other bachelors were able to continue the conversation with me the unexpected incident occurred that whirled me in an instant from obscurity to fame on the Third Day of the Fourth Earth-Month of the Seven Hundred and Forty-Second Sun-Week of the Zero Point Zero Zero Third Evolution in the Eleventh Cosmic Capital Year of Virgo, in the Geodrome which, unless I was mistaken, was the central plaza of the entire inhabited globe. When the incident began I couldn't believe my eyes. On the night sky of this remote present of the future, on the blackboard of the "Evening Stars"

I saw my own name emblazoned in stellar type—my own name, augmented by the prepositive "Io," the word that indicated personality, that distinguished man from all other creatures. Pale with terror I read this name from which I had taken leave one night incredibly long ago, for an eternity, as I thought. For my true, indestructible ego could not be covered by a single name and consciousness any more than an adult body could be covered by a handkerchief. I was shaken with embarrassment and confusion. But the worst was still to come. In phrenetic journalese the "Evening Stars" anounced that the "Committee for the Greatest Debate of All Times" had the unusual pleasure of offering the esteemed public a rare surprise—namely me—and not only as a primeval Seigneur, a sufficient surprise in itself, but as an intellectually vigorous Seigneur, a glaciationist, an antediluvianist, a pre-solar-transparentist versed in all philosophical tricks, who would consider it an honor to act as umpire in the last round between Sophistes Io-Sum and Sophistes Io-Clap and, on the basis of a just and Mentally well-founded decision, to award to the victor the prize of the pale yellow wrist-rosette. I was thunderstruck. My mouth opened and closed spasmodically. Suddenly I tried to escape on my whizzing Mercury shoes. But the members of our household formed a solid phalanx about me, led by the gold-helmeted Bridegroom whom this incident seemed to provide with a welcome thrill.

"What shall I do, B.H.," I whispered and felt that I was even paler than was fitting for a ghost.

"No nonsense now," B.H. whispered in reply.

"Imagine my embarrassment," I whispered.

"Take it easy," he whispered back, "and follow your impulses. The more zigzag, the better."

"Where are we going?" I asked a little louder, feeling my courage grow.

"To the Uranographer," they answered in unison.

And there he was, the Uranographer, the skywriter, the editor-in-chief of the "Evening Stars." He was standing at a wobbly table out in the cool night air. In front of him lay nothing but

two or three scraps of dirty paper. Every time he scribbled a
few words on one of these yellow sandwich wrappers with a
gnawed stub of a pencil, the stars began to hop around and to
form words and phrases. How did it work? Well, that was the
optic maneuver. The Uranographer looked up at us with the
unspeakably bored expression that constitutes an important part
of the journalist's stock-in-trade. For the true journalist inclines
to the conviction that facts in themselves do not exist at all and
that they only come into being when he reports them. After he
has reported them, to be sure, he accords them a little more
respect, for they are now a part of himself. He is consumed by
a creator's arrogance, and his only safety valve is his bored and
obviously harassed self-sufficiency. So the Uranographer looked
at me with harassed self-sufficiency, as though a materialization
from the forties of the twentieth century were not only an every-
day, commonplace phenomenon to him, but also a questionable
one. After his eyes had thoroughly impressed me with his professional nil admirari, he asked me in a low, grumbling voice,
"Have you made your decision, Seigneur?"

The Uranographer's bored air and his indifferent voice were
probably intended to express his utter disbelief in me as well as
in all the other facts that he wrote on the sky with his gnawed
stub of a pencil. But this air and this voice, while they offended
me, filled me with fresh vigor and energy.

"The trains of thought of Io-Sum as well as of Io-Clap," I said,
"are both quite conclusive and both fully defensible."

A pale glitter of interest gleamed in the Uranographer's
eye.

"Does that mean, Seigneur," he asked, "that you declare the
contest a tie?"

"No," I replied with slight emphasis. "I declare the contest
decided in favor of Professor Io-Sum."

The Uranographer yawned. He was the first person of this
era whom I caught in the act of a physical reaction to fatigue.

"And upon what grounds," he asked, "do you base this un-
appealable verdict?"

"Upon very simple and conclusive grounds," I said slowly, carefully choosing my words, and my heart glowed warmly with the oxidizing consciousness of being right. "Sophistes Io-Sum employed only sixty-four words for the formulation of his thought, while Sophistes Io-Clap required one hundred and fifty words to achieve the same degree of condensation. Io-Clap's thought, which, moreover, is not an independent hypothesis but a rebuttal, is therefore eighty-six words weaker than Io-Sum's thought. If we count ten words as one point, then Sophistes Io-Sum won eight and a half points in the final round and has accordingly won the match over Sophistes Io-Clap by a score of twenty-three and a half to seventeen."

The Uranographer's pencil stub flew over the sandwich wrapper so that the crippled table wobbled even more than before. As a completely disinterested editor he faithfully recorded the arithmetic of my verdict without either accepting or rejecting it. Of course I was very proud of my decision as umpire. The formula of my judgment sounded in my ear like a Newtonian formula: "Of two truths serving for the elucidation of the same theme, the one requiring the smaller number of words and syllables for its utterance, is to be awarded the prize of the yellow wrist-rosette."

Today, long after my return from that future present into our present present I find the popular approval of my verdict unintelligible as well as exaggerated. The idea of using the number of words as index to the truth was really a frivolous joke rather than a serious principle of philosophic research, particularly in view of the lofty character of the controversy. Be that as it may; in the bright starlight of that evening I was filled with cheerful satisfaction that I hadn't made a fool of myself, that I had acquitted myself nobly, and, to top it off, I had established a new principle. The strange thing was that this principle—the philosopher who uses too many words is sunk—made a big impression on the crowd in the huge Geodrome. Applause and the metal stamping of thousands of skates had an elemental ring. This Mental era, that shrank from all violent contact with the intellect and the emotions, approved particularly the pointed, ironic nature, the lightly clad earnestness of my verdict. Furthermore, they had a greater appreciation for the equivalent of Attic salt and Gallic spice than for the Germanic thoroughness that Sophistes Io-Clap seemed to have inherited over the decamillennia. The applause I received may even have reflected the antipathy for professors in general and for the theme of this everlasting debate. One thing, however, I must reiterate: today— I mean the time in which I am writing these pages—today the public discussion of such a subject before a world-wide audience would be utterly out of the question. Today only a few exceptional people have the education, vocabulary, freedom from prejudice, and intellectual capacity to follow a philosophical deduction. At that time—I mean the evening that will come a round hundred thousand years from now—practically everyone possessed this freedom from prejudice and the necessary education; from days immemorial time and leisure had been identical, and after the conquest of nature mankind would simply have died of boredom without intimate intercourse with the spirit realm and the realm of the spirit.

But the matter of this unexpected success of mine was still more complicated. I had been required to choose between two types. Of these two types Io-Sum represented simplicity, faith, and inspiration; Io-Clap represented intellectualism, unbelief, and skepticism. These two types, it soon dawned on me, were the symbols of an ancient feud that was still alive in the present age. I had awarded the crown to Io-Sum, the inspired. Very soon the ill-concealed bad humor of the Spokesman, the House Sage, and the Permanent Guest made it evident that the verdict had gone against the wishes of these new friends of mine. The bachelors all belonged to the older and oldest generations. In the course of the dinner Io-Fagòr, the father of the Bride, had paid his great-grandmother, the lovely Ancestress, a compliment to the effect that only during her youth had people known how to live. At the same time Io-Fagòr had recognized the decadence of modern youth in the fact that they were no longer devoted to pure play but threatened to relapse into long-conquered emotions; similarly, the sensible irongray sod covering the globe burst open here and there into those curious Jungles with their "roosters and clucking hens" and with what B.H. had called the "swinish hubbub." Bridegroom Io-Do with his martial collection and with his mania for trans-shadow-disintegrators and powderguns had furnished me a surprising instance of relapse into long-conquered emotions. So I began to suspect on the very first evening of my visit that the older people were mourning the passing of a sort of rococo, an ancien régime, which had preferred pastel shades (the light green and pale blue of the travel globules), while the younger generation now began to smuggle in heavier and darker hues, who knows, perhaps even real blood-red.

While all these paradoxes flashed through my brain, which was quite clear in spite of all hardships and which proved equal to the demands of the day in spite of the long period of training-less nonexistence, we—the members of our household and I—whizzed back and forth across the central plaza through the applauding, waving multitude. After a fashion, it was like reviewing a parade, just as distinguished visitors of yore used to do, kings, presidents, princes, marshals, prime ministers, who with their retinues, inspected the guard of honor. Bridegroom Io-Do seemed to derive the greatest satisfaction from my success; after all, he was directly responsible for it and could credit it to the account of his wedding days. The master of ceremonies at the moment, however, was not the Spokesman, who was still sulking because I had played a dirty trick on skepticism and agnosticism in my verdict, but the Permanent Guest, the one who looked like a baroque aristocrat in his plastic silver wig. He sped along at the head of our troop. Now and then he raised his hand and we had to interrupt our flight. In an instant we were then ringed by a curious crowd. One of the novel phenomena of this Astromental era for me was the fact that everybody appeared to know everybody else. The human family must have shrunk to a very few millions; no doubt to the exact number that mature judgment deemed necessary for its perpetuation. At any rate, everyone greeted everyone else and was greeted in return. The extremely formal and ceremonious salute reminded me somewhat of the manner in which the Chinese in my age had greeted each other, and also of the greeting of Prussian officers when entering a room; for they inclined their heads, at the same time keeping their torsos rigid, in order to avoid the broken line. B.H. explained the ceremonious intimacy of all with all by the fact that men had learned to treat each other with a higher degree of mutual respect because of the complete awareness that they were not members of an animal race which happened to be the survivors in the struggle for existence, but of the only human race, and therefore the center of the universe. The mere fact that one was human made him an acquaintance. And failure to salute an acquaintance was equivalent to showing him disrespect and hostility. So we stopped now and then whenever the Permanent Guest gave the order. I inclined my head and kept my torso rigid, and accepted similar salutes, although I belonged to this generation only through the vagaries of the time dimension and not in any sense of contemporary space, and I could be recalled at any time—a fact that I felt very clearly and with some amusement at this moment. Again and again I was asked questions that have remained unchanged since the beginnings of mankind and that will remain unchanged until its end.

"Is this your first visit to the Geodrome, Seigneur?"

"Yes, my first."

"And were you really as deeply impressed as the 'Evening Stars' just claimed you were?"

"I'm tremendously impressed."

"We're delighted, Seigneur."

Why should they be delighted with my few empty words of praise? Why were they so vain? Were they so very poor? Could it be that even in this day and age they were suffering from an inferiority complex?

"Tell us frankly, Seigneur, do you notice that we have made any progress?"

"Progress is too weak a word for the mountain heights of development that you have reached."

"And did anyone in your day, Seigneur, foresee these mountain heights?"

"No! In my time the complete subjugation of the forces of nature by means of technology was the epitome of all dreams of the future. They also included the struggle for a little social justice. An Astromental civilization of the sort you have today lay beyond our powers of imagination and beyond our wishful dreams."

"You don't say so, Seigneur!"

Reciprocal stiff bows concluded the conversation.

They were insecure, very insecure. Io-Sum's "in spite of everything" gnawed at them.

Suddenly puffy little Io-Solip began to get worried and thoughtful. "I have just been called up by my in-law, Io-Fagòr," he said.

I looked at the good-natured little father of the Bridegroom to see whether I could discover a tiny telephone or radio receiver in his hands. There was nothing of the sort. "How and by what means were you called up?" I asked curiously.

In order to silence my childish ignorance B.H. explained in a disparaging tone, "We call each other up Mentally," he said. "That will have to suffice for you. It takes a considerable amount of education and practice. You have to develop the ability to interrupt the stream of inner ideas and images at will and to evoke the image of the person you want to call with the greatest clarity. I'll practice it with you later."

"We are to come home at once," said Io-Solip, betraying a certain nervousness. "Io-La, the Bride, Io-Fagòr's lovely daughter, is getting very impatient and annoyed. She wants Seigneur to be introduced to her."

"The young lady's wish is my command," I said with old-fashioned courtliness; in reality I could hardly wait to get "home" and rest. I was filled with the hope that, after absolving my duties with regard to Io-La, or Lala, as the young lady was called,

I might be permitted to sit down somewhere, preferably in the amber of the little parlor where B.H. and I could be fossils again. But my hope was quickly shattered. The Official Guide of the Era approached at the head of an obviously official group. The Committee for the Greatest Controversy of All Times had made a decision about me which did not take into account my longing for the broken line. I was to be taken to the Global Major-Domo at once in order to receive a reward for my philosophical verdict.

"Global Major-Domo?" I asked. "Major Domus Mundi? Is this designation to be traced back to the ruling satraps of the time of the Merovingians and Carolingians?"

No one could answer. B.H., who probably could have, seemed disinclined.

"Is the Global Major-Domo the head of the state?" I asked.

"He is the Geoarchon, the World-President," B.H. replied.

"I beg your pardon," I said hesitantly, looking at my friend. "But I think that tomorrow, if I am still alive and here, I will be much more presentable than just now."

They outdid each other in assuring me that I could not possibly be more presentable than I was at the moment. Not even the argument that the lovely Lala, the day's Bride, was impatiently awaiting me, had any effect. The chief of the global state had commanded my presence.

"Gentlemen," I said, "you see this moderately honorable decoration here on my breast. The state which awarded it to me was dismissed from world history three weeks later until further notice. It's an evil omen. Unreliable people, who work in such imaginary realms as I do, should not be honored with medals and decorations like soldiers, solid government officials, politicians, and industrialists. Adroitness in literary expression is a gift but not an accomplishment, and least of all a virtue."

They scolded me for my superstition and tried in all seriousness to allay my worries. Every child knew, they said, that united humanity lived in a state of equipoise that only a cosmic catastrophe could shake.

Without attempting to suppress my sigh I asked, "Is the Government Palace near by? Will I have an opportunity to wash my hands before I appear before His Excellency?"

B.H. looked at me angrily. I was terribly sorry to disgrace him again and again.

"Government Palace!" He shook his head. "The Global Major-Domo lives in the Sentry Booth!"

* * * * *
* * *
*

NO, THE OFFICIAL RESIDENCE of the World-President or Geoarchon was something more than a Sentry Booth. It was a sort of guard-room in a crudely constructed shanty, reminiscent of military cantonments such as I had known only too well back in my day. Only its coat of paint—pale green and pale blue stripes—might have conjured up a dim recollection of the word "Sentry Booth" in the memory of my reincarnated friend; a recollection of round or square, wooden or stone boxes, intended to afford shelter in bad weather to the sentry on his post. The Sentry Booth of the Global Major-Domo was situated on the northern elevated rim of the platter in the midst of the architectural structures, whose purpose was still not clear to me, and whose symbols and ornaments towered much more solidly over the earth's surface than had been apparent from the center of the Geodrome. Compared with these structures, the intentional, exaggerated inferiority and humbleness of the highest official residence struck me very forcibly. It was almost a consolation to think that the World-President of the Era probably also occupied a splendid, roomy dwelling in the bright and airy labyrinths under the ground. Directly behind the uncouth guard-room, or, to preserve the wrong but more effective name, behind the Geoarchon's Sentry Booth there rose a high, wide dome of vitreous material, so that the interior of this opalescent cupola could be seen. On reclining chairs arranged in a circle, with the foot-ends turned toward the inside, lay about thirty motionless individuals who were either actually sound asleep or who seemed to be dozing while they took a healthful ray treatment.

"A sanatorium?" I asked B.H.

With a smile he shook his head. "On the contrary, my friend, those are the Harmonizers."

"Probably state officials—pardon me, world officials—who are taking the evening off?"

"Actually the most important world officials, F.W. Perhaps their unusual title will make it clearer to you. They are the Symphronists or Harmonizers. They Mentally harmonize the Keenly Directed Desires and thus regulate traffic. You can imagine that it's no small matter to harmonize something like ten thousand trips per minute, for lots of people move the same objective toward themselves simultaneously. It takes pretty complex higher mathematics to avoid collisions."

Although the mirror surface of the Geodrome sloped upward at a very gentle angle, we had to describe loops and arcs continuously, like regular ice skaters, in front of the Geoarchon's Sentry Booth, to avoid sliding back from the edge of the platter in the direction of the Monument of the Last War. The multitude kept at a fair distance from our little group, which had been augmented by the Official Guide of the Era and two or three committee members. As a child of my time I began at once to worry about the fact that the World-President's ridiculous Sentry Booth was entirely unguarded and unprotected. The striped door stood wide open. No bodyguard, no sentry, no detective, no policemen, not even a common, ordinary doorman was there to restrain a would-be assassin. The office of Global Major-Domo thus seemed to be neither envied nor sought after. I tried to steer my skates as near as possible to B.H.

"What is the name of His Excellency, the incumbent Geoarchon?" I asked.

"He doesn't have a name," B.H. answered softly.

"I mean, what's his actual name, what is he called in private life?"

"The Global Major-Domo isn't called anything. Neither actually nor in private life. At the time of his investiture his name is solemnly expunged from all records. He even has to sacrifice his 'Io.'"

"That must be very unpleasant," I blurted.

The House Sage, who had heard my exclamation, stopped directly in front of me. "It is a part of my duties, Seigneur, to give you a summary of the constitution——"

That was as far as he got, for the Spokesman rushed up abruptly (what suppleness at his age!) and interrupted him. "Your duty is pure speculation. On the other hand, the presentation of things in writing and orally is the Spokesman's duty——"

"Not the Spokesman's duty, for he is only a house speaker," rang the raucous, oratorical voice of the Official Guide of the Era, who suddenly towered above all the others and looked exactly like an unforgotten reading acquaintance of my youth, I mean the Egyptian Isis-priest Arbaces in Bulwer-Lytton's "Last Days of Pompeii." "Whose duty is it to guide a stranger who is not only a house visitor but a world visitor?"

They stood ashamed and silent. No one dared to question the authority of this ranking bureaucrat.

"The election of the planetary Archon," the Official Guide began dryly and at the same time impressively, "takes place by authority of our constitution through the medium of equal, direct, and secret universal suffrage. . . ."

The concept of "equal, direct, and secret universal suffrage" sounded familiar to my ears, too familiar, I must confess. The political speeches and newspapers of my own youth had been full of it, and the people of my own country had rejoiced when this principle became law, replacing franchise by classes. We, the students of that serene time, the week-end of world history, before 1914—I mean B.H., myself, and all our friends—had paid very little attention to politics and politicians, whom we scorned as representatives of uncultured, beery vulgarity. These same beer-bellied politicians, for their part, scornfully referred to us as "inexperienced esthetes." And that is exactly what we were,

in the firm conviction that we soared high above ordinary mankind because we regarded poems as more important than wage
disputes in industry, tariff boundaries, and the language question
in Irredentist states. When, after the week-end of history, the
bloody week-day dawned again, we soon learned our lesson.
But now, countless centuries after those forgotten battles for
democracy, which were lost and won, over and over again, when
I heard the faded, archaic phrase "equal, direct, and secret
universal suffrage" from the lips of the Official Guide, I felt
something of the disappointment of a tourist who had expected
St. Peter's Cathedral in Rome to be larger and more mystically
holy. At the same time I relived something of the estheticized
scorn of my youth for the deadly earnestness of politics. A
moment later, however, I found out that the election laws of this
era were not as beer-bellied and archaic as the sound of the
phrase led me to think.

"Every man and every woman," the radio voice of the Official
Guide continued to instruct me, "every bachelor and every spin-
ster, in short, every Io who has attained the thirty-third year, is
entitled to vote. Only eleven depersonalized persons, however,
are eligible for election. These are the Selenozusians, the Lunar
Consecrates. . . ."

In the interests of brevity I shall interrupt the Official Guide's
lecture and shall try to paraphrase this strange business in my
own words. I must admit that I was unable to make any notes,
and if I had, I could not have brought them back with me;
consequently, I could not possibly recollect all of the twenty-one
conditions necessary for Selenozusia or Lunar Consecration,
although I recall an essential portion. (The term "Lunar Consecration" seems to imply a retrogression to the mythological era of
the human race, long before the universal suffrage of my youth;
this implication is erroneous, however, and does not do justice
to the facts.) The eleven Selenozusians who, without knowing
it themselves, were candidates for the highest world office, were
chosen by a secret commission on the basis of certain legally
prescribed physical characteristics and spiritual qualities, and

their selection took place at the tender age of five years. From their fifth year on they were constantly but imperceptibly supervised. The number of such unsuspecting candidates could at times reach a hundred and ten; in case of necessity—that is, when the office of World-President was vacated—this number was sifted by the secret commission to the constitutionally prescribed eleven. The commission was engaged in a perpetual search for young children who possessed the required aptitudes for the highest office of the united human race. It was with regard to this discreet searching, testing, and choosing that the election was called "secret," and by no means with regard to secrecy of ballot. As these disclosures were being made I had to look at B.H., who was probably reminded even more forcibly than I of the search for the youthful Dalai Lama, the reincarnated Buddha, in the forbidden city of Lhasa. Thus all historical motifs recur, notwithstanding the passage of time. But I kept my mouth shut, mindful of B.H.'s ambition to be entirely up-to-date and without any yesterday.

Following are the physical characteristics, as I remember them, by which the commission, according to traditional precepts, recognized the genuine Selenozusians and global-presidentables: The ring-finger of the left hand had to be more than one centimeter longer than the index finger and, if possible, even longer than the middle finger. The thyroid gland had to function at a slower than normal rate, so that many of the presidentables tended toward slight corpulence, without, of course, offending against the normal esthetic standards. Furthermore, the perfect Selenozusian not only had to develop a higher capacity for sleeping than the average man, but he had to sleep with his mouth open. The reason for the latter was said to be a septum deformed by a curvature to the right, hindering the sun-breath that was inhaled through the right nostril, but permitting free passage to the moon-breath through the open left nostril. So much for the physical characteristics.

The mental and spiritual qualities that I enumerate here are more than incomplete: Slow but, if necessary, penetrating thought processes. An inclination toward day-dreaming and absent-mindedness. Bashfulness, timidity, a passion for solitude, a tendency toward broad generalizations and abstractions. All these qualities presupposed a definite deficiency in factual sense and in instinct for power. This particular deficiency was (or, more correctly, will one day be) required of the chief executive, probably in order to prevent the power-hungry type from attaining power, to spoil the honor for ambitious persons, and to destroy completely any propensity for tyranny and despotism in human nature. As I write this I recall one more biographical condition required, or at least expected, of the Lunar Consecrated candidate for the regency. This was not only simple celibacy but a definitely unhappy love affair (a great rarity at that time, as the reader may imagine) which the presidentable had to experience at the civil turning point of his life—a real, old-fashioned, unhappy love with all the trimmings, including a tear-soaked pillow and sirupy lyric poems. Only after this final revelation of a sensitive and vulnerable soul, resulting in celibatarian resignation, was the complete fitness, that is, unfitness, for the highest power established.

Now just a few words about the voting procedure itself, as far as the elucidations of the Official Guide clarified it. The term of office of the incumbent Major Domus Mundi was for the duration of his life. It ended only with his departure from existence. The secret of this departure, in connection with which the word "death" was always assiduously avoided, cannot be revealed, as I have said, before I come to the end of my visit. The Permanent Guest, the one with the baroque physiognomy, had prematurely revealed the fact that this departure was made "voluntarily and on foot." I myself will reveal nothing further at this time, and I insistently implore the reader not to turn to the conclusion of the book. (The relation between reader and author, too, must be based on mutual confidence.) The voluntary nature of the last journey excluded the likelihood of a precipitate and unpredicted exit from life for the average citizen, and of course that was even more true of the world's most prominent citizen. And yet in the

case of the most prominent citizen, only the secret commission
was informed of his start upon the final journey. The general
public found out about it only when the election was announced.
In the very hour, however, when the aged but ever youthful
Global Major-Domo departed, the eleven candidates for the succession were thrown into a sort of monastic prison, where they
had to await the result of the election in solitary confinement,
darkness, and asceticism. It would be a great mistake, however,
to assume that the eleven presidentable Selenozusians complained about their imprisonment and their privations. The only
thing they complained about was the misfortune that would soon
overtake one of them, namely, to be elected to the highest rank
among men. Again and again they implored the wardens and
the members of the commission to permit them to escape and to
sink back into obscurity, or even to keep them forever in dark,
solitary confinement. They sought to escape only a single danger,
the danger of becoming the focal point of mundane distinction.
For the gentle reader this attitude will be just as unintelligible
as it was for me and for the entire world into which I returned
from there. Our kings, presidents, vice-presidents, ministers, sec-
retaries of state, governors, undersecretaries, mayors, and village
magistrates are glued to their respective thrones and chairs. They
cling to the arms of these seating accommodations with such
desperate claws that nothing but a swift kick or a revolutionist's
bullet can dislodge them. If it is an elective office that they hold,
they would be delighted to be elected for twenty successive
terms, if only to avoid the disgrace of returning to the ranks of
the insignificant and nameless. For the politician is only a para-
site of fame. A truly gifted man earns his name by the exceptional nature of his character and accomplishments; the politician
gets his name surreptitiously by the most commonplace commonplaces, in caucuses and conventions, in party congresses and
meeting halls, in back rooms reeking of intrigue, cheap tobacco,
horse trading, and corruption. The possession of power must be
depressing, crushing, breath-taking beyond words! Must not a
moderately moral human writhe in perspiration and in night-

mares of terror before every weighty decision that depends upon
his signature? And yet the mighty flourish wonderfully in the
civilization of the twentieth century. They grow old, they have
steady nerves and rosy cheeks, and the best among them dine,
wine, and smoke with visible relish. It seems as if they are sus-
tained beyond the measure of ordinary humans by the steel
corset of demoniac arrogance, by an orgiastic turgescence which
fills the remotest corners of their being with perpetual lust, that
can only be debilitated by loss of power. And loss of power is
indeed a tragedy from which they wither like actors, only faster;
for they too live only by the sound and fury that their short-
lived names stir up.

So much for the rulers of our century, I mean the twentieth;
and I wasn't even speaking of the power-mad despots, the dicta-
tors and their subordinate devils. It was utterly different with the
Selenozusians of the remote future in which I was now living.
They fell to their knees before the commissioners and begged,
implored, to be released from the nightmare of power, of position, of honor. The only amelioration of the misfortune lay in the
fact that the chosen candidate would no longer have a name, so
that at least only a nameless, hence unidentifiable, person would
bear the burden of elevation. Meanwhile, in the course of the
election procedure, the names of the presidentables were announced by the hand of the Uranographer in the "Evening Stars"
on the night sky, along with their records and a pitiless charac-
terization and biography, so that the voters might have a clear
picture of each candidate. This was repeated nightly for an
indefinite period. Then the people were informed of the date
fixed for the election. But they were not informed whether the
candidate receiving the largest number of votes or the one receiving the smallest number would be declared elected. This was
decided by a small quorum of Cosmic Sages. So the voters remained in ignorance as to whether their ballots helped to steer
the chosen candidate into the Sentry Booth of the world's highest
office or excluded him from it. Today, after my return, this
frustration of the voters seems incomprehensible to me; at that

time, that is, in the most distant future, when I first heard it
from the mouth of the Official Guide, it struck me as the bold
answer to a riddle or the clever solution to a difficult mathematical problem.

When I first heard the word "Sentry Booth" in connection with
the term "Global Major-Domo," it occurred to me that this civilization intended to degrade the function of power in the person
of its highest representative both visibly and symbolically. I
mention this idea only in order to emphasize the awe-inspiring
reality of this mighty man who abhorred might, this recipient
of honors who wanted no honor.

The Official Guide had already disappeared inside the august
shanty and my household group shoved me gently after him
through the open door into the brown dusk. The first things I
distinguished were two little lamps on the floor, two night-lights
—I almost said funeral lights—whose glow barely penetrated the
gloom. They were the first "natural" sources of light that I had
seen in this world of invisible and variegated modes of illumination; flat little lamps with long beaks, of antique design, dating
from Babylonian or earliest Roman time, little receptacles filled
with oil and with a floating wick. In the pale beam in the room
of the present Geoarchon unutterable antiquity and unutterable
modernity mingled with the eternally human. It was probably so
intended as a symbolic expression, for in the eternally human
nothing is more persistent than the wish to invest reality with a
dual meaning and to give trite things a divine background. The
so-called realistic eras that stubbornly refuse to acknowledge
the divine duality of reality—as, for example, the twentieth century, to which I have meanwhile returned from the Geoarchon's
Sentry Booth—are as corroded by their own meaningless, self-
sufficient reality as by vitriol.

Finally I began to see more clearly. Between the two archaic
lamps from ancient Rome or Babylon the couch of the World-
President of the beginning of the second hectomillennium bulked
solidly against the background of the narrow guard-room. The
head-end was considerably elevated so that the sleeping figure,

wrapped in the violet veil of regency, was visible from head to foot; the ageless face of yellowish ivory color stood out as sharply as that of a body lying in state. He was asleep, the most important, the most prominent man of the period, the only nameless one, the only one of living Ios not identifiable with himself, the uncrowned crowned head. He slept as Selenozusians should sleep, breathing evenly but with his mouth half open. It was easy to see that this sleep was not the customary infirmity of our depraved twentieth-century nature that required restoration and invigoration, but a sort of official sleep, in the course of which a part of the mysterious business of government was being transacted. I had to think of the Harmonizers in their reclining chairs under the heavy glass dome, the high officials who had to harmonize the Mental traffic of the entire globe. They too did it in their sleep, yes, even by virtue of their sleep, although their office was far below that of the world-chief in rank, dignity, and importance. *The utilization of sleep for the purpose of increased mental vitality*—this principle was now disclosed to me as a completely unknown and inexplicable field, in which man had made the greatest advances up to now. We—I mean the reader and myself—we spend about one-third of our average of seventy years sleeping—in other words, about twenty-three years—whereby our average span shrinks to an insignificant forty-seven years. But these people here had learned to be something more in their sleep than at best victims of a sham life of dreams. By means of their formative spirit they influenced events as vitally as though they were awake, although actually they appeared to be unconscious. They lived the full hundred and eighty or ninety years of their mundane existence without any deductions.

The distinguished gentleman who had forfeited his name at the time of his investiture slept an alabaster sleep that lay on his features as thin and as diaphanous as a layer of present absence. Under this pellucid film he seemed to be working on the soul of the world and on his own soul with the highest degree of calm concentration. In my recollection it is still an unforgettably admirable sight. Even Bridegroom Io-Do, who had boasted before

the Monument of the Last War that he would personally waken
the Global Major-Domo, stood there absorbed and silent, as
though on tiptoe. It was obviously impossible to waken anyone
from such a sleep of farseeing hyperwakefulness. Behind the
head-end of the couch stood two ministrant Mutarians. The
glistening bald head of the Official Guide was bowed in a listening attitude at the right hand of the sleeper. At his left hand,
bowed in a similar manner, was another bald head; presumably
that of the attending Chamberlain.

Suddenly the sleeper opened his eyes. They were splendid,
dark, deep, thoughtful eyes, the most beautiful I had ever seen,
but they were brimful of indescribable grief. How was it possible
that these eyes, shiny with grief, watched over a world whose
highest ideal was simple, aimless play? Suddenly I was startled
to discover that the eyes of the Nameless One were fixed unwaveringly and searchingly on me, and had been for some time.

"Your Excellency," the head at the left began to speak, "the
time for the Oracle of the Day has come. The Uranographer is
waiting."

The ruler of the planet made no reply. The word, of course,
wasn't "Excellency" any more than it had been "Professor" a
while ago. That is only my poor translation. Now the hoarse
oratorical voice of the Official Guide of the Era rang out.

"Your Excellency, Seigneur, from the beginnings of mankind,
has arrived to receive from Your Excellency's hands the badge
of merit for his verdict in the greatest controversy of all times."

The eyes of the Geoarchon looked at me steadfastly; and as
if they, and not his gentle, somewhat too high voice, were speaking, I heard the words: "The stranger who comes home, does not
make himself at home, but makes home strange."

This was a very pretty Oracle of the Day; the constitution
required one such to be published daily in the "Evening Stars."
It was couched in the style of a Delphic dictum, but it was
spoken lightly and dryly, in the manner of the judge of a royal
court mumbling the routine phrase: "In the name of His Majesty,
the King, I declare the court in session." At the moment I had

no idea that this was not an empty ceremony but a prophecy that applied to me, the fulfillment of which I would experience.

The Nameless One had made a gesture. Thereupon the bald head at his left rattled off a couplet:

"The Sleeper will now step down to the ground.
All tactful witnesses turn around."

Everybody turned around. Since I was a little confused, B.H. had to give me a shove to make me do the same. It was not considered good form to look when a dignified or a prominent person arose from his couch. The transition from one bodily posture to another was regarded as unlovely and embarrassing, except in the case of very young people. Now the bald head at the left rattled off another couplet that turned us back to His Excellency again. Since I have forgotten this verse I can't repeat it without inventing one, and I am doing my utmost to avoid any invention in this narrative.

Although I had turned around again after the second couplet, I kept my eyes cast down in order not to offend the noble Selenozusian's profound embarrassment and his uneasy touch-me-not attitude that made the air vibrate perceptibly. As I looked up now, his unbelievably sad eyes gazed at me even more intently and more steadily than before. The figure in the violet drapery, elegant in spite of its slight corpulence, now stood directly in front of me. I knew that my gaze had to withstand his without flinching. It was not easy. Gradually, however, I felt and knew that the overfull eyes were speaking to me. This is not the trite fictional phrase; the eyes of the world-chief were actually speaking to me in the language of eyes and thoughts. Since everyone understood the Monolingua, and the silent language of eyes and thoughts was intelligible only to the person immediately addressed, the latter had, in the course of time, developed into the only means by which discreet information and secrets could be communicated. After a few nervous and anxious moments even I, arch-idiot that I was, understood or believed that I understood what the Major Domus Mundi wanted to confide to me. It was pretty distressing for me and, translated into articulate language, ran about as follows:

"Why did you come here, Seigneur? It's not only unhealthy for you but also for us, as I hinted in the antithesis of my Oracle of the Day. Man is the creature of only his own century and nothing more. He should devote himself entirely to that which constantly melts away while it continues to exist, that which he calls the present. If he visits the past in the musty medium of documents and epitaphs, he is committing a slight sacrilege, for the past of the historical delver can never be the genuine past. But if he sticks his nose into the future, into the musty medium of an absolute vacuum in which there are no documents and not even graves, then he is committing a very great sacrilege, a sin before God, even though a prophetic dream or death may·whisper many true things in his ear."

It must be admitted that the things which the language of these sad eyes communicated to me with increasing clarity were indeed more than embarrassing. I was definitely being kicked out. The world-head was handing me a summary dismissal from a present into which I had entered by the wrong door. And how right the Geoarchon was! I didn't belong here. But was it my fault? What could I do? Not a thing, for, as the reader already knows, I hadn't learned how to dissolve. Instead I did something downright nasty. By means of vigorous rolling of my eyes as well as urgent motions of my head and fingers I drew attention to the reincarnated B.H. and put all the blame on him for my presence at this forbidden time in the Eleventh Cosmic Capital Year of Virgo. Of course it was his fault, consciously or unconsciously, for he had drawn my name from the alphabet. But B.H.'s·fault did not exonerate me. Was it proper for me to commit such a treachery against my old schoolmate and best friend and to squeal to the teacher with rolling eyes and stabbing index finger, even though he was guilty and I had gotten into a jam through his fault?

I don't know how much of all this the noble Selenozusian noticed. His eyes had not followed my index finger. They rested

on me with charming, ineffable sadness without speaking any
more. Nor did these eyes waver when the Geoarchon's hands
suddenly tore a long rip in his violet veil drapery, as the Ori-
entals do when they are mourning someone's death. I did not
understand the significance of this ceremonial act at once. Not
until the Official Guide and my other companions had nodded
and blinked at me with appropriate gestures, did I extend my
left arm with its disgracefully frayed shirt cuff toward the
Global Major-Domo. The sad, marvelous eyes released me. Unnaturally slim, slightly trembling ivory hands fastened a strip of
the violet veil loosely about my left wrist. I had received a high
distinction. The violet badge of honor assured me the best of
treatment, even special preference, on the part of my uncontem-
poraneous contemporaries. The badge was undoubtedly more
significant than the provincial medal on my left breast. I had
brought the medal here with me. Would it be possible for me
to take along the rosette of honor as a piece of evidence to
wherever I would have to go from here? During the entire time
that I spent in the present of the most distant future I always
had the feeling that I was only a visitor; I never thought for an
instant that I would be permitted to settle here permanently.
But where would I be going from here? Since I had come from
the dead, as I believed, I would have to return to the dead, along
with my medal and rosette. It was B.H.'s fault that I had to die
twice. Serves him right, I thought with a sneer, that I pointed
my finger at him before.

I looked at the nameless, Lunar Consecrated world-chief intently, in order to impress the nobility of his features on my
memory forever. I regretted that I would never see him again.
How could I know that I would see his sublime face once more?
. . . In a tragic hour.

The Eighth Chapter

WHEREIN I FINALLY APPEAR BEFORE THE
BRIDE AND, IN THE COURSE OF A LENGTHY
CONVERSATION, AM TEMPTED BY THE HAND
OF THE YOUTHFULLY BEAUTIFUL ANCESTRESS
TO COMMIT AN ACT WHICH WILL HAVE
DISASTROUS CONSEQUENCES.

THE THINGS THAT happened to me upon my return "home"
and which I record here, were not particularly dramatic at
the outset but they made up for it by being highly significant. When we landed in front of the clump of trees at the garden
gate—the starlight was still bright but more subdued than over
the Geodrome—Io-Fagór, the lord of the manor and father of the
Bride, was awaiting us with the greatest impatience. The gentle—
and, I hope, still well-disposed—reader knows very well that the
preceding sentence does not correspond exactly to the facts, for
ordinarily I purposely reiterate, perhaps to the point of boredom,
everything new and unusual that I encountered. The reader
knows, therefore, that it was not we who landed at the garden
gate but that we moved the gate, along with Io-Fagòr's interesting personality, toward us by means of the Mentelobole
puzzle; he also knows that the trip required activation of the
kinetic intellects of the sleeping Harmonizers, who co-ordinated
our Keenly Directed Desires with those of thousands of other
travelers by means of some super-mathematics and physics that
were far beyond my comprehension but that functioned per-

141

fectly. And from now on, no matter what objective I may move toward myself, I shall refrain from mentioning the Mentelobole and its operation, on the supposition that the reader's highly developed gift of imagination will spare me the trouble of describing this familiar as well as unexplained procedure in connection with every change of location.

Io-Fagòr received us with a gentle reproach to the Spokesman for our delay. But when he saw the violet ribbon on my left wrist that the Major Domus Mundi had torn from his own veil garment as a mark of distinction, the father of the Bride bowed his golden head approvingly.

"You have brought great honor to my house, Seigneur," he said. "I followed the course of events in the 'Evening Stars' with pride. Your verdict was the product of a truly playful spirit and of a fine sense of tact. I congratulate you upon the highest class of wrist-rosette that can be awarded by our world-executive."

Once again I looked down along my figure and noted with disgust the old grease stains on the silk lapel of my evening coat, the wretchedly dangling medal, and the frayed left cuff that I had instinctively pulled down over the violet rosette in order to conceal it. I shrugged my shoulders. It was not a haughty gesture but one of painful embarrassment.

"I know, Seigneur," Io-Fagòr said and emphasized his words with a smile, "that such distinctions and decorations not only mean nothing to you, but are probably annoying——"

"Not at all, my dear host," I contradicted him. "Unfortunately that is not the case. Since I have had the vivid experience that not only our human ego, together with its body, is indestructible, but even the worn dress suit that clothes the body, I must now make the disagreeable confession that the vanity of this ego is likewise indestructible. I am much prouder of the veil-rosette that I received from His Excellency, the Geoarchon, for a mediocre joke, than of this metal thing for which I had to work incomparably harder."

"It wasn't a mediocre joke at all, Seigneur," said Io-Fagòr seriously, "it was the most astounding adaptability, for which all of us respect you highly. Your accomplishment seems all the greater to me when I consider how long you rested and only counted the empty beats and measures of an orchestral part during which the instrument must remain silent."

Io-Fagòr, a highly gifted man, had used a musical metaphor that lay outside the realm of my experience, although it was quite ingenious. He compared the rest between death and resuscitation with the empty measures of an orchestral instrument, during which it must remain silent because the composer had marked them "Tacet." The musician, however, who plays this orchestral instrument is required to count out the empty measures so as not to miss his cue. Up to now I had had too little leisure to meditate about the state of my ego between that final, vague night and my appearance on the irongray sod a few hours ago. But in any case it was not comparable to a musical rest during which one counts measures and stares at the conductor.

"Timelessness," I strove to explain the unexplainable, "is by no means a rest, a void, a gap; in fact it is not the absence of anything that continues to exist without it. It neither stops nor does it pass. It is like frozen lightning, an instant that rushes away incessantly without vanishing. It is——"

"Don't exert yourself, Seigneur," Io-Fagòr interrupted me solicitously. "You are getting pale and you're perspiring, as you always do when you make too many demands upon your instrument of existence. I myself have nibbled around a bit in the marvels of timelessness; years ago I took the advanced layman's course for Chronosophers and Starrovers. I'll see to it that you are admitted to the elementary Lamasery of the Chronosophers."

"That would be very kind of you," I breathed.

Io-Fagòr winked at me significantly. We let the others precede us through the garden gate. The leathery foliage bristled stiffly in the starlight. The sickly giant magnolias hung limply white, robbed of their pale pink or yellowish tints. But my eyes seemed to distinguish far more different kinds of blossoms than before. Around the stygian flora of the Mental world fluttered pale-winged Lepidoptera as large as birds which produced a pleasant twittering sound that sometimes rose to a dry trill or fell to a rustling sob. Its relationship to birdsong was the same as that of a noiseless laugh to genuine laughter. I assumed I was listening to the lay of the nightingale of the Mental era.

"Did you notice anything?" the father of the Bride asked me softly but earnestly.

"Why? Was I supposed to notice something?" I whispered in return so that the others would not hear me.

"You became acquainted with the Mononation out there in the Geodrome, didn't you . . . ?"

"What is that—the Mononation?"

"I mean the human race, naturally, the indigènes of our planet."

He used the word "indigène" as a foreign word. That gave me the courage to address him in the same language as "chum."

"Oh, you mean the people of this day and age, Compère. I'm sorry my eyes are so bad. But I thought your indigènes of today were perfectly marvelous. A fluttering of veils of changeable pastel shades; and they applaud by clapping and stamping just as they used to do, and the babies in the arms of their mothers or nurses even cry. That's what I liked best. That made me feel right at home."

Io-Fagòr stood still and looked at me with strange melancholy. "I didn't ask you, Seigneur, whether you liked the indigènes of our planet. I asked you whether you noticed anything particular about them."

"I'm not sure that I understand you."

"Did you notice any kind of tension, Seigneur? Any kind of uneasy bitterness or sneering dissatisfaction under the changeable pastel veils?"

"None whatever, not a trace of it," I declared to the best of my knowledge and belief. "The spiritualized human race, Mental mankind, seems to be in the very best of order. No more chaos of any sort. That is, if I'm to be entirely honest, the only strange thing I've observed up to now is your future son-in-law's predilection for old weapons of war."

Io-Fagòr sighed deeply and raised his noble, yellowish right hand slightly to silence me. All gestures in the Mental era were quite restrained.

"That's enough, Seigneur," he whispered. "Not another word about that."

I had no time to interpret Io-Fagòr's deep sigh, for at that minute the Mutarian, Io-Fra, had appeared and in complete silence had communicated something to the Bridegroom. Io-Do turned to us, obviously upset. "You'd better hurry, Seigneur," he urged. "I've just heard that Io-La, my enchanting Fiancée, is in tears because you stayed away so long. She's been waiting for you since dinnertime. And now the first night-vigil is almost ended."

"It isn't my fault, Fiancé," I protested. "A stranger like myself has to follow the program that his hosts lay out for him."

"It's my fault alone," said Bridegroom Io-Do, "and that's the worst of it."

❊ ❊ ❊ ❊ ❊
❊ ❊ ❊
❊

ALL THE MEN, INCLUDING BRIDEGROOM IO-DO, had to remain behind. They were not permitted to enter the women's quarters, particularly during the festal days preceding the solemn union of husband and wife. It is certainly surprising, but in this day and age, in this remotest and most enlightened future, there were again segregated chambers for women, as in the medieval period of chivalry or in the Islamitic Orient. This arrangement might have resulted from a stricter code of morals or from a crafty desire to increase the sweet tension between the sexes. I had asked that my reincarnated friend might accompany me. Whenever the companion of my youth was not at my side, I felt indescribably deserted, although my vaunted adaptability, which Io-Fagòr had recently praised, had actually helped me to get pretty well accustomed to the time and its people. So they made an exception of B.H. and permitted him, contrary to cus-

tom and usage, to precede me to the chambers of the Bride.
B.H., reincarnated as he was, and with too much memory of the
past, really didn't belong here anyhow. He was, as we already
know, not a full-fledged citizen but an outsider in the era.
Even though he had been living with the others for one hundred
and seven years, he was counted among the "born bachelors";
I, too, as an unmistakable ghost, would be numbered with them
if my visit chanced to extend over some time. And so B.H. was
permitted to walk ahead of me to the bridal chamber, which lay
at the end of a long corridor smelling of a beech forest.

As we crossed the threshold, voluptuous June moonlight flowed
about us; it quivered on the walls and floor as though screened
through swaying foliage. It was the light of the honeymoon that
would caress the young married couple two nights later when
they retired to their bridal bed. This bridal bed, higher and
wider than all the couches in the house, stood in the center of
the room. B.H. permitted me to enter first. A sudden reticence,
a shy timidity—or was it a deeper premonition?—restrained me
at the door, where B.H. also stopped. Before I could distinguish
the individual persons in the room by the extremely pleasant but
not very revealing moonlight without a moon, the dog Sur sprang
toward me and honored me with an address that occupied my
attention for some time, as I was trying simultaneously to understand him and to fend him off. It was the same old naïve babbling
behind which his discomfort and fear in my presence were only
ill concealed.

"'Scuse please, Saysur"—of course he couldn't pronounce
foreign words like "Seigneur"—"I'm not scared. Sur not scared
at all. Good evenin'; goo' night. Hope you stay long time. One
more dinner an' 'nother dinner, then it's over. Then we're moving, Sur with Papa and with Big Mamma. Little Mamma's crying,
see, Saysur. Little Mamma——"

"Will you be quiet, Sur," Io-Rasa, the mother of the Bride
ordered. She was standing at the foot-end of the bed and was
arranging sprays of rusty-red blossoms that looked like tragacanth

flowers; I had noticed these unsatisfactory substitutes for our roses the first time I entered the enclosed grove.

"Please come in, Seigneur," Io-Rasa added. Her rebuke sent the eloquent dog into hiding somewhere with a prolonged grumbling, for in spite of his frantic assurances to the contrary, my presence made him extremely nervous.

"Please do come closer, Seigneur, along with your dear friend," another female voice chimed in. But it could not be the voice of the Bride. It was a splendid contralto voice with a definitely dusky quality that was not the result of age but of conscious, wanton, and worn-out licentiousness which could find gratification only in the deepest and most shameless depravity. It is unnecessary to say that this contralto voice belonged to the Ancestress, Io-Fagòr's great-grandmother, and thus the great-great-grandmother of the Bride. The old lady, with whose impeccable youthfulness and beauty we are already acquainted, was standing near the wall by the huge bridal bed—that is, she was not standing, she was leaning, or practically lying on a contraption like an ironing board that could be folded down from the wall and that seemed especially intended for the use of those who corresponded to our tired, infirm, or aged people. It was a very comfortable support that permitted one to stand and lie at the same time. I, with my black-and-blue bones, was profoundly envious of Madame Great-great-grandmamma.

Before I turn to the true heroine of my narrative, I must first devote a few words to the wall from which the above-mentioned support projected. In the rooms which I had entered up to now, my attention had been far too exclusively centered on the people to permit close observation of objects and things. Even Bridegroom Io-Do's wall-filling collection of weapons had not caught my eye. In a fast-moving novel the hasty reader is frequently inclined to skip the most beautiful descriptions of scenery and rooms, which the author sometimes extends beyond appropriate limits not for the sake of the reader but of his own pedantic honesty. The great dramatists of the past, on the other hand, treat the problem of description, of stage direction, with consummate boldness. Calderón, Lope de Vega, Shakespeare, simply write: "Night. Castle-yard." And if it's a stage direction in Macbeth the author doesn't have to add: "Cloud-racked sky, wind. A hoot-owl is shrieking." All that and many other things are included in the two words "Night. Castle-yard." Every additional syllable would diminish the author's greatness. An author of a book of travels, as I am called upon to be, deserves a certain degree of indulgence. His main business is not action, plot, intrigue, and solution of a conflict, but—hideous to contemplate —description and more description. An explorer, for example, who is writing about the Antarctic, is not permitted to confine himself to the subjective impression that the two volcanoes Terror and Erebus made on him. He is obliged to report their geographic location, their absolute and relative altitudes, their geological formation, the cycle of their activity, and all that in objective words and exact figures. That is the task of the explorer in space, where everything is more or less permanently fixed and subject to verification; moreover, he has at his disposal a lot of good atlases that he can consult whenever he doesn't trust his memory. But the reporter sent ahead into time has no such aids and crutches for a lame memory. There are no reference books on earth about the Eleventh Cosmic Capital Year of Virgo. The snowy wastes of Fridtjof Nansen Land below the North Pole are far less untrodden than the Geodrome, the central plaza thronging with tens and hundreds of thousands. That doesn't mean that I feel sorry for myself on account of my hard task; it is merely meant for the nervous reader as an explanation of the reason that I continually relapse into the hated form of description without being capable of painting a Shakespearean picture in two words. A picture is intelligible only when it is a copy of a model. Do I have a model—now be honest—that represents the Eleventh Cosmic Capital Year of Virgo?

The moon-daubed walls of the bridal chamber were disturbingly alive. Was it a continually changing, dynamic wallpaper that covered them? Or was an endless film being projected from somewhere, a breathlike film that always showed the same landscape, varied only by perpetual changes of light, wind, and shadow? No. My eyes convinced me that both explanations were erroneous. In the background of the pictures running around all four walls several mountain ranges appeared, distinguishable from each other only by the lighter or darker shade of blue that the moonlight poured over them. But how did the memory of these mountain ranges and of these nocturnal tints get into this subterranean dwelling? Millennia ago the gray-carpeted planet had forgotten that such mountain ranges had ever risen from its surface and that one shade of blue behind another could fade away in ever hazier layers. And besides that, they were mountains of my own recollection, the mountains in whose shadow I had breathed and worked for twenty years of my relatively short life. How did this landscape come to be on the walls of Io-La's bridal chamber in the form of visionary or dynamic wallpaper? Was it a gesture in my honor on the part of the Mental era, where everyone knew more of his neighbor's inner life than was good for him? Was it I myself who cast the beloved landscape on the blank wall out of my inner storehouse and at the same time made a little, despondent gesture in order to express my nostalgic astonishment? In the foreground of the visionary wallpaper, whose perspective was more plastic than any stereoscopic photograph, the shadow designs of the pliant branches of larch trees played gently in the faint night wind, and there stood the decaying observation tower of the Kreuzberge.

"Do you see the same things that I do, B.H.," I whispered, "there on the wall?"

"What do you see, F.W.?" He smiled. "Each one of us has a different wallpaper, you may be sure."

Then I suddenly knew that during the hundred thousand years of my death man had acquired the ability to develop, fix, and project his own inner pictures on the wall. The pale confusion of the imaginative faculties of former times had increased

infinitely in power, sharpness of definition, and clarity of elabo-
ration. Everyone was his own painter and poet and could read
his visions in clearest details on the walls of his subterranean
house. The false moonlight and the artificial odor of the forest
had awakened powerful memories within me, which were now
reflected as complete images on the dynamic wallpaper.

"It's hard to see you there, Seigneur, because you're standing
in the shadow," the dark contralto voice said. "Do come closer—
still closer. My little great-great-grandchild has been shedding
tears about you, haven't you, Lala? They promised you an unusual entertainment, and the unusual entertainment kept you
waiting for hours on your evening of honor."

The youthfully beautiful Ancestress accompanied her words
with a strangely golden but toneless laugh. And I stepped shyly
toward the huge bridal bed, on tiptoe—God knows why. Io-
Rasa had meanwhile finished her work. The bed was completely
covered from top to bottom with the stiff, scentless straw flowers,
the ersatz-roses of the age. Under them the Bride lay—even in
Mental style I can't find any other description—on her stomach.
Her face was buried in her arms, and from time to time her
lovely back, gleaming faintly through the traditional dovegray
veil drapery, seemed to be shaken by obstinate sobs.

"My stubborn darling," Io-Rasa cajoled her, "my little Lala,
don't torment yourself any longer. Seigneur is here. Seigneur is
standing right next to you."

"Is he really standing next to me?" The voice of the Bride
sounded muffled and unnatural from between her folded arms.
"Is he really here or are you fooling me again?"

"We've never done that, my sweet Lala," the Bride's mother
rebuked her gently. "We have suffered from your unruliness and
nervousness that's quite unfitting for the sacred bridal time. My
heart is very sad. Don't be so childish any more, even though
you are still terribly young."

"Please don't say that I'm young," Lala's voice grumbled
morosely. "You know I can't bear to hear it, I can't bear it!"

"Much too young," the Ancestress criticized pitilessly. "Not even twenty-six years old. In my day they used to chase the twenty-six-year-olds out to the Worker's Park to grow, instead of getting married——"

"Don't be impolite, little Lala," the mother of the Bride interrupted, "and do turn around. You can't keep on showing your back to Seigneur."

"He kept me waiting so long!" Lala's voice sounded from below in an offended tone and with a suppressed sob.

"My very dear young lady," I heard myself saying in my most embarrassed and polite manner, "I am entirely new here. You understand that I am a rank newcomer, a greenhorn who finds it very difficult to get along. It's not my fault that I kept you waiting to the end of the first vigil. They drew me out of the alphabet and summoned me here without my knowledge or consent. I am entirely dependent. Your father and your Fiancé plan my program, not I myself. I'm sorry that I made you impatient. But I must decline all responsibility here and now not only for my tardiness, but for everything else that might happen later."

This I said in dignified language but at the same time I could not rid myself of a bitter feeling of discomfort. I felt like a pedantic ass who wants to vindicate himself in the eyes of a woman for all past and future offenses by a dry statement of fact.

"So you're really here beside me," said Lala from under her arms, but the tone sounded different.

"Yes, he's really here," fluted the mother of the Bride with exaggerated delight, and it sounded as childishly coaxing as though she were speaking to a five-year-old instead of with a twenty-six-year-old. "And now our baby won't hurt our feelings any longer and she'll turn around."

"I would consider it an honor," I declared as dryly and stiffly as ever. At the same time I reluctantly felt that Lala had involved me in the battle.

"Who says that I'm not afraid to look at you," the Bride exclaimed suddenly and hugged the wooden bolster. She sounded at once honest and meek. The voice of Sur, the dog, whined out of some hiding place, "Afraid, of course, yes, yes, Lalala, afraid, Little Mamma, Sur knows all about it."

Io-Do, the Bridegroom, won't have an easy time, I thought. I was getting tired of this business; worse than that, I was getting sick of it. On the one hand, I thought, they make the stars hop around and they project their dynamic tapestries on the walls. On the other hand, their women are just about as old-fashionedly hysterical as those of the mauve decade. At twenty-six our girls were fully mature. Of course, this age today corresponds to our fifteen-year-olds or even younger. So I had better be prepared for further childish naughtiness. If the brat had had some duties, or anything at all to do, she would have been more reasonable. Apparently their highest accomplishment, the abolition of work, was also their greatest curse. There must be a natural law in accordance with which the coefficient of failure in life, that which religion calls "evil," remains constant in quantity and intensity under all conditions and changing circumstances. This important thought began to worry me. My eyes were staring at the wall where the visionary wallpaper grew fainter and fainter. When I looked back toward the couch, the Bride had turned around long ago.

If it is desirable at any point in this story to call on the Muse for assistance, this is the point. Every experienced reader—and this word generally implies the feminine gender—knows perfectly well that the author's printed statement to the effect that someone, man or woman, is remarkably beautiful, means very little and makes only a faint impression on the imagination; an impression that becomes fainter in direct ratio to the display of enraptured descriptive words. Beauty is not even an immovably motionless fact in the eyes of God. For man it is an animated process that takes place between the beautiful sight and its observer. It is similar to that between the sun and a burning lens. A flame is generated only when the sun's ray finds the focus of the lens. That does not mean, however, that the beauty of the girl Lala set me on fire. I was a temporarily revived ghost, a revenant, whose body had been returned to him thanks to the wicked arts of unbelievably developed spiritualism. This body did not function any worse than formerly, but could I be quite sure of it? I wasn't exactly old, but still I wasn't young enough, rash enough, immoral enough, and tactless enough, to feel, along with confused surprise at her beauty, any of the vague, irresponsible desires that any handsome woman tripping down the street arouses in any normal man. As a matter of fact, I can honestly say that the reverse was the case. I was quite indifferent, quite unaffected, and without any sensual aspiration. (It should really be unnecessary to state this self-evident fact.) I felt no sort of attraction to Lala, neither a paternal one, nor one in an avuncular guise. My indifference was tempered only by shocked surprise that in this age of youthfully beautiful Ancestresses a girlish face could still contrast with such unbelievable charm. Even though I didn't and couldn't burst into flame, the ray had touched the focal point. A while ago I said that among all the agelessly beautiful people whom I had met so far, there hadn't been a single "radiant beauty." Here I had found one.

Just as Bridegroom Io-Do wore a golden helmet, so Io-La, the Bride, wore a close-fitting, ebony-black one that imitated the waves and curls of youthful hair in stylized form. The color of her face was pale and white. She lacked the old-ivory pigmentation which had made me suspect that colored races too had been absorbed in the planetary populace. The Major Domus Mundi, the Selenozusian, had had wonderful dark eyes that I couldn't forget. Lala's lovely eyes were blue, and if I would now add "blue as," the Muse I almost called on a moment ago would turn up her nose. And these big cornflower eyes had long, genuine, black lashes, while many other faces, in spite of their general beauty, showed albinistic features with painted eyebrows and glued lashes. Lala's ebony helmet, the arched brows, the radiating lashes, a generous, gay mouth, made a delightful contrast with the luminous blue of her eyes that ebbed and flowed like the tide. But the most significant factor for me was not the girl's beauty, although it did touch my focal point at once, but rather the fact that Lala's lovely face seemed less strange to me than all other human faces, in fact almost familiar. I concluded, therefore, that certain human values, of which beauty is not the least, are less subject to the transformations of time, evolution, and history than many other things. Lala's very beauty reminded me of beauty that had once left me breathless. How strange! Back in the years of my youth the sight of feminine beauty had filled me with a despondent feeling of strangeness. Today it filled me with an inhibiting feeling of familiarity.

Lala looked at me sharply. My unusual origin seemed to make no impression on her. I noted that she didn't even do me the honor of evincing female vanity. She did not wipe away the traces of the tears that the pampered brat had wept in her ill-mannered rage. The deep blue eyes regarded me somewhat aloofly with searching gravity. But then they became clearly more sober, and I was shocked and ashamed to notice that they reflected a growing merriment which seemed to be compounded of ridicule, youthful high spirits, and amusement. And suddenly, Io-La, the lovely Bride of the occasion, burst into long, unrestrained laughter, undoubtedly provoked by my appearance in the dress suit, so that Io-Rasa and even the hardest-boiled of all stylish great-great-grandmothers were plunged into embarrassment. And this hilarity was by no means a shrill, hysterical reaction, but the most childlike, natural, healthy laughter that only the sight of a ridiculous woebegone figure can evoke.

Now I must confess that I am particularly vain and sensitive on this point. On a few isolated occasions in my life I got into the embarrassing position of the involuntary comedian. When I think back to those moments of my youth, I still feel cold perspiration on my brow, I stamp my foot, shut my eyes, and utter foolish words of confusion. I'm no Rousseau and I don't want to make myself out any better or any worse than I am, but this "Index of Little Humiliations" that made me the butt of ridicule constitutes a more cruel memory for me than my "Index of Great Sins" for which God may one day not deliver me from Mors Aeterna, the Eternal Death.

Lala continued to laugh in spite of the exhortation of her mother, who tried to save the situation and to pretend hypocritically that this insulting merriment was not aimed at my absurd appearance but was caused by one of the many unfathomable and unpredictable whims of her daughter. But I, with the painful sensation that I had turned red as a beet, looked down along my figure to see whether anything was not in proper order. Perhaps my fingernails were hideous, black claws—after eons without attention it wouldn't have been surprising. But no, my fingernails gleamed and even showed a rosy tint; the California mortician had had me manicured. It was a first-class job. Perhaps a button? No. Or maybe my hair was long and unkempt? Hair is said to continue to grow after death. I ran my hand through it. It wasn't very thick, but otherwise felt normal. Maybe it was my hair after all that made me impossible. If they had only given me one of my berets to take along! Goose-pimples of mortification ran up my back. B.H. was still standing modestly at the door. I called to him, loudly and emphatically, "Was this necessary, my friend? Now let's go."

"Oh, please, no, Seigneur, don't go," Lala said very quickly, and the hilarity on her features abruptly changed into an expression of deepest alarm. This expression gratified me uncommonly. It gave me a splendid sensation of victory that warmed me through and through. I wanted to stretch out my victory in order to enjoy it longer. So I drew myself up to my full height and made a mendacious little speech.

"I know very well that I'm not worth much, young lady. I know that my suit is full of grease spots, that a few buttons are missing, that the hair on my head is very old-fashioned, and that all this may look very funny. Unfortunately my whole existence is full of such grease spots and missing buttons that can't be justified. And my hair is what it is. But does that give you the right to make fun of me? Doesn't a life that has been lived have a claim to some respect? And besides, Mademoiselle, you're just a young pup and I am, at least, an elderly person."

Io-La continued to look at me in consternation, and now

she had tears in her cornflower eyes. I was thoroughly content.

"I wasn't making fun of you, Seigneur," she stammered. "I wanted you here terribly and I was so terribly afraid of you. And I was laughing because you're not frightful at all. I should like very much to touch your garment, Seigneur. May I?"

Without awaiting my answer and quite contrary to the usage of the time she stretched out her long-fingered hand and began to feel the worn material of my swallowtail. In an era of diaphanous veil garments it must have been an odd sensation to rub the heavy, coarse textile from the beginnings of mankind between one's fingers. Lala kept her eyes closed. She seemed to test the material with her hand as a blind girl would.

"Elderly person," the Ancestress repeated derisively, leaning back on her ironing board. "Why an elderly person, Seigneur? I know that good manners forbid such a question, but an Ancestress can ask anything, can't she? How old are you then, or were you, if you haven't forgotten it?"

"I am, or I was, around fifty-two," I said, giving myself the benefit of a little margin; for if time hadn't stopped for me when it did I would have celebrated my fifty-third birthday within a few weeks. I was annoyed with myself for this petty, womanish correction. Why should I want to appear younger than I was, I asked myself, especially on the opposite shore of time?

"Fifty-two years," the contralto voice yearningly drew out the words. "Fifty-two years. Why, then you're still a vigorous youth in your best years. Why, you're still an Aikmetant, Seigneur."

"And a Eumelieur," Io-Rasa, the Bride's mother, added.

Lala, stroking the silk lining of my coat, repeated with an ironic inflection, "You are an Aikmetant, Seigneur, and a Eumelieur."

Now I remembered these two words of the Monolingua with the greatest accuracy. They are, so to speak, among the very few objective documents that I brought home from my trip. The philological scrutiny of these words required a great deal of time and effort in the days after my return while I wrote this record. A friend of mine, seeing my distress, gave me for this purpose a venerable, moth-eaten dictionary entitled "Greek-German School Dictionary, by Doctor Gustav Eduard Benseler. Seventh Enlarged Edition, prepared by Doctor Georg Autenrieth, Principal of the Gymnasium in Zweibrücken, Printed at Leipzig, 1882." This dictionary contains approximately a thousand pages and indicates specifically that it covers the vocabulary of the following authors: Homer, Herodotus, Aeschylus, Sophocles, Euripides, Thucydides, Xenophon, Plato, Lysias, Isocrates, Demosthenes, Plutarch, Arrianus, Lucian, Theocritus, Bion, Moschus, and the New Testament. All first-class and expensive material, as anyone can see. And yet all my searching and studying was in vain. Not a single one of the above-named immortal authors, including Bion and Moschus, of whose existence I confess my ignominious ignorance, carried an "aikmetos" or a "eumelios" in his cargo. Doctor Gustav Eduard Benseler led me around by my nose. He told me that "aikáloo" meant "I flatter" and "aiké" was "violent urge, impetus." That seemed to be an important hint. But this hint was confused at once by the word "aikía" which meant "unseemly treatment, physical humiliation (contumelia)." With Io-Rasa's word "Eumelieur" I had the same experience. The Benseler unabridged proved a labyrinth. But since I was convinced that these two loan-words in the Monolingua were of Greek origin and not meaningless caricatures, I betook myself to an eighty-nine-year-old professor who had emigrated from the University of Tübingen, worked his victory garden with surprising vigor and with red cheeks, and for seventy of his eighty-nine years had been interested in nothing but Homeric philology. The nimble old gentleman aroused my envy, for his wily buoyancy proved how healthful it is to limit, concentrate, collect one's self in a narrow field. One-sidedness, monomania, or whatever you call it, is the art of getting into focus, whereas roving universalism is dangerous because an immoderate intellect remains forever out of focus. From the garden gate I shouted to the old man, "What is an 'aikmetos' and a 'eumelios'?" — "Double nonsense," the Homeric graybeard replied. But suddenly he leaned thoughtfully on his spade and began to spell in his high, pinched voice. "Perhaps you mean an alpha–iota–kappa–mu–epsilon–tau–eta–sigma, 'aikmetés,' and an epsilon–upsilon–mu–epsilon–lambda–iota–eta–rho, which spells 'eumeliér.' Is that it?"—"And there really are two words like that, my dear Professor?" — "Not only that, but the two are identical." — "Did I understand you correctly, Professor? 'Aikmetés' and 'eumeliér' mean the same thing?" — "They don't refer to a thing, you philological barbarian, but to a person, a spear expert, a man who knows how to use his spear. Anything else?" And he pushed his spectacles back up on his forehead and turned over a spadeful of soil in the vegetable bed.

In the moonlight of the bridal chamber I didn't know, of course, what the ladies meant by an Aikmetant and a Eumelieur and that they were conferring a special honor on a warrior in his fifties by calling him a spear expert. But how did a Homeric concept get into a bridal chamber of this superfine Mental era, that preserved a memory of war only in the form of a warped celestial globe? Idle questions. If I had caught on I would have been pleased, and my debilitated self-confidence needed a little encouragement. But even I understood enough to realize that among a hundred-and-thirty- to a hundred-and-ninety-year-olds, a man of around fifty was practically an adolescent. Lala was still stroking the silk lining with attentive fingers.

"This inside," she asserted, "feels very agreeable, like— like——" She found no comparison.

Naturally. She had never touched silk before. I withdrew the swallowtail gently from her hands.

"And please remember, my dear young lady, when this shabby coat was tailored, the official date of the year had only four digits while now it has six. And the sorcery that summoned this coat out of the void into your house, along with its seams and threads and stains, that sorcery seems to be something quite commonplace nowadays."

"Who practices sorcery? We don't practice sorcery. We live in an enlightened era," said the Ancestress.

"I know, Madame, that it is improper and impertinent to contradict you," I rejoined. "But isn't the Worker, who produces everything centrally, a sorcerer? And what is the travel-toy, and the Harmonizers on their couches? And what is the Uranographer, whom the stars obey as the lead in the linotype obeys the compositor? And what about calling up people by means of unaided thoughts? We, at least, used for this purpose telephone instruments with great, big, thick cables, or radio tubes with the pertinent short or long waves——"

"My dear F.W.," my friend, who was still standing by the door, interrupted the conversation, "your telephone and radio would seem like greater sorcery to these people than their Mentelobole. Nothing to which one is accustomed is sorcery."

He stopped suddenly and then added with embarrassment, "I happen to know something about the radio and telephone from my studies."

"Stuff and nonsense," said the Ancestress with the horrible obstinacy and animosity of old people who will listen to no arguments, not even those in their favor. "We don't practice sorcery, we're too progressive, too enlightened, too superior. You're the one who practiced sorcery, Seigneur. We learned in school, for instance, that you used to begin a new year by sacrificing a suckling pig to your dog-headed house-god at midnight for good luck. Then you used to wash in the blood of the little beast, and after that you devoured it, skin, bones, and all, at the same time continually yelling 'Happy New Year.' And what's more, you really did get good luck and strength out of it, and that's what I call sorcery. Isn't that so?"

"That is definitely an exaggeration, Madame," I replied and turned to my friend. "Isn't it, B.H.?"

He merely shrugged his shoulders and remained silent.

"That's what science says," the beautiful GR³ declared stubbornly. (That seems to be a good mathematical designation for Lala's great-great-grandmother, who belonged to an enlightened and scientific generation.) And she concluded, "If science says so, it must be true."

"In my time," I said with a bow, "science was often nothing

but a game of mediocre imagination under the guise of exact dullness. Men remain pretty much alike, but, as I see, one era can never understand another."

Lala looked at me with wide eyes. But there was not a trace of disgust in them. "Is it true, Seigneur, that you sprinkled yourself with pig's blood to cast a spell for a lucky new year?"

"I swear to you, Demoiselle," I retorted full of exasperation, "there isn't a word of truth in that. I never sprinkled myself nor anyone else with animals' blood on New Year's Eve."

"But you drank it, didn't you, Seigneur?" the Bride asked with obvious curiosity.

"On such festive occasions we drank champagne," I replied. "I should be delighted to offer the ladies a glass. It's a sparkling beverage that makes you cheerful and confident, for instance Pommery or Mumm Sec or Brut or Gout Américain."

"It would be interesting," Lala smiled dreamily, "and I should like to try it, especially if it had a drop of pig's blood in it."

"But Lala," the Bride's mother shrieked indignantly, "you don't say horrible things like that even in fun. And you said it on the first evening of your Holy Days."

Lala paid no attention whatever to her mother's rebuke. She turned her eyes from me. She seemed to quiver with uneasiness and anxiety. Suddenly she moved her whole body in a gesture of annoyance, so that it shone through the dovegray veil garment.

"I hate these flowers," she exclaimed.

And she shook the sprays of rust-red tragacanth blooms from her bed where Io-Rasa had spread them as a foil to her beauty.

"I understand you very well, Io-La," I said. "You are right. All these flowers appear artificial. I have to say it, although I know that it is improper to be frank in a negative sense. But I do wish, ladies, that you could have seen our roses, a delicate heart-red La France, a Marechal Neil, a yellowish tea-rose. The latter has the aroma of tea only for dull senses; in reality it is redolent of decaying foliage, the sad essence of sunny autumn days. But what do you know of seasons?"

I don't know why I got so worked up over the roses that I

raised my hands, palms upward, like a preacher. At that point the ironing board, the support of old age, folded back into the wall and the Ancestress moved toward me with her triumphantly rhythmic stride. The gait of a goddess, I thought, if you discount the distasteful self-assurance of people who have experienced everything. The Ancestress indicated that she wanted to look at my hands. She subjected the palms to a careful scrutiny. By rights she should have produced a lorgnette or perhaps a monocle for the sake of elegance. I don't even dare to mention spectacles. I wondered when and how these clumsy, archaic instruments had disappeared. Even hundred-and-ninety-year-old eyes were so keen in the Mental era that they required no aid from an oculist. Up to this point I had succeeded in concealing the violet rosette of honor. I hid it, not because I was bashful, but because I was tired of telling or even thinking about, the whole story. But now my coat sleeve had slipped back from the frayed shirt cuff and the decoration became visible.

"Io-Do will never win the violet wrist-rosette in his life," Lala commented pensively.

"A bride should never give in to such moods, I beg your pardon," I retorted to her remark, which had been made in the most indifferent tone. What was the matter with me? More pedantic drooling? And I heard my voice continue, "Your Fiancé is an active young man of wide interests and a great connoisseur in bellology and the history of armaments. A bride like you is to be congratulated on such a bridegroom, and vice versa." (What was wrong with me, what was the matter with me? But with fatal inevitability I became involved further in dry-as-dust eulogies.) "Furthermore the Bridegroom is responsible for my decoration, for I owe it solely to his energy that I went to the Geodrome, gave the verdict, and paid my respects to the Major Domus Mundi——"

"Just take a look at his palms," the Ancestress interrupted me when she had completed her examination. "What a maze, a labyrinth of lines, back and forth, large and small!"

"Is it different with you people?" I asked in surprise.

The Ancestress, Io-Rasa, and Lala opened their palms and showed them to me. They were as smooth and unmarked as those of wax dummies. There was nothing to be seen except the three main markings: a very well defined head-line, a very faint heart-line, and a tremendously long life-line running up to the forearm. Only the mounts of the planets at the bases of the fingers and the depressions between them were present. The doll-like emptiness of the palms of these Mental people impressed me very strangely. The Ancestress asked for my hand once more, and then I also had to show it to the Bride's mother and the Bride.

"Why, you have flashes of lightning in your hand, Seigneur, and whiplashes and streets and anagrams and checkers! What does all that mean?" asked Lala.

"That means," B.H. at the door replied for me, "that in his lifetime he had many vicissitudes to overcome, physical, mental, and spiritual. On the earth as it is today, there are hardly any more vicissitudes."

"Why are there no more vicissitudes on earth today?" asked Lala, and her question sounded highly critical.

"Thank God, my child," answered B.H., who had had his share during many a reincarnation. "Prometheus has almost conquered fate."

"Is that really a good thing, if it is true?" the Bride queried skeptically. "And what is a vicissitude, anyway?"

"That's the balance that's left over when the division doesn't come out even," B.H. muttered. "Cloud, dust, storm, cold, Jungle, and the like."

The Ancestress asked permission to touch my hand. I respectfully surrendered it to her icy smooth fingers which, no matter how impeccable they looked, felt horrible.

"What currents, what waves, what forces are in such a hand!" GR³ mused. "It surges and pulsates and thrills you like the medicinal rays that the Worker delivers to our houses. And all that results from friction with the vicissitudes of life, as your

dear friend says. Would you permit me, Seigneur, to hold
your hand a few minutes every day as long as you honor us with
your company?"

I bowed silently. But the ancient lady still did not release me.
Then I saw a glitter in her deep-set eyes. They were now
definitely old eyes in the otherwise youthfully smooth face.
What was it that glittered in these eyes? Lasciviousness? Malice?
An old witch's craving to create confusion and then to watch
that confusion, to warm herself by it, to avenge herself because,
in spite of all cosmetics, her day was drawing to a close and she
had nothing more to look forward to except the "voluntary
journey on foot"? I can't answer these questions. I can only repeat that the deep-set eyes of the Ancestress glittered with something that looked like malicious lasciviousness.

Her icy smooth fingers drew me closer to the bridal bed.

"The primeval forces from the beginnings of mankind are
still in your hand, Seigneur," she raved. "Give us a little of them.
Let us taste a bit of them and bring some fun into our lives.
Suppose you put your hand on our little girl's heart for just a
few minutes. She'll become stronger and happier through your
blessing."

"I am prepared to obey any command," I said uncertainly
and felt myself grow pale. "But I will do only what the Bride
herself wishes."

With affected leisureliness the smiling GR[3] exposed Lala's
breasts with one hand while she hung on to me with the other.
The girl looked at me unmoved and said calmly, "I don't know
whether your primeval forces from the beginnings of mankind
are good or bad for me, Seigneur."

"I shall do whatever you wish," I repeated, and I felt my
old weakness of character get the better of me that prompted
me to avoid all decisions and responsibility today just as it used
to do back in the beginnings of mankind. An inner voice, however, warned me more and more insistently against obeying
the glitter in the old lady's eyes.

"Seigneur's blessing and touch will surely have a good effect,"

Io-Rasa said hesitantly with an attempt to combine tact with mother instinct. "We know that much about you. But shouldn't we consult her father first?"

"Her father—her father," the Ancestress mocked angrily. "What does a father know, a man whose hair is still golden, about such women's affairs?"

"Put your hand on my heart, Seigneur," said Lala with regal indifference. And the Ancestress pulled my hand down with a light but unyielding pressure, as though I were resisting—which I wasn't—and laid it carefully, almost tenderly, between the little bare breasts of the Bride. The fragrant, yet somehow fleshless hand still made no move to release mine. It seemed to relish the contact with me, the hundred-thousand-year-old ghost, and Lala's barely unfolding youth, vibrantly, like a forbidden thrill.

"Touching the heart was an ancient sacramental custom of certain Islamitic mendicant orders," I said idiotically in a didactic tone, as though in explanation, mitigation, and justification, while I felt the unbelievably soft, cool, Mental skin of the girl under my rough paw like a delightful reproach. But was it really a reproach? Wasn't it something else? I felt—and I don't think I am mistaken or falsifying the truth in retrospect—I felt the girl's velvety, pliant, Astromental body flexing, breathing, nestling its way into my hard palm which was scarred by the runes of a hundred vicissitudes. At the same instant Lala wrinkled her smooth forehead and exclaimed angrily, "Take your hand away. It annoys me. It's so hot and heavy."

I withdrew it at once, genuinely offended, for I had just figured out a sort of benediction that I wanted to say. I brought my hot and heavy hand up to my forehead.

"It's not true at all that my hand is hot, my dear young lady," I exclaimed. "You're quite unjust, for I'm not feverish at all any more."

Somewhere below, Sur, the dog, began to whine and to nag vociferously. I didn't understand a word of his balbucinations.

The Ninth Chapter

WHEREIN, DESPITE MY EXHAUSTION, I DO
MY UTMOST TO AVOID SLEEP, AND FROM
B.H., WHO LOYALLY SHARES MY SOLITUDE,
I LEARN A FEW ODDS AND ENDS ABOUT
THE HAPPENINGS IN THE WORLD SINCE THE
LAST TIME I WAS RASH ENOUGH TO FALL
ASLEEP.

B.H. HAD VOLUNTEERED to spend the night, my first in the Astromental era, with me.

"That's very decent of you," I said, "and I thank you for your kindness. For it's no small sacrifice that you're making. But you know, I wouldn't have stayed alone under any circumstances."

"I seem to remember, F.W.," my friend smiled, "that you used to be a regular crank for solitude."

"Yes, so I was, B.H. But only to devote myself without interruption to my thinking and my work in lonely mountain hamlets and fishing villages. Goodness me, that wasn't even diluted twenty per cent alcohol of solitude. Once you've become acquainted with the hundred per cent variety, with the genuine, unspeakable loneliness from which I come, it makes you afraid to spend a night alone."

At these words B.H. looked at me a little startled and perhaps even a little guiltily, and he said nothing. We were in a spacious guest room that wasn't at all uncomfortable although

165

its furnishings consisted only of a few reclining chairs, a
fair-sized couch with a raised head-end and a hard bolster, and
a small buffet that rather resembled a medicine stand, in whose
circular holes glistened the crystal egg-cups filled with varicolored juices and soups, with which we are already familiar.
They were more numerous than those served at the dinner. When
the lady of the house had said good-night to me she had promised
me a little "nightcap." Measured by Mental standards, however,
it appeared to be a sumptuous supper. I felt a slight urge for
nourishment, a very gentle and timid sort of appetite, but at the
same time I feared the intellectual exertion connected with the
incorporation of such substances as "the sea," or "hunting
grounds," or "billowing cornfields." Then B.H. opened a little
compartment in the buffet and took out a regular old-fashioned
crock, from which he filled two white cups without handles, for
himself and for me, with a thick, steaming, creamy liquid.

"Just try that. I think you'll like it."

I did. It brought a warm glow to my exhausted limbs, flattered
my stomach, and oiled my nerves.

"Don't tell me. Let me guess," I requested. My lips, tongue,
and gums eagerly tasted the flavor. "I believe I know that. At
home we used to call it a Tom and Jerry. It's made of sweet
wine or cognac with egg yolk and sugar."

"Once in a while the Worker slips one over, you know," B.H.
laughed. "He milks the capricornettes, the tiny animals that
graze in the meadows of his Park. And he gives the milk—just
imagine, honest-to-God milk—to some of the children or brides
or old people for whom he has a special liking. He has a soft
spot for Lala. She got this real milk from him and they made
our nightcap out of it. It's really a forbidden delicacy and contrary to the food laws."

"So much the better, B.H., so much the better." But then I
asked him, "Why does the Worker show a special preference for
Lala among a thousand other brides—there must be that many?"

"Is that so hard to understand, F.W.?"

"On the contrary, I understand it very well, B.H. Lala is

pretty as a picture; and the most beautiful thing about her beauty, for me at least, is the fact that she isn't strangely beautiful or inconceivably beautiful. You could occasionally—not often but once in a while—bump into such a Lala on Rue St. Honoré in Paris or Kärntnerstrasse in Vienna or Fifth Avenue in New York. When you first look at her you gasp for breath. But when she opens her mouth she seems a little underdone intellectually, capricious, and—and those empty palms, like a wax dummy—!"

B.H. looked at me strangely. "Intellectually undeveloped?" he asked. "Are you serious?"

"I'm not serious about anything, old man. How could I, in my situation, give a serious opinion about anybody or anything. So you claim that Lala is neither capricious nor intellectually undeveloped?"

B.H. made an evasive answer. "Culture," he said, "is the tricky art of understatement and of avoiding the issue. Remember that, F.W., in your intercourse with our Mental society."

"Would you be so good as to pour me another half a cupful, B.H.?" I requested.

"As you wish, F.W.," he complied. "But it's very filling."

I pushed the refilled cup aside after the first swallow.

"You're right, B.H.," I confessed. "Being what I am, I have to be temperate and careful in my pleasures. Incidentally, it's strange that in my present condition I still distinguish the flavors of food so clearly, and not only that, but I derive a distinct satiation from the food. Back in my lifetime, whenever I used to dream at night about sitting down at table with a huge appetite, I always woke up at the instant that I put a bite in my mouth. Now I don't wake up, B.H. Consequently I must be something like an overexposed spirit. You exposed me too long to the light, like a photographic plate, so that my picture has become very dense and very black. So don't be surprised if I ask a very delicate question: where do I go if I feel the call of nature?"

"Do you feel the call of nature, F.W.?"

"No, old-timer, thank goodness, no. Not yet. But I've been worrying for some time about this anti-Mental possibility."

"Well, don't worry, you won't feel anything," B.H. laughed. "We take care of that once every five days."

"You don't say so!" I exclaimed in relief. "What a wonderful short cut! What a saving of time when you have practically no work to do!"

"Listen, F.W.," my friend said tactfully. "I notice that you wince every time I say something about the 'beginnings of mankind,' to which we both belonged, as I can't deny. Of course they weren't really the beginnings of mankind; I know that better than anyone else; they were really highly differentiated conditions, after several millions of years of evolution. I use that phrase which sounds so shocking to you merely from the present-day perspective, and mainly to enhance the pleasure of my contemporaries in materializing a real aborigine. You know me. I'm no progressivist ass. Furthermore I know that a hundred thousand circuits of the earth about the sun are a mere shift of the shadow of history. And yet, in spite of his limitations, man has progressed in the biological sense."

"No doubt about that, B.H.," I guffawed. "Using the toilet once every five days is really something in the way of biological progress."

"Please don't laugh, F.W. It's not a smutty joke," B.H. reprimanded me. "Dirty stories aren't as funny any more as they used to be in your time."

"In my time there were various kinds of medium-sized snakes that used to gulp down a mouse once a month and pass it. Turtles and other reptiles and amphibians would hibernate for several months without exerting their bowels a single time."

"Your reptiles and amphibians, my dear F.W.," my friend retorted with a superior air, "were so constructed physiologically and never changed. But we humans, we did change biologically; more than that, we have become refined. In your lifetime you had an intestine that was twelve yards long when it was unrolled. Meanwhile, thanks to the ethereal nutrition of the entire human race, it has been materially shortened. In your lifetime the organ of male erotic power had the degrading name of "urethra." Isn't that a shocking expression for the organic symbol of procreative potency? But that's different now, since the secretion of urine no longer takes place through the organ of erotic power but through the intestine."

"I was quite wrong to laugh, B.H.," I said meekly, pondering his serious words. But then I stretched out on the couch, since my limbs had become practically numb with exhaustion. "Yes, indeed," I said with a relaxed sigh, "that's more than progress. That's a sanctification of man. It's too bad that I personally won't profit by it any more."

"It is a sanctification, F.W.," my reincarnated friend said almost angrily. "You see, God corrects Himself——"

"God corrects Himself," I repeated, sitting up, tired as I was. "Didn't you say that once before? Back in those days. . . ."

And I saw the two of us, the nineteen-year-old B.H. and the nineteen-year-old F.W., engrossed in conversation, walking along the Belvedere hill-road and looking down on Prague with its hundred towers and baroque bridges stretched out in the sun-drenched haze to the "Royal Vineyards" on the horizon. And the student B.H. explained his metaphysical philosophy to me, the attentive F.W., and now I remembered it word for word, and it seemed much more cogent and much more solid gold than that of Sophistes Io-Sum and Sophistes Io-Clap combined. And since I remembered this philosophy so exactly, I recalled it to the memory of its originator, who shook his head as he listened and was surprised at my excitement.

"This is what you taught me, B.H.: God is the perfect Being. Creation is only an expression of this Being. The expression of a Being can never be identical with the Being that produced it. It is not even a fraction of this Being but only its partial revelation, just as a word, a sigh, a laugh is not a fraction of man but exhaled common property, namely air. Even if God represents eternal and perfect Being, yet His expression, creation, is necessarily highly imperfect, that is, inferior to Him. The difference between the perfect, infinite Being and its expressed, imperfect and finite Being is that which the world calls 'Evil' or 'Wickedness.'—Do you recognize your philosophy, old-timer? It must have made a tremendous impression on me to remain in my memory for more than a hundred thousand years."

"When we're very young," said B.H. diffidently and defensively, "we incline toward lofty thoughts and broad generalizations."

"Don't underestimate yourself," I argued. "The recognition of evil as the hydrostatic gradient or as the difference in potential between perfect, primary Being and expressed, secondary Being is a real philosophical discovery and an elegant formula in the greatest controversy of all times. You're the one who should have won my verdict, although the Church would certainly have branded you as a heretic because you blame the fall of man at least partly on God as a result of the act of creation. But you went even farther. What you said a few minutes ago, you said away back in those days, that's what you did. 'God corrects Himself.' Your voice is still in my ear, the way you improvised that phrase: 'A part of divine activity is correction, polishing His expression.'

"You see how callowly anthropomorphic such ideas are," B.H. interjected. "God correcting His lessons like a schoolboy or like an ambitious hackwriter!"

"But you uttered that sentence just a few minutes ago, at the age of one hundred and seven years. I shouldn't think that was a callow age even today. And this sentence, my dear B.H., further implies that you define natural history and the history of mankind as a history of divine correction. For unless we are atheists we must admit that a higher, logical, and purposeful will shortened our far too long intestine and refined and ennobled our crudely bungled sexual organ."

By this time B.H. had also stretched out comfortably in one of the low reclining chairs. The word "chair" is really a misnomer, as these pieces of furniture were intended to be used in a recumbent position and by no means "in a broken line." Only the back was propped a little higher than on the ordinary couch with its bolster. I had spoken a little expansively, perhaps even excitedly, because I was pleased with the excellent functioning of my memory. B.H. sought to calm me. He seemed to feel some anxiety about me.

"It's really remarkable, F.W.," he sighed, "how well you remember those old philosophemes that we concocted during the endless afternoons of our youth. In my case, of course, it was only one youth among many other youths, don't forget that. Still, I believe I could retaliate by reciting one of your poems. Do you want to hear it?"

"For heaven's sake, no, B.H.," I declined. "It's very good of you, but I'm afraid any of my verses would be bad for my nerves and would fill me with deepest remorse. You know, esthetic remorse is just as painful as the moral kind. Besides I'm quite sure that some of my poems, the expression of my Being, are better than that Being, that is I-myself—just the reverse of the case of God."

B.H. cleared his throat before asking abruptly, "How do you feel in your Being, in your old body, F.W.?"

"Perfect," I replied. "That's to say, for the past several hours every muscle in it has been aching with indescribable exhaustion."

"That's what I thought, old man," he nodded. "You mustn't forget that only the spiritual act of will of a certain circle of persons reconstructed you and your body out of the hidden reserves of matter, out of the secret wardrobe of invisibility, and called you back into life. You can't treat your body as we did at the age of twenty. You have to take care of it, good care. But instead of doing that, you get excited and you overdo. I suggest that you keep your mouth shut for a while."

"Good, let's both keep our mouths shut."

I sighed deeply. My breath came from the very bottom of my lungs, a good sign for my renovated body. Then I looked about the room. Io-Rasa, with the kindly intention of making me feel at home, had not switched on the illumination that reflected the lofty moods of nature, no moon-magic nor gold-dripping forest green, no glistening ocean-silver nor melting snow of cloud-racked early spring—all the moods that had vanished from the earth's surface—but she had placed two pale, frosted glass lamps on a low table that produced the atmosphere of a cozy study. I turned my eyes to the bare walls, curious to see whether I would be able to project a visionary wallpaper as I had done in the bridal chamber. There was nothing. Presumably my exhaustion was too great. Now I noticed for the first time that the wall was fitted with a window, the casements of which were wide open toward the inside. No doubt this room had been assigned to me because of its artificial window to make me feel more at home. And truly, it seemed to me as if a grandiose Sierra or Carpathian night were peering into the window like a pitch-black she-bear. A faint breath of ozonous mountain air fanned my face. What more can a person ask for, I thought to myself.

Then I heard B.H. say, "How about a little barcarole?"

"What sort of barcarole?" I asked suspiciously.

"Don't be silly. I think a little sleep in six-eighths time would do us good. Don't you want to try it?"

Electrified with terror, I jumped to my feet. "Sleep? Out of the question, B.H., entirely out of the question. I'll never risk sleeping again, I'll never dare to fall asleep."

Startled by my wild reaction, B.H. also arose. "What's the matter with you, F.W.? Why don't you dare ever to fall asleep again?"

My heart was pounding in my throat. I gasped for words. "Do I have to explain that to you? Don't you understand?"

"No, F.W., now I don't understand you at all."

"My Lord," I groaned, "if you had only thought it over before you brought me into this situation that even you can't understand!"

He took my hand and pushed me gently down on the couch. "Calm yourself, my friend," he implored. "I'll do everything possible for you; I'll even do the impossible. But why are you afraid to fall asleep? Every normal person sleeps and needs sleep."

It took quite a while before I could actually hear the words that tumbled out of my mouth: "Certainly, a normal person, I know. When a normal person falls asleep he sinks down into his body, he is submerged in his vegetative base. Now don't tell me that the Selenozusian hovers above his base as he sleeps. He is a conqueror, a chosen individual. The happy, normal sleeper turns to earth, turns to a planet. But the planet revolves around a higher order, around the sun-star. Moreover, it revolves about itself. Thus it has a day-side and a night-side, which the sun does not have. The night-side is to the planet as sleep is to man. The sleeper stands in his own shadow in order to rest from the light of the spirit. But why does he do that? Because he can depend on his vegetative base, his body, his planet-likeness. But I can't do that, B.H.; no, no, horrible as it sounds, I can't. Only a few hours ago my body was thin air, thinner than air. It wasn't even a shadow, not even an ectoplasmic phenomenon, it was like a brutally murdered person whom the murderers buried in the cement of a basement, and after a few years the police stop looking for him because nothing recognizably characteristic of him remains, and the murder of F.W. is expunged from the police records and forgotten until doomsday. Just try to visualize that completely, B.H., that vanishedness, that lostness, that forgottenness. Right now, of course, my body seems to be normal. But who will guarantee that that's no illusion? You yourself warned me against exertion, even against the moderate exertion of talking. You yourself said that they reconstructed me out of 'the hidden reserves of matter,' out of 'the secret wardrobe of invisibility.' I think that's altogether terrible. You don't experiment with things like that. No, I won't complain. What's done is done, and I won't reproach you for it. Besides, why should I reproach you when you've given me something to enjoy? For, you know, in keeping with my unprincipled character, I'm really enjoying even this absurd form of existence in the fullest measure. And that proves Io-Sum's hypothesis that God's love is expressed in the preference of His creatures to be rather than not to be. I don't know whether I can consider myself a genuine creature today, but the will to be, which is God's love, is in my heart. That's the reason for my terror, my fright. Can I depend upon my basis, which—horrible to contemplate—I owe merely to a spiritualistic circle? Where will I sink, where will I be submerged, if I fall asleep? Do you finally understand me, B.H.? If I don't succeed in staying awake I will lose myself. That's not strong enough. If I fall asleep I shall lose myself in the wilderness of an unexampled and nameless lostness. That's what I feel. That's what I fear. That has nothing to do with real death. That's death raised to an unheard of power. I'm familiar with real death. It's simple and plain and solid, and death shouldn't be pictured as a bony specter with a scythe but as an old peasant gazing speculatively at the sunset. But to give up one's ego a second time because one falls into the trap of sleep, that's too much, far too much."

"I have given up my ego many times," said my reincarnated friend after a pause, "but I understand you, F.W."

"Watch and pray," I breathed. "At least, let's watch. Can I have another swallow of the Tom and Jerry?"

"I wouldn't advise it," B.H. declared. "It's definitely a soporific."

He had sat down on my bed. For a long time we were silent. Then he made a suggestion. "People still play chess nowadays. Shall I get a board and chessmen?"

"Awful," I replied. "In my real existence I had a perfect antipathy to chess."

"Well, maybe you'll think of something else," he said obligingly.

"'Swing low, sweet chariot, coming for to carry me . . .'" I chanted to myself.

"'. . . coming for to carry me,'" he repeated my singsong dutifully, as though he were obliged to remember a little old song but didn't know which one.

"What I mean is, that I want you to tell me a few things, and perhaps even answer a few questions. In the course of your various existences you must have experienced, seen, heard, learned many things that I ought to know. . . . 'Swing low, sweet chariot . . .'"

"Now you've got me," he laughed bitterly and two sharp creases framed his mouth. "You, my boy, don't have any trouble remembering, for you possess only a single inventory. Please consider how different it is in my case. I'm not always such a literal-minded snob as you think whenever our common recollections don't click with me at the first try."

" 'I looked across Jordan and what did I see. . . .' "

"Well, I'll try it, F.W., I'll do the best I can. Where shall my chariot carry you? Where do you want to start the interview?"

"Let's see. . . . When was it that I fell asleep? It must have been in the spring of 1943. And what about you? I imagine you outlived me by quite a while?"

"Just a moment, my friend!" he interrupted me. "You still haven't the slightest idea how difficult it is for me to focus my sense of continuity sharply on a particular one of my past existences. It's a lopsided comparison, but every one of my reincarnations, that is, every concluded existence from A to Z, is a dust-covered volume of an encyclopedia in a dark library. Even the best system of mnemonics doesn't alter the situation. The empirical part of every soul that has experienced various reincarnations consists of many such dust-covered and faded volumes. But mark well, I said the empirical, and not the essential, part. It is the task of my imperfect collective consciousness to find the right volume in the dark, to brush off the dust, to open it, and to find the proper section without becoming addled by the odor of spiritual decomposition of inconceivably old books. That requires great concentration. Please remember that I now have to fetch the first and most faded volume from the shelf. Remember also that the Transparency of the Sun runs through the memory of mankind like a dividing line. You and your time lie far on the other side of the Transparency. I beg you, therefore, to ask your questions slowly."

"I asked you," I repeated distinctly as one speaks to a deaf person, "how many more years you lived after 1943, post Christum natum?"

He closed his eyes and lowered his head. I could see how pale the effort of reopening his old life made him. Perhaps my presence was of some help to him.

"It seems to me that I lived to a fairly ripe old age at that
time," he finally began haltingly. "It was a pretty good accomplishment for that generation, I believe, especially if you consider that I served in two armies, the old imperial Austrian and
the royal British army."

"What? How could you serve in the English army?"

"I did, that's all there is to it," he said, and added with a deep
breath, "Of course I don't remember the exact date, but it's
quite likely that I was still alive in the first half of the nineteen
hundred and seventies."

"Almost thirty years longer than I, B.H.," I nodded approvingly, "and in a most interesting period historically. That certainly puts you under some obligations to me. So please pull
yourself together and do your best. Are you ready for Question
Two?"

"Question Two," he repeated after me and added, "Very well,
I'm ready. But slowly and patiently, if you please."

"Did you live to see the Third World War?" I drew the words
out.

"I believe," he replied, paler than ever from concentration,
"I believe that I never saw any more peace in those days. You
probably recall even better than I that human superstition of
that time made the happiness of nations dependent upon two
economic systems that were both wrong. Both led to serfdom of
the individual: one under the heel of the ruling classes, the
other under the heel of the ruling masses. It was the most stupid
either-or in world history, which always develops by virtue of
such alternatives. How could there be peace in my old age
as long as two systems existed side by side that hated as well as
envied each other? No, no, the more I think about it, the more
distinctly the roar of bombing planes rings in my ears."

I raised my voice again. "And what became of the German
nation after its defeat? That's Question Number Three. Shall

I repeat Question Three or would you rather have me write it down?"

"It's not necessary, F.W.," he declined. And as if to gain time he chanted to himself: "The Germans, the Germans. . . . What became of the damned Germans?"

Suddenly a sly grin spread over his pale face and with sardonic exaggeration he began to recite headlines from the newspapers of those days.

"Listen, this is going to be good," he said, "for this really happened: 'World Friendship Day in Cassel.' . . . 'All Hearts Sympathy Week at Gera.' . . . 'Universal German Festival for the Propitiation of the Jews at Halle-an-der-Saale.' . . . 'Union of German Pantheist Women for Surrender to Love and Life in Every Form.' . . . These and many similar things I see before me as I read in the oldest volume of the encyclopedia of my early recollections. Between World Wars Two and Three the Germans took the lead in humanitarianism and good-will. The combination of the words 'humanitarian' and 'nonsense' was forbidden under penalty of two days in jail or a corresponding fine. And most of the Germans were really quite serious about their concept of humanitarianism and good-will. For centuries they had tried with blood and iron to become the world's pet. Humanitarianism and good-will now seemed the best way to this end. They even found it far more convenient than heroism and racial science."

B.H. kept his eyes closed. I felt that the stream of memory produced by his adjuration of the past was constantly becoming broader and swifter. Now and then I threw in a brief remark in order to stimulate him, as one does with a medium. The dim, distant past was now rising to the surface so forcibly that at times he seemed to forget my presence entirely.

"I remember," he continued, "a famous book by a German-hating German, a familiar alibi-type of that time. One moment, don't interrupt me, the author's name was—now wait—I've got it, his name was Carl Egon (von) Ausfaller. With a little more effort I might even recall the title of the book, but I had better save my strength for more important things. I'm sure the book was published before 1960. Ausfaller claimed that there were two kinds of Germans, 'the Brownies and the Imps.' [Translator's Note: In German these two breeds of fairies are known as Heinzelmännchen and Wichtelmännchen, respectively. The former are "good-natured goblins, supposed often to perform important services around the house by night, such as threshing, churning, sweeping." The latter are "young or inferior devils; little malignant spirits; petty demons." While their English-speaking cousins have less sonorous names, they have comparable qualities.] The Brownies were good, helpful, tireless, industrious workers who stubbornly appeared everywhere, whether they were wanted or not, to atone for their guilt. If, for example, the workers had walked out of a factory anywhere in Europe, the Brownies arrived on the scene at night and drudged unobserved until the dawn, even though the labor unions of the country in question stormed with rage. They helped everyone in every way and they demanded no other reward except a little forgiveness of what was regarded as the eternal disgrace of the German people. I personally met a lot of these Brownies in many different places and I felt very sorry for them, although I didn't forgive them. They were the inventors of the thankless ethics of 'Altruistic Officiousness.' By way of recreation the educated ones among the Brownies gave philosophical lectures in university extension classes, in Protestant churches, and even in Reformed synagogues, and their monotonous theme was always devoted to the fraternal duty of man. They couldn't get along without 'duty,' since the German's basic concept of life was the 'Veneration of the Disagreeable.' In a word, they were genuine sheep in sheep's clothing. But since they were so frantic about it, nobody believed them and they were regarded as wolves. These Brownies made up the greater part of the German nation.

"The other, much smaller group, the Imps, played a far more interesting role. They weren't good spirits, but wicked ones, unregenerate hobgoblins in hundreds of disguises. They never

appeared in their fabulous primitive form as hunchbacked dwarfs
with long white beards. For that they had too much racial
pride. Whenever it was halfway possible they preferred to take
the form of Nordic warriors; nevertheless, even when they were
tall and lean, they could not quite lose the facial expression of
spiteful, narrow-minded dwarfs who were chronically offended.
They served all masters and all ideas in the world, for true
Impdom regarded all masters and all ideas as interchangeable,
since the Imps had never had an idea of their own except that of
'protest.' Even their secret society which they called 'The Mes-
sengers from the Grave' or 'The White Vampires with Red
Lips,' the would-be terror of Europe around 1950, was simply
plagiarized from the Italian Maffia of 1848 and from American
horror motion pictures of darkest antiquity. But even here, as in
all other regards, the Imps made up in excessiveness what they
lacked in originality: to become a 'Messenger from the Grave'
the neophyte had to chop off his left arm and substitute for it an
artificial limb equipped with a built-in electric battery capable
of producing fatal shocks. The Imps, no matter where or whom
they served, were the first to live an underground life, the cul-
mination of which you can observe in today's Mental civilization. By virtue of their phrenetic energy and their meaningless
self-immolation they undermined the capitals and large cities
of all nations with their scientifically contrived labyrinths. And
they did that while the victorious powers had disarmed and occupied their country, and while they, the Imps, were not to be
distinguished from the Brownies on the surface. Moreover, the
Brownies had such weak characters that they frequently could
not resist the temptation to become Imps. The Imps were also
the inventors of the subterranean monuments, one of which you
saw today. In their weird labyrinths they erected hundreds of
such monuments to an idol by the name of Heiltier, a wretch
who wasn't even a real German Imp, but was said to be a
low-down mixed breed and a dirty border product of some
sort——"

"The name isn't right, B.H.," I was constrained to interject.

"What is the right name, F.W.?"

"Too bad, I had it on the tip of my tongue just now."

"It may be," B.H. mused, "that his name was Whilter. They longed to return to their 'Folk Community,' an automatic form of life which this Whilter had introduced, in which everyone was permitted to be accuser and accused, torturer and tortured, executioner and executed, all at the same time. Anyway, they not only erected monuments to this Whilter, but for decades after his disappearance they wrote 'Heil Whilter' on the walls of their public latrines. This was a magic act of repetition. For it was by this same practice of scribbling 'Heil Whilter' on the ammonia-scented urinal walls that the Imps had previously gained dominance over the Brownies and had almost achieved world dominion."

"And were the Imps successful the third time, B.H.? That's Question Number Four."

"That I can't answer from personal experience," came the ready answer. "Whether they did or not really doesn't make a damn bit of difference, for the next time I returned to life on the planet there weren't any more Germans. Only the German language still existed and was spoken here and there, especially among the colored races. But it was called the Mödling language, and not German. Mödling was said to have been a suburb of Vienna."

[Translator's Note: As a philologist I cannot refrain from commenting on this curious fact. Mödling, a suburb of Vienna, as I recall it, was a missionary center, the headquarters of the Brothers of Saint Gabriel, the most powerful and most active Roman Catholic missionary organization. Obviously it was through the agency of the missionaries of the Church that the German language—the Mödling dialect—was preserved among the colored races for centuries after its extinction in Europe.]

"Those are really aspects that I never dreamed of," I commented. "And what happened to all the little nations, B.H.? That's Question Number Five, if you can stand it."

"The little nations," he replied without hesitation, "disturbed the scene for a little while longer and then they were absorbed by the so-called primary nations. It's too bad, because some of the little nations were more congenial and more useful than the primary nations."

"And what was the fate of the primary nations?" I insinuated a subordinate question into the interview.

"The European primary nations were fused with each other and vanished. Not only the Germans, but also the French, the Slavs, and finally even the English. Strange to say, the British Empire still existed long after the last real Englishman had disappeared. The last national remnant was an enclave of the Italian people, and that resulted from the fact that Rome, as the seat of the Roman Catholic hierarchy, proved to be imperishable. But the primary nations of Europe suffered the same fate as the nomadic tribes of their ancestors, from which they had sprung in Roman antiquity. They fused into a greater unit, the oldest Continental Nation in the Old World. The nationalistic world wars that preceded this fusion were nothing but the final convulsions of an outmoded, provincial tribal system. The united Continental Nation of Europe, however, declined into a long period of sterility, while the cultural sun rose over entirely new Eastern nations, of whom scarcely anything had been heard so far. And which one of the primary nations do you think it was that first applied to the Central Psycho-Surgical Bureau for extraction of the national feeling?"

"Well, maybe the French," I guessed, "since they were the ones who introduced nationalism, with the aid of Joan of Arc and of the English."

"You're wrong," he laughed, "the Germans were the ones. The ultimate extermination of the pestilence of nationalism goes to the credit of the Germans, after they failed something like seven to fourteen times to become the world's number one darling by blood and thunder."

"I should have guessed that, B.H.," I said abashed. "Obviously it could only have been the Germans who finally protested against protest."

"The simplest answers are usually the most difficult," he consoled me.

"And the Jews?" I asked. "I assume that's Question Number Six."

"The Jews," he answered, "tried desperately at that time to be a small nation among small nations; but in keeping with the divine plan of salvation they were not permitted to be absorbed."

"So the Jews continue to exist," I said, "just like the Catholic Church?"

He looked at me sharply and then replied briefly, "Let's not go into that. You will probably have an opportunity to examine these phenomena and you'll find them incredible."

B.H. had stretched out on one of the deck chairs again and had folded his hands under his head. I wanted to keep him from falling asleep. I could stay awake only if I succeeded in keeping him awake.

"I know it's terribly selfish of me," I said, "but would you permit me to continue the interview? I have two or three more questions."

"This will be Number Seven," he murmured and opened his dark eyes good-naturedly.

"'Swing low, sweet chariot . . .' swing over to Russia. . . ."

My friend's forehead puckered with concentration.

"When I was a very old man," he began, "I passed through Russia several times, from east to west and from west to east. I have never seen more intoxicating religious pomp anywhere than in Moscow toward the end of the twentieth century. It was in the Red Square. No mistake, it was still called the Red Square, and the old party, hoary with age, and as conservative to the core as London Tories, had control of the state. But the bells pealed from all the cathedrals. The orthodox clergy paraded in Byzantine splendor. In their midst the ancient Metropolitan walked behind the sacred icon of the Black Mother of God. Of course, in these Russian mass demonstrations of that time it was always hard to tell whether or not they were making a historical film, since the state was willing to spend untold millions on this form of national glorification. The Marxist clergy too, whether they liked it or not, had donned their red dalmatics and their balloon-shaped miters, adorned in antique letters with the words: 'The Welfare of the Greatest Number of Microorganisms is the Purpose of the Cosmos.' But although the rival procession from the Kremlin was magnificent and the young Marxist minis-trators swung censers of disinfectant vapor (formaldehyde) and intoned hymns of rhymed statistics, it still could not touch the splendor of the other procession that had issued from an un-pretentious frame church in Sokolniki that had weathered the storms of the godless era. They were celebrating the so-called 'East-Roman Compages,' a compromise of the schism, a practical and dogmatic rapprochement of the Greek Orthodox and the Roman Catholic Churches. It was a clever trick that the Metro-politan had played on the Muscovite Grand-Boyard, which was the official title of the Socialist Dictator during the period of romantic reaction. But it was only the beginning of the great Catholic unification that I personally didn't live to see. In the closing years of my life, however, it became more and more evident that the results of the Reformation and the Renaissance were declining. This clarification was really initiated by Whilter and his Imps. Some of the Christian sects were absorbed into so-called Communism. Of the latter very little had survived except the memory of a great national victory, a closely knit central bureaucracy, superstitious veneration of science on the part of illiterates recently converted to literacy, and the normal progress of the denizens of the planet. The other Christian sects were absorbed by Catholicism——"

I could not refrain from interrupting. "Your interesting com-ments remind me that on the last evening before I fell asleep, I was saying to a friend that the Second World War was nothing but the resumption of the Counter Reformation after an interval of some two hundred years, with slightly altered roles and with confused arguments."

"Your observation was quite correct, F.W.," the reincarnated

B.H. stated. "The second half of the twentieth century witnessed a temporary victory of the metaphysical tendency over skepticism, and that can very well be regarded as a victory of the Counter Reformation."

"I felt this victory in my bones long before," I said.

"I know it," he smiled. "After all, we all contributed our bit. The yokel's solution of the riddle of the universe always offended our intellectual arrogance. And in your case there was esthetic arrogance besides."

Under the screen of my numbing need of sleep I felt a radiant happiness. "It's true then," I mused. "The great naturalistic stupidity and its consequences were finally conquered?"

"Nonsense, F.W.," my reincarnated friend shook his head scornfully. "Don't you know that nothing spiritual on earth can be conquered, not even the anti-spirit? Both principles have their eras of expansion and contraction, and that's all. And a spiritual principle is never more powerful than when it is powerless, and never more powerless than when it is powerful. Besides it's childishly absurd to assume that the nineteenth century was the first to think in terms of naturalistic skepticism and that the exalted mysteries of Christianity were less preposterous a hundred years after the Crucifixion than eighty thousand years later. I've seen a great many things. At one time I was born into an age of ultramodern polytheism: they believed at that time in a large number of coexisting but utterly dissimilar universes, each of which was unknown to and unsuspected by every other. Each universe had its own gods. It was believed that these gods were spirit, but that spirit was nothing but primordial universal matter in the nervous state preceding creation, at the instant before it begins to radiate into its cosmic space. In other words, the gods in which people believed at that time were corporeal and spiritual at once; that is, the material worlds of stars and atoms merely represented a higher, that is, degenerate, degree of density of the divine existence. It was the most refined form of pantheistic materialism that I ever met in the course of my reincarnations. But when I made my appearance again a little later, I found myself in a most commonplace era of atheism. In the immeasurable curve of human intellectual life, science and technology reached their historical zenith in that age. Even the sequence of Popes, which had never been interrupted since the time of Peter, was broken for several generations. The Pope merely reverted to a plain Roman bishop and presided over a mendicant sect of physical and spiritual paupers. The Church wasn't even persecuted; it was nothing but a laughingstock. But this in itself sufficed to make it great again and to usher in an era of new triumphs. The deluded Jews too, who wanted to get rid at last of their mystic past, burned their Torah scrolls, prohibited the use of the Hebrew language, and implored the entire globe to adopt Anglo-Saxon as the Monolingua. It was all in vain, for the Bible could no more be destroyed by flames than could the works of scientific naturalism. The latter had just reached its greatest height and therefore faced its deepest fall. For the most illustrious astronomer of all ages, who flourished at this particular time, proved with adamantine certainty that the entire universe, despite its infinite polyphony of movement, revolved exclusively about the earth; and that, of all the planetary heavenly bodies of all the star systems, our earth exclusively and alone possessed the necessary conditions for higher organic life and thus for a rational human race. But I believe I've already told you about that. The consequences of this theory of Ursler's, entitled 'The Infinitely Mobile Central Point of All Conceivable Orbits,' were without historical precedent——"

"Wasn't this theory," I interrupted him, "devised by Pascal, who defined the universe as a sphere, the center of which was everywhere and the perimeter nowhere?"

"Not at all," he indignantly spurned my question, "the naïve individual you quote conceived of the universe as infinite; Ursler's theorem of the 'Infinitely Mobile Central Point,' however, refers to a necessarily finite universe. But it wasn't so much my intention to speak of this mathematical law which restored the earth to the role of protagonist of the universe, as in the Ptolemaic conception, but rather of the tremendous impression of this novel discernment upon the spirit of mankind."

"Oh, I can very well imagine," I said, "that after endless eras of the generally accepted naturalistic conviction that our earth was the most insignificant mote of the cosmos, the sudden knowledge that it really is the center of all centers, must have upset the human intellect completely."

"You can't even begin to imagine it," he retorted sharply. "Compared with the Counter Reformation which this knowledge provoked, yours was a mere trifle. After the first few decades of bitter controversy, during which the new astronomical theory had to battle against the indignant attacks of the reactionaries, a strange wave of ascetic mysticism swept over the human race. Since the days of the early Christian Thebaists, the anchorites in the Egyptian desert, the like had not been seen. Invisible gyroplanes, pilotless, crewless transport rockets, which attained a speed of two miles per second, whizzed across the sky. And who sat under this sky, on the highest towers, projections, and copings of skyscrapers, sat motionless and in utter silence for years and decades? They were the neostylites, the modern pillar-saints who, by self-renunciation and self-abnegation did penance for the boundless sin of arrogance of animated matter. For the trip to the three-hundredth floor and higher they had used the express-suction-lift; for the return trip, however, they needed no elevator. When these neostylites, who subsisted solely by ingeniously inhaling atmospheric vitamins, were shaken from their perches by the winter's blizzard or the summer's hurricane and tumbled to the pavement, they were as desiccated as dried prunes and shed scarcely a teacupful of smiling blood——"

"Just a moment, B.H.," I broke into his flow of words. "I can see your neostylites distinctly. But for some reason they don't have the features of penitents from the Egyptian desert; somehow they seem to have bold, almost Indian lineaments with wrinkles fanning out from the eyes."

"You're not bad at riddles," he laughed. "The home of this new

mysticism, believe it or not, was North America. To the surprise
of all boneheads, this matter-of-fact continent suddenly revealed
its deeper strata. Not without good reason had Columbus been
a Christopher, the strong ferryman, who carried the Christ-Child
over the water. The Christian revival began in America, the
revival that was rooted in the theorem of the 'Infinitely Mobile
Central Point,' in other words, in the victory over antiquated
science that regarded man only as an animal and the earth-planet
as a mote. But long before this time America had played an
important role in sciences and arts. Of course, that was not until
the use of the expressions 'Entertainment Industry' and 'Amusement Business' with regard to literature, drama, and music was
forbidden under penalty of heavy fines. These fines were particularly heavy where such works as Dante's 'Divine Comedy,'
Wagner's 'Parsifal,' Joyce's 'Finnegans Wake,' and others were
concerned, in connection with which any reference to the pro-
ducer's industry or the consumer's amusement is indeed misleading."

"The continent of pure commercialism?" I marveled.

"There was a time when various neural diseases made their
appearance in America," he resumed, "for example, 'tachyphobia'
and 'plutophobia,' as they were called by old-fashioned medical
science. The Americans were suddenly no longer able to stand
any degree of speed. In any form of locomotion that exceeded
twenty-five miles per hour they fell victim to a critical cerebral
anemia that assumed epidemic character. Passenger airplane
traffic had to be abandoned and gradually even the dear old
auto disappeared from the incredible highway system of the
continent. The aversion of the present Mental era to wheeled
vehicles is possibly a result of this tachyphobia. In order to
understand this epidemic of tachyphobia correctly, we must not
forget that all these ultrarapid means of locomotion were invented not so that man could be fast but so that he could be
slow, so that he would have more time to waste."

"And what about plutophobia?" I asked.

"Plutophobia," he explained, "was a skin disease, a sort of

allergic psoriasis that was induced by the sight of drafts, stocks,
bonds, mortgages, but especially of long, complicated contracts.
It was a curious mixture of disgust, loathing, and boredom which
led to plutophobia and eventually brought about the abolition
of all commercial activity. They became so ashamed of the
evaluation of things on the basis of their market value that they
awarded prizes in an annual 'Competition of Worst-Sellers.' The
Congress in Washington was obliged to adopt an amendment to
the Constitution by virtue of which the economic law of supply
and demand was declared null and void. Of course, in America
where every acre of prairie and desert produced untold wealth,
the principles of Neocommunism had meanwhile been victorious; these were summed up in the official slogan 'Everyone a
Stinking Millionaire in his own right.'"

"And what did the active, naïve, ambitious, impulsive, energetic, competitory, statistical-minded Americans do with all their
time?"

"The great scientific idea of the Djebel," B.H. replied mysteriously, "a real American idea, began to project its shadow
ahead. The first primitive principles of Chronosophy, of Cosmic
Calisthenics, and of Starroving go far back to the plutophobic
era. At a similarly early time we find the first efforts that finally,
after countless millennia led to victory over old age and early
death. It is said that even way back in the beginnings of mankind it was not unusual for a group of octogenarian American
ladies to shout cheerfully to a group of robust American gentlemen of the same age: 'Don't you boys want to come over here
and sit down with us girls?' This feeling of never being grown
up that was characteristic of the Anglo-American race contained
within itself a premonition of later fulfillment. At the same time,
when the high tide of mysticism had receded, the idea of pure,
meaningless play as a purpose in life was conceived for the first
time. From our host and from our Spokesman you heard a few
words today on the subject of meaningless play. Here's a good
example of it from most ancient times: the plutophobic Amer-

icans, who had given up all buying and selling, nevertheless clung tenaciously to one commercial branch, namely the advertising business. But the trick was that they were only permitted to use their customary gaudy superlatives to advertise persons and objects that really didn't exist. . . ."

I lay still and listened attentively to my reincarnated friend, in order not to miss a single detail; for no one had ever been fortunate enough to be permitted to take a course in world history like the one that I was taking. I, who was present with body and soul in the Eleventh Cosmic Capital Year of Virgo, was in addition granted the privilege of hearing with my own ears about events that took place decades, centuries, and millennia after my death. A new breath of ozoniferous mountain air cooled my brow. Perhaps morning was not far off. My exhaustion had decreased in weight but not in intensity. Now it seemed to me that the black she-bear of night outside the artificial window had moved, had raised her paw. At the same time, however, I had lost the thread of the discourse and had missed many, many things that B.H. reported regarding the centuries and millennia that he had witnessed. I began to speak, but I had the feeling that my ears were full of sawdust.

"You've no idea, B.H.," I said, "what a satisfaction it is to know that all the things I've just learned from you are not empty prophecies and predictions but solid facts from the past!"

"I wish they were more solid," he replied. "Not only the prophet is forced to distort his visions when he reports them, but also the reincarnated historian. It's a well-known fact that he is nothing but a prophet in reverse, for the receding past becomes just as unreal as the approaching future. The images of events are unrelentingly refracted in the stream of time."

"They are even refracted in space, my friend, in the cosmic space through which we roam—what's that, B.H.? Who is whispering in my ear in purest Latin, 'Animula vagula, blandula, pallidula'. . . . You'll have to help me, B.H. . . . Even today, after ever so many reincarnations, you're still the better Latinist; and of the two of us, you always knew the answers and I didn't. . . . So tell me, who is whispering to me, 'Animula vagula, blandula, pallidula' . . . ?"

"'. . . rigida, nudula,'" B.H. concluded, and his large head quivered and the ecstatic smile of poetic connoisseurship lay on his features. "Yes, who is it that is calling you 'blandishing little soul, restlessly roving, deathly pallid, icily rigid, nude'? It is Emperor Hadrian who is whispering his death chant to you."

"Yes, and I quite understand him, your Emperor Hadrian," I sighed. "He wants to warn me with the death chant that he crooned to himself on his deathbed with tears in his eyes, the sentimental tramp. He is warning me against taking off my old dress suit and this starched, frayed, crumpled shirt. For underneath it there's probably nothing but a sensual, blandishing little soul, ready to rove restlessly, deathly pallid and icily rigid. . . ."

B.H. lay still and said nothing more. But I continued to talk, and I told him all sorts of things—at least so it seemed to me—although my voice seemed to come out of the bottom of a mine shaft, a mine shaft that was I-myself. Just relax, B.H., listen, just relax, as the famous American dentist said to Dame World as he was about to extract her upper left wisdom tooth. And it was a good suggestion. But then somehow I was next in the chair and I wasn't scared at all, for by this time it was all over. Just drop your shoulders, he advised, and I thought they were golden words, although, distrustful as I am, I had long suspected that I had no shoulders at all. But I sat solidly and comfortably in the torture chair, I can't deny it, although I no longer existed at all. And behold, I had a deep, deep experience: although I didn't exist at all, I was being moved. For the torture chair was a wheel chair. Being moved is the last thing one knows. But since being moved never ceases, the knowledge of being moved, the final consciousness, also never ceases. If Io-Fagòr should ever quiz me on the subject of timelessness again, I would reply: Just imagine, old man, that you are nothing but the empty space inside a vehicle fabricated out of time, out of time-metal. The door slams relentlessly behind you and off you go. You move, no, you are moved, you are being moved, timelessly in time through time. Being moved means being a Moved Being. A marvelous motto for a travel agency. But whoever thinks that the timeless empty space that is being moved is really empty, knows nothing of the truth. There is no absolute emptiness, just as there is no absolute death. There's always something in me, even in the ninth power of the ninth power of my nonexistence. And how strong that something is in me just now! How strong that something that speaks and stammers and blabs and blathers and babbles and blurts! And what is it, and who is it, but the young-old precocious tattler, the syllabic Sybarite who can't keep her mouth shut, forever and ever, amen. And is that the animula vagula, blandula, the rigidly, frigidly immortal soul? And isn't it simply too, too absurd that Caesarean butchers in the hour of their death become lyric asses, who feel terribly sorry for themselves and for their blandishing, wheedling little souls? Why feel sorry? Just drop your shoulders, but don't drop yourself. As long as the eternally garrulous is being moved through space by the eternally mobile, everything is all right. And that's the congenital situation in our family, in the Sun-family. Where are we going, pray tell? We're going to visit grandma, my dear child. Is grandma the Ancestress? Shame on you, you bonehead, grandma isn't a youthfully beautiful pervert; she's a wrinkled old lady full of crotchets and funny stories. Does grandma still have her goiter? Shame on you, don't you know any better than to speak so bluntly? No, this is the older grandma, the oldest grandma. Well, what do you know, there she is, with her hair slicked back and parted in the middle, and with her jolly martyr's eyes, and with her pinched mouth. Grandma, what jolly martyr's eyes you have! The better to weep for you. Grandma, what a pinched mouth you have! The better for you to understand man's last language. What's happening to me? This is awful! Now I've learned man's last language, which is also his first. It certainly isn't the Monolingua, that hodgepodge, that Esperanto from the Mental attic.

No, no, just raise up the bells of your ear trumpets, I'm speaking the Protoglossa, the language of the First Day of Creation, that still echoes in the ears of the hydrogen atoms. I understood the Protoglossa—don't think I didn't—the day the midwife slapped me on my back. And I understood the Protoglossa again when they were preparing me for my last, involuntary final journey, a journey on which I didn't move but on which I was moved. What a wonderful language it is, this Protoglossa of ours! It lies far back of the tipple language and the nipple language and the soaked-diaper idiom. It lies beyond all swoon-babbling and all narcosis-blabbing and beyond the fast fading death cry. It is the red thread that grandma embroiders into her tapestry of organdy, yes, of organdy. But now I have to be careful not to slip too far back into the Protoglossa, like old immigrants who keep on backsliding because they can't become accustomed to the language of their new environment. Use your head, old man, and stay with the Monolingua, that's your duty right now. All right, I won't step into any snares or on any trap doors. And now, let's move on please. Or rather, let's be moved on, please. This Mental traveling is a terribly poor excuse for our traffic. What we really need is a conductor with gold braid on his cap and a locomotive with a bell and a whistle, and a porter who yells, "All aboard." For we're children of the railroad, world without end, and we'll never get over it. Just look at me, the three-year-old over there, staring up at the viaduct, and rapturously shouting at the steaming locomotive in nipple language, "Injin!" The children of the railroad know that all darkness in the world is caused by a tunnel and therefore it passes. And whoever is a Lovejoy, as I, a Christian I. Lovejoy, he begins to see the light in the middle of the tunnel. But beyond the tunnel lies the Park of the Worker. And that's where I'm going the first thing in the morning. And even if I'm lying far below the surface of the earth and staring into the dark, yet I know that the sun has risen. For where could the sun rise, but within me . . . ?

"Our wakening drink awaits us," B.H.'s cheery voice rang clearly.

"It's only a morning drink," I replied, "for you see, I held out, and I don't have to be wakened."

Part Two: THE SECOND DAY

DJEBEL AND JUNGLE

The Tenth Chapter

WHEREIN I VISIT THE PARK OF THE WORKER,
AM ENTERTAINED BY HIM IN THE VALLEY
OF SPRINGS AND FORCES AND TAKE PART
IN THE DANCE OF THE DOVEGRAY BRIDES
UNTIL A DARK FIGURE COMES TO CALL ME
AWAY.

ONLY A PERSON who has for a long time been deprived of the sight of nature's color, green, knows what it means to the human psyche. Although my sojourn in the Mental era had so far been a scant half day and a full night, still the notion that I would be surrounded everywhere only by the iron-gray sod of the present age along with the black, leathery trees, the tragacanth roses, and wax magnolias, had plunged me into a mood of depression. Despite all the artificial moonlight, meadow brightness, and forest gloom, the illuminating art of the subterranean apartments did not make up for the absence of natural green. Although I had been something of a house plant all my life and had climbed mountains and roamed the woods only on rare occasions; although I had loved the landscapes of my life with my eyes rather than with my feet, yet the awareness of a nature still untamed had circulated in my bloodstream day and night. The highly advanced, that is, desolated, nature of the Astromental world filled me with a sensation of desiccation and atrophy; and while my living contemporaries of the future ap-

195

peared to feel no privation, I, the ghost from darkest antiquity, suffered like a plant from want of fresh water.

And so I don't need to describe my relief, my exuberance, my satisfaction, in short, my spiritual and physical delight, when I stepped through a narrow gate in a dilapidated wooden fence into the Park of the Worker, which lay before me as a unified, green landscape. This time I was alone. It was fun to move about freely in the Mental world for the first time and to elope from B.H. by means of the travel-puzzle. Over the decaying fence a sign was affixed with the words "The Park of the Worker," and beneath it, in small letters: "Whoso touches his back will carry away the virtue that goes out of him."

The quotation seemed vaguely familiar to me, still I assumed it came from some later author of whom I knew nothing. A few days after my return into the twentieth century, however, when I chanced to pick up the Gospels again, my Testament opened to the eighth chapter of Luke, and my eye fell on the passage where the woman having an issue of blood touched the border of Jesus' garment and was healed. I read: "And Jesus said, 'Who touched me?' When all denied, Peter and they that were with him said, 'Master, the multitude throng thee and press thee. . . .' And Jesus said, 'Somebody hath touched me: for I perceive that virtue is gone out of me.'" I merely mention the inscription above the decaying gate of the Park of the Worker and the corresponding words in the eighth chapter of Luke without understanding their connection. It may be that the inscription contained an allusion to the Gospel, but perhaps I am wrong.

The first thing I did when I had gone about two hundred paces into the Park and stood in a flower-covered meadow, was to throw myself full length onto the grass and inhale the unspeakably familiar fragrance with distended nostrils. Lying flat on my back, as I had so often in my old life, I looked up at the sky. It was empty, desolate, fiery. It radiated that strange cold heat that had made me chilly when, as an invisible spirit, I first met B.H. on the irongray sod. It was indeed the Mental sky above me.

But it did not seem to be the Mental earth beneath and around me. Beneficent powers had breathed the green of spring over it, had covered it with long blades of grass between which, slightly varied but recognizable, familiar wild flowers blossomed—anemones, bluebells, buttercups, dandelions, larkspur, and others. When I had rested my head on the bare ground for a while, I had a little shock from the distinct feeling of its magnetism, which threatened to devour me, incorporate me, digest me as though it were the stomach of an enormous cow. The thought flashed through me: had the earth-planet become more compact during my absence, had its power of gravity increased, or was I less compact and less resistant than of yore? I certainly didn't want to run the risk of being dissolved, of being lost in the great lostness, although on this familiar meadow I was much less afraid of it than last night in the guest room of the strange subterranean house. At the moment, however, I felt more curious and more inquisitive than in need of rest. I sat up with a jerk and gazed about me.

The Park of the Worker, thank goodness, was no level plain like the inhabited earth round about, which, as I had been told, consisted of a single, endless city. It was pleasant, hilly country. Through the little valley between the low knolls crept a tiny brook—and the word "brook" is really too flattering for this very insignificant trickle at whose banks the light green deepened into somewhat richer shades. There, among ferns and all sorts of shrubs, were also a few trees that differed most agreeably from the low, leather-leaved boughs above the houses. These were all slender, fairly tall trees with quaking, smoky, or silvery foliage. They appeared to be descendants or imitations of our birches, silver poplars, aspens, and alders, feminine and ghostly species, which obviously fitted into the Mental landscape much better than oaks, elms, maples, or giant redwoods. In the selection of these surviving trees I recognized the cogent logic of nature. And they filled me with great happiness, these slender successors of the silver poplars, aspens, and birches.

It took quite a while before I became aware that even this

natural nature was unnatural in a faintly provocative manner. But then I ask myself, is there really such a thing as natural nature? Assuming that the patient reader and I were not sitting at this moment in the Park of the Worker, in the Eleventh Cosmic Capital Year of Virgo, but that we were sitting in the Euganean hills near Padua between the years 1300 and 1400— wouldn't nature, as Giotto and his successors painted it in their frescoes in the form of background landscape, seem just as unnatural or, putting it more mildly, stylized? The truth is that there isn't any natural nature, for nature always wears the historical costume in which the human eye clothes it. A person in the year 1943, looking at landscapes by Renoir, Pissarro, or the later Impressionists, may well be surprised that only thirty or forty years earlier sensitive souls actually fainted before these highly stylized compositions because of the brutal naturalism of their portrayal. But this secret is most completely revealed in the fact that even the photographic lens is not objective, and that the pictures which it records are as much bound to the historical style of their era as those of the painters.

It is not easy to find a suitable parallel to the landscape of the Worker's Park. It reminded me most nearly of the weak classicism of the Empire period, or of early Romanticism, when people used to hang Aeolian harps on willow trees, when you had to be careful not to stumble over artistically scattered fragments of pillars, when the poet strolled in an "ideal landscape," as the Spencerian letters under the colored engraving coyly announced. I gazed at this meager ideal spring landscape, the languid, smoky, quaking green of whose trees and shrubs I seemed to inhale with every breath. I had been deprived of it too long. I thought of nothing. I dreamed of nothing. My hands plucked blades of grass with hundred-thousand-year-old feelings of childhood. Now and then I put a long stalk in my mouth and sucked at its pallid sweetness, which took me back over endless ages.

I had almost forgotten the Worker and my curiosity when I suddenly felt sharp jolts against my legs from all sides. I cringed

with fright before I even dared to look. But when I looked,
I was confronted by a strange and unexpected sight. In the
course of the night B.H. had told me about the "capricornettes"
that the Worker milked for himself and his favorites. In spite of
the diminutive, the word could mean nothing but goats or goatlike creatures with heavy udders, as we knew them. And without
doubt, they were goatlike creatures that now flooded the meadow
by the thousands, although on second thought they could just as
well have been something halfway between a chamois and an
ibex. But the astonishing thing was not the species. In the eras
that had passed during my absence, the goat family had shrunk
to about the size of our squirrels or smaller varieties of rabbits.
Around my legs pranced and played well-shaped, dun-colored,
living toys of ibexes and nanny-goats, an immeasurable flood of
capricornettes, that sniffed at me, pushed inquisitively against
me, rubbed mischievously against my legs, and belabored me
with their tiny horns. I was in a serious fix unless help came
quickly. I jumped to my feet and considered calling up B.H.
Mentally, especially as the active little beasts, excited by my
violent movement, were now leaping up on me and were beginning to rip my venerable pants with their miniature horns. I had
to kick wildly in all directions in order to clear a small space
about me. Suddenly a moderately loud shout rang out and the
high tide of goats receded at once. I was free.

Slowly and deliberately the man who had shouted came
nearer. He was much larger and clumsier than the ordinary run
of Mental people. At first I thought he was the Worker in person.
But soon I noticed that he was not wearing a beard, but that his
naked breast was completely covered with brown hair which he
did not conceal. In this respect, whether of his own free will or
under compulsion of some regulation, he departed far from the
usual standard of dermal smoothness. Furthermore he was not
wearing any sort of veil material but a fringed, leatherlike apron
which hung down to his knees. On his head perched a cone-
shaped felt, something between an Alpine hat and a coolie
sombrero. In his hand he held a knobby stick that could have

only a symbolic meaning in the age of the Mentelobole, while over his shoulder hung a sagging something that might either have been a water-sack or a bagpipe. At his appearance the multitude of capricornettes calmed down immediately and gave voice to a bleating of welcome that ebbed away far behind the crests of the hillocks, although the volume of this bleating was in exact proportion to the shrunken stature of the goat species. It was not quite bleating, but rather a bleating squeal, and from the opposite hillside a baaing squeal replied, for there the so-called ovettes were grazing, the surviving race of lambs, ewes, and rams, which had suffered the same diminution as the billy-goats and nanny-goats. Thus I found in this most modern of all worlds the two varieties of Biblical animals, sheep and goats, that symbolize the legal situation of the human soul at the right and left of the Seat of Judgment on Judgment Day. The horses, on the other hand, had long ago become extinct. The cattle that still existed did not come under my observation, and I am there-fore unable to report whether they too circulated only in abridged editions.

Now the relatively clumsy, half-naked figure of this man was standing in front of me. He kept his eyes lowered, for he seemed to be timid by profession. Probably one of the Worker's head shepherds, I concluded.

"Have you been sent after me?" I inquired, trying to find an opening for a polite conversation.

"I knew it," the supposed shepherd nodded, "I knew it." And a broad smile suffused his features. I hesitate to call it a grin, for it had an element of veiled pain in it.

"Then you know who I am?"

"Seigneur, our welcome visitor," the man replied.

"Unless I am mistaken, you have charge of these capricorn-ettes, these cunning, mischievous little beasts, that almost tore up my only pair of pants. Are you perhaps an animal specialist?"

I didn't want to say "shepherd," a word that was too remi-niscent of the beginnings of mankind and that might have offended him. The clumsy fellow shook his head for a while, then lowered it sadly to his breast and answered softly, "No, I'm not a specialist. I'm the Idiot of the Era."

"The Idiot of the Era?" I echoed in surprise, for the man was looking at me with deep and intelligent eyes which seemed not a whit more stupid than the eyes of Bridegroom Io-Do or of his father, timidly pompous Io-Solip.

"Does your title have any official significance?" I asked politely.

"I'm half-witted," he replied frankly and sadly as if he were showing a wound. "My head isn't any good for learning."

At this point, of course, I should have kept my mouth shut and not forced him to further disclosures. But since I had bumped into what might be called the official moron of the Mental world in the person of this man, I wanted to discover his limits, and I did my duty as an explorer at the risk of being rude.

"How far did you get in school?" I asked him.

"Only as far as the binomial theorem and integral and differential calculus, and not a bit further," he answered in a choked voice and pointed at his goitrous throat.

"For us that would have been pretty good," I remarked in great surprise. "Most of us would have been very proud——"

He looked at me incredulously. "But that's kindergarten stuff," he sighed and added, "and that's not the worst of it. The Commission decided that I don't use enough hypothetical conditional sentences."

It sounded as though a patient said, "I don't have enough red blood corpuscles."

By this time I was completely upset and asked, "What are hypothetical conditional sentences?"

The capricornette herder's forehead was creased with the furious exertion of thinking. After a while he blurted, "If the Idiot of the Era were not so idiotic, he too might dance with one of the brides today!"

Yes, it was a genuine hypothetical conditional sentence and besides it was a lyrical eruption that demanded silence. I motioned to the Idiot to precede me and show the way. He started.

I kept hard on his heels, for the capricornettes didn't seem to be very fond of me yet. Whenever they could play a goatish trick on me the little fellows did it. Once I almost fell down. But then the Idiot of the Era raised the leather sack to his lips. I thought he was drinking because there was no sound of a bagpipe. The nasty little beasts, however, formed in rank and file and pranced along nodding their behorned and bewhiskered little heads in rhythmic unison. So far I hadn't found out anything about Mental music.

* * * * *
* * *
*

THE WORKER, WHOM I NOW FACED amid surroundings of greenest green, was a real giant and not of this time at all. He was close to seven feet, but his radiant stature had nothing in common with that of the miserable giants that we used to see in the cities of deepest antiquity as doormen of movie and vaudeville theaters and sideshows. Those hypertrophic statures usually resulted from a diseased pineal gland, and their bearers looked as unhappy and uncouth as if nature's checkroom girl had given them the wrong body for the right check and they hadn't noticed it until too late. Not so the Worker. All of his seven feet were genuine and healthy and downright jolly. The reason for his exuberant well-being was his extremely salubrious profession, the tending of the mysterious sprinkling system on which the economy of the Mental era was based. Everything in the vicinity of this system was green and parklike, flourished and burgeoned. That this was not the case with the capricornettes and ovettes and that they remained stunted, was no contradiction at all but had evolutionary reasons of its own. Other animals, however, and particularly the most typical species of Mental fauna, the insects, had grown alarmingly in size. I am not speaking of Lepidoptera, butterflies and huge silver moths and dragonfly-like biplanes which played the role of songbirds in the now familiar house gardens; I am speaking of the bees in the

Park of the Worker. They were as large as hummingbirds, and I was told that they not only buzzed about the wild flowers in the valley and on the hills, but that they also sucked the insipid sweetness from the wax and candy blossoms in the vicinity to make their honey. Man, to be sure, had no use for this honey. The children in the Worker's Park were not afraid of the stingless giant bees but pointed at them with enthusiastic fingers and crowed in a mixture of ancient Greek and nipple dialect, "Melissili, dada, melissili!"

Well, the secret is out: the Worker was surrounded by children. They were mostly tiny children, hundreds of them. And they were being pushed in regular gocarts, the only wheeled vehicles that had survived, as the billiard table had, but with better reason. I can't express the deep gratitude I felt in my heart, the tender satisfaction, at the sight of so many perambulators that moved in loops and circles about the Worker. The young mothers pushed them over the worn, light green lawn, and a babble of voices rose that was composed of a hodgepodge of squalling, squawking, enraged squealing, stubborn screaming, prattling, and prating, punctuated by feminine scolding and comforting. The Worker, who looked exactly as I had imagined the first time he was mentioned, appeared to play the part of a biological Helios, a sun god in overalls, who unfailingly radiated health, strength, and well-being all over the neighborhood. They all thronged about him, they all wanted to touch him, heedless of the elegant Mental custom that made all physical contact taboo. As I expected, he wore a short, dark-blond beard which was beginning to show a few strands of white. His good-natured, roundish face was very sunburned and wind-tanned, as though he were a sailor or fisherman, a Worker of the sea rather than of the soil. Fun and laughter were hidden in the wrinkles and crow's-feet about his eyes—eyes of the same cornflower blue as Lala's. And the Worker's laughter missed no opportunity to erupt. It was never a laugh, however, that released a witty tension, but simply the resounding symbol of physical super-well-being and spiritual balance. If the Major Domus Mundi was the epitome of delicate and sorrowful selenity, the Worker was the epitome of powerful and benevolent solarity. At sight of him I realized the wisdom of the Astromental constitution in assigning rule and government to the gentle man of night, while it left work and husbandry to the vigorous man of day, even though by this assignment of duties it reversed the old order of things. Both the man of day and the man of night, however, far excelled the present standard of mankind, the one physically, the other spiritually. Together they formed the poles of the axis that ran through the age. At the same time the Worker had not lost the characteristics that his name expressed. He was jovial and condescending as befitted his gigantic growth that forced him to stoop down to everything and everyone. But he was not jovial in the manner of a prince or a commander, but jovial as an experienced foreman, a locomotive engineer, or a master miner, in short, as a successful proletarian of the remote past, who on Sundays was dressed exactly like the industrialist, his employer, and yet stepped aside and tipped his hat to him when they met. The Worker was without any doubt a superman, yet he succeeded in expressing in every gesture the fact that he had come up from below, and that he knew it.

The Idiot with his capricornettes had left me alone. Now I was standing in the midst of the gocarts, babies, and young mothers who were crowding about the Worker, and I was ashamed of myself. How should I call the giant's attention to my person? I heard his mighty voice outlaughing the jagged up-and-down of feminine chatter in a leonine yellow key of C-major. What I referred to before as his overalls was really a big blue apron tied around his waist in the manner of shoemakers and carpenters of former days. I expected my extraordinary figure in the black evening suit to frighten one or another of the women. They were, however, so engrossed in the salutary sight of the Worker that he had wind of my presence before they. Suddenly he made an expansive gesture with his right arm above the golden heads of the young mothers and beckoned to me.

"He comes, he is coming!" his voice rang out. "He's long over-due. Take care how you treat him, he's diff'rent from you."

That was undoubtedly a little verse in which he commended me to the kind treatment of the women and children. After a few excited exclamations, a little caterwauling of babies, and the wordy remonstrances of several dogs that happened to be pres-ent, everyone was silent and stared at me. The Worker's habit of lapsing occasionally into rhymed speech was merely the result of the increased joy of living that filled him especially in the morning hours and that expressed itself not only in primitive verse but also in humorous proverbs, spoonerisms, and puns. As I stood on tiptoe next to him, I felt repulsively small beside his towering height and unspeakably frail and feeble beside his resounding soundness. Never during my sojourn in the Mental world did I feel more hopelessly like a cheap, underdone, half-baked materialization than at this moment when I stood next to the Worker. He, however, whose laughing blue eyes became attentively serious for a fraction of a second, seemed to feel and to know what went on inside me. He embraced me with his tremendous left arm and pressed my head gently against his breast. At the same time he spoke to me softly, or rather, he growled something golden, and it was in verse again.

"Think calmly, draw your breath deep and slow! Your Creator would have you do it so. Red sun is your blood from crown to toe. Each minute counts seventy beats of your heart. Let your ego be child, your body its gocart. Pressing the diaphragm in, is bad and wrong. The solar plexus is the seat of life's morning song."

His golden lion's growl was wonderfully hypnotic. I felt my body relax from the cramp that so often seized me on account of my excitability. After a few deep breaths I felt wonderful; if it weren't so absurd in my case, I should say that I felt reborn; I felt reborn with a new, unspeakably satisfactory constitution. My nerves no longer tormented me by alternately overexpanding and overcontracting my blood vessels in successive emotional thrills. With my head resting against the Worker's enormous chest, his huge reddish-brown hand on my hip, I suddenly experienced an equilibration of my being such as I had never felt before. I relived the long-forgotten bliss of childhood when we rolled in the grass or looked at the sky from between our legs. My physical comfort was so overpowering that I scarcely noticed that we had been walking for some time and that we had left the playground with its babies, gocarts, and young mothers far behind us.

"So you're the Worker," I said, just to be saying something, and pressed close to his force-radiating person.

"The Worker works from dawn the whole day through," he rhymed in reply. "But only shoddy work makes tired and blue."

"Of course, anyone as big and strong as you," I declared with enthusiasm, "couldn't ever get blue and tired."

"I'm not so big and strong at all," the Worker finally dropped into prose. "You ought to see my sons. They're much bigger and stronger and stigger and bronger."

"What's that?" I marveled. "You, as an official of the Mental world, have sons?"

"Certainly, twenty-two sons, all told and tall old I have twenty-two," he said. "So I have. And the twenty-two have two hundred and forty-two sons, all told and tall old. And the two hundred and forty-two, they have, let's see, they have all told one thousand three hundred and ten sons and they're my great-grandsons."

"And all your sons," I ventured to inquire farther, "and your grandsons and great-grandsons, they're all Workers like you?"

"All of us together are the Worker," he explained briefly.

Now I understood. The Worker was the exact reverse of that which the grammarians call a "plurale tantum"; they were a plural that linguistically appears only in the singular. The situations of the Official Guide and of the Idiot of the Era were probably similar. The Worker, against whose chest I was peacefully leaning, was the head of a tribe in which certain physical and spiritual powers and virtues were propagated by means of selective breeding; and this tribe or clan was thus qualified for specific services that the average Mental man was no longer capable of rendering. I should have liked to ask the Worker how many parks like the one under our feet, tended by his sons, grandsons, and great-grandsons, existed on the planet. But since he was loudly singing the "morning song of his solar plexus" at the moment, I didn't dare to interrupt. I was in a position, however, to draw the definite conclusion on the basis of my research, that the distant future not only linked certain occupations and callings to castes, but to specific clans and tribes with particular, highly bred, organic, almost magic characteristics. Moreover, the wives of the Worker, despite the general infrequency and the lengthening of pregnancy, appeared to have been given a continuous fertility that set them apart from the rest of humanity without, at the same time, degrading them. Incidentally, the wealth of children was another proletarian and peasant element of antiquity that had been preserved in the Worker. In him elements of primordiality combined in a most natural manner with elements of highest evolutionary advancement.

So remarkable was the cosmic contentment which flowed through my veins from the physical contact with this giant that I uttered a little cry of pain when he released me in order to open another lattice gate above which a worm-eaten wooden sign announced "The Valley of Springs and Forces." We entered a broad hollow in which the tall grass, interwoven with flowers, was almost malachite green. This hollow—quite different from the bowl of the Geodrome—was fairly deep, and I assume that the malachite color resulted not only from exalted fertility but was in keeping with the strange daylight down here. The farther we descended into the hollow, the paler and more transparent the sky became, until finally, even with the sun nearing the zenith, a few stars became visible. Considering the relentlessly burning, dry sky of the era, this Valley of Springs and Forces was the most pleasant outdoor spot that Mental nature had to offer.

"And here's the first spring," I heard myself exclaiming in a completely strange, boyish voice, and I wouldn't have been a bit surprised if I had discovered that instead of my old dress suit I was wearing one of my even older sailor suits with short pants, and stockings. My legs developed an irresistible desire to skip, and now and then I yielded to it without the least consideration of my dignity. What not only I, but anyone else, would have taken for a spring, a medicinal fountain in a health resort, was nothing but a fine, large alabaster bowl that stood at about the height of my chest on a thin glasslike column fixed in a stone pedestal. I stepped up to it quickly in order to examine the bowl and was surprised to find it quite smooth inside without either inlet or outlet for water.

"Please, Mr. Worker, won't you turn on the fountain?" I heard my excited boyish voice asking.

"My boy, your wits must have gone awry," the blue-aproned giant rhymed cheerfully. "Nothing springs from below, it comes from on high."

The concept of a medicinal spring, a bubbling fountain, as I had often seen, was so strong in my mind that I completely failed to understand the Worker, and I began to get annoyed at the light and shallow nature of his pert jingles. After all, they were only the silly afterdinner verses of a damn fool, even if this damn fool had at his disposal the magic powers and the deep nature instincts of a pagan demigod.

Meanwhile the Worker had walked over to the fountain, had rather solemnly bared his arms, and now began to rub his powerful paws just above the bowl, gently at first, then more and more vigorously, and finally as a surgeon who scrubs his hands for dear life. And while he washed himself without water in the subdued light of the hollow, his tremendous hands suddenly began to phosphoresce and then to glow in a steady ghostly light, and when he finally raised them, the ghostly glow did not leave them but faded toward the sky in the form of a pale greenish ray.

"I too, please, I want to do it too," my boyish voice exulted, but my intellect was still mature and understood that this was not a planetary spring but a stellar one that was not derived from below but was brought down from above to serve man. Man had transferred his industries into cosmic space and employed the forces of the stars on a piecework basis for the satisfaction of his needs. And in so doing he had realized only one of his primordial perceptions that is engraved in cuneiform characters on the famous Sumerian stele of Bab-el-Nazdr: "Everything that is below, is also above." This sentence declared the unity of cosmic material to the early Assyrians and Babylonians, and invited them to reach up to the skies for their sustenance. While all these thoughts ran through my mind, the Worker had taken hold of my hands and had showed me the proper way to rub and wash them in the sidereal ray. But it wasn't as easy as it looked, for the ghostly glow became heavier and heavier, and it seemed as though the rubbing hands had to bear the weight of the star. When I was about to lower my hands under this weight, the Worker suddenly commanded:

"Close your fists, quickly!"

I closed my fists convulsively, but I couldn't get them quite shut, for some sort of force pressed from inside and irresistibly opened my clenched fingers. When I finally looked at my two open palms, a pair of tiny, white baby shoes lay on each one. It was this pretty machine product that I had wrested from the ray of the star. The Worker shouted with laughter, and I too laughed and laughed. I didn't inquire about the why and wherefore, I didn't ask whether the Keenly Directed Desire sufficed or whether something else was necessary to induce the union of the appropriate atoms to manufacture a pair of baby shoes. I didn't ask by what determining power these atoms were torn from their moorings nor where, on their radiant road through space, they were condensed into the desired article. Let's be honest with each other: did I understand anything about reinforced concrete structure or about the secrets of the chemical industry? Did I have the slightest idea of the construction of a radio and of the long and short waves which it catches out of the atmosphere and pipes through a moderate-sized box into the human

ear in the form of sonorous campaign speeches, advertising
slogans, jazz cacophonies, and noble symphonic movements? No,
I understood just as little about the radio as about the manufacture of pretty baby shoes by stellar rays. More than a hundred
thousand years ago I had made up my mind to accept the existence of the radio and all the rest of the technological developments with an arrogant lack of understanding. Why should I
now take the trouble to ask for a scientific explanation of the
mathematical, astrophysical, kymatological, and other requirements for the Mental manufacture of goods, and waste a lot of
valuable time? Perhaps I was lax in the performance of my duties
as a journalist and travel reporter; with a little intellectual exertion I might have been able after my return home to give some
sort of account of the unknown principles of astral garment
manufacture and thus shorten humanity's rocky road toward the
subjugation of matter. But in the first place, I am not a utilitarian
world benefactor and I don't believe in shortening a road that,
by the measure of human experience, is endless. In the second
place, I was a simpleton of my own era and, unlike the capricornette herder, I never even got as far as differential calculus.
And in the third place, I don't believe that the Worker could
have given me an adequate explanation of the genesis of the
baby shoes. After all, he was only a Worker, a magician of
handicraft, not an inventor and not even an engineer. He was
still laughing so hard about my surprise that his gigantic frame
shook from head to foot, and I too was convulsed with healthy
laughter.

Of course, the baby shoes were not the end of it. We went
from one fountain bowl to the next, and they were without
number. But the principle always remained the same no matter
whether our hand-rubbing produced larger or smaller household
goods from the pale green, blue, rose, or lilac beams that suddenly and mysteriously appeared between the bowl and the dim
sky above the spring. Naturally the coloration of the rays was
human handiwork, since they lay far beyond the infrared and
ultraviolet bands of the spectrum. Occasionally the Worker set

concealed mirrors into motion and thus magnified the play of the rays into a tremendous illuminated fountain. The pale-hued ghostly streamers leaped high up, united with each other, formed round and pointed arches, and we could see them scintillate far out over the surrounding country. (I assumed that at the same instant all the necessary supplies were trickling into cupboards and larders through the roof gardens of countless underground homes in Panopolis.) Now and then the Bearded One quickly passed his hand through a ray and then attentively licked his finger. I imagined he was tasting some of the soups that were being prepared for people—for the better families even according to private recipes. Or, with the gesture of a prestidigitator, he reached into another ray and drew out a cambric-like fabric and tested it between his fingers as a good shop foreman tests a piece of finished goods before he lays it aside. Yes, his name fitted him. He was really the Worker.

Finally, when all the bowls were in synchronous operation, he grunted with satisfaction, sat down in the grass, and drew me down beside him. I could not turn my eyes from the indescribably glorious spectacle of the stellar rays working in broad daylight. He, however, reached into the pocket of his apron and pulled out an old-fashioned lunch package. He unwrapped it with a great rustling of paper, and I saw to my surprise that it contained a large chunk of goat cheese. Apparently the Worker derived his nourishment from the inferior sources and not, like his customers, from the superior ones. That was something to think about. He, who was more intimate with the sidereal rays than anyone else, was more deeply rooted in the planet than his Mental fellow-men. Now he broke the capricornette cheese in half and handed me a big piece. I bit into it joyously and began to eat fervently, for I too, being still an inferior human, had been deprived too long of solid food from below. After we had chewed in silence for a while the Worker slapped the ground beside him lazily. At once two thin streams of water gushed forth. I needed only to open my mouth to drink the sweetest icy mountain water that I had tasted since the mountain climbing tours of my youth. Goat cheese and spring water—that was the first of three significant lunches to which I was to be treated this forenoon.

* * * * *

* * *

*

FAR BE IT FROM ME TO CREATE THE IMPRESSION that man, the most fraudulent of all microorganisms, was fed and clothed in this era exclusively by rays from the heavens. To regard the temporally and spatially infinite cosmos as a colony of the tiny solar satellite Earth, would mean to fall into the opposite extreme of error and to simplify falsely the delicate geocentric doctrine of the "infinitely mobile central point of all conceivable orbits." The earth was still the chief source of all raw materials for human needs. The sidereal forces merely supplanted the tools and machinery of primitive eras by relieving the human body and human time completely of expenditure of energy on work. The deep, malachite-green hollow in which I was lying with the Worker, eating the savory capricornette cheese, was undoubtedly not the only Valley of Springs and Forces on earth. There must have been a large number of them, including also such that did not bring down the streams from above but that captured the forces from below by means of ingenious devices. But I didn't give it much thought. The indescribable creature comfort which this place imparted to the human body and the human consciousness was much too all-embracing to permit the exertion of any intellectual activity. So I never even thought of thinking; I surrendered to the paradisiac lullaby of the Springs and Forces about me and dozed luxuriously.

But as I nodded peacefully I suddenly noticed a steadily growing throng of young men silhouetted against the clear sky on the crest at the right side of the hollow. These young men appeared to be decked out for a special occasion. Their golden headdresses were festively taller than ordinarily. Otherwise they were attired only in that peculiar blurred nakedness that seemed to be an optical specialty of the age and that was actually worn as a garment. Their torsos gleamed like bright bronze in the sunlight.

"The dandies, the fops, make me madder than hops," the Worker growled. He had finished his meal and was folding up the paper with a disapproving rustling; then he stowed it away in the pocket of his blue apron as an exaggerated symbol of his domestic economy.

"What dandies?" I asked in surprise.

He bared his strong, slightly yellowish teeth. "The dandies up there make me want to swear."

As I looked at him attentively, the Worker began to twist the syllables and sounds in his golden, leonine growling, "The dandies, the fops. The fandies, the dops. The doppies, the fands. The dondies, the faps. . . ."

The golden growling became onomatopoetic and more and more nonsensical, or perhaps the Worker was speaking a dialect of the Monolingua that I didn't understand. The reader will probably be as surprised at the man's jingling, versifying, and spoonerizing as I was. In the old days I had observed it as a characteristic of musicians rather than of plumbers and electricians. Remember the letters of Mozart that are filled with "silly" sound play. The spirit of the musician combines and varies everything; he takes it apart and puts it back together as with notes; for that is the character of composition. Mozart's silly word plays are not so much eruptions of humor as musical pieces made with different material: theme and variations. The Worker's puns, on the other hand, were, as we already know, expressions of his enormous well-being that was not even reduced by anger and annoyance. My own body—which I always regarded with suspicion as merely a poor copy of my body—could testify to the salutary effect of fleeting contact or mere proximity of the Springs and Forces upon the feeling of health. How much more must this Worker, this giant of a fellow, have profited from his constant professional contact with these Springs and Forces!

He was still growling to himself when the crest opposite to that of the dudes, fops, and dandies was suddenly populated with a gracefully swaying rank of dovegray shapes. It was so beautiful that I jumped to my feet.

"Look there," I exclaimed, "I'm astigmatic, but I'll eat my hat if those aren't young girls."

"Sit down, son," the Worker ordered, and continued in a fluent rhyme, "Today is the day, as you may suspect, of the Dance of the Hundred Brides-Elect."

No further explanation was necessary. In spite of the dubious nature of my existence I was by no means so stupid as not to understand at once that the hundred preferred brides-elect of the city, the county, the state, or whatever this administrative unit of "California" was called, assembled in the Park of the Worker and in the Valley of Springs and Forces on the eve of their matrimonial union in order to partake of the salubrious virtues and impulses that emanated from the pale, starry sky and the malachite-green floor of this valley. And whether it was a question of a real blessing or of a mere symbolic ceremony, I fully understood it. What I did not understand, however, was the presence of the dudes, fops, and dandies; maybe the Worker had given them these derogatory names only out of envy, and they were probably thoroughly respectable young men, who knows? Meanwhile they streamed down the hill and lined up expectantly in a semicircle near us.

"What do these gentlemen want?" I asked, "and why are they lined up here?"

"Dance and ladies' choice," the Worker growled, and I had the feeling that in spite of the sublime monogamy of the Mental era he was jealous of every woman, every girl, and particularly of every bride-elect. With his tremendous physique, his explosive health, and the biological impulses necessarily resulting from these factors, it certainly wouldn't have been surprising. The Worker, with his twenty-two sons (number of daughters unknown), his two hundred and forty-two grandsons (number of granddaughters unknown), and his thousand three hundred and

ten great-grandsons (number of great-granddaughters unknown),
along with his entire clan, was an exciting exception in this regard too, and he wasn't a bit ashamed of it. Little by little I
learned the following: it was the legally prescribed privilege of
every bride-elect—a privilege which, in recent generations, had
developed into a ceremonial duty—to choose a young man as a
dancing partner and escort in the Park of the Worker on the
second day, the preparatory day, of her wedding festival. This
young man (chosen from the chorus of dudes and dandies) had
to be her cavalier of honor for two hours, that is, for the duration of the dance and the picnic following it, which was held
at the source from which all good things came. The chosen
cavalier could be anyone except the bridegroom. All prospective
bridegrooms were legally expressly barred from this ceremony,
which dated back to archaic times and was regarded by some
historians as having originated even before the time of the
Sun-Transparency. This fine, frank practice must have had its
beginning at the conclusion of a polyandrous era, when women,
who had had a male harem, considered the return to strict
monogamy a serious hardship. To preserve the illusion of a free
choice just once after the socially correct decision had already
been made, that was what they wanted! To pretend just once
more that the way was still clear for chance, for the god of love
himself, the way that, after the first successful kiss, would prove
to be the eternal road of destiny of soulmates. Ladies' choice
at a dance—the last shadow cast by the unquenchable longing
for freedom.

The gracefully swaying rank of brides had come nearer. The
dovegray veil garments billowed with the tiny advancing and receding dance steps. Under them the bright maidenly bodies
gleamed in the chastely subdued light. It was the famous Dance
of the Hundred Brides. I wondered whether the lovely Lala
from our household was among the chosen dancers. To my
unpracticed eye, however, the girls all looked so much alike
that I couldn't tell one from another. I sensed the tight nervousness that gradually took possession of the young men. Since

there were twice as many of them as of the brides, a hundred unwanted cavaliers would either have to look on as disgraced wallflowers or retire with feigned mockery. The vain fright, the frightened vanity, of the dudes lay like a bank of fog over the transparent air of the malachite-green hollow. To what sort of music, I wondered, were these brides dancing their ballet, which was strangely reminiscent of highly refined primitive dances? With all this Mental progress, how much primitivism kept eternally bobbing up! What was that? I heard no music of any sort. But presently I spied, at a great distance from my position, a sort of a melancholy gypsy lad with a hand organ (don't forget the billiard table in Io-Do's anteroom), which seemed to be authentic nineteenth century but which, in spite of most assiduous grinding, didn't emit the slightest sound. But in the great silence, in the absence of music, I gradually began to feel the music that lent rhythm to the limbs of the young girls. Next to the hurdy-gurdy man stood the Idiot of the Era, now surrounded only by a small cluster of capricornettes, and blew into his toneless bagpipes with flushed and puffed cheeks. Occasionally he lowered his leather sack, stared with tearful eyes at the dancing rank of brides, and stretched out his arms toward the girls without restraint so that I could feel his unbridled, eternally unquenched desire.

The Worker had left me alone after a few more disgruntled puns and rhymes about the dudes and fops. Evidently, in addition to his normal duties, a good deal of extra work was demanded of him today. He had to use all his skill to raise the output of the terrestrial springs and sidereal forces to their utmost capacity, and at the same time he had to prepare the festive picnic for the hundred brides and their hundred cavaliers of honor. Soon the network of luminous fountains on all sides grew higher, and I stood in the darkened daylight under a complex arch of ineffably delicate, colored rays that came from above and rose again from below to lose themselves in the infinite. By virtue of the Springs and Forces, so it seemed to me, my body lost as much of its ordinary gravity as in water; my lungs expanded more

freely than ever; my blood coursed more easily through my
veins; and as a result of the reduced organic strictures and frictions, an imponderable spiritual cheeriness unfolded within me,
the very memory of which brings tears to my eyes.

Now the crank of the silent hurdy-gurdy stopped turning, the
ballet of the brides dissolved. On the other hand, the ranks of
dudes and dandies froze into a solid wall. The signal for ladies'
choice had evidently been given. And, in fact, the brides began
to walk along the line of young men, first in one direction, then
in the opposite. They made up their minds very circumspectly,
and only after lengthy consideration. I stepped closer, for it
was a pleasing, a stimulating, spectacle. I was so engrossed in
the charming scene that it took some time before I noticed that
one of the shining, dovegray brides was standing timidly beside
me. The intuitively alert reader needs no hint as to her identity.

"For heaven's sake, Lala," I exclaimed as a galvanic shock
ran through my nerves, "you do me too much honor by greeting
me here."

The cornflower eyes looked at me earnestly and searchingly.
Then Io-La bowed her head gracefully and ceremoniously, so
that I could admire her ebony black helmet under the bridal
veil. A faintly perceptible, sweet, living fragrance—I can find no
other name for Lala's perfume—shyly insinuated itself into my
senses.

"I didn't come here to greet you, Seigneur," said Io-La, "but
to choose you for the dance."

I thought I had misunderstood her. "Whom are you choosing
for the dance?"

"You, Seigneur," said Lala, "that is, if you don't mind."

"You're joking, Lala," I protested, shocked down to my solar
plexus which was no longer the seat of a morning song. "You
know who and what I am and where I come from."

"Why should I be joking, Seigneur?" she asked, and her eyes
were genuinely puzzled at the question.

But my heart was beating so violently that the words tumbled
jerkily over my lips. "My dear Bride," I said, "there are two

hundred young athletes. Two hundred choice male specimens of your generation, even though the Worker may call them dudes and fops and dandies. And tomorrow, Io-La, you start upon your true and loyal married life with Io-Do, who will then no longer be your fiancé but your husband. This is your last day of liberty, that offers you a chance of spending two carefree hours dancing and dining with a handsome cavalier whom you have chosen to serve you; who has not been assigned as your permanent playmate by command of the stars and by a long process of testing and trying. You are free to forget him or to remember. And what, Lala, are you doing with your last bit of liberty?"

"I am choosing Seigneur as my Chevalier d'Honneur," the Bride interrupted me with complete candor. Then she looked at me. "The music has begun. Just put on your gloves, I'm waiting. . . ."

Without knowing exactly how it had happened I was holding a pair of white, fairly clean kid gloves in my hand. I had taken them from the tail pocket of my coat where they had peacefully survived the eons along with the repeatedly mentioned overworked handkerchief, some small change, and an empty matchbox. I tried to recall whether I had worn these gloves at my reawakening and had taken them off later. No, surely not. They, like the handkerchief, were relics of the sloppiness of the ancient mortician, who had neglected to empty the pockets of my coat before he dressed me. But as I reflected, I suddenly remembered when I had worn these white kid gloves for the last time. It was at the church wedding of a couple of my acquaintance, who had done me the honor of asking me to stand up with them. My services as best man had unfortunately not proved a boon for their married life, as they were promptly divorced at the end of a disagreeable year. This recollection of my failure as best man struck me as an unfavorable omen with regard to the lovely Bride at my side. At any rate, I possessed the white kid gloves prescribed for a formal dance so that I would not need to touch my partner with my bare hand. As I nervously pulled on the kids, I was suddenly shocked at the memory that yesterday, tempted by the Ancestress, I had let my hand rest between Lala's naked little breasts, for the express purpose of transmitting some of the primordial virtues of the twentieth century to this beautiful child of a late age who had no vicissitudes in her life nor lines in her palms. I felt myself grow red—disgracefully, considering my years—and perspire at the roots of my hair. I was paralyzed with confusion. Suddenly I knew that I had reached for my gloves only to avoid touching the girl's naked body once more. The Ancestress was right. The contact of such disparate elements could not be without consequences. And upon my honor, I wasn't thinking of myself, I was only thinking of Lala, whom I wanted to protect from my ancient, fateful, crisscrossed hand. At the same time I knew in my unspeakable confusion that Lala was aware of everything that went on in me. Even without the clairvoyant powers of Mental man she would have guessed everything, for neither the brides nor the dudes and dandies were wearing any sort of gloves of veil material or cambric. I bit my lips with embarrassment. Lala looked attentively at my hands but gave no hint of knowing my thoughts. At that instant the seams of my gloves split apart. You really can't blame them, considering the enormous longevity they had attained. And now I hoped to God that Lala would laugh as she had done yesterday, the more mockingly the better. Her laughter would have angered me and relieved me. But she didn't laugh; she remained calm and dignified.

"Which dance do you like best, Seigneur?" she asked, emphasizing the distance between us by a girlishly sly deference.

"Please, please," I implored, "consider what you're doing!"

"Does that mean that you reject me, Seigneur?"

"No man could do that, even if he were another hundred thousand years older than I." How I suffered from these words that offended me even more by their trite compliment than my pedantic dryness had done last night. That was the reason I now became abusive toward Lala.

"I only hope," I declared with excessive bitterness, "that your

snobbishness or bluestockingism isn't going to cheat you out of
two pleasant hours of your life. Even though I may be a rare
museum piece for your friends, I'm not worth such snobbery."

"Which dance would you like, Seigneur?" Lala repeated, paying no attention to my tactless words and placing the indescribably light fingertips of her right hand on my almost insensitive
left kid glove, while she rested her left hand on the right
shoulder of my dress coat with a trace of more intimate pressure,
ready for the dance.

"I was never much of a dancer, my child," I stammered.
"When I was your age, the world that came to an end during
my lifetime was chiefly addicted to a dance that was called a
'waltz.' Even at that time it was definitely an old-fashioned
dance, since the couples had to whirl in alternating step, that
pumped the air out of their lungs and drove the water from
their pores."

"And what sort of dances did they dance later on, Seigneur?"
Lala inquired, as serious as ever.

"Later on, let's see," I mused aloud, "later on they didn't
really dance at all any more. It was a sort of a walking up and
down in couples, a kind of an indolent promenade of the sexes
on an overcrowded dance floor. I'm not saying anything against
it. It served its purpose. And it was accompanied by a persistent carpet beating and by moaning, groaning music, the ille-
gitimate offspring of the African jungle memories of civilized
Negroes and Anglo-American languid crooning technique."

"In that case, Seigneur," decided Lala, smiling at me for the
first time, "we shall dance a waltz."

"But how?" I argued. "And where's the music?"

"The music is about to begin," said Lala. "You only need to
listen closely to yourself, Seigneur."

Obediently I closed my eyes in order to listen closely to myself. And sure enough, Lala was right, the music had begun
inside me. It was a very tenuous, infinitely old, music-box waltz
melody, which developed more and more distinctly in me with-

out any recognizable source—for the silent hurdy-gurdy and the silent bagpipes were obviously only props—until its three-fourths time communicated itself irresistibly to my legs. And my partner had the same experience, for without being particularly aware of it, we began to whirl in waltz time. But the best of it was that the whirling, whether to the right or to the left, was no strain at all, since the Springs and Forces of the malachite hollow had reduced the specific gravity of my body. It was by far the most satisfying dance of my conscious existence, including the almost fifty-three years of my past life. The word "dance" is too weak. It was really floating, the epitome of light floating, mingled with a still lighter floating, a dual floating. I hardly noticed the other couples and foursomes who moved about us in various rhythms. How strange that all these different rhythms seemed to originate in the same hurdy-gurdy, and that at the same time this poly-rhythm did not produce a disorganized effect. But why bother about the others? Passively floating, I understood what I had never known in my lifetime—the seriousness, the solemnity, of real dancing. After a few minutes Lala stopped without, however, releasing me. With the characteristic sensitiveness of elderly gentlemen I suspected that the girl did not wish to overtax my feeble strength. But she appeared to have something else in mind, for she made the following confession:

"I made a nasty remark about your hand yesterday, Seigneur. But I didn't mean it. I was only so terribly mad about Great-great-grandma."

"Madame is a very distinguished person," I commented with admirable nonchalance, for I had to control myself in order not to press a burning kiss on Lala's hand. Her words proved that she knew why I had put on my gloves, that she held the Ancestress responsible rather than me, and that the memory of the incident of last night was not repulsive to her. I was inordinately happy when we resumed the dance. Suddenly I observed that the Idiot of the Era had been following us for some time. He held the bagpipe in front of him without blowing into it. His features were distorted, his eyes blinked. I felt how much he envied me, who was even more outlawed and excluded from the privileges of living life than he.

To this day I don't know why, to spite myself, I said to my partner, "There is one who would give his life to be in my place."

"Only one? Only that one?" she asked, and I realized at once that I had made a terrible faux pas. A moment later Lala gave me a strange look and asked politely, "Do you want me to dance with the Idiot of the Era?"

At first I was dumfounded at the thought. "How can I wish," I replied contritely, "that you dance with anyone, Lala, although, or perhaps because, everyone else has a better right to it than I?"

"If you wish, Seigneur," Lala repeated with the insistent stubbornness that I already knew. "If you wish, I shall even dance with the Idiot of the Era, because——"

She suddenly stopped in the middle of the sentence and of a step, took her hands from me, and drew back a little. I was sure that I had seriously offended her. I was overcome with a desperate feeling of guilt, as always when I had "done something to" a lady without knowing exactly what it was. What difference did it make whether I was right or not, when a woman stepped away from me, turned her head away violently, bit her lips, and choked down the tears? No matter whether woman was the primeval temptress, for me she was always the touchstone of male guilt, for the sake of the natural suffering that man causes her. Had I offended Lala because I had mentioned her in connection with the Idiot, who was a pariah because of his boorish deficiency of hypothetical conditional sentences and his goiter? Or was my crime even deeper and more complex?

"Forgive me, Lala," I implored. "What a brute I am, rewarding all your kindness and indulgence with stupid blunders."

I tried to put my gloved hand reverently about her waist and to resume the waltz step.

"The dance is over," she declined with a very serious mien, "for we have been interrupted."

That could only mean that she was tired of my company.

"So you've reconsidered after all, Lala," I said with spuriously accented bitterness. "Too bad it's a little late. You will have to choose among the dudes that were left over."

Io-La shook her head and stared past me as though she were watching someone who was still concealed from me.

"No, I haven't reconsidered, Seigneur. And I won't choose anyone else either."

"Well, well," I misunderstood. "So I didn't pass the test, my child."

She raised her hand a little as though she wanted to keep me from speaking. "The test, Seigneur, that you will have to pass, is still ahead of you: to see whether you are on the right or wrong side."

Although I didn't get it at all, I felt the horror that lay in her words. "And if I'm on the wrong side?" I asked her with suddenly rising defiance.

"Then you'll not return, Seigneur," she said, but, as though frightened by her own thoughts, she added quickly and gently, "Of course you'll return."

"I won't even go away," I sulked. "I want to go on dancing with you, Lala. After all, you selected me as your Chevalier d'Honneur."

"But now the priest is sending for you, the Grand Bishop," Lala replied in a soft voice that sounded sad.

"I don't give a tinker's damn who is sending for me, the Grand Bishop or the Global Major-Domo or the Official Guide or the police, in case you have anything like that. You don't seem to realize, my dear girl, the extent of my liberty, independence, and sovereignty in this miserable world. My will has never so completely been my law. Shall we dance?"

Lala did not react to these words but continued to stare past me. Then I couldn't resist any longer and turned around toward the person whose presence behind me I had felt for some time. It was a little man in a black cowl, a monk or a lay brother. His head was bowed so low that I could not see his face but only his glassy smooth skull on which a wreath of hair had been painted with black paint about a tonsure, and in the center of this tonsure were the intertwined Greek letters "X" and "R," the name of Christ.

"Don't be in a hurry, please," I said to the little man in the cowl. "Life is short and I've been invited to dance."

The Grand Bishop's messenger did not raise his head from its humble posture, evidently to indicate that he had not received permission not to hurry. When I turned around irresolutely toward Lala, she was already gone.

The Eleventh Chapter

WHEREIN THE PRIEST PERFORMS A POWERFUL EXORCISM UPON ME WHICH LEAVES MY PHYSICAL AND SPIRITUAL STATE UNCHANGED AND CLEARLY PROVES THAT I AM NO CACODEMON, NOR AM I HARBORING ONE.

IT WAS A moderately large, bare, cold, prosaic hall, not quite as underground as the dwelling houses, but projecting above the surface of the earth, so that daylight fell through the light green, round windows. We would have said the chapel lay below the street level. But since there were no streets in Panopolis, only the gray universal sod, this expression would be meaningless. That this bare room, in spite of its barrenness, was a Catholic church, was attested by the high altar which had preserved its form unchanged through the decamillennia and was crowned by a tall, gold, gleaming monstrance. It was only my first personal impression that this was merely a large chapel, the private chapel of the Grand Bishop. It may be that the metropolitan cathedral of the prelate was just as unadorned as his private chapel; at any rate, I, who had grown up in baroque surroundings, found it difficult to become accustomed to the complete absence of images in this Mental church. Today—that is today, as I write these lines—I incline to the view that the clergy, in their dogmatic defense of the divine likeness of man, preferred to forego all imagery rather than permit any form of "abstract" or "analytic" art to cross the threshold of the church.

The cruciform ground plan as architectural symbol had remained the same as in the time of Romanesque, Gothic, and baroque churches. What struck me as strange was the absence of all pews or other furnishings to accommodate the kneeling worshipers at mass. The moderately large nave of this chapel was merely an empty space, divided in about the middle into two sections by a tall, ornate railing of some dark metal like old silver. I had no idea of the reason for this division. It reminded me of the time of the primitive Church when the Christian congregations consisted in part of people already baptized and in part of catechumens who were being prepared for acceptance in Christ, but who were still heathen. Both groups, converts and catechumens, took part in the service in a room divided by a rail similar to this one. Let by my little cowled guide, I approached a narrow open gate in the railing. Before I had reached it, however, I felt myself restrained gently. And now the scales fell from my astigmatic eyes. The raised platform upon which the altar stood was not empty, as it had appeared to me at my entrance. In the choir benches on both sides of the Holy of Holies sat black-robed padres who, no doubt, belonged to the same order as the lay brother who had interrupted my dance with Lala, had disrupted the festival of the brides, and had brought me here at the command of the Grand Bishop. I said the monks were sitting. That is neither a lapsus memoriae nor a lapsus calami. I didn't write it absent-mindedly or in error. I really saw the fathers sitting. The priests of the Catholic Christian Church that had survived all eons took no exception to the broken line as prescribed by the affectation of Mental manners.

In the midst of the monks, on a raised throne, sat the Grand Bishop in pale green vestments that did not differ from those I had known. His features beamed plainly and placidly in the sober daylight of the church. It was a smooth face but an old one, and the sight of age nobly acknowledged filled me with peculiar satisfaction. Three of the fathers had now approached the little gate at which I stood. Their figures were much taller than those of the average contemporaries, but extremely slender. They almost equaled the Worker in height although they contrasted sharply with him in all other respects. The one in the middle was the tallest of the three and also the oldest, but by no means advanced in years. It seems to me now that I have never seen narrower, more spiritualized faces. In the features of these clerics the high degree of asceticism that their saintly life had attained in this quite unascetic Astromental world was evident. The two younger monks, to the right and left of the one with the tallest stature and the finest, most ascetic features, each carried a burning taper in his hand. But I was much too strangely excited to greet these burning candles with the friendly sentiments that I felt toward all old familiar objects that had somehow found their way into the Eleventh Cosmic Capital Year of Virgo. The oldest of the three priests, the one in the surplice, had a tiny book, no larger than a postage stamp, in the palm of his left hand; in his right hand, however, he carried the aspergillum. He looked at me sadly and penetratingly before he rather softly chanted the Gloria:

"Gloria Patri et Filio et Spiritui Sancto."

After he had solemnly made the sign of the cross he addressed me in an ordinary and polite tone, "If you are able, please make the sign of the cross."

Obediently I did so, although I was very much surprised at the form of the request. Why shouldn't I be able to make the sign of the cross? The monk observed keenly while I touched my forehead, breast, and both shoulders with my right index finger. It seemed to astonish him more than a little that I succeeded in making the gesture without unfortunate consequence for myself. From the bishop's dais there sounded a long-drawn "Oremus!" This was followed by the soft intoning of prayers.

"In nomine Patris et Filii et Spiritus Sancti," the speaker began anew and then he asked me in a solemn, liturgical cadence, "Quis tu es? — Who are you?"

I answered loudly and distinctly as I had so often in my

life answered this inquisitorial, albeit less liturgically stylized question, in schoolrooms, in barracks, in public offices, in police stations, on witness stands, in consulates and at border control posts when one country had thrown me out and the next was in no hurry to take me in. The two younger monks stepped slowly through the gate, took their posts at my right and left, and held their tapers close to my face so that it could be more clearly seen, at the same time increasing my agitation. The priest in charge was now standing in the very center of the gate, his head touching its top, not more than three feet from me.

"Quounde venis? — Whence do you come?" he asked, this time lowering his head.

Although I did not feel the slightest constraint to answer any personal questions, and although I was sensible of a growing anger with this unexpected clerical tribunal that had cheated me out of my dance with Lala in the Park of the Worker, still I found it quite impossible to remain silent, as I had, for a moment, intended to do. And so I replied not only truthfully but also in detail.

"I appeared in this world yesterday afternoon at about the fourth hour. I have no memory and no idea of the manner of my appearance. It seems most likely that I stepped out of some dark, medieval gateway, that I traveled a fairly long distance in a somnolent condition, in order finally to meet my old friend B.H. somewhere on an utterly strange, irongray lawn. I recognized my friend at once and he recognized me, although I was totally invisible for at least half an hour, even to myself. That is the truth, the whole truth, and nothing but the truth. Regarding the mode of operation of this technically advanced necromancy, the Reverend Fathers can no doubt give me more accurate information than I can give them."

A certain amount of ironically bitter, even impertinent defiance must have vibrated in my words. I felt it in the silence of the clerical assemblage. Their heads seemed to droop lower, as though the hope for a happy ending of this affair were fading. In the deep silence round about, the priest who had questioned me strode back to the altar where he remained on his knees for a long time. Again the long-drawn "Oremus" resounded, followed by the intonation of Gregorian prayers: "Deus coeli, Deus terrae, Deus angelorum . . . Deus qui potestatem habes donare vitam . . . humiliter supplico . . . per Christum Dominum nostrum. . . ."

At the conclusion of the prayer the speaker arose, came slowly toward me, stopped at the gate in the railing, and called to me—I don't want to say "yelled at me"—in a loud, admonitory voice, putting a staccato accent on every single syllable, as if he had to make himself clear not only to me, but even more to the being that was concealed inside of me.

"In the name of the Father, the Son, the Holy Ghost! If you belong to the Demon, to the corrupter from the beginning, to the corrupter of human kind; if there resides in you a spirit of the evil spirit, then I command him in the name of Jesus Christ, Our Lord: Begone, come thou out of him, get thee behind him, betake thyself hence, so that he in whom thou clothest thyself may again be what, by the will of God, he was! *Discede seductor, cede, cede Deo!*"

Let me assure the astonished reader who has never experienced the like of this procedure, that it is no small matter even for the most enlightened and most liberal person to become the unwilling and unexpected object of an exorcism, a casting out of the Devil. I was fairly conscious of my innocence. But what is innocence? And what is consciousness? Does the soul know exactly whether it is aligned on the side of good or the side of evil? Everyone, including the Devil himself, nurses the sincere conviction that at the very spot where he stands, the good resides—or, at least, the just cause, the only good that the wicked understand. Self-consciousness cannot regard itself as entirely base, any more than the will to live can entirely negate itself. That is, the will to live can entirely negate itself only in the act of self-destruction, suicide. And in the same way self-consciousness can negate itself only by perpetual, penitent sanctification, whereby, as this word indicates, it ceases to be an expression of evil. In general, however, self-consciousness is to a large extent identical with self-pity. Self-pity, like everything sweet-sour, has a spicy taste. Of course, my self-pity came as a much later reaction. At the beginning I felt as though the floor were heaving under my feet like burning cardboard. Cold shivers ran down my spine. A sweeping consciousness of guilt began to vibrate within me, and the possibility that I was a spirit of the Evil Spirit seemed to become more definite certainty from moment to moment. I expected to shrink down to the ground along with my dress suit, my gold medal, my purple wrist-rosette, and my good old breathing body, and be transformed into a heap of loathsome reddish-brown worms. I looked at the Father Exorcist as tensely as he looked at me. Not even he could banish the dark question "What will happen?" from his disciplined eyes. Nothing happened. I remained standing, undoubtedly with a very scared and sheepish expression on my face. At this instant I felt four drops of holy water strike my face at the exact terminals of the cross, on my forehead, cheeks, and mouth. They were doubly intended—to weaken the resistance of evil within me and strengthen the resistance of good. Father Exorcist, who for a time had vainly awaited the effects of his first attack on the demon incorporated in me, began anew with an invocation to the Triune God, and then went into the details of exorcism, literally as follows:

"If you are of the discipleship of Simon Magus; if you hold with Basilides who proclaims the rule of Archon, the chief angel in the nethermost realm of spirits; if you are subject to Valentinus who preaches that this world is only symbolical and not real, because it is created by demiurges; if you render homage to Marcion according to whom the Creator knows only justice but not love; if you owe allegiance to the Ophites who worship the son of Ialdabaot and Sophia in the form of the house-serpent that curls about the sacred wafer and drops its venom on the Eucharistic Lord; if you have consorted and still consort with the unrestrained hordes of Cainites, Sethites, Adamites, and Manicheans who believe in two gods, one of Ormazdian brightness and one of Arimanian darkness; and if you acclaim their accursed successors, the Priscillians, the Paulicians, the Bogomiles in the mountain fastnesses of the Haemus, the Messalians, the Euchites, the Neo-Enthusiasts, the Borborites who call themselves the Filthy because they spill their semen upon the Bread of Heaven; if your path was and is that of the unchaste Nicolaitans, the Carpocratians, the Montanists, the Valesians who mutilate themselves, the Patricians and Circumcellions who, in pessimistic madness, mutilate not only themselves but others; and if you had intercourse with the Catharists who, stinking with pride, call themselves the Pure, although their true name is derived from Catto, the Tom-Cat of Hell, whose backside they kiss in adoration—then begone, come out of him, get behind him, betake yourself hence, discede seductor, cede, cede Domino, demore . . ." and so on. . . .

I became more composed and calmer as word after word, name after name, fell on my ear. And quickly I lost the spicy, the sweet-sour self-pity that had taken hold of me on account of my preposterous fate of first being summoned from the sleep of death and then exorcised on top of it. My conscious catalogue of sins was of quite another kind, more subtle and more personal than this, which consisted of an enumeration of Gnostic and post-Gnostic heresies that had had their origins in a strange mixture of early Christian theology and Neoplatonic philosophemes. But was it pure chance that Father Exorcist connected the evil spirit, of which he suspected me, with these long-forgotten false doctrines? No, it couldn't be chance. What was it then? Suddenly it dawned on me. In the last few days and nights before I fell asleep, I had been reading a very musty old volume about the Gnostics with the greatest interest. I could, for example, have answered the Father Exorcist's question, "If you are subject to Valentinus," truthfully and warmheartedly: "I am not subject to Valentinus, Reverend Sir. From your remote point of view, his and my era appear to coincide, however, that's nothing but false perspective. Among my contemporaries only a few learned theologians and scholars even knew his name. But that did not keep me from being strangely moved by this noble, profound, and highly poetic spirit when I chanced upon his quite forgotten doctrine in that old book. The only thing that's remarkable, Reverend Sir, is that you knew about this fleeting emotion of the last few days of my life and that you used it as the foundation of your attempt to exorcise the evil spirit in me. But I can assure you that my interest in the Gnostics and in Valentinus was of purely academic character and that, as far as heresy is concerned, we went a lot farther than the Catharists with their miserable Catto, the Tom-Cat of Hell, whose hind end they kissed." Naturally I didn't utter a word of these pert jokes, but stood at attention like a soldier at roll call. But in a moment I was to discover how far I had underestimated the Father Exorcist. His information was utterly boundless, and no matter to what decade of the past hectomillennium I might have belonged, he would not have been at a loss in the history of heresy. He cast only an occasional glimpse at the tiny book that lay open on the palm of his hand. Without the slightest pause there followed the names of the heretics and heresies with which I, or the exorcised demon inside of me, might have been in league. Although I was not quite inexpert at this historical material, still a great number of the cited names were strange to me, who was much nearer to them than the Father Exorcist. When, for example, a hypothetical conditional sentence credited me with membership in a sect that had nothing better to do at the end of the twelfth century than to engage in perverse practices with Herodias, I could not refrain from shaking my head, and when we had finally reached the Waldensians and their Black Masses, I almost had an attack of vertigo. For two minutes I feared that I really might have belonged to the Waldensians, and that divine vengeance would now descend on me. But vertigo and headache remained unchanged and I with them. I closed my eyes and paid no attention for a while in order to gain strength to survive this thoroughgoing exorcism. After a period of absent-mindedness new and more familiar names recalled me. I became aware how far we, that is, the exorcist and the exorcised, had advanced in the history of heresies, and that I hardly needed to worry about being an evil spirit, since I myself had been engaged in battle with more than one of the heresies that passed in inexorable review.

". . . do you belong," the voice sounded loudly and monotonously in my ear, "to Voltaire and to the others who substitute their own overweening pride for God in the name of 'human justice,' and who do not know that justice without mercy is hell-fire; are you permeated by the teachings of Immanuel Kant and his philosophic heirs who confound created reason with divine reason, and therefore maintain that their philosophy and science are unhypothetically critical; do you follow the wild hosts of Saint-Simon, Proudhon, Karl Marx, Friedrich Engels, and Vladimir Ilich Lenin who invented the most despicable human hatred in the guise of ice-cooled philanthropy, they who, with the traitorous and dreadful word 'masses,' libel the souls destined for redemption and salvation, they who liberate the poor and the oppressed by thrusting them into an even deeper and darker dungeon, whose tyrants and keepers, of course, they themselves are; do you side with the populous tribe of those who follow Darwin, Huxley, and Haeckel, the tribe of nature enthusiasts who are divided into the 'wearers of sandals' and the 'wearers of galoshes,' to those who confound the divine depths of nature with a lottery in which only 'the fittest' draw the lot of survival; do you consort by night with occultists, parlor-Buddhists, and theosophists who make an unholy brew of the holiest secrets mixed with their own insanities; do you consort by day with Sigmund Freud and his psychoanalysts who revere the sexual appetite, libido, the reincarnation of the ancient Astaroth, as the ruler of the ruler, the Logos; do you adhere to the philosophers who call themselves Positivists because they are convinced of nothing but the great Negative; to Auguste Comte and Spencer and Dewey, to Schopenhauer who denies God out of self-pity, to the rebel Nietzsche who, rage and rant as he may, is chained with chains of iron to the cross of the Crucified from beginning to end, wherefore he may be called the watchdog of Christ who barks at the faithful; or do you even worship that Stefan George, may his name stand for all domineering calligraphers, or others of his ilk, who wear modishly cut coats instead of sackcloth and ashes, who parade in flowing Ascot cravats and pseudo-Dantean locks, who swing their shoulders and their hips while they publicly proclaim a sick homosexual youth as the Holy Savior and hand brassy spiritual poverty around in costly containers until their dupes finally fall into the net of the most brutal and most bloody of all devils; and do you join the cause of Reinhold Ebermann Kotitzky, the orthobiotician, who came long after all these and who preached that life itself was the only purpose of life and that Paradise meant nothing but harmonious metabolism——"

At this point I could no longer restrain myself. I raised both hands in a defensive gesture, stepped forward from between the two candlebearers, and interrupted the Father Exorcist in a loud voice.

"You needn't bother to go on, Your Reverence. My answer is no, no, and again no. And as far as Reinhold Ebermann Kotitzky, the great orthobiotician, is concerned, he came not only after Stefan George but also after me. I've never heard of his name nor of his heresy. Not even I, in my helplessness, can be held responsible for the past future."

"Oremus," came the long-drawn-out order from the Bishop's throne, and a louder and more detailed intonation of prayers followed. I, however, trembled with rage so that tears came to my eyes and I could no longer see the Father Exorcist and his assistants. Only when the Grand Bishop, descending from the dais, in his mild green stola consolingly put his arms about me did I gradually become calmer.

"Your Lordship," I blurted out, still struggling for composure, "I don't object to being taken for a potential evil spirit; every man with a little spirit is a potential evil spirit. But what have my sinfulness, my daily defection from God, my unfaithfulness to men, my transgressions of the Commandments, to do with this damned history of heresies, in which I have just had far too long a lesson?"

"My dear son," the Grand Bishop answered gently, "when you entered the Geodrome last night the secular authorities, in accordance with custom, examined the contents of your soul"—it sounded exactly like "contents of your stomach"—"and they found the names of Basilides, Valentinus, and other heretics. You must remember that your presence in this world is unusual, to say the least."

"Basilides, Valentinus, they were the subject of my last reading in life, that's all," I replied angrily and was on the point of losing my composure again. "Is that the sanctity of private life in the Mental era? And does the Church recognize the Cacodemon by nothing more characteristic than by absurd and long-forgotten errors?"

"There is nothing more characteristic, my son," the Grand Bishop said softly, "for error springs from evil, just as evil springs from error."

* * * * *
* * *
*

"AND THEN THERE'S ANOTHER THING," the Bishop murmured, carefully closing the two doors of his library into which he had led me, "yes, another thing, my dear Sir and friend. Our Father Diocesan Exorcist, as you have noticed, is a tremendous scholar. He took exception to the fact that you are being addressed as Seigneur."

"I didn't select this title, Your Lordship," I rejoined a bit angrily. "I was astonished and not exactly pleased myself when I was first honored with it yesterday. I am well aware that the title Monseigneur is appropriate only for a prelate of the Roman Church and not for a poor soul like me."

"That's not it, my dear son," the Bishop interrupted me with a vague gesture. "But there is an opusculum in the Sephirodrome, the original of which must have appeared about in your lifetime, somewhere between fourteen and fifteen hundred post Christum incarnatum. The little book is entitled 'Fortalitium Fidei,' and in the chapter on 'Deception of Women by the Demon' the author, Alphonse de Spina, describes the atrocious worship of the great billy-goat, Elboche de Bitche, on dark new-moon nights. And that goat was addressed as 'Seigneur' or 'Monseigneur.' "

I erupted into loud and unseemly laughter and, after a moment of astonishment, the prelate good-naturedly joined me.

"Well, there really isn't much of Elboche de Bitche or any other demonic beast about you," he finally said. "We found that out very soon; but your black coat with its tail-like appendage at first aroused our suspicions. Well, all good spirits praise God. I bid you welcome, my dear son."

From a small cupboard the Bishop tenderly lifted a jug gleaming with golden wine and a basket of white bread.

"You won't get this anywhere else," he said with a smile as he set these gifts of God on a low table. He was right. Wine and wheat were raised only in the episcopal plantations. A part of the yield was intended for consecration, the balance was divided among the clergy.

I sipped the wine, which was fierier than any white Burgundy I had ever tasted; I ate of the bread, for, alas, I had a great longing for bread and wine, as I had for all other things that belonged to my own time. (I never even tried to explain to my clerical host that I did not belong to the fourteenth or fifteenth but to the twentieth century, since even the learned Father Exorcist had made a silly mistake in localizing, that is, temporalizing, me.) Moreover, the fact that the Bishop and I sat in armchairs in his Sephirodrome without appearing ill-mannered, was a great comfort that I consciously relished. But the thing that pleased me more than anything else was the environment of books, products of the intellect, a doubtless well-sifted selection of the world literature of past millennia and decamillennia, that filled the cases and shelves of this room. But my intelligent reader, who is quite right in checking up on me from time to time, objects: "Now look, that's getting just a little thick. Do you really expect me to believe that the entire literature of the world for more than a hundred thousand years could find room in the private library of a prelate, especially when it includes such

unusual rarities as that 'Fortalitium Fidei' that the Bishop referred to? With all due respect to the Eleventh Cosmic Capital
Year of Virgo, you can't make me believe nonsense like that."

To that objection I will have to reply truthfully: there was,
indeed, in this library a little handful of hoary original editions
that my eye and the reader's would have recognized as books.
None of these antique originals, of course, was much older than
twenty-five to thirty thousand years. That was about the limit
of durability of even the best materials in which the recorded
intellect expects to become immortalized. But most of the books
for the cultured reader—I mean the relatively modern editions—
were published in Imaginoprint, which was utterly incomprehensible to me, in tiny volumes, the size of postage stamps, or on
narrow tape, like reduced microfilm. And all of it was recorded
in ideograms involving condensations and omissions which saved
so much space that, for example, an entire chapter of the Bible
was contained in a single, intricate symbol remotely resembling
Arabic script. Modern Imaginoprint or Fulguroprint (lightning
script) was based upon the almost superhumanly developed capacity of the Mental intellect to assimilate entire series of concepts by skipping them. Only the evening news recorded by the
bouncing stars appeared in demotic, extensive characters, so
that not only the simplest child of the time, but even I, was able
to read it. In the presence of the Grand Bishop's little books and
rolls, however, I turned out to be the most ignorant analphabete,
and I admitted it to him at once.

"But you make up for it by your command of Greek, Latin,
and Hebrew," His Grace overestimated my accomplishments,
"languages which so many of our learned clerics only pretend
to understand," and he added with a glance at the door, "except-
ing, of course, the Reverend Father Exorcist."

The prelate pensively lowered his handsome old face (in spite
of the Mental semblance of youth, it was a genuinely old face).
I felt that he was struggling with himself.

"You will probably wish to ask me a few questions, my son,"
he began after a lengthy, irresolute silence.

"If it won't inconvenience Your Lordship," I took up the thread.

"Later, later," he declined. "First I have to ask you a question. I realize that in asking this question I am almost exceeding the bounds of my authority, and that I am acknowledging a thing that I, as a Bishop, have no right to acknowledge. And yet, you are sitting before me in the flesh. And I am not only the shepherd of my numerous ovettes, but—but—what was it you called yourself before, my dear son—a poor soul? Yes, that's what I am and that's what I can call myself. But you, my child, although apparently much younger, you are a poor soul of vastly greater experience than I. That is . . ."

And now he reduced his voice to a breath, and it seemed to me that he was trying to conceal his words from the all-hearing Father Exorcist.

"Please answer this one question, my child. How does it feel to be dead?"

I lapsed into startled silence. The Grand Bishop too appeared alarmed and rubbed his brow in embarrassment.

"I expressed myself a little improperly, my child, I know," he stammered. "In the doctrines of eschatology our creed informs us clearly what fate our poor souls must expect when God has taken the burden of the body from them. Far be it from me to subtilize the eternal truths about the ultimate or to try, with culpable curiosity, to unravel what the Lord in His merciful wisdom conceals from mortal ken. Still, even in our shamelessly sinful age it doesn't happen every day that someone appears who was already at home in the beyond." He sighed deeply and added anxiously, "You probably don't know, my friend, that the central sin of my contemporaries is intimately connected with the question that I have just asked you."

"Your Lordship, I shall try to find an answer to your question," I replied willingly, "although I have not yet had time to recall to memory clearly the facts of my dropping off to sleep and of my reawakening and of the things that lie between. I not only had no time to think about it, but a certain timid dread restrained me, except perhaps last night when I approached this question in uncontrolled associations of ideas while I was struggling to stay awake. Yes, it was really a great dread."

"Then you must obey your dread," said the Bishop, "and let us change the subject."

"No, no, Señor Gran Obispo," I said eagerly. "I'll have to get this problem clarified sometime anyhow, and with whom could I find more understanding, mercy, and grace than with Your Lordship?"

After these words I leaned far back, dropped my shoulders without being asked to do so, and the thought ran through my mind that not only was I investigating this strange era but the latter was even more thoroughly investigating me. Again and again I faced the same problem as at the dinner at Io-Fagòr's house when I had to render an account of the manner in which we had experienced life in our day. And now I was to testify before this noble and gentle theologian and prelate on the experience of being dead and, if possible, without offending his devout sensibilities. The peculiar thing was that in the first few minutes I not only had nothing to say about the condition of being dead, but I noticed to my horror that my intellect was completely paralyzed. Aha, I thought, just relax. Don't get all cramped up. Let yourself go. And then thoughts and words began to rise to the surface like the subterranean rivers of the wild and jagged Carso Mountains.

"First of all, Your Lordship," I began my attempt, "there's where I fell asleep and here's where I awoke. What lies between is certainly not a void. That much I can say without difficulty. What lies between is a duration, a span. But when I look back at this span, which actually lasted for more than a hundred thousand years, I must confess after searching self-examination that these hundred thousand years did not last a timeless instant, as the lay world might imagine, nor any sort of eternity; no, in my subjective feeling this span lasted some five or six hours."

The Grand Bishop raised his head, looked at me sharply, but said nothing. In contrast with the mild moon-eyes of the Geoarchon he had mild sun-eyes. These eyes bade me continue.

"Unfortunately the act of falling asleep," I resumed my effort, "the actus moriendi, is just as blurred in my present consciousness as the process of waking, which I reported to the best of my knowledge and belief to the Reverend Father Exorcist. Something inside me conjectures that I re-entered life at approximately the same geographic spot where I left it. But how I left it, whether in torment or in gentle detachment, whether in lonely struggle or hand in hand with my beloved wife, completely escapes me. Perhaps the last feeling devoted to the world that I remember is one of dismay that I was about to cause grief and that I was leaving behind dust-covered disorder neatly camouflaged to give a false appearance of order. At the same time, however, this feeling of dismay was mingled with something vainly pleasant, as if what was happening to me was a sort of personal heroic deed, for which my bereaved relatives owed me increased recognition. These are things that I remember, or seem to remember. What followed then was a drama of loneliness, a drama in several acts."

"So now we've come to the loneliness," the Bishop nodded as if he knew the melody, and suddenly I suspected that I wasn't telling him anything new at all but that I was being subjected to a test, and a much sharper and trickier one than that to which the stern Father Exorcist had exposed me. But I didn't let it worry me and I continued to grope for the real and true interpretation of my experiences.

"Death," I went on, "particularly death in the first stage, is by no means pure nonexistence, as I have already reported, but only an illusion of nonexistence, because of the absence of contrasts. Consciousness, it is true, gradually ceases; it languishes, it withers, with all its nerve-fiber roots which lie far beneath the surface. But this too is only an illusion, and the most illusory of all, for it is not consciousness that languishes but only the duality of consciousness, the abundance of the Thou in the I, the reflecting vis-à-vis of existence. The ego no longer faces itself and can therefore no longer be aware of itself, as a human face becomes aware of itself in a mirror. The ego disappears in the ego, in itself, as water in water."

"So it is," nodded the Grand Bishop and closed his eyes, partly in satisfaction, partly in disapproval of my abstract language.

"But how does this disappearance of the ego in the ego come about?" I asked myself more boldly. "Along with natural life, the soul is deprived of images. It receives no more nourishment from images. From the psychological point of view life is nothing but an uninterrupted series of images from the first awakening of the infant to the last sleep of the moribund man. Death, as an experience of the soul, is first of all a great fading of images. Everything that only recently raced past us, drops and is no more. When we used to sit in a motionless railway train back in my day— Do I make myself clear in such parables, Your Lordship?"

"You make yourself clear, my child. Don't be afraid."

"So when we sat in a motionless railroad train while another train passed us, we had the illusion that the latter was standing still and we were moving. This illusion is gone now. Nothing passes the pure ego any more. There is nothing to bring it out in relief. Just as the geometrician and physicist teach us that a single point in space cannot be computed without a point of reference, so the pure ego cannot experience itself. And with that it enters upon the second stage of death, which might be called the infinite loneness without any point of reference and without any background."

"The infinite loneness," the Bishop repeated slowly and, like a kind examiner, he briefly summarized my exposition in order to put me on the right track. "When the images no longer pass in review before the soul, when everything is eclipsed that the soul might address as 'Thou,' and when at last no definite opposite is left by means of which the soul might become conscious of itself—well, what does the poor soul do then?"

"I don't quite understand Your Lordship," I hesitated.

"I had hoped, my dear son," the Grand Bishop replied with a shade of displeasure, "that you would be able to express the entire truth. In the natural order, being dead certainly means infinite lonesomeness. But in the supernatural order does not this infinite lonesomeness mean infinite twosomeness? By the very fact that the vivid play of the temporal vis-à-vis vanishes, the play which creates mundane consciousness by distracting the soul from its true aim; by the very fact that the shade-mottled wall between the soul and the sun collapses, this spiritual sun, the eternal light, the Triune God Himself, becomes the permanent vis-à-vis, the essence of the Thou, through which the pure ego receives its new, boundless, ecstatic consciousness."

"Your Lordship," I said, deeply moved, "if my poor soul had won this new, boundless, ecstatic consciousness, I would not be sitting here. I can only speak with complete sincerity of my own personal experience of death without adding or omitting anything, though the temptation to do so is certainly great. It is not only possible but probable that I can remember neither the actual unconsciousness of my poor soul nor its twosomeness with God, or, at least, I cannot reproduce them, since neither can be expressed even in the Protoglossa. Isn't it, moreover, a necessary premise of life that the soul can't remember its twosomeness with God before birth and after death? I do not regard it as impossible that my poor soul spent the past hundred thousand years in a place of torment, a form of existence for which there is no comparison and therefore no memory. What really happened to me in the few hours to which these hundred thousand years had shrunk, all that I recall objectively and that I retained as the experience of death, was—well, the passing train on the next track had vanished and now the train in which I was sitting began to move for the first time. How shall I express it, Your Lordship? I myself was the infinitely immobile, the infinitely apathetic, the infinitely quiet, that was being carried away by something indescribably mobile, full of intention, purpose, energy, actually full of the noise of wheels. It seemed as though the dead man whose senses were no longer dulled by the busy activity of his body—circulation, metabolism, internal secretion, breathing—as though this dead man were now being borne away by the vibrant activity of the planet and of the entire cosmos——"

At these words—and I was far from finished—the Grand Bishop arose brusquely and his mild features were very serious. "You have never been dead, Sir," he said in a voice that sounded almost scornful, at least reproachful.

"But how could it be possible?" I objected.

A tired gesture silenced me. "You began your description of the state of death quite accurately. But then, despite sufficient profundity and more than sufficient eloquence, you described a condition that is premortal and nothing more."

"I spoke the truth in every word, Your Lordship."

"You undoubtedly spoke the truth, my son. But this truth is, you were never dead."

"But then how did I get here, in the Eleventh Cosmic Capital Year of Virgo," I asked in astonishment, "in this distant Mental era of history, without first having been dead?"

"That you will have to straighten out with yourself, or rather, with your friends," replied the Grand Bishop.

We had sat down again. I drank my second glass of wine slowly, relishing its bouquet.

"I am drinking," I said pensively after I had put the glass down. "I drink, therefore I am."

"This conclusion is quite warranted," said the Grand Bishop with an approving nod, "but I too am drinking."

"What does Your Lordship mean by that?" I asked suspiciously.

"That only one of us can drink, my child."

He bent his pale face far forward, so far that the light green bishop's cap which he was now wearing instead of the miter almost touched me. Then he added, "Yes, and that only one of us can dream that he is drinking, either you or I."

An impulse of warmth and admiration for this priest moved me to the words, "I know that you are the genuine one of us two, Señor Gran Obispo."

He looked at me sadly and then confessed, "I wish nothing more ardently than that I were only the product of your sinfully vivid imagination."

"Why, that's almost making a concession to Valentinus and his demiurge," I exclaimed, impolitely jumping to my feet. "May a high dignitary of the Third, the Spiritual Church doubt his own reality? Wouldn't that offend the Father Exorcist? Isn't the conviction that this world is this world the foundation of all faith?"

The Grand Bishop's serious eye forced me back into my chair. I slapped my own mouth. "Forgive me and have pity, Your Lordship. Who am I to say such things! I was only trying to express the astonishment of a primitive man at the fact that Your Lordship seems to be dissatisfied with a vastly improved and advanced world in which you have the good fortune to live and to rule."

"Vastly improved and advanced world," the Grand Bishop repeated in a dragging cadence.

"Your Lordship should consider," I resumed, "how the day of an archbishop of my time, the nineteenth or twentieth century, passed. His heart was weighed down by worry about ten thousand neglected, lousy, rickety children, who grew up in dreadful shacks and tenement houses, and who had no other choice in their years of puberty except to become either wretched wage-slaves or whores and gangsters. Tuberculosis, syphilis, and moral nihilism wasted the fiber of youth. The wars had pulverized entire cities and generations. What was left was a black fog of hatred and reproach that lay over the peoples like the reeking coal smoke of hell. They lived in a world of slovenly dead-end streets. The icy chill of the materialistic spirit made it impossible to solve even the simplest problem because it was stated wrong to start with. And in the midst of this world of spiritual and physical ruin the Church and its priests had to fight for the truth. But how is it now, Your Lordship? A Worker and his family feed all mankind. War is nothing more than a dilapidated, ghostly monument, a rusty armillary sphere in a hole. Poverty, physical and spiritual misery have become mythological concepts.

In proof of its supernatural founding and mission, the Church has not only outlasted the eons but has, moreover, re-established its original unity—a realization of Christ's prediction that my former contemporaries would never believe if I could report it to them. And you, Most Reverend Sir, you will not admit and you deny to my face that the world has vastly improved and has progressed beyond belief?"

"What you call progress, my dear son," His Grace said in a tired voice, "is nothing but the desperate superstition that something that falls could fall upward."

"I beg Your Lordship to be patient with me, who am not yet an Astromental man. This paradox is not clear to me."

"It is no paradox," said the Bishop, "but a simple parable."

He paused a while; then, putting the fingertips of his hands against each other, he directed this question to me, "Are we agreed that our forefathers sinned in Paradise?"

"Our forefathers seem to have done that," I replied, "else we wouldn't always have to start over again."

"Well, if we are agreed on the first point," the Grand Bishop continued, "then we must also agree on the second, third, and fourth points. We are agreed, therefore, that all human history is the history of the consequences of the fall of man, that is, the history of progressive alienation from God. No matter how pitiful the conditions in the nineteenth and twentieth centuries may have been, they were still better by a hundred abysses, by a hundred millennia, than those of today, that have impressed you so deeply. For we have fallen just so much lower and are just so much farther alienated from God."

"What, Your Lordship," I exclaimed almost bitterly, "man's tremendous effort to overcome the archangel's curse of labor and dispersal, man's effort to make the earth more habitable and himself more intelligent, this effort, you say, is no return to God but an even colder and more insolent apostasy?"

"The old civilization of which you spoke, my son," the Grand Bishop answered, "at least bore suffering and death and thus accepted the curse of the archangel. Today's civilization, however, in which you are moving, which calls itself Astromental, is a deceitful and tricky attempt to escape that curse by insidious intrigue—the curse that enjoins us to eat the bread of the earth in the sweat of our brow and in sorrow, and to return humbly to the dust whence we came."

The old man lapsed into melancholy, yes, painful, meditation, so that I did not dare to speak for some time. Did he really regard Mental civilization as an illicit attempt on the part of man to transfigure, to sublimate, nature in his own improper way? Curiously my eyes clung to his hands. I should have liked to know whether his palms were also as unmarked and inanimate as those of a store-window dummy. But I couldn't decipher a thing, for his waxen hands lay in his lap, clenched into fists.

Suddenly he sighed deeply and murmured in conclusion of his thought, "Yes, return to dust and await resurrection."

Then I could no longer restrain myself and asked the pointed question, "Was Your Lordship perhaps thinking just now of the road of which my friends boast that it is traveled voluntarily and on foot?"

The Bishop made no reply. His eyelids had drooped. His eyes were covered by violet shadows behind which, as with the Geoarchon, the vital activities of sleep seemed to be going on. (Was this too only a further alienation from God?) I had risen and was about to sneak on tiptoe out of the Sephirodrome. But the priest's gentle voice recalled me.

"No matter what may be the true interpretation of your phrase 'I drink, therefore I am,' I ask that you place your hand on mine in a solemn vow."

I obeyed and placed my hand softly on his.

"Promise me," he murmured, looking around, "promise me that you will come to me for advice and help *if a certain demand*—you understand me—should ever be made of you."

The Twelfth Chapter

WHEREIN THE JEW OF THE ERA FOLLOWS ME, INVITES ME, ENTERTAINS ME, AND INTRODUCES ME TO HIS SON.

IN ADDITION TO a very small number of truly new phenomena, every world and every era contains an incalculably large number of repetitions, modifications, and paradoxes. The Astromental era was no exception to this historical law, which is based upon the limitations of human capacity to make combinations. The reader who has accompanied me voluntarily to this point—I am beginning to look upon him as a magnanimous friend who shares my intellectual curiosity as well as my disdain of journalistic nonsense—this friend knows that, and why, Mental dwellings had to be underground. Although I had already seen a number of notable exceptions to this rule, still I was not prepared for the sight that met my eyes when I finally emerged into the daylight from the archiepiscopal palace after climbing an endless, narrow, steep cellar stairs. This steep flight of stairs, which the clerical dignitaries were forced to climb for ascetic reasons, corresponded exactly to the lowly Sentry Booth in which, for humility's sake, the secular dignity of the Geoarchon, or Selenozusian, was domiciled. I had left the Grand Bishop wrapped in gloomy thought, and I had refused to be accompanied on the way out either by him or by one of his padres, since I knew very well that it was inappropriate for him and his

clerics to be seen in public with the queerly clad result of spiritualistic machinations.

I arrived on the surface a little out of breath from the arduous
climb, and I had to keep my eyelids closed for quite a while in
the pitiless sunlight. When I opened them again I could scarcely
believe my eyes, for I was standing in front of a fairly high
gateway on whose Romanesque arch were chiseled the words
"Former Eastside District" in broad, familiar letters. The ground
was covered partly by cracked cement, partly by wooden blocks,
and partly by paving stones between which the irongray sod
sprang up as the green weeds had formerly done. But the
strangest thing was that there were two regular streams of pedestrians going in opposite directions. For some reason these people
either possessed no travel-puzzles or preferred not to use them
because they wanted to reach their near-by destinations on foot.
I was unable to divine, however, the nature of these destinations.
One of the streams of pedestrians originated not far from the
ruined archway in which I was standing; the other came from
just behind a similar arch which jutted up against the noonday
sky about a thousand paces distant. Between these two gates,
beyond which the remarkable traffic ebbed off at once, there
extended something that could easily have been described as an
old-fashioned trading alley, a lane of secondhand stores and
pawnshops, or an Oriental bazaar, if only there had been dilapidated little houses, shanties, or even rickety booths on the right
and left. In reality, however, this picturesque alley with its
bartering nooks and whispering crannies consisted simply of two
long, fairly low parallel walls that had no apparent reason for
existence. By standing on tiptoe I could easily look over the wall,
and what I saw there was nothing but endless irongray lawn
with a few scattered house-garden islands in the distance. Yet
I had the impression that I was standing in the most densely
populated borough, in the Whitechapel, Ottakring, Wedding,
Saint Cloud, or Lower East Side of the Astromental metropolis.
This impression was intensified by the human faces and figures
that passed me without greeting each other as the custom of

the time required. They all looked serious and grouchy and kept their eyes cast down. It was clear that the people of the Former Eastside were the weary and heavy-laden, that is, of course, only relatively weary and heavy-laden. But does the qualifying word "relatively" really reduce the fact of weariness and heavy-ladenness? Had eternal youth or agelessness, had the manufacture of all commodities by the Worker, had the elimination of all want and probably of most diseases, had the extension of life to the limits of boredom, actually reduced the static sum of human unhappiness? Or were these gloomy people who had conquered nature in an incredible fashion no happier than we, just as we had been no happier than the cavemen? That might well be the second-greatest controversial question of all times. The Grand Bishop had answered it just a little while ago. But his answer was dictated by his office.

All through my life—pardon me, all through my past life—it had been one of my greatest pleasures to drift with the throngs along the splendid avenues of great cities or through dingy and disreputable alleys of slums and foreign quarters. Even when I had no conscious intention of making observations, ten thousand mosaic fragments of human fates formed patterns in my soul. Without hunting for adventures I bumped into them at every step on such strolls. Here too, in this out-of-the-way corso of the Mental world, I felt the old, electric urge to mingle with the throng. I had not felt this urge in the central plaza, the Geo-drome, where I had been forced to play the role of a curiosity. Here, on the other hand, not even my ridiculous formal garment of the twentieth century was conspicuous enough to attract attention. It was a great relief to be totally disregarded by the crowd. That might have been caused by the fact that the men and women streaming back and forth here were not in "normal" dress either, that is to say, they were not wearing veils or cam-bric-like draperies over their blurred, gleaming nakedness; in-stead they were garbed in duller, coarser, so to speak, more dismal, materials. It's hard to find a parallel, but their garments might best be likened to Bedouin burnooses of dark brown, sand color, or ashgray. Moreover, I didn't see a single gold or silver headdress such as was worn by the average citizen. In the Former Eastside the robes were drawn up to cover the head; this not only intensified the impression of the Orient but also gave rise to the suspicion that these unfortunates were still supplied with an ample hirsute crop that banished them to a lower degree in the order of human rank. Here, beyond a doubt, lived the despised "prolific" families whose physiques—horrible to contemplate—had remained so primitive that their women were able to give birth to more than two children. Only the Worker's bright race of giants could afford its tremendous fertility since it occupied a mythical position of distinction in all respects.

I tried to study the faces of the passers-by, although most of them kept their heads lowered. Their complexions, tan or copper-colored, differed from the ivory pallor of my friends. The origin of the unified race from the fusion of white and colored peoples was more evident here in the Eastside District than elsewhere; however, I noticed no deviation from the general standard of beauty and agelessness, discounting the more melancholy, more somber, and occasionally more irascible facial expressions. The Grand Bishop lived in this neighborhood, and somewhere in this vicinity, probably half underground, was his metropolitan cathedral. Was the Church obedient to the words of the Gospel by its location near to those who labor and are heavy-laden, of whom there seemed to be many even in this age without economics and social frictions? Or did its situation in the Former Eastside express its exalted reactionary conviction which, in the words of the Grand Bishop, regarded Astromental culture as an aggravation of the fall of man and a further alienation from God, and for that reason it attached itself to the "delinquents"?

These questions were running through my head when a slight prickling of the nerves in my back informed me that someone was looking at me intently. I stopped and turned around. The someone behind me stopped too. He was a small, slim man, wrapped in black cloaklike material with which he covered half of his pale face in ritualistically solemn fashion. I moved on. He moved on. I stopped. He passed me slowly. After we had covered about thirty paces in this almost creeping manner—I had the feeling that he was leading me to a definite objective—he stopped again without warning. Unless I wanted to repeat the entire maneuver, I now had to pass him. I did it rather emphatically, keeping my eye firmly fixed on him. Then, like a conspirator, he briefly uncovered his pale face, paler than those of my acquaintances, with gaunt cheeks and a trace of black beard that looked as though it were painted on. Gloom-shaded eyes—no, I must modify the word—relatively gloom-shaded eyes fastened themselves on mine. He was Rembrandt's "King Saul," who, deeply moved by young David's song, tries to conceal his tears by drawing a drape over his eyes. This gesture wasn't necessary now since there was no young hero singing nor were there tears in his eyes. It is only natural that Rembrandt's King Saul looked much brighter in this Mental world than in the original. He looked at me with gloomy irony out of eyes that were neither moon- nor sun-eyes, but star-eyes. They blinked at me as I passed him so that I felt constrained to greet him in a whisper.

"King Saul, peace be with you."

"Quite right," he whispered even more softly in return, "my name is Io-Saul Minionman." But when I tried to open a conversation, he made a conspiratorial gesture and gave me a plain sign to stay near him but to do it inconspicuously. Without opening his lips he hissed, "Can't you see you're being watched from all sides? Why do you have to consort with the Jew of the Era?"

Aha, I thought, another inverted plural, and that makes him an official. King Saul nudged me in passing. He muttered from between his teeth, "Hundred paces, then turn left. Follow me unobtrusively."

* * * * *
* * *
*

OF COURSE, NO ONE WAS POOR. The word poverty had lost its meaning as far as it referred to material goods and necessities of life. In these labyrinths of the Former Eastside too, everyone could satisfy his appetites with the most exquisite substances, if he was sophisticated enough to enjoy them. Here too, he could get the most delicate, diaphanous textiles from the celestial fountains and terrestrial forces of the Worker, unless he preferred crude and dull materials. Here in the Mental slums too, the dwellings were as spacious as the splendid villa of my wedding party, the couches were as luxurious, the illumination just as fanciful, the walls of the rooms just as ready to reflect dynamic wallpaper, that is, projections of inner images. And yet, in spite of this identical, refined comfort, I clearly felt that I was visiting in the congested nooks of the poor and the despised who congregated here because they didn't belong there, because they sought warmth, companionship, confinement, and because they suffered less in crowded conditions than the others. Suddenly I acquired an understanding for which I had been far too superficial and positivistic in my lifetime: poverty is much more than the result of want, nor does it disappear with the latter. Poverty is a karmic limitation of the soul, based upon the inequality of everything that constitutes life. Poverty and wealth are not so much the individual results of economics as their causes. The truly poor and rich are born poor and rich respectively, in the sense of natal characteristics, just as one is born with blue or brown eyes, with a gentle or violent temper. In a word—and this is important for the understanding of all economic revolutions—poverty remains even when it is abolished. After all, the Idiot of the Era was really idiotic, even though he had gotten as far as the binomial theorem and differential calculus.

Now all of this doesn't mean that Minionman, the Jew of the Era, belonged to the poor, the weary, and the heavy-laden. He was just as far removed from these as he was from the others, the Io-Fagòrs, the Io-Dos, the Spokesmen, and the Permanent Guests.

The large room into which he conducted me differed from all other rooms I had seen so far in that it was crammed full of memories. Is that strange after more than a hundred thousand years of historical continuity? I wasn't in the least astonished, for I knew beforehand that in the home of Rembrandt's King Saul I would find all sorts of scrolls, ancient tomes, seven-branched candelabra, spice boxes with copper pennants, rugs, brown paintings, and ancient materials. But of course I hadn't known in advance that everything would be covered with a thick layer of dust, when there couldn't be any dust in the Mental climate except that of the millennia, and that everything would smell strongly of decay as well as of camphor.

At any rate, it was very pleasant that Saul Minionman offered me an armchair, as the Grand Bishop had done, and that no snobbish ironing board was folded down from the wall to rest weary bones. I dropped comfortably into the armchair and yielded to the relaxation of the broken line. The Jew of the Era disappeared into the next room and returned a little later with an antique silver salver. It looked ancient enough to have come from the tabernacle of Shiloh. On it were two white porcelain jugs. He placed the salver on a taboret that stood between us and began to speak in the bitter, witty, reproachful, and self-ironizing manner that I and every other knowing person would have expected of him. King Saul's subordinate clauses were like shadowy valleys in which the aggressive thoughts of the main clauses were obscured.

"You've just been to see the Grand Bishop, haven't you, Doctus? You'll notice that I call you 'Doctus' and not 'Seigneur.' 'Seigneur' is fatuous, an expression of hopeless ignorance. Of course, 'Doctus' doesn't exist any more either but at least it's in good taste. Well then, Doctus, you were with the Grand Bishop in his Sephirodrome. Before that you were in his church and you were getting a little preparation for burning at the stake.

Don't conceal anything from me, don't tell me anything; I know too much for my own good already. Did he give you something to eat?"

"He did," I nodded. "I drank two glasses of wonderful wine, and for the first time in a hundred thousand years I chewed on earthly bread."

"If only it had been plain earthly bread," Io-Saul sighed ambiguously, leering at me. "Did you enjoy the bread and wine?"

"Very much," I replied, "just as much as I did the Worker's cheese a little earlier."

"It is goat cheese," commented Minionman with obvious disgust, turning up the palms of his hands. "Heathenish, epicurean, unrefined goat cheese. Enough to turn one's stomach."

"Isn't that prejudice, Rabbi Saul?" I asked. "And you even seem to have an aversion to bread and wine."

"Not in the least, Doctus," he said with a twinkle in his eye. "Bread and wine are the second-best things on earth. The only objection I have to them is that they're hard to get."

"I think I understand you, Io-Minionman," I nodded. "You too come from the beginnings of mankind, as I do. My friend B.H. doesn't like to be reminded of it. So you'll forgive me, for an ancient lineage seems to be anything but a patent of nobility. The Mental soups and creams taste better and are more substantial than anything that we used to eat, but while they delight the palate, they occupy the attention of the imagination at the same time and so reduce the old animal pleasure of eating. But bread and wine, you see, is bread and wine, no more, no less."

Minionman gave me a satiny look of reproach and his mouth twitched with half-concealed scorn as he turned up his palms in an extravagant gesture.

"Bread and wine is bread and wine," he said in a singing tone, "if it doesn't happen to be body and blood."

"Aren't you people finished with that yet?" I smiled. "After so many eons?"

King Saul drew the black burnoose more tightly around his slim body. He avoided my eyes and shrugged his shoulders.

"Finished with it? I? What's it to me? I never started with it. The Others didn't finish with it. Well, their abstruse, ineradicable superstition isn't the worst thing about them. But do you think it's in good taste to treat a stranger, who had just been exorcised as a heretical emissary of Satan, to the potential substance of the sacrament in both forms?"

"Who would ever think of anything like that when he is drinking wine or eating bread?" I said, shaking my head. "But what is the worst thing about them?"

"Nothing at all," Minionman evaded me. "I get along all right with them. They often protected me from the goat-cheese eaters, after they slowly, slowly realized that they would not have found an adequate god without me."

"Won't you tell me, Saul Minionman," I insisted stubbornly, "what, in your opinion, is worse than superstition?"

"I have to get along with them, Doctus," said the Jew of the Era. "I have to get along with them, for we've been neighbors since time immemorial."

After these words he looked around suspiciously, just as the Grand Bishop had done. Then he continued more softly, "I'll tell you what the worst thing is, Doctus: self-deception that justifies itself instead of correcting itself. From the very beginning those Others built the most complicated buttresses around their faith instead of laying a new foundation for the sake of truth. The truth they received from us, great and simple and plain and easy and credible, for children as well as for wise men. But they mixed and messed up the truth with outgrowths of Moab and Edom."

"And what is this truth?" I asked, a bit irritated.

"The Lord our God," he sang in a Hebrew melody, "and God is the One and Only."

I leaned forward so that I was close to his face. "Does not the Church," I said, "today, after a hundred thousand years, still pray to the God of Abraham, Isaac, and Jacob at mass, to our God who is the One and Only?"

Rembrandt's King Saul pressed his chin with its trace of beard characteristically against his chest. "How, pray," he asked, "can that which is One have three units, that which is Only, embrace three persons?"

"Father Exorcist," I said, "can prove to you much more cogently than I, that every Oneness is a unity and that every Whole possesses various aspects."

King Saul nodded his head emphatically as he said, "He not only *can* but he *must* prove it, Doctus. That is his weakness. Again and again he has to prove in words that the impossible is the truth. I don't have to prove anything. He can't bear the complete ultramundanity of the God I gave him. That is his greatest weakness. I can even wait for the Savior with all my being and at the same time I can be certain that He will never come. That is my greatest strength." Contrary to his ordinary effete tone, Io-Minionman had spoken these words with great fervor. Even his star-eyes turned red. In this most distant future I had unexpectedly become involved in a medieval disputation, a religious argument such as had developed between Dominicans and Jews in Spain in the fourteenth century. Contrary to my intent I had been assigned the role of the ecclesiastical speaker instead of the reverse. King Saul, on his side, used the same arguments that his Spanish ancestors had advanced with far greater caution, for they, in their time, were risking their necks.

"Can a thing that is not fundamentally true," I resumed the Toledan disputation, "outlast the ages as the Church has done?"

King Saul shook his head slowly and smiled discreetly.

"Again something has to be proved, Doctus," he said, "and this time by means of durability. Every rock is two million times more durable than the Church. And what is the meaning of 'fundamentally true'? The game of chess has outlasted the ages too because it is fundamentally true and although it is superficially neither true nor untrue."

With these words he rose; from a shelf he took a bowl, a twirl, a large and a small wooden spoon. "The Church will live as long as we live," he continued while he assembled these utensils, "to testify for Abraham, Isaac, and Jacob, who first acknowledged the true God."

"To my knowledge, Saul Minionman," I replied, "the Church makes this statement in reverse. The Church says Israel will live as long as the Church, that is, to the end of things, to testify for the Messiah."

"That takes care of both of us," Minionman nodded, reconcilably irreconcilable. "Infinite distances are equally long, and we can patiently wait to see who will testify for whom. But now my welcoming drink can't wait any longer."

With these words he definitely concluded the disputation as he carefully poured thick milk or cream from one of the jugs into the bowl. From the other bowl he added a golden fluid that spun out into a long thread which he broke with his finger.

"Milk and honey?" I asked expectantly.

"Milk and honey," he confirmed; "the milk of the pure animal in which no demon resides and the honey of the busy little workers, not the brazen melissae in the Park of the Worker. Doctus, I offer you our mystic mundane food, milk and honey, that is consecrated by God and cannot be changed into anything else."

"Milk and honey," I asked, "perhaps from the land where milk and honey flow?"

"Yes," he agreed, "in the consecrated land we have kept some ten thousand acres exactly as it used to be. Our fathers insisted on that when all the world and all mankind were leveled off into uniform gray-in-gray."

King Saul stirred the milk mixture with the wooden twirl so that it became thicker and finally began to foam. Meanwhile he continued pensively, "Do you know what our wise men say of milk? What spring water means to 'Eretz,' inanimate nature, milk means to 'Odom,' animate nature. It is the spring water of breathing life. And do you know what they say of honey? In the collected blossoms of the earth, God feeds us on the thought that moved Him to create summertime."

King Saul spread his hands over the dish and murmured the blessing that dated still farther back in the beginnings of mankind than I. Then he pushed the bowl over toward me and handed me the smaller wooden spoon. But I was filled with solemn thoughts as I tasted the honey-sweet whipped cream, and I felt like a child at confirmation. And suddenly I understood for the first time the religious food interdictions, the meaning of "cleanness" and "uncleanness," and that the taking of food is intended as the incorporation into human nature of the divine idea of creation.

Minionman contentedly observed my enjoyment. He did not wish to disturb me. He remained silent until I resumed the conversation.

"You call yourself the Jew of the Era," I said. "Does the singular form have the same meaning as in the case of the Worker?"

"The meaning of the word itself indicates," he explained, "that there are always ten who simultaneously answer to the name of Minionman. They represent the race that, by the will of God, must not die out."

"And why ten, Io-Saul?"

"Ten are a congregation and a community of prayer. Ten is the limit of condensation of communal piety."

"Forgive my curiosity, Io-Saul," I inquired further. "Are these ten single and unattached persons or are they ten heads of families?"

"Ten single persons," he answered, "ten chosen persons, husbands of wives and fathers of children and sons of mothers and brothers of brothers and sisters, and brothers-in-law and fathers-in-law and cousins and uncles and nephews. I am very happy, Doctus, that you liked my lunch even without alcohol."

"I like it sincerely, sincerely," I said dreamily. "May I ask for a tiny bit more?"

When he had served me I resumed the thread of conversation. "Husbands of wives, fathers of children, sons of mothers, broth-

ers, sisters, brothers-in-law, **fathers-in-law**, cousins, uncles, nephews—that's quite a bit of family, it seems to me."

"Quite a bit of family," King Saul said earnestly, "that has
always been our speciality."

At this moment I unconsciously assumed the complete role of
travel reporter and interviewer; and so, at the risk of being im-
portunate, I continued to inquire. "And in this world leveled off
into uniform gray-in-gray, as you called it, for what ultimate
purpose do these ten Minionman families segregate themselves
and make their own lives difficult?"

"Is there any other ultimate purpose on earth but to keep the
commandments and——" He hesitated and paused, so that I was
forced to interject a curious, "And——?"

"And wait," King Saul concluded with a melancholy smile.

I leaned back and pondered about the word "wait." Yes, they
were indeed the people of pious waiting and therefore the
people of hope, these ten Minionmen. Lost in thoughts that
spring from our most intimate experiences and that are therefore
obscured when they are cast into words, like bedside lamps
darkened by veils in sickrooms, I completely forgot my surroundings and did not notice that Minionman had stepped behind my
chair.

Suddenly he whispered sharply into my ear, "Don't believe
them. I know them all. And how I know them! Don't believe any
of them. I warn you."

I was startled by his voice. Only a moment ago I had admired
Saul Minionman as the unbreakable vessel of hope. I had admired him, who believed in the coming of the Messiah while he
was convinced that He was not coming; I admired him who
turned the empty time of waiting into a pious time, when I was
suddenly confronted by quite a different Saul Minionman, a
person of extreme nervousness and extreme impatience, who was
struggling like a gasping fish in the net of passing time.

"Do you know, Doctus, when our troubles began?" he asked,
staring at me with almost demented eyes. "When men foolishly

began writing from left to right instead of from right to left, as we do. That's when life was reversed for us. Listen: the Greek word for life is 'bios.' But we had to read it in reverse and it became 'soib' or 'sob.' When we settled among the Germans almost two thousand years later we read their word for life, 'Leben,' backward and it was 'Nebel,' which, as you know, means fog and vapor, and it exactly fitted the situation. Then, by means of a tremendous persecution, God transplanted us to the world-dominating realm of the English language. And there we found the verb 'live,' and you can turn that around for yourself."

Obediently I turned it around but then I interrupted him for fear that I might be required to read fifteen hundred more words for life backward.

"Against whom are you warning me?" I asked rather sharply. "Whom am I not to believe? The Grand Bishop?"

"Who cares about the Grand Bishop!" Minionman muttered and crouched down in his armchair. "I mean the Others. All the Others."

Now he really had the eyes of the Biblical Saul, Saul of the benighted spirit. With an exaggerated gesture he seemed to push away the entire world. But suddenly something reared up in his eyes like a team of horses at a thunderbolt. Minionman stared at the door.

"And don't believe him either," he grumbled, "and let me warn you against him too, although he's a very distinguished golden-head."

The dark door opened.

* * * * *
* * *
*

SAUL MINIONMAN HAD IMMEDIATELY RECOVERED his ironic sadness as he introduced the young man who entered the room:

"Io-Joel Sid, short for Sidney, my oldest son, but no Minion-

man, for he sold his birthright, and for something less than a
mess of pottage."

The first thing I noticed about this youth—who, strangely
enough, for reasons of some forgotten tradition answered to the
Anglo-Saxon name of Sidney, shortened to Sid—was the fact that
he was dressed in the customary Astromental fashion and not
with a cloak drawn over his head like his father and the others
who lived between the two ruined gateways of the Former Eastside. He even wore one of the close-fitting, marcelled, golden
headdresses of glittering material that the young people preferred to the baroque wigs of the older generations. The young
fellow was characterized by a bulging brow and myopically
pinched, almost lashless eyes that fairly screamed for strong
glasses, and, in addition, by a strangely frantic indifference and
artificial indolence. A case of extreme assimilation, I thought, a
person who has to be constantly on guard, who has to keep a
tight rein on his emotions. But what sort of emotions? Behind
the front of accentuated indifference it was not difficult to detect
a tortured arrogance, a stubborn will to be superior, that could
grow only from the root of an almost physiological sense of
grievance. Why was Io-Joel grieved and offended to the depths
of his being? His father was not. King Saul was a little dejected,
a little sardonic, now and then a little unctuous. He evinced no
arrogance but only the pride of one who voluntarily accepts isolation. Io-Joel Sid had apparently cast off this burden to assume
another. I wondered whether he lived in his father's house, among
the weary and heavy-laden, or whether he only came to visit,
having become a Mental man through and through. I was inclined to assume the latter. These and many other questions ran
through my head as I tensely watched father and son. With
pretended indifference Io-Joel avoided Io-Saul's eye, while the
latter devoured his son with an indescribable look, a contradictory mixture of anxiety, love, paternal pride, disavowal, indignation, and sometimes even hatred. After watching these two for
only a few minutes I had to think of Io-Solip and his son, the
Bridegroom of the day. And for some reason I felt at once that

Io-Do and Io-Joel were two antitheses that had to fight to a finish because they were in reality two identities.

"Well, been out picking flaws in the world again, son?" Minionman greeted the new arrival maliciously, and I was aware that an uncanny compulsion moved him against his will to choose taunting and insulting words that hurt him as much as his son. Not the slightest tremor in Io-Joel's faintly albinistic face betrayed any resentment against his father's familiar disdainful greeting.

"You must know, Doctus, that he is a radical analyst," King Saul added, and it was impossible to tell whether it made him proud or furious.

"Whoever wants to make changes, must first recognize and define," Io-Joel said in a dry pedantic tone that sounded much more provocative than his father's passionate jeering. Could he know that I would understand this maxim? I understood it only too well, for it had been the familiar slogan of those who regarded themselves as revolutionaries around 1920. Oh, how well I knew that impertinently icy tone that maintained, on the one hand, that the human spirit was nothing but a bubble produced by material evolution and demanded, on the other hand, that this helpless bubble should come to the aid of sovereign, material evolution. It was as logical as though the ocean were to ask the buzzing roar of the sea shells to come to its aid. So that was to be found in the Astromental world too, I thought in surprise, this vindictiveness of unfounded but insatiable arrogance, mendaciously masquerading as world reform.

"This is Doctus," Minionman finally presented me to his son, "whom the Others call 'Seigneur.'"

"I had the pleasure of observing Doctus and Seigneur in the Park of the Worker at the Dance of the Brides," Io-Joel declared with stiff, supercilious gravity. At first I didn't know whether this gravity was impertinence or not. Later I found out. It wasn't.

"What business do we have in the Park of the Worker?"

Minionman raged, and the dark ruddiness of fury and disgust colored the classic pallor of his hollow cheeks.

"I go walking there." Joel-Sid addressed his pedantically calm reply to me and not to his father. "I like to go walking where one can get firsthand information."

"Information from the goat-cheese eaters," his father growled, became calmer, hesitated, and concluded with a forced joke: "It would be better for you not to go walking in the Park of the Worker but to sit down here in your father's house——"

"I don't sit," Io-Joel declared briefly and flatly.

"What's good for your father isn't good enough for you?" Minionman flew into a new passion.

"One shouldn't try à tout prix to be different in trivial things," the son turned to me again with the greatest courtesy. "And, moreover, sitting is a reactionary posture."

"I suppose your Jungles aren't reactionary," King Saul ejaculated impulsively. I felt that he was fighting a losing battle for his self-control.

"The Jungles are footholds for social reform and for the conquest of Mentalism that natural evolution itself offers us." Thus spoke Joel-Sid with the most pedantic equanimity, and his gift of crisp formulation intrigued me so that I quite unintentionally took a hand in the argument.

"My sojourn here has been far too short," I said, "for me to have visited the Jungles that you mention. From what I have heard about these Jungles, however, I judge that they represent a strange retrogression on the part of nature, including the human phenomenon, to conditions long outgrown. I fail to understand in what respect 'swinish hubbub' on formerly swampy soil, poultry farms, carnival booths, merry-go-rounds, and the like can be 'footholds for social reform.' I'm not afraid of the word 'reactionary.' In some cases it may mean something quite desirable. But I don't understand why merry-go-rounds are less reactionary than, for example, these nice armchairs in which we are sitting in your father's house. King Saul and King David and all the Caesars and later emperors sat on thrones; all the Popes, probably including the current Pope, sit on the Sedia gestatoria, and the Lord God himself is represented by painters as sitting on the Judgment Throne, that is, in the broken line. If you want to conquer Mentalism, why do you acknowledge the validity of this one particularly snobbish detail of regarding the broken line as a reactionary posture?"

"That's giving it to him," Minionman giggled delightedly.

"And why do you want to conquer Mentalism at all?" I asked in conclusion.

"Everything that exists must be conquered so that something new can come into being," the youth decreed. And now he sounded a little uncertain and the cool young man seemed immature.

"A sharp little goldenhead," King Saul muttered, and the comment might have been either praise or scorn. But I took advantage of my opponent's weakness.

"What you have just said is an empty, purely formalistic principle that places a moral value on the mere fact of sequentiality. This principle was invented away back in my time by the vain, lazy, unfeeling mob of political and artistic Bohemians. They were the people who easily conquered everything that stood in the way of their vanity, except themselves."

"Didn't you subscribe to similar principles yourself more than a hundred thousand years ago, Doctus and Seigneur?" asked Io-Joel, who had quite recaptured his provocative apathy.

"Unfortunately, yes," I replied reluctantly, taken aback, "yes, at least for a time. But I am convinced that we had a better right to be revolutionaries back in my day. At that time men exploited each other savagely. People with a heart rarely lived longer than fifty years. Many never even attained this age because they were driven into wars again and again. And if they were sick and stayed at home with their women and children, they perished in the ruins of their houses or died of hunger and disease on the highways as fugitives. But today. . . ." And I began, as I had done several times before with more or less verve, to sing the praise of the Astromental world and its accomplishments.

Io-Joel fixed the myopic stare of his pale eyes on me and mercilessly let me finish my speech. Then he asked, "So it was compassion for mankind and indignation against its tormentors that prompted you to stand up against the conditions existing in your youth, Doctus and Seigneur?"

I confess that Minionman's son had made me more uncertain than I had made him. "A part of our revolutionary conviction," I finally answered hesitantly, "was certainly based on sentimental and generous impulses, in which we basked in the arrogant belief that we were better and nobler men. But the hateful, chief incentive of us revolutionaries grew out of an obscure feeling of frustration, from which many young people suffered."

Joel-Sid folded his hands with a gesture of depressing patience, while Rembrandt's King Saul eyed us curiously as though we were engaged in a prize contest.

"Pardon me, Doctus and Seigneur," Io-Joel inquired with unvarying courtesy, "is your knowledge of the Astromental world so complete that you regard this world as final and perfect? Do you believe that, because eating and drinking are no longer a problem and because we don't depart in a filthy fashion, we don't suffer from frustration?"

"I fail to see," I rejoined violently, "any political power or institution that could be held responsible for this frustration. Moreover, there can't be any such thing as frustration in a world whose ideal is aimless play."

"Isn't life itself frustration?" the youth asked without twitching a muscle. This question, I thought, is the offspring of Satan, although there's something in it. King Saul was so delighted with the skillful fencing of his hated darling that he broke up the discussion with a long burst of laughter.

"You won't get the better of him, Doctus," he guffawed, "of this cold, warped, shameless little goldenhead! He suffers when he doesn't need to, ha-ha, he suffers from pure officiousness. The

Others stop suffering the minute the pain ceases, but he goes on suffering."

"And so the Jungles are definitely the footholds for social reform," Io-Joel summed up the argument, unaffected by his father's laughter. "If you should extend your visit, Doctus and Seigneur, you may perhaps be a witness of it."

"Don't worry," muttered Minionman, who had recovered his poise, "goldenhead promises that every day."

But suddenly he broke off and sagged down in his armchair, and his face seemed to shrivel up as he said to me with gloomy foreboding, "He only promises it, but the Others will bring it to pass."

The Thirteenth Chapter

WHEREIN THE GREAT ASTRAL EPISODE OF THE DJEBEL BEGINS, WHICH TAKES ME FIRST INTO THE ELEMENTARY CLASS FOR BOYS IN THE SCHOOL FOR CHRONOSOPHERS, AND THEN ALONG WITH THE CLASS INTO INTERPLANETARY SPACE.

THIS IS NOT only an account of an exploration. If I call it a travel novel I am not falsifying truth just to keep the reader's interest. While an account of an exploration is a simple circle, a travel novel is an ellipse with two foci. The second focus is the traveler's ego, which not only passively accepts things and events, but is often drawn involuntarily into the strangest adventures and occasionally even becomes the reluctant instigator of well-nigh insoluble complications. But I must repeat again and again that the author of this travel novel did not undertake his task for the sake of thrilling adventures, nor for the sake of constructing and dissecting characters, but solely to acquaint his readers with an unknown world, with a completely blank spot on the map of the most distant future.

Since I never lose sight of this principle and since I am now approaching an extraordinarily important chapter, the subject of which far transcends everything novelistically and humanly interesting, I take the liberty of merely touching upon the events that follow immediately.

My hosts had missed me. B.H. had become quite anxious, since

he regarded a sudden retrogression on my part into invisibility
within the realm of possibilities. We had become very much
attached to each other since last night. Since B.H. knew that the
Worker was the first item on my day's program, they looked for
me in the Park among the young mothers and babies and later
in the Valley of Springs and Forces. As the dance and picnic of
the brides was already over, it took some time before they discovered my trail leading to the house of the Grand Bishop.
But at that point they lost me.

Meanwhile I was still sitting in King Saul's strange room full
of antiques, listening to the violent argument that divided and
united him and his son Joel-Sid. Io-Joel was still carrying on his
battle indirectly, by addressing his polemic replies to me instead
of to his father, the Jew of the Era. It seemed odd to me that
both Minionman and his son were convinced that the Mental
world had to be "changed." The father's reasons were of orthodox
nature although they differed from, and even contradicted, those
of the Grand Bishop. He declared, for example, that the Grand
Bishop's doctrine of the fall of man was a forced interpretation
of the Biblical text and represented at once a grotesque overrating of man and a blasphemous underrating of God.

"Those Others," Minionman complained, "are so talented for
the things of the world and so untalented for God. If they had
only let us manage things with God they would be better off."

In contrast with this self-assured assertion, however, he ad-
jured his son Joel-Sid not to "meddle" and to refrain from all
dealings with the Others who openly expressed their dissatisfaction.

"Things are bad," he said. "Don't I know better than anyone
else how bad they are? But the bad is *their* bad and not *our* bad.
What's it to me? This question has saved me a lot of trouble.
You ask yourself too: what's it to you?"

Confronted by such monstrous isolationism, Joel-Sid seemed
on the point of losing his pedantic apathy. His eye took on color
and for the first time looked sharply at his father. Even the
golden headdress, with which he mimicked the fair world of the

Others, was shoved askew. His answer would have been packed with venom if Minionman had not suddenly become uneasy; he tugged at his trace of black beard and rose. I rose also and asked a question that surely no ghost before me had ever asked.

"Have I stayed too long? Do I disturb you?"

"By no means, Doctus," King Saul replied, "but the Bureau of Missing Persons is sending out calls for you."

"And what do I do about it?" I inquired.

"You shout loudly 'Here I am,'" said Minionman but at the same time raised his arm entreating me not to do it.

"Please, Doctus," he said, "don't call 'Here I am' in my house."

Joel-Sid laughed for the first time at this gesture and at these words. He laughed noiselessly and without moving a muscle of his face. It was a laugh that didn't bode well for the future.

"Is it for your sake or for my sake that you don't want me to do it?" I asked expectantly.

"Why should they catch you with the Jew of the Era?" King Saul grumbled.

"He doesn't want you to do it on his account," said Joel-Sid pointedly and slowly; "he doesn't want to change the world but he wants nothing to do with it. That's in his blood."

"And you," King Saul sputtered, "you're panting to have something to do with the world, although it isn't in your blood."

"Quite possible," said Joel-Sid with feigned indifference.

Although I had many more questions on my tongue I silently followed Io-Saul-Minionman, who led me through musty halls and up dark stairs out into the open air. We were quite a distance from the parallel walls of the Former Eastside.

"Any time they demand something impossible of you and you need me, simply set your desire on the Former Eastside."

I was startled. It was the second time this morning that someone had promised to get me out of a jam. I waited until Minionman had disappeared. Then I called loudly, "Here I am."

In less than two minutes my hosts and I met out on the gray lawn. Although both they and I were objectives of travel being moved toward each other, the illusion of a casual meeting was

complete. The delicacy and tact of the modern method of transportation was a source of constant surprise to me. As a runaway
and gadabout I expected to be greeted at least with a reproachful chilliness. Nothing of the sort. The greeting could not have
been more joyful and warm. No one even chaffed me about
my unconfined roaming. Only B.H., reincarnated as he was
and carrying with him a residue of the nervous twentieth century,
besides feeling a sense of responsibility for my existence,
whispered into my ear, "Thank God that you're still on earth.
I've been sweating blood."

In the search party were Io-Fagòr, the Spokesman, the House
Sage, and the Permanent Guest, as well as our ever-apologetic
Io-Solip. The latter at once called up his son to tell him that I
had been found. Io-Do was required to spend the day, the eve
of the wedding, alone in quiet and meditation; for the evening
was to be devoted to a festive Sympaian, which I took to mean
a musical and theatrical performance. Of course, when I heard
that the young man was engaged in solitary contemplation, I
pictured him standing in front of his collection of arms rubbing
incurable rust from ancient tommy guns. Io-Fagòr and the others
invited me to go home with them and eat a good meal.

"Gentlemen," I declined, "that would really be too much, for
I have already been treated to three mystical meals in the course
of the forenoon. First I had heathen cheese and spring water,
then bread and wine, and finally milk and honey. I've had
enough."

"And what else may we offer you?" asked the Spokesman.

"The sun is high in the heavens, and I am thirsting for knowledge," I said, and it didn't sound as funny as I had intended.

"How about the seminar of Sophistes Io-Clap?" the House
Sage suggested.

"Why be so hard on me?" I asked with a laugh.

"You get the silliest notions," the Spokesman sternly reproved
the House Sage whom he regarded as his most superfluous rival.

"Didn't you say something about 'Chronosophy' yesterday?"
I inquired of Io-Fagòr.

"As I was quite sure of your interests," the father of the Bride said pleasantly, "I have already made all arrangements. We will go to the Djebel at once. Are you ready, Seigneur?"

"But please consider," B.H. interrupted with obvious anxiety, "whether a chronoelastic or chronogymnastic drill period would not be extremely dangerous for a completely untrained soul? Perhaps we should first consult a physician."

"But B.H.," I said indignantly, "what do you mean by an untrained soul? Wasn't my absence and return sufficient training?"

"The competent authorities," declared Io-Fagòr, "have thoroughly examined and considered everything. Seigneur will participate in the elementary instruction of the youngest boys."

* * * * *
* * *
*

SO THIS WAS THE FAMOUS "DJEBEL" IN ALL ITS SPLENDOR, before which we, Io-Fagòr, B.H., and I were standing. The Djebel was a huge artificial mountain of more than four thousand feet altitude, constructed of partly transparent, partly highly translucent, vitreous or crystalline material, and the word "constructed" seems entirely inappropriate for an artificial phenomenon whose size and grandeur far exceeded all natural phenomena on the leveled planet. In the Djebel, aspiring humanity (aspiring away from God, according to the Grand Bishop) had almost attained the idea of a "transfiguration of nature." The mountain covered an area no less than that of a medium range of the Alps. It was remarkably well graded and tapered, in such a fashion that the symmetrical character of its architecture was always concealed behind the asymmetry of imitated nature. Canyons and valleys furrowed the entire circumference of the Djebel. From these canyons streams gushed down into the plain. In the upper reaches of the prismatic crystal peaks, however, these streams descended in iridescent cascades and scintillating bridal-veil falls. On the whole, the Djebel impressed me far more as an optical creation than as an imposing structure of solid material. By the term "optical creation" I mean something composed of light, highlights, shadows, rays, refractions, spectral phenomena, color scales, and chromatic variations. This infinitely changeable light was sometimes unbearably blinding, sometimes dimmed and heavy with color. Yet the Djebel consistently maintained its cathedral-like, tapering mountain shape. It was a Pikes Peak, a Mount Whitney, a Mount Shasta—not as high as these American summits, but miraculously constructed by human hands of materials that appeared no more substantial at a distance than pure light in the refractions of the spectrum.

With definite satisfaction my friend B.H. and my host Io-Fagòr read the speechless admiration on my features. It was the first time that I had been speechless, for the hopping and skipping of the stars for journalistic purposes had aroused my irritation rather than my astonished admiration. But confronted by the glittering and glistening, the flickering and flashing, of the Astromental mountain, I had really lost my surfeited composure.

"In our Djebel," Io-Fagòr informed me, "all three Lamaseries of the Chronosophers are housed."

"But how is it possible," I stammered, annoyed at my own lack of self-possession, "for the bodies and nerves of Mental men to exist amid such cataracts of light?"

"Don't be silly, F.W.," replied B.H., shaking his head at my foolish question. "Naturally the chronoelastic and chronogymnastic laboratories of the Starrovers, the assembly halls of the Marvelers (Thaumazonts), the cognition-cells of the Foreign-feelers (Xenospasts), everything, from the dormitories of the students down to the Office of the High Floater, is located in quarters filled with pleasant twilight and normal house illumination. I am ashamed to say that I know all this only from hearsay, for, in spite of my age, I have never been in the Djebel."

"And you, Seigneur," Io-Fagòr added, "will become acquainted with a darkness such as you never even dreamed of in your absence."

Suddenly I had a queer notion. Was the Djebel perhaps an enormous, unimaginably complicated reflector telescope that transported the human eye out into cosmic space beyond all previous concept and that projected the genuine image of cosmic reality into our consciousness? I was on the point of divulging this idea when I happened to recall that even toward the end of my life the mammoth telescopes of Mount Wilson and of Arequipa might have become outmoded and might have been replaced by tiny electric iconoscopes or by televisionary apparatus. Two or three decades after my departure it was undoubtedly possible to carry the actual moving picture of the starry sky in one's vest pocket like a watch, and to turn it on and run it off after a quiet dinner at home like an amateur film of a vacation trip. Two or three historical eras later, in the course of the eternal change of all things, astronomy might well have returned to mammoth instruments.

My readers know by this time that I explain nothing that was not explained to me or that I did not grasp even when it was explained, for the simple reason that a mind from the beginnings of mankind did not have an adequate background. I made no attempt to explain the travel-puzzle and its operation; I wouldn't even think of trying to explain the Djebel although, as the reader will notice, I was repeatedly tempted to suspect that I was in the middle of a telescope. These suspicions, however, were only momentary. In a short time we shall all enter interplanetary space without doubting the reality of our experience; and if we have to refrain from visiting the intergalactic and internebular spaces, it will be only because our hosts and the chief Chronosophers do not trust our strength to penetrate so deeply into space-time and time-space without endangering our lives.

Meanwhile I again felt an icelike mirror surface under my unexpectedly skate-shod feet. By daylight this surface gleamed bottle-green and had the appearance of oceanic depth, although it consisted by no means of frozen water but of a material similar to that of the Djebel itself, for which I used the word "vitreous" or "crystalline." In a few minutes of invigorating motion we had covered the considerable distance that separated us from the foot of the Djebel. Now we skimmed through one of the hundred and eleven giant pylons that served as entrances in the south wall (were there a hundred and eleven? How can I be so sure?— Author's note). In both directions young men whizzed past us, wearing around their necks tiny books strung on cords, like sea-shell necklaces of South Sea islanders. They were day students and auditors. They teased and chaffed each other, laughed and were noisy, just like the boys of my own schooldays. Very likely they belonged to the lower grades of Chronosophic students. In order to assure us free passage without interference from gatekeepers or janitors, Io-Fagòr had unfolded a little blue flag with the inscription: "I am a sponsor and patron of Chronosophic and Astropathic instruction."

The word "instruction" really does not do justice to the facts as I learned them. It was an understatement. Nor would the word "science" adequately describe the exalted activities that went on in the three chief Lamaseries. Instruction, such as I had had in my youth, was a well-done dish of knowledge that was assimilated by means of the memory and eliminated through the forgettery. More or less vague traces of learning remained in the mind. The social trick of combining these traces of learning into all sorts of mosaic patterns was called "culture." Mental acquisition of learning, however, as the very word "Lamasery" indicates, had little in common with the superficial school routine of darkest antiquity, to which, fortunately, I have now returned. Lamaseries were great, monastic boarding schools, which one entered as a boy and left at the age of two hundred, when life came to a close. But when that time had come, most of the adepts in Chronosophy, Starroving, Marveling, and Foreign-feeling complained that they had scarcely acquired the elements of learning and that they were departing from the cosmic spaces as high-grade illiterates. The essential difference between the Astromental school and our ancient intellectual school lay in the fact that learning was not disconnected piece-work, carried away in the form of lecture notes, but a definite form of being, a mysterious essence that had become existence, with which the adept saturated himself physically, intellectually, and spiritually from the first day to the last.

I stated a moment ago that Astromental acquisition of learning had nothing in common with the school routine of our beginnings of mankind. I maintain that this statement is accurate, although, after some rambling in the courts and corridors of the Djebel, I presently found myself in a regular classroom, which might well have been my own classroom in the Piarist Public School where I had learned reading and writing. There was the blackboard, the platform with the desk of the teacher, the whitewashed wall, a cupboard with various globes, in short, everything except the school benches and desks. In place of these, cots with raised head-ends stood row on row. But the strangest thing was that on the cots lay sleeping-bags of diaphanous, rainproof material. At least I had the mistaken impression that they were sleeping-bags. Around the room, among the cots, stood a number of young boys who looked exactly like my fellow-pupils of old, except that they had tight-fitting leather caps with ear muffs on their little bald heads. They looked at me curiously and suspiciously, just as we would have looked at an intruder or visitor back in my day. They had interrupted their horseplay; they were silent and embarrassed, like B.H. and me. My friend had insisted on accompanying me on my seemingly harmless schoolroom adventure. I felt that our presence was beginning to strike the boys as very funny, and that we might sooner or later expect an outbreak of derisive amusement on the part of the class. To be on the safe side, I exposed my purple wrist-rosette, which at once produced excited and respectful whispering among the boys. I should not have believed that this honorable appendage, which I myself had hardly appreciated at first, would impress even these Astromental schoolboys. And then the teacher entered the classroom with a typical long teacher's stride.

The teacher was every inch a teacher. His appearance proved that certain basic types of mankind remain untouched by the

most extreme mutations and developments of history. Even the
black official cowl, in which he nervously wrapped his shivering,
pale, slim frame, was schoolmasterly. Schoolmasterly too were
his mannerisms of suddenly twitching, staring blankly at his
wrist, drawing up his mouth with disapproving scorn, letting his
eyes rove suspiciously over the class to discover some mischief in
the last row that filled him with schoolmasterly grief, schoolmasterly anger, or schoolmasterly anxiety for the future of the
miscreant. He carried a long pointer in his right hand which he
was inclined to use at times as a support, at times as a weapon,
at times as a conductor's baton. Sometimes he brandished it
menacingly in the air when the shrill whispering of the youngsters or a particularly stupid answer exhausted his patience. The
teacher's archaic character was a definite relief for me. Why
should I conceal it? I looked forward to my first Chronosophic
lesson with some anxiety, or, to be more exact, with a kind of
cosmic fear. (What I call cosmic fear was a childhood heritage,
acquired when I received my first enlightenment on the true
nature of the heavenly bodies.) I would have been pleased if the
teacher had quizzed me once in a while as he did his other
pupils. That would have given me a feeling of confidence. He,
however, treated me not only with exquisite courtesy but even
with a sort of timid reverence, as though I were an official school
inspector who was to render a weighty verdict on his pedagogical
fitness.

At first we all stood in front of the teacher's desk, B.H., I, and
the entire class, consisting of about twenty boys, aged, according to my judgment, somewhere between ten and thirteen years.
I had no way of telling how old they actually were by Mental
count. The teacher, with the facial expression of a sovereign,
counted noses twice and then murmured ritualistically, "We now
take our places at the right hand of the couches of rest and
motion!"

In a burst of noise, giggling, and scuffling the youngsters
obeyed. B.H. and I, however, stood there embarrassed. Then the
teacher descended from the platform and, with a stiff inclination

of the head and an affected smile, led us to the two longest reclining chairs, or cots, in the first row.

"These two couches of rest and motion," he said, "have been reserved for you, gentlemen."

Meanwhile a crescendo of schoolboy chatter arose. The teacher raised his head with a start and shouted angrily, "Quiet back there! Let's have a little seriousness and soberness, for which I plead with you daily, particularly today when we have the honor of entertaining distinguished auditors with the purple wrist-rosette." He bowed to me and to B.H. without interrupting his philippic. "We are about to ascend into cosmic space and you are acting like the babies in the Park of the Worker. Even though we are only going to romp through the 'Minor Cosmos,' the 'Lower Intermundium,' with our kind guests, still I must insist that it be done seriously and soberly. Seriousness and soberness are the lamps that burn with true inner joy. We must be filled with inner joy when we ascend into the Intermundium!" He stopped suddenly and with an almost malignant schoolmas-terly eye looked around for a victim.

"Even if usage permits us to say 'ascend,' is this word logical and correct? Io-Scram, you have so much to say to your neigh-bor, answer the question."

"No," said a reluctant voice from the back of the room, "no, sir, it is not logical and correct to say 'ascend.'"

"And why not, my dear Io-Scram?"

"For various reasons, sir," replied the pupil even more reluc-tantly.

"Well, well," the teacher laughed a little spitefully. "Scram seeks refuge in generalities. Wouldn't you oblige us with at least one of your various reasons?"

A long pause. Finally the answer came haltingly. "Because . . . one ascends downward . . . just as . . . one descends upward. . . ."

The class broke into one of those gales of derisive laughter, of which everyone who has ever been a schoolboy has at one time or another been the victim. I was astonished and pleased at this echo of our own life, and I winked and smiled at B.H.

"Quiet!" the teacher exclaimed in a voice of thunder. "You're laughing at the wrong time. In his uncouth fashion Scram gave the right answer. We shall continue. Where did we stop yesterday?"

A babble of boyish voices eagerly replied. I needed only to close my eyes to be transported to my own schooldays. But I didn't have the slightest idea what these answers meant.

"Yesterday we had Mary Magdalene, sir . . . and then we had The Baptist, but only for a moment——"

"One after another, if you please," the teacher chided. "We are not at the Riddle-Soirée in the Geodrome, but in the Djebel, in the Lamasery of the Chronosophers, of whose outer court we have the honor of being members."

I gave my Vergil a startled look. He leaned over toward my ear and whispered, "Don't worry, F.W. You knew the planet Mary Magdalene by the name of Venus and the reddish Baptist as Mars. And the Apostle Paul was once Saturn with his rings. After the Last War of the Planet—you remember, the war that lasted three and three-tenths minutes, that had broken out between the Blues and the Reds about the naming of the stars— the Conference of Tao-Tao decided to Christianize the planets and the galactic constellations. They are now named after prophets, apostles, and saints."

"I get it, B.H.," I said like a ventriloquist with closed mouth and with an eye on the teacher. "We're not supposed to talk."

The teacher, now standing on the platform again, drew a wavy line in the air with his pointer and announced, "We shall follow an informal program today, in honor of our esteemed auditors."

"Oh, great, an informal program is always fun," the boys cheered, and there wasn't a bit of seriousness and soberness in evidence.

"We shall now put on our space-diving costumes," the teacher ordered dryly, putting an end to the cheering.

Motion and loud rustling were all about me. The boys were slipping into the sleeping-bags of waterproof, or rather space-proof, material that lay on the school cots. They weren't sleeping-bags, however, but real diving costumes with helmets of thick glass; that is, it was too light for glass, and must have been some other sort of transparent substance, perhaps the same of which the Djebel was built. The teacher, in person, helped me and B.H. into the odd outfit and screwed down the helmet over our shoulders. If one of my former contemporaries could have seen me— in a dress suit and diving costume—he certainly would have rubbed his eyes. Fortunately I could see, hear, and breathe even better than before in this hermetically sealed, utterly weightless casing. The spaceproof material and particularly the transparent substance of the helmet seemed to intensify all the senses, even hearing.

"Do you know," I said to B.H., "that I have the most peculiar palpitations of the heart?"

"I shouldn't be surprised," he replied, "for I'm taking part in a Chronosophic drill for the first time myself, and I've been living in this time and world for one hundred and seven years."

"Well, then, at least, I don't have to be ashamed," I laughed.

"Each one of us will now stretch out on his couch of rest and motion," the teacher directed, and his instructions were carried out by the class with unnecessary noise and giggling. Hereupon he loudly repeated his motto, "Seriousness and soberness, if you please!"

I agreed with him. My heart was beating irregularly. I was filled with more than seriousness and soberness. It was fear and trembling. After all these preparations I had no doubt that we were actually, physically and not only figuratively, ascending into the cosmos.

The teacher's voice now rang like that of the captain of a ship giving final orders for departure, "I shall appoint the pupils Io-Hol and Io-Rar as Respondents. Do not lose sight of our esteemed guests."

Two obedient voices answered from the rear, "Yes, sir, we will stay near them."

Now the teacher suddenly vanished from sight, since he too had stretched out on his cot on the platform. At the same time,

however, he seemed to have switched off the illumination. For
the murky twilight that had filled the schoolroom until now,
changed into darkness, quite ordinary darkness, incidentally.
The next occurrence too wasn't at all unusual at first.

The "couches of rest and motion" on which we reclined began
to roll forward slowly. We rode through the ordinary room darkness as though there were no walls to resist our progress and to
limit our movements. I reached for B.H.'s hand and found it.

"You see," I said with a note of triumph, "it's always a matter
of being moved, and the Grand Bishop thinks I wasn't dead at
all."

"Let's wait and see, F.W.," said B.H. "Besides I don't think
we're just being moved, we're being flown, and that's quite
another thing."

He had hardly spoken these words when our couches began
to cut all sorts of capers. Their speed increased alarmingly and
slowed down just as alarmingly. We described wild circles and
spirals. We whizzed straight up and shot abruptly down, like the
scenic railway at Ocean Park. Yet I had the definite sensation—
God knows why—of always returning to the same spot, or rather,
of making no progress whatever, despite the most violent and
most labyrinthine movement.

Still I couldn't tell whether it was a matter of being driven
or being flown. If it was a ride, it was certainly free from all
material friction. I felt nothing of the surface under the vehicle
nor of the draught that our motion must have produced.

It was very much like the great ride of death with which I
had become acquainted ages ago. Just to hear my voice I said
to B.H., "Isn't this just like the Grimm fairy tale where Jack
wants to learn how to be frightened? The bed rides and rides."
I was surprised to find that I had to strain and pant to utter
these words. But the voice of the teacher just in front of me was
smooth and calm.

"What is the Chronosophic drill Roman Numeral One, small
a? Answer the question, Io-Hol."

Promptly and clearly came the reply from the mouth of the prize pupil just behind me, "Drill Roman One, small a: Confusion of the sense of space."

* * * *
* * *
*

THIS, HOWEVER, WAS NO LONGER ORDINARY DARKNESS. God knows whether we were still in the schoolroom. Perhaps, perhaps not. But this was certainly no longer ordinary room darkness. Ordinary room darkness, after all, isn't anything but the temporary dimming of normal conditions. It isn't darkness at all but only darkening, a blackout. That is also true of the darkest earthly night, which is brought about only by the relative absence of enduring sunlight. The same distinction exists between earthly darkness and genuine lightlessness as between human death and genuine nonexistence; I should certainly have explained that to the Grand Bishop. But here—wherever that might be—there was undoubtedly some vestige of primordial darkness, that is, lightlessness, that existed before Creation. In this lightlessness there was no right or left, no up or down. Drill Roman Numeral One, small a, seemed to have been a complete success. If the teacher had now asked me: "Pupil F.W., where is your right hand?" I would have had to think long and deeply about this problem. The left hand was the one where I was wearing the rosette, that much only was clear in my consciousness. But why wasn't I lying in a prostrate position any longer, as at the beginning of the blackout? It was vital that I should be lying on the bench, on the narrow cot, on the couch of rest and motion, otherwise I would fall down into the void. No, I was filled with the physical consciousness that I could as easily fall upward as downward. The most disquieting fact was that my back no longer touched anything. But there was still greater ground for concern. For I hadn't the slightest idea whether I was right-side-up or up-side-down. At the same time I was firmly convinced—and again it was a purely physical conviction—that I could whirl around my longitudinal axis many hundred times per minute without any effort at all, or spin my rigid body around the hub of my navel, like an airplane propeller. At this moment, however, the idea of converting my ego into a prima ballerina gave me no pleasure whatever. Practice makes perfect, not only on earth, but also in the Lower Intermundium, where I now believed myself to be. More and more clearly I became aware that the unusual darkness, of which I was a part, was not night. Oh, how black, how pastose, how sonorous were the darkest nights I once knew. But this darkness that surrounded me was not black, pastose, sonorous, it was completely and totally colorless, like the blindness of one who was born blind, who does not know when and how night comes, or morning. I would probably have done well to play truant from this class period. Shame on me. Even a thoroughly experienced dead man is a deserter from life. Our shabby instinct of self-preservation extends beyond our factual existence. Wasn't this my best chance to dissolve, to be lost in cosmic space? Now or never. . . .

"How do you feel, F.W.?" I heard B.H.'s voice, and it had no resonance. I could not have told from where it came, right or left, above or below, from behind my being or before my thought. It rang from everywhere at once, but the word "rang" is a misrepresentation, for, as I said before, B.H.'s voice had no ring, nor had my own voice or that of any of the others.

"I'm pretty fair, B.H.," I hastened to answer, although a feeling of great uneasiness, almost nausea, had seized me. "If I only knew where I left my good old hundred and sixty pounds."

At once the teacher's voice sounded in the void, a toneless voice too, comparable only to a faint hissing. In the same instant I knew that I was closely surrounded by the class and it was a tonic for my nerves although I could not localize anything or anyone. But the mention of my weight had given the teacher a good cue

"Io-Rar," came the unlocalizable hiss, "where did Seigneur leave his weight? Answer the question."

"In the Djebel, sir," responded Io-Rar, whereupon the class, whose nearness was now more noticeable, giggled a little. I didn't know why. It sounded like steam hissing from a leaky radiator.

"Respondent Rar, I didn't expect any silly jokes from you," hissed the teacher. "I shall answer the question myself: Seigneur and all the rest of us have no weight of our own here. Our good old hundred and sixty pounds or less are our exact share of the love of our Mother Earth with which she holds—or held—each one of us, as the case may be."

The thought "So I'm right after all" thrilled me from crown to toe. We were outside the earth's gravitation. Our weightlessness clearly proved it. But the teacher's poetic parable annoyed me. If my Mother Earth's love for me weighed only a hundred and sixty pounds, then I was a neglected stepchild in comparison with every fatter and heavier man.

"Respondent Io-Hol," the teacher directed, "define our location. Where are we?"

"We are——" the eager but unlocalizable boyish voice began but then hesitated and stopped.

"Any dunce knows that we are," the teacher scoffed. "I want to know where?" When no one replied he hissed after a pause, "Others can cover a hundred light years before my pupils can answer the simplest questions. We are in the Gray Neuter. The class will repeat!"

The class chanted in unison, "We are in the Gray Neuter."

The teacher did not explain this expression, nor was it necessary. The Gray Neuter probably meant the section of the Minor Cosmos in which the fields of gravitation of the various heavenly bodies are neutralized, that is, inoperative, and which is not penetrated by any light rays.

I confess that I am a great astronomical ignoramus, and that when I entered the Chronosophic elementary class I knew almost nothing about the Minor Intermundium and nothing at all about any of the Major Intermundia. I mention this circumstance only because it is an embarrassing disadvantage for me, but an agreeable advantage for my readers with their undoubtedly superior educations, that I am not in a position to bore them with scientific discussions and prolixities but that I must confine myself to the factual experiences of my poor senses. I know perfectly well that my empiricism is entirely out of place, but I don't want to pretend. We have to cut the suit to fit the cloth. And so I can't chat any more learnedly or wisely about my visit to interplanetary space than about a Sunday afternoon picnic in the environs of my hometown back in the horse-and-buggy days.

Among the boys in the class of which I was now a member the youngest, smallest, handsomest, and most agile was called by the familiar nickname Io-Runt. Despite the seriousness and soberness upon which our teacher properly insisted in cosmic space, he too used this nickname, although in his mouth it sounded more like a term of endearment. For the little fellow with his bright, attentive face and strangely spherical head was decidedly his pet, particularly because he was regarded as a model and master in Comet Calisthenics.

"Ready now, Io-Runt," hissed the teacher's toneless voice, and then followed a brief explanation that was undoubtedly intended for B.H. and me, the two novices who came out of the depths of time and yet had less knowledge of time than any of these Chronosophic first-graders. Every body, we were told, that was located in the heavens, that is, outside sidereal gravitation, became eo ipso a heavenly body. We were therefore privileged, nay, we were absolutely required, to assume the form of heavenly bodies. Now the only form that came into question was that of the comets, the rambling stars that trail a tail. A hundred and sixty pounds of earthly matter, the teacher said, half of it, a quarter, a tenth, a hundredth, was amply sufficient to make a respectable comet, with a gleaming head and a tail millions of kilometers in length. Since, however, we were not only matter, but also spirit and will, he said, we were free to determine our heavenly corporeality, its expansion and its contraction, without running the risk of being hurled into interstellar space or being inadvertently caught by a planetary field of gravitation as a meteor. We could move in any direction according to our wishes. On the basis of this exalted harmony of matter, spirit, and will, the teacher concluded, the founders of Chronosophy had established the important children's discipline of Comet Calisthenics.

"And since we have distinguished and very strange guests with us today," the teacher finally remarked, "we will not indulge in any nonsense. Remember that, Io-Scram and a couple of others. We shall therefore not extend ourselves beyond the modest length of twice the polar radius of the earth. And how much is that, Rar?"

"Twelve thousand seven hundred and thirteen kilometers," came the Respondent's answer promptly.

"Less two hundred meters," the teacher carped, hissing like a recalcitrant steampipe. "Silly jokes and no precision. You'll have to do better, Io-Rar." He paused in the approved manner of all schoolmasters to give his prize pupil time and space for proper contrition. Then his voiceless voice again penetrated the unresponsive void, but with a little more cheeriness.

"All right, let's go, my dear Io-Runt."

The Gray Neuter, as far as I could gather, seemed to resemble the terrain that infantry tacticians call the dead sector, namely the portion of the target area that cannot be swept by projectiles. In other words, this realm, where there was no up and down, no front and back, was a blank space, an offside corner, that was not reached by the rays of the near sun nor of the distant stars. The result was that one not only could see nothing at all, but that the very idea of seeing, which is necessarily connected with the existence of light, became pure nonsense. Since the human soul, and particularly my own, adapts itself to existent conditions with unprincipled fanaticism, I had almost forgotten, here in the Gray Neuter, that there was such a thing as light. My astonishment was all the more agreeable when gradually a faint and gentle phosphorescence began to glow before my eyes.

It was Io-Runt's diving helmet that emitted this breath of

light, and the graceful form of the boy became ever more distinct as he whirled about his own axis, like a top, with arms extended and legs crossed in a dancing pose. As I have said before, I had no idea of the materials of which our space-diving costumes and helmets were made. But they must have been the right materials, for lo, with a sudden jerk the whirling form of our handsome little classmate extended itself, became a streak, and finally a faint beam that reached from one end of the Gray Neuter to the other without a beginning and without an end. I could no longer survey our dear little Runt who, at the teacher's order, had stretched himself out to a length of twelve thousand seven hundred and thirteen kilometers, less two hundred meters, while I was still only one point sixty-nine meters, provided earthly measurements, other than weights, had some lasting significance. So this was Comet Calisthenics, the Chronosophic exercise for little children. I could not help but wonder what kind of drills and accomplishments were expected of more advanced students, not to speak of the masters. At sight of our Runt who had transformed himself into a faint beam in the twinkling of an eye, I felt a surge of cosmic playfulness (in contrast with my recent cosmic fright), an itching urge for unparalleled astral adventures. Without any real plan or purpose I began to spin about my own inclined axis with gracefully extended arms and crossed legs. A few shouts of approval from the class reached my ears but then my utter imponderability accelerated the rotational velocity to a point where I lost consciousness for a few moments. When I recovered my senses, I too was nothing but an infinitely long streak, a faint beam with a little glowing head, rocking in the stagnant space of the Gray Neuter like a log in a lagoon.

Need I give the imaginative reader a description of the joy of being a beam, an almost immaterial streak of radiant energy? No, I am convinced the reader can feel this joy with me. But the strangest and most important thing was that the transformation of my shape, the well-nigh infinite attenuation of my body, had made no change whatever in my consciousness, not even in my physical feeling. In my inner self-consciousness I was exactly as I had been before, and that is particularly remarkable considering the uncertain character of my existence since I entered the Mental era through some dark gateway.

Not I seemed to have changed, but the void on which I lay as a heavenly body alongside the other heavenly bodies of my classmates; and by our presence and our gleaming we changed the void into space that had directions. My phosphorescent head in its vitreous helmet was now floating right next to that of Io-Runt, who was performing all sorts of evolutions that I tried to imitate. More and more streaks and beams with glowing pinheads appeared beside us. The fundamental Chronosophic exercise of Comet Calisthenics was in full swing.

Following Runt's example, I repeatedly contracted myself to my normal shape and, with the speed of an electric current, expanded myself into my celestial bodily form, increasing my chronoelastic capability with each of these exercises. As thin cometlike streaks we were a species related to sunlight, with a wave-length of about one twenty-fourth of a light-second. That means that we could move through the Gray Neuter at a velocity only twenty-four times less than a ray of the sun.

Please don't get suspicious. I didn't figure that out myself. My classmates Io-Rar and Io-Hol, who had to answer the teacher's questions continually and were constantly criticized for their inaccuracy, made the statement. If their figures were only approximately correct, we were truly endowed with a fearful freedom. Assuming our position in the Gray Neuter to be in the latitude of the earth, we—the schoolboys of the Chronosophic elementary class, B.H., and I—could have made the journey from here to the center of the orb of the sun in one hundred and ninety-two earth minutes.

Well, our position in the Gray Neuter was actually much nearer the source of all light, even though our round trip, breathtaking as it was, was to be confined to more modest limits. But the one thing about Comet Calisthenics that remained most viv-idly in my memory was the strange dual physical consciousness that I have already mentioned.

Although the good thick solid matter of which I was normally composed had become attenuated almost to the vanishing point, yet I felt wonderful. In fact, I felt even better than I had felt in my invisible state on the preceding day when I met B.H. for the first time in the Mental world. With my hundred and sixty pounds extended to the length of the earth's axis I tried to cough and to speak and, much to my surprise, I did it as well as the others.

Again I had the suspicion, as I had several times later on, that I was the victim of an illusion of a Mental demonstration, and that I was actually in the midst of complicated reflections in the depths of the Djebel, reflections that easily brought the In-termundium down to earth. I almost yielded to this suspicion and I was foolishly on the point of mentioning it, when the divinely beautiful occurrence that now took place completely destroyed all my doubts of the reality of our experiences. Not even the perfectly justified objection that a cometlike heavenly body is obliged to keep on moving and mustn't lie around lazily in space like a log in stagnant water, can convince me of the opposite. After all, the teacher had repeatedly spoken of the "free will" of the Chronosopher to move in any direction or to rest, as he is spirit of the Spirit.

It began with music. Of course, if music is what it is, namely the resounding organization of lapsing time as man experiences it, then this was less and yet much more than music. It was the resounding organization of lapsing time as a planet experiences it. Imagine the approach of the heavy summer droning of count-less swarms of bees. No, it's not enough. Imagine the distant rasping chirp of octillions of crickets. No, it's too one-sided. Imagine an orchestra tuning up, an orchestra composed of ten times as many musicians as there are living beings, and each one, lost in thought, blows, fiddles, flutes his own passages, his own phrases. The upper limit of the instruments does not end with

the piccolo and the E-flat clarinet but continues infinitely beyond
the audible spectrum. Similarly the bourdons continue far below
the oscillations of the contrabassoon and the contrabass tubas.
A tuning orchestra is chaos waiting for redemption. There is
nothing more exciting. But suppose redemption has been injected
into chaos, inconceivable order into apparent disorder? Suppose
the tuning world orchestra is playing from a score, is playing
hundreds of thousands of symphonies at the same time and in the
same space? Oh, let's forget all these comparisons, for they are
only comparisons and therefore worthless. Let us rather listen to
the approaching hum of chromatic thunder that draws all the
stops of acoustic nature, yet is not loud but, rising scarcely beyond a full mezzoforte, despite its crushing grandeur, never loses
the veiled nobility that not even he suspected who invented the
word "Harmony of the Spheres." And matched to this approaching, divinely gentle, thunderous hum from pedal to treble, was
the vision that now appeared at the edge of the Gray Neuter and
grew majestically toward us. At first there was a heralding glow
of pale silver light pulsating through the void. And then there
rose the disc, no, the orb, and it became more and more an orb,
a spheroid, for we cometlike celestial bodies saw it in relief.

"Mary Magdalene," whispered the Chronosophic schoolboys,
who were mere swaying streaks of light. And suddenly the voices
of their tiny glowing heads held a note of deep emotion.

"Stay close together and stretch," the teacher warned; the
seductive gravitation of the approaching Venus planet might
easily have lured some of the pupils from the Gray Neuter. Although we were larger than the diameter of the gliding queen,
she outgrew all dimensions and, for an instant, completely filled
our field of vision. Mary Magdalene, Venus, and formerly Astaroth; her light is infinitely subdued, penitent, mystically renun-
ciant. Mary Magdalene has taken the veil. Her body is not visible. We saw only thick white clouds, the impenetrable mist of
her atmosphere in which she is eternally clothed. The bank of
clouds, her stately pleated gown, was restless; it surged and un-
dulated as though the starry body beneath it were suffering

grievous pain. Only at the fuzzy edge of the spheroid the misty ghostly light brightened into a suggestion of golden nakedness.

When, as a child of six, I saw the ocean for the first time, I fainted. A year later, when I had my first view of an ice-capped mountain, I held my eyes shut. Now, when a planet moved across my field of vision at close range, filling the heavens before me, I began to tremble. I was a faint, endless streak, and the whole length of me trembled. But since I also had eyes and nerves and a heart, I began to sob wildly. No matter how hard I tried, I could not control my tears, for I soon discovered that it was not I who was weeping. Everything in me that came from God wept in sweet emotion and in ineffable delight at God's creation, and because even in the stars the masculine and feminine could be distinguished from each other.

* * * * *

* * *

*

FOR THE SKEPTIC MY EXPERIENCES up to this point would still not constitute final proof of my physical presence in the Minor Cosmos. The next events in my Chronosophic lesson, however, will make it more difficult for him to maintain that I, with the teacher and his class, did not actually leave the Djebel. Be that as it may, I must reiterate that the examination, analysis, interpretation, and explanation of human attainments is not a matter for me, an ignorant layman, but a problem for the specialized scholar. One indisputable fact, however, remains; namely, that in the course of our Comet Calisthenics the teacher and his class visited two planets, two splendid celestial bodies, whose orbits not only lay millions and millions of kilometers apart but whose physical characteristics were, moreover, utterly different. I cannot say how it was possible for us in the course of a single school hour to surmount distances for which a rocket plane traveling at the rate of a thousand kilometers per hour would have required several decades; nor can I say why our feather-light equipment

sufficed to withstand the horrible cold and the lack of atmosphere
of the Lower Intermundium as though it had been a fresh, yet
mild, spring night, not to speak of the flaming heat of the place
we were to visit in a few minutes. I'm not in the least interested
in an adventure fantasy à la Jules Verne nor do I have the slightest intention of composing one. Moreover, my narrative deals
with an Astromental world and not with a technically materialistic one, such as that of the ingenious Frenchman. I am relating
what happened to me and what I experienced, and nothing more.
But we must never forget that the final aim and purpose of the
Chronosophic doctrine, as developed by the Astromental masters
in the Djebel for hundreds of years, were the very concepts that
we, of the beginnings of mankind, find it so difficult to grasp:
intensification, spiritualization, deification, or, to say it in other
words, the annihilation of the feeling of time by daily intercourse
with the sidereal universe.

The initiative, of course, came from our Runt, teacher's pet.
Io-Runt had a particular predilection, an almost childish enthusiasm for one of the phenomena of the Lower Intermundium. This
was the Mare Plumbinum, a huge ocean of molten lead, located
on the last of the three innermost planets, that is, those nearest
the sun, of which our earth is the third. I am speaking of the
star formerly known as Mercury, the Hermes of the Greeks, the
Nabu of the Chaldeans, who had recognized his intellectual,
prophetic character at an early time: a being strangely compounded of frivolity and brooding, for which reason they dedicated him to the writing profession, since they evidently were
familiar with the windy character of writers. Today (I mean the
Mental today) Mercury was no longer named after the caduceus-
bearing messenger of the gods, but he was baptized in the name
of Christ's favorite disciple, John Evangelist. The renaming of the
heavenly bodies had been done with a great deal of inductive
and deductive profundity. The Evangelist John, the prophet of
the Apocalypse, who reveals the divine mysteries, corresponded
exactly to Hermes and Mercury, the messenger of the esoteric,
the mystic among the gods on whose staff are entwined the heal-

ing serpent of Aesculapius and the harmful serpent of temptation. At the same time, however, this planet, never wavering from
the side of the sun, symbolized John, the favorite disciple, who
never left the side of the Savior.

So it was Io-Runt who wheedled permission from the teacher
for a few special stunts. We were allowed to whirl even faster
about our inclined axes and to stretch ourselves even longer than
before. Not only I, but also B.H., had gradually learned the unimaginable joy of Comet Calisthenics. At one time my normally
sedate reincarnated friend could not restrain himself and uttered
a long, hoarse, exuberant shout that hissed away in the hollow
unresonating void. Now we extended ourselves into streaks and
beams of inconceivable length and rushed ceaselessly forward.
And since the entire planetary system was moving toward us, as
the passage of Mary Magdalene had proved, it happened suddenly and unexpectedly, and was scarcely perceptible to more
than a fringe of our hypnotized consciousness, that the Mercurial
disc of John Evangelist glared, shrilled, screamed toward us,
grew to proportions that overflowed the heavens; and in the same
instant we drilled and spiraled our way into the world-wide bowl
whose horizons engulfed us with their immense height. The inexplicable thing—that is, inexplicable for all but the full-fledged
Chronosopher—was that no one was hurt. As soon as we were
within the compass of this new gravitational force we ceased to
be celestial bodies, we did not explode into a lot of shabby meteors, but we landed as intended and planned on the silvery Mare
Plumbinum, very near its shore, and began at once to splash each
other, like children in a pond, with the molten lead that didn't
burn us in the least. It must be remembered that most of us, after
all, were children.

Although I splashed, laughed, and gamboled with somewhat
feigned playfulness, and at every jump the strange elasticity of
the viscous molten metal tossed me high in the air (which, of
course, didn't exist here), I really didn't feel so playful and
frisky at all. Heavy, silvery-black steam billowed up to the sky
from the lead sea. If we had unscrewed our glass helmets with

their self-replenishing breath of life, we would not only have suffocated, but would have died at once of acute lead poisoning. Although lead is a metal which, as everyone knows from childhood experiments, melts in relatively low heat, still the temperature on the steaming Mare Plumbinum must have been far from salubrious. Fortunately our space-diving costumes were so constructed that, no matter where we were, the temperature was about that of the Mental houses. I was not informed until later that John Evangelist, like our moon, does not rotate on his axis but keeps his face turned to the sun in constant fascination and eternal adoration. For this reason the terrific noonday and summer heat on his light-side can never be cooled. But the questions and thoughts that agitated my soul as I absently dipped my hands into the lead sea or let myself be tossed aloft by the waves were not of a scientific nature.

I was thinking that I was the only human born in the nineteenth century privileged to set foot on another planet. I had a vague feeling that this fact imposed certain responsibilities on me, although at that time I could certainly not know that I would ever be permitted to render an account in the presence of ears that understood my language. (But it was strange that from time to time, and again at this moment, I had half a notion that I was on a voyage of exploration.) So I tried to compose myself, and I firmly resolved objectively and coolly to collect all the impressions that the strange planet made on me, and to engrave them accurately in my memory. The latter was not as simple as it sounds. The human memory resists incongruous impressions. It therefore ejects everything that is not earthly because it is incongruous. For the sake of the proper climax of my account I shall begin with the minor things; this is the exact reverse of my experience in this new world, for the greatest of all greatest impressions came at the very outset.

The lead steam had collected on our helmets like silver soot and protected our eyes, and that was very fortunate. For only through this dense precipitation was it possible for us to endure the insane intensity of light that prevailed on John Evangelist.

Instinctively I kept my face averted from the monstrous source of light that stood permanently and unalterably between the zenith and the western horizon of this planet. I kept looking in an easterly direction toward the extended coastal range; it consisted of black granite cliffs with interspersed porphyry walls, but I can't guarantee the correctness of this mineralogical diagnosis. These two exaggerated fundamental colors, gleaming anthracite black and intense bloodred, as well as the jagged formation of this moderately high but very forbidding coastal range that extended far beyond my range of vision, bore only a remote similarity to our earthly geography. A world other than our earthly world had produced these rocks of glistening scoria; I should like to call it a world with a different soul. I knew at once that it was a dead world, but only in our mundane sense, since it could not possibly have supported organic life, like that of our earth, at least not on its eternal day-side. In its own sense, however, the world of John Evangelist was anything but a dead world. In these minutes I felt with unexampled clarity the presumptuousness of conceding the quality of life only to the green life of our planet. The landscape that I viewed through the pleasantly subduing screen of lead steam expressed something that I did not understand, but I understood that it expressed something. How different are the characters within a single human family! The characters of these first children of the sun, however, the planets, are not only different but are contrasts of an indescribable sort. In my mundane consciousness I could never have imagined the existence, anywhere in the universe, of this thousand-peaked range of glistening black and bloodred rock, bordering a steaming sea of dull silver under a sky that was not blue but that consisted of unbearably blinding mother-of-pearl and opal fish scales, behind which lurked the blackness of space.

The molten lead rolled against its rocky coast in long, slow, viscous breakers only a few hundred yards distant from us. The rhythmic surf made a loud, cracking, splintering sound, not comparable to any earthly sound. I don't know why there should have been rollers in the lead sea when it was not affected by any rotation on the part of the planet, nor do I know why clouds of silvery soot steamed to the heavens when there was no atmosphere. To be sure, the speed with which this strange world moved about the sun was terrific compared with the pace of our earth. Could it be that the particles of this strangest of all oceanic substances were hurled into outer space in the form of metal clouds by the force of the reckless speed of revolution? Who am I to answer this question? I never even asked it, nor did I wonder why I did not sink in this sea of molten lead instead of frisking cheerfully on its surface, nor why I did not burn my hands in the flowing metal when I dipped them into it as into greasy, lukewarm dish water. As far as the eye reached coastward, it saw only myriad jagged peaks of patent-leather black and bloodred. An ocean of thick, glutinous, dull, silvery molten metal with long rollers like wrinkles in a heavy velvet blanket, under a canopy of argent clouds of soot particles—that was the landscape of John Evangelist that I can scarcely conjure up before my earthly eye today.

More significant by far, however, than the strangeness of the Mercury landscape was the strangeness of my presence in these surroundings. Compared with the impact of this feeling of strangeness, Comet Calisthenics seemed like a good old custom. Up there in the Gray Neuter I was imponderable. Complete imponderability, however, cannot be experienced. Here, on John Evangelist, on the other hand, I was light. And lightness is a most startling experience. Since I was astronomically probably more ignorant than the Idiot of the Era, not to speak of the youngest Chronosophic schoolboy, I did not know that Mercury was the smallest, paltriest, and weakest of all planets, weighing scarcely one-fourth as much as the earth. For this reason my hundred and sixty American pounds were now worth hardly eighteen European kilograms. The velocity required to escape from this miserable field of gravitation was only a little over three kilometers per second, a bagatelle, even for us beginners in Chronosophy. I'll have to confess that I acquired all this cheap science of weights and measures, of figures and fractions, much later. While

I was exercising on the Mare Plumbinum of John Evangelist—we bounced around on the molten metal as on a first-rate spring mattress—my lightness was a completely unique experience. My weight had melted down to that of a child; the strength of my muscles, however, had not changed. With a light shove against the elastic surface I could bounce a hundred times as high as a bounding rubber ball and then land gently and reluctantly like a moderately heavy snowflake; or, in a horizontal direction, a single, flying pace carried me far out into the lead sea, to my shocked surprise, almost out of range of our party. Of course I leaped back at once, for I could not rid myself of a terrific fear of being left behind alone in this deadly solitude.

I really can't say that my lightness was an experience of un-alloyed pleasure, as it was contrary to the nature of our body which was constructed for quite different purposes. Only Io-Runt, the cosmic dancing genius, enjoyed the reduced gravitation and the absence of atmospheric friction to the full. He whizzed past us like a flash of lightning and disappeared behind the horizon of the sea; he described loops, circles, curves, figure eights, spirals, and designs of such complexity and elegance that even our teacher watched him with surprise. Finally, however, the teacher ordered him to end his performance, as it was high time to conclude our planetary visit. Moreover, he said, the class had not yet devoted itself sufficiently to the ultimate and highest contemplation. In connection with this admonition he intimated that a lengthy sojourn on the planet was dangerous for the character of earthmen. The courage and gigantic fortitude of the great masters in the cognition cells of the Marvelers and of the Foreignfeelers were all the more to be admired, these men who had traversed millions of light years in their lives and had withstood even the remotest nebulae. The danger of such a visit, the teacher said, lay in the fact that two planetary natures in man came into conflict. And I felt this very thing in myself even before the teacher pointed it out. I felt myself becoming more Mercurized from minute to minute. My senses began to adapt

themselves to the changed conditions. My instincts became mixed
up. My consciousness became confused.

The teacher cast a glance in my direction and then ordered,
"We will form a line and hold hands. We will not move, but
devote ourselves to high contemplation with all the seriousness
at our command."

I took hold of Io-Runt's hand on the left and B.H.'s on the
right. We did not have to raise our heads in order to contemplate
the greatest thing in the Minor Cosmos, the highest in the Lower
Intermundium; nor did we have to turn aside, for the clouds of
metal were so thick and our helmets so covered with silver rime
that we could even look into *this* sun without becoming blind.
This sun, however, the sun of the favorite disciple and Apocalyp-
tist, was, at a modest estimate, eight or nine times as large as
the same sun seen from our earth. But the size was not the important thing, although even this was almost unbearable. It was hard
to hold one's head erect without bursting into tears of overwhelming grief. This sun had nothing in common with the earth sun that
beams kindly from the heavens, harmoniously well-balanced,
greeted by playing children and by chilly old folks in the city
park; a star that reveals its true nature only during an eclipse,
when the good people stare at it through smoked glass from their
rooftops. This sun, that disclosed itself to us in clouds of lead
steam, was not our good old accustomed sun, it was not Helios
and Apollo, the star of divine symmetry: it was a surging golden
fleece; it consisted of bristling curls, of flaring flakes, of whitehot
wool; it quivered in mad raptures of procreation, it writhed in
labor pains, it leaped in frenzied eruptions, it tore open its heart
in bloodred protuberances, it cast aside veils of flame that threatened to strangle its self-wastefulness, it burned in a hurricane of
inconceivable activity, its energy never diminished; it enacted
the drama of being from beginning to end before God and itself.

Only seriousness and soberness? It wouldn't have sufficed for
any of us. I could feel B.H. trembling in his space-diving suit,
but the Mental Runt was beside himself too. Tears ran down his

feverish, burning cheeks. As though to recall us from the frailty of the physical to the sovereignty of the spiritual, the teacher improvised an examination.

"Who can tell me Ursler's fundamental paradox?"

One of the Respondents quickly collected himself. He knew the answer and rattled it off like a good fellow: "When the energy of a star is greater than itself, then the star has to sacrifice itself, that is, destroy itself by apotheosis."

When energy is greater than itself. . . . I closed my eyes in order no longer to look at the ninefold sun of John Evangelist. I stood in an inverted bowl of blazing scarlet. I no longer knew where I was. But these words, whose meaning is not quite clear to me any more since my return, I understood at that time down to their very foundations. If energy is greater than itself, then the hour for sacrifice has come, the hour of the Phoenix who is consumed by his own fire. The life of the sun, in its deepest meaning, is an act of sacrifice, an eternal, world-sustaining love-death. If beauty is more beautiful, if love is more loving, art more artistic, holiness holier, than itself, then the moment of the miracle is at hand. . . . In the midst of the blazing scarlet I blessed Ursler, the learned man who, long after my time, had formulated the first fundamental paradox. And more than the man himself I blessed his lofty insight which I fully understood then, as a man of the future, but which I only vaguely feel now, as a man of the present—the fundamental insight that a quantity can be greater than itself. At that time, however, in that most remote future, as I stood on the lead sea of John Evangelist, my heart beat with rapture, and I felt that I had to hasten back to my old contemporaries and bring them this truth that applies not only to the sun but also to the freest child of the sun, mankind.

The Fourteenth Chapter

WHEREIN THE PRECEDING CHAPTER IS CON-
TINUED ON ANOTHER GLOBE, APOSTLE
PETER, AND I AM EXTRICATED FROM AN
ALARMING SITUATION BY THE INTERVEN-
TION OF MELANGELOI, IN ORDER AT LAST
TO BE UNEXPECTEDLY CONVEYED FROM
INTERPLANETARY TO INTERATOMIC SPACE.

IT SEEMED TO ME that I was awaking from a sluggish, utterly
terrible sleep. But perhaps I had not been sleeping at all, but
had merely been lying stretched out on this sirupy something,
on this gooey ground swell, this rusty-red, squashy morass that,
strangely enough, did not swallow me, any more than the lead
sea on John Evangelist had done. I instinctively felt that this
time it was some sort of ore that had not yet solidified. How was
I, in my ignorance, to know that the unstable surface of Apostle
Peter, the old planet Jupiter, consisted of entire continents of
magnetized iron swamps, continents that were larger than all
the continental areas of the earth? This and many other things
I learned much later, in part not until my return to the past
present which still continues, immeasurably enriched, here and
now at my desk. My condition on this, the hugest, massiest,
heaviest, and at the same time thinnest of all planets, can be
described in two words: I lay. Of course, it wasn't any lying
such as we know on earth. I lay squeezed down to the ground,
pressed out flat, there could be no doubt about it. Won't some-

one ask who or what squeezed me down flat? The answer is, I was squeezed flat by myself, by no one and nothing else. The ingenious space-diving suit of the Chronosophers could protect me from the deadly cold of the Gray Neuter and from the blazing heat of John Evangelist; it could shield me from the unceasing, agonizing rain that pounded down on me from the eternally murky sky of the king of planets, to be transformed as soon as it landed into lukewarm steam; but the space-diving suit could not compensate the incompatibility between my weak telluric physique and the terrific gravitational force of Apostle Peter. As I lay there—I get dizzy at the word "there"—I weighed a good eight hundred pounds. So I lay there on top of myself, so to speak, with the weight of a healthy young hippopotamus. It was a good thing that I lay on something soft, something indefinite and spongy, for I lay on this morass of reddish, not yet solidified iron ore that yielded without giving way, something like a pillow.

I tried to remember how all this had come about. But with this terrible weight ratio on Apostle Peter every slightest movement of the hand or foot was an athletic feat, as the reader will believe; not only that, but every exertion of the will, whether it was feeling, thinking, or remembering, was accompanied by immediate exhaustion, faintness, and profuse exudation from the pores.

Unless I was mistaken, we had left John Evangelist with the speed of thought; and to the displeasure of the humanists I am forced to comment that the average human thought is one of the moderately speedy means of locomotion in the cosmos, since even the quickest thought can be conceived only through the medium of language. As a rule this medium is the Monolingua and only in rare, inspired cases, the Protoglossa. But light, and therefore also the eye with its images, is incomparably faster than language.

Io-Runt performed some of his trickiest pirouettes above the lead sea; we imitated him, and at the same instant we were borne aloft as though John Evangelist had no intention of attracting us but was trying to repel his uninvited earth guests as quickly as possible. Transformed again into heavenly bodies in the Gray Neuter, we found Comet Calisthenics a pleasant relaxation from our recent adventure on the Mare Plumbinum. It was B.H. who expressed the fatal wish to balance our excursion to the lightest and smallest planet by a corresponding visit to the largest and heaviest one. Such a visit, he argued, would be a most exciting change for him, since circumstances and other interests had kept him from having adequate Chronosophic experiences up to this time. For me, however, as a visitor from the beginnings of mankind, he said, this excursion represented an urgent, a compelling necessity. For nothing could give me a more brilliant picture of the progress of Mental mankind than its command of the starry realm by means of Chronosophy. Although I was only a faint streak of attenuated star dust, I cleared my throat loudly in order to give B.H. a hint not to shove me into the foreground. The teacher, however, replied that he was entirely at Seigneur's service, and that there was nothing whatever to prevent our setting foot on Apostle Peter, the hugest of the planets and fifth in line from the sun. Although Peter's orbit, he explained, was fairly distant, he was nearer than usual at this hour, and besides he was located in the extension of our own axis. He, the teacher, would like to call our attention to one thing, however: his class consisted of cosmically hardened youngsters; furthermore, the boyhood years just before puberty were best suited for Chronosophic propaedeutics. Twelve-year-olds had the inestimable advantage of spiritual apathy, while the nervous system of adults reacted much more violently to everything ultramundane and was therefore much more imperiled. The earlier one began Starroving, the better. Apostle Peter, the star of Jove or Marduk of antiquity, was not as simple a matter as John Evangelist, Mary Magdalene, or The Baptist, formerly Mars. He, the teacher, however, would never think of suggesting a visit to The Baptist because, from time immemorial, amateur clubs and stodgy Babbitts had used this planet for their family outings.

"But," and these were the teacher's actual words, "Peter is a manic-depressive being. He is a personality of the highest divine value, but he is not yet mature and settled. In the starry realm the greatest mature slowly and gradually. They remain subject for a long time to stormy transitions, of which adolescence is the most painful. God alone knows what sort of a future awaits Apostle Peter. At present he is full of emotions, violence, and turbulence, and he treats the visitor to surprising manifestations of his melancholy. Unfortunately he is very unreliable, a quality which he has in common with his god-fathers, both Jupiter, the seducer, and the prince of apostles who betrayed Christ before the primeval cock crowed thrice. I don't know whether to advise for or against a visit——"

"Of course you should advise in favor of it, sir," I interrupted his reflections. "I don't like to be the object of worry and solicitude. No living person has been through my experiences. What have I to fear from Apostle Peter?"

At these words the teacher shrugged his comet shoulders and with a muttered, "As you wish, Seigneur," moved to the van of our party. Now our speed accelerated beyond any pace that our talented Io-Runt had set. The teacher immediately undertook exercises of the boldest dimensions, and although time, space, extent, location, and direction "up here" were empty concepts for me, yet it seemed to me, as we expanded and contracted with lightning speed, that we were now covering distances ten times as great as those at the beginning of the school period. And at this point my memory became defective. The last scraps that I could still patch together included the angry, leonine, growling rumble of bass drums and the vibration of double organ-bourdons that announced Jove-Peter's music of the spheres at an infinite distance. It blotted out life and consciousness, although, with all its awfulness, it was never loud and never rose above a turbulent mezzoforte. For the drumming, trumpeting, harping, came from the atmospheric envelope of the planet, but the partial vacuum, the tenuous, material medium of the Minor Cosmos, transmitted only an infinitesimal part of the vibrations and sound waves.

My last visual impression was that of a vast soup tureen,

glowing with eerie reddish light, filling the world from horizon to horizon, its great bowl open to receive us. The gleaming porcelain of the tureen was miraculously patterned with long, crimson, yellow, and violet bands. I heard the teacher instruct us to enter the world-wide opening of the soup bowl head first and land in that fashion. Aha, I thought, so the material of our helmets is more durable than that of our bones. And the last clear notion that flashed through my head was this: we land head downward on the planet Peter because the Apostle was crucified head downward in Rome.

That was the end of my recollections. I have no idea what happened between this last thought and my first bewildered awareness of a bodily weight of some eight hundred pounds. I only knew I was lying there. I knew that in a more ponderous manner than I had ever known anything. But the worst part was that I was lying face down in the rusty-red, squashy, wet, iron mud. The familiar odor of the ferric compound even penetrated my space-diving suit. My immediate plans were necessarily very limited. The first thing to do would be to roll over, that is, turn over on my back. But that was just as difficult for me as the reverse operation for a giant tortoise of New Guinea. Everything that I touched was soft, rain-soaked mud; no, the definition isn't quite accurate. It wasn't ordinary mud but a kind of modeling clay, putty, a mass that was much more cohesive than mud, like something artificial, that could be stretched like rubber. The high degree of cohesiveness of this earth-mass—pardon me, of course I should say Jupiter-mass—seemed to be responsible for the fact that I was not swallowed up and sucked down into the morass, as well as for the fact that the rain that had been raining for millions of years formed no puddles, ponds, and lakes, but only served to keep the modeling clay moist. It occurred to me that this was an ideal place for sculptors. But this quality of the soil of the unstable planet Peter thwarted my first efforts to roll over on my back. I felt the full weight of the giant raindrops that spattered on my space-suit like machine-gun fire on an armored tank.

So far I had no sensation of fear or loneliness. The primary pedagogical purpose of Chronosophy, to dissipate the earthly consciousness of time and space for the sake of a higher and more inclusive reality, proved effective in my case. I couldn't tell, for example, whether I had been lying on this spot on the mammoth planet for several days and nights (Jupiter days and nights, of course, which, as I learned to my great amazement, were less than ten hours in length, all told) or for only a few short minutes. Not by the verdict of my addled instincts but purely on grounds of reason I decided in favor of the latter, that is, a few minutes. I believed firmly in the authority, the prudence, and the superior ability of our teacher, who had so far guided us safely through the Lower Intermundium. Under the leadership of such an experienced Chronosophic pedagogue it was out of the question that a cosmic accident could happen to one of his wards. I was sure that the teacher would appear in a few minutes and collect all of us, including B.H. and me, and give us a little lecture about maintaining discipline and staying together. But suppose we had spread out in landing in a "cone of fire," like a burst of shrapnel? That was an old wartime memory that flashed through my brain. In that case we might be separated by hundreds or thousands of miles. But I banished the thought at once, in complete confidence that no conscientious schoolmaster would ever expose his pupils to such danger and that no sensible school board, let alone a Lamasery, would ever give such powers over life and death to the teacher of an elementary class. No, no, this isn't a case of shipwreck, I thought, bolstering up my own spirits and courage. And then I tried to raise my head.

To my amazement I succeeded after several attempts. An unexpected and astonishing thing had happened which indicated that I must have spent more than a few short Jupiter minutes in this precarious situation. Just as John Evangelist had begun to gain possession of my body on the Mare Plumbinum by means of assimilating Mercurization, in the same way the infinitely stronger Apostle Peter was now Jupiterizing me. This Jupiterization was manifested not only in the revaluation of my weight in conformity with local conditions, but also in a countermeasure on the part of nature, seeking to balance the discrepancy between my overweight and my insufficient physical strength. At this moment as I experienced it in my own body, I did homage to the sacred urge for compensation, the innate, unerring will of all creation to restore equilibrium, one of the most Godlike and God-conscious traits of life. If material life is based upon the electromagnetic laws of attraction and repulsion, then spiritual life is based upon the law of compensation, the restitution of balance.

The countermeasures of the compensating forces in this case consisted of a sudden, novel, and miraculous suppleness and pliability of my body. It seemed as though the substance of my body were trying to assume the puttylike adaptability of Jovial substance. I could, for example, undulate my arms and legs in serpentine movements, and I enjoyed doing it. The normal rigidity of my bone structure was gone. I could not only turn and raise my head, but I could twist it almost completely around its axis. Moreover, my body suddenly seemed to have become accustomed to a creeping, crawling mode of locomotion, as though I had never known any other. Undoubtedly this form of movement was best suited to the physical conditions that prevailed at present, in the Eleventh Cosmic Capital Year of Virgo, on the slowly congealing surface of the planet Peter. If there had been any advanced form of fauna here, analogical with that on earth—but as far as my eye reached I did not even see the lowest form of plant life—it would probably have consisted of gigantic reptiles, writhing through the warm, rubbery modeling clay in peristaltic undulations. At this moment, however, I was not thinking of ugly lizards and pythons, but of our Runt, and I was curious to see the graceful and elegant manner in which the little star dancer would manage his weight and his pliant bones.

Meanwhile my Jovization seemed to have progressed to a point where I felt that my body had been flattened and spread out as though it had been worked over with an invisible cosmic rolling pin, like cake dough. I had the feeling that I could fold my two symmetrical halves together like an omelet. Much of this may have been imagination, but, at any rate, with a tremendous effort and with arms spread out like the feet of a lizard, I succeeded in worming my way out of the dimple that my plunge had made in the rusty-red iron morass. And sure enough, I had hardly squirmed out of the indentation when it filled out with a juicy smack like a rubber air-cushion. I lay still for a moment, took a deep breath to collect new strength, and then threw my tremendous weight toward the right with a well-calculated swing, overcame the center of inertia, and landed on my back. The force of my motion and my own weight luckily caused me to slide down a slight incline, so that I finally came to rest at a very comfortable angle, head up and feet down, with a broad panorama before my eyes.

It was a gloomy November twilight. At least so it seemed to me, and I decided on the basis of mundane experience that the time of day was either before sunrise or after sunset. Soon, however, I was to recognize my error. What appeared to me as the grayest of gray dawns was really full Jovial daylight. The vast, utterly strange sky of Apostle Peter was covered with just as vast and just as strange clouds. These clouds, mostly of a reddish brown or dirty violet color, raced along at a very great height in the permanent hurricane of the upper Jupiter atmosphere. The word "race" is much too weak a word, for the motion of the clouds was so swift that the eye could not follow it; at the same time the cloud formations changed shape at the same speed, so that the eye could not observe their evolutions. Today I assume (with the modesty of a layman) that this incomparable storm and this vertiginous racing of the clouds are related to the rotational speed of the gigantic celestial body, which requires only ten hours to turn once on its axis, while the earth, which is only a thousandth part as large, takes a full twenty-four hours. The indescribable storm, of course, raged not only in the upper reaches, but also on the surface, at least in the form of an echo.

The storm was, so to speak, the fundamental atmospheric factor on Peter the Apostle. But since there was nothing on the boundless rusty-red morass, literally nothing, that the storm could have seized, shaken, tousled, I could gauge its strength only through the medium of the diagonal, whipping, projectile-like gusts of rain. No, again it's not quite right; there was something on the rusty-red swamp: I was there. My body was there. But this body resisted the force of the hurricane with such ponderous weight that I felt it less than a normal earthly disturbance, not to mention the fact that I was completely protected by the space-suit. Thus the storm manifested itself only in the racing of the clouds and in an unceasing roar which entered the consciousness as a single, protracted organ tone.

I could survey only a part of the sky from the vantage point of my putty wave. Now and then the rain diminished slightly. At one time the canopy of clouds was even rent for a few moments because Jupiter's eternal storm had changed its direction for unknown reasons. A fairly large lake of navy-blue sky (neither day nor night) appeared, and in its center floated the sun. But what had become of the golden fleece, the whitehot wool, that I had observed with trembling and with sobbing in my throat from John Evangelist in this same unfinished Chronosophic study period? Where was the bursting, titanic aegis, where was the hurricane of flaming activity that acted out the great drama entitled "I am" before God and itself? What? This faint little bicycle lamp was the sun? It was. If there had been any mythology here on Jupiter, Helios would have been reduced from the exalted charioteer to a bicycle rider. The disc of the sun was not even as large as a distant bicycle lamp, and in spite of its corona of rays I could fix my eyes on it without blinking. I said a moment ago "the sun floated"; that was a very incautious expression in view of Jupiter's sky. The sun flew. The sun fled. The sun raced. It was not only an illusion produced by the racing storm clouds, but the sun actually moved more than twice as fast as it seems to move on the earthly sky. It had scarcely appeared on one edge of the navy-blue lake when it disappeared on the other. Only a few minutes later, I calculated, it must have set behind the horizon of the great moor. But it made no difference whether the faint bicycle lamp was above or below the horizon. There was no distinction between the twilight of day and the twilight of night. Absurd as it sounds, but I am at present the only living witness in the twentieth century to the fact that night on Peter the Apostle, alias Jupiter, was brighter than day.

I regret to say that I did not have the opportunity to see *all* the moons of Jupiter during my anxious exile. There are, take my word for it, plenty of them, nine or ten, if I'm not mistaken. The four major ones play a role in human history, since Galileo discovered them one night with his ridiculously primitive telescope, a moderately good opera glass, and thus founded modern empirical astronomy. Very soon, however, I did see three of them simultaneously, gleaming through thin spots in the cumulus storm clouds. One of them was a regular cartwheel but the other two were also larger than our good earth satellite, about whom I had wept so bitterly the night before. And again the cosmic blues rose up in my throat. I ask you: was man born to see three moons at once in the sky? Certainly not a man of earliest antiquity, as I am. All the animal qualities in our nature are frightened to death at three simultaneous moons in the sky. What a nightmare! Where are you, great holy mother of the world? I want to hide my little head in your skirts. . . .

But that only lasted a breath or two and then I became quite calm again, thanks to my repeatedly mentioned lack of principles, otherwise know as adaptability. I even had to laugh a little as I suddenly remembered an expression of an English humorist who spoke of the "cozy little universe" in which we live, in contrast with the nihilistic nature philosophers who revel in astronomic trillions in order to make man a louse. Right now I was living evidence of the correctness of the expression "cozy little universe." For in the course of my very first Chronosophic lesson I had not only raced through considerable reaches of space and time, but had also visited two very different worlds, in one of which I weighed less than forty pounds, in the other

more than eight hundred. At this instant I felt particularly content, I had almost forgotten my unique and frightening situation,
and tried to make myself believe that the beneficent effects of
Chronosophy were at work in my blood like an opiate, dissipat-
ing all measures of time and space and augmenting my feeling
of sovereignty.

Reason prompted me to utilize this bold exhilarated mood for
a special effort. I had scanned the section of empty, flat, slightly
undulant moor as far as my eyes could reach. I had even shouted
repeatedly at the top of my lungs for my friend B.H. And, according to Mental custom, I had added the identifying words
"Here I am." To my surprise I heard my shout reduplicating
itself again and again in the dense Jovial atmosphere and con-
tinuing into the infinite in radiolike waves and ripples. Why that
happened, God alone knows at this moment as I write; later on
the scientists will have an explanation for it, but it will be a
different one in every generation. Far, far away, at the limits of
my range of vision, where dirty violet, presumably magmatic
clouds hung on the horizon, my shout died away. There was no
answer. I assumed that B.H., our teacher, and the entire class
were in a similar predicament as I and that they had also temporarily lost their mobility. The whole crowd was probably
behind the putty bank on which my back was resting fairly
comfortably. At the same time it became more and more apparent from second to second that something very strange was
going on behind my back; I could hear dull rolling and rumbling,
fearful panting, groaning, and grinding from far and near. There
could be no doubt that the landscape behind my back (if the
word "landscape" could be applied at all to Peter the Apostle)
was far more interesting than that which I faced. I trusted our
teacher with all the faith in authority innate in the son of a
baroque and feudal country, and I was sure that he would have
selected the more interesting side, the more characteristic panorama, for purposes of instruction and examination, and that he
would have his pupils form a circle and hold hands as they
engaged in contemplation. (How he managed that was his busi-

ness.) Perhaps he hadn't even noticed my absence. Since the
Chronosophic propadeutics were already beginning to show their
effects on me, and my time and space sense had become completely confused, I could not distinguish between long and short,
early and late. The fact that the sickly bicycle lamp of the
Jupiter sun had already set, told me nothing at all.

So I pulled myself together, in the most literal sense of the
word. I accomplished it as follows: thanks to my new serpentine
pliancy and suppleness I bent my flattened torso without much
difficulty until I assumed a position something like a U-shaped
pipe. My arms, considerably foreshortened by this maneuver,
and my hands, which struck me as extraordinarily small, I
planted sidewise, like the feet of a lizard. I braced my feet
against two solid lumps of iron ore, many of which lay scattered
round about. My helmet, which for some reason had become
hard as flint, I shoved down into the putty with all my might
until the latter ceased to yield. In this fashion my surface had
been reduced to a minimum and with it the element of friction,
while, at the same time, the leverage that I could exert on my
own weight had been materially increased. Of course, I tried and
failed at least twenty times before I managed to combine the
right position with the proper application of force and before I
could drag myself slowly upward by using my helmet as a fixed
center of gravity, shoving it into the damp putty bank higher
and higher up. Finally my lizard hands in their spaceproof
gloves gripped a rough surface. One more shove, and I had
reached the top of the hummock. But the most incredible thing
was that I was no longer lying. I was sitting. I was sitting on my
hind-end with a ponderousness that pushed my buttocks down
into the modeling clay as into an air-cushion and made them
into a fixed pivot. As soon as I succeeded in raising my feet a
little—no simple matter at all—I could spin around on my hub.
I became, so to speak, my own piano stool. And now I turned to
the interesting side.

The first thing I did was to close my eyes, for I wasn't equal
to the spectacle that greeted me. Up to this instant I had been

supremely confident that I would find B.H., our teacher, and
my classmates on this "other side," which I expected to be more
interesting but not different in character from the rusty-red,
desolate moor that was beginning to bore me. Well, it certainly
was more interesting. But it was also quite different, as different
as land and sea. I said and wrote "sea." And it was a fearful
ocean that surged here before me. But more fearful than the
ocean itself was the fact that it did not consist of water, but of
the same rusty-red mud or putty as everything else. Only this
putty appeared to be in a somewhat more fluid, or, let us rather
say, in a more agitated, more turbulent state. And the worst blow
for me was that I was right in the middle of the ocean. I had
been there from the beginning, lying on a temporarily torpid
wave, an inactive drift, a dead calm in the midst of the mael-
strom, which would certainly be swallowed up in the course of
the next half hour by the mountainous red waves all around.
The unstable surface of this world was in tidal movement. The
nether powers raised and lowered it, presumably under the influence of the ten moons, the invisible and the visible ones,
whose ivory light broke through the constantly shifting and
changing tumult of storm clouds. The image of the storm-tossed
ocean is weak and inadequate, for the most fantastic waterspout
in the Pacific cannot be compared to this surging, seething red
moor. And this commotion produced a racket, a tumbling clatter,
crashing, gurgling, and smacking that literally—and this is no
figure of speech—made the senses reel. Whenever the red waves
receded, invisible crevices opened from which lava steam rose
to the sky. At the constantly shifting horizon behind the clumsy
waves of heavy mud, stood several completely immovable sultry
red and dark violet pillars of fire that seemed to support the
Jupiter sky with its skull-pale moons and its ceaselessly storm-
whipped clouds. The most striking feature of the glutinous and
depressing drama, however, was the unending display of fireworks of white- and red-hot lumps of iron and of black lava,
which were tossed up from all over the moving surface, to be
audibly crushed as they fell back.

There I squatted with my broadened, flattened, hunched back, squashed by the inordinate gravitation. I squatted and looked. This is something I never asked for, I thought, when I had gained a modicum of composure. Perhaps I even uttered the words, adding, "This would be something for a Wagnerian rather than for me." This objectivity in the midst of my cosmic shipwreck can be explained only by the fact that my earthbound consciousness refused to regard the magnificent drama of the surging moor as congruous to me, in other words, to regard it as real. A part of my panic-stricken soul was even bored by this drama. That's why I thought: this is something I never asked for. I had a much greater affinity for John Evangelist. There, confronted by the riotous revelation of the sun, I had not doubted my physical presence. Here and now, at this most precarious of all instants, I again fell prey to the old suspicion: Had not Mental men devised a hundred and one means for neutralizing the incompatibility between man's limitless inner capacity for experiences and his tellurian, physical bounds? Wasn't that the purpose of their mode of travel, of the Uranographer's star writing, of their dynamic or visionary wallpaper which everyone could project from the treasury of his memory at will, and of many other things? Astromentalism could actually be defined as the art of materializing the infinitely mobile images of our soul and projecting them into time and space. In view of the optical crystal mountain of the Djebel I had had, as the reader will recall, an almost "technical" suspicion. Had there not been, even in my day, such a thing as electronic photography? Or did I merely imagine that? Had it not meanwhile become a perfectly simple matter to synchronize a man, lying in a trance in ordinary room darkness on his couch of rest and motion, with an endless reel of film of John Evangelist or Apostle Peter? Was it not possible that this synchronization could be so perfect that this same man was not only present in the film of the planetary landscape but actually, by one of their Mental tricks, experienced himself there? In the materialistic twentieth century I, for my part, never believed that our images, in particular our photographs, the two-dimensional proofs of our presence, were something dead. I have often expected a photographed person to step out of his two-dimensionality and to give word to the emotions that were frozen in the picture. Why shouldn't I now be experiencing the things I was experiencing as a plastically photographed figure in the plastically photographed Jupiter landscape, synchronized there by means of Mentalism and, though only an image, awakened to consciousness? I promised to make no explanations, and I am breaking that promise only because these thoughts actually flashed through my mind. And I am revealing these thoughts chiefly because the event that took place just a moment later could not possibly have been recorded by the most sensitive Mentalized film in the optic center of the Djebel.

As I sat there squashed and hunched on my putty dune, I became more and more certain that the inert portion of the iron moor was diminishing from moment to moment. Soon the uninteresting side that I had been facing before and that was now behind me began to rumble, clatter, thunder, and groan. How long would it be before I too would be tossed up into the air and crushed by the putty jaws that might be soft but that never yielded when the limit of their elasticity had been reached? It proved once more that men and materials of steel were less dangerous than those of rubbery elasticity. As though the undulant dance of the moor were not sufficient, a new phenomenon topped all the others. It suddenly became darker and darker. Beneath the normal storm clouds of the Jupiter sky, very low, nearly black, tattered cloud-rags rushed in from all sides; they galloped toward each other with leveled lances, ghostly sotnias of stampeding black horses, mounted by mythological Cossacks clinging to streaming jet manes. An instant later I knew they were not clouds. It was Jupiter soil, ripped to shreds, whipped through the atmosphere. The squadrons of unstable planetary soil crashed into each other, and the most incredible of all thunderstorms began. Between the putty clouds, of the same consistency and density as the ground beneath them, crackled constant, persistent, frozen flashes of lightning, a network of discharges, as between

Leyden jars of inconceivable dimensions. The hope that I was only a synchronized photograph experiencing itself vanished. Frankly, all power to think vanished in my growing panic. I forgot everything, my former life, the hundred thousand years of my absence, my surprising reappearance, all the strange circumstances that really entitled me to an attitude of ironical superiority toward fate, I was nothing but a Jupiterian Robinson Crusoe—oh, what conceit—I was nothing but a human being in dire fear of death, a wretched realist with not more than two impatient Jupiter minutes behind me and two before me. In the second minute that still lay before me the dune on which I was sitting contracted with an unforgettable groan, its crest became pointed, it grew upward . . . upward . . . toward the crackling flashes of frozen lightning. I felt myself rise, tried to burrow deeper into the wet clay; one more breath and the wave would throw me off like a gigantic red horse. In the last second I thought of the divine power that had saved my life more than once, and for the first time since the creation of the world a human mouth on this huge unstable planet uttered the Latin words, "Ave Maria, Gratia plena, Dominus tecum. . . ."

* * * * *
* * *
*

I KNEW ONLY AS MUCH ABOUT ANGELS as everyone knows who has read a little in the Scriptures. I knew, for example, that they were divided into four classes or orders, although Dante recognized nine, and some of the more meticulous theologians went so far as to classify them into twenty-four categories. At any rate, the four classes that I know are called Choirs, Dominions, Highnesses, and Thrones, and I have no fixed concepts that connect with these lovely words. Moreover, these lovely words constitute the sum of my knowledge. Frankly, I had never been a very firm believer in the existence of angels. In that regard I did not differ materially from my former con-

temporaries who were just as fanatically willing not to believe in
invisible angels as they were to believe in equally invisible
protons and electrons. Well, I don't regard myself as the most
skeptical of men, still I would never have thought it possible
that I, in person, would appear in a Mental world of the future,
first in invisible, later in visible state. This fact was certainly no
less strange than the two indistinct beings whose presence I now
felt behind me. But where was the Mental world and where was
I? I was shipwrecked on Apostle Peter, the largest of all planets,
as old as our earth but remarkably retarded, while we had already
arrived at Astromentalism. But what did I know about early or
late, these childishly human categories that we apply all too
boldly to the celestial bodies? What did they mean to me at this
moment when I expected to be thrown from the rearing ground
wave and to vanish in a smoking crevice with my crushed body?
What really happened, however, was that my ground wave
hesitated and, after a period of perceptible deliberation, became
calm again, like a person who was about to lose his temper but
thought better of it. It ebbed back and froze again, while all
around me the surging, rolling, and seething of the oceanic moor
continued with increased violence. Lightning flashed and thunder crackled endlessly, and the whirling chunks of red-hot iron
hissed through the thick atmosphere. The three visible moons,
including the cartwheel, raced along, now concealed, now exposed, while the sultry red and dirty violet pillars of fire on the
horizon jutted immovably, and their tops, on which they seemed
to support the heavens, were Corinthian capitals with volutes of
smoke and acanthi of steam.

It was at this moment that I felt the presence of the two
Dominions or Highnesses beside me. I was not afraid nor even
thrilled, as I had been the few times in my life when the supernatural had revealed itself to me. I was lying on my back again,
as in the second stage of my visit to the planet. Not from fear
but from a new sort of joyous reverence I refrained from the
slight effort of turning my head in its crystal shell to look at the
two beings whose presence by now was quite distinct.

In the midst of the explosions of doomsday I asked softly and, if I am not very much mistaken, in my German mother tongue, "Did you come to me, Your Highnesses?"

They answered my question in the same language and not in the Protoglossa. Sometimes they spoke in unison, now and then the one finished the sentence which the other had begun.

"We are here," said the one.

"We are on our way," said the other.

"Then perhaps I am fortunate enough," I whispered, "to have met with real angels."

"We are known to ourselves as Melangeloi and we belong here," they said in unison.

"Melangeloi? Dark Angels?" I asked, a bit startled. "Does that mean Evil Angels?"

"Evil angels are unknown to us," said the one.

"Our brightness is not yet fully bright," said the other.

"And are you corporeal beings, Your Highnesses?" I asked, becoming a little bolder.

"Incorporeal beings are unknown to us," replied the Highnesses or Dominions or Thrones.

"Then perhaps a very sensitive film could catch you," I thought out loud.

But the two beings rejected my opinion. "We can only be caught if we want to be."

"And you don't want to," I returned. "That's perfectly clear."

At this point I became conscious of the fact that I was no longer on the rusty-red moor but floating through the twilight between the two Highnesses or Dominions or Thrones. Ungrateful, like most people whose lives have been saved, I gave little heed to it. I was far too much concerned with the unanswered question of the corporeality of these Melangeloi and all angels. It occupied me so thoroughly that I failed to pay the least attention to the space we traversed, and I can't say, therefore, whether we were still within the precincts of Apostle Peter or had already left them. I did not even observe the mode of my locomotion, whether my two companions carried me or whether

I was doing Comet Calisthenics, a form of movement that had almost become second nature. At any rate, I've forgotten. I was concentrating with all my power on the correct formulation of my questions, for I was aware, with all the nervous susceptibility of my nature, of the unspeakably noble but equally sensitive character of these angels. A wrong adjective and one of these Highnesses or Dominions might be miffed for good. Constant association with the Logos is likely to make one impatient and easily annoyed with an improper choice of words.

"The people down there on earth," I began very cautiously, "photographed the spectral lines of unknown elements and the electronic hail of burst atoms untold millennia ago."

In their reply to this provocative scientific remark I noticed for the first time in the intonation of these Melangeloi something like good-natured amusement.

"There are no spectral lines on us," they said in unison, "and no hail of electrons, and no other idols of the human cerebellum. . . . Wouldn't that be something. . . ."

"But then how can you be corporeal, Your Highnesses," I argued, "if you don't even consist of light or radio waves? Isn't matter unified, from the hardest diamond to the sunbeam refracted in it?"

"Take a look at him," said one of the angels, "he doesn't know what's revealed and written."

"He doesn't know," said the other angel, "that we are the predecessors and the successors."

"It is known to us," said the one, "that we are made of the same stuff as this world, only a little less perishable."

"It is known to us," said the other, "that we were in this world before it existed."

"It is known to us," said the first again, "that we will be in this world when it no longer exists."

"But only in this world," they joined in unison, and in their words lay something like the melancholy of finitude.

I had drawn them out. And it hadn't even been difficult. I had to be careful to conceal the note of triumph in my voice.

"I understand you, Your Highnesses," I said with restrained happiness. "You are created of materia prima et ultima. You were there before the words 'Let there be light' rang out, when something of infinitesimally short wave length streamed down into the Gray Neuter. You are simply Ultras and Infras and you don't leave an image on even the best celluloid. But I know that's the reason you can so easily assume all sorts of shapes. You appeared to the youths in the fiery furnace in a mantle of flame and to old Abraham as pilgrims with girded loins. Oh, how I love and revere you, Highnesses, when you appear as pilgrims with girded loins or as mail carriers or policemen or ambulance drivers."

With these words I dared to turn my head for the first time and to squint curiously at the two beings who persistently accompanied me. Fully convinced that my retina would see nothing of the materia prima et ultima, I was most pleasantly surprised when I saw something after all. Of course, I didn't see two pilgrims with girded loins as Father Abraham in his day. And yet the two Highnesses, Dominions, or Thrones—I forgot to inquire to which class the Melangeloi belonged—were something halfway between the inconspicuous vision that called on Abraham and the conspicuous vision that visited the three youths in the furnace. Above all, I saw no wings on these angels, and that filled me with greatest satisfaction. I have always regarded angels' wings as a human invention, and a poor one at that. Either arms or wings. The useless swan's plumage, attached to human shoulders and not supplied with adequate muscles to set it in motion, is nothing but an anatomical absurdity. Nothing can be more horrid than this insipid burlesquing of the winged bull of the Babylonians, chiefly because it is impossible. In order to believe in angels—and in gratitude for my experience I should like to contribute to this belief—we must imagine *possible* angels. They must be protomaterial, ultracorporeal beings, who use their substance at will, who can disguise themselves on behalf of their fallen half-brother, man, at times.

If I am to describe the Highnesses, my two companions—and

it isn't easy at all—then I must say that in the familiar utter
lightlessness of the Gray Neuter I saw two very subdued brightnesses, whose coloring ranged somewhere between a delicate
lilac and a faint pink. But the essential thing was the form of
these brightnesses. I might best describe them as two moving
cloaks or draperies that swept along at my side in utter silence.
But what a joy, what a satisfaction, it was to see that these
faintly gleaming draperies seemed to conceal human forms, and
magnificent forms at that. At times the drapery outlined a
pointed knee, a powerful thigh, a small foot, a melodious elbow,
a masculine Michelangelesque chest, and as quickly the drapery
concealed it, as though this fraternal approach to the anthropomorphic were more than enough. Tintoretto and especially the
Toledan El Greco had had the idea. I could not distinguish
faces, or let me rather say, the two beings did not express themselves to that extent. Now and then, however, I had the impression of noble heads behind veils, of heads with streaming crimson hair of flame.

The Highnesses had just heard me mention the pilgrims with
girded loins who had appeared to Abraham. They seemed to like
that because it wakened splendid memories.

"It is known to us that we are pilgrims with girded loins," said
the one.

"And always on our way," added the other.

On your way, I thought, of course you're always on your way.
In that respect you don't differ from sunbeams, planets, and
atoms. For this purpose you might as well be materia media and
not Ultras and Infras. Who knows, perhaps even dead space is on
its way, the Gray Neuter, the Nothing, the yawning void between
flaming activities. Actually we humans are the only ones that are
not constantly "on our way," for God has given us the refreshing
illusion of rest. In death this illusion vanishes, and that is the
secret of "being moved." But a pleasant little afternoon nap,
when the work of fiction has dropped from the relaxing hand,
when body and soul are lulled in equilibrium, while in reality
every single cell of the body is restlessly "on its way"—this illu-

sion is granted to us humans alone. And another thing: when we humans are on our way we have a destination, a limited but definite goal. The planets in their monotonous orbits certainly have no destination and the sun and other stars probably have none either. The angels, however, the men of the Intermundia, must have a destination.

"Your Highnesses," I said loudly and probably in a very affected manner, "I know that even among humans only the rude ones ask their acquaintances on the boulevards 'Where are you going?'"

The brightnesses beside me, the pale lilac and faint rose draperies, began to undulate and to billow, and the hint of human forms became more distinct, even to the delineation of strong masculine faces framed in fluttering red hair. I had the feeling that this phenomenon indicated hearty laughter on the part of the Melangeloi. They answered my question regarding their destination with two terse words: "Rosarium Virginis." Then they stretched out horizontally, turned into faint beams, and I no longer felt their presence beside me.

What I felt, however, was a lump of weeping emotion in my throat. The Melangeloi had named their destination: Rosarium Virginis. I translated it as the Virgin's Rose Garden. Perhaps that meant the constellation of Virgo in the zodiac, belonging to the same system as our sun. Or was it more? Was it the Virgin herself, the queen of the stars and the angels, who kept court in her rose garden? They flew in from all sides, the predecessors and the successors, those with hair of flame and those with locks of white heat, the great and the tiny, that were created before the stars—they came to do homage to the earthwoman out of whom had issued the spirit whose passion had liberated God in man and man in God.

✳ ✳ ✳ ✳ ✳
✳ ✳ ✳
✳

AT THE SAME INSTANT I WAS BACK IN THE MIDST of the class at Comet Calisthenics. The Melangeloi, the good St. Bernard dogs of the Intermundium, had picked me up and brought me back. My shipwreck on Apostle Peter and my absence must have taken practically no time at all, for neither the teacher nor B.H. had missed me. They were both of the opinion that I had not been out of their sight for a moment. Now I was a long streak of star dust again with a gleaming pinhead like my classmates'. As I lay in space next to B.H., I could not restrain myself, in spite of my intention to the contrary, and blurted out the great experience.

"Don't you know, B.H., that I was lost? And that a pair of genuine, materially existing angels, called Melangeloi, saved me and brought me back to you?"

B.H. turned his helmet toward me and looked at me as we whizzed on our way.

"What are you talking about, F.W.," he hissed voicelessly. "What sort of angels saved you? Why did you have to be saved? God knows I didn't see any angels or similar nonsense. You were simply knocked silly by our brief glance at Apostle Peter. So was I, but don't tell anybody about it."

"No, B.H.," I argued, "It's not a matter of course at all that I found you again. On the contrary, it's a little miracle, a miracle of second or third degree, let's say. I had a very informative conversation with two Dark Angels."

"What's all this drivel about angels?" B.H. asked, annoyed.

The teacher, who had overheard our conversation, came near as though to calm me and to forestall a quarrel. "We are on our way home, Seigneur," he hissed like a leaky petcock. "The first Chronosophic lesson is always tiring, particularly for adults. But these angels that you mention must be a strange trick of the imagination that you brought along from your earlier life."

Not another word, an inner voice warned me. Undisciplined as I am, I did not obey but became offensive instead.

"Why shouldn't there have been any angels? Don't you believe in angels? Aren't angels good enough for the Mental intellect?"

"I'm no scholar but an insignificant schoolmaster for elementary instruction," said the teacher modestly but obviously offended. "I know this much, however, that for many generations all images of man's outer and inner world have been catalogued in the Lamaseries of the Starrovers, the Marvelers, and the Foreignfeelers. We possess a complete inventory of everything that exists inside and outside of man. There are no angels in this catalogue of external and internal images, Seigneur."

"They can't be on this list," I rejoined bitterly, "for they belong neither to the external nor the internal images of man."

"That's perfectly clear," the teacher replied nervously, forgetting all about his speeding class. "But it's a concession that there are no angels, Seigneur. For what could exist that belongs neither to the external nor to the internal world?"

"Many things, sir," I replied pointedly, "there can be many such things, for example, God."

"Well, all right, God," the teacher admitted reluctantly, "but nothing else."

"Why not?" I inquired as I contracted and expanded with particular enjoyment. "Can't God have created any protomateria? As a matter of fact, He surely created it. That's what lies between Him and the words 'Let there be light.' That's what existed before all else existed that still exists. You see, sir, that's the spirit realm which includes the angels which are not in the catalogue."

With these words I was sure that I had proved the possibility of the existence of angels, if not the certainty. But the teacher had not been listening closely to my arguments, for an unexpected incident—a bit of cosmic monkey business on the part of our tumbling genius, Io-Runt—had distracted his attention and made his crystal helmet quiver with rage.

On our way home from Apostle Peter to the Djebel we could not avoid a planetary orbit that was much more densely populated than all other elliptical circuits. Along its path, according to the most recent census, there moved more than eleven thou-

sand objects, or, to be less cold-bloodedly scientific, more than
eleven thousand genuine planets. These tiny planets, which were
called "Asteroids" back in the beginnings of mankind, had their
origin in the disintegration of a great planet between Apostle
Peter and Mars, the star of The Baptist, a celestial body that was
named Judas Iscariot at the time of the Christianization of the
firmament. Since time immemorial there had been an esoteric
belief that this planet, the fifth in line from the sun, the most
beautiful and most highly developed of all, had not simply been
the victim of a sidereal traffic accident, but that it had purposely
committed suicide by getting too near the danger zone of a
superior field of gravitation, that of Apostle Peter. He had done
the same thing as Judas, the man from Carioth, had done on
Hakkalama after he had betrayed Jesus for thirty pieces of silver.
Whether there was a grain of truth in this legend or not, the
Asteroids, which had formerly been named for Greek goddesses,
were now combined under the single name of Judas Iscariot.
We could tell that we had entered the precincts of Judas by the
faint hint of lunar brightness that suddenly quivered through
the Gray Neuter, as well as by the ineffably soft, spidery, high-
pitched sound that chirped all about us. Now and then a pale
planetary disc appeared at the outer rim of our field of vision,
passed us, and vanished. But I closed my eyes each time in
order to see no more, for I must confess that my soul was sated,
it could no longer bear the grandeur of creation. After all, it was
an earth soul and no cosmic soul or angel's soul. And I could not
help but admire the boys round about me who took all these
Chronosophic experiences and exercises in their stride as though
they were potato races on the public playgrounds.

When I opened my eyes once more I saw a spectacle that I
shall not forget to the end of my days. I mean the end of my
present days in the twentieth century. One of the Judas planetoids
was passing very near us. The more conscientious among my
readers, whose sense of time and space is probably just as
confused by now as mine was then, will understand that I could
not possibly form an opinion of the size of this planetoid at

first. Not even my own length as a comet could serve as a standard of comparison, and so the dimensions of the little star that floated along near us depended solely upon its distance from me and upon the perspective foreshortening which I could not determine. Instinctively I knew that the little thing was near enough to touch. This instinctive knowledge was contradicted, on the other hand, by the miraculous perfection of the softly shining star, which served as evidence that the gigantic Judas Iscariot must indeed have been a splendid planet before its destruction. By the words "miraculous perfection" I mean to indicate that this floating orb was a genuine globe with a day-side and a night-side, the day-side illuminated by the sun that was invisible to us, the night-side covered with deep shadows. Like the earth this spheroid had icecaps on both poles. And if my memory serves me well, its light surface showed various formations, planes, and shadows that could only be continents, oceans, deserts, and craterous mountain ranges. If the bright side of the thing had suddenly grown into a space-filling disc, then into a concave dish, and finally into an illuminated world-wide soup tureen, I shouldn't have been a bit surprised. But it remained as it was; it didn't grow larger or smaller.

Suddenly one of the gleaming streaks peeled off from our formation and shrank to his normal boyish stature which, to my greatest surprise, however, far exceeded the size of the floating planetoid. I have already revealed the fact that the culprit was Io-Runt. The size of the little fellow in proportion to the starlet was approximately that of a playing child to a big bright toy balloon, extending about from the child's knees to his chin. Our graceful but spiritually undeveloped Runt regarded the globe from the ruins of Judas Iscariot as nothing more than a delightful cosmic toy. Consider the incident from a child's point of view: a real star, with all the genuine attributes of a planet, and yet so tiny that you could catch it and take it home with you, like a giant tropical butterfly. Io-Runt's exultant shouts drowned out the thin, almost inaudible whirring that constituted

the starlet's contribution to the universal music of the spheres.
And Runt stretched and contracted and hovered above and
below the sphere and extended his arms and dodged away play-
fully and wove a wooing dance about the tiny orb in a coquettish
pas-de-deux palely illumined by the starlet's reflected daylight.
The little planet, however, floated along imperturbably on its
sacred orbit, ordained by God just as that of the sun or of Sirius.
For up here the only ones free to follow their own devices were
we infamous cometians and Chronosophic will-o'-the-wisps, in
a word, we humans who were not ashamed to reach for the
stars. I still recall clearly that the Asteroid made me think of a
young girl going about her business with quiet dignity, taking
no notice of a boulevard wolf trying to force his attentions on
her.

For a while the teacher was speechless at the cosmic impertinence of his favorite pupil. Then he began to tremble with
anger. Finally he abruptly contracted himself to his magisterial
shape, brandished his geographic pointer in the Gray Neuter,
and his hissing voice broke in outraged accents.

"If that doesn't top everything that's ever been seen since
the creation of the world! A Runt, a nothing, an insect reaches
for the stars. Will you stop that at once, you wretch, you—you—
Haven't you any sense of propriety? On your way! Get going
before I lose my temper. Is that your idea of seriousness and
soberness? Get going! On your way!"

And he stretched out and flew in pursuit of the malefactor.
And the rest of us stretched out just as far in order not to be
left behind. Io-Runt, however, frightened and clever as he
was, managed to keep his distance, and by more than a neck.
As for the teacher, he was not only tricky but he knew the lower
Intermundium with all its traps and pitfalls. He knew the Lower
Intermundium even better than the greatest specialists among
the Starrovers and Marvelers. For he had been moving around
in this elementary space with the youngest beginners for more
than a hundred years. The classes were promoted, year after

year. But the teacher flunked, year after year. That's the way it's always been, and Mental pedagogy didn't seem to have changed anything.

Suddenly it seemed to us that the absence of light in the Gray Neuter had become even blinder, and that the splendid freedom of movement which our cometlike bodies had enjoyed had suddenly been limited. I can't quite express it, but I felt as though I were aimlessly cavorting about in a coalbin whose walls did not consist of stone but of inhibitions and prohibitions. This too was probably a Chronosophic exercise, for our teacher was a real teacher, who knew no passion other than his subject. Well, now he had cornered the culprit. Poor Runt, I thought. But what did a naughty pupil have to fear from a teacher who was worried about him?

Then I found that my troubles weren't over yet. Even this coalbin of the Lower Intermundium was not uninhabited. I firmly closed my eyes and swore that I wouldn't open them again until we were back in our schoolroom in the Djebel. Without a doubt I had seen something new again, and that was too much for me. It looked like a sort of astronomic Maypole dance. A good-sized, faintly luminous heavenly body, suspended in space, constituted the central figure, and around it revolved a number of satellites that appeared and disappeared at a much higher rate of speed than ordinary planets. Although the central globe diffused rays of its own, a comparison with the sun or any other star would have been ridiculous; for its radiant activity was moderate and dull, and the satellites that danced around the Maypole were dark, flat, unsubstantial, and unreal. Another conspicuous characteristic was the complete absence of even the slightest sound of music of the spheres from this apparently enormous star and its companions.

"Io-Runt," came the wrathful examiner's voice of our teacher, "what do you see here? Classify and define it."

As I had expected, the question was followed by a deep, guilty silence on the part of Io-Runt and then a hint of boyish tears.

Now the teacher erupted in typical schoolmasterly anger. "So, when it comes to playing tricks on the universe, you're right there. But when you are asked to define the simplest phenomenon you can't open your mouth. You should be ashamed of yourself, Io-Runt. You will write on the blackboard one hundred times in extensive script: 'I must not reach for stars.'"

Runt's suppressed sobs filled the inhumanly stern space. At the same time, however, I felt how the teacher's heart ached because he had had to punish his pet. Merely in order to relieve his aching heart he hissed at the two Respondents, the model pupils Io-Rar and Io-Hol; "What do you see? Classify and define it. One, two, three."

"We are faced by a phenomenon," one of the star pupils began in the mendacious roundabout way of an ignoramus who is trying to gain time with empty words.

"Don't stall, Io-Rar," the teacher interrupted him sharply. In the same way he silenced the other Respondent, Io-Hol, when the latter began to stutter something about a self-inclusive system. Followed a long pregnant silence. Then the teacher's voice whistled with unconcealed scorn, "Next time I'll call on the Idiot of the Era for help!"

From the rear rank of our class came a reluctant, cautious guess, "Perhaps a unicle, an achad, a monad."

"Well, at last," the teacher growled with a note of satisfaction. "That's very good, Io-Scram; keep it up."

I pushed my gleaming head close to B.H. and whispered, "For heaven's sake, what is that, a unicle, an achad, a monad? We didn't have anything like that in school, did we, B.H.?"

"I believe we did," my friend replied. "Weren't those things called atoms? A wrong designation, by the way, for they're anything but indivisible; even at that time they were divided into nuclei and electrons. It's just as wrong to call them unicles or achads or monads, for I see not one object but nine, one large one and eight small ones."

Behind me sounded a rebellious hissing from the class. "That's a trick—a dirty trick, sir. You played us for suckers."

"Ha-ha," B.H. laughed softly, "the boys are right. He really did play us for suckers; by some dirty Chronosophic trick he steered us out of cosmic space into a fleabitten microcosm, into the atomic network of a speck of dust or some such thing, where we're now coasting around in the form of subcomets."

"But we haven't lost any of our speed," I marveled.

"A trick, teacher, a trick," the boys sizzled more rebelliously than ever.

"Quiet there," the teacher commanded. "Trick is an ugly and disrespectful word. Don't you see with your stupid eyes that there are stars even in *this* infinitesimal yet infinite space? That means that seriousness and soberness are required everywhere. What is the index of our speed now, Io-Runt?"

The little fellow with the round head gulped and snuffed into the void, "We now have—a negative coefficient."

"Very well said, my boy," the teacher praised him, only too glad to comfort the culprit. Then he turned to the entire class. "You accuse me of playing a trick on you. In spite of the ugly and disrespectful word, I admit it. I made use of a peda-gogical expedient that only a few teachers know, to take my pupils from one extreme to the other. But why did I do that, my dear young friends? I did it so that you might acquire the princi-ples of Chronosophy in an organic manner as early as possible, that is, in your very first schoolyear. These irrefragable princi-ples are as follows: the infinitely great is infinitesimally small, just as the infinitesimally small is infinitely great. What does that mean? It means: nothing is large and nothing is small. Nothing is long and nothing is short. In the light of the spirit all these words are illusory. Man alone is great, if he can cover the distance from the infinite to the infinitesimal and from the infinitesimal to the infinite within himself. That is ancient wisdom, almost a banality, and Seigneur will corroborate me. The only difference between the ancient sages and us Chronos-ophers is the fact that we are not satisfied to carry the cosmos into ourselves but we carry ourselves into the cosmos. How much bolder are we than the sea, air, rocket, stratosphere, and moon navigators of dark antiquity! First we visit the planets and become acquainted with their characters and approach to within a short distance of our life-giving sun bursting with vital activity. The most important thing is proficiency of movement in the Lower Intermundium, swiftness in Comet Calisthenics, for this is decisive for all further progress. Yes, my dear young friends, you will soon leave me and take the entrance examination to the Lamasery of the Starrovers. Then you will ascend—as we mistakenly say—into Outer Space; then life becomes serious. At first you will immerse yourselves in the galactic realm, of which we ourselves are a part. You will progress from the nearer constellations to the miracles of the distance. Then, however, after further difficult and rigorous tests, you will venture out into the unspeakable oceans of space that lie between the universes of the nebulae. And so some of you may rise to the summits of mankind, from the Starrovers to the Marvelers, the Thaumazonts, and from the Marvelers to the Foreignfeelers, the Xenospasts. And who knows, perhaps one of you is chosen to be the High Floater of his era in the domain of the Silver Spiders."

During this fine speech we were moving constantly along the walls of inhibitions and prohibitions which made me feel as though we were banished to a coalbin. At the last words about the High Floater of his era I had the impression that the teacher foresaw his pet, Io-Runt, elevated to that dignity. The whole speech, however, particularly the part dealing with the greatness of man, made me think of the Grand Bishop and his doctrine of the growing alienation of mankind from God, brought about by the mere passing of time. Was Chronosophy too, only a symptom of this alienation, an indication of the gigantic arrogance of the human race? Suddenly I forgot my promise to myself and opened my eyes. We still seemed to be caught in the atomic network of B.H.'s conjectural grain of dust. Although we diligently expanded, contracted, and expanded, the coalbin still held us captive, for the clumsy, faintly glowing orb with its family of planets continued to reappear in the distance.

All at once—did my eyes deceive me?—I saw white cloaks and draperies detaching themselves and streaming away from these starlike, ultimate components of matter, defying the laws of attraction and repulsion, moving in accord with their own free will. No matter how far from me they flashed along, I saw, or rather I felt, human forms under these snow-white cloaks and draperies, and I had an impression of flaxen hair which fluttered in their flight. There could be no doubt—they were Choirs, Highnesses, Dominions, and Thrones, and they were not Melangeloi but Leukangeloi, Bright Angels or White Angels, that issued from the atom. Albertus Magnus, Bonaventura, Scotus Erigena, or whoever else wrote on the subject, had underestimated reality when he maintained that only three hundred thousand angels could dance on the point of a needle. There was room for many more on the point of a needle. Where were these beings streaming, like flashes of white lightning? Were they too assembling in the Rosarium Virginis? In my exaltation I was about to shout, "Good Lord, B.H., look, look there—real angels!" But this time I restrained myself and kept quiet. There were experiences that a man had to keep to himself even in the Astromental era, simply because it was too soon for them. My heart was still pounding with its sweet firsthand knowledge when the teacher turned on the normal rainy daylight in the classroom.

The Fifteenth Chapter

WHEREIN A TOUR THROUGH THE LAMASER
IES OF THE STARROVERS, MARVELERS, AND
FOREIGNFEELERS CONCLUDES THE DJEBEL
EPISODE, CLIMAXING IN THE CELL OF THE
HIGH FLOATER, WHO ACQUAINTS ME WITH
THE TRUE SHAPE OF THE UNIVERSE AND
WITH THE MOST IMPORTANT MOMENT OF
MY FORMER LIFE.

THE TEACHER HAD handed B.H. and me honorary Chronosophic diplomas, richly ornamented little cards, crediting
us with several million kilometers and several decades of
space travel, certifying our inspection of John Evangelist and
Apostle Peter as well as our successful visit to the interior of
an oxygen unicle along with the appropriate negative measurements. We also received excellent grades in macrocosmic and
microcosmic Comet Calisthenics. Although it looked more like
a bank statement than a school report card, it was the most
creditable document of the sort that I had ever received. But
what good is it to me, when I can't display it today? It's worth
no more and no less to me than my high and unmerited badge,
the purple wrist-rosette.

More important to me, however, than the written certificate
from our dear pedagogue, was the fact that the period of instruction and the vast distances in space and time that we had
covered had not fatigued me in the least and that I felt even

more vigorous than before, more inquisitive than ever, and practically transparent with concealed enthusiasm. I had done more than just take a look into interplanetary and interatomic space. In the days of my youth anyone could take a look into the cosmos if he strolled in the evening through the park where a shivering old man had set up a shabby telescope and sold a peep for a few pennies. Generally the star salesman with the inadequate overcoat offered you Jupiter, because even the poorest instrument revealed this titan as an imposing disc with four moons. But I had planted my flattened hind-end on the putty waves of the rusty-red morass as I faced certain destruction, just as I had bounced like a rubber ball through the frictionless ether on the molten lead sea of Mercury. I had been the only one privileged to see the divinely extravagant life of our sun not only with the eyes of imagination but with my physical eyes protected by clouds of dull silver. In orderly and pragmatic fashion I described how all that came about. Can anyone expect more of a travel writer? I say no, emphatically no. Undoubtedly the critical and intelligent reader is ready to offer various explanations for the crystal miracle of the Djebel, as he thinks about televisionary iconography by means of which a celestial body can be brought down from on high at will to be reconstructed here in any desired dimensions. I myself have repeatedly voiced these suspicions as they befell me in the course of my experiences.

As we take off our space-diving suits now and lay them neatly on the school couches, one or another of us would probably like to examine the diaphanous, oilclothlike material for spots of rusty-red mud or congealed particles of lead. I do not deny this possibility by any means. It is more than likely that we brought along traces of planetary substances. But I look every curious reader straight in the eye and ask him softly, "Isn't it far more important that I met genuine angels, my friend? And genuine angels can't be caught on a photographic plate." My hypothetical interviewer will perhaps grumble in reply that he regards a meeting with angels in the Intermundia as unimportant and scientifically unprofitable. To that I will answer boldly, "Let's disregard the spiritual and metaphysical meaning of the Melangeloi and Leukangeloi completely. Let's confine ourselves to natural science. Isn't it of scientific importance that there is such a thing as *transcendental matter* that lies outside the realm of electrons but this side of the pure spirit, an intermediate substance, so to speak, capable of assuming all disguises, filling the voidest void of creation? And isn't that particularly the realm where we dead live and from where I was lured without thought of consequences?"

Notwithstanding this imaginary conversation, I resolved never again to mention the word angel to B.H. or to anyone else. I suspected that many an era would have to pass over the Djebel before the existence of angels and the character of transcendental matter would be recognized and investigated. My visit to the cell of the High Floater, however, was to convince me that my pessimistic conclusion was in error.

But not only I, whose mind was filled with angels, was elated in a strange, transparent manner. My reincarnated friend's face beamed and his dark eyes gleamed with deep exultation when the teacher had finally freed him of his helmet.

B.H. thanked the schoolmaster in the following words: "It seems to me, sir, that in addition to all my other lives I have now lived two more lives."

That was a real compliment from one who had been frequently reincarnated. Our good pedagogue was visibly pleased and muttered some modest phrases about "propadeutics," about his "insufficient powers," and about "much too simple a problem." Thereupon I hastily assured him that if we were ever privileged to take another trip to the Gray Neuter we would not think of going with anyone but him. As I was paying him this compliment I had already forgotten my shipwreck on Apostle Peter as well as the fact that I would never have found my way back to his class except for the help of the Melangeloi. But past dangers are even more immaterial than past pleasures. The teacher bowed stiffly, in accordance with the custom, rubbed his hands, and asked us to honor him with another visit as soon as possible.

The Minor Cosmos or Lower Intermundium, he said, was at our disposal daily from eleven to twelve, along with all its heavenly bodies. Although he was only a plain elementary teacher he had far greater surprises in store for us than the ABC of Mary Magdalene, John Evangelist, and Apostle Peter. There was, for example, Peter's neighbor, Apostle Paul, formerly Saturn, a highly intellectual, soulful, complicated, very energetic, but slightly epileptic planet personality, for whose superficial inspection he, the teacher, ordinarily took more than one hundred school periods.

While we conversed and while the teacher invited us to visit the most remote outer planets, the boys frolicked around the schoolroom in the old familiar way. Only Io-Runt was writing line after line of extensive letters—the same kind that the Uranographer used in his edition of the "Evening Stars"—on the blackboard with chalk: "I must not reach for stars." As he wrote, the tip of his red tongue wiggled between his lips. I wondered why the calm face of the boy attracted me so deeply and strangely. Then the recess bell rang. Things really hadn't changed except that the pupils roamed among the stars instead of among Vergilian hexameters. It was time for the class to take its required mind-invigorating bath in the sulphur pool. The teacher explained that it was a dry bath and invited us to participate. But at that moment B.H. was called up by Io-Fagòr, who informed us that the Official Guide of the Era had just arrived in the Djebel to conduct me through the Lamaseries and, if fortune was kind, to present me to the High Floater among the Silver Spiders.

* * * *
* * *
*

HERE I AM BACK AGAIN AT THE CRUX of all travel writing, namely description. And this sort of description is even more difficult to manage than the kind that deals with sightseeing. Is there anything more boring, I ask myself, than sight-seeing? Certainly not for me, to be frank. Whenever I was in a caravan of sightseers, in the Catacombs of Rome, in Pompeii, in the Temple of Karnak, on the Acropolis of Baalbek, in the Cathedral of Chartres, I always managed to sneak away, to drop behind, in order to escape the monotonous voice of the guide and the stolidly staring herd limping in his wake, at the risk of learning even less about the sight than they. But I was even more unwilling to read about it in the guidebook. The description of a sight is like the shadow of a shadow, the epitome of a footnote, that you can read or omit without missing anything.

Now I assume that a few of my readers are particularly good-natured, an entirely unpermissible assumption. Readers are not good-natured. They are and should be the author's pitiless creditors. They went to a bookstore in good faith and spent as much money for a book as for a mediocre meal in a mediocre restaurant, not including a bottle of wine. Their investment en-titles them to a full equivalent in return from the intellectual restaurant keeper, the author. Since intellectual nourishment has a much lower market value in our world than physical pabulum, the reader's demands upon the author include the following: several day and night hours of intensive suspense; entertainment of a refined sort of which one needs not be ashamed later on; genuine emotions; soft smiles and belly laughs, occasionally spiced by tears; greatest comprehensibility; appealing char-acters; swiftly moving action; and above all, as little description as possible. I have no intention of arguing about these just de-mands on the part of the reader. They are the immutable law that I and every other author have to obey. And yet I am postulating a good-natured reader, or let me rather say, an understanding, a tolerant reader who is aware of certain diffi-culties of my material and who speaks to me encouragingly: "Our Chronosophic exercise in planetary space was nothing but a sightseeing tour after all. Of course, I should have preferred Saturn to Jupiter—those rings have always aroused my astronomic curiosity—but still I've experienced and felt a number of things that lie outside the normal realm of imagination and that you don't read about in ordinary novels."

Being a fretful and worrisome author I naturally pounce upon these encouraging words of the good-natured reader—who, unfortunately, is only an invention of mine—and reply: "On this sightseeing tour of the Djebel you will also meet only persons and phenomena that lie outside the normal realm of your imagination and that are not to be found in any novel that has ever been written. Since I cannot, without lying, communicate to you directly the experiences, feelings, emotions, and thrills of the great interstellar and even nebular spaces, I can at least show you the men who have had these thrills in their short mundane lives and who have penetrated to the bounds of the most distant heavens, the faint radiation of which is barely perceptible with the most delicate instruments or perhaps not at all. You will meet the *cosmic man* of the most remote future who has made himself master of time and space, and for whom near and far, moment and eternity, are almost as identical as for the Creator. You will see the strange consequences which incessant tension produces in the bodies and souls of cosmic men. And finally you will hear the solution of world riddles from the lips of the High Floater, a solution that has never been confided to any mortal. That too is included without extra charge in the price of a mediocre meal. On top of all that, I promise to conduct you through the cognition cells of the Djebel much faster than the relentlessly thorough Guide of the Era conducted us. For even I am getting anxious to leave the Djebel and to get back to our friends, to Lala, to Io-Fagòr, to Io-Do, to the Ancestress, and to the Mental world where, if my feelings do not deceive me, a catastrophe is brewing."

*   *   *   *   *
*   *   *
*

THE DJEBEL, A MIGHTY ALPINE RANGE from the outside, was an even more gigantic and richer world on the inside. It would have taken a lifetime to comprehend it completely. Let me say one thing right at the start: it required relatively little time to get around in the vast interior of the artificial mountain in spite of the very considerable distances. Just as in our own era of very early antiquity good hospitals "air-conditioned" their wards, so the corridors, runways, ramps, and passages of the Djebel had "conditioned gravitation." That means that within the confines of the Djebel the gravitation of the earth could be turned high or low at will. (Without knowing it, we had had our first introduction to this regulated gravitation when we were riding around in the frictionless labyrinthine darkness on our school couches.) This conditioned, or rather modified, gravitation prevailed not only in the corridors but also in the interior of the various Lamaseries, as for example, in that of the Starrovers, the Astropaths, through which we were now passing.

Starroving meant the first advanced grade of Chronosophic study, if the concept of a study is applicable at all. Everything in the Mental era, and especially in the Djebel, was so utterly different from the content of our former, that is our present, life, that I purposely stress the analogies in order to make the differences in character more obvious. The great multitude of Starrovers corresponded to college students of our time, or rather, to students in a theological seminary, or still better, to the youthful monks in the gigantic Buddhist monasteries in the mountains of Tibet. B.H. mentioned this analogy at once, and it was for this reason that I chose the word "Lamasery" to give the right impression. While the children in the Chronosophic elementary school did Comet Calisthenics and frolicked around in the Lower Intermundium, the students of Astropathy were assigned to the Major Cosmos of the First Degree. This technical term referred to the cosmic realm that included our solar system and is popularly known as the Milky Way. All this is easily said and written, but the amount of cognitive material which the

Starrovers had to acquire was immense, and the effort required
by their course of study was superhuman, in laudable contrast
with the current lackadaisical Mental attitude. While, for example, a few brief hours of instruction with our good, serious,
and sober elementary teacher sufficed not only to lay eyes on our
entire planetary system but also to set foot on it, it would have
required millennia at the same chronoelastic rate of speed merely
to take a fleeting peek at the intergalactic spaces. If a visit to
Apostle Peter was comparable to a short stride from your bed to
the table, then a trip to any of the more respectable stars in the
Milky Way would have been equivalent to several complete
circuits of the globe. My own experiences in the Lower Intermundium coupled with the inconceivable figures which the
Official Guide recited down to their last decimal point in his
histrionically raucous voice, filled me with frightened admiration
for the courage and accomplishments of Astropathic students.
If I am not mistaken, our nearest neighboring star, Alpha
Prophetae Iesaiae, formerly Alpha Centauri, moves in an orbit
four and three-tenths light years away, a ridiculous bagatelle
in the cosmic timetable. More remote individuals in the same
Milky Way move at distances of hundreds of thousands and millions of light years. Not to insult, but merely to remind the reader,
I mention the fact that a light year is the product of one hundred
and eighty-six thousand miles (or three hundred thousand kilometers) times the number of seconds in a year. The resulting
vast figure gives us a faint idea of the physical and psychic
difficulties of the Astropathic course of study.

First of all I want to speak of the physical, the gymnastic,
course of study, which had been tried and tested for many
hundreds of years and occupied much more of the student's time
than intellectual instruction. It was the doctrine of Chronosophy
that the course of truth ran from the outside to the inside, from
experience to judgment, from the surface to the center, from
perception to cognition, from the body to the spirit. Well, this
doctrine was anything but new, and B.H. remarked that he had
been familiar with the venerable teachings of Yoga as early as

the twentieth century, and the practical mysticism of Yoga was based on this principle. Yet even he could not conceal his astonishment and admiration as we skimmed through the upper rooms, the attics, so to speak, of the Djebel (where the lowest classes were housed), and witnessed the Astropathic gymnastics. These "attics" consisted of an endless flight of spacious rooms, most of which were eerily illuminated by the sheen of collected and then disintegrated starlight. In each of these cognition halls, chambers, and cells, a large or small group of students was engaged, under the direction of a master, in adapting their own bodies to the individuality of a particular star or constellation by means of appropriate exercises. It was a strange feeling to see a room, for instance, in which there was not a single ray of earthly light, but only the unspeakably faint dark-lilac tint of the star Betelgeuse (Alpha Orionis), a titanic, reddish sun of the Intermundium of the First Degree. We were not permitted to enter any of the star chambers, chiefly because in many of them the force of gravitation had been turned up so high for practice purposes that it would have hurled us to the ground and crushed us, inexperienced and untrained as we were.

Assisted by reduced gravitation, we flew along a sloping corridor, a ramp, leading between transparent walls, stopping at times when the Official Guide wanted us to look more closely at one or another astrogymnastic exercise. Of course I failed to grasp the significance of these various exercises, and the Guide's explanations and interpretations would not have helped much either since I lacked all prerequisite understanding. But fortunately he didn't say anything. Why should I have tried to grasp the meaning of the exercises analytically? The very sight, sometimes in the form of ecstatic beauty, sometimes of grotesque distortion, had in it something of mysterious meaning. There, for instance, lay a well-formed youth on the mirrorlike floor and slowly stretched his naked body longer and longer until B.H. and I both uttered exclamations of fright. When the Astrogymnast had stretched his body to about fifteen feet in length without tearing his sinews or breaking his bones, he suddenly snapped back to his former stature and shape. And this was not done in the complete imponderability of the Gray Neuter, like the Comet Calisthenics of the children, but under the added handicap of increased gravitation. The star which he served had been named by the Arabians Unuk-al-Hay, meaning "neck of a snake." In another room I saw a young fellow who did nothing but stand on tiptoe with his head thrown far back and his arms extended in the world-embracing gesture of one crucified. In this instance the star in question, Albireo was its name, demanded nothing of its adept but expression, the expression of universal sympathy and sacrificial surrender.

"He is going to be a splendid Starrover," said the Official Guide, pointing at the young man, "for the beauty of his posture is already developing into beauty of soul."

In the adjoining room the reddish gloom of another star prevailed, a star, judging by its color, thousands of times larger than our sun. The demonic character of this star—it was Etamin, or Caput Draconis, "dragon's head"—induced its study group to engage in most unusual Astrogymnastics. With disgusted surprise I saw a number of handsome youthful bodies entwined, twisted, and crumpled into something that I can only call a nest of snakes. Each of these fine young bodies formed an elastic, tangled knot from which a far larger number of slippery limbs writhed forth than it really possessed. In this room, the Official Guide declared, the highest experimental gravitation in the entire Lamasery prevailed. Not far from it, however, he showed us a huge hall where the gravitation had been reduced to the lowest degree. Here, in the bluish, bright, collected rays of an entire star cluster, hundreds of naked youths—each one of them a cosmic dancing genius like our Io-Runt—combined their bodies into all sorts of fantastic structures that changed so rapidly from one to the next that my eye could scarcely catch them. The scene reminded me of a fanciful vaudeville act or a pantomime. At one instant the shining, whirling bodies formed a kind of Gothic cathedral with two tall spires, a rose window spinning like a wheel above the portal, and many nodding waterspouts; in the next instant the cathedral had been transformed into a fabulous beast with seven dragons' heads and twelve long tails of white human bodies that whizzed through the air and wrapped themselves around the central figure; and then suddenly the whole thing was a dead, rigid pyramid. Nothing about these evolutions, however, was intended, planned, or rehearsed as a spectacle for admiring eyes. Their sole purpose was to make the human personality independent of the earth, to raise it far above its planetary and solar limitations, and to bring it into relation to the strangest star natures by means of tried and tested symbols, which are nevertheless quite incomprehensible to us. The surmounting of the physical barriers of time and space was only the first purpose of Chronosophic science, not its second, third, hundredth, or last. It involved much more. It involved an incredibly audacious attempt to enrich the cognitive content of planetbound man and extend the limits of his experience to the edge of eternity. Again and again during this hour I had to think of the Grand Bishop. Was man really trying to take the place of God by carrying himself into the universe whereas he had formerly carried the universe within him? Was the Djebel the most modern human expression of the "Tree of Knowledge," of which the Tower of Babel was the oldest?

On our winged way through the corridors of the Astropathic Lamasery we met many groups of students who were bound for their solitary meals or who were using their intermission for other purposes. They were ordinary young people of the Mental world, perhaps even a shade handsomer than the average I had seen at the Geodrome, but otherwise not distinguishable from them. It struck me that these young Starrovers were cheerful and did not give the impression of vagueness, absent-mindedness, or dreaminess, although they were under the constant spell of the Major Cosmos of the First Degree. But just as Chronosophy and Comet Calisthenics were partly tedious lessons and partly practical fun for the boys of my elementary class, just so these youths regarded the boldest of all sciences more from its technical than from its intellectual side. So far they naïvely accepted what they were taught. So far they whizzed through the galactic spaces with youthful audacity, at speeds far exceeding that of the light-ray. It would require many decades before the effects of Chronosophy—the desirable as well as the deplorable ones—would become evident to them.

In the Lamasery of the Marvelers, also known as the Thaumazonts, which occupied the central portion—I almost said floors— of the Djebel, the desirable effects of Chronosophy could be observed. While the upper part of the mountain of stellar knowledge housed the ambitious youths, the middle part was appropriately devoted to adult men in their best years, the years between sixty and one hundred and twenty, when the men in the Mental world outside were entitled to wear golden headdresses. When I inquired whether there was a Lamasery for women, the Official Guide replied in the affirmative. Since successful Chronosophic practice, however, required strict asceticism and absolute celibacy, men and women were not permitted to see each other and were scrupulously segregated. Incidentally, the Guide added, women rarely advanced beyond the fundamental principles of Starroving, and they were naturally inclined to devote themselves to the study of the stars that had feminine names.

The Thaumazonts were mature men, and it would seem reasonable that they should now reap the rewards of their fifty years of Astropathic study. This assumption, however, was only half correct. Unlike the scientific studies in the beginnings of mankind, the Chronosophic course of study never came to an end. There never was a time when the Chronosopher took his final examination and was graduated as a finished master and scholar. Every final examination that he passed was another entrance examination and made him a student again, though on a higher level. In this way a humble equality of all in face of the eternal problem was preserved. Our cicerone said that even the Chief Chronosopher, the personage who was known as the High Floater (a title that had a magic attraction for me), had to pass an oral examination from time to time, in which the youngest boy in the Planet Class was the examiner. So the testing of the oldest, the highest, the most advanced Chronosopher by the youngest, the greenest beginner completed the Chronosophic cycle.

In the Lamasery of the Marvelers a much more mundane variation of light and shadow prevailed than in the astrogymnastic rooms of the Starrovers into which the rays of the individual stars were conducted and diffused by myriad prisms and light filters on the craggy peaks of the Djebel. That was because the profession of the Thaumazonts was more contemplative than active. The older ones among them had trained their bodies and their spirits in more than a hundred years of work and had adapted themselves to the stellar spaces. They still "ascended" at regular, but always greater, intervals. The objects of their intermundial visits, however, were not only the more remote regions of our Milky Way; the Thaumazonts were the first to be accorded the honor of crossing the unfathomable oceans of space separating the spiral nebulae from each other, the separate universes which together make up the universe. I could form no concept whatever of that which the Marvelers experienced "up there." It could not be expressed in gymnastic evolutions like the ballets of the Starrovers. It was entirely their own affair, and I was told that they never wrote and rarely spoke about it. But one thing had gradually trickled through and had reached the lay world in the form of a rumor: even if the fundamental laws and fundamental formations of these star nebulae are the same as those of our own star nebulae, the Milky Way, yet the "expression," the "genre," the "style," or, if you like, the "soul" of each of these universes is radically different. Well, I'm not a bit surprised. And perhaps my reader isn't a bit surprised either—and by this time I can call him my loyal reader—for he has experienced the radically different characters revealed by Apostle Peter, Mary Magdalene, and John Evangelist, and he has a vivid recollection of the glorious Phoenix and Christ-nature of our sun as we observed it from John Evangelist.

While the youthful Astropathics were constantly getting ready

for a voyage, and their return meant nothing to them but preparation for their next "ascent," the Thaumazonts divided their
lives between departure and return, and from year to year the
accent was shifted more strongly to the latter. This fact was
clearly revealed in the totally different manner of life and work
in the intermediate Lamasery.

As we flew through the corridors we saw no great chronogymnastic rehearsal halls but an incalculable number of small studios
and thinking chambers, in which the Marvelers, alone, in pairs,
or in groups of three to six, applied themselves to contemplation,
research, or discussion. Decades of intercourse with the stars,
daily contemplation of the substance of creation in its fundamental forms, the addition of infinite quantities of time and space
to their own lives—on the basis of their travels many of these
Marvelers were millions and millions of years old—all these
factors placed an indelible stamp on human habits. In former
days a scholar pushed aside his book and pen, his microscope and
test tube, and along with them his intellect and spirit, to appear
at his club or his favorite bar as any other insignificant Babbitt.
These men, on the other hand, were immersed in their study day
and night, for every cell of their bodies was impregnated with
their tremendous experiences. We saw one of them, for example,
walking up and down in his studio. He was a very handsome
man. He was shaking his head, slowly but incessantly, so that
my former contemporaries would certainly have taken him for an
idiot. In reality he was a sage of high degree, a "Marveler" in the
truest sense of the word, for as he walked up and down, shaking
his head, his heart was ready to burst with divine amazement at
existence and creation. He had "returned home" only a few
hours before.

In another studio we saw a large powerful man holding a
pebble, a sea shell, and a flower on the palm of his hand. I
assumed it was just an ordinary wild flower from the Park of
the Worker. But I never imagined that the features of a human
face were capable of bearing such an expression of spiritual
absorption. This face was almost concave with concentration.

It was white as death from the weight of the gargantuan thought that unfolded behind it. Suddenly tears began to stream down the man's cheeks. He never even noticed when they fell on his hand and on the little flower.

We saw a third Marveler, who was preparing to set out from the Djebel into the world of Mental men. That was his privilege. He was one of those who had brought home the Amor Dei from the cosmic world and whose love of the world and of his fellow-men impelled him to share his radiant knowledge. Such men as he appeared unexpectedly in the houses beneath the surface and spoke to the people of the thrilling breath of the Intermundia; they freed their fellow-men of earthbound shackles and taught them to distinguish between the important and the unimportant, and to think and feel as an integral part of the whole.

Not all of the Marvelers shook their heads constantly in divine amazement like the man whom we watched in his studio for several minutes; but they all wore expressions of disconcerted astonishment which had earned them the ancient Greek name of "Thaumazonts." The spiritual overwhelmedness of the Marvelers was most clearly revealed in their common room or assembly hall or hall of worship, or whatever you want to call the huge, brightly lighted arena in which we found several thousand of them together. There were so many of them and they were so absorbed that no one seemed to notice us intruders when the Official Guide bade us enter. He informed us in a loud tone of voice that for countless centuries the brilliant light of universal noonday had pervaded this hall and that, like the light, the perpetual sacrifice of the Lamasery of the Marvelers was never interrupted by day or by night. It was, of course, no pagan sacerdotal sacrifice nor a Christian sacrifice of the mass, but an incessant offertory of hymnic poetry that was never recorded and never repeated. The strangely rough choral chant streamed forth directly from the distraught souls of the returning wanderers. (Nowhere in the Mental world, except from the Worker, had I heard such rough voices.) In black festive veils adorned with gold tinsel, the Thaumazonts formed processions and moved about in circles and loops in a strange esoteric pattern. Each of these star processions carried a varicolored banner of veil material. While these mature, powerful men marched, rude words and cries broke from their ecstatically compressed throats. Each one contributed his own word, his own poem, and yet, I don't know how, the chorus was harmonious and unified.

The crude hymn of the returning Thaumazonts that had not ceased for centuries and that was renewed every three hours by other Marvelers, the wild poem of humans awakened and trained to full cosmic consciousness, resounded in our ears for a long time as we sped down the endless incline leading to the lower parts of the Djebel. There was much more space between the Lamasery of the Marvelers and that of the Foreignfeelers than between the attics of the Starrovers and the quarters of the Marvelers. They were far from each other in every sense of the word. The Foreignfeelers devoted themselves to the state of having returned home, to the harvesting of their experiences. Ascensions to the bounds of the universe were included in the exercises of Xenospastics but they were made only rarely and with fear and trembling. The reason for that was not so much the age of the Foreignfeelers, who were in the last sixty years of Astromental life; the reason lay rather in their keener consciousness, their increased sensitiveness, and a strange susceptibility, one of the unfortunate consequences of Chronosophy. Whenever man transcends his limits—and he is the only creature capable of doing that—he always finds a barrier that stops him. In the beginnings of mankind, when the first experiments with X-rays were being made, the technicians lost their fingers. Later on they learned to protect themselves against the deleterious effects of the rays. In this instance the barrier could be moved farther. But I ask myself the mysterious, unanswerable question whether Zingarelli, Beethoven, Smetana, and many another musician did not lose his physical hearing because he transcended the limits of inner hearing. However that may be, the Foreignfeelers, the veterans of interstellar and internebular worlds, were afflicted with a disease that partially or wholly

crippled and paralyzed many of them. I have forgotten the
name of the disease. It seemed to be a sort of cosmic arthritis.
Its victims could no longer "ascend."

But even the healthy ones in the Lamasery of the Foreignfeelers did not wear the same expression of divine amazement on
their features as their colleagues in the upper stories of the
Djebel, the mature Marvelers. Their facial expression was quite
different and much harder to describe than that of divine astonishment. It was the expression of men who feel permanently,
unalterably, almost professionally strange. This feeling of foreign-
ness never left them, but now and then, in some cases daily, it
became intensified into violent attacks, so-called Xenospasms.
No one of us has ever heard of a "Xenospasm." The word is
unknown, but the thing itself is a familiar human condition.
Ordinary nostalgia in its double form, for example, yearning for
a distant place and longing for a past time is a typical case of
Xenospasm. This familiar sensation is much more complicated
and is much more capable of intensification than one is inclined
to imagine. The nostalgia of a retired old sea dog for his ship
that is still seaworthy, is a fairly simple matter. The nostalgia of
a refugee for his fatherland is much more complex, because he
knows perfectly well that what he has lost changes with every
passing hour and therefore becomes irretrievable. The impossibility of its real appeasement is the spice of every respectable case
of nostalgia, just as the hopelessness of retrieving what is gone
and lost is the pungent spice of exile.

The paroxysms of the Xenospasts were not foreign to the emotions of a life in exile; I drew the analogy for this reason. At
the same time I want to make it clear that the Chronosophers
were by no means homesick for the cosmic spaces which they
could no longer visit. Their nostalgia had no object or aim. They
looked upon the entire material universe as a place of exile.
Xenospasm was exactly the same as the ecstatically hymnic state
on a less active but spiritually higher scale. It surpassed the
state of approving ecstasy, which deceived itself because it knew
no limits. The Xenospasts, however, who had penetrated to the

limits of creation, often felt these limits more strongly than
creation. As we stood before one of the small musing cells far
beneath the surface on the lowest levels of the Lamasery, we saw
an old Foreignfeeler standing there with lowered head and
tensely motionless features, heedless of us and of his surroundings. Our Guide gave us an explanation in loud tones—he knew
that the Xenospast would not hear him—that moved me deeply
and at the same time provoked me to laughter. This man, he
said, had devised and worked out to the last detail ninety-seven
creations, all of which were better than the existing one. He was
constantly engaged in impressing his deductions and arguments
on his mind, so that he would be able to explain and defend his
point of view to the Creator of the world if he should have the
opportunity to do so in the beyond.

"I'm afraid," I said softly to B.H., "that even less important
creators than the Creator of the world neither welcome criticism
nor accept suggestions."

This, I must say, was the only case in the entire Djebel that
might be open to suspicion of irreverence. Most of the sages
whom I observed had unspeakably gentle, deeply moved, resigned, and pious smiles on their faces. Some of the Foreignfeelers, like the Marvelers, occasionally left the Djebel and went
down into the houses of men. They brought with them not the
vital counsel of the enthusiastic Marvelers, but the moderating
words of those who knew the limits.

As we passed a certain spot in the lower regions the Official
Guide remarked, "And now we have entered the realm of the
Arachnodrome."

I noticed that the lower down we went in our inspection of
the Djebel, the less there was to see. In the upper reaches that
belonged to youth, our eyes had been held by the astrogymnastic
exercises, pantomimes, and ballets. In the central regions we had
been permitted to enter the eternal light of the Hall of Hymns
and to see its unending festive procession. Down here, among the
Foreignfeelers, there was practically nothing to see but the faces

of silent men, smooth and ageless like all the others, and yet consumed by unequaled emotions.

At the word "Arachnodrome" I pricked up my ears. The Monolingua was a bit careless in its use of the Greek ending "–drome," which is really supposed to express "running motion." The word "Sephirodrome," for example, meant library, although books are rarely in the habit of trotting around like horses in the Hippodrome. By analogy, therefore, Arachnodrome probably meant something like "realm of spiders." And that was what I found it to be, down here in the depths of the Djebel, in the final corridors of the Xenospastic Lamasery.

We had already noted in the world outside the Djebel that no variety of animals had undergone such remarkable development as the insects. It's not up to me to explain this fact biologically; I have my hands quite full merely trying to describe what I saw on my brief visit to this strange world. It is evident, however, that the available food supply for animals had been materially reduced. I don't know what varieties of mammals could have subsisted on the pasturage of the irongray grass. The capricornettes, ovettes, and whatever other diminutive ruminants might disport themselves in the Park of the Worker and his clan, seemed to me to play the role of goldfish rather than of useful domestic animals, in spite of the excellent sweet milk which they supplied. We know that the birds of the air had long been extinct. The air, even in its lower strata, was much too pure and clear to be as hospitable as it once had been. The dogs, amalgamated into a single mixed breed, chattered in the Monolingua with humanish eloquence. Concerning the family of cats we will hear an incredible episode in just a little while. It was said that there were even a few wild, that is, undomesticated, animals in existence. But since the entire inhabited earth had been transformed into a city, an underground Panopolis, even a poor little fox in his concealed burrow had become a city dweller. And if there still chanced to be such a thing as a forest on this leveled globe and if there was still a deer in this forest, it was undoubtedly another inverted plural, like the Worker or the Idiot or the Jew, namely the Deer of the Era. Many indications pointed clearly to a victory of the insect class. Insects could subsist very well on the irongray sod. But they also had at their disposal the gardens with the dark leathery foliage and the thick waxy blooms, as well as the houses themselves with hundreds of filmy robes and other nourishing textiles. In view of this luxuriant food supply no zoologist will be surprised to learn that certain varieties of insects and related orders had increased remarkably in size and beauty. And among the most highly developed of these was the order of spiders.

Many a reader will no doubt be filled with loathing at the thought. That's simply because he does not have the Astromental man's attitude toward the spider but connects it with all sorts of horrid nursery tales and obsolete superstitions. For the cosmically expert sages in the Djebel, however, the spider was almost sacred, a hieratic animal. Why? In the first place, the spider is the physical image of the star in the animal kingdom; its body consists of a rounded core from which its long limbs radiate in all directions. The spider is unique among animals in respect to this form. In the second place, from its inwards the spider emits a white thread by means of which it fashions a net in which it hangs like a star in its network of rays. The spider thus symbolizes the creative process of the emission of "radiant energy," the scientific name for light. In the third place, suspended in the center of its radiating web, the spider calmly waits for its victims, flies, gnats, and moths. It never moves, for its prey is bound to fall within its grasp. Thus the spider symbolizes the star's force of gravitation, the fundamental universal force called "attraction," that maintains the original creative impulse in motion and balance. Because of these characteristics the Chronosophers revered the spiders as astrosymbols and kept a few particularly splendid varieties in the quiet rooms and halls of the lower Djebel, feeding and breeding them as the Brahmans did their sacred cows. The reader, whose loathing has not been dispelled by the above arguments, should remember that these spiders had practically no resemblance to those which he knows and detests. The largest of them were about the size of a human palm. Their circular bodies gleamed like silver, like moonstones, or like opals. They looked like bright jewels on the dark walls. The snow-white webs swayed slowly and majestically from the gloom of the vaulted ceilings. Each of the giant spiders had the name of a star, and the oldest Xenospasts, whom we met down here, proudly and eagerly pointed out individual ones to us.

As I stared at the ceiling B.H. suddenly nudged me. I noticed a group of men gliding smoothly and weightlessly past us. The leader of the group was a medium-sized, slightly corpulent gentleman who concealed his face in his violet veil robe. The Official Guide stood aside with inclined head. The others too had recognized the Geoarchon. Only grave anxiety could have roused him from his couch in the Sentry Booth and driven him to the Djebel. He was obviously returning from a consultation with the High Floater. The next one to be received in audience, they told me, was—I.

* * * * *
* * *
*

EVERY HUMAN HAD THE LEGALLY PRESCRIBED PRIV-ILEGE of seeing the High Floater of his era once in his life-time and to ask him three well-considered and keenly focused questions. At the "Chancellery Gate," also known as the "Office-Door," the Official Guide proudly informed me that I had been granted the same privilege by court verdict, although my existence was of dubious nature. He warned me to give serious thought to my three questions. It was the exact reverse of the legend of Oedipus and the Sphinx and of all similar legends. The knowing monster did not question the ignorant wayfarer, but the ignorant wayfarer questioned the knowing monster. Besides, the whole business of the questions had no tragic consequences as it did in the antique tales. The High Floater did not have to kill himself, unlike the Sphinx, if only for the reason that there was no conceivable human question that he could not have answered. I have repeatedly mentioned that I was quite unaware of my duty as an explorer and I never thought for a moment of the possibility of a return home from this most incredible future into an equally incredible past. Still I made up my mind at once to prepare three questions of decisive significance. To my great satisfaction the Official Guide gave me a legal interpretation on the subject; he said that it was not merely a matter of three brief formal questions, but that everyone was entitled to elucidation of three subjects that were close to his heart. For this purpose it was permissible, within discreet limits, to ask a few secondary or subordinate questions of importance.

Finally I found myself all alone in the locality known as the "Chancellery" or the "Comptoir." Relying on my old acquaintance with these words, I had expected something totally different. I had expected a sober, reasonably light room with a few desks and a bierlike couch for the High Floater, in short, something corresponding to the Sentry Booth of the Geoarchon and Selenozusian. My expectation was not entirely unjustified, for I understood enough about Astromental society to know that there were four hierarchies that functioned side by side: the ecclesiastical, represented by the Grand Bishop; the political, in the person of the Geoarchon; the economic, managed by the Worker; and the cosmological, administered in the Djebel by the Chronosophers and their head, the High Floater. For the explorer the last of the four hierarchies was undoubtedly the most original of all; still I don't want to minimize the unusual character of the Worker and his malachite Valley of Springs and Forces. But the room that was called the "Chancellery" or the "Comptoir" was not at all what I had expected it to be; even the illumination was not moderately bright but dusky and shadowy. The room was not a sober cube but a sort of grotto carved from faintly luminous rock. I had seen rooms like this, that gave the impression of caves, in medieval houses and castles in the world from which I had come. Of all human handiwork that I had seen in the Mental world, this Office seemed to be the oldest and the most unartificial. I assumed that we were deeper in the bowels of the earth than the deepest mine shaft of my day, and that they had left the living rock in the mighty foundations of the Djebel in its natural state without desecrating it by smooth, manmade walls. The room was indeed much larger than even the most spacious office and particularly much higher. It was as high as the nave of an ancient church. I noticed at once that the gravitational force was turned up fairly high, for I could scarcely drag myself across the room with bent back and sagging knees to the big wooden cot that stood in the center of the office, flecked with silvery light and flickering shadows. I dropped on the couch and stretched out on my back immediately; it was the only way to neutralize my overweight. My eyes swept the rock walls in search of the door through which the High Floater would enter. But I could not even find the narrow Office-Door through which I had entered.

Gradually I became aware that this room was not really an office in which the activities of the Lamaseries were coordinated, but rather a treasure chamber, the treasure chamber of the Arachnodrome. Wherever the pale silver twilight flickered over the walls and arches, gossamer webs hung, and in them the rarest, strangest, most beautiful spiders that the Mental world brought forth. Among them were not only splendid specimens of the great silver spiders that I had seen in the Lamasery of the Xenospasts, but many other entirely new and unusual species of the victorious star-arachnids. I was struck by the extraordinary beauty of the webs, which hung far down from the vaulted ceiling like fishnets or hammocks of light beams. They swayed back and forth in a slow rhythm, an indescribably sovereign motion that held the eye of the observer. Firmly convinced that the High Floater would have to enter the room through a door like anyone else, I paid no particular attention to a round dark bundle that I could barely see through the spider webs in a shadowy corner of the vaulted ceiling. This big bundle which, for no good reason, I took at first to be a huge kettledrum, clung firmly and motionlessly to the vault so that it almost disappeared in the shadows. I never suspected for an instant that this dark, immovable spheroid could be a man and that the word "High Floater" was not a figure of speech.

Of course I was familiar with the concept of "levitation," mysterious elevation in space, as I lay on the Office couch, breathing deeply in order to offer more resistance to the increased gravitation in the room. There are countless documents irrefutably attesting this peculiar phenomenon throughout world history, which of course ends for me with the twentieth century. Damis, the companion of Apollonius of Tyana, as early as the first century of our era, assures us that he saw certain highly developed Brahmans in India cheerfully floating ten ells above the ground while the crowds bartering in the bazaars close by were not particularly disturbed by the sight. The Neoplatonic philosopher Iamblichus around the year 300, an antagonist of Christianity incidentally, is the first Roman citizen of whom it was reported that he could rise to a height of four feet from the ground in the course of his meditations. Stephano Maconi, a skeptical layman and medic, says in an eyewitness account of Saint Catherine of Siena (1347-1380) that "whenever her soul was exalted in prayer for something divine, her body was also lifted up, and in this floating condition she was seen by many people, including also me." This phenomenon of levitation is ascribed, however, not only to Buddhist initiates, Neoplatonic mystics, and Catholic saints, but also to quite ordinary persons, as for example, to Anna Fleischer of Freiberg, concerning whom the Protestant Dean Möller relates as follows in his description of the city of Freiberg: "She was an epileptic and subject to violent hallucinations. In the presence of Messrs. Dachsel and Waldinger she was suddenly lifted up from her bed, body, head, and feet, to a height of two and a half ells and remained thus floating freely, so that those present cried to God, seized her, and dragged her down, for it appeared as though she were about to float out the open window."

It would be a simple matter to augment these random examples of attested mystic elevation by a hundred more (as, for example, the manifestations of the famous Scotsman Home in the seventies of the nineteenth century), and yet they would not have the slightest bearing on the sort of levitation from which the High Floater of this era derived his curious but appropriate title. His elevation in space was not caused by any mystical or strangely epileptic abnormality of the human body, but, if I may express it so, it was the natural result of a century and a half of inspired and completely devoted Chronosophic exertions. The High Floater was so thoroughly at home in the Intermundia of all degrees that his final repatriation on our planet was not a complete success. For a long time his body had been incapable of coming to terms with Mother Earth's gravitation. The forces of attraction of the most remote stars pulled and tugged at him and sought incessantly to steal him away from the earth. No matter in what part of a house he might be, he always flew up to the ceiling like a toy balloon and nestled in a corner up there with his face always turned to the wall. I never suspected that the round dark bundle, the abnormally large kettledrum hanging up there in the cruciform vault, was a living being until I heard a deep sigh and saw a smooth, gleaming, bald head peering for an instant from the mysterious bundle.

In a flash I saw it all. The High Floater of the era had not even noticed my arrival in the Office. Presumably they had chosen the worst possible moment for my audience and had not even noticed that the chief of all Foreignfeelers was just suffering a violent Xenospasm. I was very much embarrassed. Was it proper for me to lie on my back in the presence of the High Floater up there? But I was incapable of standing politely erect in this immoderately high gravitation. On the other hand, this excessive degree of gravitation was the only means of making mundane life even reasonably bearable for the Archixenospast, although it was still not turned up high enough to entice him down from the ceiling and make him feel at home on the floor like other people. I meditated: Is it my right or even my duty to call his attention to me? Or would I be tearing the gossamer web of his lofty thoughts and feeling? After two minutes of indecision I did as every customer in a little store does when he finds that the proprietor has stepped out into the next room; I cleared my throat and coughed loudly and hypocritically a couple of times, meanwhile keeping my fascinated eye fixed on the large round bundle up there. The latter began to move slowly. The shiny pate protruded as from a snail's shell, remarkably short limbs appeared, another deep sigh proved the existence of a painful life, and then a soft, high-pitched voice said, "Please don't go away. I'm coming."

As though it were being lowered by an invisible thread, the queer spherical figure floated down toward me and remained suspended a short distance over the foot-end of my cot. I recognized at once that the High Floater was a cripple with bulging deformities on his chest and back and with withered little hands and feet which were probably quite useless. He had presumably been crippled by astral arthritis, the disease whose name I have forgotten. But perhaps this disease was only a process well known in all natural history that caused the gradual atrophy of organs that are no longer used and have therefore lost their purpose. Naturally the High Floater had no practical use for his arms and legs, since he never walked but floated in the air. Celestial gout might be a very painful malady, yet it pointed toward a rationalization of the human body for new purposes. Perhaps the Djebel and the practice of Chronosophy were even now laying the foundations for a much, much later radical metamorphosis of mankind, a race of men who would live underground like Mental men, but who would go about their business floating around in the air like toy balloons. Of course, this would require a corporeality adapted to a floating existence, indications of which were already present in the spherical cripple hovering above me. I quickly shoved the idea aside, for not I, but

B.H., the professional reincarnatee, would have to test my theory in some dim future, perhaps not before the Thirteenth Cosmic Capital Year of Virgo.

The High Floater came to rest about a foot and a half above the foot-end of my cot. He did it by paddling in the air from time to time with his atrophied hands and feet, in a manner similar to that of a good swimmer treading water; but he curiously reversed the swimmer's motion and paddled upward instead of downward in order to avoid being carried up into the air. These motions, his bulging chest and back, his perfectly round, smooth, and shiny head without eyebrows and lashes, his light, slightly reddened, convex eyes, and his wide mouth drawn down at the corners with concealed pain—all this combined to give me the impression of a divine sun-fish.

I tried to rise to indicate my reverence. He made violent paddling motions with his little hands to bid me to lie still. At the same time he kindled a friendly smile in the depths of his goggle-eyes, a smile that courageously conquered his astral gout, his Xenospasm, and his cosmic indifference and inattention. As a living witness of the beginnings of mankind I might be a five-star hit at a Mental wedding feast; for him, I and my hundred thousand years were at best an annoyance and at worst a torment. What could I give him? What did I know that he didn't know? We, that is, I and a few readers, will feel a shudder of awe in a few moments to realize that he knew far more about me than I knew about myself, and by no means in a groping psychoanalytic fashion, but practically and factually.

Since he did not permit me to rise from the couch where the full force of intensified gravitation held me prostrate, I saluted him with a nod of my head and a grateful glance.

"The first question is expected," he said in his high, toneless voice that reminded me of the radiator hiss of voices in the Gray Neuter. I knew that I would have to collect my wits in order not to abuse his suffering patience. I tried, therefore, to formulate my three questions as tersely as possible. The form of address that I would use in speaking to the High Floater pre-

sented a somewhat knotty problem. If I had been an Englishman
or an American I would have solved the quite insignificant problem with a coolly distant, official "sir." Being neither an Englishman nor an American but a Central European, born in a mon-
archy, and having long outgrown my revolutionary adolescence,
I regarded it as boorish to withhold appropriate honors and titles
from an official personage. Suddenly I remembered the humble
old chaplain of a Bohemian aristocratic family who could not
bear to have the Count call him "Your Reverence," while he was
supposed to address his illustrious employer merely as "Count."
In his distress the old Czech priest became creative and invented a form of address that actually didn't exist at all, namely,
"Your High-Grace." No title seemed to me more appropriate for
the Chief Chronosopher of the era. And so I prefaced the first
of my three questions with the address "Your High-Grace" and
said, "Are there any angels and is there such a thing as infinitely disguisable protomaterial from which they are created?"

As I spoke these words, timidly and with palpitations, I noted
for the first time the noble, refined beauty that radiated from
the High Floater in spite of his deformities, his spherical skull,
his bulging eyes, and his pale, too smooth Buddha face. He
looked at me sadly, and I felt that he was weighing my worth
and found me too light. He had been drawn up a few feet
higher and he had to tread air and paddle a little to get near me
again.

"Why does one wish confirmation," he asked, "of that which
one has seen with his own eyes?"

"Because one lacks the courage of one's convictions, Your High-
Grace," I replied.

The Floater revolved about his own axis a few times, and it
looked as though he were sitting on an invisible piano stool with
his short little legs. He was not attired in pastel-colored veils
like average Mental men but in a dark cowl such as I had seen
not only on official dignitaries but also on Mutarians as well as
on Marvelers and Foreignfeelers. I failed to understand the tired,
mechanical twisting movement of the High Floater, but it had a

hint of Comet Calisthenics in it. Quite a while elapsed before I saw what I was to see. Something was dancing around the pale Buddha head, something that only an astigmatic without glasses could take at first for insects, large moths, Lepidoptera, or even small bats. Very soon, however, even my poor eyes recognized that these supposed little animals were nothing of the sort but that they rather resembled the little sun ringlets and cringlets with a black dot in the center that glide across our field of vision when the optic nerve has been irritated by pressure or glaring light. What I saw, however, did not vanish but grew and became more distinct. It moved in columns from the Buddha head obliquely toward my own. And suddenly I observed flowing cloaks and draperies in the moving columns. They were strangely rigid and inarticulated, to be sure, and they moved as though they had no autonomous motion but were being moved, almost pushed, from outside. At the same time I knew and saw that similar phantoms were moving in serried columns from my head to that of the High Floater, among them also these rigid, unfinished, flowing cloaks and draperies.

"Are those perhaps angels that we two are sending out?" I exclaimed excitedly.

The Floater paddled a little, staring at me from the goggle-eyes between the reddened lids. I couldn't tell whether he was smiling because he was in pain or because he was bored.

After a brief pause the high, toneless voice rang again, and in the single sentence which it uttered I felt the urge to clarify the subject with the utmost precision and the opposite urge to shroud it in a manner appropriate to the arcane. The High Floater spoke thus: "We send out toward each other what stirs within us. Only the wise man perceives what is not to be perceived."

Then I blurted out the question I could not repress. "Does that mean that the angels in the Intermundia are the impulses, the emitted thoughts, feelings, concepts, desires, and fancies of God——"

"The angels in heaven," the High Floater interrupted me with a definite note of pedantry, carefully avoiding the word "God," "the angels in heaven are communications of that which is outside the world with that which is inside the world."

"Then the self-assurance of the Melangeloi was no self-deception," I exclaimed in a loud voice.

"The first question is answered," said the High Floater and, "The second question is expected."

He was right. The first question was fully answered. Although the purport of the High Floater's reply about the angels was exactly the same as the official answer in any catechism and differed only in form, still I felt wonderfully satisfied, as though an impenetrable truth had been proved to me mathematically. I knew—no, more than that—I had seen the visible fact with my own eyes that our thoughts, feelings, concepts, desires, and fancies are angels that man sends out as communications, as a spirit realm of our own productivity, and it was this fact that made me so happy. We too, like the Creator, emitted plastic protomaterial. That was the real basis of all higher activity of life and of the spirit. How I longed for an hour of contemplation in order to absorb fully this truth that the High Floater had given me. But I had the definite feeling that I ought to hurry; without a doubt the divine sun-fish suffered torment when he had to answer questions instead of nestling up against the vaulted ceiling like a toy balloon. I therefore immediately proceeded to question Number Two, "What is the shape of the universe?"

That was short and to the point, perhaps a little too short and snappy. Displeasure crossed the Buddha face, and the corners of its mouth sagged even farther while the little hands paddled angrily.

"Why does one search out secrets?" the High Floater asked.

"Do the dead know this secret?" I parried.

"The dead are the reunited. They do not know it, but they are in the midst of the secret," he retorted.

"I was dead until just recently and therefore in the midst of the secret. Doesn't that give me a right to question Number Two, Your High-Grace?"

The High Floater was silent. I tried to build a bridge.

"So the whole does not have the shape of the parts," I groped along, trying to interpret his silence, "that is, not the shape of the star, the spheroid, the orb flattened at the poles, the form of greatest tension with the least surface?"

His silence grew oppressive. I was on the point of canceling the all-too audacious question that I had asked the mortal who had penetrated to the bounds of space. My mouth was already open to utter question Number Three when the high, toneless voice unexpectedly said, "The whole has the shape of man."

Now it was my turn to be silent, thrilled by an unknown emotion that constricted my breath. I do not know how much time passed before I asked one of the permitted subordinate questions, "Does that mean that we live in the heart or navel of a human figure consisting of moving stars and star nebulae, just as we consist of moving unicles, achads, and monads?"

"The whole has the shape of man," the toneless voice retorted with a definite hiss, as though it were unnecessary to vary a reply that covered and explained everything. I, however, became stubbornly entangled in more subordinate questions.

"Does that confirm the vision of the Prophet Ezekiel who saw a human figure hovering over the throne of God? Or has Chronosophic science verified the profoundest insight of the Cabalistic Book Sohar, which speaks of Adam Kadmon, the cosmic Adam, who is identical with heaven, the first creation of God?"

My excitement gave voice to a cataract of questions. For the High Floater, however, these secondary and subordinate questions were mere redundancies that he was not legally required to answer, for he now repeated the all-embracing sentence for the third time, "The whole has the shape of man."

I closed my eyes. I collected my wits. I felt that my next secondary question would have to be very carefully phrased, lest I appear as a shabby opportunist. The cosmos in human form had been one of the earliest dreams of my youth, long before I had heard anything about Sohar or about the Cabala and its celestial human, Adam Kadmon, whose body consists of

stars and universes just as ours consists of protons and electrons.
And now, a hundred thousand years later, I found my youthful
inspiration confirmed by the empiric science of Chronosophy,
after I had regarded it as ludicrously fantastic throughout my
entire adult life. Furthermore, it furnished the natural explanation of the expansion and contraction, the breathing of the universe. But weren't there still many difficulties to surmount before
we reached the pure truth? First of all, was our human shape
fixed and final? By no means. Descriptive anatomy and phys-
iology were not to be disregarded, and they had taught us eons
ago that there were tremendous differences between the human
form of Pithecanthropus erectus and the human form of modern
man. Could the cosmos possibly have a face with a horribly
receding forehead and with cannibalistic jaws? I opened my eyes
and looked at the High Floater who was maintaining his balance
by treading air diagonally above me. And suddenly I knew that
we earthmen were still far from having attained our final cosmic
human shape, and that even the High Floater with his spherical
Buddha's head, with his atrophied extremities, and with his body
that was in the process of metamorphosis for the purpose of floating locomotion, had not yet attained the final goal of this development. A certain timidity, however, prevented me from
basing my next subordinate question on this important group
of ideas. I passed on to another phase of the subject.

"If the whole has the shape of man," I enunciated carefully,
"then there must be two entities, there must be a male and a
female universe."

"The whole is wedded to itself," the High Floater declared
with surprising promptness and without his customary reluctance.

For the flashing fraction of a second these words revealed
the basis of the sacramental sanctity of human wedlock and the
reason why true marriages are made in heaven, as the proverb
says. At the same time I asked a rather impudent question and
I fully deserved and expected to be snubbed.

"If the whole is wedded to itself, doesn't the positive or negative electric charge of all things indicate the sex distinction of matter?"

"The second question is answered," the high, toneless voice rebuked me. "The third question is long overdue."

All right, you asked for it, I thought to myself; for despite my reverence for the High Floater I had prepared a question with which I expected to trap him. Aren't all question and answer games contests, and isn't that the only thing that makes them attractive? I had just heard the solution of world riddles from the lips of the Chief Chronosopher. But since I had only been permitted to visit the elementary class for boys in the Lower Intermundium, I would never be able to make a personal test of the accuracy of his solution. It would be a simple matter for me, however, to test the correctness of his answer to my third and last question, just as it would be much more difficult for him to find this answer than the solution of the world riddles. So I asked my third question and repeated it a second time, "What was the most important moment of my life?"

I asked myself this question at the same time and applied the full power of my imagination to the stream of recollections that passed in most vivid review before the eye of my soul. If the High Floater would make use of one of these recollections, then I would win the contest, then I would have trapped him, for Mental progress was largely based on thought transference and clairvoyance. In order to convince me he would have to startle me with something utterly unexpected; he would have to tell me something that I had irretrievably forgotten. But what scenes and images did I conjure up in the search for the most important moment of my life, an undertaking that had never attracted me before now? Naturally I knew that the great dramatic occurrences, emotions, and decisions are not the most important moments, and that tiny, insignificant, barely perceptible causes frequently produce momentous consequences. Yet I cannot say why these particular things occurred to me instead of something equally important or unimportant; at any rate, the incidents that reached my consciousness astonished even me.

I saw myself, for example, as a twelve-year-old, standing on the slippery quai of the absurdly small river harbor in my native city. At times this harbor was visited by skiffs and tugboats that came "directly from Hamburg," from the sea, from the ocean, perhaps from America, the America of James Fenimore Cooper and of the Leather-stocking Tales. One day a fairly good-sized tugboat lay moored there that gave me an impression of perfectly overwhelming seaworthiness. It had been freshly caulked and smelled intoxicatingly of tar. It had a beautifully curved deck cabin and splendid brassbound bull's eyes, and a "genuine hatch" through which one could reach the interior by way of a "genuine companionway." My heart pounded wildly—and that's no mere figure of speech—at sight of this ocean-going vessel. Few things in my later life attracted and lured me as the thought of an ocean steamer in my boyhood days. I frequently played hooky in order to hang around the inland harbor of our wide but shallow Moldava River. On this particular day a young woman suddenly stepped out of the door of the beautifully curved deck cabin. She was pretty well curved herself; she had a broad, vulgar face, a short nose, thick lips, and carelessly pinned up black hair. As I lay on my cot I could visualize this face with all its character-istics of cheap prettiness. The young woman was wearing big ear bangles, her dress was slovenly, and she was barefooted. This fact merely enhanced her siren qualities. She must be a Spanish woman, I thought with a thrill as I hugged my schoolbooks to my chest. At this moment the "Spanish woman" noticed me, puckered her lips, and motioned me to come to her. Although I was timid by nature I ran up the gangway without any hesi-tation and for the first time in my life I felt the planks of a sea-going vessel under my feet. The only later sensation that sur-passed this experience was when I felt the boards of a stage under my feet for the first time. The woman seemed to understand what went on inside me, for she laughed and pressed me to her capacious bosom. She smelled strongly of sweat and of a vile perfume. For me, however, the mixture was intoxicating. "Come along, young man," she said, and it didn't sound Spanish at all but like good plain Saxon dialect. It was the old story of the cabin boy. But nothing could have kept me from going along, not the thought of my father and mother, of school, or of my future. I threw my bundle of books aside in order to have my hands clear for any work that might be demanded of me. My fate hung in the balance, for never in all my later life was I ready as at this moment to vanish utterly, to alter my life radically— and probably more on account of the beautifully curved cabin than on account of the beautifully curved lady. A vehement old seaman with a Hindenburg mustache decided the matter for me by chasing me ashore with a volley of curses, but that did not change the fact that I had lived through an important moment of my life.

Why I brought the following recollection up out of the depths as I lay on the couch in the High Floater's Office is even more incomprehensible to me. Mean and shabby as my moral failure was in the case of the young Frenchman Benoît, I will have much worse things to answer for when the big balance sheet is made up at the end of time. We were both more than nineteen years old, Benoît and I, and we had blown in a lot of money; that is, we had blown in Benoît's money, for my father wasn't very liberal with me and my pockets were usually empty. While we were having our good time—and it probably wasn't as good as we tried to make ourselves believe—I had given Benoît my word to return the money to him down to the last penny. Then I went back home and thought no more of it. It was the middle of August. At the end of September I was to enter military service. Suddenly Benoît put in an appearance. He reminded me of my promise in an amiable manner and suggested that I make a full confession to my father so that he might settle my debt. I knew that Benoît was a pedantically precise person but I didn't believe that he actually needed the money. As far as my father was concerned, he was a good father. I know that much more deeply today than in my youth when he often annoyed me with his fully justified but bitterly carping criticism. In the matter of making debts, however, he was not to be trifled with. He him-

self had suffered a severe reverse through a debt which he had
not contracted himself but which he had innocently assumed
from the bankruptcy of his own father, and with the excitable
pathos of a fortunately stable era he had regarded this reverse
as civil shipwreck. I put Benoît off from day to day because I
didn't have the courage to tell my father that I had contracted a
debt, wantonly and unnecessarily, merely for the sake of illicit
pleasures, when he had innocently assumed the debt of another.
Those were terrible days. Benoît's thoroughly justified scorn
became more and more apparent. One evening it happened
that my father, Benoît, and I were eating dinner together.
Benoît's eyes rested more and more accusingly on me and finally
he began to make indignant signs that I was finally to open my
mouth and speak up. My father seemed to feel the tension. He
raised his head, looked at us intently, and finally asked, "Is
something not in order between you two?" Consciously or unconsciously he built a bridge with these words and anyone who
would not take advantage of it was a stinker and a louse and a
dirty coward. And I was all three of these things, and whenever
I think of my quick, evasive answer, "No, Papa, nothing," I always
grind my teeth at the recollection of this permanently frozen
moment that passed judgment on me for all time to come, even
though I gathered up my courage later on and made a confession.

These were only two of the many moments that passed in review before me as I lay on the cot in the Office of the High
Floater. Even more numerous were the disconnected images and
fragments of tableaux flashing through my mind, all of which
had been of significance in my life. I looked, for instance, through
the garden gate of the Home for Incurables on the Vyschehrad
and saw the goat-man standing there on all fours, with his fox-
red whiskers and his shamelessly elevated hind-end—a sight that
first opened my eyes to the terrible abyss and the demonic possibilities of nature. But I'll say no more of such loathsome images,
moments, inspirations, and experiences; it will be better to take
them back to the grave with me as secrets. For another, more

complete story demanded the attention of my memory, an incident that I believed I had forgotten long ago. But now, as I lay heavily on the couch in the High Floater's Office, it suddenly seemed to me not only a highly important moment in my life, but also most suitable for testing the Chief Chronosopher by setting a trap for him. The occurrence was of external rather than psychological nature, and its details began to take on such vivid clarity that I was sure any ordinary mind reader, not to mention the High Floater, could pick it out of my mind with the greatest ease.

At that time too I was lying stretched out. I was stretched out in my sleeping bag of black oilcloth. My sleeping bag and I were lying on a bed. It was a wretched bed in a tiny, smelly room. I had rented this room shortly before from a Polish widow by the name of Pozñanská who moaned all day long about her houses that had been destroyed by the war. The house with my room had not been destroyed although our Austrian front had run right through the middle of this little Ukrainian town for some time. Ordinarily I have a very poor memory for rooms. This time, however, my recollection was so vivid that even after these endless years I could have put every object in this miserable hole-in-the-wall in its proper place. Perhaps that was because on this memorable night an extravagant full moon was beaming through the open window. This full moon was probably also the reason for a secret order we had received from Division Headquarters the day before to the effect that our entire "Northern Artillery Section" was to be on the alert because the full-scale offensive of the enemy, the Russian General Brusilov, was expected at any moment. Presently forgotten names from the First World War began to pop into my mind. For weeks we had been attacking and counterattacking around the famous "Worobiowka Heights," Hill 310, about two kilometers from my sleeping quarters. I saw my uniform blouse hanging over one of the two wooden chairs. The red collar tabs with the three white stars gleamed in the moonlight. They signified the rank I had finally attained, that of Sergeant in the Imperial-Royal Heavy

Field Howitzer Regiment No. 15, attached to the Northern Artillery Section.

I distinctly remembered an unessential detail which I elaborated in my fancy, partly to entice the High Floater more deeply into my story and partly because it reawakened a definite feeling of pleasure. On the stool next to my bed stood an alarm clock. In spite of the moonlight its phosphorescent dial gleamed. Phosphorescent dials were a fairly new invention at that time. And here was the most pleasurable sensation in the life of a soldier: the clock told me that I had a few more hours of sleep. At five-thirty I would have to wade through fifty yards of bottomless mud to our telephone shanty and relieve my partner at the switchboard. There's nothing more wonderful in the midst of a hard and strenuous life than to awaken with the feeling that morning has come and to find that it is still the middle of the night and that there is still an eternity of sleep ahead. Sleep, especially the deep sleep of youth, is man's sweet self-embrace. I wasn't afraid of the barrage that might start at any moment of this fine night. I wasn't afraid of the infantry attack of the reinforced Russian army that was to drive us across the endless beet fields of this countryside in disorderly retreat only a few hours later. I was not even afraid of captivity, although I mechanically felt for the leather pouch that hung from a cord around my neck. In this pouch my mother had sewed a few gold pieces in case I should be taken captive. I distinctly remembered falling asleep again, cheerful and carefree, my head on my arms.

And I remembered just as distinctly that much had changed when I wakened, or rather, when I was wakened, an hour later. The dial of my clock no longer glowed, for the moon shone into the room even more brightly than before. But that was not all. Not only the moon and ticking time shared Pani Poznańská's hole-in-the-wall with me. Someone had climbed in through the open window, had moved one of the wooden chairs next to my bed, and sat there looking at me. It was a soldier. Who else could it have been? Outside of Mrs. Poznańská and a couple of ancient Jews there were no civilians in this front-line town. It was a mud-

bedaubed infantryman who had come straight out of the trench
that ran along the edge of the village. The man had a typical
trench-beard, the kind that grew even on the youngest men,
stubby, bushy, matted, blond in spots, brown in others, and both
in the same square inch. Such uninhibited, luxuriant facial vegetation always reminded me of rolled-up, rusty barbed wire.

The soldier sitting at my bed was in full kit. His rolled pack
bulged above his shoulders. Suspended from two dirty bands
crossed over his chest his canteen hung on the left, his ration
bag on the right. He held the rifle between his knees. He had
drawn the short, sharp bayonet from its scabbard and, much to my
surprise, he carved off a good solid hunk from a loaf of sour-
smelling black bread. The remainder of the loaf he stowed away
methodically in the ration bag. Now he held the thick slice of
bread in his left hand, and with the bayonet in his right he made
painstakingly regular incisions in the slice. I was fascinated by
the skillful manner in which he handled the dry, crumbly, rye-
and-corn war bread so that not a particle fell on the floor. And
now he pushed the first cube of bread into his mouth and began
to chew slowly and thoughtfully. At the same time he kept staring at me intently, unwaveringly, from two very deep-set eyes.
Or rather, he didn't stare at me with any kind of eyes, but with
two attentive, shadowy, black spots. It was a horribly dismal
stare. I felt the man's hatred in every slow, taunting motion.
More than hatred. The man was a reproach personified. And
this nameless reproach was directed against me personally, as
though I were responsible for everything, for the grime, the
war, the barrage, and death. I remembered with great clarity
that I accepted the intruder's reproach with all my soul as I lay
there in the moonlight, I, who wasn't any more than he, a common ordinary soldier. I didn't wonder a bit why he had climbed
in my window, of all people, instead of into that of the command-
ing general, or at least of a major or a lieutenant-colonel. Without shifting his gloomy, eyeless stare from me he shoved the
next cube of bread into his mouth with the same hand that held
the bayonet. The man stank of filth and mud and weeks of un-

washedness and also of iodoform, as though he had been
wounded and had a bandage under his uniform. His overcoat
was no longer fieldgray, or rather fieldblue, as Austro-Hungarian
Army regulations prescribed, but yellowish brown, like a plowed
field or an open grave.

I tried to break the spell that held me, to utter a word, to
move my hand. I couldn't. Then I was almost certain that the
soldier here beside me was a dream soldier. Despite the consciousness of danger I closed my eyes for a few seconds in order
to give the dream a chance to dissolve. When I opened them
again the infantryman had leaned his rifle against my bed and
had risen to his full skinny height, as though the time for action
had come. He was no longer chewing. He was only staring. But
his stare was no longer the horribly dismal stare of personified
reproach; it was an objective, calculating stare from small, pale,
real eyes. His right hand was behind his back. His left hand lay
on my chest. It was fingering the leather pouch with the gold
pieces. It was tugging at the cord.

Then I understood at last. I was lying under the knife of a
murderer. And then I managed to scream, "Who are you? What
do you want?"

It is a terrible thing to be lying under the murderer's knife.
Anyone who hasn't experienced it and survived the experience
cannot possibly comprehend it. I lay helpless in the sleeping bag
that prevented me from struggling. As I screamed I knew perfectly well that my scream forced the murderer's hand, that it
compelled him to plunge the concealed bayonet into my breast.
I expected the thrust with deadly certainty.

But the soldier turned his head toward the window. He had
heard something that I had not yet heard. "Military patrol. Room
inspection," he said briefly with a foreign accent.

"Military patrol" was our word for Military Police. I recalled
that I heard these words with relief. My window had been open
and the Military Police on their rounds had checked to see who
was sleeping here. Everything was in order. But in the next
second I knew that this man in the filthy, stinking uniform, in

front-line kit, without a brassard and corporal's insignia, could
never be in command of a military patrol. At last I untangled
myself from the sleeping bag. I leaped to my feet. To the window.
He could be only a few steps away. Many soldiers were running
around outside, buttoning their coats, strapping on their pack-
rolls, shouldering their rifles. "Military patrol," I shouted, but no
one paid any attention, for the Russian barrage had already
begun. A few moments later it had grown into an unbroken, inarticulate roar. The first shells began to drop. The black trees that
were explosions grew out of the ground. A house at the other
end of the street received a full hit.

I dressed calmly. General Brusilov, whose shells whined
through the air, had saved me from the hand of a murderer. It
was really quite illogical that the murderer should have been
frightened off by the artillery fire. In the tumult of battle he
could have gotten my gold pieces with much less danger to himself. At any rate, this was not only a weird but a very important
moment of my life, for life itself had been at stake. This was the
story that I had brought to light and that I spun out in great detail in order to offer it to the High Floater in its full realism.
The recollection had so enthralled me that for a minute or more
I forgot my surroundings.

Now I looked for the High Floater with a curious glance, for
he had moved away meanwhile. He was no longer hovering over
my feet but over my head and he was upside-down so that his
Buddha face stood in the air parallel to my own. Suddenly
something took place that I can illustrate only by invoking a
comparison with a painting by a Spaniard of the baroque school
that hangs, if I am not mistaken, in the Rijksmuseum in Amster-
dam. This painting represents a saint in a state of levitation whose
heart is joined by a silver-white, very substantial ray of light to
the heart of Jesus Christ, who is leaning down from heaven above
him. I was horrified to see a yellowish white thread of some sort
emanating from my breast, and the High Floater was winding
this thread with amazing dexterity on a glass hand-spindle in his
crippled fingers. In this way he very quickly produced a wide

spider web that hung down from the spindle, and it became evident that the thread was no thread at all but a limp, preserved, I could almost call it greased, ray of light. That, I thought, is the most important moment in my life. He is reeling it right out of my heart, and of course it isn't the silly anecdote about the ocean steamer on our little river nor the disgusting confession concerning Benoît, but it's the murder story of the infantryman that I skillfully unwound for him out of the tangled skein of my life. God knows why I picked this one. And now he's going to read it back to me verbatim as I dictated it. All the really important moments seemed to have gone into hiding, like bats at the break of day. Meanwhile the fabric hanging down from the glass spindle had become about as long as a small lace shawl. The High Floater, now hovering five or six feet above me, dropped it, so that it slowly drifted down upon me, much more slowly than an autumn leaf. When the preserved light reached my face, I was. . . .

* * * * *
* * *
*

I WAS . . . WHERE WAS I? First of all, of course, within myself. But this I-myself was no longer what it had been. My tongue did not touch gold on the upper left but a normal line of teeth. I was younger, I was young. I could tell by the beating of my heart, by the tension of my muscles, and for a flashing instant it was a satisfying feeling. Then at once it became a matter of course and was forgotten. Next—long before I saw or heard anything—I discovered a shy embarassment in this new I-myself, a growing nervous torment. What was it that drew me with powerful longing and at the same time made me wish that I were ten thousand miles away from "Here" and many years distant from "Now"? So far I had no idea where this Here and Now had combined. I only knew that I felt like a murderer.

The first thing I saw was the white door that I closed behind me with infinite caution as though by doing so I could postpone

reality a little longer. I had reached this door by way of a long
corridor and I had hesitated for a few long heartbeats before I
knocked and turned the knob. I was expected. I entered into a
deep silence, a much deeper silence than that outside. A bare
white room. Many flowers. A small hospital room. The window
was open. It was in August, four o'clock in the afternoon, and the
humid air of a metropolitan summer day was oppressive. On the
white enameled hospital bed lay the woman whom I love. She
could barely move. She greeted me with a look that combined a
smile of happiness and the horror of the last few days. Her long
blond hair streamed over the pillow. Her face was whiter than
white but her beauty was never more glorious. The woman whom
I love was not my wife, not yet. I was even obliged to act strange
and indifferent in this terrible situation. A nurse was bending
over the crib in which the child lay. I had to restrain myself
to keep from groaning aloud. How could a person be so convinced of his own depravity as I was and still go on living? At
other times I had defended myself against myself by saying: It
takes two. But now I knew that the woman, even as a sinner,
is the heroine and the victim. I was nothing but a frivolous,
thoughtless, irresponsible exploiter of the intoxicating feeling I
called love. How could it be love? Love only begins at the point
where one has something at stake and something to lose. What
did I have to lose? I was a Bohemian or something like that. I
wrote poems and plays, and upon this cheap and ambitious
activity I and the likes of me based the strange claim of ex-
emption from "the civil order." Even at this instant I was sure
that other standards applied to me. At the same time, however, I
was convinced more icily, more cuttingly from moment to
moment, that we two had offended not only against the civil
order but against a higher world order. Man—woman—child—
the holy meeting of these three should not have been like this.
I should not have entered this white room with a smiling nod,
with controlled features like any friend or acquaintance. The last
time we had seen each other was in the lonely house on that
terrible night when she became deathly ill. Three weeks had

passed meanwhile, three weeks when she hovered between life and death, three weeks of operations climaxed by this premature birth. And today, after three terrible weeks, I had finally received permission to see her again, as a good friend like other good friends. I was afraid to look at her, for my self-control was exhausted. One of us would finally have to say something. And then she spoke. But not to me. She was sending the nurse away on an errand. I waited, listening, until the inner door closed, then the outer door, and I sank down on my knees by the bed. This combination of expectant waiting and sudden kneeling struck me as theatrical and made me unhappy, like everything else that I did during these lagging minutes. Her hand stroked my hair. She said: "The child. . . . Your child. . . ."

I rose. I walked on tiptoe to the little crib at the foot of the bed. Was the nurse listening outside? Why was I thinking of the nurse? I was afraid to look at the child. The physician whom I had asked downstairs had shrugged his shoulders. "It can hardly be expected to live." But now I was surprised to find this premature child a complete human, an incredibly developed personality, completely limited by its tiny body but no more identical with it than a painting with its canvas. I looked at the well-formed little hands and fingers. I looked at the delicate, pallid face, the high forehead, the extraordinarily round skull with its pulsating fontanels. And I became absurdly convinced that in this spherical little head there resided a unique, characteristic, independent permanence that was older than twelve days, that was as old as the world. I was the father and this was my little son. I was the cause and here was the effect, and this chain of cause and effect went back to the beginning of things. I should now have felt a solemn attachment, the miracle of the nearest relationship on earth, the poignant pain of impending loss. I felt nothing of the sort although I made a feeble effort to talk myself into it. Ordinarily I was an easy victim to autosuggestion; now I was quite incapable of producing the reactions that the difficult situation demanded. Strangeness and embarrassment were my only sensations. And it was a double embarrassment: once before God and a second time before the independent individuality in the body of this infant. The child was quiet. If it would only cry, everything would be easier. The child was still feverish, its big blue eyes roved. I knew that I had to say something hopeful to its mother. I wanted to give myself some hope too. "We'll get through all right," I said, or something like it.

Once more, one last time, I bent over the round little head. Suddenly I had a feeling of kinship. I knew this feverish little boy. The nurse had returned to the room. I put on my mendaciously innocent face. The woman on the bed said in a soft voice, "When you stepped into the room before, funeral music was being played outside. . . ." These words gave me a chance to walk over to the open window and look outside. The street in front of the hospital was deserted; the trees in the little park were wilted in the drought of the late summer.

"I don't see a thing," I said.

"Please close the window," said the woman.

I closed the window. A silent, dry sob rose in my throat. I pressed my face against the pane. As my forehead touched the cold glass, I was. . . .

I was . . . there's no need to say where.

The High Floater had risen a little higher. He paddled with his little arms and tread the air vigorously, but still he couldn't stay as close to me as before. I couldn't say how much the word "before" meant; that is to say, I didn't know how much time had passed. For all the moments that I had conjured up, and this final moment that I had relived through the High Floater's power, did not run on the tracks of ordinary astronomic clock-time but were spun of their own heterochronic time. The moment might have lasted for hours or for seconds.

"It was just so, just so," I murmured, "my every thought, my every feeling, I mean, my every lack of feeling. . . . And nothing has passed——"

"Passed?" asked the hissing voice of the Intermundia. "What is that?"

The High Floater's triumph over me and my traps was so complete that I couldn't bear to lie still, in spite of the intensified gravitation in the Office. I pushed my heavy feet down from the couch and sat on its edge, hunched over and breathing with difficulty. The Chief Chronosopher of the present world had reeled the faded light thread of a long-forgotten moment from my innermost recesses, a moment I had overcome long ago, but one for which I will have to answer on the day when all light will be collected. I had to think of Ursler's Seventeenth Fundamental Paradox which the Official Guide had quoted as we flitted through the Lamasery of the Starrovers: "Time and space originate through light. Light does not originate through time and space." Light, the navigable stream of all phenomena, would carry this moment along with all others to the river's mouth.

"It is a terrible moment," I said. "But why is it the most important?"

Once more I received an answer. "Because the moment of greatest continuity is the most important."

I understood that. But suddenly I understood much more. It struck me like a high voltage current. The High Floater's naked Buddha's head was round as a ball. The naked little head of the child in the crib was round as a ball. And still another head was round as a ball—the head of the little star dancer, the head of the future High Floater. And more than that. The face of the star dancer was the perfect image of the face of the child in the crib. Was this the *wealth of continuity* of that moment?

Breathless and hoarse I gasped, "Is the boy whom they call Io-Runt mine?"

"The third question is answered," came the stern reply.

I held my hand in front of my eyes. I didn't dare to speak any more. When I looked up a little later the High Floater had disappeared. That is, he was again clinging to a remote corner of the vaulted ceiling, high above the hammocks and fishnets of the silver spider webs, a dark bundle, a strange kettledrum, pressed hard against the rock. He was suffering from an ailment that was unintelligible to me, a primitive man. He was no longer interested in my life, no matter what it might be, although he knew a hundred times more about this life than I. The webs of the miraculous star spiders swayed majestically in the vault of the Office-grotto. Now I knew that the spider webs of the Arachnodrome were the archives of well-preserved occurrences, recorded in the Office.

When I left the Djebel some time later, I was a changed man. It was not so much a moral change as a complete change of my feeling of life. I am still under the spell of this change as I finish writing this page in an early and fairly primitive world.

The Sixteenth Chapter

WHEREIN I STAND AT THE EDGE OF THE
JUNGLE OF THE MENTAL ERA AND WITNESS
THE EXODUS OF THE DOMESTIC CATS AND
THE FIRST BLOODSHED.

THE UNEASY PREMONITION that had not left me during my
visit to the Lamaseries of the Djebel had not deceived me.
Something unpleasant was brewing. At first I attributed
my worries to the house and circle of my new friends. Fortu-
ately I was wrong. The impending catastrophe did not concern
any individual family but the entire world conurbation, all Panopolis, whose inner borders, as I had been told, were only spiritual
and therefore unmarked. The unification of mankind was not
without its disadvantages, for it was perfectly obvious that if
anything started in one place, every other place would be
affected, from pole to pole. I was quite astonished at my feeling
of relief that nothing had happened "at home." I hope the
reader will be astonished with me at the venality of my character, or perhaps of human character in general: I felt at home
already, a hundred thousand years away from myself. I was
already attached to some utterly strange, incomprehensible
creatures who clothed themselves either in blurred nakedness or
in iridescent veils; who sipped bright-colored juices and soups
prepared for the whole world by the Worker in the Valley
of Springs and Forces by means of sidereal powers. I had become accustomed to all these things and I took them as a matter

378

of course, just as a change of diet while traveling in my former
existence. This assimilation had taken place with uncanny
rapidity, even for an impressionable person like myself, considering especially that exactly twenty-four hours had elapsed
since I had first set foot on the irongray sod of the Mental era
and that I had meanwhile bounced around on the elastic Mare
Plumbinum of Mercury and had suffered a veritable shipwreck
on the undulating red moor of Apostle Peter. Incidentally, my
visit to the Lower Intermundium had only served to make our
good old earth, that is, the new Mental earth, more familiar and
more homelike. I was really looking forward to my return to the
house of the wedding party. I gave no thought to the morrow
and to the future. I was never more carefree. My sense of time
was completely anaesthetized, no wonder. The only thing that
worried me after a fashion was the surprising attachment that
began to bind me to my new friends. In the last few years of my
former life I had developed a sort of self-protective resistance
against meeting new people and making new attachments. This
resistance even extended to animals. I gave away a beautiful
dog before I had become accustomed to him. When a person
has passed his fiftieth year he has no more desires and fears
nothing but new love.

B.H. was waiting anxiously behind the Office-Door. The
Official Guide had suddenly been called away on business. With-
out our conductor we strayed through the labyrinth of the
Djebel, through halls and corridors, up and down ramps, past
pits and shafts, flying along on the wings of regulated gravitation.
If Io-Fagòr had not finally personally piloted us out of the maze,
God knows when we would have found the exit.

Our host had covered his anxious, serious mien with a charming smile. Refined people of the distant future, like those of the
distant past, do not readily expose their worries.

"I trust, Seigneur," said Io-Fagòr, "that you are taking home
three striking answers from the Djebel?"

Before I could reply, B.H. looked at the Bride's father in surprise and inquired, "Did something unpleasant happen?"

"Your question," Io-Fagòr answered, "should be, 'Is something unpleasant about to happen?' The proper authorities have just made this inquiry at the place that our friend has just left."

"Judging by my experience in the Office," I commented, "there is nothing from the Day of Creation to the Day of Judgment that His High-Grace could not reveal."

Io-Fagòr somewhat sternly rejected my comment. "The High Floater is no revelator, but a sage," he declared. "He can only make suggestions regarding the future, for the future of men is concealed even from him. Every passing instant, as an old proverb says, is a juncture of many roads which man arbitrarily chooses."

B.H. was still looking intently at our host. "Something has happened after all," he said.

"And something not very interesting is happening right along," Io-Fagòr said with a smile. "But don't expect too much, Seigneur." He turned his handsome, gold-crowned head in B.H.'s direction. "Has your friend been informed?"

"If you're talking about the Jungle," I interrupted, "I've had a little information about it." I was thinking of my conversation with Minionman and his son.

"I hope you're not too tired, Seigneur," Io-Fagòr demurred.

"On the contrary," I laughed. "Chronosophy takes up a lot of time and space, but it is one of the most refreshing sciences I have ever encountered."

"That's true at the start," my host nodded. "After the fourth or fifth lesson you would change your tune. If you like, Seigneur, let's go to this place where things are happening."

* * * * * *

* * *

*

THE IRONGRAY SOD THAT WAS EVEN AND DENSE everywhere else became constantly shabbier and mangier. We were walking—and how I enjoyed it—across a narrow swale

which I called the "Valley of Indecision" in my own mind, because the soil seemed undecided whether to retain its Mental
character or to relapse cheerfully into outmoded vegetation.
The Valley of Indecision consisted of sandy soil in which a few
miserable unfamiliar thistle and cactus plants managed to eke out
an unhappy existence. Here and there a few timid spots of green
grass and weeds cropped up. About fifty paces farther along we
climbed up a fairly steep embankment that was definitely green.
At the top of this embankment a rampart of huge blocks of
stone barred our way and cut the world in two, for it extended
in both directions as far as the eye could see, like the Great Wall
of China. Obviously unauthorized persons were not permitted to
approach this rampart. At considerable intervals we saw guards
whose duty appeared to be to keep trespassers away. The guards
were not actually armed; weapons were not produced by the
Worker, and those that were still to be found in considerable
numbers came from excavations, like Io-Do's interesting collection. And so the guards, standing there stiffly and looking very
important, were armed in the manner of medieval mercenaries
or of the Swiss sentries in the Vatican, with lances. But the iron
points and barbs had been removed from the lances so that they
looked like the long alpenstocks that mountaineers used to carry
in my boyhood.

At regular, widely spaced intervals, broad, square, lookout plat-
forms projected from the wall. A few steps ahead of us a number
of persons were crowded against the balustrade of such a platform. I recognized Io-Do and his father, gentle little Io-Solip.
The Spokesman, the House Sage, and the Permanent Guest
were also there. My respect for these three bachelors with their
conventional, rationalistic intelligence had dropped considerably
since my great experiences in the Djebel. The only lady present
was our youthfully beautiful Ancestress. I confess that I was
disappointed not to find Lala, the Bride. But I was told that
according to custom she and her Bridegroom were not to appear
together in public before this evening. All the others who were
congregated here, staring down excitedly from the lookout plat-

form, were strangers to me. As usual, they made room for me with polite respect. Everyone seemed to be informed concerning my origin and my nature.

When I reached the parapet I remained rooted in surprise. The first thing about the Jungle that deeply moved me was the perspective, the blue distance of old times, of my times. While I had spent a scant twenty-four hours in this world, its flatness, its uncontrasting surface, its unlimited uniformity had depressed me more than I can say. I had made several remarks to B.H. on this subject, but he had consoled me with the unanswerable declaration that the Mental spiritualization and enrichment of man was intimately connected with the fact that the earth had become so uninteresting and boring. He asked me whether I didn't think that the regions that had been carefully prepared for the tourist trade in the twentieth century were just as uninteresting compared with the wandering mountain ranges and the roaring volcanoes of the antediluvian period. Culture, he said, was in all respects progress from the crude spectacle to delicate, spiritual differentiation. No doubt he was right. But that did not alter my feeling of discomfort at the fact that nature was no longer real nature, not even in the Park of the Worker. And now I was seeing mountains again, genuine mountains!

"Better close your mouth," B.H. warned me with a smile. He probably had reason to be ashamed on my account again. And the reader too may object that I really had no reason to wax too enthusiastic about mountains, when only a few minutes ago I had turned around for a last look at the glorious sight of the Djebel with its torrents of rainbow refractions; and only two and a half hours before that I had feasted my eyes on the anthracite-black and bloodred coastal range of John Evangelist. What a mistaken objection. The Djebel was the work of human hands, the most amazing of all future history, more noteworthy, larger, but not different in character from the Temple at Karnak or the Eiffel Tower. And the red-black coastal mountains of Mercury did not belong to me. Even now I had difficulty in visualizing them. But these mountains were mine, they were the mountains of my earth, and the light, cool, woodsmoke-laden breeze that they exhaled almost drove tears to my eyes.

The mountains rose toward the west. The sun—no golden fleece and no bicycle lamp but our good old earth sun—was be·ginning to decline and poured its afternoon gold over their slopes. The peaks grew up one behind the other in various tints and shades. The last range was properly snow-covered, although the snow-line seemed to have moved lower in the course of the millennia. That might have resulted from the gradual cooling of the earth's surface, or the sun might have lost some of its heating capacity since the Catastrophe on that thirteenth of November, or the reduction of humidity in the pure Astromental atmosphere might have prevented the accumulation of the heat to which we are accustomed. Greater purity always seems to go hand in hand with reduced warmth. I mentioned all these phenomena briefly soon after my first appearance in the new world. I repeat them at this point because I felt and understood everything more clearly—I should like to say, more planetarily—after my Chronosophic experiences.

Familiar as the lines of these mountains seemed to me, I felt as though I were looking down upon them from a point in the Gray Neuter. Furthermore, they didn't remind me so much of the tree-clad slopes of my former home as of the Apennines or other ranges near the Mediterranean or the Pacific Ocean. And that was quite appropriate for, after all, we were near the Pacific. The thing that surprised me most was the enormous extent of the island of vegetation which the citizens of the Mental world quite incorrectly called a Jungle. If it was true, as they confessed to me, that there were more than a hundred such Jungles on the leveled globe, then there was indeed imminent danger that the latter would sooner or later lose its irongray monotony. The low parapet certainly could not prevent the vegetation from spreading and from stealing more and more Panopolitan land. Even though the name Jungle was misleading, the phenomenon itself must have been most unusual and depressing for Mental eyes. I understood Io-Fagòr's concern much better than I had yesterday. Suddenly I recognized pine, and olive trees and clumps of palms in the near foothills, and, scattered among them, handsome white cubes.

"For goodness sake, those are houses," I exclaimed.

"Horrible," replied a voice in the group surrounding me. It was the Spokesman's voice. "What a horrible thought that humans live in such boxes, and on the surface, at that."

"You can't call those creatures humans," was the indignant remark of Bridegroom Io-Do, who looked particularly handsome and dignified today in his golden helmet and black festive garb.

"Unfortunately they are humans," said Io-Fagòr. "I would be less worried if they weren't humans. They differ from us only in that they are more sunburned, that they wear barbaric costumes, and that they work with their own hands. It's a small difference."

At this point the charming Ancestress entered into the conversation. She was leaning gracefully on the arm of the House Sage on the right and on that of the Permanent Guest on the left. She had been tenderly swathed in many veil shawls, for while old age did not affect beauty, it manifested itself in a certain susceptibility of the respiratory organs.

"I remember my own great-great-grandmother," said the Ancestress. "She was one of the most beautiful women of her era. When I was a child—I won't tell you what century it was—I heard a great deal from her about the Jungle of her time. Naturally it was smaller, less pretentious, and less developed than today, but it was beginning to get fashionable. There were certain ladies who ran away and disappeared in the Jungle. But the Jungle men were much more sunburned then and wore much more barbaric clothes than today——"

"My dear lady," her descendant Io-Fagòr interrupted in harassed but courteous tone, "you should treat your velvet voice with greater consideration in the open air."

"And I still say they aren't human," the Bridegroom insisted. "Humans don't live on the surface."

"We lived on the surface, my friend," I retorted somewhat sharply, "and in houses just like those."

Now B.H. intervened. "Well, my dear F.W., let's not forget that the cathedrals, castles, imperial palaces, skyscrapers, airplane factories, Egyptian temples, and American suburbs of your lifetime were something quite different from these things."

I did not answer him. It seemed to me that we were standing on top of a mighty fortress wall, for the parapet ran along the edge of a steep, probably artificial precipice, about a hundred yards high and very difficult to climb. At its foot ran a wide green moat or something of the sort, that separated the Jungle from the "World." I had the impression, however, that this dividing line was a symbolic rather than a real obstacle, and that both parties, Mental men and Jungle people, had no desire to have any traffic with each other. That was strange, of course, and contrary to all historical precedent. Beyond the wide green ribbon that I called a "moat," the terrain began to rise gradually in steps and terraces, and not only the vegetation but life in general became more dense from step to step.

My annoying astigmatism again prevented my unaided eyes from seeing all that there was to see with perfect clarity. But I saw what I saw, and I haven't added anything to it. Nearest us at the edge of the mountain fastness, slanderously called a Jungle and libelously accused of harboring a "swinish hubbub," I saw a number of small parcels of land neatly divided by fences, reminiscent of those on the outskirts of cities in my time. In those palmy days they were called "victory gardens"; in the period of World Wars, food shortages, and black markets they served to supplement the scant rations by supplying vegetables and perhaps even a few chickens. Behind these victory gardens there was a wide expanse of weeds and brush, probably intended as a barrier. Beyond this strip of brush I could distinguish a few plain white houses. There was also a small church with a low steeple and a cross on top of it. I saw a lot of other things, but I don't want to be accused of straining my astigmatic eyes. I saw a few fields, for instance, real, genuine fields, with grain that was still green. A little farther up the slope I saw a very primitive sort of fairground, with a running merry-go-round, a few swings, and a climbing pole, where screeching children were at play. In the clear air I could even make out the tanned, skinny limbs of the children in their wretched peasant smocks, and the thick growth of hair on their heads, ranging from coal-black to blond.

So much for the facts. In connection with their interpretation I must remind the reader of the word that my reincarnated friend used the day before while we were sitting in the little parlor like a pair of fossils in amber. The word was "backsliding," or recidivism. Undoubtedly this oasis with its vegetation and its human population was a case of backsliding, a relapse of nature into a past stage of earth history. It should not be difficult to imagine my feelings when I saw our earth, right in the middle of the Eleventh Cosmic Capital Year of Virgo, relapsing at this spot into a form of life approximating that of my former existence. I don't mean to say, of course, that the Jungle was a perfect replica of a village in the twentieth century. It could just as well have been the seventeenth or the fifteenth century, provided that these centuries had simple merry-go-rounds, as they probably did.

There are many precedents for backsliding of the human race. There are, for instance, the dark ages between classical antiquity and the Renaissance. Moreover every outbreak of a new volcano, the vanishing of an island, in fact, every great earthquake is a relapse on the part of the earth into its age of puberty. The relapse of the earth into the moderate vegetation of the neat, orderly Jungle might well represent the hundred thousand years of its added age. The parallel existence of various stages of civilization was not only attested by history, but by my own experience, for I had seen a good slice of the earth in my day. But the genesis and segregation of a primitive society in a leveled and unified world was an unprecedented phenomenon. The natural magnetism of a higher civilization which irresistibly assimilates and absorbs a lower one seemed to be inoperative in this case. In order to appraise these enclaves that had grown up on swampy soil which suddenly erupted from the irongray Mental sod, we must imagine great primeval forests springing up overnight in the vicinity of London, Paris, and New York, peopled with tribes of timid pygmies hiding in caves and hollows. Of course, we—I mean my former contemporaries—smart and hard as we were (that is, are), would have cleaned up these primeval forests near London, Paris, and New York, including the pygmies, in jigtime. In the present era, however, such barbaric "liquidation" was out of the question, for homicide, not to speak of mass murder, was not only abhorred since time immemorial but was actually regarded as an impossibility. For this reason the anomalous condition had to be tolerated, and the only countermeasure was complete and inexorable segregation. The thriving fields of grain and the vegetable gardens proved that the Jungle people lived as ancient tillers of the soil and received no food from the Worker and from his Valley of Springs and Forces. The coarse smocks of the children indicated that no veil materials or other textiles of sidereal manufacture were furnished in the Jungle. The Jungle people not only had to plow, sow, and reap, they also had to spin and weave. In short, they had to labor. I had to think of Io-Joel's curious opinion that reform had to come from the Jungles. What mad snobbery! But the Grand Bishop also inclined to this view in his theory of the alienation from God aggravated by the mere passage of time.

While these thoughts and many others like them assailed me at sight of the familiar mountains, gardens, fields, and houses, I was suddenly roused from my reverie by an exclamation of loathing uttered in chorus by the group about me. When I looked around I saw all the youthful, handsome faces distorted with disgust. About thirty extended arms pointed at something in the moat as though an incredibly detestable thing were going on there. Many choked voices were shouting, "Just look, look there!"

It took some time before I grasped the cause of their disgust: a number of chickens had made their way through the lattice fences of the victory gardens. At first glance they were simply roosters, hens, and chicks, as far as I was concerned. So what, I thought. At second glance, however, I recognized that chickendom had undergone some imposing changes during my absence,

and during their own absence, for they owed their resuscitation
to the Jungle. While this change was not as tremendous as its
reverse had been in the transformation of sheep and goats into
ovettes and capricornettes, the chickens, and particularly the
roosters, seemed to have grown far beyond their former size. I'll
not say that they had attained the stature of ostriches, but they
were well on their way. Well, let's not exaggerate. They were a
good third taller and considerably heavier than our chickens in
the beginnings of mankind. Animals are always the incarnation
of a single characteristic, except perhaps the dog, versatile copyist that he is. The single characteristic personified by the rooster
was never particularly attractive. Back in my day he had resembled a vainly strutting hidalgo. Sir Hotspur, that was the
rooster. Here in the moat between the Jungle and the World, the
roosters were no wiry cavaliers in glinting feather armors. They
were bloated Bohemians. The combs on their silly heads were
flabby and fat, and under their beaks wobbled enormous, baggy,
fiery-red Ascot cravats. They no longer watched over their
nodding, pecking henfolks as sternly as of yore. They put on an
air of bored absent-mindedness. Occasionally one of the roosters
crowed; it was no longer a tenor cockadoodledoo but a disillu-
sioned, baritone croaking. Occasionally one of them climbed
languidly on a hen but stopped in the midst of his performance
as though an important idea had suddenly struck him.

While it was quite true that chanticleer had changed for the
worse, still there was no call for the exclamations of loathful
disgust and the shuddering revulsion of the Mental people. I
wondered what these sensitive gentlemen would say if they could
see a buzzard, a vulture, or a condor slowly gliding down to a
good meal on a dead horse. Meanwhile the number of chickens
in the moat increased remarkably. The cackling of the fat hens
became louder and louder and also the croaking of the worn-out
tenors whose cockadoodledoo had slipped an octave lower. The
sky began to change color, and the hour was at hand in which one,
as the saying is, goes to bed with the chickens. The irruption of
the feathery tribe into the moat impressed me more and more as

an intentional arrangement. I was sure I detected a satirical purpose of provoking the nervous dread of my high-toned friends at
sight of the honest egg-producers. A moment later it became
evident that my suspicion was well founded. At first a few
gleaming eyes and faces stared out of the heavy shrubbery over
there. Then the bushes parted, and people appeared, singly and
in groups, and walked to the fences of the victory gardens, leering furtively up at us. The Jungle people were by no means
pygmies. On the contrary, their powerful figures towered well
above their Astromental contemporaries. My more skeptical
readers may perhaps, rightly or wrongly, mistrust the evidence
of my astigmatic eyes, but these primitives looked to me like
something halfway between the motley gypsies described by
Victor Hugo and other Romanticists, and the former Monte-
negrins or Albanian Skipetars whom I had seen with my own
eyes. The men wore their glossy black hair in braids that hung
down over both shoulders. Some of them wore red caps with
tassels. Their jackets glittered and clinked with silver buttons,
medals, and braid. Their faces, necks, hands, and forearms looked
as though they were carved from the knotty rootstocks of the
live oak or olive. I saw black, gray, and white mustaches and
the shriveled faces of two or three toothless old women, wrinkled
as witches. I saw no young women. But the children came running
down from the playground and squeezed in among their elders.
I could have imagined that I was looking down from an Albanian mountain on a (remarkably clean) village near Scutari.
But the curious thing was that the Jungle people, in spite of the
chicken trick on their Astromental neighbors, manifested no
vindictiveness against them, if anything, only scorn. The reaction
of my friends on the platform was all the more incomprehensible.
They watched the primitives down below with disturbed, hate-
distorted faces and with ill-concealed fear. There was genuine
loathing even on B.H.'s features.

For these dainty, bald, eternally young, and eternally beautiful
Olympians the sight of the gypsylike aborigines, who owed their
existence to some obscure crossbreeding, was obscene and re-

pulsive. For me, an aborigine myself, it wasn't anything of the sort.

"Why do we stand for that?" I heard Bridegroom Io-Do say with that sullen voice that had surprised me a number of times before. And then the "interesting occurrence" began to take place, that is, it began to recur after a pause of several hours.

The sun was now directly above the snow-capped mountains. The sky turned green and violet as it had done over the Geodrome yesterday. The parapet with its battlements began to cast overlong shadows on the slope behind us. More and more Jungle people congregated in the victory gardens, and suddenly their excited fingers began to point in a certain direction and they began to chatter in swift syllables, undoubtedly a hill-billy dialect of the Monolingua.

"There's the phenomenon again," said Io-Fagòr seriously. He was standing directly behind me.

"After it had ended abruptly directly after sunrise this morning," the House Sage supplemented. And being a precise man, he added, "That's what the Custodes report."

"We all know that. Why keep repeating it?" the Spokesman snapped with an exasperated look.

I strained my eyes in the direction in which everyone was staring, intent upon getting a good look at the "phenomenon" that caused so much disquiet among the Astromental citizens. To start with, the phenomenon consisted of nothing but a cat, an ordinary, spotted gray and black domestic cat, which crouched on the parapet about twenty paces from us, hesitant and alert, its tail switching. The cat was of medium size, no larger and no smaller, no uglier and no handsomer than ordinary house cats in my day. As a resident for many years in an out-of-the-way nook on the Canale San Polo in Venice, I can claim to be something of an expert on the subject of ordinary cats.

So far I failed to understand why this trivial animal that had retained its ancient shape through the millennia with commendable steadfastness should be regarded as a phenomenon and why the group of people on the observation platform should look

on with reserved earnestness, and the Jungle people down below
with curiosity and pleasurable excitement. The cat itself, crouched
against a projection, seemed to waver, seemed to consider.
Suddenly it arched its back wickedly, its electric fur bristled, it
leaped from the parapet to the bare rock, skidded down a natural
groove into the moat quick as a flash, and disappeared at top
speed through the fence of one of the victory gardens. Violent
shouts from below and even a few from up here accompanied
this apparently insignificant occurrence. I was about to turn
angrily to Io-Fagòr or B.H. and demand an explanation of why
this was called a phenomenon, when both of them impatiently
pointed in the same direction again.

This time there were four cats, four plain ordinary cats with
reddish tiger markings, hesitating on the parapet with bristling
fur and switching tails before they took the leap and slid down
the rocky bank like their predecessor. I caught a flash of a staring,
icily impersonal feline eye as one of the animals turned its head
toward us. The cats that followed didn't even hesitate. For a
while there were individual groups but then, incredible as it
sounds, a solid, serried army of cats leaped over the parapet in
closed ranks, whizzed down the precipice, crossed the moat, and
disappeared into the Jungle.

I must confess, Io-Fagòr was right. It was a phenomenon. And
if there hadn't been so many sober heads about me as witnesses
of this phenomenon, I could easily have taken it as an attack of
delirium on my part, or more politely, for a vision. Cats are
highly individualistic animals. They bask in the sun alone on our
doorsteps. A cat purrs when it is feeling good, content with its
own company, and exhibits an ostentatious absence of interest
in its surroundings. Its egocentricity is unalterable; for this reason
it is the most solitary of hunters. It permits no hunting colleague
to participate in the pleasures of the chase or in its bag of mice.
Its self-veneration and self-justification are so complete that a
mother-cat will reject her kitten if another cat has licked it.
That's the cat for you. Now I ask you, who ever saw a drove of
cats? The sight of an army of cats is breath-taking. All of us stood

in deep, uncomfortable silence. The Jungle peasants too were still. Even the silly giant hens had stopped cackling.

"Can it be that the cat has become a social animal in the Astromental age?" I marveled out loud.

"A cat's a cat," said Io-Fagòr. "It's probably never been different. It's not educable, not gifted for speech, not communicative, not congenial like a dog, but a damn sight more talented."

"But what we're seeing there," I continued to wonder, "is a joint undertaking of the cats. I should never have considered it possible. A collectivistic undertaking of the instinct must have a purpose. Is the purpose known?"

"The purpose is quite simple," Io-Fagòr replied. "The cats are leaving us."

I shook my head. "Have the people of today become such great cat-lovers," I inquired, "when the species hasn't improved a bit? On the contrary, in my day there were much finer varieties, like Angoras and Persians and Siamese. Are these ordinary cats going to be missed on account of their usefulness, since people live underground where there may be all sorts of surviving and possibly enlarged rodents?"

"Who cares about that?" said Io-Fagòr with a curt laugh. "The phenomenon is a general telluric omen and is being reported from most of the other Jungles."

"Omen?" I exclaimed. "In my day it used to be said that the rats left a sinking ship, not the cats."

"We'll not talk about that, Seigneur," said Io-Fagòr, suddenly proud and aloof. I had gone too far.

Io-Fagòr had been quite right in his remark about the educable, speech-gifted, communicative dogs. Gradually a whole pack of Surs gathered on the parapet. That is, our own house companion Sur wasn't among these dogs at all; fortunately the humane society hadn't yet initiated the dogs of the era into the use of the travel-puzzle. It almost gave me a feeling of embarrassment to see how little these dogs differed from each other in color, fur, muzzle, and other physical characteristics. The unification of all breeds of dogs had made it necessary to remember their physiognomies in order to distinguish one dog from another. Their uniformity concealed the same pretension as their barking command of the Monolingua. I must repeat the word "humanishness" that I used once before to express this conceited as well as empty simulation of personality. It occurred to me that the cats showed a much higher degree of personality by the very fact that they had not learned the Monolingua, had retained their soft, expressive mewing, and were as sharply differentiated in fur and color as ever. The cat, a domestic animal like the dog, had resisted man through all the millennia. Its staring, icily impersonal eye looked past him and through him and owed him nothing. Io-Fagòr was probably thinking of the unbroken spirit of the cat when he credited it with greater talents than the dog.

As the hour advanced the number of dogs grew constantly larger, and they were evidently very excited and very angry. Their mood seemed to be composed of jealousy, envy, and an indefinite fear of something impending. They ran in and out among the people on the platform, dashed back and forth on the flat top of the wall, formed yapping committee meetings, shouted short, insulting words at the cats but did not dare to go near them. If I wanted to understand the chatter of one or more of the dogs I always had to wait a while until the flat barking and growling sounds became differentiated into words in my ear. For this reason I can't repeat their invective verbatim but can give only the general sense of the interjections and exclamations that they hurled after the emigrating cats.

"Look at 'em . . . there they go, with their famous instinct. . . . Grandma had a bad dream. . . . Sure, they're full of instinct but what about their loyalty, what about their fidelity. . . . You dastards, you bastards, are we ever glad to get rid of you. . . . Into the Jungle, haw, haw, where you won't get any soups or creams, no pistachio green ones, not even saffron yellow ones. . . . But you'll have plenty of hairy papas and mammas. . . . That's where you belong . . . not with us in the world of culture, culture. . . ."

I distinctly remember that they dragged out the word culture in two long syllables, culminating in wild, inarticulate barking. The cats, slipping over the parapet in supple waves, didn't pay the slightest attention to their rivals. They never even looked around. They probably felt the admiration concealed behind the invective, the discontented, envious admiration of the domesticated, the Babbitts, for those who had the courage to escape. A female dog named Melba had ventured nearest to the tribe of emigrating cats. God knows where she got her name, a name that had been very famous in the days of my youth. As we already know, all dogs referred to themselves by their names and spoke of themselves in the third person, a practice common to children and primitives. I admit that I may have misunderstood the name and that the animal may have been called Malba. Melba or Malba, whichever it was, stood there with her muzzle raised and her head tilted, in the manner of dogs barking at the moon. In this case she was howling at the sinking sun. I distinguished two exclamations that she kept repeating: "Melba is homesick. . . . Melba wants to sing. . . ."

The dogs seemed to understand her howling better than I. An enraged, vicious snarling rose dangerously behind her. "You bitch. . . . You daughter of a bitch. . . . Get out. . . . Beat it. . . . Scram . . . into the swamp. . . ."

The reader will notice that the dogs used the word "bitch" as an obscene insult. The strange practice of using one's own name as an insult was not an invention of the dogs. All despised, ridiculed, persecuted people have done that from time immemorial. If prostitutes quarrel, one of them invariably calls the other a whore. And I recall a professional comedian, who, ill-tempered and surly like all of his ilk, shrugged his shoulders in speaking of another comedian, and said, "What do you expect of a clown?"

As the last quarter of the sun glowed red over the snowfields of the mountains and a pine-scented flood of crimson light filled the air, the exodus of the cats seemed to have reached its height. Endless swarms of them disappeared into the terraced landscape of the Jungle. The slender body of the bitch Melba or

Malba on the parapet was shaken by convulsive trembling. She tugged on an invisible collar that seemed to choke her, then she reared like a horse. Suddenly she tore herself loose from the imaginary leash of her Mental dog morality, leaped over the wall, slid down the precipice, and, with incessant howling, galloped alongside the flitting cats like a sheepdog with a flock. In a matter of seconds she had disappeared in the brush behind the victory gardens. The other dogs almost lost their command of the language. A hysterical yapping, yowling, and yelping in every conceivable pitch ensued, and I am sure Io-Fagòr or some-one else would have chased the whole kit and caboodle of them away with a stern reprimand if another occurrence had not attracted everyone's attention.

For some time I had been aware that the strange parade of speeding cats was not as homogeneous as it had been at first. Among the domestic cats with mostly light-colored fur I discerned occasional darker, clumsier, stranger animal shapes, some of them smaller and some considerably larger. Concerning these animals that had joined the exodus I can only say that they were certainly quadrupeds and probably mammals. Since there was no rule without exceptions in the Astromental era, the irongray sod of the unified, continental Panopolis must have covered countless hiding places, forgotten wastes, concealed gorges and hollows, in which all sorts of timid game might still find shelter and food. Some of these wild animals living in the vicinity seemed to be making use of the welcome opportunity of escaping into the Jungle in the throng of disloyal cats. Some of the higher species of animals possess a definite capacity for logical action. This capacity had probably grown in the course of time. If the cats who, as everyone knows, are attached to their home but not to man, left their homes, why shouldn't the untamed animals with their vastly keener instincts also sense that there was some-thing in the air? The beasts that mingled with the cats here and there were unfamiliar to me and probably originated from various crossbreedings and combinations of the past. I couldn't have named any of them. There were some foxlike creatures, some that looked like minks, some like raccoons, but most of them appeared to belong to the cat family. That slender animal with the round, flattened head and sand-colored fur could very well have been a wildcat, a lynx, or even a small mountain lion. I recalled that California in my day was still well supplied with the latter. Of course there weren't any mountains any more outside the Jungle. And yet that graceful, dangerous looking animal certainly resembled one of the extinct mountain lions. As I watched it intently, it slipped sinuously down one of the rocky grooves. But while the domestic cats raced through the moat without a glance to right or left, this elegant, leonine stranger made a detour, pounced on the fat giant hens, and in the course of a few seconds staged a perfect massacre among them. The beast did not succeed, however, in carrying off its prey, for the Jungle people came running with fence pickets to protect their chickens. They uttered shrill martial shouts. The buttons on their jackets gleamed in the dying crimson light. The marauder fled without his booty. Plaintive cackling followed him. One of the worn-out roosters let out a futile baritone croak. Finally the only sound was the faint cheeping of the four or five big hens that lay dying in their own blood. There was a moment of silence. Then suddenly and without any prelude the roosters and their clan pounced on the wounded hens, cackling and beating their wings, and, with a horrible show of bloodthirstiness, tore them up and devoured them. It didn't take a minute. Nothing remained but a heap of gory feathers and bones on the blood-spattered grass. The Jungle people drove their fowls home with angry shouts, taking no notice whatever of the Mental spectators. The latter, pale and silent, stared at the bloody remains of the chicken massacre. I assume that not one of them had ever seen naked blood, that is, blood spilled in anger, any more than the average citizen of my lifetime would have attended an autopsy. To me, of course, the horror of the Mental people seemed ridiculous and exaggerated.

"Chicken's blood," I said after a while. "I wonder whether that's a symptom?"

No one replied, not even Io-Do who stood right next to me. I recalled the question he had asked me yesterday about war—"How does it feel when a fountain of blood gushes at you?"

The dogs had run away with their tails between their legs. The absurd silence made me garrulous. I turned to B.H.

"I once saw a little volume entitled 'Egyptian Dreambook' at the home of an old woman I used to know. In it you could look up the meaning of fish blood and chicken blood and you could even find the exact significance of the entire scene we just witnessed. It's an old story that chickens tear up a bleeding fellow-chicken, but it has a deep meaning. The interpretation is in this 'Egyptian Dreambook.' Don't you remember, B.H.? You know all the books of the past and present. I've always admired you for it."

"It's called 'Dreambooklet,' F.W., not 'Dreambook,'" B.H. corrected me gently. "Let's not talk about it; it was pure nonsense anyhow. Not even lovelorn servant girls believed in it."

"Who can say whether it's nonsense?" I insisted foolishly. "Even Ursler says in the Seventeenth Paradox that time and space are creations of light and not vice versa. Consequently blood, as a subdivision of time and space, is darkened light. Hold your hand against the sun and you'll see that it's translucent and red."

"The sun's gone long ago," someone said sullenly.

The sun had set. Twilight spread quickly over the mountain region they called the Jungle. But the sky was still so saturated with color that only three pale stars gradually emerged. The brightest of them, the evening star, was certainly Mary Magdalene. The second, just above the ridge of the Sierra, near the vanished sun, could be no other than John Evangelist, the favorite disciple. The third gleamed with a placid blue light; it did not scintillate; it had to be a planet. Was it Peter the Apostle? Oh, if only one or another of those who are my companions in spirit on my journey could feel the reverent thrill that shook me at sight of these remote heavenly bodies on which I had sojourned only a few hours ago. My emotion was so strong that I had to lower my head in order to recall myself forcibly from the starry realm to my mundane surroundings. A quick glance around convinced me that the exodus of the cats had stopped temporarily at least. Only the shadows of a few stragglers were still flitting over the parapet and vanishing in the victory gardens.

I turned away, toward the world of culture. And the others did as I. In the deep twilight something that gleamed faintly came from below and plodded up the slope where the guards with their alpenstocks stood stiff-legged and black. It was a man. Then it was a little man in a cowl. And finally it was Io-Fra, the Mutarian. I wasn't a bit surprised that his small, dainty figure glowed a little in the dark, like certain varieties of phosphorescent wood. Why shouldn't he glow, a Mutarian who had taken the vows of blindness and deafness and who therefore had the gift of inner sight and hearing? Io-Fra had come to fetch the Bridegroom whom he served. The first nightwatch had begun. Now he had to prepare himself appropriately for the second festive vigil when the bridal couple were to appear publicly at the Sympaian. Everyone hastened to reach the edge of the irongray sod, for the Astromental method of travel operated only when the feet were planted on this groundcover. As we hurried across the sandy margin that separated us from culture, night fell, quickly as in the tropics. It was my second night in the Eleventh Cosmic Capital Year of Virgo. The bright bluish spirit light of the stars that covered the sky in dense array seemed more familiar. They were so dense because the anthropomorphous breast of the universe was in the process of "inhaling," in contrast to my former lifetime, when it had been "exhaling." I shook my head in astonishment at all the tremendous doctrines I had learned in the past few hours. No one will believe me, I thought, perhaps not even I myself.

Not far from our little group I noticed a young man who was dawdling along all alone, not in the company of any other group, with a certain air of contemptuous indifference that attracted my attention. It was Io-Joel Sid, Minionman's renegade pet. I was curious to hear his opinion about the "phenomenon" that had cast a pall of silent gloom on my friends. I called to him. He stopped. I don't know whether his mocking, superior expression was genuine. I do know that he didn't enjoy being stopped. In my embarrassment I made a conventional gesture toward Io-Do and said, "May I make you gentlemen acquainted with each other?"

Io-Do bared his teeth in a forced smile. But he didn't have a chance to say a word, for Io-Joel anticipated him.

"It's not necessary, Doctus and Seigneur," he said adroitly; "the gentlemen know me and I know them."

The Seventeenth Chapter

WHEREIN, IN THE COURSE OF A FESTIVE
SYMPAIAN, THE GREAT MUSICAL-DRAMATIC
IMPROVISATION OF THE ERA, THE CALAMITY
TAKES PLACE WHICH PROVES TO BE THE
TURNING POINT OF ASTROMENTAL HISTORY.

AT THE OUTSET of this chapter which begins with a drama and ends with a tragedy I must confess without reservation that I felt better than ever. The reason for my well-being was the fact that I felt clean; I was washed and shaved and my clothes were pressed. I had spent about thirty hours among the living after an eternity in dead storage in the wardrobe of invisibility, where I had been carefully put away in moth balls like all others of my kind. In the course of these thirty hours I hadn't had much opportunity to get dirty, yet I was uncomfortably conscious of my crumpled linen and my mussed suit. This consciousness went so far that I asked B.H. privately whether it might not be possible for me to appear at the festive Sympaian in the customary veil draperies of the Mental world. B.H. replied promptly and sternly that it was out of the question. My dress suit, he said, made a far greater impression than I. Without this "genuine, remarkable antique" I would look like any ordinary person who was unlucky enough to be pretty hairy and in need of a barber. Incidentally, B.H. went on sotto voce, having assured himself that no one was listening, the cosmetic tough luck of being hairy was far more general than one might suspect; even among the youngest and most beautiful brides there were some who concealed a heavy growth of blond or black curls under their helmets. Finally B.H. pointed out that he himself was running around in the disguise of a prehistoric doughboy on my account. There wasn't any answer to this argument.

I sighed and said that I had always been accustomed to change my suit and my linen in the evening before going out socially. B.H. laughed out loud. Did I really forget to help you, poor fellow? All you need to do is stand under an Astrotonic shower. No sooner said than done. The dry shower not only gave me the delicious feeling of being washed, massaged, and shaved, but in a jiffy it laundered, starched, and ironed my shirt and restored my swallowtail to the state of pristine impeccability in which it had been delivered by my Viennese tailor. Need I add that this remarkable dry-cleaning method not only renovated the body and garment but also refreshed the soul and spirit in the twinkling of an eye?

After a late but substantial meal, similar to the one of the night before, we started for the evening's entertainment with the bridal couple in the van of our party. My heart was filled with uncurbed curiosity, as though I had not paid a visit to the Park of the Worker, had not survived a thorough exorcism, argued with King Saul and his son, had not done Comet Calisthenics in the Gray Neuter, bounced around on Mercury's Mare Plumbinum like a rubber ball, had not wallowed like a hippopotamus on Jupiter's red morass, scuttled around on the inside of a unicle, learned about the shape of the universe and the most important moment of my life from the High Floater, taken a look at the Jungle from the outside and witnessed the exodus of the cats and the massacre of the chickens—not bad for just one day. I remembered how tired I had been yesterday from the first few hours of my new life after I had had a pretty good nap for several eons, and I was surprised to feel so ambitious now in spite of my sleepless night. Apparently I was still the same old night owl as of old.

* * * * *
* * *
*

THE LARGE THEATER IN WHICH I NOW FOUND MY-SELF was a real, genuine theater, just as the schoolroom of the elementary class in the Djebel this morning had been a real, genuine schoolroom. I wasn't in the least surprised. Essential requirements permit little variation in the outer form of certain things. The Sympaian Theater was located, unless I am mistaken, among the many public institutions and state buildings that encircled the outer rim of the central plaza or Geodrome. The justifiable objection may be raised that the word "building" is inaccurate. There was nothing above the surface of the earth except a large, empty, vaulted hall that marked the place and its purpose; in the description of the Geodrome I used the word "shadow architecture." Right now I can't even be certain whether this hollow entry hall had a roof or whether the stars looked in from above. I need not mention that this opera house—pardon the old-fashioned expression—was far beneath the surface. It consisted, as the word "theater" indicates, of an auditorium, an orchestra pit, and a stage. The auditorium rose in the manner of an amphitheater and, like an ancient circus, was divided off into boxes or loges. The boxes were very spacious and were separated from each other by low railings. Instead of armchairs they contained roomy couches with raised head-ends, each affording ample room for six people side by side. Toward the rear the boxes rose to the height of a balcony, assuring excellent visibility. Presently we will discover, however, that good visibility and acoustics were not the primary requirements of a modern theater. Every box contained three couches rising in steps behind each other, so that there was room for eighteen persons. Since today's Sympaian was dedicated to the hundred most distinguished bridal couples of the state, the front row of the first ring of loges was reserved for them, giving each couple the exclusive use of one of the wide divans. The latter were covered with magnificent veils, pillows, and rugs, and were literally loaded down with the familiar rust-colored roses. The lovely brides in their dovegray, bluish veils, under which gleamed the blurred ivory of their naked bodies, the young men in close-fitting black with their glittering gold helmets, each lying next to his bride and holding her hand in a formal, solemn fashion—all that made a tableau of indescribable charm and beauty. Still, with all my admiration of this exotic scene of the future, I will have to admit that a première of, let's say, Puccini's posthumous opera "Turandot" at the Vienna Court Opera House or at La Scala in Milan was no less brilliant than this Sympaian here several eons later.

Be that as it may, the cream of Astromental society was assembled in the House of the Sympaian. What's that? Did I hear somebody plaintively say the word "democracy?" Well, there really can't be much argument about my hundred noble brides and fiancés. Moreover there can't be much argument about the repeatedly stated fact that these people were not only living in a perfect democracy but in the most ideal form of communism. But for the very reason that democracy had become an absolute matter of course since untold millennia, it had ceased to exist. For democracy is one of those relativisms of life that ceases to exist as soon as it is realized. As long as the just demands for material and potential equality of every citizen of the globe had not been fulfilled, politicians and journalists could make a living by reiterating these just demands. But when, after endless battles, victories, and defeats, democracy finally triumphed, the much deeper inequalities than the material ones came into prominence: inequalities of beauty, of strength, of will, character, idiocy, cynicism, indolence, cleverness, talent, acumen—all those things for which God and nature can be held responsible, but no ruling party. I devoutly hope, however, that my report from the most remote future will not create a panic among our radical politicians and give them the deleterious notion that the only hope for their business lies in the secret soft-pedaling of material and potential inequality.

It should be evident, therefore, that the theater was filled with the sort of people who were once called the "two hundred families" in France, along with their retinue of Spokesmen, House Sages, Permanent Guests, and another category, not previously mentioned, the Body Gardeners or Recreators. The latter were hygienists or, if you like, private physicians, and were kept only by the most distinguished families. Of course, the medical practice of the era consisted chiefly of preventive rather than therapeutic medicine, since diseases had practically vanished down to a mere symbolic remainder. I also recognized the athletic dudes, fops, and dandies whom I had seen at the dance, although they were now dressed in festive costumes instead of in glistening nakedness.

So I repeat, it was high society that had assembled in the theater. It is obvious that I had by this time acquired an eye for social distinctions although they were much less crude and apparent than the gross contrasts of my own day. In my description of the audience I must not forget the Mutarians, that strange brotherhood that had become blind and deaf by a sacred act of will in order to serve men more unselfishly at the great turning points of their lives. Every bridal couple had their Mutarian with them; in the case of ours it was Io-Fra. (I almost wrote Fra Angelico.) The latter lay with a rapt smile I shall never forget at the feet of Io-Do and Io-La, ever ready to jump up, look for something, run an errand, call someone, or only listen for unexpressed wishes with his inner ear. The greater part of the audience was still on their feet, craning their necks to admire the horseshoe of bridal couples. Today's Sympaian was the climax of the season. Jewelry, furs, and gowns, furnished a very unsatisfactory topic of conversation for the ladies, since the habiliments were fairly uniform despite their various nuances. I am ready, however, at any time to withdraw this statement, as it may be based in part on my ignorance of Astromental styles and in part on my astigmatism.

It was customary that on this particular evening every bride-groom appear with the implemental insignia of his favorite occupation. Since actual work was a thing of the remotest past and even excavating, masonry, and carpentry were done Mentally without benefit of human hands, it was only natural that dilettantism and hobbies of all sorts took the place of the deadly seriousness of labor of the past. We have been told that the ideal of aimless play prevailed. Even the most exalted expression of the Astromental spirit, Chronosophy in the Djebel, did not have the remotest notion of usefulness or of practical utilization of its discoveries. Men indeed emulated the gods. And what purpose in life do the gods have besides the full enjoyment of their own existence?

The tools which the bridegrooms were carrying as evidence of their aimless playfulness were of various sorts. One of them held a huge guitar in his hand, an instrument, incidentally, without strings. In this manner the youth indicated that he was interested in a particular sort of music. There were quite a number of painters who appeared with clean palettes, maulsticks, and bouquets of unused brushes. There were not nearly so many sculptors and architects—the latter with gigantic dividers and T-squares—for, after all, painting is the least utilitarian of the formative arts. I had the impression that about one-third of the bridegrooms had chosen one of the arts as their hobbies. Among the others there were some remarkable occupations. One young man had appeared with a sprinkling can, a spade, and a rake; he had made his garden independent of the central gardening system and took care of it himself. Another brought an old-fashioned spinning wheel. Who could know that this antique instrument belonged in the hands of women? A third was carrying a sort of hall-tree hung with countless tiny parchment rolls. It was the symbol of philological dilettantism. A fourth had his hand clenched around a billiard cue as though it were a lance. I still don't understand why my suspicions were not aroused by the fact that there were at least fifteen others besides Io-Do who collected weapons. Our Bridegroom had a clumsy old single-action re-

volver slung over his shoulders by a strap, the same old Wild
West persuader dating from the nineteenth century that I had
noticed in his collection last night. He was especially proud of
this piece, much prouder, of course, than of his insignificant
trans-shadow-disintegrators.

The semicircle of the hundred bridal couples was brought
into prominence by a soft illumination of its own while the rest
of the auditorium was wrapped in pleasant dusk. Everyone stood
facing the flower of Mental youth. No one became tired of looking. The flowing dovegray draperies faintly revealing the
shining maidenly bodies, the black festive robes of the youths,
their golden helmets, the narrow ebony-black headdresses of the
brides which lent a bright glow to their faces, their necklaces and
ear-pendants, their bracelets and anklets with large, pale gems,
the grace of their stylized manners, the silvery twittering of
voices—all that pelted down upon me like a blissful blizzard of
light and sound. It seemed to me that I was young myself and
belonged in their midst instead of being a revenant of unfathomable antiquity. I had been given the place of honor directly behind our young couple. I was to recline between B.H. and Io-
Fagòr, while the places at the sides of the broad divan were
reserved for the Bride's mother, Io-Rasa and for the Ancestress,
GR³. I owed B.H.'s presence beside me to the particular courtesy
of considerate Father Io-Solip, who had yielded his proper place
so that I might have my Vergil by my side. Io-Solip contented
himself with the couch behind us, which he shared with the three
bachelors. I must confess that an exciting little interlude contributed to my pleasure. When all the bridal couples, including
ours, had simultaneously entered their boxes and the storm of
applause that greeted them had died down, Lala had turned
around with searching eyes. I knew she was looking for me. When
she saw me she smiled most graciously and even winked at me
just the tiniest bit in memory of our dance this morning. My
nerves reacted in a perfectly adolescent manner that I would
not have expected of them any more; I twitched with excitement
like a twenty-year-old—and that's just about what I was by

Astromental measurement. And like a twenty-year-old I felt impelled to express my feeling of happiness in some surreptitious way. So I invented a little verse and whispered it into B.H.'s ear:

> "A heart, resigned and tired, blooms anew
> Beneath the sunshine of a woman's smile. . . ."

"Who wrote the ghazel beginning with these verses?" I asked hypocritically, "which one of the Persian drunkards—Hafiz, Firdusi, or Omar Khayyám? I've forgotten, but you my friend, will recognize it, just as you recognized Emperor Hadrian."

"Oh, Lord, F.W.," said B.H., shaking his head, "can't you ever get rid of all these infantile things, especially now, when you are to experience a Sympaian for the first time?"

"Of course, the Sympaian." I pulled myself together. "I'm looking forward to it. What piece are we going to see?"

"Perhaps each of us will see a different piece," replied B.H. cryptically. Then he turned around and nodded to the Spokesman behind us. "I don't want to anticipate your explanations—"

"The Sympaian," the handsome old gentleman began with a flattered air, "the Sympaian is a composite work of art——"

"A composite work of art," I interrupted him, startled out of my composure, "I've heard that word before. Moreover, it seems to me I've heard the thing itself before. It generally lasts five hours. Steam rises from a trapdoor along with magnificent music that has no beginning and no end, and the bearded singer in a wolf's pelt nervously shifts his long spear from one hand to the other——"

B.H. quietly put his finger to his lips. It was a sign of ill breeding to interrupt a Spokesman in the very first sentence of his causerie. The latter, however, continued imperturbably.

"The Sympaian is a composite work of art," he repeated, "for the creation of which a poet, a musician, and an audience join in co-operation."

I must have looked so dumfounded that Io-Fagòr smiled at me encouragingly and said, "Let's not bore Seigneur with a long causerie on the modern Sympaian. Just let him ask the questions that are on his tongue. This is a thing that's related to his own profession."

I felt sorry for the Spokesman who had once more been deprived of his professional privilege to make a few well-chosen remarks. But I availed myself of Io-Fagòr's offer and asked, "I don't understand why the audience should be named as co-author of the composite work of art. Don't they perform a piece that has already been written and composed, that has either already made a name for itself or, in the case of a new composition, will have to make its name tonight?"

They all looked at me with indulgent smiles.

"But, F.W.," my reincarnated friend said mildly, as he would to a child, "those times are long past when you could serve the audience a petrified cake."

At this point GR³ threw in a remark with her sonorous but suggestive contralto. "I remember those petrified cakes distinctly. I liked them better than the Sympaians of today."

"I'm no barbarian, Madame," said Io-Fagòr. "I know that there is much to be said for the older, elaborated method. But don't forget that the difficulties that were placed in the way of the poets exceeded the limits of permissible artificiality. Every verse had to have twenty-one syllables and three rhymes, at the beginning, the middle, and the end. It took ten years of hard work to complete a piece under such conditions."

Now the classicistic Spokesman succeeded in making himself heard. "This sublime artificiality, my esteemed pater familias," he said, "was only the result of the shameless, unbridled realism that preceded it. A poet who wanted to describe a fractured leg had to produce an official certification that he had broken his own leg."

"You're quite right, my friend," Io-Fagòr nodded graciously. "But after all, it was tiresome to observe in all the fields of art how School A followed School B and School B followed School A."

"What, my dear, do you mean my School A and School B?"

asked Io-Rasa, and I suspected that her question was intended
to give her husband a chance to scintillate. It turned out that I
was right, for Io-Fagòr replied with an epigram that he obviously
kept on tap for such occasions. I didn't mind, for I know artists
and writers who do the same. He said, "The shallowness of
School A is so deep that it seeks in vain to make itself intelligible,
and the depth of School B is so shallow that it seeks in vain to
make itself unintelligible."

"Bravo, Compère," I applauded politely, although I don't have
a very high regard for such antithetical puns. "Even we barbarians
were familiar with these two schools that regularly alternated
with each other. We called the contrasting tendencies of School
A and B naturalistic and symbolistic. But sometimes Schools A
and B mixed the faults of both styles and the result was a swinish
hubbub that called itself futurist or expressionist or surrealist
or some other kind of –ist." Everybody looked at me unapprecia-
tively. What could such high-flown designations mean to them?

"Ladies and gentlemen," I resumed, "the thing that worries
me is not the question of style, but the method, just the bare
method. You tell me that the Sympaian we are about to witness
has been neither written nor composed at this moment. The
people back of the curtain there have no libretto and no music,
there's no score for the conductor and no parts for the musicians
in the orchestra."

"But you're dealing with other brains, old man," B.H. reminded me, "with brains that can think and dream a great many
things synchronously that could formerly be thought only con-
secutively."

"That's just what I'm thinking of," I replied somewhat dis-
heartened, "and I've been afraid right along that I won't get
much out of it."

"Don't worry, Seigneur," Io-Fagòr encouraged me; he was the
most tactful person I had ever met on either side of the grave.
"The method about which you're inquiring is the simplest thing
in the world. You see, it was discovered long ago that the creative
geniuses have been flimflamming the public since time imme-

morial. The great works of art of the past are not so much the
fruits of genuine inspiration as of the critical intellect. The
masters of the arts whose names are still enshrined in the
archives twisted their words and sounds back and forth hundreds
of times, scratched them out, changed them, rewrote them, and
tested them in the strongest acids of the intellect before they
ever reached the public."

"That's more than true, Compère," I agreed. "The nobler ones
did it amid pangs of torment in order to reduce the weaknesses
of their work; the ignobler ones did it with cold calculation in
order to enhance their chances of success. And between them
were the 'Highbrows,' the 'Advance Guard,' the 'Bohemians,'
consisting chiefly of unruly juveniles who passed directly from
adolescence to senility by some sad physiological freak."

"What is this queer word 'Bohemians'?" they asked me.

"Well, ladies and gentlemen, by way of comparison I should
say they were the Jungle creatures of the beginnings of mankind, who lived a phantom life in cafés, bars, studios, editorial
rooms of newspapers and magazines. They were a conceited
clique in the disreputable sections of all the cities of our world.
Their painting and writing were motivated by the consuming
ambition to outdo each other in absurdity. This absurdity was
capable of every conceivable disguise. Today it might parade in
the garb of ecstatic madness, tomorrow in that of shamelessly
sophisticated objectivity, day after tomorrow in that of grinning,
idealistic classicism. But the very moment when one of them
gained the advantage for which he had passionately striven, he
fell behind the others to the exact extent of that advantage. For
the Bohemians were subject to the principle of the merry-go-
round in which you drop behind as soon as you get out in front."

"The merry-go-round is in vogue in our Jungle too," the
House Sage commented darkly.

And I concluded my historical discourse with the words, "In
the beginning the politicians' diabolical craving for power corresponded precisely to the artists' diabolical conceit."

"It is very fitting, Seigneur, that you use these two expressions,"

Io-Fagòr complimented me. "Craving for power and conceit. By the elevation of the Selenozusian our constitution tamed the craving for power. In the same way it tames the conceit and the craving for recognition of the artist by forcing him to rely on inspiration alone and by depriving him of the weapon of the critical intellect. We insist upon pure nourishment, upon unclouded inspiration, upon the divine afflatus, without any admixture on the part of ambition."

"But how is that possible?" I asked.

At a sign from Io-Fagòr, B.H. assumed the duty of interpreter. "You must know that the poets and musicians of the Sympaian are selected and sifted exactly like the final eleven Selenozusian candidates. For these offices only tested and proven inspired persons are chosen, and there are far fewer of these than of genuine Lunar Consecrates. The competent commission unfailingly recognizes the born improviser by certain signs and qualities. The born improviser, for instance, is scared to death to undertake an improvisation, and after it's over he is so ashamed of it that he usually goes into hiding. Nothing makes him happier than to have his work forgotten at once instead of being recorded for posterity. He doesn't even read the reviews that appear on three successive days in the 'Evening Stars.' If he is permitted to experience an instant of ecstasy in the moment of the inspiration itself, he is adequately punished by the eternal torment of self-rejection."

And all that, I marveled to myself, is taking place at the very spot where they used to manufacture the synthetic Sympaians of the films, without any inspiration or improvisation, only with cold calculation, like chemical fertilizer.

"Well, you mustn't go too far, Io-B.H.," Io-Fagòr put a damper on my friend. "Our Sympaianists are permitted a little vanity. It would be a cruel hardship to deprive an artist completely of vanity. After all, he occupies a different position from that of the Selenozusian or the Mutarians. He's a buffoon who produces something that doesn't exist."

"That's why he may be identified with himself and is permitted to have a name," said the Permanent Guest with the baroque wig.

During this conversation, which fascinated me without entirely revealing the nature of the Sympaian, all sorts of waxy blossoms were scattered over the bridal couples, and the air about them was perfumed with pungent scents. We, the audience, were handed cold drinks, the color of mercury, which were supposed to enhance our capacity for productive co-operation. All at once an excited stir ran through the crowd. Three black-robed persons on wheel cots were pushed down to the very front to the space between the boxes and the orchestra pit. This space was almost completely filled by the dudes and dandies, the gilded youth of the Mental world, who were lolling indolently on rugs and mats. The fops and dudes turned right and left in an affected manner in order to attract admiring eyes. They were athletic figures but belonged in the lightweight class. I couldn't help noticing again and again that mankind had become weaker and more delicate in the course of the eons. No one paid any attention to the gilded youth, however; all eyes were riveted on the three black figures on the wheel cots. You could have taken them for corpses if they had not occasionally uttered a distinct sigh of boredom.

"Have they been iced yet, the three of them?" GR³ inquired in her deep voice. She didn't miss a thing.

I looked at B.H. for help. He lowered his eyes. I had caught him with a question he couldn't answer.

"They are the three Critics of the Era," Io-Fagòr came to my aid. "Shortly before the beginning of the Sympaian their emotions are anaesthetized. That is, all their sympathies and antipathies are paralyzed so that they may judge by their critical intellect alone. Moreover, their powers of expression are reduced to a minimum so they will not be tempted to indulge in stylistic escapades. It's just the reverse with the Sympaianists; they have not been permitted to spend a minute alone in the past three days so that their critical intellect would have no opportunity to fashion any idea that they might have had."

"Poor fellows," I sighed, "I hope they at least get a chance to sleep."

"They are put into a dreamless sleep every night," Io-Fagòr replied.

But I was not only worried about the Sympaianists; the black-robed critics down there worried me even more.

"Pardon me, old man," I whispered to Io-Fagòr, "is the icing of the emotions really successful every time?"

"The elimination of the good emotions, that is, the friendly, the favorable ones, can be counted on as sure as fate," was the answer.

"And what about the elimination of the bad emotions, that is, the unfriendly, the unfavorable ones?"

"No, Seigneur," said Io-Fagòr, "the bad emotions can never be completely paralyzed, for the critical intellect itself is a bad emotion, or rather, two bad emotions."

"Two bad emotions?" I repeated in surprise.

"Yes, Seigneur. Envy, because the critic is the critic and not the author; and malicious pleasure because the author is the author and not the critic."

"But then all reviews must be unfavorable nowadays." I exclaimed.

General surprise greeted this comment.

"But reviews are naturally unfavorable. Do you mean to say that there were favorable reviews in your day, Seigneur?"

"Hm, our reviews were softened by commercial considerations now and then," I declared, shamefaced and confused, adding, "I refuse to give any further information on this subject, since I write Sympaians myself and am therefore dependent upon the reviewers of our former age."

As I spoke these ill-considered words I noticed Io-Joel, King Saul's firstborn son. He was the last one still on his feet in the gigantic auditorium, standing with his back to the orchestra and letting his apathetic, myopic gaze rove over the festive house. He wore the same formal garment as the bridegrooms. I noticed something peculiar about him and around him, as though the air that enveloped him were trembling. He differed from the dudes and dandies and the other young men in some indefinable manner, although externally he looked exactly like them. He was standing at the farthest right edge of the orchestra pit, near the door which even in this day and age bore a glowing red sign "Exit." The house lights faded. The bridegrooms in the wide horseshoe took the hands of their brides with a formal, affected gesture. Io-Do made a remark to Lala. It seemed to be an angry remark, for the young man's back and shoulders definitely expressed annoyance. I would have bet that the remark concerned Minionman's son. Lala laughed a little. If I keep looking at her, I thought, I won't fall asleep at this Sympaian.

* * * * *
* * *
*

AS THE CURTAIN ROSE I SAW many members of the audience assume a posture that I had observed more frequently at a football match than in a theater. It was the posture of the goalkeeper on a soccer team who stands crouched with extended arms, intent upon catching a flying ball. This gesture proved that the enjoyment of a Mental show no longer consisted of the passive acceptance of the offering, and that the role of the Sympaian audience had improved, had become more important and more vital than formerly. Some of my readers may object that they see a contradiction in this tenser participation of the Mental audience, since the entire world had developed in the direction of reduced effort and painless enjoyment. What the rising curtain revealed was therefore all the more disappointing and disillusioning: a huge empty stage with three bare white walls. The smallest summer amateur stage of our day in the process of scene shifting was a breath-taking world of enchantment in comparison with this. The light that flooded the stage was just as bald and cold as the stage itself. But I knew at once

that this baldness and barrenness were not a part of the performance. Two utterly absent-minded gentlemen stood in the right
and left foreground, respectively, and their gleaming bald heads
and black cowls indicated that they were officials of the era.
Farther upstage six or seven ladies and gentlemen in ordinary
dress were chatting in undertones. They seemed to have dropped
in by pure chance, and apparently had nothing to do with the
Sympaian, least of all with the audience. It would be difficult
to imagine anything less dramatic than this little group of citizens.
When actors in my former life arrived on a rehearsal stage in
street clothes, laughing and wisecracking, it was a thrilling
scene compared with this. I couldn't understand why the theater
revealed itself stripped of every illusion in a world that had a
particularly strong sense of ceremony and formality. I thought
of the ballets and pantomimes of the youthful Starrovers and
whispered my comment into B.H.'s ear. He reprimanded me in a
similar tone.

"In the first place, the Chronosophers don't put on shows but
seek truth. In the second place, the people of today don't need
any childish illusions suggested to them from outside. They
would be bored by anything that they didn't produce themselves. And in the third place, wait!"

B.H. had not yet finished when the lone gentleman standing
at the left side of the proscenium began to make swinging motions with his arms, like a freezing cabdriver at a taxi stand who
tries to get warm by stimulating his circulation.

"Is that the inspiration hitting the poet?" I asked impertinently.
But I really didn't intend to sound quite so ironical.

"The poets always stand on the right," Io-Fagòr corrected me.
"The musicians stand on the heart-side."

"That's really the least they can do," I muttered, "although in
my day the better poets stood pretty far to the left."

Suddenly the musician made a funny little jump to the edge
of the orchestra pit. His smooth face beamed with such honest
ingenuousness that a ripple of sympathetic laughter ran through
the audience like a glissando. The maestro paid no attention

whatever to this unintentional effect. As an improviser he was so involved with himself that the reaction of the people was a matter of utter indifference to him. He frowned as he surveyed the orchestra. The latter consisted of about one hundred men. All had bald pates and wore cowls. I shall not waste my time with a description of the instruments. Some of them differed from ours in shape but the principle was the same. No matter how old mankind gets, I thought, they will always make music in the same way, by singing, fiddling, plucking, blowing, and by striking on tuned strings or taut skins. My Lord, how mistaken I was. The instruments in the orchestra only appeared to be wind and string instruments. In reality these Mental descendants of violins and harps had no strings at all; they were simply props, like the bagpipes of the Idiot and the hurdy-gurdy in the Park of the Worker this morning.

So far the orchestra showed no signs of attentiveness, but now the composer looked sharply at one of the woodwind players, who rose with an indolent smile. A series of messages transmitted by their eyes passed between the two men, then the player raised the prop oboe to his mouth and the maestro began to beat time with the index finger of his left hand. I heard nothing. Other instruments joined to accompany the oboist whose body was swaying back and forth in rhythmic motion. The actions of the orchestra gradually began to reflect the picture of music more and more. The audience heard it plainly. And suddenly my inner hearing opened, in very much the same way as the ears open when an airplane has finished its glide down from a considerable height. The music, created by the spirit of the master, was now recreated by our own spirit through the medium of the silent orchestra, every member of which played his part with the greatest emotional intensity. The secret of Astromental music did not lie in mere suggestion, avoiding material sound, but in the release of the inner, active, musical life of the audience. It represented a tremendous step in advance in the direction of spiritualization. I don't know whether it is so, but I regard it as likely that Mental throats and lungs and muscles no longer had the strength to produce sonant music, such as we knew, for an hour or more on end. It is a fact, however, that I don't remember hearing a single breath of song and that even the Monolingua often sounded like a mere rustling of dry leaves. This dynamic participation in the music was also responsible for the attitude of the audience; they did not sit there laxly and apathetically like subscribers to a symphony series, but reflected the motions and emotions of the orchestra in their sparkling eyes. The most significant thing I can say about the music is that even I, who had missed an entire eon of progress, was able to reproduce it in my own mind under the direction of the composer. I am ashamed to confess that back in the beginnings of mankind I had been far less competent to keep up with musical progress.

It is quite clear by this time that the Sympaian had little in common with our beloved opera. The music, important as it was, was not intended to produce feelings of rapture on its own account. Singing itself had withdrawn from the joyously vibrating vocal cords to the more intimate realm of thinking and feeling. Music was rather intended to emphasize the passage of time. It served to carve the drama out of the sphere of time. But where was the drama?

The gentleman on the right side of the proscenium, the author's side, had been wiping the perspiration from his forehead with a veil kerchief for some time. Presently he walked slowly, with bowed head, toward the chatting group of actors, who gradually stopped talking and turned to the dramatist. A long silence ensued. Breathless suspense gripped the audience too. The music stopped abruptly, for suspense is not properly the object of musical expression. The dramatic author inclined his polished pate to the right at an almost plaintive angle. Finally he nodded to one of the actors. The latter was tall and broad-shouldered beyond the average. Again there was a brief exchange of glances, supplemented by a few muttered words. Then the author returned to his post without taking his eyes from the chosen artist. The actor first retired into deep thought, or more accurately, he fell into a deep reverie that could be felt at a

distance and from which he had trouble rousing himself. Then
he began to walk up and down along the footlights with crossed
arms and tightly closed eyes, traversing the entire width of the
stage each time. With every turn his step became heavier and
heavier, boorishly clumsier. The composer on the left side watched
him with the keen immobility of a hunter before he signaled the
make-believe orchestra and unleashed a muffled accompaniment
that made me think of a rope with many knots. Suddenly the
actor stopped his boorish pacing and rearranged his ordinary veil
garment with two angry jerks; then he resumed his walk, but now
more rapidly and with an air of agitation. I have no explanation
for the things that happened next. Since I was lying there
stretched out it was no wonder that I was overcome by weariness now and then. Whenever this danger threatened I quickly
looked at Lala, whose profile I could clearly see in the semi-
darkness. This time, when I turned back to the stage, refreshed
and a little more wide awake, the actor had undergone a complete change. He had been transformed into a magnificent
Jungle man, a Romantic gypsy, or rather a Montenegrin or an
Albanian Skipetar. Tiny bells jingled on the ends of his tremendous black mustache. A red cap with a long tassel dangled on the
back of his head. Silver buttons glittered on his jacket. His feet
were shod with authentic peasant boots. And yet it wasn't all
quite as simple as that. The actor seemed to be a hybrid, a
changeling. Sometimes the black veil garment which he was
actually wearing broke through the barbaric costume of the
Jungle man which his powerful imagination forced on our
senses. But the strangest thing was that his true face never once
broke through his assumed face, his mask. The power of this
actor made me think that perhaps in one of his next reincarnations B.H. would meet people who had several bodies and heads
at their disposal, and not for theatrical purposes.

And now, rack my memory as I will, I find it utterly impossible to describe the manner in which this magnificent Jungle
man spoke and sang or did not speak and sing. It is quite possible
that the actor uttered no sound at all but that he caused his

speeches to originate directly in us, his listeners, in the same
manner in which the dead musical instruments produced their
music. This, however, is less important than the fact that the
text of the speeches, which the actor received from the mind of
the author, was beautiful, simple, and intelligible even for the
slow wits of an aborigine like myself. Incidentally I had adapted
myself to the situation very quickly; I learned to hear the words
and sounds solely with my inner hearing, and in a few moments
I caught on to the action and began to enjoy it. The Sympaian
seemed to differ from the theater of my day in that it was less
interested in dramatic conflicts than in problems of the soul
expressed in the form of monologues. Naturally I have forgotten
the words and verses spoken by the Jungle man in elegant
Monolingua. In abridged and attenuated form they probably
expressed the following:

"I am a son of the Jungle. Like my father and forefathers
I love our blue mountains and fragrant valleys that give me food
and happiness. Like my father and forefathers I never thought
of breaking the proud prohibition that we set for ourselves—
until yesterday. Although I am a man, a Christian, a son of the
Church, like the Others, yet I never dreamed of going over to
them, the associates of the stars, the rulers of space, before whose
omniscient spirit I would be crushed, poor peasant and shepherd
that I am. But since yesterday. . . ."

Aha, just as our authors used to exploit the "social problem,"
so these exploit the Jungle. I thought this as an "aside," while
the play was developing in me with the full co-operation of my
attention. The capacity of the Astromentals to become conscious
of several intellectual processes simultaneously was gradually becoming part of my equipment. I was painfully aware, for example,
of the acute discomfort which the author's choice of material
engendered in Io-Fagòr. I also felt that this choice of subject
had touched a neuralgic spot in almost the entire Sympaian
audience. Suddenly I became shockingly conscious of the dangerous game which we authors of all eras had always played merely
for the sake of the sentimental effect. Certainly the Jungle fur-

nished brilliant material. There was nothing more tragic in the
present world than the contrast between the recidivism of nature
and man on the one hand, and Astromental accomplishments
on the other. But I felt the stress at once which the author gave
this improvisation. This stress served for the romantic glorification of the Jungle and, strange as I was, I sensed its Rousseauist
spuriousness. As an impartial observer I could easily tell that
it was the Djebel and not the Jungle that needed defending. Yet
if I had not been born a hundred thousand years ago but only a
hundred, like the mirror-skulled author down there, I would no
doubt have glorified the Jungle with the same romantic sentimentality. It's a great privilege to be a man living beyond the
bounds of history; it's more than a privilege, it's an impossibility.
At the moment I was the incarnation of that impossibility. Unfortunately I didn't enjoy it.

While I was thinking all these "asides" the stage had become
very animated at the inner command of the improviser. By
virtue of the agitated projective force of three thousand nerve
centers, colorful stage settings had developed which could have
been called "dynamic" or "visionary" backdrops, if the entire
stage had not been burst open and extended into infinity. The
same people who, only a few hours ago, had looked with disgust
at the *reality* of the Jungle during the cat phenomenon were now
gazing with rapt attention at their *vision* of the Jungle. For this
situation too I quickly found analogies. Hadn't the most reactionary bourgeois and capitalists of my day frantically
applauded the plays of the "revolutionary dramatists" when literary snobbery happened to bring them into vogue? They did it
because they were firmly convinced that the revolutionary dramatists weren't serious about it at all, and they were quite right.
A vain, self-centered literary ego can't be serious about anything
except about the impression which it creates. And so, night after
night, the theaters of our great cities were resplendent with
jewels, glittering evening gowns, and white shirt-fronts, while
misery, hunger, depravity of body and soul paraded on the stage
and wild imprecations were uttered against those who had paid

big admission prices for the privilege of being cursed because
they believed that these curses were not directed at them but
belonged to the "realm of art." The poor people, on the other
hand, crowded into the motion picture houses in order to stare
rapturously at the jewels, glittering evening gowns, white shirt-
fronts, and lucrative eroticism on the silver screen. Right now,
in the Eleventh Cosmic Capital Year of Virgo, there was no more
money, of course, no social distinctions, and, above all, no misery.
But in place of that they had the Jungle, and the Jungle, which
couldn't be mentioned in polite society, seemed to have become
a sort of romantic abstraction in the hearts of idealists like Io-
Joel and the authors of the day.

The improviser brought new characters into the action. Now
a young lady had changed before our eyes into the hero's Jungle
wife with an embroidered peasant bodice, and an elderly gentleman had become his father with a snow-white, jingling mustache.
It pleased me to discover that my inner eye and ear were beginning to react much more rapidly to the stimulus of the author
and actors than at the start of the play. The wife and the father
advanced cogent arguments in their effort to dissuade the moon-
struck hero from exchanging his green island for the irongray
desolation outside. But the arguments were unavailing, even
when two curly-headed children were superfluously conjured into
our consciousness and clung to their father's arms. The young
Jungle peasant wrenched himself away from his family and his
crackerbox house to embark upon his adventure. Whenever the
action became tense the music faded, only to become more
prominent during the speeches and monologues.

I was quite disappointed. "They didn't have to summon an
improviser down from heaven for this sort of thing," I whispered
into B.H.'s ear. "That stuff is old as the hills—the contrast between city and country, between rustic simplicity and decadent
culture. They did that a lot better back in our eighteenth
and nineteenth centuries, of course, with the help of the
intellect."

B.H. was offended.

"You shouldn't judge prematurely, F.W.," he grumbled. "You can't possibly grasp all the nuances and overtones yet."

"Don't underestimate me, B.H. I can tell you now, for instance, that a beautiful young lady, a dovegray bride, is about to appear. Our husky aborigine has seen her at the Mental parapet, and she is drawing his emotions out into the other sphere. Not a particularly original idea. You see, I'm improvising the improviser."

"You are improvising the improviser because he improvised the dovegray bride into the subconsciousness of the audience, including yours, at the very beginning of the play. You can only guess what the improviser wants you to guess, and you're not even guessing everything."

"Great is the Djebel," I muttered, whereupon Io-Fagòr at my left, who had heard my words, sighed deeply.

From this moment on I was disturbed and felt so indescribably ill that I should have liked to leave the Sympaian if such an affront hadn't been unthinkable. I must confess that I felt something worse than nervous hypertension. I felt fear, strangling fear, and I couldn't explain it. I tried to calm myself with the thought that the Astromental audience around me would feel a three times greater fear if my premonition of coming disaster had any foundation. Or could it be that my recent audience with the High Floater had made me more sensitive for the moment than these clairvoyant people of the future? I closed my eyes in order to escape the Sympaian. I didn't succeed. The terrible thing was that the Sympaian became unbearably intensified behind my closed eyelids. Since this form of art was no external process but one projected to the inside, its power was doubled and trebled when the physical senses were turned off. I tried to force my thoughts into other channels. I thought of her whom I love and whom I had had to leave eons ago. It made me infinitely sad to think that she no longer had a destiny. I began to fidget like a nightmare-ridden sleeper, so that B.H. reprimanded me repeatedly. I didn't even want to see Lala again. I pressed my hand against my eyes. The music became still louder, the action

shriller. In addition to everything else my nerves were tortured
by the suspicion that the improvising author had tackled a problem which had no solution. My critical intellect ran ahead of the
play. The improviser couldn't possibly let the Jungle man conquer Astromental mankind. But if he even had him perish in tragic
beauty, the Jungle would be right and the Djebel wrong. Any
way you looked at it, it was bound to end in a terrific mess.

The author at the right side of the stage had finally produced
his dovegray bride (who had been deposited in all of us from the
start), and now he gave her and the Jungle hero a great scene.
I recall that at the end of one of the speeches in which the
actor declared that life would have to be "renewed" (Io-Joel's
words), the bride took off her black helmet and showed that it
did not conceal a shiny little bald pate but a head of lovely,
tabooed blond hair. It seemed as if the deep bell-tone of ocean
surf reached my ear. An invisible force drew my hand from my
eyes. I looked at the audience. It had changed radically. Many
people glowed negatively. The dusky loges were marked by these
pale emanations of light. It was clear to me at once that this
glowing represented a predominance of the Astral in the Astromental composition, a dangerous ascendancy of the emotional
side over the intellectual. This optical expression of the aroused
temperament did not strike me as remarkable or strange for an
instant. Among all these faint light emanations, however, two
persons not only glimmered but actually glowed like star-trans-
parencies. The word glow is not a metaphor in this case, but an
actuality that I witnessed. One of the glowers was Io-Joel, King
Saul's son. He glowed a panting bright red from head to foot, in
the exact manner of an overheated stove. Who would ever have
believed that he, the frigid, ironical, superior creature, was
nothing but a torch of primeval fanaticism? It was plain to see
that Io-Joel was sending out the rays of his red heat to the hero
on the stage, stimulating his acting to a frenzy.

The other glower was not far from me. In fact he was hardly
two paces away. I am speaking of Io-Do, the Bridegroom, of

course. He glowed in exactly the same ominous colors as the pillars of fire on the horizon of the Jupiter moor: brownish-violet. His fervor had less illuminating power and probably also less heat than that of Joel-Sid. It seemed, however, to be all the more consuming inside him. And then there was still another who did not glow but shone instead. It was Io-Fra, the Mutarian, who had lain at the feet of the bridal couple until recently, but who had now risen and was standing at the outer corner of the box. He was shining, and this word is to be taken just as literally as the bright red incandescence of Io-Joel and the brownish-violet glowing of Io-Do. The Mutarian's face emitted mild, pale rays of the same silver-gold that the old masters used to paint the aureoles of saints. No one will ever see a holier face than that of Io-Fra in the last few seconds before the catastrophe. His eyes were closed and shadowy, his nose prominent and pointed, his mouth was smiling in ecstatic expectation. Turning his back to the stage, he slowly spread his arms.

Lala used both her hands, trying to pull her Fiancé back to the divan. Io-Do, however, wrenched himself away with quite un-Mental brutality and jumped on top of the cot. All but the Ancestress in our box rose to their feet. Io-Do began to wave his ridiculous nineteenth-century revolver around in the air like a madman—this choice specimen from his collection and the symbol of his historical spleen. It's a good thing, I thought, that there's no life left in the silly toy, otherwise it might go off, because the damn fool is holding his finger on the trigger. I had not even finished thinking this relieving thought when the silly toy did go off. It was a stupid, clumsy, exaggerated, old-fashioned crashing explosion accompanied by much powder smoke. Io-Do had aimed at the Jungle man or at the glowing red Io-Joel. That's what I assumed. But he had hit the Mutarian right in the middle of his shining face.

* * * *
* * *
*

AMONG THE FEW THINGS THAT HAD SURVIVED from the beginnings of mankind was this grain or two of gunpowder, sealed airtight in a rusty cartridge that chance or fate had preserved in the chamber of ancient roscoe, and it had now forced its lead projectile through the rifling of the barrel. The effect of the soft-nosed bullet was terrific. It had completely shattered the shining face. The loge was spattered with human blood and brains. For generations the civilized world had not witnessed a homicide. Only a homicide? As far back as the memory of this civilized world reached, people who had attained the extreme limit of ageless old age and whose satiety and weariness exceeded all other emotions, had voluntarily betaken themselves to the institution called the "Wintergarden." Even the death of animals went unnoticed. For dogs and cats there was an annex to the Wintergarden. The dogs had rapidly become accustomed to it, but the cats had not. Oh these miserably ungrateful cats! They had shown themselves far more clairvoyant than Astromental men and had emigrated at the right time.

It took a little while before everyone in the theater became conscious of what had happened. The improvising author and composer, wrapped up in their creative activity, did not even seem to have heard the crashing explosion. The scene ran on for a full minute before the visionary stage setting faded, reality broke through the costumes and masks of the actors, and the distorted music in our minds became silent. Here and there a musician still played a soundless vibrato on his make-believe instrument. The Sympaian did not come to an abrupt end. It was a mangled, frayed, unraveled end. The pause of deep silence following the last note as it slithered away was all the more horrible. And then came a cry from three thousand throats, a little, short, not very loud cry, but one that was charged with hysteria and that betrayed the fear and terror still living in the enlightened human soul. In my century this cry would inevitably have been followed by panic. After a slight quivering of the scales, however, it was followed by something quite different. Mental discipline, rooted in refined individualism, withstood the urge to mob insanity. In the depth of the renewed, awestruck silence the people, one after another, covered their heads with the loose, flowing veils which they wore as garments. It was an exceedingly antique, sublime gesture, although its motive was not grief or reverence in the face of death but the unspeakable dread of these people at the sight of spilled blood and corpses, a sight which only a very few in each generation ever saw. I, in my dress suit, of course, could not cover my face, nor could B.H., in his field uniform, cover his. Only one other person stood beside us with uncovered head and courageously faced the mutilated body that lay slumped in a corner of the box. It was Io-Fagòr, his face yellow as wax. He was gently holding the head of Lala who had sought refuge with him.

Slowly, solemnly, the audience began to clear the House of the Sympaian without breaking the silence by a single audible breath. We, however, B.H., the Io-Fagòr family, and I waited until a group of Mutarians approached noiselessly, picked up the body of their brother, and carried it away with the supersensual sureness that they had acquired by sacrificing their senses. For the Mutarians were familiar with death and the dead. They and, of course, the priests and friars of the Church, as well as the Chronosophers of all the Lamaseries, and a few other eccentrics did not voluntarily betake themselves to the Wintergarden. They regarded dying and death as God-ordained destiny, and they served each other before and afterward. The Church, moreover, rejected the Wintergarden, just as, in the beginnings of mankind, it had rejected euthanasia, by means of which the physicians had sought to ease the final way for incurable invalids. The Church administered the dying sacraments only to those who were no longer able to go "voluntarily" and "on foot."

Upstairs in the strangely unfinished, roofless entry hall the people still thronged with terror-wide eyes. But outside, in the vast Geodrome, a crowd of hundreds of thousands surged about. The news of the tragic shot from a forgotten blunderbuss had made its way around the inhabited globe with incredible speed.

Murderous death, bloodstained Mors had irrupted into the era of peace after a holiday of several historical eons. But now Mors and murder were again identical. What good was all my logic that told me Io-Do could at worst have been charged with manslaughter in our courts, and he couldn't even have been convicted on that charge because he didn't know the danger of the firearm that he had waved around so carelessly. But what about his intent? Perhaps that weighed more heavily in Astromental jurisprudence than the fact itself.

Suddenly it seemed to me that the whispers of the throng were amplified to a roar by a concealed loud-speaker: "The Sympaian was no improvisation, it was prepared. . . ." "The Commissions will have to act at once. . . ." "All engagements have just now been broken. . . ." "This is the constitutional end of the Geoarchon. . . ." "The High Floater has been asked to float here but he refused. . . ." "Not only the collectors of weapons are in the conspiracy. . . ."

Now I realized that it was not a matter of a tragic accident but of a political development which could be decisive in the destiny of the world. The how and why were beyond me. But I had no doubt about it. Suddenly many of Io-Fagòr's dark, anxious remarks became clear to me. Why hadn't they informed me more clearly of the dissension in the world? Even B.H. had been ashamed to confide in an outsider. And as I became more and more conscious of all this I almost collapsed with horror for I realized with a clairvoyance that I cannot explain: I myself shared the guilt. The eyes of the Major Domus Mundi had accused me; his Oracle of the Day had expressed it in dark words. I felt that I was the catalyst, the instigator of the tragic catastrophe. I was to blame simply because I was a wrong, that is a premature, admixture in this future present; because, as a man of the twentieth century, I was unsuited physically and spiritually for the Eleventh Cosmic Capital Year of Virgo; because I had found out a few things that I and my century were not yet permitted to know.

Crushed by this feeling of guilt in my heart I stood among my new friends. Io-Fagòr had maintained his proud composure and said nothing. Lala still kept her face covered. So did Io-Rasa, her mother. Io-Do had vanished. Dear little Io-Solip, only half-conscious, leaned on the arm of the Spokesman. The latter, in agreement with the other two bachelors for the first time, was giving them some whispered instructions. Poor B.H. was completely crushed, on my account and on the family's account. But everyone knew that something incalculable was brewing. Everyone knew that the pebble had begun to slip that was destined to grow into an avalanche. Least concerned of all was the aged Ancestress. In her eyes gleamed the curiosity of indestructible life.

As soon as we arrived at home I fled to my room. I wanted to be alone. Even the companionship of my best friend, upon whom I was so dependent, would have annoyed me tonight. After all, I was a stranger and they left me in peace—perhaps because they were ashamed, perhaps because they had important things to plan. But I felt that men were walking up and down in all the houses of underground Panopolis, talking things over. All night long I heard the light, bare, tapping steps of the conspirators and the defenders above, below, beside, and in me.

The Eighteenth Chapter

WHEREIN THE BRIDE STEPS TO MY BEDSIDE, ROUSES ME OUT OF PURGATORY, AND MAKES ME AN ALLURING PROPOSITION THAT PUTS A SEVERE STRAIN ON MY MORALE.

I SHOULD HAVE liked to spare my readers what follows now. But inasmuch as I haven't concealed ever so many strange and unusual emotional complications, I can't swallow this oddity either, although it doesn't concern anybody except me. Only me? Every once in a while I get the queer notion that every human soul experiences everything, both outwardly and inwardly, that the world has to offer in the way of experiences. If that were not so, there would be no equality before God. The difference between souls does not lie in their ability or inability to have experiences but only in the degree of articulation with which they become conscious of these experiences. Even those who are simple enough to discount the more mysterious conditions of our soul as "extravagant fancies" are filled and permeated by them. For this reason the hope springs eternal that even the most ineffable inner experience will strike a responsive chord in someone who will exclaim in brotherly surprise: "I've had exactly the same experience."

In my understandable fear of sleep I had stayed awake with B.H.'s help all of last night. Today, with the second night of my sojourn well advanced, I had forgotten my fear of "being lost";

or, more accurately, after the tragic occurrence I was much less concerned with my own importance, and my fear of being lost had shrunk in proportion.

This was the reason that I boldly took off my swallowtail, removed my shoes, and dropped on the couch. I turned my eyes to the open window through which the now familiar mountain night peeked into the room, while faint, pleasant whiffs of wind breathed coolness over my face. And then it happened that I, who had only recently been drawn from the alphabet by B.H. and newly reconstructed both physically and psychically out of the arsenal of death by the highly developed spiritualistic technique of my modern contemporaries, fell apart again. No, that's an exaggeration and is bound to be misunderstood. I didn't actually fall apart into various components, I merely broke in two. To be perfectly exact, I became double, thus giving every trained psychologist the opportunity to regard me as a poor schizophrenic and breathe a sigh of relief.

So it came about that I split into two halves that were infinitely distant from each other. And now I must request the reader's kind indulgence while I try to describe my condition with inadequate words, a condition which every bright, healthy mind, including my own, will refuse to accept. For I broke up into a Mr. F.W. who was located practically nowhere and knew nothing of himself, and a second something, something very fragmentary, very limited, that seemed to have no other function except to know about the sinister Mr. F.W. This other thing, this second thing, that knew about Mr. F.W., wasn't really a person with a body, a soul, and a will at all. It was nothing but a pang of conscience floating in space; it was a concentrated, glaring consciousness of guilt; or, if you like, fear floating freely in space, fear that the crime will finally out. Good Lord, what crime? — Every real crime includes murder. — Who was murdered? — Mr. F.W., of course. — But I'm Mr. F.W. — Not just as you think. — And who murdered Mr. F.W.? — The thing that knows about him, the thing that was left over, the thing that is afraid of being found out. — I never committed suicide. I was always too easygoing, too easily glowing. — We're not talking about suicide, we're talking about murder. — That might be, because I not only killed Mr. F.W., but also Messrs. A.B., A.C., A.D., and a few other XYZ's. — They're all buried next to Mr. F.W. — But I'm only a jot of painful knowledge. Am I answering myself? Who's answering me? — Hello, hello, this is the sounding board speaking. — Does that mean that everything is recorded from everlasting to everlasting? — Silly question. — To hell with your police government. Doesn't anybody ever get free of police government from everlasting to everlasting? When I think of all the files of cause and effect I'd like to be the devil. — All right, you've got your wish. — Aha! So this is hell, and I'm back from furlough. I'm not quite clear about it, but I know I had some kind of furlough. — No, this isn't hell. — Of course it isn't hell. Pardon me, dear sounding board. How could I be so stupid? Hell is much more final. I only had a furlough from purgatory. Please, sir, do you think it's too late for a little moral improvement? — No answer. — Do you suppose I could clear away the corpus delicti and the other corpora delicti that I buried? I remember it distinctly now. — Burying them meant clearing them away. — And moral improvement means digging them up again, is that right? — Right you are. On your way. Look. Find. Dig.

I have tried to render in the form of dialogue what went on in the incorporeal consciousness that I called a pang of conscience floating in space. But it wasn't a dialogue at all. It was a kind of ebbing and flowing, a rhythmic, breathing brightening and darkening of the conscious but almost an abstract part of my existence. The unconscious but concrete part, the sinister Mr. F.W., lay far away, somewhere nowhere. But the important thing was his state of being murdered and buried. I was getting more and more certain that I was no longer on furlough but that I had been taken back into the great absence. This absence was really and truly purgatory, as I had always suspected. I had returned to the condition that I had quite forgotten during my furlough, a condition of dull uneasiness that had to do with my person and its misdeeds that were separated from me. So this is purgatory, I thought, the state of which the living haven't the slightest notion. Purgatory is not in the Intermundia nor in the Gray Neuter. It lies beyond space in its own space and beyond time in its own time. The horrible thing about purgatory was that there was no diversion; that there was no intercourse with any other being; that—if I may speak personally—it consisted of an unimaginable solitary confinement; that the egocentricity of life was surpassed and punished by an ulterior egocentricity precluding any association with other beings. As Dante's travel report indicates, there were probably many kinds of purgatory. But since the life of the soul, no matter what it may be, can never be anything but life, it is subject to the primary principle of life, mutability. As a man of the twentieth century I obviously had to undergo a different kind of purgatory from a man of the fourteenth century, not to think of one of the Eleventh Cosmic Capital Year of Virgo. Moreover my solitary confinement was probably only intended for the "upper tenth," for the so-called "intelligentsia," whose chief fault is egocentricity.

But there was one good thing about purgatory, that there was a chance; and as I floated in the great lostness in the form of a pang of conscience, I wished that a new Swedenborg might come to tell mankind about this chance. For suddenly I knew deep down inside me that I was permitted to wander and search and find. Yes, I was permitted to go look for Mr. F.W., and an innermost hope told me: the moment I find him and dig him up, he will no longer be dead, but free and sprightly along with all his victims. But how to find him? When all is darkness. In what direction to look for him? When there is no direction. Let's go, I said to myself, and now I really began to move. I can't tell you how. It certainly wasn't any floating. And it wasn't any lazy "being moved." It was an eternal dragging along, the crawling of a centipede in a pathless wilderness, with only hope to guide me. I still thought I was crawling when the soft beam of light was already shining on my face, when I was no longer split into a jot of painful guilt and the distant, buried, unself-conscious

Mr. F.W. For by this time I had been perfectly reconstructed
and was lying on the couch. Where? On what couch? In Bedford
Drive? Or in Madame Poznanská's hole-in-the-wall? For heaven's
sake, that was a long time ago. That was in the Chancellery of
the High Floater. In the meantime something terrible has happened. An ancient revolver exploded. Io-Fra was sacrificed. All
engagements are broken. I protest. It's not my fault. In spite of
the Oracle of the Day.

"Who's here?"

* * * * *
* * *
*

IT WAS A CONVENTIONAL EXCLAMATION. It sounded
like a character in a childish story who awakes from a faint and
asks: "Where am I?" I had known for quite a while who was
here. And the question on the tip of my tongue was one that is
more frequently heard in operas and musical comedies than in
real life: "Is it a dream?" But I couldn't trill a pretty aria in
reply. "It is a dream, it is a dream, oh, vision of heav'nly bliss. . . ."
The floating, creeping pang of conscience in the void of purgatory might more properly have been diagnosed as a dream, although I can't even say that with twenty-five per cent certainty.
At first I kept my mouth shut and stared and stared. The Bride,
who stood at my bedside and who had saved me from purgatory,
was real, she was flesh and blood, breath and fragrance. She had
not yet taken off her dovegray formal garment although her
wedding had been bloodily ruined. As a matter of fact she
seemed to have put on fresh finery. On the palm of her left
hand she carefully held a white object that looked exactly like
a large egg. But it was a boudoir lamp, or rather, a source of light
for, without shining itself, the egg diffused a mild glow about its
bearer. The first thing I did was to pull my veil cover up to my
chin because I was embarrassed to be lying there in shirt sleeves.

"Pardon me," I muttered in confusion.

Lala said nothing at all as though, despite her Mental training in polished, indirect conversation, she disdained to say anything empty and formal at this moment. Her magnificent blue
eyes gazed at me intently. So I was forced to speak.

"Did something happen, Lala? Another calamity?"

"Much is happening," she answered briefly and equivocally.

"Is that why you're coming to me?" I asked.

"No, that's not why," she said.

"I believe you're not permitted to come to me at all," I
whispered, as though we were in danger of being overheard, "to
me, an utter stranger. After all, you're still a bride. What are the
women's quarters for? What would your father think if he knew
that you are visiting me so late at night?"

Lala's reply to my pedantic question was a queer little laugh.

"I'm no longer a bride," she said dryly after a lengthy pause.

But I, to my own disgust, relapsed once more into the didactic
tone that had cropped up once or twice before quite against
my will in my talks with Lala.

"That you're no longer a bride is only your subjective conception, Lala. But what is the objective legal situation?"

"My subjective conception is the objective legal situation,"
said Lala with the astonishing wit of which young girls are
sometimes capable in moments of stress.

"Is your Fiancé in the house?" I asked suspiciously.

As she replied, Lala's eye was keenly searching. "Io-Do packed
up his weapons and left the house."

"And do you know where he's gone, Lala?"

"To horrid people, Seigneur."

"What sort of people, Lala?"

"To the conspirators. To the other collectors of weapons."

"Aren't they harmless fools?"

"They dream of using their weapons."

"Aren't you being unjust to your Fiancé, Lala?" I admonished
her. "He's more to be pitied than blamed. He didn't know that
living death was in that antique revolver, and besides it's absurd.
That's even more unbelievable than the mummified grains of

wheat that were planted after five thousand years and that bore
full ears of grain."

Lala dissented and shook her head. "It isn't quite like that,
Seigneur. Io-Do always hated and tormented Brother Io-Fra.
And he deceived me, because I never knew anything about the
big conspiracy."

Despite her revelations I was determined to continue my
defense of Io-Do to the bitter end.

"Lala," I said, "I'm very familiar with the type to which your
Fiancé belongs. They flourished in my day. The first time I saw
Io-Do and his collection of weapons I felt it at once. In its time
this widely prevalent type was called fascist."

"What does this word mean, Seigneur?"

"Fascists, my dear child, were party members who destroyed
the old world order by defending it. But let's forget this moldy
nonsense. After all, the anti-fascists destroyed the new world
order by establishing it. Unfortunately history repeats itself
like the weekly bill of fare of a small-town housewife. Let's
speak of Io-Do. He will return to you, Lala, a better man as a
result of this calamity. A year from now you will celebrate another wedding, and I won't be here to see it."

Lala interrupted me with a gesture as if she wanted to stop
my mouth. But I continued to take Io-Do's part all the more
stubbornly.

"You two were destined for each other from early childhood.
The stars approved your union. Therefore everything will still
turn out well."

"Never," said Lala softly but emphatically and repeated it
twice.

Then I gave up and lay still. All at once she placed her light,
Mental, girlish hand on my breast and left it there while she
brought the luminous egg close to my face. I distinctly felt that
it was a cosmetic light which falsified my appearance by smooth-
ing my wrinkles, removing my double chin, and making me years
younger.

"I shouldn't have done it, Lala," I groaned.

"What shouldn't you have done, Seigneur?" she asked with overtones of tenderness.

"I shouldn't have put my hand on your naked little heart the day before yesterday . . . but your great-great-grandmamma tempted me to do it."

"It's too late to talk about that now," said Lala, and suddenly her mouth was just like GR³'s.

"But I'm much too old for you, Lala," I stammered, bravely suppressing a thousand volts of blissful ecstasy.

"You're only fifty," the girl smiled at me happily.

"A little more than fifty," I retorted very inaccurately.

"So we fit together splendidly, Seigneur," she said. I shut my eyes in order to keep my strength.

"It's not a matter of the silly fifty years at all, Lala. In my day and especially in this country, there were plenty of older fools than I, fools of sixty and sixty-five, who married brats of eighteen. Why not? But my fifty years are antique fifties and not Mental fifties. We'll have to do a little problem in proportion therefore, and very likely it will be wrong anyhow, because I'm a very poor mathematician, even compared with the Idiot of the Era. Now let's see, a hundred and eighty years—that's the average length of life—is to your twenty-six years, Lala, as my relative age, X, is to a little over fifty, my absolute age. Now what's the answer? Oh, Lord, won't you help me, darling?"

"About ninety-three," said Lala without stopping to think. A wonderful accomplishment of Astromental youth, mental arithmetic. Then she added, "But I don't understand what you mean, Seigneur."

"I mean that I am subject to entirely different laws from you."

"What are your laws to me?" she laughed.

"They do concern you, these laws of mine," I tried to explain in a dignified tone. "The difference in our ages isn't really important, Lala, I admit that. I feel young. I even feel much too young. My friend B.H. was quite right today when he called me infantile, that is, hoary but immature. I'm not afraid of you, Lala. As far as youth is concerned we'll get along fine together, whether I'm over fifty or ninety-three. No indeed, I'm concerned with quite another matter."

"And what is this other matter?" she asked in a singing voice while her hand stroked my shirt-front very gently.

"Don't you know," I blurted, "that I'm only a dead man on furlough? Don't you know that I'm rooted in darkest antiquity while you're living in the remotest future? On the very first evening of our union, Lala, you'll not be able to bear the gaps that you'll hear in every word of mine. And besides, don't you know that I only exist subject to recall? Do I have to tell you all these things, Lala?"

The girl looked at me calmly. My disclosures hadn't frightened her in the least.

"You didn't need to tell me anything, Seigneur, for I know everything. And it doesn't change a thing."

"It's madness, Lala," I almost yelled. "You don't know a thing, nothing at all. You haven't the slightest idea, just as your dear sweet little hand hasn't any lines."

Quickly and deeply ashamed she took her hand from my shirt-front. "You're right, I haven't any lines in my hand," she said, "but I have something else that no one knows except Father and Mother. And I'm going away with you and I'm happy that my Fiancé is gone."

"You want to go away with me, you want to go away with me," I whispered, and my composure melted away.

"Yes, we're going away together, Seigneur," said Lala and handed me my swallowtail from the reclining chair with child-like, feminine resoluteness. She picked up this fantastic, ancient, male, formal garment not like one who is only familiar with veil draperies but like a real wife who is entirely at home in the ward-robe of her husband. It was charming and touching, but I had no time to think about it. She stood there ready to help me get into my coat after she had laid aside the egg that diffused light and smoothness. I jumped up from the bed, stepped into my shoes, and slipped into my swallowtail. And to think that I didn't even possess a comb and brush, shabby old sloven that I was.

"What do you intend to do, Lala?" I asked. "Where——?"

"Is there another place for me but the one?" she answered my question with a question.

I had been trying to straighten my dry, tousled hair with my bare hands.

"Why should there be only one place in this world for you, Lala?" I cried indignantly.

"But it's the very place where I want to go," she said emphatically and then added quietly, "Isn't it your place too?"

Now I saw it all. She had chosen the Jungle. And when she said that it was my place too she was speaking nothing but the truth. The Jungle was my place. It was the refuge of everything that was past, ancient, backward, primitive, familiar in my make-up. It was, so to speak, my own time in the midst of the strangest future. Furthermore, it seemed the only way for me to escape from the adventures of my voyage of exploration and to remain alive. We would live in one of the little white houses that I had seen from the parapet yesterday, so my thoughts ran on. It will be easy. We will live on bread and milk, and perhaps even on eggs. By and by Lala will even become used to the chickens. I could be a schoolteacher or a storyteller or town crier or public scribe, for the Jungle would probably be full of illiterates. My dress suit would be most appropriate for all these occupations. Yes, there was no doubt, I was at home in the Jungle. But was Lala at home in the Jungle? What a comedown for her.

"Lala," I heard myself exclaim. "Use a little discretion; you don't belong in the Jungle, in the swinish hubbub of antiquity!"

In answer the girl took the ebony black helmet from her head with a strangely resolute gesture and held it above her crown for the space of three breaths. To speak of an abundance of black silky hair would be crude. It was an aura, a halo, an intimation of dark hair that Lala showed me for two seconds. But I need not say that this self-revelation of a touching, Mental infirmity robbed me of the last vestige of my composure. Lala's radiant beauty had not only become much more beautiful in my eyes so that her forbidding strangeness melted away in this aura of feminine hair, but the total effect was far more than a mere intensification of her sensual charm. I felt indescribably closer to Lala historically. A sweet companionship had opened between us. I knew something about Lala that only her father and mother knew. She had surrendered her secret in order to prove that she belonged to me rather than to Io-Do and to the dandies and fops of this era. In the midst of this Sirius-strange world into which I had dropped willy-nilly, a fellowship, an intimacy suddenly bloomed, such as only a woman can give to a strange man. The result was—I lost my head. I thought the clock had struck 1920 or 1930. I drew Lala into my arms; I kissed her and received her kiss.

For the sake of this kiss I unfortunately have to interrupt the novel in order to do justice to the travel account. My duty compels me to record the most significant differences between the beginnings of mankind and this very distant era. No one will deny that a kiss is as important a phenomenon as, for instance, the formal dinner right after my first appearance, to which I devoted a detailed description in the fifth chapter. In the first place, it will be a matter of gratification to a good many people to learn that the exchange of a kiss between man and woman had not been abolished as a result of a hygienic taboo of physical contact. Since I enjoyed the quite unexpected honor and the quite undeserved, dizzying good fortune of a kiss from an Astromental girl's lips, I can, in all fairness, not content myself with a simple account of the sentimental transaction, but I must interpolate a brief, yet circumspect analysis. In my day people were rather impetuous and uncontrolled in such things. But when I held Lala in my arms so suddenly and unexpectedly, my congenital impetuousness quickly faded. Again, as on several previous occasions, I felt that I, the ghost, was the crudely material and brutal factor in this Astromental community. The girlish body that lay in my arms was as ethereal, as imponderable, as delicate, as overrefined as the eye alone could never have guessed. And the kiss also was not a primeval, primitive, passionate squeezing and squashing of the lips, et cetera, but a mere delicate, breathlike, elfin touch, that left the soul to experience the satisfaction which the bodies denied themselves. I hope no one will object to the comparison, but it seemed to me that the kiss revealed the same principle that I expounded in connection with the Mental soups and creams; namely the distinction between matter and substance: as much substance and as little matter as possible. The kiss itself, as long as it lasted, was little more externally than a blending of breath, an accontiguity of the physical peripheries; the spiritual reaction, however, that was induced by this chastely restrained kiss was so overwhelming that I finally had to tear myself away from Lala and turn aside in fear of a swooning fit. Yes, I turned away and stared convulsively at the empty, false night at the window, simply because I couldn't look at the girl. Although such confessions on the part of persons of mature years are very embarrassing, I must admit that I was literally trembling from head to foot. A man who was born in the nineteenth century may possibly get away with kissing a girl around the year 1950, if he has the courage; but to do the same thing in the Eleventh Cosmic Capital Year of Virgo, that's absurd, that's—that's God-awful.

The ineffable delight of the kiss had logically changed into burning pain. I threw myself down full length on the couch and forced myself to look away from fair Lala. If I didn't, I was lost. And now I made a long, pedantic, dry-as-dust speech, and all the arguments that I advanced were cogent and idiotic.

"I musn't look at you, Lala," I began, "because otherwise I would go away with you at once. But do I dare go away with you? Please consider. It's true that I didn't come voluntarily into the house of your parents, the house of the wedding. Your circle summoned me without first asking my consent, but that doesn't relieve me of any responsibility. For even the things that happen to you are included in the final accounting. I'm a guest in the house of your parents, a terribly strange, embarrassed, and bashful guest. God alone knows to what extent my presence is connected with the calamity that took place. But I was in the absence beyond long enough to know that such concatenations are not as unthinkable as the little, weak, distracted, human minds assume and wish. After all, this world is the shadow of the other world, and not vice versa. But whether my presence has any connection with Io-Do's shot or not, it would be disgraceful conduct on my part to take advantage of his misfortune and to steal his Bride even before the dawn of the wedding day. A thing like that would have been most disgusting even in the very first beginnings of mankind, in the days of the bow and arrow, long before the good old railroad. Whenever I speak of my age, Lala, you laugh your silver, Mental laugh. But I don't have the right any longer to make my own happiness and my own infatuation the focus of the universe. Oh, I did it all my life, again and again. I don't renounce the privilege of being in love with you, my sweet. But I no longer have the privilege to draw selfish consequences from this fact. As a revenant I am obligated to forget everything that went on between us, even the kiss, which I shall never forget. It's your future that's at stake. Still I'm just the least bit worried about myself. Do you know what you did with your shining egg just a little while ago, my sweet child? You roused me directly from purgatory. That's where my actual residence seems to be. That's where a piece of me is hanging in space in the form of a pang of conscience and another piece is crawling around as a centipede of guilt in order to dig up myself and my other murder victims that I've buried somewhere. Even if I don't look like a seducer with my little pot-belly, believe me, Lala, back in my day a man turned into a Bluebeard without half trying. Even right now you're not the one that's seducing me, as I would like to make you believe, but I'm seducing you, for the man is always the seducer, simply by his covetousness. But I don't want to bury anybody else, no one at all, and least of all you, fair Lala."

While I stammered these words with confusion in my mind and pain in my heart, my eyes riveted on the white wall, I seemed to hear the trampling of many feet. And they didn't stop when I stopped speaking, they wandered up and down in the labyrinth outside and inside me. On the other hand, the room in which I lay was derisively silent. Suddenly I was seized by wild panic that I had rejected the most divine opportunity of my life.

"Let's go, Lala," I cried and jumped up from the bed.

But where was Lala? My moralizing, vinegary speech had driven her away, and how right she was. The divine opportunity was gone forever. My respectability as a guest and as a man of principle was safe.

*　*　*　*　*
*　*
*

I STARED INTO SPACE WITH SLEEPLESS EYES. God knows how long. A resolution grew more and more firmly within me to put an end to my Astromental adventure. I had no idea how to go about it. Only one thing was certain: I must go away. I couldn't stay in the house of the wedding party. I'll simply walk and walk and walk, and finally I'll get somewhere. That was the only clear thought in my turbulent brain. I'll see no one and speak to no one, least of all B.H. For my reincarnated friend, my best friend, would convince me, would persuade me, would force me to stay here, although my presence had become useless for all concerned, useless for the canceled wedding and useless for me, because I had seen and heard enough. In a handful of hours I had seen, heard, and felt everything that was new and significant in this Astromental world, particularly the Djebel and the universe it enclosed. The only thing I had not seen was the institution that was mysteriously and probably euphemistically called the "Wintergarden." As I tested my most intimate feelings I found that I was still curious to become acquainted with this institution in which the era seemed to culminate, though I couldn't even guess how. But now that Lala was gone, no sight and no piece of information seemed important enough for me to expose myself to new conflicts and to burden my poor soul in its accustomed purgatory with newly acquired troubles. Over all these murky lucubrations there hovered a restless torment which I can only describe as an aimless urge to flight. I

felt the travel-puzzle in my pocket but I had no intention of
using it. I wanted to walk and walk. A few seconds later I was
standing in the garden under the trees with the leathery foliage
and the motionless waxy blossoms. The giant moths fluttered and
twittered excitedly at this hour. I stepped through the garden
gate into the open, that is, into solitude.

It was about five o'clock in the morning. The first signs of
dawn were in the sky. The emptiness of the Mental world was
stifling. It required a strong imagination to picture the labyrinth
of the living Panopolis under the irongray sod from horizon to
horizon. I almost lost my faith in the existence of the universal
city, even though I had just emerged from one of its houses.
Never had the earth impressed me so much as a lonely planet as
it did in the dawn of this April day. Despite the millions of people
under the turf on which I walked, and their highly developed
powers of mind and spirit, Gaea or Eve seemed more deserted
than John Evangelist and Apostle Peter. How I would have
welcomed two Melangeloi of the earth planet as my companions.
But the angels were otherwise engaged at the moment. Then I
thought of the Jungle. Maybe the Jungle was really a new experiment that God was making with mankind, after Experiment
Number 7958 (Astromentalism) had failed. Was Minionman's
son right in regarding the Jungle as the basis for renewal? My
hand reached for the travel-puzzle. The Jungle was my place.
Lala had been right. No, no, the Jungle was old stuff. I had three
other possibilities in case of need. The Grand Bishop and King
Saul had offered me refuge, and the High Floater would certainly
not turn me away. While my thoughts turned confidently to these
three persons, my feet had discovered a narrow, worn path in the
irongray sod. Along this path they walked with morning brisk-
ness without knowing where they were going.

A silvery haze, such as I had never seen before, rose just
ahead of me. It was not the damp morning fog that used to rise
from the earth before sunrise. It was the exhalation or emanation
from the gray sod, a kind of electrically nervous dew, reminiscent
of the vapor over the Mare Plumbinum, except that it billowed

up much more thinly and more slowly. I had long ago learned to understand the meaning and purpose of the omniprevalent turf. Superficially it appeared to supplant the good old green grass of olden days, but actually it played a much more important role: it was the common "conductor" for all nerve impulses, thought flashes, exhibitions of feeling, and adhibitions of will that Mental men sent toward each other. Within the realm of this heavy turf, which had the same color as nerve substance, everything human was spiritually united. The Keenly Directed Desires were transmitted to the Harmonizers, since the bottle-green vitreous material of the Geodrome amplified and separated all the currents that the turf carried. This was the reason why objectives outside the realm of the irongray sod, that is, outside the civilized world, could be moved toward the traveler only with great difficulty or not at all. The hills and mountains of the Jungle, for example, as we will soon witness, had to be climbed under one's own power or by some other old-fashioned means of locomotion.

As I strode along in the silvery morning haze of Panopolis, heedless of the path and ignorant of its destination, a dainty figure suddenly began to take shape not more than thirty paces away against the brightening horizon, calmly awaiting my approach. I was certainly not prepared to meet the Ancestress out in the open at this hour. I must admit that I never in my life saw a beautiful woman dressed in such perfect harmony with time, place, and light as GR³ in this early dawn. She was all wrapped in silver veils, as though she were the incarnation of Mental pre-dawn mood. I must not forget the long, stylized shepherd's staff on which she nonchalantly leaned. It was decorated with a bouquet of the rusty-red roselike blossoms.

"Your Elegance has already risen," I said with an embarrassed bow. "Madame is no longer sleeping?"

"No, Madame is no longer sleeping," GR³ replied in her deep alto voice, the most colorful voice in the Mental world, and if I understood Her Elegance rightly, she meant that sleep was entirely superfluous at age two hundred.

"I don't wish to disturb Madame on her morning walk," I said with another bow and tried to go on, mindful of Io-Fagòr's warning that the Ancestress was to take care of her respiratory organs out in the open air.

"Disturb?" the dark contralto cooed, restraining me. "She who retires late and rises early knows more than the others and lives more than the others."

I replied with strained gallantry that Madame would know and experience incomparably more than all the others even if she did not retire late and rise early. The youthfully beautiful old hag looked at me with deep-set eyes in an enamel-smooth, unclouded face. I couldn't tell whether the expression in her eyes was derisive, sad, rigid, angry, or merely extremely myopic.

"I know, for example," she said, "that our little one has run off."

"Our little one? Whom do you mean, Madame?" I stammered, although I knew exactly whom Madame meant.

The Ancestress rearranged the folds of the silver veil about her immaculate body. It was the characteristic gesture of the modern lady of fashion.

"Our little one ran off directly from your room, Seigneur, just as she was, but not as she had been before."

I felt myself grow rigid and pale.

"Lala," I exclaimed impulsively. "What does that mean? She's run off? Where to?"

"Why ask something to which you know the answer?" said the Ancestress, and her voice was dark velvety with feigned moral indignation. "She went the way of the free kittens, the way of Melba."

"But she musn't," I cried, "she musn't be permitted to, she must be stopped."

"Who's to stop her, Seigneur?" the Ancestress sighed deeply.

"There's no other way," I said. "I'll have to bring her back. I will bring her back."

"Good, good, good," the horribly charming old woman cooed. "Better do it before the house awakes, before the city awakes, before events begin and end."

It was one of those moments in which one gropes as in a labyrinth. The Ancestress knew that the Bride had spent a part of the night in my room. She intimated that she believed the Bride had been a different woman when she left me. Whatever she knew or claimed to know would be common knowledge of the whole house, the whole city as soon as they awoke. Quite innocently I had become an infamous scoundrel who abused hospitality, who raped his host's daughter, the virginal betrothed of another man, in his room, when he couldn't even lay claim to being a genuine, living human. All that was implied in the words with which GR³ blackmailed me, and left me no choice. She had the whiphand. At the same time, however, something else vibrated in the words and in the tone in which they were spoken. It was a lecherous, pandering invitation to seize the divine opportunity, to follow Lala into the Jungle, and to vanish there with her forever. What a situation for me. I had the choice of two roads, one moral, the other immoral. But both roads, the moral and the immoral one, were the same, for they both led to Lala. It would have taken a stronger character than that of Benoît's debtor to avoid the moral road in this instance because it was a subterfuge for the immoral one.

The sun rose, parting the unfamiliar haze. Never during my entire stay was I less conscious than at this moment of living in the anticipated present of the remotest future. It was a pure present all about me, for Eros knows no other tense. I blinked up at the sun. How about a little heart attack right now, or a Transparency, or better yet, self-destruction in accordance with Ursler's First Fundamental Paradox? But the sun did not react to my suggestion.

I turned around. Something had forced me to. With rhythmic little steps GR³ was moving toward our house garden, swinging her flower-decked shepherd's staff. In the silvergray veils, on buskins, and with her tall headdress she resembled one of those well-known eighteenth-century engravings representing Greek goddesses, nymphs, and dryads. I sent a powerful evil impulse after her. My powerful evil impulse hit her right in the middle of her slim back. She tottered weakly—after all, she was two hundred years old—and I thought she would fall over. But guess again, she didn't fall over. I hadn't counted on the forceful vanity of Astromental mankind incarnated in the person of Lala's great-great-grandmamma. The youthfully beautiful old lady regained her balance at once and skillfully transformed her tottering and swaying into a brisk, cheerful little dancing and prancing. She didn't even stop to catch her breath.

But I reached into my pocket for my travel-puzzle.

Part Three: THE THIRD DAY

FLIGHT

FROM THE WINTERGARDEN

MOTTO:

"There are two fundamental species of angels. The ones helped man from the beginning to make the earth habitable. The others prevented him from doing it. Mankind is still far too immature to be told which of these angels are the good ones and which the bad ones."
—Valentinus the Gnostic, cited from the *Syntagma* by Hippolytus, *ca.* 170 A.D.

The Nineteenth Chapter

WHEREIN I GET A CLOSE-UP VIEW OF THE
PREPARATIONS IN JUNGLE-MOUNTAINTOWN,
BID FAREWELL TO A TRANSFORMED LALA,
AND AM QUITE UNEXPECTEDLY APPOINTED
AS NEGOTIATOR.

AND THERE I sat, once more in familiar surroundings, at a genuine oak rathskeller table, in a huge, smoke-filled, public restaurant, and I have the definite impression that it was called "Central Beer Parlor."

If I could begin the following chapter with this lively sentence, we would both be better off, the reader and I. But that's just the trouble. I am not permitted to plunge in medias res with such animated and ruddy-cheeked sentences. That is contrary to the fundamental law of this travelogue, which requires me to avoid the epic illusion and to take the reader behind the scenes again and again for the sake of the unpleasant truth.

On my desk lie many scraps of paper filled with rapidly scribbled notes. I'm not silly enough to try to make anybody believe that I brought these notes back with me. Still they are among the oldest documents of my journey, no matter how you define it. For these notes concerning my visit to the interior of the Jungle are some of the memoranda that I put on paper in the first few days after my return into the year 1943, written, for the most part, in a hand that I can scarcely decipher today. I quote the following selections at random.

451

"Don't forget that Jungle-Mountaintown was really a mountain city in the heart of the Jungle; it may have been called 'Montin' or something like that, I don't quite remember. But the essential and surprising thing that I do remember is the fact that Mountaintown was not antique or Italian or Spanish or Mexican, although I might well have expected it to be Mexican, with a population of Indios and Mestizos, since we were in California. But it wasn't as logical as that. Mountaintown was rather Slavic or perhaps Scotch, plain and prosaic, while the peasants in its environs for unknown reasons resembled Albanians." — "I had been blindfolded. They thought I might be a spy from the Mental world." — "How can I best describe the quintessence of this vision? The question that still worries me most is this: How could the Astromental Panopolis (dull, gray nerve substance) and the Jungle (old-fashioned, beer-drinking, rustic, enchanting) exist side by side on the same earth? This coexistence struck me as unspeakably remarkable. Any attempt to bridge the contrast—as, for example, a discussion of the question why Mountaintown looked gray under the eternally blue sky—would diminish the validity of the experience." — "Mental time seemed to differ from time in the Jungle in spite of the fact that they shared the same sun. Likewise weeks and months seemed to separate the Lala of this morning from the Lala of last night." — "I can't recall whether it was a funicular railway or a cable car that brought me to Mountaintown or Montin. Although I dozed off at once I had the feeling of sitting in a scenic railway or a roller coaster. At any rate, it moved like the wind."

These quotations are a scant and entirely casual selection from the hundreds of notes that I jotted down while the memories were still fresh. Meanwhile they have hardly faded at all. And now, under the reader's very eye, I shove aside this mountain of notes because it brings back too many details which would only stand in the way of a concise account of my mission in the Jungle. The word mission has just slipped out of my pen. I would have been the last to suspect that my moral purpose of fetching Lala home or my immoral purpose of living with her in the Jungle could have developed into a mission, and a political mission at that. My eye falls once more on the scrap of note paper on the top of the discarded pile. It contains two questions: "Why had the guards with the alpenstocks been withdrawn?" — "Who was it that blindfolded me like a go-between with a flag of truce?" — I can't answer the first question. But it proves that I missed the guards along the parapet when I climbed down through the moat. It may be that treason was involved.

The second question is easily answered. A group of Jungle peasants in their Sunday best seemed to have been waiting for me. In a crude hill-billy dialect of the Monolingua (which I understood very well, however) they explained apologetically that they had been commissioned to blindfold me and to conduct me to Mountaintown. "Go right ahead," I laughed, "I don't mind being blindfolded, if you'll only get me to the distinguished Bride Io-La as quickly as possible." They told me that quite a number of the erstwhile dovegray brides was assembled in the Central Beer Parlor, and that the trip would take only a few minutes since there was no point in using the slow observation car when the express coach was waiting for us. "All the better." One of the brown-skinned Skipetars or high-class gypsies unfolded a red silk kerchief and bandaged my eyes.

When they removed the cloth in front of the Central Beer Parlor in Mountaintown I had a chance to cast a leisurely look all around. I had the impression of being in a rather cheerless provincial town, built on hilly terrain, with narrow, precipitous streets. The gray, three- and four-story houses with perfectly plain fronts were quite without character; their only mildly noteworthy features were the windows, which were not transparent but consisted of a greenish, opaque substance intended to protect the inmates against the glaring sunlight of the era. If I had had an experienced historian of culture with me, he would probably have established the fact that this recidivism, which Astromental men unjustifiably termed "Jungle," had reached a state of development roughly equivalent to the year 1860, the early period of Victoria and Francis Joseph, of Darwin and of world industrialization. And yet, in spite of certain obvious analogies, Mountaintown had an entirely different mood from the era of my grandparents, an echo of which I had felt in my youth. The restrained, repellent, even menacing temper of Jungle-Mountaintown—as foreign to me as that of the Astromental world —stifled my momentary suspicion that I had been materialized into two different historical eras in the course of my involuntary voyage of exploration. No, there could be no doubt that the Jungle was not only located on the same earth with Panopolis, the Geodrome, and the Djebel, but it was also running on the tracks of the same historical period.

The simple Junglemen with their plaids and red tassel caps took leave of me with old-fashioned handclasps and two men in city dress took me in charge. But for the life of me I can't describe the details of their city dress from memory. It was probably so commonplace to my eyes that I paid no attention to it, and I assume, therefore, that it must have looked like the normal dress of my former life. In the same way my black formal and burial suit attracted neither attention nor derision. We walked through a wide, dark vestibule, crowded with people going in and out, and descended a flight of worn stairs into the great hall of the beer house. Despite the early morning hour most of the tables were occupied. Perhaps it's a market day, I thought. For I hadn't a moment's doubt that we were back in an "economic world," a world of cheerful, wretched buying and selling. There —and now the time has come for the first sentence of this chapter, the poor sentence that I left miserably dangling a while ago.

And there I sat, once more in familiar surroundings, at a genuine oak rathskeller table, in a huge, smoke-filled, public restaurant, and I have the definite impression that it was called "Central Beer Parlor." I saw that the customers all about me were drinking brown beer from earthenware mugs and I looked forward passionately to this unforgotten and long-missed pleasure. My companions read the craving in my eyes and smiled at each other.

"The carrier will be here in a moment with your drink," said one of them, whereupon they both took leave of me. The second one, however, turned around once more and called to me in a low tone, "The General wants to see you, of course."

The General, I thought, this is going to be good. But I didn't have much time to wonder about the General who wanted to see me because I was distracted by loud choral singing. Perhaps it was only a vocal quartet or maybe a sextet that was singing on the distant stage; at any rate, it was resounding music and not inner music, which marked a difference between the Jungle and the world of the Sympaian. I surmised that it was the customary beer-hall chorus that entertained early drinkers in Jungle-Mountaintown. A few of the tipplers at adjoining tables hummed with the music or kept time with their hands or feet. But the melodies of the singers proved that my impression that the Jungle was a relapse to the year 1860 was a mere illusion. All these choral tunes (and their tonal system) were slow, ruminant, indolently mournful and belonged to a totally strange era.

A moment later a mug of foam-crowned dark beer stood on the table before me. I took a long, passionate draft. The wild satisfaction that this drink produced was not comparable with that which I had felt yesterday after the heathen meal of water and cheese, the Christian one of wine and bread, and the Jewish one of milk and honey. I was just about to reach for the stein again when I noticed that the carrier was still waiting at the table. I assumed that it was customary here to pay for the drinks at once, a suspicious and distrustful habit of second-rate restaurants. (Here, in the Jungle of the Eleventh Cosmic Capital Year of Virgo, we are plunged back into the most archaic economics; it's these little things that make it obvious.) I remembered that fortunately but carelessly a handful of quarters and smaller coins had been left in the trouser pockets of my dress suit, and that these had been reconstructed as meticulously as the birthmark on my right arm and the gold tooth in my upper left jaw. I reached into my pocket and pulled out three quarters, intending not only to pay for my beer but also to give the carrier a good tip. The superiority of American legal tender over all other varieties of money had been such a dogmatic experience in my former life that I was quite sure that the carrier in the Central Beer Parlor of Jungle-Mountaintown would accept my three quarter dollars with humblest thanks. But chance or my awkwardness caused one of the coins to drop through my fingers and to roll under the table. As I stooped for it the choral music rang particularly loudly in my ears. Then I saw a pair of small, beautifully formed, ivory-pale feet in golden buskins. I arose slowly. I knew who was standing beside me. Lala was no longer wearing her dovegray bridal-veil but a sort of peasant costume with a lot of gold braid and stylishly modified. Today she's enjoying it. But what about tomorrow? That was my first subconscious thought as I exclaimed, "Lala! What have you done? Now you're suddenly entangled in economics. You poor little thing!"

"Why poor?" Lala asked, surprised.

"You don't understand what economics means, Lala. It means no service without its equivalent. It means that you have to sell yourself in one way or another only in order to eat and drink."

"But I like it here in spite of your economics. Besides I always liked to play at buying and selling." A note of stubborn defiance lay in Lala's words.

I laid the three twenty-five cent pieces on the table.

"Now I almost gave you a tip," I muttered. "Isn't that awful, isn't that terrible?"

"Why terrible?" she asked, and her deep blue eyes were innocent and at the same time glittered with cupidity. "Please give me the silver, Seigneur."

She didn't even wait for my reply; her fairylike Mental hand reached for the money, caressed it, and quickly hid it in the breast of her gold-embroidered bodice.

"Don't you know that it's you who have been paid now, Lala, not only the beer, but you yourself?" ·

"What is 'paid'?" she laughed. "I think being paid is very nice."

She sat down on one of the low chairs at the table. In her decision to sit down, to form a "broken line," I felt something purposeful and stubborn. My head was so heavy with undefined sadness that I had to rest it in my hand. Many bitter words came over my lips. But perhaps I only imagined that I was speaking while I was silent in reality.

"It's a good thing that, outside of my friend B.H., there aren't many reincarnated people who remember. Otherwise they would go crazy over the history of mankind. You've finally conquered economics, you no longer need to sell yourselves to more powerful people or to the state, you have a central Worker with a golden, growling voice, who provides your soups and clothes and toothbrushes and baby shoes and household furnishings—and you've no sooner attained all that when a Jungle crops up, full of swinish hubbub and paved streets, and the hands of the most glorious brides reach out for small change. Three steps forward and two back might still be evidence of the existence of God. But two steps forward and three back, there's no sense to that, that's madness."

Lala looked at me uncomprehendingly since I had probably only moved my lips. But I struck the table with my fist. "I'm completely on your father's side, Lala," I shouted louder than necessary. "Get yourself ready at once. I'm taking you home. We can still get there by the time your parents awake."

The beer-hall chorus was just having an intermission, so that a deep silence reigned in the restaurant, and the dull eye of many a tippler turned toward us attracted by my loud excited voice. But Lala only inclined her lovely head, wrapped in a gay shawl, and said, "No. Never." And this "Never" had the same note of irrevocability as it had had a few hours earlier at the time of her nocturnal visit to my room. And now I felt what I quoted a few pages back from the notes made immediately after my return. The brief hours that lay between Lala's visit to my room and these moments in the beer parlor of Jungle-Mountaintown had the weight of weeks and months. Lala was radically, utterly changed. The Jungle had swallowed her. Mindful of my own experiences on John Evangelist and Apostle Peter, I should have been less surprised. The former had Mercurized, and the latter Jupiterized, me much more rapidly than the recidivous life in the beer parlor had absorbed the girl Lala. I must confess that I was deeply grieved, although I really should have been pleased that Lala's incredible adaptability to the Jungle brought her even closer to me historically. But that's where the trouble lay. I clearly felt that her greater nearness was at the same time a barrier. And there could be only one reason, and I knew the reason. As I asked the following questions I did it with the perverse pleasure of a wounded person who rubs alcohol on his wound to make it burn still more.

"Did I understand you to say, Lala," I began hypocritically, "that you intend never to return to your world, to the house of your parents, that you never want to see your loved ones and your home, that you want to disappear forever in such dens as this one?"

I purposely paused in order to give her time to shake her head violently to emphasize her "Never!" Her face had become ghastly pale. Now I went on with my second question.

"So you don't intend to return. That means you want me to stay here in the Jungle with you and live with you?"

Lala was so obviously shocked at these words that I gave the rack of my voluptuous torture another deliberate twist.

"I gave a lot of thought to your visit, dearest, and to all the things you said in my room. More than that. I came here at the advice of your wise Ancestress, from whom you seem to have inherited many qualities. All my moralizing arguments at home were untruthful and cowardly. I hereby officially retract them. The difference in our ages, Lala, is a bagatelle. And even if I were ninety-three years old, as you figured out, what does that mean? I could be a good twenty years older without having to renounce you. My life is perfectly regular although I don't know exactly how I came to be reconstructed. The main thing is that I'm an Aikmetant and a Eumelieur. Look: when I flex my biceps you can feel the muscle through the heavy material of my dress coat. Does a ghost have muscles like that? The same thing is true of my morale. I don't owe the slightest consideration to your father or your mother, to your Ancestress or to B.H. On the contrary, I didn't summon anybody, they summoned me. Furthermore, you know perfectly well that I didn't court you by any seductive wiles, not even by a single glance. When I touched your breast, Lala, my thoughts were timid and chaste. It is true that the hand of your Ancestress placed my hand on your naked little breasts in order that the primitive forces of antiquity might pass over to you. Whether that happened or not, it was a dangerous gamble in any case. You've made your decision and carried it out. Now I'm doing the same thing, Lala, for I can't live without you. That's why I'm here. I accept the proposal you made last night."

Lala slowly lowered her head. I moved closer to her and took her hand.

"You haven't forgotten," I said, "that you kissed me?"

Lala's mouth quivered once or twice before she said softly, "They've given me some work to do here. And I'm so proud of it."

"Work, dearest, yes, work," I nodded with satisfaction but with clenched teeth. "Things certainly move fast. In the wink of an eye people get Mercurized or economicized. Five hours ago the word 'work' was as strange to you as the word 'death.' Your Astromental ancestors liberated you from work, Lala. But back in the beginnings of mankind, where I come from, men and women had to work. And that was a good thing, else they would have chewed each other up even more frequently than they did. I admire you, Lala, for working as a waitress. And I'll find some work too, for now we're all tangled up with economics again, with this primary consequence of the fall of man. But first of all I'll find us a place to live. Maybe the General can help me."

I knew exactly what I was doing when I injected the word General into the conversation at this point. Incidentally, this designation is no linguistic makeshift and no mere substitute for some concept in the Monolingua. This general was really called General. I knew everything. The clairvoyant powers of advanced mankind had not left me untouched. My foresight and prescience had increased remarkably. When Lala heard the word "General" from my lips she raised her eyes and gave me a long look. And suddenly she began to weep.

"Tears?" I asked in malicious, feigned surprise. "Why tears? Isn't everything smooth as butter? Just a day or two ago you wept from pure stubbornness. And after just a few hours in the Jungle you bawl from genuine grief."

"That's not true," she said and glared at me coldly. "I didn't weep and I didn't bawl. I'm just not used to this biting smoke."

"You'd better get used to this biting smoke, Lala. For not only was I a heavy smoker all my life but the General still is."

"It isn't true," she blurted out; "the General just promised me to give up smoking."

"Thanks," I said, "that's all I need to know."

With these words I rose from the table. I was so hurt that my hands trembled. My throat was swollen and I could hardly speak.

"I don't deny," I finally said, "that I'm in love with you, Lala. I don't deny that you have deeply hurt me by your behavior. You're not the first woman to deceive me or to be unfaithful to me. But your fickleness breaks all known records. Nature worked for a hundred thousand years on the refinement of the female sex, even to the point of monopedia, and three hours in the Jungle are enough to make you what you are right now."

I stopped because I had to cover my eyes in order not to betray myself. I clearly felt that I shouldn't speak as I did. I was disgusted with myself beyond words. Whatever was it that had compelled me from the very beginning to preach to this girl again and again? Did I have any claim to her? A claim to jealousy? Because of the General, who was probably a fine, husky, robust specimen? I wish I could say that I made myself so detestable for moral reasons, in order to alienate Lala entirely. I seemed to have succeeded completely in doing that; every nerve told me how loathsome I had become to her and how much she wanted to get rid of me. At the same time I suffered agonies that her assimilation into the Jungle had progressed so rapidly. At this moment I adored Mental civilization and cursed Jungle-Mountaintown, where they drank beer and sang quartets, where there were generals and money had regained its value. Without being in the least ashamed of the curious drinkers at the adjoining tables, I placed my hands on Lala's shoulders and raised my voice excitedly.

"I implore you, Lala, come back. I'm not begging on my account, I'm begging for you. I know that your nocturnal visit doesn't give me the slightest claim. But I don't want you to be vilified, to be Junglefied, to relapse a hundred thousand years. I want you to be forever much too good for me. Come, let's go, let's run away quickly. Maybe the General took your travel-puzzle from you, but I still have mine."

As I spoke the customers at the near-by tables looked at us curiously with bleary eyes. Lala kept her face turned away. I firmly believed that it was on account of the effect of my words, but she was actually looking at two men who were approaching me. The choral music broke off in the middle of a song. The men politely requested me to follow them.

*＊＊＊＊

＊＊＊

＊

THE ROOM LOOKED EXACTLY AS THE TEMPORARY OFFICE of a military commander of any era is supposed to look. A bare room with two windows. A plain deal table with two documents on it, three colored pencils, a clumsy watch, and a half-empty coffee cup. I don't want to be too certain of it, since I have no notes on the subject, but it seems to me as I write that there was a big relief map on the wall and on it was written, either in Greek or at least Cyrillic letters: "Subterranean Dwelling Network. Southern California Sector." I am definitely certain about one thing, and that is that I read the words "Southern California" on the wall of the office. This fact made a strong impression on me because it proved that this particular Jungle was actually located in what had formerly been California. I was led to the conclusion that each of the inhabited sectors of the earth had its own Jungle and its own local danger.

On the other hand, I was worried by the many paradoxes that I found on my brief visit to this future world. Wasn't it logical to expect that a Jungle located so close to what used to be Mexico might be populated by brownish, small, lazy, mild-eyed, flat-nosed Indians or Mestizos rather than by these tall Balkan-esque people? No, it wasn't as simple as that anywhere. Un-expected confusion lurked everywhere. Even the morphological laws that govern the creation and extinction of the planet's dreams seemed to have been revised with the changing climates and altered conditions. Perhaps the Jungle of the Balkan sector now harbored flat-nosed Zapotecans instead of eagle-beaked Skipetars.

And there was the General, sitting at the table, absorbed in one of the two documents and expertly ignoring me. I don't know his name. As far as I was concerned, however, he couldn't possibly be called anything but Constantine. During my military service in the lowly grade of a sergeant I had sometimes been required to deliver messages to high-ranking officers. And in all cases the situation was invariably and monotonously the same. The general or colonel or lieutenant-colonel was always sitting at a table absorbed in a document and paid no attention to me standing there before him, until I felt as though my cramped rigidity were shaking me back and forth like a man who hadn't found a seat in a rocking streetcar. In spite of changing times some of life's repetitions resemble the stereotyped staging of second-rate films. The hapless director knows only one routine: General sits at table—reads document—pays no atten-tion to anything else. Even the Chronosophic schoolmaster wav-ing his pointer at the pupils was an eternal stereotype, as I realized at once yesterday.

General Constantine was definitely a primitive phenomenon. A quarter-inch haircut merged gradually into the bald spot on his square, undistinguished, gleaming skull. His red cauliflower ears stood out from his head. His violet, crisscrossed bull neck was encased in a sort of blouse-shirt. Pale blue eyes under very blond brows, a short nose, and the brutal mouth required by a resolute profession spoiled the picture of a gaunt, gray-haired, Roman type that I had had in mind since I first heard the word General. And did I have to be summoned from purgatory after a hundred thousand years just to take a look at you, Constantine? I realized that the history of the swamp-bred Jungles and of their ill-begotten inmates was far too brief to produce more distinguished generals. Wasn't it sufficient that there were generals at all? This fact may surprise the reader more than me. I took it as a matter of course that the historical stage represented by the Jungle required the maintenance of soldiers and officers, and for that reason I accepted the word General without any qualms. Since the Jungle had produced roosters, why shouldn't there be soldiers to wear the tail feathers in their caps? Furthermore, I didn't find it particularly astonishing that the highest ranking ones among these soldiers had taken steps at once to secure the dovegray brides who had eloped to the Jungle by the dozens in the course of the last night. But the thing I couldn't stomach at all was Lala's poor taste. This coarse Constantine fellow, nothing but a hunk of old-fashioned male muscle, gave orders to the most glorious of Astromental brides and she obeyed him. Lala had demonstrated the greatest delicacy of feeling and understanding at the dance in the Park of the Worker yesterday when I refrained from touching her without gloves. Only a few hours ago she had lain in my arms, chaste as a breath, and I, unworthy of her ethereality, had scarcely survived the ecstasy of her kiss. But Constantine would kiss her as you kiss a barmaid or any other Jungle woman. And the worst part was that he would be right.

The General shoved the papers aside and turned around.

"What do they call him?" he asked his adjutants who gradually materialized before my astigmatic eyes. Beside his chair stood none other than Io-Joel Sid, Minionman's son, who was still wearing his Astromental garb. He was the only one in the room with a golden headdress and dark veil costume.

"They call him 'Seigneur' over there," said King Saul's son, leaning a little in the direction of Constantine's protruding ears.

"Then I'll call him 'Gospodar,'" growled the General. He was undoubtedly speaking the Monolingua, though with a harsh foreign accent.

I understood him, as I understood everyone during my visit, not so much as a result of outward linguistic ability as of an inward willingness to understand. Constantine turned once more to Io-Joel, who looked extremely Mental here in Jungle-Mountaintown, while he had looked highly anti-Mental in California's Eastside. It was particularly clear to me at this moment that he belonged neither here nor there. And as this thought ran through my mind I felt that he became uncertain and suffered from it.

"Explain the situation to him," the commandant ordered.

"Seigneur and Doctus," Minionman's son began, and his distress and embarrassment became more and more obvious. "You know the fact. But you do not know the significance of the fact. The fact is spilled blood. The significance is blood to be spilled."

"Why shouldn't I know the significance of this fact?" I replied, firmly fixing my eye on Constantine and not on Io-Joel. "Spilled blood cries to heaven and demands that blood be spilled, especially after such an unnaturally long time of peace."

I squinted at Io-Joel from the corner of my eye. His slightly albinistic face was pale. The freckles and blemishes of his skin became conspicuous. The young man had lost the self-assurance and the cold sarcasm that had been so much in evidence at our meeting in the Former Eastside District. Here in Jungle-Mountaintown, in the office of the primeval General, he seemed to suffer from a sense of his own inadequacy. I knew lots of people like him in my lifetime. He was one of those fanatical idealists who hate the moral state of their own class and therefore look up to all lower classes. Io-Joel, overfed with star substance and with milk and honey, admired the beer drinkers in the Central

Beer Parlor for their virility, their strength, their unfamiliar, boorish well-being; he admired them so timidly and humbly that all the arrogance with which he hated Astromental culture evaporated here in the wilderness. In Minionman's son I had long ago recognized the tendency of intellectuals which had formerly manifested itself from Rousseau to the Deutero-Marxists as a sentimental hatred of their own origins.

"Please don't misunderstand my role, Doctus and Seigneur," he said. "I am no advocate of blood to be spilled, as you might imagine after our conversation in my father's house. No, I am not. And neither is the General. We have an entirely different idea of the renewal of the world."

Aha, I thought, that sounds familiar too. In the last minute before the action begins he wants to crawfish. Those are bourgeois scruples that the real revolutionaries will settle without batting an eye.

"Pardon me," I said, sitting down boldly on the General's desk and letting my legs dangle. My audacity made Constantine furious but seemed to impress him at the same time, for instead of reprimanding me for my impudence he growled at Io-Joel, "When the Jew of the Era appears, facts dissolve into words."

Deeply offended the young man straightened up and announced with exaggerated pride, "Not I, but my father has the honor of being the Jew of the Era."

The General, forgetful of his promise to Lala, lighted a long thin cigar, bent like a horn, and began to puff so that I was shaken with envy.

"Go on with the information for the Gospodar," he ordered and leaned back. I could see Io-Joel pulling himself together and forcing himself to be coldly casual.

"What is going on in this Jungle, Doctus, is going on simultaneously in all Jungles on earth. The shot which, as you know, was intended for me as a representative of reform, was only a signal. The conspirators everywhere were listening. But calm yourself, Doctus. The conspirators are not on this side, as you believe, but on the other side. The fiancés and the dandies and fops have been collecting weapons on the craziest pretexts for a long, long time and have had them put into working order by experts, weapons that are effective at great distances, with which they could easily destroy the Jungles."

General Constantine's big red fist hit the table so hard that I slipped down from it.

"Boy," he yelled, foaming with rage, "who has given you the right to call our civilized society a Jungle? The Gospodar here regards Mountaintown as a city and not as a primeval forest and he knows that our good beer isn't ditchwater. You are a licensed interpreter and not a Sophistes. Stick to your job!"

"That's what comes from being born above class distinctions," Io-Joel muttered with white lips.

"It would have been more modest to say 'between' class distinctions," I criticized although I felt sorry for him. Incidentally, this almost geometrically compulsive tactlessness was an old, old story. But Io-Joel, a morally sensitive character, now apologized for the wrong use of the word "Jungle" on the ground that it was commonly current in the cultured world outside.

"I understand," I began, "it's a question of who will attack first, the conspirators or the General."

"Quite right, Gospodar," Constantine laughed, addressing me directly for the first time.

"And besides," I continued, "it's clear that a General has to keep the initiative."

Constantine was obviously pleased.

"There's just one thing I don't understand," I concluded. "The use of arms, as I have heard, is an impossibility for Astromental people and is not provided for constitutionally."

"But the possibility lies in this impossibility," Io-Joel declared, perhaps a little too captiously. But I understood his legal train of thought: a thing that is so impossible as not even to be mentioned in the laws, becomes possible by that very fact.

"And for what purpose am I being drawn into your political confidence?" I asked the General.

"Because you are a natural-born umpire, Doctus and Sei-

gneur," Io-Joel resumed as interpreter. And he couldn't refrain
from adding a questionable joke, "As a matter of fact it is even
an exaggeration to say that you were born."

"Ha-ha, he's only living subject to recall, ha-ha," the General
chimed in. Apparently he liked to hear himself laugh. And I, unprincipled as I am, joined in with his laugh and found only the
following comeback.

"Sometimes that's an advantage."

Of course I could have said, "I'm only living subject to recall,
gentlemen, but you're not living at all yet and still you manage
to act important." I can think of such bon mots by the dozen
today but they're only afterthoughts. In the course of that conversation I felt offended and bitter, for my consciousness of
reality wasn't a whit weaker at that time in Jungle-Mountaintown, in Lala's vicinity, than it is today at my desk where I am
recording a part of my experiences.

". . . and that's the reason I'm entrusting this mission to the
Gospodar," I heard General Constantine completing a sentence,
the beginning of which I had missed because of my ill humor.

"A mission as a negotiator, presumably," I said.

Constantine cleared his throat and summarized. "You will tell
them to consider the following: For the present the General of
Mountaintown isn't in the least interested in plowing up your
world. But he has the means to plow up your world, little old
means that you don't know anything about because you neglected studying. And if your young men so much as make one
false move today—what is today?"

"The fifth day of the fourth month," several of his aides
obligingly shouted.

"—then there won't be any more Geodrome or any more
Djebel on the evening of the fifth day of the fourth month.
Or perhaps there will still be a Geodrome and a Djebel but
you'll be moaning about something else."

A deep silence followed these terrible words.

"That's quite an errand for so early in the morning," I said and
wiped the perspiration from my forehead.

Io-Joel had come closer and whispered into my ear, "Don't ever believe, Doctus, that the people over here have more to worry about than the ones over there. You know the dandies and fops, Io-Do and his buddies. They're amateurs. They have collected and repaired the most archaic trans-shadow-disintegrators with which they can easily level out a few mountains and forests. But these people have the will to live and the General has psychic artillery at his disposal, about which I am not permitted to tell you anything. If I were you I would hurry."

This warning showed me that Minionman's son was worried about his father although he was eternally at swords' points with him. Lala, on the other hand, had given up her family easily.

"I accept the commission," I said so loudly that my ears rang. "I'm not doing it because I'm interested in the will to live or in the future. I wouldn't know what to do with any more future than I've already had. I am doing it for the Djebel, for the Starrovers, Marvelers, Foreignfeelers, for the High Floater and for Io-Runt, the star dancer, who will some day add to the knowledge of the shape of the universe and of the most important moment of mankind."

"Gospodar is dismissed," said Constantine and picked up a paper, terminating the interview.

I was annoyed that he treated me like an orderly, just as all the officers in my former military career had done.

"Stop," I cried, "I demand that my mission be facilitated."

"What kind of facilitation?" growled the General without looking up.

"I demand the immediate repatriation of the dovegray brides," I said, finding it a little difficult to put this bureaucratic terminology into the Monolingua.

Io-Joel looked at me derisively with his pale eyes. "I doubt whether you are doing the dovegray brides a favor. Possibly within the next few hours it will be safer here in the Jung— pardon me, here in Mountaintown than over there. Don't forget about the cats."

"It's not a question of safety," I insisted, "but of justice, law, and the constitution."

At these ill-considered words of mine Constantine jumped up furiously. "Constitution," he barked at me and his square skull and his cauliflower ears became red as the revolution. "The Constitution was always against us and it's the General's business to protect the freedom of the will."

"What is the General's business?" I asked calmly and deliberately. "I can't believe my ears. It used to be the business of our generals to protect the unfreedom of the will. And sometimes that was very important, Constantine."

"Bring the girls here," the General yelled. "They can tell him whether they want to go home or not." The General's rage helped me to retain my equanimity.

"You talk of freedom of the will, Constantine," I said, "of the miracle that permits man to break the laws of nature. And you haven't even enough miracle in you to throw away your Cigarohorn for the sake of your new sweetheart."

Unfortunately my audacity went unnoticed because at this moment a group of the brides crowded into the room. Some were still in their dovegray bridal finery, some in peasant dress with embroidered bodices, like Lala's. Only a small number of them managed to get through the door, the rest milled around in the corridor outside. Lala was probably among the latter, for I didn't see her. I could almost bet that I also noticed a few furry gray pussycats prowling around among the young girls.

Constantine rudely addressed this bevy of vastly superior Astromental youth and beauty, perhaps to impress me: "The Gospodar here has come to take you home, Female Ios. He is doing an important errand for me. You will facilitate this errand and help your people at home if you go with him. Whichever ones of you don't want to stay here can pack up your junk and get out."

A long silence followed Constantine's incredibly plebeian words. Then the silence was broken by a strange mewing moan from the brides in chorus. Once more the General had proved that he knew his business.

"That will do," I said, bowing to the ladies, and then I couldn't see any more for they had already put the red silk bandage back over my eyes. As I was led outside my ears rang as from the sound of marching columns and clanking artillery. But that was simply imagination.

* * * * *
* * *
*

THE PERSON WHO HAD BEEN LEADING ME by my hand took off my blindfold. I knew at a glance that I was standing in the central square of the little border village that I had seen yesterday, where the merry-go-round and the primitive swings now stood deserted. The Skipetarian Jungle peasants in their Sunday suits, who had whisked me up to Mountaintown and back again, were disappearing in the distance. Their red tassel caps gleamed in the distance for a moment and then vanished around a corner.

But one person was still holding my hand. It was Lala in her gold-embroidered bodice and shawl that did not go properly with the golden buskins at all. Had she accompanied me? Or had she followed me? It flashed through my mind that she wanted to go with me. She wanted to go home with me. And at the same instant I was astonished, even a little terrified, to realize that I didn't want that to happen. My delight in Lala had vanished along with my infatuation. It was not that the intensity of her image had faded for me; it was only that the background of the picture and the frame had become more prominent.

In these minutes as I stood in the little square in front of the village church I felt more circumspect, I almost said "more double" than ever before. I knew what fate inevitably awaited the world. I knew that Lala and all the brides were safer here than in the houses of their parents. I knew that Lala would not leave the General, for in Constantine she had met for the first time the elemental male force which the Astromental world had

not known in eons. But alongside of all this sensible knowledge
ran a strain of embarrassment rooted in my masculine feeling of
guilt which always crops up when a man begins to lose his
concentrated interest in a woman. In spite of my infatuation
and enchantment I was beginning to withdraw from Lala. I
could easily have ignored my feeling of guilt in this instance,
since it was the girl who had jilted me and not vice versa. But
my embarrassment was more honest than I and so I became
entangled in a final feeble effort to persuade Lala to go home
with me. But I had not counted on the refinement of the soul
of an Astromental girl, who could not be "deceived" at all in
the same sense as her sisters of early or later antiquity. (This
point represents a truly respectable advance in the relations
between man and woman which, on the other hand, means a
remarkable impoverishment since it excludes a lot of colorful
novel and comedy plots.) I had hardly uttered my first few
persuasive words when Lala nervously put her finger on her lips
and shook her head a little, as though she feared that I might
make a clumsy mistake at the last moment, spoiling everything
and degrading myself forever. With her right hand she pointed
at the little village church. Then she walked ahead of me in that
direction with the rhythmic, rested step that women had acquired in a world of pure play. At the portal she whispered to
me, "I want to show Io-Effdoubleu something."

It was the first time that she had not addressed me with the
coldly conventional "Seigneur" that always had a slightly derisive
sound to my ear; she had addressed me with the sounds that she
took to be my personal name because my friend used them.
This form of address made me feel very strange. Lala had kissed
me under the aegis of the name "Seigneur." But I understood
that I had only now become human in her eyes, a real living
person, not merely an interesting phenomenon to parade in
public. She made me feel that our relation had only now become
real and genuine.

We were now standing in a baroque rustic church, as I and

any of my well-traveled readers might have expected. Of course
it was a variety of rustic baroque that neither my readers nor I
have ever seen, compounded of the remotest outcroppings of
human powers of expression, a mixture of styles that will dawn
in thousands of years and fade and dawn again. Still it was
recognizably rustic baroque, in pleasant contrast to the abstract
severity of the Astromental church. I saw images of saints with
eyes fervently raised toward heaven, and a golden, voluted
canopy over the main altar, and a monstrance in the shape of the
sun, and everything was as quiet and simple and rustic as it ought
to be. Lala was holding my three quarter dollars in her hand.

"Where can I make an offering?" she asked.

I pointed at the almsbox.

She stepped up to it and awkwardly laid the three coins next
to the slit. How could she be expected to know what to do with
money and how to give alms? We walked on silently and stopped
in the transept before a fairly large statue of the Madonna and
Child. In the traditional reverence of the Jungle peasant for
unattainable Astromental beauty, the artist had given the Blessed
Virgin the form of a dovegray bride. You could plainly distinguish the ebony helmet and the characteristic folds of the veil
garments produced by the Worker.

"Is that the holy Mother of God?" Lala asked.

"Yes, the Mother of God with the Child, Io-La; the same that
stands as a work of art in your father's house."

"And do you believe in her, Io-Effdoubleu? Do you believe
that she lives above the Intermundia?"

"'Believe' is the wrong word in my case, Lala, for I 'know'
that she helped me, wherever she may live."

"Then I want her to see what I am going to show you now,"
said Lala, and with a determined little gesture that was proud
and bashful and sad all at the same time she opened the palms
of her two hands. It was gloomy in the little church for it had
no windows at all, only small slits under the ceiling arch. So I
saw nothing at first and had no idea what Lala wanted. But
when I put my hands under hers and drew them nearer to my

eyes I saw that they were no longer the empty palms of a show-window dummy like those of her mother and of her Ancestress and of all other people over there. Overnight these waxen, rose-tinted palms had developed a few delicate lines and signs and runes which crossed the three main markings and began to fill the former void with touching new life. These few delicate lines woke compassion in my heart like fresh wounds. They were not the stigmata of a saint, they were the stigmata of a real human, who is born in pain, lives a fateful life, and dies in pain without avoiding these three discomforts. Over night Lala had won her stigmata, no matter how plain and scanty they still were. I almost expected her to say, "Now do you understand, Io-Effdoubleu, that I can't go home with this disgrace, which is my pride, and that I have to stay in the Jungle with the General, who smokes his horn until my eyes begin to water?"

Fortunately she said nothing of the sort, for as long as Lala lives she will always be an Astromental fairy, cool, innocent, impervious to any sentimental impulse. No matter how deep the lineation of her palms may become, she will be eternally different from us who lived before.

Lala said nothing awkward. She merely asked with a little smile, "Can you read what is written in my hand?"

"I'm not trained to decipher this writing," I replied, "but I understand the general outlines."

"And what do the general outlines mean, Io-Effdoubleu?"

I knitted my brow and pretended that the simple hieroglyphics were hard to translate. Finally I spelled out, "You will be happy through misfortune and unhappy through good fortune, dear Lala."

"And is that bad?" she asked attentively.

"No, Lala, I believe that's good."

After these words I bent my head over her delicate, fragrant hands and breathed a kiss on the scars of her normalization, that is, her recidivism. And so I said farewell to Lala who, of all the women of my more intimate acquaintance, will always remain the one with whom I was least acquainted.

The Twentieth Chapter

WHEREIN I TRY TO CARRY OUT THE NEGOTIA-
TOR'S MISSION, MAKE A SOUNDLESS SPEECH,
AND SEE THE ORANGE FLAME WHICH
WILL ONE DAY, CONSUME THE MOON.

"YOU'RE ALL WRONG, it isn't coldness and indifference," said
B.H. when we were alone for two minutes. "The only
coldness and indifference is the pretense of grief in order
to torture the others."

"Do you mean GR³?" I inquired. "Wasn't Lala always her
favorite descendant and didn't she always guard her like the
apple of her eye?"

"GR³ envies Lala to the point of hatred, for one of the consequences of eternal youth is that strong women never know
when they are through. Io-Fagòr and Io-Rasa are deeply grieved,
although you could never tell by looking at them."

It was true as B.H. had said that Lala's parents showed nothing. One might almost have believed that they never thought of
criticizing their daughter and that they had already gotten over
her loss. They did not even avoid speaking about her. They
spoke about her with impersonal sympathy. It was an admirable
attitude which the human race had acquired since the days when
erring children were cast out and cursed and their names were
torn from the parents' hearts. And yet in these days of monopedia a child was worth ever so much more than back in the

474

times when many women were pregnant almost year after year. Since a premature and involuntary death never occurred (except in a few unusual instances), parents could lose their son or daughter only through life and to life. Even that occurred only rarely since the economic and social frictions of the ancient world had disappeared and there was no dissension over rank or inheritance; the only things that might disrupt a family were emotional clashes or philosophical differences of opinion. But in this case it did happen. Io-Fagòr had lost his daughter and Io-Solip his son. What went on among the conspirators, incidentally, where they had their headquarters, and how and since when this Maffia had developed, all that was religiously concealed from me on account of a general feeling of shame. This concealment was not particularly advantageous for the fulfillment of my mission.

It is easy to imagine my painful embarrassment as I stood before Io-Fagòr, Io-Rasa, and the entire household to render an account of my unsuccessful attempt to lure Lala home. Even my Vergil was shocked by the precarious situation into which he had brought me by drawing my name from the alphabet. By comparison the real Vergil had plunged his protégé into far less serious difficulties, for he remained quite untouched by the calamities of hell on his visit, except for some slight twinges of compassion. Dante observed all the cruelly famous episodes as an interestedly disinterested bystander and was not personally involved in any conflicts. Perhaps that was because he moved among the dead as the only living person while my case was exactly reversed. Of course, it required the mighty poetic genius of a mighty era to create the "Divine Comedy," the millenary best-seller, out of a mere "sightseeing tour," without any personal involution, without intrigues, complications, eroticism, or any other consideration of the more or less reading public, and to do it in adamantine terza rima at that. Somebody should try that today.

The strangest thing was that the Ancestress had kept her mouth shut. Lala's parents seemed to know nothing of their daughter's nocturnal visit to my room, or at least they pretended to know nothing. GR³'s discreetness gave me the most uncanny feelings. I recoiled from the thought of sharing a secret with her. For this reason, distasteful as it was to me, I divulged the secret of Lala's clandestine visit without, of course, carrying my honesty too far. Naturally I kept quiet about Lala's proposition and about my own infatuation, for which no one can blame me, and I spoke only of Lala's request that I accompany her as far as the Jungle. To be sure, I could not quite justify myself on the charge of not having given the alarm at once. But no one accused me of that, for the decisive factor lay in Lala's passionate yearning for the Jungle. For Astromental people an inner longing and an outward realization were practically synonymous. How much easier it was for us in the twentieth century, when the road from the wish to its fulfillment was narrow and rocky, when an ocean of inward desire produced only a few driblets of realization, and when we could practice mountainous deceit on ourselves and others without being found out by our own clairvoyance and by that of the world at large.

I had no means of measuring how much of the truth my friends knew after I had given my account. But in our few minutes of private conversation I revealed the entire truth to my friend B.H. At first he looked at me horrified but then he thanked me and opined that I might have brought even greater disgrace on the beginnings of mankind. This private report occupied only a very few minutes. More important things were at stake. We started out at once. I hardly had time to gulp down a crystal cupful of some sort of juice.

* * * * *
* * *
*

IN THIS DECISIVE HOUR I became the unfortunate victim of a strange indisposition which proved that people like me are not suited for any kind of political missions and that the world must be in bad shape when such a mission is entrusted to pianists, professors, theologians, lyric poets, or any other kind of virtuoso. My psychologically gifted reader, who by this time is not only acquainted with the Astromental period but unavoidably also with me, will probably have wondered back in the General's office why I should have been chosen as a negotiator in this life and death matter—I, a private individual, a stranger from the beginnings of mankind.

The word "indisposition" that I used just now is quite inappropriate but I couldn't find a better one. I wasn't taken ill, I had no dizzy spell or any other discomfort that might be traced to the stein of dark beer that I had guzzled too rapidly; no, I lost my voice. Some of us will possibly remember that in the first hour at Io-Fagòr's house I had suddenly lost the ability to understand and to speak the Monolingua. My present affliction was not a repetition of that. I understood everything. I made a perfect speech. But as I made it, to my horror not a sound was audible.

I can't say why that happened to me. Perhaps the pathetic situation was to blame. We were in the hall where the Senate sat in session. Everything, simply everything, about this sentence is wrong. The word "Senate" is made up out of thin air. I could as well have said "State Council" or "World Council" without being a shade more accurate. As in the case of the words "Professor" and "Excellency" I am forced again and again to paraphrase these experienced realities with familiar but inexact analogical terms. Perhaps I was told the real name of this assembly under the chairmanship of the Geoarchon, but I don't remember it. I'm sorry, because I'm not one to regard a name as mere sound and fury, signifying nothing. On the contrary, I know that very often the name is the thing itself. But to say that the Senate "sat" in session is so wrong as to be entirely misleading. Anyone who has only turned the pages of this book knows that if the Senate did anything, it "stood" in session. So I really ought to say "we were in the Standing-Hall of the Senate," or, if I weren't afraid of sounding too abstruse, I should like to call it a "Distance-Hall." For the essential thing about this assembly

was the wide interval that separated the individual members
from each other. Since events were now moving so rapidly, I was
unable to get definite information on such details of secondary
importance, but it seems quite certain that these wide distances
served to reduce the influence of the Astromental mandataries
upon each other. The "insulating parquetry" under our feet undoubtedly had the same purpose. As soon as I entered the hall
I felt a certain inner dullness and nerve deafness, exactly the
reverse of the condition induced by the irongray sod. I find
myself at a loss, however, to explain why the floor of this colossal
auditorium was an inclined plane sloping upward at a sharp
angle to the place where the Selenozusian stood; I can only
conjecture that the "road upward" was to be made symbolically
and practically difficult and perilous, for there was great danger
of slipping on the steep grade. I myself experienced this danger
for, although Io-Fagòr and Io-Solip supported me on the right
and left, I hardly managed to get to the top and kept slipping
back.

When I had finally arrived at my post pretty well winded,
Io-Fagòr and Io-Solip left me since they did not belong to the
State Council. I stood alone and felt deserted. But no matter who
or what I was, my violet wrist-rosette not only gave me the right
to appear in person in the House of Lords (again a wrong
designation), but also to be pushed up to the first row. So I
stood alone in the first row of this assembly that was arranged
like the men on a chessboard, each individual, lost in deep
thought, occupying a vast, separate square. No one glanced aside
to look at his neighbor and I too obeyed this important rule.
Only on the arduous way up I had observed that the Senators
were not dressed in cowls, like the officials of the Astromental
world, but in pale violet (heliotrope), richly pleated veils, in
contrast to the dark violet robe of the Major Domus Mundi.
The latter stood on the uppermost, steepest slope of the inclined
floor, and immediately behind him the hall merged into a strange
adjacent room, the entrance to which was indicated by a rounded
arch of moderate height. This dark room could have been taken

for an oversized fireplace or an enormous oven, if it had not been too ridiculously large for both purposes. And so, as I pondered over this mysterious cavern, I finally yielded to the suspicion that it must be a darkened stage, used for certain state actions, for coronation ceremonies, but chiefly for solemn state funerals. The illumination in the tremendous hall itself was of the sort that I have repeatedly designated as rainy weather light, a form of illumination which the Astromental civilization seemed to prefer for rationalistic and intellectual purposes.

The reigning Selenozusian's portly and yet graceful figure was leaning against a metal pillar, the only one in the hall, which rose white and slender from the sloping floor. The fact that he did not stand unsupported like all the others I took as a sign of his greater age and of his moon-born fatigue. From the first moment on the face of the nameless aristocrat reminded me of the expression of the Mutarian Io-Fra as he awaited his bloody death in fully conscious awareness in the box of the theater last night. To be sure, the Selenozusian did not gleam the least bit, he never even glowed. He was no saint. He was only a sage and a sufferer. He smiled to himself. But this smile with half-closed eyes included such contradictory ingredients as defiance, scorn, and irony.

To the right of the Geoarchon's pillar a lectern was bolted to the slanting floor. On the lectern lay a huge folio volume, which struck me as a clumsy anachronism until I recognized its true nature. But this occurred quickly enough. The man at this desk, who can best be designated as a "Reporter," was turning the pages of this volume and appeared to be reading aloud from them with monotonous rapidity, like a parliamentary secretary. The pages, however, were not book pages at all but frosted mirrors or specially treated plates, which emitted a faint light and dimly illumined the bald pate of the officiating state functionary. It took me about a minute to discover that the Reporter was not reading from the reflecting mirror pages but that he was observing events taking place simultaneously and reporting them to the august assembly and its chief in rapid, monotonously flowing words. Something about the expert, galloping speech of this Reporter reminded me of the radio commentators of my own lifetime, who specialized in the description of state receptions, Olympic Games, football matches, horseraces, and Hollywood premières, and dished them up with colorful eloquence for the lazy listeners in their homes. He too was reporting events as they occurred, but he did it without eloquence and with impartial indifference, although these events concerned nothing less than the fate of the world. In a moment I will tell why I could not give my undivided attention to this Reporter; still a few sentences like the following remained in my memory, particularly because of the words "diabolical expert teachers" and "Eurasian Peninsula."

"The arms collectors have mounted their trans-shadow-disintegrators at many points. It is surprising how many of these pipes and pipettes the young men managed to collect. There can be no doubt that since time immemorial diabolical experts have been traveling around the world renovating and repairing these old weapons and instructing promising candidates in their use. The activity seems to be greatest in the three administrative districts of the Eurasian Peninsula. The Jungles are dangerously calm, although prolific families, inhabitants of the Former Eastside Districts, vagrant bachelors, and stranded individuals are crossing the boundaries everywhere. . . ."

I have compounded this speech from various parts of the report. The reason I could not follow it in its entirety was the man at the other lectern, at the left of the Selenozusian. In view of his activity this functionary could be called by no more accurate title than the "Analytic Annalist." He too had an enormous folio on the desk before him. But the mirror pages of this volume were turned from left to right. While the reporter went along with time as it passed, the Annalist pursued time backward from the current moment. He was the historian who read off the unknown interrelations of the past as they were revealed by the progress of events. Unfortunately I was too inexpert in the art of the polyphonic perception of words, so that the Annalist only kept me from understanding the Reporter without making himself clear to me. The only thing I understood was that he was exposing the threads of causality which led, on the one hand, to the shot at the Sympaian and, on the other, to the world-disrupting consequences of the shot.

It would be a simple matter for me at this point to yield to the temptation of putting a few sentences into the Annalist's mouth and to tie the events together with a logical string where they appear disjointed even to me. I can think of no course of action that I would regard as more detestable. There was many an unsolved riddle in the catastrophe that I witnessed. As a transient visitor in a very distant, vacillating, and sometimes unintelligible future, I am not obliged to solve these riddles, and my sensitive reader will not want to be insulted by clumsy solutions as in detective stories. Truth above everything else! Particularly in a realm where truth and falsehood cannot be distinguished from each other. I stake my honor upon this motto. It is for this reason that I have acted contrary to my own interest as an author from the very beginning; I have disturbed the reader, I have engaged him in conversation, I have implored him not to confound "spiritual sight" with dream turmoil or, still worse, with the bold play of fancy, difficult as it is to keep these elements separate. I have told many realistic stories in my life but I have never served the cause of truth with such painful care as in this quite unverifiable account. On the first day of my visit we saw Io-Do's collection of arms without guessing that it meant more than a mere playful hobby. We heard the Geoarchon's Oracle of the Day, we witnessed Io-Fagòr's gloomy forebodings and a number of incidents that pointed toward serious developments: the visit of the Selenozusian to the High Floater, the exodus of the cats, the massacre of the chickens, and so forth. We were present when the shot was fired at the Sympaian and all sorts of mysterious whisperings came to our ears. Finally we stood eye to eye with the General in Jungle-Mountaintown and we heard the unexplained word "psychic artillery." That's all, and it looks like a jig-saw puzzle with half of the pieces missing. But now, when I might have had the opportunity to increase my understanding of the underlying causes of events through the rapid and unaccented accounts of the two mirror analysts at the right and left of the world-regent, their duetting merged and blurred like poorly applied water colors.

In addition to these there was a third baldhead in a black official cowl who stood like a shadow behind the Lunar Consecrate, and since I don't know his title, I now baptize him "Moonshadow." Moonshadow stepped forward now and then to pound with a small hammer on the thin white pillar, which emitted a horrible, hollow sound that I shall never forget. Simultaneously he directed a few warning words to the Geoarchon each time, as for instance: "The stream of time is doubling its flow. Earth minutes are no longer earth minutes."

Or the following sentences which I find among my notes: "If the stability of the world is imperiled, the Lunar Consecrate must guard the Constitution." — "The moon will one day vanish in an orange flame." — "The Constitution gives the Lunar Consecrate the choice of letting the disturbers of the peace vanish in the orange flame or of doing so himself."

These were a few of Moonshadow's warnings, accompanied by the hollow gong sound of the lone column which still rings in my memory. The Astromental custom of revealing facts by concealing them in portentous words was more reminiscent of the Eleusinian or Oriental mysteries than of the twentieth century with its laudable preference for simplicity and precision. Still I thought that I understood the warnings correctly. All of us, my readers and I, have experienced the doubling and trebling of the flow of time in highly dramatic hours of world history in our own era of World Wars. Since time is far more human an expedient than space, which exists independent of the consciousness, the Chronosophers had long ago discovered that time can stampede like a frightened horse. These same Chronosophers, and probably the great Ursler before them, had long ago calculated the cosmic year and the earth hour in which the moon would end its existence in an orange flame. I regarded the refer-

ence to this flame, in which either the disturbers of the peace or
the world-regent would have to vanish, as merely an ominous
Astromental metaphor. Presumably the Constitution gave the
world-chief the right to do away with dangerous criminals, that
is, by arresting them, paralyzing or anaesthetizing them, or
neutralizing them in some other gentle and highly cultivated
manner. How mistaken I was!

Other thoughts oppressed me. I clearly saw that the Lunar
Consecrate was unable to make up his mind. This moment of
imminent peril showed the weakness of the tricky election system that placed the highest power into the hands of a sensitive,
contemplative visionary who had no ability to exercise power nor
pleasure in wielding it. I don't recall whether it was B.H. or I
who formulated the "Conservation of Evil in the World." That
is to say, no matter how much you turn things upside-down and
put one thing in place of another, the fixed measure of failure
can never be reduced. The Astromental Constitution was perfectly adapted to a cool, unemotional, playful human race and
to a cosmically oriented mode of life on a high plane, but it was
utterly unfit to provide a barrier against the bloodred passions
that had suddenly erupted from the depths. Who could have
guessed that these passions still existed? An archaic shot rang
through a puff of powder smoke, the most genteel brides eloped
into the Jungle by night, and the destructive frenzy of the conspirators had a sufficient, you might almost say, a reasonable,
incentive to strike. The Lunar Consecrate, leaning leisurely
against his white pillar, smiled with ironic expectation. Moonshadow behind him struck the column with his little hammer:
"The stream of time has trebled its flow."

Despite the insulating parquetry I felt that the Senators, the
motionless, heliotrope chessmen (a countless number of rooks
and knights), were becoming more and more agitated. I heard a
low grumbling behind me. The duet of the Reporter and the
Annalist accelerated to a galloping presto. Moonshadow struck
the pillar a clanging blow: "The existence of the world is imperiled. Let the Lunar Consecrate guard the Constitution."

The Geoarchon smiled an ineffably mild and knowing smile.

"The Constitution gives the Lunar Consecrate the choice of letting the disturbers of the peace vanish in the orange flame or of doing so himself."

The irresoluteness of the world cunctator settled over the assembly like mildew. (Is irresoluteness the right word? Wasn't it rather a secret resolve to bring about the end?) I felt myself torn back and forth. One idea after another to save the Astromental world flashed through my mind: stop all travel by removing the Harmonizers; deprive the conspirators of all food and provisions from the Park of the Worker. But I rejected all my plans as inadequate. It became ever clearer to me that the Lunar Consecrate had to destroy the criminals physically, without a second's delay. Death without mercy. There was no other expedient. Meanwhile a group of the heliotrope chessmen had climbed to the top of the inclined plane and surrounded the Lunar Consecrate. I did not understand what they were murmuring to him but I assumed they were trying to goad him into action. The Geoarchon gave no heed to the whispered suggestions of his advisers although his moments of grace were running out rapidly. I felt a sudden pang. I had been recognized. The Lunar Consecrate languidly raised his right hand. He had called me. I had to step forward. With clenched teeth I managed to clamber up the steepest part of the sloping floor without slipping and falling. Straining to keep my balance, I stood about five feet from the white column and the World-President. I now had the floor as negotiator. It was my duty to bring about a compromise in this last desperate moment between the Jungle and the world of culture. Whenever my profession required me to face the public my excitement vanished and I felt calm and collected. This was also the case now.

"First of all, Your Excellency and Notables," I began firmly and with conviction, "first of all, it seems necessary to abolish the word 'Jungle' officially. It is not only inaccurate but it is also highly offensive to the mountain and city dwellers over there. I propose that a deputation be dispatched at once to give them the solemn assurance of the abolition of the word 'Jungle.' In this manner the World Government will prove its fairness and its good intentions and will show its disapproval of all aggression. But the most important thing is this: beware of any halfway measures, of temporizing, or of appeasement, as we called it in our day. Make it perfectly clear to the collectors of arms, the conspirators and aggressors, that your reply to the first criminal act will be the merciless physical extinction of the criminals, regardless of all Astromental prejudices and attainments. . . ."

It was about at this point when I noticed that, while I was making a very intelligent and well-considered speech, this speech was resounding only inside me and not a single tone was audible outside. It was neither a physical nor a nervous impediment that prevented me from speaking, nor was it a spasm of the vocal cords or any other debility. I spoke quite normally, but what I said could not be heard. The heliotrope chessmen were making embarrassed signs, a few came nearer to me, others desperately cupped their hands to their ears. The Lunar Consecrate smiled knowingly as though he had expected nothing else. I tried to shout, I yelled at the top of my lungs. But although the yelling hurt my throat, it was just as inaudible as my whispering. It might be surprising that all these Astromental dignitaries (many of them no doubt habitués of the Sympaian) were incapable of comprehending an inward speech, especially one that was made with so much emphasis, almost with convulsive effort. Even I had reached a point where I knew, or at least felt, a considerable portion of the thoughts and unexpressed intentions of others. To this very day, after my return, I am still making use of the ability which I brought back with me; I enjoy, for example, watching people on the crowded boulevards and predicting whether they are going to turn off into a side street fifteen paces farther on. And here, in this assembly, where there were also a few Mutarians, was no one able to understand a silent speech? No one was. Perhaps the insulating parquetry was sufficient to prevent any communication of souls. And another thing: it was not intended that my arguments and proposals should avert the coming catastrophe. I suspect that the author of world history is no improviser as the authors of Sympaians are supposed to be. He prepares his manuscript with emendations, deletions, and corrections, and there is no greater leeway for freedom of action than there is for the imp that spirits typographical errors into a book. In my lifetime there were several despots who, by the most incredible dispensations, escaped from a remarkably large number of minutely prepared attempts at assassination. It bordered on the miraculous. No, it was miraculous. The gentlemen were spared for the final scene as provided in the script.

I tried once more to resume my speech. It was in vain. Not only my voice was inaudible but now my thoughts were also dead. I was not permitted to send out my little Leukangeloi. Then I lowered my head and, if I am not very much mistaken, I sobbed aloud.

My only consolation is that it would have been too late in any case. A deep silence still pervaded the Senate when the irreparable event occurred. There was a sharp sound of crashing and splintering. The mirror pages of the Reporter's folio were shattered into a thousand fragments. The book literally exploded like a bombshell. The volume of the Annalist who was tracing events backward was also damaged, but it remained whole, like the past itself, which can indeed be marred but never destroyed. The Selenozusian smiled a smile of pensive gentleness. Defiance and irony had disappeared from his features. I knew what had happened. Explanations were not needed. The most insane and the most wanton of all wars had broken out. It had begun over the heads of unsuspecting Astromental mankind who would have expected another Sun-Catastrophe rather than this anachronism which seemed to have been safely buried forever in the pit of the Monument of the Last War. And now the hotheads of Panopolis, the arms collectors, the conspirators, whoever they were, would have their fun and their revenge. There was no longer a multiplicity of nations, there were no frontiers, no social distress, no economic crises, no imperialistic ambitions, there was nothing but the mild contrast between the Jungle and the world of culture. And yet a single murder had sufficed to unchain the old furies in this highly advanced, star-allied race. War was not the result but the cause of all conflicts. War was the subconscious craving for bloodshed, no matter on what pretexts it was waged. War was Adam's son, the Cain in man. In frightful passion the roosters tore to shreds the hens whose blood they had seen.

Now, after unnumbered millennia, the trans-shadow-disintegrators were at work again. The recoil of these unfamiliar weapons, consisting of thin pipes and pipettes, was so terrible that it had shattered the Reporter's mirror folio into tiny splinters as it reflected the distant events. Perhaps the mountains and hills were already in flames, and the white house-cubes, the village churches, the merry-go-rounds, and the capital cities of the oases that were called Jungles. But perhaps—and I hoped I was right —the various Constantines with their officers, engineers, and strategists had not only devised new offensive weapons but also defensive armament to resist the destruction. After the explosion of the current events' folio the silence in the hall became still more profound. The din of war—I doubted that there was a din —could not penetrate to this hall. Only the rain illumination became a few degrees duskier. And the same thing happened that had happened last night at the theater when Io-Do's shot shattered the skull of the ministering friar: all the assemblage slowly covered their heads with their flowing veils of light violet. Only one person besides me did not cover his face. It was the Lunar Consecrate. (I remembered that he had left the Office of the High Floater with his face covered yesterday; he had therefore anticipated this action of grief and detachment.) Now he walked in a circle around the white column, taking very tiny steps and making a farewell bow in each of the four directions of the compass. It seemed that he wanted to say something; but irresolute to the last second, he said nothing. His smiling glance came to rest on me and held me. His glance plainly said: Remember my Oracle of the Day, "The stranger who comes home does not make himself at home but makes home strange." I lowered my head under the weight of his glance and of the

Oracle of the Day that rang through my soul. Once more, very softly, Moonshadow's hammer struck the hollow column. Ominous words were whispered: ". . . or the Lunar Consecrate himself. . . ."

I raised my eyes although I knew it was forbidden and that I should not look. The chessmen in the enormous room with the sloping floor stood with their covered heads deeply bowed. The white metal pillar was no longer white; it was filled with seething orange-red vapor. No one was permitted to observe the overwhelming event that took place now. I only inclined my head a trifle, like a person attending a religious ritual not his own. Of course, I had nothing with which to cover my face. And I had made up my mind to see this great occurrence despite the interdict.

With short, light steps, as though the slipperiness of the floor and the steep inclination of the slanting plane meant nothing to him, the Selenozusian had covered the short distance to the rounded arch that led to the adjacent room which I described as an oversized fireplace or a stage for state ceremonies or solemn funerals. Before the entrance the Lunar Consecrate stopped as though he were thinking about a duty that he had neglected. There was an aura of reluctance and cringing about his shoulders. Why shouldn't the Selenozusian too pay the tribute of fear to nature? But now, with an air of incomparable composure, he stepped across the threshold of darkness and disappeared after a step or two. That's all, I thought; the world will never see him again. In the same instant, however, an orange-red flame flared up at the rear of the chamber; for a fraction of a fraction of a second it took on the shape of a human being, then it was gone. The Major Domus Mundi had fulfilled the letter of the Constitution that required him to vanish in the orange-red flame of the dying moon if he lacked the strength and the will to commit those to the flame who menaced the stability of the world. The reign of this nameless one, this eternally impersonal one, who was now extinguished and forgotten forever, had ended with one of the greatest calamities in world history. But in spite of

the catastrophe that was in progress, or perhaps on account of
the catastrophe, the secret commissions were hurriedly making
preparations for an election. I could feel it behind my back.
When I turned around I saw the Uranographer hastening from
one chessman to the next. Presumably the eleven eligible Selenozusians had already been arrested and were by this time wailing and moaning in their dungeons. I couldn't blame them, for
the new World Major-Domo's berth would be no bed of roses.

The old President had sacrificed himself like—I almost
thoughtlessly said "like a phoenix." No, the sacrificial death of
the nameless, impersonal one was just the reverse of the self-
immolation of the sun-bird, the phoenix, which, according to
Ursler's First Fundamental Paradox, occurs when the radiant
energy of a star is greater than itself. It was not the exultant
flame of the sun in which the nameless one had cremated himself because he could not cremate others. It was the dark flame
that had consumed him, the flame in which the moon will one
day perish, the flame of weary knowledge, of futility, of dejection.

* * * * *

* * *

*

THE HOUSE WAS FILLED UP TO THE ROOF and the
pallid garden above it. Io-Fagòr's entire clan, even its more
distant members, seemed to be seeking his protection. The father
of the Bride had also offered refuge to his in-law, dear little
Io-Solip, and his family, in order to indicate that he did not
regard Io-Do's disgraceful conduct as more reprehensible than
Lala's flight, and that he looked upon the Bridegroom's father
as a brother in misfortune. All the talking, whispering, rustling,
muttering, murmuring in the house made my head whirl, for I
understood very little of it.

At long last, however, I was lucky enough to be alone with
B.H. in the little parlor next to the dining room where there were
anachronistic seating accommodations and where we had sat to-

gether before like fossil insects in amber. I sensed at once that B.H. had been deputized by Io-Fagòr and the clan to speak to me.

"Well, B.H.," I sighed, "how much of the world is still standing?"

My friend was trembling from head to foot, practically quaking, with alarming embarrassment. I had never seen him like this. Not even in his most nervous moments. Our hosts seemed to have put a fine burden on his shoulders.

"That's not it," he replied, gnawing at his lips. "They have dangerously underestimated the Jungle people. They're not fighting with such silly weapons as the half-baked Mental fools. You can protect yourself from the trans-shadow-disintegrators and even from the existence-extinguishers—tiny tools the size of glaziers' diamonds that were used in the Last War—by taking refuge in certain regions of the lithosphere. But, incredible as it sounds, your Constantines and their war colleges have developed super-Mental artillery in their Jungle cities. They are shooting with psychic shells, and neither you nor I can be certain whether we haven't already been hit."

"I knew about that psychic artillery long ago," I growled, and I was annoyed with myself that I hadn't investigated the nature of this artillery while I was in Mountaintown. I inquired, "What type of shells do they appear to be using?"

"They are shooting with manic-depressions and melancholias," B.H. bitterly emphasized each word. "But, please, by all means, be calm, F.W. Particularly in the face of this danger it is essential to remain calm."

"But I should like a fuller explanation," I exclaimed. "That's the least I can ask for."

"Our only salvation lies in keeping our heads," B. H. replied in anguished tones. "Do you want me to bore you with psychochemical technicalities? It's no miracle. They stole a few ideas from the Djebel and the Wintergarden and developed them in the aggressive direction that we neglected. The bad part is that there is practically no limit to the range of the depressions and the melancholias; that is, they are effective wherever there are men, in the Intermundia and in the bowels of the earth." And he added in a lower tone, "The first casualties have already been brought in and their number is growing from minute to minute."

"I'm not afraid," I declared harshly.

"Don't say that," B.H. warned me and raised his hands. "A direct hit of concentrated depression is worse than ten abdominal wounds, gas corrosion, and third-degree burns. By comparison cholera, ileus, rabies, strangulation, and being roasted over a slow fire are all perfect picnics."

"Are you speaking of manic-depressions?" I exclaimed. "Of psychic wounds? Is Constantine shooting insanity at us?"

"That's just it," B.H. hissed. "Constantine's manic-depression shells are not insanity. There are plenty of remedies for insanity, even if they are only narcotics. But these shells contain true sanity. If you're hit by a twenty-six caliber self-analysis, no opiate will do you any good. They are shooting horrible disillusionments. They reveal what must never be revealed. They inoculate the victim with the most radically negative aspect of life, so that he no longer even wishes to depart. There! Take a look!"

B.H. pointed with shaking finger through the open door to the brightly lighted dining room. A man who seemed to be fleeing from unseen pursuers rushed in one door and out the other with a moaning cry of pain. I shall never forget his Medusa mask of horror, a caricature of a face that was no longer human. But I shall not describe it either, for it stands so ghastly clear before my mind's eye that I prefer not to hold it there. If the silver baroque headdress that fell from the man's bare skull had not betrayed him, I should never have recognized the House Sage, the one of the three bachelors who was constantly intimidated by the Spokesman. The latter, as well as the Permanent Guest, Io-Fagòr, and several others came running to hold the unfortunate man and to assist him. But terror lent him wings. I heard their flying footsteps fade away in the once so quiet house. My tongue and gums were dry.

"Wounded?" I asked. "Wounded by a depression?" and my voice sounded hoarse.

"Perhaps only grazed, grazed by a panic trauma," B.H. whispered, "or by a fragment of a so-called fulfillment-disappointment. He was late getting home and was caught in a traffic jam, because the Harmonizers are no longer equal to their tasks. But what's the difference? We're not safer in the house."

I jumped up and stood rigid. "What has been decided, B.H.? What do they propose to do?"

"Take it easy, old man," my friend implored. "Strong nerves are the only protection that our organism offers. Now, please, sit down again and let me say a few frank words."

When I saw tears in his kind dark eyes I became a little gentler and more tractable for a moment.

"I am at fault, F.W., and I don't deny it," he began. "Of course it was no accident that I drew your name out of the alphabet and had you summoned."

"Forget it," I interrupted him roughly. "Why bring up that old nonsense at this time."

"What?" he asked as though he didn't understand. "It's not a matter of indifference to me at all. Certainly it's my fault that you are here. But you were probably thinking of me in the place where you were and you brought yourself to my attention."

"As far as I know I thought of you for the last time in April 1943, and with a pricking conscience at that. Quite a while ago, wasn't it? Whether I thought of you in purgatory—that seems to be my permanent address—God alone can tell. That locale is made up of nothing but depressions and melancholias, but I have a feeling that it's bearable and that we have a few chances and an objective. Under the present circumstances, at any rate, it's a much better address than this one."

"Why, Io-Fagòr and his household have exactly the same opinion," B.H. exclaimed and smiled in pretended surprise.

"What sort of an opinion?" I grumbled.

"I'm not speaking of the divers conceptions of the various

members of the household concerning the afterlife. I am speaking of the fact that they have unanimously decided to leave this life; a little prematurely for most of them, but in a perfectly legitimate manner, voluntarily and on foot. The last part of the way to the Wintergarden, you know, is always covered on foot. In spite of your theories about being moved, F.W., in view of the unspeakable horror that confronts us, I consider this decision entirely reasonable. As far as the deeply humiliated parents of the bridal couple are concerned, the decision is comprehensible, even disregarding the terrors we face. But in any case an aristocrat like Io-Fagòr could not possibly survive the fall of the Astromental mode of life."

"Isn't that a sort of suicide?" I inquired suspiciously.

"Suicide means taking one's own life," B.H. replied quickly. "In the Wintergarden no one takes his own life. The Wintergarden offers the only possible, cultivated, comfortable, luxurious end of human existence. All evil, all wickedness, all inherent failings of nature, about which we have so often philosophized, F.W., are eliminated in the Wintergarden by the power of the searching spirit. The worms no longer celebrate their field day. We no longer feed the earth with the manure of our once animate body. We no longer yield our remains to the cremating flame to be melted and charred to dirty ashes in a furnace along with boards, sawdust, and other filth. But more important than all that, we don't die. I use the word frankly. We don't succumb, with death sweat on our brow, to apoplexy, to thrombosis, and to malignant ulcers. In place of all these horrors mankind has introduced a pure and holy procedure, which is so beautiful that those who have passed through it are sorry that they can't repeat it."

"What a paean of praise, B.H.," I said without trying to conceal my derision.

"I have told only the truth," he retorted briefly.

"And what have you decided to do, B.H.?"

"The question is what have you decided to do, F.W. You are the chief problem, not I. All of us are agreed on that. But no matter what your decision may be, I will remain with you. In any case, you ought to see the Wintergarden, just as you saw the Djebel."

"You don't need to work so hard to sell me your Wintergarden, B.H., I've already bought it. I accept the unanimous decision. What else can I do?"

My friend turned with a start and looked at me sharply.

"When you say 'what else can I do,'" he said, "you're going at the thing the wrong way. The voluntary character of the last journey requires genuine agreement and a certain amount of joyousness. These distinguish the civilized man, who knows when he's had enough, from the barbarian, whose appetites are never sated."

"Listen, B.H.," I interrupted, "don't kid yourself and let's be realistic. I have no desire to be wounded by depressions and melancholias, or by panic traumas and fulfillment-disappointments. And what else do I have to look forward to in this dreary world that is on the point of destroying itself again? To hell with your genuine agreement and joyousness. For me the Wintergarden is just a way out of a mess."

My reincarnated friend propped his head sadly on his hands. "I feel terrible about it, simply terrible," he confessed, "that this thing has turned out so badly. I was happy beyond words to see you again. I thought we would have a perfectly wonderful time and you would enjoy everything and be enchanted with everything."

"That I am, my friend," I consoled him. "I am completely enchanted with many things, in spite of everything. As for the rest, it isn't your fault."

"Too bad," B.H. sighed once more.

Then he led me into the next room where I had first appeared to the Io-Fagòr clan. They were all assembled. B.H. did not need to say a word. They could tell by my face that I was ready to join the family on its last voluntary journey. An air of brotherly warmth greeted me. I was one of them. All these youthfully beautiful men and women, most of them of mature years, stepped up to me and embraced me in the delicate manner required by Astromental custom. Io-Fagòr even drew me to his breast. Only GR³ acted strangely. She stayed in the background and her deep-set eyes roved restlessly from one to another. Meanwhile Io-Fagòr had produced a small, gleaming key with which he opened a concealed door leading to a long corridor.

The Twenty-First Chapter

WHEREIN THE EPISODE OF THE WINTER-
GARDEN BEGINS IN THE INTERIOR OF THE
PLANET, AND I ENTER THE INSTITUTION
WHERE INGRESS IS MOST CONVENIENT BUT
EGRESS IS HIGHLY INCONVENIENT.

IN THE "dark ages" which, according to my Astromental friends,
includes the century from which I came, men had accumulated
a remarkable wealth of information concerning all "external"
things, while they knew very little about all "internal" matters.
Even the Sumerians and Chaldeans had a good deal of more
than theoretical knowledge of the planets in the Minor Intermundium and of the galaxies in the Intermundium of the First
Degree. My report on the excursion to the Gray Neuter and
my sojourn on John Evangelist and Apostle Peter would scarcely
have aroused their astonishment; and Babylonian, Egyptian,
and Hindu neophytes would certainly have felt more at home
in the three Lamaseries than students of Heidelberg, Oxford,
or Harvard between the years 1920 and 1940.

But the case is quite different with regard to "internal"
matters. First of all, by "internal" I don't mean anything psychic,
spiritual, or mystic. I merely mean everything that lies on this
side of, that is, inside, our skin. We'll have to admit frankly that
we children of the twentieth century were really quite uninformed about the things that went on inside us; after all,
only a historical moment had passed since the wise English-

496

man Harvey discovered the circulation of the blood around 1650. Just imagine, in my younger days medical science knew practically nothing about gland secretions, about biochemistry, and about the electric charges of the nervous system. What is true of the restricted interior of our bodies is also true of the greater interior of our planet. We did not shrink from audacious calculations regarding the strange universes of star nebulae but we managed only to penetrate a scant three miles into the interior of the earth. This proves beyond a doubt that man stands in much less awe of the world about him than of the world within him and that he is much less afraid of the distant infinite than of the immediate infinite enclosed within himself.

Everyone who recognizes the accuracy of this reasoning will comprehend my pleasure at having visited not only the Lower Intermundium above our planet but also the interior of the planet itself. It is true that artistic convention recommends the progression from the lower to the higher rather than the reverse. But, as in many previous instances, my duty as a travel writer interferes with my freedom as a novelist. I do not guide events; they guide me. The fair-minded reader will decide in the end whether the directional anticlimax was also an anticlimax of suspense.

What follows now is the report of an eyewitness, not of a geologist. Here in this mighty chamber in the earth I shall remain true to my unscientific principle which stood the test of the Lower Intermundium, although it is much easier to describe Comet Calisthenics in the remotest realms of celestial space than the adventure in the Stygian domain. In school we had learned that the temperature in the interior of the earth increases by thirty degrees Centigrade for each kilometer and that it makes very little difference whether you penetrate the surface at the North Pole or at the Equator. You would accordingly reach the boiling point of water at the end of the third kilometer in depth, and sixty kilometers farther on you would attain a temperature of 1800 degrees Centigrade at which even granite melts. Geological facts seemed to bear out this formula based upon practical observation. It was attested by countless volcanoes that hurled fiery, molten matter to the surface in the form of lava, as well as by the geysers that puffed clouds of hasty, heavy steam to the sky. Volcanic and tectonic earthquakes reminded us that the firm crust of the earth, on which the tragedies and comedies of history unfold, is not even comparable to an eggshell, but at best to the skin of an apple.

Now I do not presume to assert with a layman's audacity that this theory is wrong. On the contrary. My experience on the unstable surface of Apostle Peter tells me that it is right. The only thing that I can report on the basis of my personal knowledge is that the theory is incomplete. Just as the sight of the more densely sown stars and the authority of the High Floater had taught me that the universe expands and contracts as it breathes, so my physical presence down here taught me that the interior of the earth contains at least one cavity of enormous dimensions (probably, however, several), and that this cavity is filled with breathable atmosphere and suffused with a milky twilight, bright enough to distinguish people and things clearly.

Two questions, however, puzzle me. First: Did such cavities in the bowels of the earth always exist or were they created by the gradual cooling of the planet? I never discovered the exact six-digit number designating the year in which I was privileged to spend three days. The "Eleventh Cosmic Capital Year of Virgo" was a cyclic denotation, probably embracing an entire eon, by which the ancients meant approximately six thousand years. On the other hand, whenever I speak of a hundred thousand years or more than a hundred thousand years that I spent among the dead, that is merely a conventional figure that B.H. and I used in our conversations and does not represent an exact number. But no matter what this six-digit number of revolutions about the sun might have been, it meant a mere instant, half a breath, in the life of a heavenly body, in the course of which the cooling process could hardly have progressed appreciably, unless we were dealing with some unknown effects of the

Sun-Transparency. For my part, I incline to regard these cavities in the earth's interior as ancient formations, whose origin far antedates the real beginnings of mankind. All known mythologies inform us of realms beneath the surface of the earth. And even our most prosaic historians know that mythologies are no idle fantasies but actualities seen as visions and interpreted.

The second question is: Was the Tartarus surrounding the Astromental Wintergarden naturally or artificially lighted and ventilated? My lack of information on this important point is the result of the unpardonable neglect of a poorly trained reporter. But if you consider my state of mind, the gloomy agitation that made my dubious body quiver as it approached a second dissolution, my negligence will appear more comprehensible. Although I can't prove it, I should like to assert frankly that I regard the ventilation and illumination of this vast earth chamber as the work of human hands. After all, Astromental civilization had accomplished greater things than to supply light and air to a place that lay two or three hundred miles beneath the surface.

The concept of "two or three hundred miles" is also scientifically quite unjustified and is merely the result of an instinctive conjecture of my sense of time and space. Unfortunately we had no Chronosophic elementary teacher with us in the Camera Caritatis which lowered us into the earth almost imperceptibly, nor any Respondents like Io-Hol and Io-Rar, from whose mechanical and sometimes inaccurate babbling I might have derived some slight enlightenment. And so I arrive at my own conclusion independently on the basis of my own sense experience and surmise that a fairly thin and probably not continuous layer of molten magma lies directly beneath the appleskin or eggshell—to stretch a point—that we call the earth's crust. The small amount of heat that radiates upward seems to bear this out. Otherwise every living being on the skin of this baked apple, the earth, would evaporate in a puff of steam, and the well-known glacial periods could never have established entire continents of moving glaciers on the shell of this red-hot egg.

This appears to be simple and cogent reasoning and leads to the assumption that the hell-fire that supplies the volcanoes can only be a very tenuous stratum between fixed layers of rock of varying elasticity. Far, far below these there may be a liquid or gaseous core of magnetic iron which is said to form the inner-most heart of the earth.

According to my "feeling," therefore, this wondrous world lay beneath the lava floor but still in the upper stories of the earth building. I couldn't tell how much time our descent consumed because I didn't even notice for a long time that we were moving at all. We hadn't put on any light protective gar-ments like the space-diving suits in which we had visited the Lower Intermundium. The absence of all preparations kept me from discovering that we were well on our way to the starting point of our finish. I suppose that B.H. wisely refrained from telling me the purpose of this room which was commonly called "Camera Caritatis." Incidentally, I'm not at all certain that this remarkably large parlor at the end of a long corridor was actually called "Camera Caritatis." I'm inclined to think that this circular room with separate compartments fanning out from the center was not called "Chamber of Mercy," but "Chamber of Equality," in other words, "Camera Paritatis." It reminded me in one way of the waiting room of a successful quack doctor, in another, of a beauty parlor. The compartments were intended for couples who wanted to spend the last hours of their lives together. The Camera Caritatis—let's leave it at that—was so overcrowded on our trip that intimate conversations were out of the question. It goes without saying that Io-Fagòr and his household were not the only ones who had made this fateful decision. The Camera Caritatis didn't serve only a single house but a number of them—I don't know how many—that composed a "neighborhood," the smallest administrative unit of the urban community. Some seventy or eighty people in festive dress were crowded and jammed into our round parlor which provided couches for only twenty-odd. The women, even the oldest ones, wore the dovegray veils of their bridal days, for a charming, archaic custom required both men and women to wear wedding garments on this last voluntary journey. Our Ancestress too was no exception to the rule. She looked splendid in the bluish dove-gray, and the ebony helmet in place of the silver headdress made her look even younger, if that was possible. I had a curious little interlude with her that didn't strike me as significant at first, although it really was. The Ancestress and I were the last to enter the Camera Caritatis. Behind us was no one but Io-Fagòr, the head of the clan, who was counting his flock to see that none had been left behind. While Io-Fagòr was looking through the open door, occupied with his duties, GR³ invited me to enter with a vehement, annoyed gesture. Of course, I was reluctant to walk through a door ahead of a lady, and particularly an eminent and venerable lady of the ancien régime, and I emphasized my refusal with a superfluously gallant motion of my hand as I bowed the Ancestress into the Camera Caritatis. I have never received a look of more inimical despair than that which stabbed me from the eyes of the graceful hag. I was aghast, because I didn't have the slightest idea what I had done.

After a brief conference of the heads of the various house-holds the door of the parlor was ceremoniously and cautiously locked with several big bolts. Now I assumed that this was a secret conclave in which we would be told what to expect and how to conduct ourselves. But nothing of the sort happened. No one made an instructive speech. Io-Rasa, who was now as radiantly lovely as her daughter Lala, even though her beauty was tinged with ineffable sadness, took her husband's hand and held it. Her blue eyes were large and moist and were fastened on the eyes of Io-Fagòr. In the presence of all this youth and beauty it seemed absurd to think of the end. The other couples did the same as Io-Fagòr and Io-Rasa. Most of them were silent. They seemed to be reviewing their past life. You could almost see it glide across their bright, smooth brows like shadows of clouds. Strangely enough the bachelors, who were present in large numbers, appeared far less composed. These household officials strode up and down morosely and nervously without uttering a word. B.H. had closed his eyes and slept standing up, or pretended to sleep in order to avoid my questions.

While the people were silent the dogs spoke. There were perhaps seven of them in the Camera Caritatis, among them naturally our dog Sur. And at last the moment has come for me to conciliate my dog-loving readers who have been irritated for a long time. At least I shall make the attempt. In the first place, I am anything but a dog-hater. How often have I looked into the great sad eyes of our shepherd dogs and Irish setters and have immersed myself in the dour depth of the animal's soul until my heart began to pound. For me every beautiful dog that shared our life was a kind of enchanted fairy-tale prince. That was because the animal form of good dogs contrasted sharply with the intelligent, soulful expression of their eyes. There was an overabundance of expression, a love-filled struggle for attention, concentration, and memory, which transcended animal nature, at the same time betraying and denying it. Man had found a creature on earth that could love without being inconvenient. In his insatiable desire to be loved, venerated, deified, and imitated as a master, man drew this creature to him, fed it, cherished it, instructed it, and thus made it into the hopeless renegade of the animal kingdom. My dear dog-lovers, at the risk of spoiling my attempt at reconciliation I must say frankly: the dog is one of the sins of man. Isn't the measure of love and kindness in our hearts so lukewarm and so small that we should not spend it on convenient objects while we deny it to our inconvenient fellow-creatures? The history of the future supplies the answer to this question. Our excessive cynophilia turned out badly for men and still worse for the dogs. In the course of time man corrupted the dog by robbing him of his true character and making him a copyist by virtue of his constant proximity. As a perfectly logical result the dog developed into a babbling, pseudo-artless creature, in short into Sur, whose character and mannerisms are repulsive to all dog-lovers among my readers. And finally I must confess that I had the misfortune of meeting a particularly affected specimen in the person of Sur. It was curious that the people paid no attention whatever to the talking of the dogs. Here too, in the Camera Caritatis, they ignored them entirely, although the dogs were the only ones who were carrying on a conversation.

"Sur is very, very faithful," yapped our dog, trembling from head to tail, "very, very faithful."

"Shut your trap," growled a bass voice; the speaker was a large, sturdy animal who, in spite of the uniformity of all canine characteristics, had retained something mastifflike about him. "We're all in the same boat."

"What goes on anyway, what goes on?" a third one squawked with silly curiosity. His tail was bobbed and was wagging prestissimo like that of a terrier. A fourth joined in the chorus of foolish questions, but he spoke incoherently, chattering like a parrot: "What's happening to Skippy . . . what's happening to Skippy . . . what's happening . . . ?"

"Morons, all of them," growled the honest old bass voice. " 'What's happening to Skippy?' . . . It's the end for us."

"Really the end?" whined Sur, quivering as though with cold. "Papa, Mamma, Sur doesn't believe it."

The other dogs, all but the one that looked like a mastiff, joined Sur in a shivering, whining chorus. A thunderous shout from one of the men finally called them to order and they moaned more softly and slunk with drooping ears in and out among the people.

At this point I lost track of events because I was busy trying to overcome a sort of nausea. I pressed my handkerchief to my lips for I felt as though I would have to vomit. No wonder, considering that we were hurtling downward through strata of liquid fire or elastic, semiplastic minerals.

"I feel as though we're moving," I exclaimed, rousing B.H. from his coma.

"Are you just finding that out," he yawned, "you old Comet acrobat and movement specialist? We've been moving for almost an hour at the rate of acceleration of an object falling through a vacuum. These splendid shafts are hermetically sealed vacuums, and it's probably around noon by this time."

I didn't succeed in avoiding a brief fainting spell. Fortunately I didn't fall over but merely leaned against B.H. He was startled and gently wiped the perspiration from my forehead. (Just a little later our circumstances were reversed and I had to take care of him.) When the Camera Caritatis stopped moving as imperceptibly as it had commenced, I felt well at once. The bolts were drawn and the door opened. The air that streamed in seemed cool and fresh. My body quickly regained a sense of well-being and along with it I recovered my curiosity, the surest sign of complete vitality. As we emerged from the Camera Caritatis its bright light yielded to the twilight of a late autumn afternoon. I had expected to see a place like the bottom of a mine. Instead, however, we found ourselves standing in a wide, open countryside.

* * * * *
* * *
*

THIS DEPRESSING LANDSCAPE, wrapped in autumn gloom, gave every indication of being located at the outskirts of a big city. The road on which we were walking—voluntarily and on foot—led toward a city that looked at a distance like one of those gigantic railway terminals built in the nineteen thirties in "modern style." At any rate, it was a two- or three-story building with symmetrically recurring square turrets and it extended as far as the eye could reach. This building, which was still two miles or more ahead of us, was obviously the Wintergarden. To the right and left of our road the terrain was bare and hilly. But perhaps they weren't genuine hills or knolls at all but only deposits of coal, cinders, rubble, and ash. Any child of my own era would have concluded at first glance that he had gotten into one of the big industrial centers, like Pittsburg or Witkowitz or the Ruhr district, where they had just closed up shop for the evening. But that was only a momentary illusion. It was raining gently. Or let's say, it was misting, for the warm, light drizzle could hardly be called rain. The Astromental people, however, seemed to enjoy the bad weather on their final journey, since they had only rarely experienced it up above under their eternally blue sky. And while we're speaking of the sky I will confess that the spacious sky over this landscape, heavy with clouds, gave me the queerest feelings. A cloudy sky in the interior of the earth? the reader asks incredulously. I admit that the word "sky" is misleading although I have never seen a higher cloudy sky anywhere, or if you prefer, a higher cloud ceiling. Suffice it to say that the distance between our eyes and the bank of clouds or steam above us was more than three hundred thousand feet, while the rain clouds or thunderheads out in the open air usually collect not much more than three thousand feet above the ground. It's no wonder, therefore, that we seemed to have an inordinately high sky above us here in the depths. The cavity in which we were walking appeared as unlimited in all directions as the earth above us. It had the effect of a strange, tragic landscape. A soft rushing sound was audible from all sides, as of distant cascades or rapids. There must be certain natural forces held in perfect balance, I thought, that keep this chamber from collapsing. The light, which was strong enough to permit us to recognize each other as well as to see in the distance, was something like the day-night or night-day on Apostle Peter. A more vigorous illumination with a bluish tinge rose from the buildings ahead of us, that I compared with a gigantic railway terminal, while occasional surges of red blossomed in the rolling landscape around us.

Low stone balustrades ran along both sides of the impeccably smooth road. I had to step quite close to these to discover that the road that led to the Wintergarden was no road at all but a bridge of incredible length. I looked down into a dizzying abyss at the bottom of which the ground seemed to heave in glutinous swells. Was it a swamp? Or was it plastic, unsolidified earth? Presently we reached a spot where a fairly wide river of lava rolled along in the depths under the bridge;

it was the source of the surges of reddish light that flared up over the landscape from time to time.

"Why, that's the Phlegethon," I said to B.H. with a childish laugh. And B.H. broke into a childish laugh too. We were both happy that the Greek mythology of our schooldays was no empty dream. We were looking at the Phlegethon, the fiery river of Hades, with our own old eyes. And it proved once more that neither Homer nor Vergil nor any other poet and prophet could ever invent anything that didn't and doesn't really exist.

This heart-warming little humanistic experience made me feel much better. I confess that my spirit reacted to a tiny touch of erudite vanity that enabled me to harmonize the most ancient with the most modern, to recognize in the realm of the Astromental Wintergarden, where death is conquered, the Phlegethon, the Styx, and the Cocytus, all empty words for those who were born too late to get a humanistic schooling. In the recognition and acknowledgment of the fact that the most ancient is the ultramodern we find a profound spiritual satisfaction, and in it lies one of the eternal roots of conservatism.

We soon became aware that human nature was so little adapted to the conditions down here that our bodies became weaker with every step. The air we breathed seemed insufficient for our lungs. We began to feel a strange longing to get to the Wintergarden as quickly as possible and to be put to rest there, no matter what the nature of this rest might be. Even if our sense of time and space was not confused as in the Gray Neuter, still we were outside our accustomed dimensions, in the interior of the planet, in one of the cavities that might have been created by the ejection of the mass that made the moon.

The bridge on which we were walking was bustling with traffic but it was not particularly crowded. I had already noticed that there were many roads or bridges like this one, converging from all sides, as well as from above and below, to a great junction.

The individual groups or clans, including our own, plodded along in silence. A faint stupor, a kind of somnolence enveloped everyone and made him lonely. Not even Sur was prattling; he crept along, dragging his belly on the ground. The journey that was made voluntarily and on foot was shorter than I had anticipated. We were already approaching the structure that I arbitrarily called a city or railway terminal. Big signboards with illuminated inscriptions in extensive script began to appear on both sides of the road. But the lettering on these signboards had nothing to do with distances, directions, or place names; instead they repeated two questions with magnificent monotony: "What do you fear? Were you afraid to be born?"

The nearer we came to the buildings, the more frequently these signboards appeared, and now there were also some with the following instructions: "Trust the Animator and the Bath Attendants!"

Simultaneously we began to pass men and women in white who leaned idly on the balustrades of the bridge and paid no attention to those who went by. Their white smocks, buttoned up to the neck, were not made of veil material and made them look very much like practicing physicians and nurses of antiquity. But the thing that struck me about them, particularly the men, was their taller stature than the Astromental average and their obese, flabby, sexless appearance. That's the result of the unhealthful living conditions down here in Tartarus, in the realm of the dead, I thought. Io-Fagòr, who was walking at the head of our party, stopped, waited for me, and told me in a low voice, "Those are the Enumerators, Seigneur."

I noticed that my tongue was heavy and that I had trouble speaking. "What are the 'Enumerators,' Compère?"

"Every Io that reaches this point is counted, given a number, and entered in the book."

"I don't like that," I grumbled. "I thought that Mental civilization had outgrown statistics."

"These are the only statistics in existence, Seigneur."

"And for what purpose are we numbered out here on the highway, like pieces of baggage?"

"Will you kindly notice, Seigneur, that the traffic on this

road runs only in one direction," Io-Fagòr replied in a remarkably savage tone.

I swallowed the bitter taste in my mouth and inquired, "What's become of the sublime freedom of the will, my friend?"

"Our thinkers, inventors, and law givers had to take human frailty into account," said Io-Fagòr. "What human would not recoil at the last moment from that which is our greatest accomplishment? You yourself awarded the prize to Sophistes Io-Sum for making the statement that God's love is manifested in our will to be rather than not to be. In other words, man must even conquer God's love in himself in order to depart this world in a clean and decent manner. It will probably be easier for you, Seigneur, than for some of us. And in order to keep the weak ones from deserting and from perishing miserably, this road may be traveled in only one direction."

There was an almost menacing tone in Io-Fagòr's words. I realized at once that in Io-Fagòr and his kind the idea of the Wintergarden took the place of religious fanaticism, the only sort they knew. In this point the Astromental probably did not differ from dervishes and fire-worshipers. So far I had no idea what would take place in the buildings directly ahead of us. In any case it was a detour around death. Io-Fagòr regarded this detour as the greatest attainment of modern mankind. Although I was quite ready to use this detour as an exit I felt that I was in a trap.

"All coercion is terroristic," I exclaimed, "even coercion for one's own good."

No one had heard me, not even B.H. We were standing before the portal that had been assigned to us. There were probably hundreds of such portals, for the fronts of the buildings stretched out interminably. The arch over our door had the following inscription: "What you are is the reward and punishment for what you are."

A moment later we were in a room that had none of the qualities of the railway terminal I had expected; on the contrary, it closely resembled the lobby of an expensive hotel or of a sanatorium for pampered neurotics. I was strangely on guard. I was permeated with a definite will to fight, as if I were not preparing myself for the end but as if I were ready to defend my dubious life—which wasn't the case at all. White-smocked persons greeted us with disarming friendliness, with cheerful cordiality, like old acquaintances. I, as the "Seigneur," received an undue share of attention. But I felt at once that this fine, warm reception had a distinct purpose. Everything was to proceed quickly, before we had a chance to think. While they smiled at us and complimented us, men and women, and particularly married couples, were imperceptibly separated. In this way they were cheated of the pain of parting. Although, as I have said, my head was heavy with somnolence, I had firmly decided at once not to be separated from B.H. All the tricks of the white-smocks failed. I demanded and obtained a joint room for my friend and me. This room with its dangerously soft couches was more luxurious than any room in Io-Fagòr's house.

"We'll try once more not to sleep, B.H.," I said gruffly.

He looked at me with half-closed bleary eyes and nodded.

* * * * *
* * *
*

I HAD STERNLY TOLD MY FRIEND NOT TO LIE DOWN.
He sat on the couch in an extremely broken line, his heavy head propped on his hands. My own head was undoubtedly as heavy as his. But in order to combat my sleepiness I walked up and down our spacious room with firm steps, loudly declaiming the while.

"Never in all my life did a hypnotist succeed in putting me to sleep," I boasted. "I distinctly remember that I almost managed once to hypnotize the hypnotist. You know perfectly well, B.H., that will power isn't my specialty and that I'm much more of a lazzaróne than a character snob. But there's one thing I won't stand for, and that is to have someone take liberties with my soul and my consciousness. Those are things that I guard like an archangel or like a prizefighter. Back in my younger days a couple of psychoanalysts tried to start impertinent conversations with me but I fixed them in a hurry, believe me, in a big hurry."

"And what about confession, F.W.?" muttered my sleepy friend.

"That's an old comparison, B.H., and a spurious one," I replied. "Confession is not heard by an individual who has to prove his superiority and who stealthily challenges you with malicious eyes, but by the priest, a steward and not a person, the administrator of a holy sacrament, who is not guided by fiendish theories but bound by stern precepts——"

I stopped abruptly for at this instant my eyes settled on a white card posted on the wall, like the price list in the hotels of ancient days. This card announced in neat lettering: "The Brothers of the Childlike Life say Holy Mass and hear Holy Confession."

A masterpiece, I marveled. The Church denies the dying sacraments to the candidates for the Wintergarden, but not confession and communion. Suddenly I recalled that the Grand Bishop had offered to protect me if that should happen which had happened and if they proposed the Wintergarden as the last chance. But what good was it? At the memory of the Grand Bishop I excitedly pounded my fist against the wall. It was a white wall and oily smooth as in all Astromental rooms in order to afford the appropriate blank surface for visionary wallpaper before the occupant of the room fell asleep. But this wall was surprisingly brittle. My bare fist had made a big hole in the wall, which must have consisted of very inferior material, for it was not crumbling plaster that trickled to the floor but sand, black soil, and ashes. Besides, the hole was much too large for the force of my blow. Now if some kind of bugs, cockroaches, or other vermin had crawled out of the hole, I shouldn't have been a bit surprised. No cockroaches or other bugs crawled out of the hole, however, but all kinds of question-

able mollusks, queer little snails, with and without shells, ring-
worms, and other repulsive gastropods, some of which stayed
so clearly in my memory that I was able to look them up and
find them after my return in Dr. H. G. Bronn's "Classes and
Orders of Mollusks" (1862-1866). For the most part they were
pulmonates or lung-snails, that were classified by Lamarck as
cephalopods and nudibranchiates, and further described as
Pupa, Bulimus, Achatina, and Planorbis. So these creatures with
the lovely names writhed and slithered out of the hole. It proved
that there had to be rich, black, nourishing soil in the neighborhood, a thing no one would have expected in this lifeless cavity
far beneath the lithosphere, for rich, nourishing earth is nothing
but the product of decaying organic life which can only exist on
the outermost surface of the planet. I'm not particularly finical
but I felt an irrepressible loathing at sight of these snails and
other mollusks. The water affected me the same way.

There was a splendid bathing saloon next to our bedroom.
I must insist on the word "saloon," for it was at least twenty feet
long and contained all sorts of unfamiliar shower and spray
equipment. It reminded me of a cold-water sanatorium of the
old days. Down here in Tartarus the dry Astrotonic ablution
seemed to be inadequate. Everything down here was old-
fashioned and out of keeping with Astromental customs. Near the
bathing saloon was a fountainlike basin with a faucet in the
shape of a fish. I moved my hand back and forth inadvertently
over the fish mouth a few times, and the electromagnetism of my
body activated the fountain. But even as the water fanned out
I was disgusted to observe that it was thick and brown with
microorganisms. Tiny tadpoles, infusoria, larvae, miniature fish,
and shells collected in the basin. I called B.H. and showed him
the hole with the gastropods as well as the fountain bowl with
the crazily gyrating water fauna.

"What do you suppose Io-Fagór thinks of this, and all the
other fine gentlemen and ladies who live on star food?"

"We're in the underworld, F.W.," B.H. shrugged absently
and yawned again.

"What about the underworld?"

"The underworld was always messy," he said without evincing any interest.

Our room had two windows with closely drawn curtains. As the Astromentals were not used to real windows, our predecessors here had probably never thought of opening the curtains. I did so over my friend's objections and pushed up one of the windows. Incidentally, the panes were broken and pasted up with paper (messy, messy!). Despite the autumnal twilight I could see fairly far.

No name, no designation, ever described the external appearance of its object as well. What we saw here could be nothing but a Wintergarden, a hothouse of infinite dimensions. The singular form is wrong of course. There were countless hothouses of varying sizes extending in all directions as far as the eye reached out into the November dusk. Most of them had appropriate roofs of glass or glasslike material, and the gleaming reflections here and there seemed to come from invisible rays that were refracted on the glass roofs before they penetrated the interior to fulfill their purpose. I sniffed the air that had a faint but sharp aroma.

"What do you smell?" I asked B.H.

My friend, whose body was not of dubious nature like mine, who was properly born into the Astromental world and had lived in it for one hundred and seven years, was not as distrustful as I and appeared to be satisfied with everything.

"I don't smell a thing," he said. "Naturally the air in the Wintergarden isn't particularly salubrious. That's an old story and you can't expect anything else. What do you think you smell?"

"It smells like—wait a minute, it smells like diapers, it smells like babies."

"Could be," he yawned deeply. "We'll smell like babies ourselves soon."

"A hell of a note," I exclaimed.

My ejaculation aroused B.H. from his apathy. "How can you

say it's a hell of a note," he said, shaking his head over and over again. "It's man's greatest attainment, it's the death of death, it's birth from one's own body. Nothing in the world is pleasanter and sweeter, so it's said."

At this point our conversation was interrupted by two white-smocked figures who had been standing in the room for some time but whom I noticed only when I closed the window with the diaper scent and turned around. In contrast to Astromental dwellings which affected a certain Spartan barrenness, the floors here were covered with heavy carpets, and besides the white-smocks sneaked about on feltlike soles so that you could never hear them coming or going. The two Bath Attendants who had been assigned to us were big, heavy individuals, like the others. Although they did not attain the gigantic stature of the Worker and his clan, their dimensions nevertheless invited this comparison which, of course, was to their disadvantage. I don't want to be unjust, and it would be, if I expected the employees of the Wintergarden to have the sun-tan, the tremendous good humor, the explosive healthfulness, and the golden lion's growl of the Worker. You really couldn't expect the attendants down here in this great cavity, who never saw the sun and probably couldn't stand it, you really couldn't expect them to harbor life's morning song in their solar plexus. In the low oxygen content of this atmosphere, constantly imperiled by the irruption of dangerous carbonic gases, subjected to unnatural pressures, exposed to the warm drizzle of this make-believe sky, the human body developed quite differently than in the dry, clear air of the Park of the Worker. These two Bath Attendants in our room had gray faces, were morbidly bloated, and looked like eunuchs in a harem. They moved slowly and languidly, spoke with high-pitched, flat voices, and exhibited good nature and patience. Their great stature and girth seemed to inconvenience them. They had too much to carry around. My impression of the white-smocks could be briefly formulated: colossi on clay feet. While I had no out-and-out antipathy for them as yet, still my entire nature was involuntarily and unconsciously on guard. B.H., on the other hand, who had had the propaganda about the "greatest attainment" dinned into his ears all his life long, showed no trace of resistance and was agreeable to everything. I was annoyed to hear him thank the two functionaries for coming so quickly to take care of us.

"We're bringing breakfast for the gentlemen," said Bath Attendant Number One, leering at me bashfully with lowered eyelids, which led me to assume that he was assigned to me. The two had carried in a small table with the familiar juices and soups.

"Or you can take it as your supper," said Bath Attendant Number Two. "You can take it for whatever you like, gentlemen." And he leered at his charge, B.H.

"How's that?" I asked sharply. "It's much too late for breakfast and much too early for supper. What time is it anyhow?"

"We don't have any clock at all," the startled Bath Attendants answered in unison. And the one who seemed more intelligent added, "Where there's no sun and no moon, there aren't any clocks."

"You're quite wrong," I reprimanded him sternly. "Clocks were invented to take the place of the sun and moon. On what kind of time do you run down here?"

My forceful manner not only appeared to intimidate the Bath Attendants but also to worry them. They looked at each other apprehensively. Their guests didn't ordinarily exhibit so much violence.

"You want to know on what kind of time we run, Seigneur?" Number One repeated my question, raising his white cap that looked like a cook's bonnet. "Well, as soon as it becomes necessary, everyone gets his own private time down here."

"Private time? What kind of nonsense is that?" I shouted furiously. "Time is the one thing that's probably least private."

"But now you're quite wrong, Chronosopher F.W.," exclaimed my friend who had been startled out of his sleepiness by my bad manners. "Don't you know that every human has his own body time, and that every human is his own body clock?"

"And when do we start looking at our body clocks here?" I inquired, slightly mollified, for, after all, B.H. was right.

The Bath Attendants again exchanged worried and apprehensive glances. Then Bath Attendant Number Two, who was a little smaller than Number One, lowered his eyes and said hesitantly like an uneducated person who is not sure of a technical term: "The private time down here begins with Anti—with Antiception."

As if to anticipate my anger, Number One began to pacify me in his high-pitched voice. "There's no hurry, gentlemen. You have all the time in the world before you make up your minds to begin your private time. In fact, you don't have to make up your minds at all. If you want to, you can become Bath Attendants or Assistant Gardeners, or Head Gardeners, or even Animators, if you pass the twenty-seven examinations."

This well-meant speech raised my ire once more. "I heard the word 'Antiception' just now, a lucidly obscure scientific term. I don't like lucidly obscure allusions. I want complete clarity and no dark light. I don't object to the gallows if it's called a gallows and not a loop-swing——"

I had to stop abruptly. My previous lethargy had developed into the most violent headache imaginable. The blood throbbed in my temples. The pressure in my forehead became unbearable.

"They say," I groaned, "that you experience only the pleasantest and sweetest feelings in the world down here. So far I haven't noticed anything of it. Oh, my poor head!"

The two white-smocks now exchanged satisfied instead of worried looks. They seemed pleased with the opportunity to help a sufferer. Such headaches, they said, as my friend and I were enduring, were regular afflictions of all newcomers; they didn't mean a thing but a passing reaction of the system to the unaccustomed conditions and the high atmospheric pressure down here in the cavity. There was a tested remedy, they said, for getting rid of the headache. After that we would feel unusually relaxed; more than that, we would feel like newborn babes. And the remedy wasn't anything more serious than a little mud bath

in the water sanatorium next door; moreover, everything was
ready for us. Before we could say yes or no the Bath Attendants
had undressed us. I still had the strength to insist that my clothes
be kept in plain sight. The Bath Attendants were very reasonable. They didn't appear in the least offended by my suspicious
attitude, not even when I demanded assurance under oath that
there would be no snails, worms, mollusks, and tadpoles disport-
ing themselves in the mud bath.

"Light," I shouted in conclusion. "I want more light in the
bathing saloon."

"What kind of light would you like, Seigneur," Attendant
Number One asked eagerly.

"June noonday sunlight," I demanded unreasonably in sten-
torian tones. My desire was fulfilled without delay.

Now this wasn't the first mud bath I had ever taken. But it
differed agreeably from my previous baths of this sort in the fact
that the thick warm substance in which I stretched my relaxing
limbs neither stuck to the skin nor soiled it. My headache vanished in a few seconds. A feeling of freeness and lightness permeated my whole body, as though the lagging bloodstream had
been given new impetus. It was undoubtedly a pleasant, a sweet
sensation of rejuvenation and alleviation that I was permitted to
experience. They really hadn't lied to me. After the numerous
hardships of my third Astromental day I gladly yielded to the
balsamic bliss of the moment and began to forget where I was
and the purpose of my presence. I don't know how long we had
been sitting in the mud bath when my eye fell on B.H.

He had closed his eyes and was smiling in perfect serenity.
As an Astromental, it seemed, he was much more susceptible to
the effects of this bath than I, a dull citizen of early antiquity.
But when I looked at him more closely I noticed that his face
had changed in an alarming manner. He seemed to have become
even younger, even more boyish. All lines and shadows in his
features had been erased. It looked as if one of the Bath Attendants had covered his face with a very thin layer of a cosmetic
preparation, removing all characteristics and leaving only this

doll-like, rigid expression of serenity. I still marvel at the strength and resoluteness with which I jumped up out of the thick mud, seized my friend under the armpits, dragged him out of the wooden tub and set him on his feet. He offered no resistance but he appeared very angry, although he didn't say a word for a long time. The consternation in his eyes, however, made it clear that he couldn't understand why I had brutally torn him out of his blissful state. I couldn't understand my own reaction. Why was I afraid of this harmless, invigorating mud bath? Hadn't I, moreover, made up my mind in Io-Fagòr's house to take this final journey as my only way out? What did I want? I didn't know what I wanted. I wanted B.H. not to smile so blissfully. The Bath Attendants One and Two stared at me, and worry creased their foreheads at the unexpected muscular strength I had demonstrated.

"Send for our Animator," I shouted at them. "Have him come here at once."

"You've asked for him, here he is," replied a lisping, shivering voice, an obsequious, hand-rubbing voice, so to speak, from between the bedroom and the bathing saloon.

The Twenty-Second Chapter

WHEREIN THE LAST OF MY SIGHTSEEING
TRIPS TAKES PLACE UNDER THE GUIDANCE
OF THE ANIMATOR, AND I MAKE THE AC-
QUAINTANCE OF THE HOTHOUSES, THE PRIDE
OF ASTROMENTAL MANKIND, AND OF THE
MOUND OF THE WET NURSES.

THE ANIMATOR WAS standing in the doorway of our bathing
saloon with an encouraging smile and was actually rubbing his hands. He was no giant. On the contrary, he was
small and perhaps a little deformed. His white smock seemed
too large for his figure. While the other functionaries of the
underworld wore head-coverings reminiscent of cooks' and confectioners' caps, the Animator displayed his bare, unusually long,
and slightly misshapen cranium. He had the only ill-proportioned
figure I had seen on my journey, for the spherical deformity of
the High Floater had, as we know, proved to be a premature
tendency of the human body in the direction of floating locomotion, a development which would be consummated in countless
hectomillennia. The slight deformity of our Animator, however—
and the word "deformity" is really an unjustified exaggeration—
betrayed no kind of biological design. It was not the result of
cosmic arthritis that the Foreignfeelers contracted in the oceans
of space between the star nebulae. As far as the name "Animator" is concerned, I'm not quite clear about its meaning. It

518

would certainly be a mistake to translate it literally as "inspirer" or "enlivener," for the bearer of the title had nothing to do with inspiring or enlivening dead matter; quite the contrary, it was his business to transform the separation of the soul from dead matter into an occasion of festive enjoyment. I am inclined, therefore, to connect the title of the Animator with the word animate in the sense of encourage. It was the Animator's business to encourage his customers. Io-Fagòr's last words to me had revealed the fact that there were many who, when the time arrived, recoiled from this festive enjoyment which they had praised so highly all through their lives; for, after all, no matter how exquisite and enjoyable and attractive the end may be, it is still the end of a long, accustomed condition. And who likes to change his accustomed conditions, even if they are not enjoyable at all?

I mustn't forget to mention an amusing trait of the Animator. He seemed to feel chilly even in the thick, steamy hothouse atmosphere down here; every now and then he would audibly suck in a deep breath as he tried to keep his teeth from chattering. I'll risk another comparison: just as the High Floater could not manage to remain in the lower regions of his Office in spite of intensified gravitation, so the Animator could not manage to keep warm in this steam bath. Occupational infirmities.

"Please pardon our informal attire, Maître Animator," I said, suddenly quite composed, forgetting that nakedness wasn't improper at all.

The Animator suppressed a shiver and replied with a slight lisp, "To the eye of the physician, Seigneur, nakedness is only another garment." As he came nearer with apologetic little steps he continued to talk to himself as if the incessant scientific monologue inside him broke through to the surface for an instant. "No, no, the skin, the epidermoid area, is anything but nakedness. Anyhow, nakedness is nothing but an illusion of lovers who rub against each other in order to make each other receptive. But the skin is the most inclusive and conclusive thing

in the world. It is the seamless garment." This time he didn't
quite manage to refrain from shivering. He surveyed me, and
then my friend, from head to foot with a brief, remarkably sharp
look of his reddened eyes. Meanwhile he continued his monologue in the manner of one who accompanies his work with
loose, meaningless talk. "The seamless garment of the High
Priest had four openings. The seamless garment of man, the skin,
has three times three openings: Two eyes, two ears, two nostrils,
a mouth, a sex organ, an anus. . . . Everything in good shape,
Seigneur, as far as the seamless garment goes, with the exception
of the tenth aperture or semi-aperture, the navel. Crude job of
binding. Must have been sinister times. Well, makes no difference now. You survived it. But we're not going to have such an
easy time with you, Seigneur, not too easy. More difficult than
with your friend, at any rate." And he smiled encouragingly at
B.H.

"What do you mean by easier and more difficult?" I asked the
Animator from between clenched teeth.

"I should like to preface my remarks," he lisped, "by saying
that I have devoted myself to the service of mankind and that I
always have only the best and most charitable designs."

This false phrase—for, of course, designs are always evil and
never good—is not to be charged to the author as an error. Not
often, but occasionally, the Animator slipped up on his meta-
phors. Perhaps these slips were the result of what B.H. had
called the messiness of the underworld.

"Somebody used the word Antiception a while ago," I said
with a trace of acerbity.

The Animator pacified me. "Don't pay any attention to words,
Seigneur, particularly not to scientific, technical words, empty
and idle synonyms in dead languages. They are nothing but
relics of outmoded times, when science consisted of nothing but
them—don't you see that the gentlemen are chilly," he turned
to the Bath Attendants, "and you let them stand there without
drying them. Hurry up, rub them down and dress them."

The two white-smocks pounced on us with wonderfully rough

towels and rubbed us off in a fairly expert manner but without
showing much muscular strength. Dressing us was a harder job
for them because they were unfamiliar with the intricacies of
B.H.'s field uniform as well as of my black formal garment. They
found the fronts and backs of the trousers especially confusing.
Moreover, I noticed at once that the order to dress us had
aroused their astonishment and disapproval, as in the case of all
subordinates who are asked to commit a breach of regulations
or conventions. The regulations undoubtedly read: When the
customer is once undressed, he is not to be dressed again.

When we were finished, we preceded the Animator into our
bedroom.

"Whatever your intentions, gentlemen," he said almost humbly,
"I am at your service."

"You know who I am, Maître Animator," I said, glancing down
at my violet wrist-rosette which I had not even taken off in the
mud bath. He inclined his head in order to indicate his sympathy.

"I am ever so sorry that your visit to our world has been so
rudely interrupted." And looking upward he added, "Things are
bad, very bad. The latest news is devastating. You gentlemen
made the only correct choice."

"Even under ordinary circumstances I would have decided to
pay a visit to the Wintergarden and to its management. After
all, I was also in the Djebel, I 'ascended' with the Chronosophers
and was received in the Office of the High Floater. The Wintergarden, it seems to me, is just as important for the welfare of
mankind and for the curiosity of a stranger as the Djebel."

The Animator looked at me, at first suspiciously, then searchingly, and finally he broke into a broad smile. "Do you really
mean that, Seigneur? Foolish question. A man like you speaks the
truth, and if he lies he only deceives the others but not himself.
You didn't deceive yourself. We down here don't have any illusions. They praise our institution as a great attainment, but they
do it timidly and in whispers. They would ignore us entirely if
they could. Yes, the Djebel shines brightly. Stars are headline

attractions. Stars are for snobs. Understand me, I'm not saying a word against the stars of all the various Intermundia. But I should like to ask you not to underrate our unassuming Intermundium of Cell Division."

"On the contrary, Maître Animator," I interjected, "I hope you will give my friend and me the same attention we received in the Djebel." With these words I pushed my rosette back under my cuff. At this instant B.H. suddenly emerged from the blissful absent-mindedness into which the mud bath had plunged him. He pulled himself together. His face showed more lines and shadows than ever. An expression of determined concentration formed about his mouth.

"We have the right to demand the same attention we received in the Djebel," he shouted in the violent tone of one who is not quite sober. "I promised my friend from the beginnings of mankind that he would get to see everything."

"I am delighted at the opportunity," the Animator smiled. "Honor to whom honor is due. I thank you in the name of the Wintergarden. Our relations with the Djebel are excellent. In an extended perpendicular directly above your head, Seigneur, is the Office of the High Floater. Again in an extended perpendicular directly above that is the Archangel Michael, otherwise known as the North Star. Directly above the latter in a third extended perpendicular is the zygotic, i.e., the fructified, star nebula, Mundus Hibernus or Winterworld. They must have told you in the Djebel of the two kinds of star nebulae, the spiral ones and the egg-shaped ones, the spermatic and the ovarian, the male and the female."

I was not only surprised but annoyed to hear the Animator talk so freely about exalted world riddles and to speak quite casually about a tremendous secret like that of a fructified universe, when the High Floater had been so reticent.

"Unworthy as I am," I said softly, "I have been told that the universe has the shape of a human and that it is wedded with itself."

"We talk about these things in less mystic and metaphysical

language, Seigneur," the Animator retorted. "We don't ascend to
the heights but descend into the depths. And the deeper one
goes, the more real reality becomes. Remember one thing, gentlemen, the universe is not androgynous, not male-female or
female-male, as a few quacks claimed only recently, that is, just
two hundred years ago. Three words hold sway over everything,
from the bright Winterworld up there to the dark Wintergarden
down here. Procreation, fructification, parturition——"

"I don't want to hear anything about it," B.H. yelled in a
sudden rage and stamped his foot. "I don't want to hear it said
that stars are the same thing as unicles, achads, and monads.
That's all lying rubbish of obsolete natural science. We rolled
around long enough yesterday on the inside of a damned hydrogen atom. Atoms aren't stars any more than poker chips are
gold pieces."

The Animator looked at me for help.

"My friend chose a figure of speech from one of his former
lives," I laughed. "You see, he's a bit excited. But I prefer his
excitement to the apathetic compliancy he demonstrated in the
mud bath."

I took B.H.'s hand. "Isn't it about time to start on our sightseeing tour, Maître?"

"Just another moment, gentlemen," the little man replied and
inclined his long, narrow skull. "I regard a few preliminaries as
indispensable. By that I mean a few explanatory remarks on my
part, so that you will understand the principle and will be able
to appreciate the miracle more fully. Man, oh, man, this certainly is a bright Sunday for me."

"Sunday?" I asked. "Do you have days down here?"

"Of course there aren't any days, Seigneur," the Animator informed me. "That was only an expression to indicate my happiness at your visit. We have the advantage of not being ham-
pered by an astronomic schedule——"

"But by private time instead," I smiled pointedly.

"'Private time' is only what it is called in the jargon of the
subordinates," the Animator answered in a tone of faint reproach.

"We, gentlemen, speak of autobiological time. And no one is forced into autobiological time."

In a low voice the Animator gave an order to the Bath Attendants. The colossi on clay feet stumbled over each other in their eagerness and returned a few seconds later. They brought a jug and three cups which they filled with fluid from the jug. While I was constantly on guard, still I decided to accept the welcoming drink. It really and truly seemed to be old cognac. At least it tasted and burned like good cognac, fiery and oily smooth at the same time.

"You will need new energy for the inspection tour, gentlemen," the Animator exhorted us. And he was right. The drink concealed no insidious trick. Whether the cup was filled with brandy or with some unfamiliar elixir, it did miracles, at least for me. Although I had no idea at this time what I intended to do and had no real doubt that I would submit to the procedure of the Wintergarden, yet I watched over B.H.'s and my physical and mental powers with the utmost concentration. For an Astromentally acute premonition told me that we would need every ounce of these powers for whatever adventures might confront us.

Meanwhile, to my great surprise, the Animator squatted unceremoniously on the rug like a son of the desert.

"You detest this posture, gentlemen," he lisped, seeing my astonishment. "But quite wrongly. Knees drawn up to the chin, little hands turned out, that's the devout posture of nascent man in utero, when he receives the gift of higher life. We should pray to the creator, whoever he may be, in this posture of receptivity, and not on our knees, as before a despot."

Since even squatting was hallowed by these words, I sat down on one of the couches and drew B.H. down beside me.

"Is that part of the principle?" I inquired in order to get the Animator to the subject as quickly as possible.

"The principle is very simple," he nodded. "Terra is not Terrus and Gaea is not Gaeos. The human spirit, which is nothing but the awakening consciousness of life, was aware even in its first dawn that its planet is a woman."

"Maître Animator," I interrupted, "if I had not become personally acquainted with the strictly masculine natures of John Evangelist and Apostle Peter I should regard your disclosure as the tritest kind of banality."

"But now, since you have yourself discovered what a barren, brutal, uncharitable creature a masculine planet is, you no longer consider this great but simple truth banal. And now you know why all of us, you and your friend and I, are troubadours and minstrels, and above all, mother's pets. You see, sometimes even dry science can get enthusiastic."

"What kind of science are you talking about?" asked B.H. He sounded dignified and hostile, and I was happy over his hostility.

"I am not *speaking* of science, I *am* science," the Animator declared, and he didn't sound as presumptuous as it looks in print. "I bring order into the millions of disorders of life, just like the honorable Starrovers, Marvelers, and Foreignfeelers up there, less spectacularly, perhaps, but with more evident results."

"For instance?" B.H. insisted on his pedantic questions.

"For instance," the Animator repeated almost tenderly, "take for instance the two gentlemen at whose feet I am squatting in receptive devotion. What are these two gentlemen physically? They are twice twenty-six trillion cellular beings, living, plasmatic discs each with a viscous droplet in the middle; and every single one of these discs is assigned to a separate group, and each group owes its existence to a different cause, serves another purpose, and assumes a different shape. Yet they are all bound together and moved by the same force and the same law that keeps the cosmos in motion. I have the honor, therefore, of squatting in receptive devotion before two cosmoses, two exalted Ios——"

"Not that," B.H. ground out through his teeth, "not this comparison, if you please."

"Don't interrupt him, my boy, when he's right," I reprimanded my friend and had another cup of cognac or elixir poured for him.

"Go right ahead and interrupt me, noble Io," the Animator fluted, "inasmuch as I don't want to bore Seigneur with ancient commonplaces about Bioelectricity and Symmetrology that had already been rejected by his famous contemporaries such as Saint Thomas, Minkowski, Aristotle, Coghill, Harvey the Great, Lactantius, Davenport Hooker, Coronios, Li-Feng Yang, and Joao Travao—do I pronounce them right?"

"Perfectly, Maître," I nodded, flattering the vain polyhistorian, "but I didn't interrupt you."

"I interrupt myself, Seigneur, by closing my eyes in order to see you better. For as I look at you with my mind's eye I succeed in retrovolving you figuratively, a faculty that has become second nature to me through a century of experience in the Wintergarden. Now I am seeing twenty-six trillion entirely different little discs, and still others, and now I skip many cycles of concrescence, and presently you are a roly-poly child, Seigneur, with big, observant eyes (why so very sad?), and then you are a postnatal baby, your seamless skin scalded red; and finally, old practitioner that I am and always fascinated over and over again by my practice, I go back to the very extreme of retrovolution, I go usque ad ovum, back to the origin."

He paused after these words, and his white face, which impressed me as almost painfully in need of a little white goatee and sharply ground spectacles, seemed to shrink with scientific ecstasy.

"Back to the origin," he repeated softly. "What's that I see? I see a globe, a globule, the archetype of all things, and possibly some day the final type. I see a globule whose unsolidified, bicellular mass is bounded and enclosed by a thin, vitreous membrane, a shell, a surface. Every being begins its existence by enclosing its bounds. And now, Seigneur, you are indebted to no one and to nothing except to your father and mother. You are nothing but a promising presumption. You are visible only to me, the Animator in the Wintergarden. The two chromosomes, the sacred color particles, the female bright red and the male sky blue, have neutralized each other in the globule—which is you—into an inextinguishable potentiality for the reception of higher life. . . ."

I stared at the Animator in profound fascination while his embryological discourse turned my stomach a little. And then— oh, no, it couldn't be—he squeezed out a tear from under the closed lid of his left eye. It beats everything, I thought, that these hellions are soft and sentimental on top of all else, and I almost missed the next words of the Animator.

". . . and so I must ask your permission to let me develop you a bit further and to make you a little bigger. About like this. Now, Seigneur, you look like a wisp of smoke or a bit of curved fluff in a palely transparent soap bubble. Let's go a trifle further. Now you have the features of a tiny little ram. But what's this? There—there, can't you hear it? The little heart is beginning to beat. It started quite imperceptibly, irregularly, giddily, drunken with sleep. So far all muscles are only faint indications, but the heart muscle has begun to pump the personality, the soul, into the tiny head. But what's the matter? Why does the little heart labor so hard? You were right to come to us, Seigneur. By your first heartbeats I can feel the negative tendency of your constitution. You were quite right. Why expose yourself to the worst of all terrors, to a sudden end, this barbarity of bygone eras? What do I hear in your left ventricle? Permit me to develop you a little further——"

"I won't permit it," I yelled and jumped up, beside myself as B.H. had been before. The Animator had given me wild palpitations and it took quite a while before I calmed down.

"You took the liberty," I finally blurted out breathlessly, "you had the unmitigated gall to retrovolve me usque ad ovum without my permission, instead of explaining the principle of the Wintergarden objectively and impersonally."

The Animator had risen from his receptive squatting posture. He seemed not only startled but actually aghast at my outbreak.

"Didn't I reveal the principle of the Wintergarden in every

one of my words?" he stammered. "Didn't the honorable Ios understand me?"

He directed his tearful voice to the two Bath Attendants who were standing in the doorway of the bathing saloon.

"Was I so very bad today?" he asked like an actor.

"Excellent! Wonderful! Brilliant! Never better!" the two assistants answered in the automatic, flattering tone in which perspiring and praise-hungry virtuosos are appeased after a performance. But then the smaller one of the Bath Attendants, it was Number Two, stepped a pace forward, blushed, and said in an embarrassed voice, pronouncing the foreign words cautiously, "I beg humble pardon. The Animator forgot about the retrogenetic humus."

I looked at B.H. B.H. looked at me. Both of us were a sorry sight.

"What is that, 'retrogenetic humus'?" I asked, and my voice sounded as though I were choking.

"It's joy beyond all joy," the Animator chattered, shivering not with cold but with ecstasy. "You gentlemen took your first bath in a weak solution of retrogenetic humus a while ago."

* * * * *
* * *
*

IN ORDER TO FOLLOW A TRAVEL REPORT from the most distant future, like this one, without resistance and perhaps even with a little profit, the reader has to free himself from the indurated thought pattern of his own era. I myself had to meet this same condition and, God knows, I didn't always succeed although I had the advantage of personal experience and direct observation. All in all I spent two and a half days and three nights in the Astromental world. But that's only a subjective statement. I don't know whether it was in reality two and a half seconds or quarter hours or just as many eternities that left the flotsam with which this volume is filled. Since we've become acquainted with so many different kinds of time—superplanetary time in the Lower Intermundium, static time in purgatory, and we are now approaching autobiological time in the Wintergarden —I must not neglect to pay my compliments to the most important time dimension in which man lives, namely "spiritual time."

This most splendid species of time is marked by the fact that it has no sequentiality, that it contains the entire course of the world in each of its parts, and that it gives him who lives by it liberty to leap without restraint from one point to another and permits him to witness the first day of creation and the Last Judgment in the same instant. Spiritual time is the source of the three virtues that elevate man to the rank of man: memory, premonition, and faith in the unprovable. And the worst enemies of spiritual time are the poor wretches who are unable to leap without restraint from time-peak to time-peak, who are not wrapped in the fabric of memory and premonition, and who do not dare to believe anything unprovable. They are the same ones who always ask the wrong questions because they want to know everything exactly, if only because they couldn't even understand it inexactly. Only the prerogative of having spiritual time within us gives the reader and me the opportunity of being present in the Eleventh Cosmic Capital Year of Virgo before it is present itself.

But we don't need any spiritual time to imagine that the congealed or half-congealed strata of the earth's interior contain cavities, which, when illumined by a dim twilight, appear as strangely gloomy autumn landscapes. That's nothing but a presumable fact, as, for example, unknown species of animals. We don't even need spiritual time in order to designate the stupendous cavity of the Wintergarden with the same words as the Animator, namely "Uterus Matris Terrae" or "the Womb of Mother Earth." It is also a presumable fact that this cavity once contained the fiery liquid core of the moon before it rose to the surface and was cast off; in contrast to the previous one, however, this is not a mere fact but one that conceals a parable: the parable of the earth-female and the female-earth. But only spiritual time, which permeates us and which realizes what has been and what will be, and even what has never been and will never be, endows us with the boldness to accept the "retrogenetic humus" and the "retrovolution of the living form" and the "Astromental vanquishing of death"—to accept them as possibilities foreseen in the dusk of distance, possibilities that nature and human reason may utilize or reject.

It would be pure nonsense for me to claim that the retrogenetic humus was a product of the cavity which the Animator called "Uterus Matris Terrae." I don't even know whether this humus was not produced up above in the Park of the Worker under the rays of the sun or of certain female stars, and was then brought down to the Wintergarden. I can't even say when it was first used and who was its discoverer. And therefore I can't put the name of this eminent biologist as a peer at the side of the great astronomer Ursler. As we entered the first of the glasshouses the Animator gave us a handful of this thick, damp, black earth that had the quality of not soiling a body with which it came in contact. In the bath I had seen it in muddy, heated form; now, as I held it in my hand, it was pleasantly cool and aroused my desire to press it against my forehead, which was beginning to hurt again.

It was much brighter in the Hothouses than outdoors. They were filled with a particularly delicate spring light. The first impression was that they served the customary purpose of all glasshouses, namely to raise flowers. In contrast with the Astromental gardens in the upper world, I saw here not only the eight or ten species of chandlers' and confectioners' flora, but a wide variety of half-familiar and unfamiliar blossoming plants of all kinds, even such things as laburnum and oversized azaleas and blooming cacti in unbelievably pale color combinations. In my archaic mind, however, this floral splendor provoked the very association of ideas which the management of the Wintergarden had most sharply rejected, the idea of a cemetery.

The glasshouses of the Wintergarden were the exact opposite of a cemetery. In an inimitably gentle manner they transferred the living being into a form of nonbeing that left no ugly traces. And yet I couldn't help it, the total effect on me, pretty flowers and all, was that of a cemetery. The persons in process of retro-volution were not in plain sight. They slumbered along the sides of the path—and again my plastic memory leads me to a funereal comparison—they slumbered in cradlelike graves. Of course, they were really slumbering, busily, and breathing rapidly. The cradle-graves were wooden vats or tubs of the kind in which we had recently taken a "mud bath." They were filled with humus of varying mixture and strength and they were imbedded fairly deeply in the floor of the glasshouses so that they did not project above the surface. Each of the cradle-graves was surmounted by a mound. Only this mound was not made up of green sod but of a grayish-white heap of something that could have been described as eiderdown, fluffy feathers, or freshly plucked lint. Flowers grew in profusion between the individual tubs, and their fragrance reduced the odor of the soil which I had sniffed at the window and had diagnosed as the scent of diapers. Down here it turned out to be a definite smell of ammonia.

We rolled along slowly between these resting places on a moving sidewalk, the Animator in the lead, Bath Attendants Numbers One and Two bringing up the rear. I was tormented by a very uneasy sense of imprisonment, while B.H. again appeared to agree to everything and listened to the Animator's discourse with sleepy approval. We encountered only a very few white-smocks and no laymen at all. Ordinary citizens of the era were not permitted to inspect this secret Astromental institution. But instead of feeling highly privileged, I was absent-minded and resentful of the manner of our guide. He had turned out to be a type of scientist or medic that I knew well and that I dis-liked. The designation "radical specialist" is inadequate as a description of the physicians who trace all diseases to "a single point," the liver, the pancreas, or the roots of the teeth, whether they are sound or not. They are people who are possessed of a fixed idea, who wear blinkers that restrict their vision to one spot, and the patient serves only as a means to vindicate their fixed idea. Radical specialism is the manifestation of human one-sidedness and narrow-mindedness in the field of science. The Animator seemed to me to be a specialist of this sort through and through, a fanatic of his profession, a troll of these strange glasshouses. Down here he had even lost his tactful smoothness. He was completely ruled by the science that he ruled. He lisped his explanations in a curiously solemn tone, with dreamy eyes, obviously quite convinced that he was doing a good job of animating us to hop right into one of the cradle-graves by the wayside.

"My researches prove," he smiled at me gravely, "that the terms 'epidermis,' 'dermis,' and 'endodermis' are as ancient as you, Seigneur. By this primitive tripartition we refer to the external, the intermediate, and the internal stratum of evolution, hence also retrovolution, that constitutes the basis of our system of Hothouses. That's an absurd simplification, of course, for there are not only three, but three hundred and thirty-three evolutional strata. For the purpose of a survey, however, we will keep it simple. Here, for example, honorable Ios, everything is confined to the external area of retrovolution; we are dealing only with cases in the primary stage. Just as the growth of the embryo takes place through rapid cell division induced by the universal forces in the amniotic cavity of the womb, just so our beneficent retrogenetic humus produces an accelerated, but infinitely gentle cell division, which underlies the most ingenious, the most comfortable, and the loveliest of all shrinking processes. By means of cell division we become what we are, and by means of cell division we again become what we were before we were —I trust, Seigneur, that this round trip will delight and enchant you."

. He tiptoed up to one of the cradle-graves, removed the heap of down and linty fluff with tender hands, and beckoned us to step closer, at the same time enjoining silence by placing his finger on his lips.

"Isn't it sweet, this sleep of childhood?" he whispered. We came nearer. I saw a polished Astromental head which lay exposed, while a boyish body was delineated under a layer of black soil, knees drawn up to the chin, hands turned out—a seven-year-old or so in the posture of an embryo. His face was not boyish but ageless as usual, and it wore the same blissful expression that had frightened me on B.H.'s features in the mud bath. His skin was a violent red, undoubtedly from fever, and his breath came in gasps like that of a critically sick person.

"This sleep of childhood," I said with gloomy frankness, "is the prologue to the sleep of death."

"How can you utter such horrid words," the deeply offended Animator objected. "It is not our task to avert the end. The end is a necessary and a good thing. But it is our task to make the end subjectively and objectively beautiful. Moreover, by brutally mentioning that word you have offended the disciplinary code of the Wintergarden."

"It shan't happen again," I apologized, "although the thing remains the same no matter what you call it."

"The process is salutary, Seigneur, the name is offensive. For that reason it is a civil offense to refer to the Wintergarden as the 'Thanatodrome.'"

He quickly covered the cradle-grave with its heap of down and fluff, and after a brief nervous pause resumed his discourse.

"All cases out here in the external area, the epidermis," he said, "are still movable. In a manner of speaking, they are still living outside the womb and are therefore fed orally."

"Why feed them at all?" I inquired rebelliously.

"Do you take us for barbarians or cutthroats?" came the outraged answer. "At first the retrovolved cases are fed by mouth, as long as they are still half-grown, and finally as postnatal infants. Only when the placenta has closed around the fetus, nourishment is introduced through the navel. Coming and going, it's all the same. As long as the heart beats it gets the necessary nutriment."

"And when does the heart stop beating?"

"At the corresponding point in the retrovolutionary process at which it began to beat."

I swallowed my resentment. A warning voice told me under no circumstances to arouse the animosity of the Animator. Besides, B.H. worried me more and more. Again he had become completely apathetic. His dark eyes listened dreamily and almost avidly to the Animator's explanations. I therefore decided to change my tactics and to conceal my irritation as much as possible.

"Cher Maître," I began with an effort at flattery, "it's almost unbelievable. It's a great pity that my own contemporaries had no idea that there would be a Wintergarden some day, with retrogenetic humus. But how about this autobiological time? How old, for instance, was the man we just saw?"

The Animator gave me a quick glance and seemed satisfied.

"The man whom you just saw in the sweetest slumber of childhood, Seigneur, arrived here at the age of one hundred and fifty-three years, according to his birth certificate. That's not old, or at least not old enough for his autobiological time to elapse rapidly. He was planted about twelve planetary hours ago."

"And twelve hours of cell division was sufficient to retrovolve him into a boy of seven years?"

"That's a fairly long time, Seigneur," smiled the Animator. "We've had cases where the whole process was finished inside of twelve hours."

"Is that possible?" I exclaimed. "And how long does it take with recalcitrants?"

The Animator's red eyes stared at me in astonishment.

"That's not so easy to say, Seigneur," he replied after an infinitesimal pause. "Recalcitrance is the only form of discomfort that the recalcitrant inflicts on himself. We've had cases that took years."

"Probably served them right," I agreed piously. "But now tell me about your most successful cases, your ideal cases, your model specimens."

"That's easy." His face beamed. (I noticed that in the incubator heat of the glasshouses he no longer shivered and chattered as he had done up in our room, nor did he rub his icy hands.

This seemed to be the appropriate temperature for him.) "A genuine Desiderium Originis," he continued, "promotes a lightning-like process, in which the blastocyst can be turned over to the Daisy Fields in a very few hours. By 'Desiderium Originis' I mean a yearning for the original state, one of the strongest impulses of man when he has grown old, tired, bitter, disappointed, hopeless, and worn out, when he can no longer resist the monsoon attacks of tedium senile, the loathing of old age for itself, even though he may still publicly parade around as a handsome, youthfully vigorous great-great-granddaddy."

As he spoke these words the Animator's goggle-eyes roved along the line of cradle-graves. By this time our moving sidewalk had carried us into at least the eighth or ninth glasshouse.

"I think I can show you a beautiful case right here," said the Animator. "It's a choice specimen, whose autobiological time began only two hours ago. This case is going so fast that it skips over entire periods." He turned to the Bath Attendants. "It's been a long time since we had anything like it as far as cell division and cell shrinkage go, isn't it?"

"Terrific," said Number Two cautiously. "The dry period will soon be over."

"It's not so easy to explain, Seigneur, how cell division and cell shrinkage can be the same thing."

"Oh, I'm used to such paradoxes from the Djebel, Maître Animator. I just think of the great Ursler."

"Here he is. Here he is, our dear good little old fellow," the Animator suddenly whispered, motioned me to keep quiet, and tiptoed to one of the cradle-graves a few steps away. This time he kneeled down eagerly and quickly removed the eiderdown and the fluffy lint that loosely covered and protected the retrovolved case. When he had finished I heard him grunt with exertion and pleasure.

"Only a little while longer and I couldn't have taken our dear good little old fellow out of the humus."

He reached into the tub and expertly removed an apparently newborn babe and laid it cautiously on his left arm in the manner of a midwife, supporting the immoderately large skull with his right hand. Beaming with pride he turned to us, at the same time prattling briskly to the infant in nipple language, "Diddle-diddle-dee. . . . Kitchy-kitchy-koo. . . . My dear good little old fellow. . . . How are we doing now?"

"Isn't he sweet with babies?" I heard Bath Attendant Number One addressing Number Two behind me.

The Animator invited me to examine the retrovolved baby. "Take a look at him, Seigneur. Isn't he a museum piece? And just think, after two brief planetary hours, one-twelfth of a revolution of the globe!"

I bent over the child with the customary vague politeness with which we inspect and praise the offspring of strangers.

"Did you ever see anything sweeter in all your life?" the Animator sighed ecstatically.

I looked at the reddish, shriveled body of the infant and wished he were wearing a nightie. But the thing that fascinated me much more irresistibly than the tiny body was the child's hydrocephalus, the enormously bloated head, and the senile face that went with it. I knew, of course, that most babies have senile features for the first few hours after birth, faces full of wrinkles and creases and crow's-feet and with the flabby mouths of toothless crones. But this was something else. This was not the senile head of an old man who was finally permitted to yield to senility after he had been kept from it for so long by the rigors of civilization. The hundred wrinkles in these features were not fresh wounds but old scars, and they reflected the Desiderium Originis, the burning desire to withdraw into invisibility and unconsciousness. The Animator blew gently on the ancient face, as one fans dying embers. Then the creature suddenly opened its eyes. And by the eyes I immediately recognized Io-Solip, the unfortunate father of Bridegroom Io-Do, who had kindled the new world holocaust up above.

"Is it possible?" I croaked hoarsely. "Are you dear gentle Io-Solip, Compère?"

"I'll say we are—hahaha, I'll say we are," the Animator answered on behalf of his charge. "Of course we're still dear good old Io-Solip, and now we're going to have our last little swig of milk and then we'll bring out the tube and get hooked up to the central circulating system and everything will get cozier and cozier and quieter and quieter and finally the whole world will just be a berceuse—just a berceuse."

The word "berceuse" which the Animator used for lullaby sounded affected and offensive to my ear. I sought to catch the retrovolved man's glance.

Most infants have the eye of timeless old age. For me the aged eye of infancy had always been a proof of the divine depth of the soul and of "spiritual time," which extends from the beginning of the world to its end and perhaps beyond it. In Io-Solip's eyes, however, there lay something quite different from the aged look of infancy. There was the desperate effort to speak of those who are condemned to silence. They were adult, intelligent eyes behind bars, eyes that could no longer make themselves understood. Undoubtedly they wanted to tell me that they had recognized me. And even more terrible than that—the tiny, sobbing wail of an infant escaped from the toothless little mouth of the old, old man. I turned away. My eyes were moist. If I had seen dear old Io-Solip as a decent corpse I would not have wept.

"Well, Seigneur," the Animator beamed triumphantly, "are you finally moved to tears? Don't deny it, there's nothing more sublime."

✹ ✹ ✹ ✹ ✹
✹ ✹ ✹
✹

FROM THIS INSTANT ON MY MIND WAS MADE UP to flee from the Wintergarden and to return to the surface of the earth, notwithstanding the trans-shadow-disintegrators and the psychic artillery. In my heart I extolled good old normal death, whether it came from without or suddenly from within, an early and likely probability for me according to the Animator's diagnosis. At all events, it was better than the Astromental detour by way of the Wintergarden, although I could hardly have summoned up any arguments in favor of normal death in preference to retrovolution, and all progressive advocates of euthanasia would certainly have been against me.

But how to save ourselves? I hadn't the slightest idea what to do. The dull pain in my head grew from one minute to the next. B.H. rode along beside me, or slouched with awkward steps when we had to walk. He never opened his mouth. I realized that in his present condition he was anything but a help to me. The only thing that gave me confidence and faith was the memory of the far more perilous predicament on Apostle Peter from which I had escaped safe and sound after all. I wasn't thinking of any help from Melangeloi, however, which was more likely to be available in the Minor Intermundium than in the cavity of the Wintergarden. The strangest thing about this Wintergarden and its gray twilight landscape here in the earth-womb was the ponderous, solid, enormous reality and the crawling inexorability that held us captive. I was forced to regard the retrogenetic humus and its remarkable effects—comparable to the therapeutic effects of radium, for example—as a development based upon biological researches with which I was unfamiliar. It was far less inexplicable than the travel-puzzle, let's say, or the space-diving suit, or the surmounting of cosmic distances in the course of a class period. My heavy head was well aware that we would save ourselves down here only by means of a good plan and of superhuman exertion. I considered myself incapable of either, not to mention B.H. in his present condition.

The Animator had spoken of people who had resisted him for years and besides he had made the remark that my case wouldn't be too simple. This sounded like a hopeful prospect to me. It was absolutely essential for us to dispel the Animator's suspicions and to gain his unreserved confidence. And so when he had reintombed dear little Io-Solip I wiped my eyes and said, "How can I help but be moved to tears, cher Maître? For you are right, there's nothing more sublime. And now, please disregard our headaches and show us everything, everything."

He immediately had the Bath Attendants hand us some of the elixir that they carried along in a jug. I found that the drink refreshed me each time. In the course of a long and painful period of time, for which there was no standard of measurement down here, we saw many more miracles worked by the retrogenetic humus. (Still they never impressed me as miracles.) In numerous glasshouses of the dermal and endodermal zones I saw embryos of all sizes and of all autobiological stages, male and female, which had been retrovolved from old age to this state. Fortunately what I constantly feared did not recur; I met no more old friends. I saw all kinds of embryos, from the fully evolved, retrovolved, prenatal child with exquisitely modeled hands and feet to the caterpillar-like hooklet with faceless, ram-shaped head enclosed by transparent membrane. The umbilical cord, leading from these tiny retrovolved human animals through the black soil to the central source of nourishment, was finally a hairlike, thin tube. The Animator's monologue flowed on without interruption. I seemed at last to have lulled his suspicions. He had found an enthusiastic ear, the ear of a man from darkest antiquity, who was still quite uninformed but intelligent enough to understand him after having gotten over his silly notions.

"Yes," he said, covering a little human caterpillar, "cell division, luxuriant, exuberant, bubbling cell division, that's the female secret of the world. The man only furnishes the impulse, the idea; and in the ancient world, as Seigneur can no doubt verify, it was the women who worked and not the men."

"In some countries that was the case," I agreed in order not to offend him.

"That's not what I mean," he shook his elongated, deformed skull. "Man's work is blazing and glowing, the residue of which is ashes. Woman's work is thriving, blooming, bearing fruit, and decaying, the residue of which is humus, as the word Homo indicates."

"And when is the female work of cell division interrupted in the Wintergarden?" I asked. "In other words, at what point does retrovolution come to an end?"

"That's a matter, Seigneur, on which I am really required to keep silent, by provision of the Constitution."

"You don't need to worry about a breach of the Constitution with respect to me," I struck while the iron seemed hot. "I'm outside the Constitution, am I not? Don't forget that I'm extra-territorial."

This legal comment appeared to impress him, as he was not only a scientist but also an official. He stared at me with his bulging eyes. Then he came nearer and whispered in my ear, "We advance the end of cell division just a little bit."

"Would you explain that more clearly, Maître Animator?"

He obviously tried to dodge the answer by asking a question. "When, in your opinion, does the embodiment of human personality begin and when does it end?"

And now something unexpected took place. B.H., who had been rolling along on the moving sidewalk next to me, silent and apathetic, straightened himself up with a jerk, clenched his fists, and something inside him creaked like the wheels of a clock. He gathered together all his energy and joined in the conversation in order to show that he was not yet lost.

"Thomas Aquinas teaches," he said, syllable by syllable, "that personality begins when the embryo receives its third soul; first the vegetative, second the animal, then the rational soul."

"Well, well," the Animator commented cheerfully, "our learned friend is feeling better. Attendant, give the gentleman another swallow, even though Saint Thomas is wrong. The first and the last thing that determines human personality is the heart. Unbelievable but true, the heart."

"Does that mean, Animator," I inquired, "that individuality, the ineffable personality, the soul, enters the embryo with the first irregular heartbeats, long before the evolution of the organs and the lowest forms of consciousness?"

"Yes indeed, and in exactly the same way the soul vanishes with the last irregular heartbeats, and not before."

"Ah, now I understand the word blastocyst," I exclaimed in sudden enlightenment, "the word I didn't understand before. Blastocyst is the embryo before it has a heart."

"Today *is* really Sunday for me," the Animator sighed with a smile of contentment.

"And you transplant these blastocysts," I went on triumphantly, "and they turn into daisies, whole fields of daisies——"

"I must ask you to be discreet, Seigneur," the Animator's voice was alarmed, "for this is not known to the general public."

"But I like the idea. It's a wonderful idea. It's a regular poem, a poem by some good primitive poet, Ovid, for instance. The departed members of mankind change into blooming daisies. I like that much better than asphodels. I only hope these daisies don't grow in glasshouses but outdoors."

"You guessed that too," smiled the Animator, "as far as we can speak of 'outdoors' down here."

"And this outdoors, is it still within the confines of the Wintergarden or beyond?" I inquired in an indifferent tone, closing my eyes so that no incautious beam or radiation might betray the purpose of my question. My anxiety was superfluous. Down here in the cavity there was no irongray sod nor any other conductor for thought and mind impulses. Here the ego with all its insidiousness was well insulated.

And so the Animator appeared not to have noticed the motive behind all my questions for he answered frankly, "At present it's still within the walls, Seigneur. But we'll soon have to move outside the gates if it keeps on like this. The congestion is getting terrible. People are all so avid for the final good fortune."

"The Daisy Fields are probably not your only outdoor institution," I fumbled on a little more boldly as though I had some further information. He looked at me askance.

"I suppose somebody tipped you off about the Wet Nurses." He turned toward the two Bath Attendants and demanded peremptorily, "Which one of you tipped off Seigneur about the Mound of the Wet Nurses?"

Before the white-smocks had a chance to utter their earnest asseverations of innocence I anticipated them. "These gentlemen are the very soul of discretion. They didn't even tip us off about the retrogenetic humus; instead of that they gypped us with a so-called mud bath."

"They only did their duty," the Animator declared.

B.H. gathered himself together once more, clenched his fists, and said thickly, with a heavy tongue, "I have heard about the Wet Nurses. . . . Up there . . . up there the mothers threaten their little daughters that they will be sent to the Wintergarden as Wet Nurses if they don't behave themselves."

"Disgusting!" The Animator flew into a passion and his voice cracked. "Everything we hear from up there is disgusting. I'll ask you gentlemen to be the judges. You shall testify that our Wet Nurses are the most beautiful, the most voluptuous, the most shapely women in the world. After all, we're all minstrels and mother's darlings and we're no pederasts and pansies; we're not afraid of genuine, well-developed, female cell dividers."

With these words the Animator accelerated the tempo of the running platform on which we were moving along so suddenly that B.H. and I almost tumbled down, but we only fell into each other's arms.

"Cheer up, B.H.," I hissed at my friend, "everything's going to turn out all right."

"You disturb me," he mumbled, and now he was sleepy again, "your vitality is simply disgusting."

Azaleas, cacti, cradle-graves, glasshouses, white-smocks, great piles of soil, and God knows what else whizzed past us before our trip came to an end. By the twilight, by the gentle drizzle from the lofty cloud ceiling, and by the more bearable temperature we knew that we were outdoors. Before us rose a round, gentle hill, a mound and not much more. Whether this round dome was shaped like a woman's breast is a matter of opinion. Much more important was the magnificent weeping willow, the largest I had ever seen, that grew from the nipple, so to speak, of the pale green hill and veiled a large area with its long silvery hair. The bodies of the young women who reclined on the hillside gleamed almost snow-white in the gloom of the day-night.

The Animator had not lied to us. The women under the tremendous spreading weeping willow on the hill that we were now climbing slowly and with heavy knees, were of great physical beauty, a beauty that is not easy to describe. They were much more rounded and more voluptuous, and apparently also considerably taller than the dainty Astromental girls. But I knew at once and without having to await the Animator's explanation that they had come to the Wintergarden as dainty Astromental girls and that they had developed here to such attractive plumpness and to such statuesque dimensions. On their well-formed faces, however—most of them were wearing turbanlike shawls around their heads—lay an expression of sullen dejection, of slatternly, staring indifference, of apathetic passivity, that was only embarrassingly emphasized by their weak attempts at coquetry at the sight of us men. I had to think of the whorehouses in the native quarters of Arabian cities, although the comparison is misleading for these women appeared well-groomed and attractive to our eyes.

The Animator took me aside. "You know," he lisped, "up there they don't know anything about the miracle of fertility any more. Just take a look at these girls. Every one of them manages to develop an unfertilized ovum in her womb up to the sixth month without any outside assistance. They're really good, these parthenogenetic cell dividers." And he clicked his tongue in admiration and approval.

These words made it clear to me that the forty or fifty naked women who were lounging in the incubator atmosphere of the Uterus Matris Terrae were the outcasts, the pariahs, of Astromental civilization. They had been exiled to the Wintergarden, just as criminals in Russia were formerly exiled to Siberia, to the Katorga. Of course, their crime consisted solely of the fact that biologically they ranked even lower than the "prolific" people, the plebeians who raised two, three, four, and in extreme cases even five offspring. These had probably been unbridled not only in their fertility but also in their inclinations. Civilization ("alienation from God by time," according to the Grand Bishop) rid itself of them as of a disgrace that was never mentioned and, if possible, never thought about. Out of the tragic fate of these girls grew the magnificent weeping willow with its drooping silver foliage.

Life in the cavity changed all those who served the Wintergarden and its ends. The heat, the pressure, the chemical composition of the air, the water, and other unknown causes had made these ostracized women what they were, simply Wet Nurses. They lolled and lounged about, given over wholly to lazy, prolific, rank growth. And yet, although the hill of the weeping willow certainly represented the extreme contrast to the Rosegarden of the Virgin, this aspect of femininity too filled me for an instant with reverent awe—reverent awe that bordered on loathing.

Some of the women were sleeping with half-open mouths. Others were crocheting or knitting huge, ridiculous, rapidly growing things of colored wool. It looked as if the internal business of cell division had been transferred outside and as if this feminine needlework were nothing but the production of parthenogenetic fabrics of wool or silk.

"Well, what's the matter, gentlemen, don't be scared of them," I heard the Animator animate us.

Awkward as a schoolboy I stepped up to one of the most voluptuous of them, made a bow, and asked in the most absurd manner, "May I inquire how you are feeling today, fairest lady?"

The girl looked at me with perfectly vacant eyes, mechanically puckered her lips to a kissable circlet, and smiled idiotically. Whether she heard me or not I can't say. But I knew at once that she didn't understand a single word.

"You mustn't speak with them, Seigneur. What do you think this is?" The Animator was having a good time at my expense.

"Our sweet ladies aren't kept here for purposes of conversation. Makes things a lot simpler, doesn't it?"

His voice dropped to a pimpish tone. "Why don't you pet her a little? Go on, she likes it. Doesn't she have magnificent breasts and cheeks?"

I stood motionless and rigid. Behind me the Animator clapped his hands. The girl stretched out her arms toward me. Apparently she wanted me to help her up. I did so. She pulled herself up by my hands with surprising ease, for she was really very large and heavy. As soon as she stood on her feet she began to pirouette before me with little dance steps like a mannequin, no, like an automaton with rosy, radiant flesh. Her breathing was strangely labored. I must confess that the figure of the girl, as she pressed nearer and nearer, exercised a growing attraction upon me which was painfully intensified by my keen sense of pity for her. The presence of the Animator, however, made me cold and unresponsive. After a while I turned my face away with an angry jerk.

Several of the women around the gnarled trunk of the weeping willow at the top of the hill were holding infants to their breasts and feeding them. In the manner of young mothers they squeezed their nipples between their index and middle fingers in order to make things easier for the babies. These babies, however, were not real infants but retrovolved adults. They were shriveled old creatures like poor little Io-Solip a while ago. In a word, they were dead. And the Wet Nurses of the Wintergarden were feeding the dead with their milk. They were undoubtedly given the difficult cases, the troublesome ones that threatened to wither away before they had reached the embryonic stage. The sweet milk of the Wet Nurses was intended to put them back in shape.

I closed my eyes in order to shut out this scene, this vision. Behind me I heard the Animator's voice. "This pleasure is always at your disposal, gentlemen. The Wintergarden is a realm of delight."

"I should like to see the Daisy Fields," I said.

"Just a few more steps," he answered.

As we turned to go down the slope I was the last one. I looked around once more at the Mound of the Wet Nurses. Then I saw one of the young women running toward me. It was the same one that had performed a little dance for me a moment ago. In each of her hands she offered me a gift. One was a big globe of crimson yarn, the other a ridiculous piece of needlework in a poisonous tropical green. I concealed both presents under my dress coat. Tears streamed over the girl's blank face.

The Twenty-Third Chapter

WHEREIN THE EPISODE OF THE PREVIOUS
CHAPTER CONTINUES IN THE DAISY FIELDS
AND I STRAY INTO FORBIDDEN BYWAYS
THAT LEAD ME TO THE TURNIP MANIKINS,
TO THE CATABOLITES, AND FINALLY TO
THE MNEMODROME, THE LAKE OF DISRE-
MEMBRANCE.

PERHAPS MY SALVATION down here in the Wintergarden lay in the fact that the twenty-six odd trillion cells of my reconstructed body belonged to some other eon than the Eleventh Cosmic Capital Year of Virgo. I don't know whether the word "allergic" is appropriate in this connection, but since everybody else uses it, I'll risk it too. I proved allergic to retrogenesis, to retrovolution. While B.H., Astromental citizen that he was, had not been able to resist and hadn't even wanted to, all the twenty-six trillion cells constituting me, a visitor from the primeval world, revolted against a process that was alien and odious to my nature. I am quite convinced that my body was not retrovolutable at all. The most concentrated retrogenetic humus would have been powerless against it. I was confronted by a single alternative: either I would succeed in escaping or I would live a miserable life as an Enumerator on the highways of the nether world or at best as a Bath Attendant. I knew it. The Animator didn't know it yet, although he was aware that he wouldn't have "an easy time" with me. I wasn't having an easy

time with myself down here in this timeless duration, this wormlike, peristaltic sequentiality, where the only clock was the body
clock. My doubtful body, which had taken Comet Calisthenics
in its stride, suffered from the incubator heat, from the lack of
oxygen in the air, and from the fantastic barometric pressure.
Only my primordial energy and my phrenetic antipathy against
retrovolution saved me from lapsing into the same state as
poor old B.H. One other thought encouraged me now and then:
I was privileged to experience a Tartarophania, a sightseeing tour
of the Underworld, such as even the authors of the "Odyssey"
and the "Aeneid" had not described. Their Plutonian visions reflected only the current concepts of their eras. I, however, was
visiting a nether world without model and without parallel, a
manmade Tartarus, which the cleverest thinkers and the boldest
dreamers of my own day could not have foretold. While I had no
clear notion in the course of my visit that I would ever be
permitted to give an account of my journey, still the mere wish
to relate what I had seen served as a powerful incentive to my
will to live. It was quite true that mankind had come very close
to the fulfillment of its eternal dream of "victory over death"
down here—despite my violent resistance I have to admit it.
The act of dying had certainly been conquered, and in a manner
that was by no means fantastically absurd to the twentieth-
century mind, since it was along strictly naturalistic lines. A
return ticket to organic evolution was certainly not in the realm
of miracles but in the realm of advanced natural science.

Meanwhile my battle with the Animator went on without
interruption. I could see that the white-smocked Pluto was
simply itching to go to work on a "recalcitrant." That would
be an agreeable diversion in his profession. But he was so
anxious that he miscalculated and made mistakes. He failed to
take into account, for example, my tough physique which dated
from the nineteenth century and not from the refined and debilitated Astromental present. He hoped to wear me down and
exhaust me by making me walk long distances. Old hiker that
I was, however, I was used to much longer walks, and besides

the conditions down here were far more bearable in motion than at rest. Our hotel room would have been much more dangerous in my present state than the endless Daisy Fields that we had now reached. Furthermore, the Animator hoped to make me drunk or relaxed by constantly plying me with the cognaclike elixir and the Bath Attendants kept serving it to me. But for some reason it had the opposite effect. My body probably still carried around some organic memories of gin and rum and whisky, and under the abnormal conditions in this subterranean cave the elixir merely served to exhilarate it, while genuine Astromental physiques would likely have succumbed.

Although my situation was almost hopeless, I was filled with a confidence that is hard to justify. Perhaps my illogical sense of security stemmed from my secret conviction that not only the Bath Attendants but all the Stygian functionaries were—as I described them once before—colossi on clay feet and nothing more. No matter how they towered over me, no matter how they stamped along like bull-necked truck drivers and piano movers, my instinct recognized that their muscular strength was not commensurate with their powerful appearance. While I had never been a boxer or a wrestler, I felt that I was a match for them. Life down here in the earth's cavity had, after all, reduced them to mere shadow creatures.

The clouds in the infinitely high ceiling had become darker, and the low fog and drizzle had changed into a definite light rain. The expanse of the Daisy Fields stretched out as far as my eye reached. The daisies were tall, straight, mostly white but occasionally yellow, flowers as large as the palm of my hand, and there were millions and countless millions of them. They sprang from the male and female blastocysts that had been removed from their amniotic cavities at the proper moment of retrovolution and had been transplanted here. When the spectator reminded himself that the flowers in these endless fields were the dead, generations upon generations of dead humans who had undergone this final and cleanest metamorphosis, it was a moving and solemn scene; and yet the strange desolation and monotony of all Astromental phenomena predominated here too. But even I, as a recalcitrant, had to acknowledge that it was more beautiful and more dignified to become a daisy in the Daisy Fields than to be shoved into a shallow hole under the earth's surface to rot.

"But why daisies?" I asked the Animator.

"Aren't they a lovely, modest species to house the last worthless remnants of men?" he countered. And he added with a giggle, "We call them oracle flowers because we ask them whether our sweethearts over on the Mound of the Wet Nurses are true to us—you know, she loves me, she loves me not. The mound of the Wet Nurses is always at your disposal, Seigneur."

"That's not the reason," I said brusquely.

"You're right, it isn't, Seigneur. We've come down in the world recently. We used to plant and raise genuine sunflowers, big as cartwheels, almost regular individuals. We humans are sun children, that's why we get chilly so frequently. The daisies are the result of a compromise. We can't expect our staff of gardeners and supervisors to do too much walking, and genuine sunflowers take up more than twice as much room."

We were walking along a fairly wide lane between the fields. I was supporting B.H., who barely dragged himself ahead. The Animator turned to face us, and it seemed to me there was a faint note of derision in his words.

"How do you feel, gentlemen?"

"Wonderful, splendid," I shouted loudly. "We won't fall down and stain your daisies red with our blood."

"You have seen something, Seigneur, that few people have seen since time immemorial," the white-smock declared with a slight bow.

"And we'll be eternally grateful to our Animator for it."

This mendacious sentence burst from me almost like a cheer. At that instant B.H. pulled himself together. His chest creaked like a slot machine and his voice imitated mine.

"Eternally grateful . . . eternally grateful. . . ."

"Fine, and now, gentlemen, I'm sure you want to go back home and have a little shut-eye, don't you?"

"Not a bit of it," I yodeled energetically. "We're just beginning to have a good time. We're Olympic champions when it comes to staying awake, both of us."

I began to move ahead at a brisk pace, for in the dim distance I had noticed a high wall, undoubtedly the outer wall, and that was where I wanted to be. What happened now was a surprise even to me. Neither the Animator nor Bath Attendants One and Two could keep up with me, although I had to drag B.H. along. They panted, grumbled, and finally began to lag behind. My superior stamina filled me with triumphant joy. It proved that I was in a position to wear out the strength of my guardians and pursuers without losing mine. At the spot where a narrow path leading to the wall branched off from the road I stopped in complete composure to wait for the others. I chuckled to myself in deep satisfaction at the sight of the Animator and the two colossi staggering and reeling along, pale and breathless.

"That's not advisable, Seigneur, not advisable at all," the little fellow panted, "you with your heart."

"You forget, cher Maître," I laughed, "that I'm a wild barbarian who doesn't care a bit if his heart suddenly stops beating. I don't feel sorry for myself at all and I'm not as afraid of death as your honorable Astromental contemporaries."

"A civilized person shouldn't even soil his mouth with that dirty and indecent word beginning with a 'D'. The heart is to stop beating when it has gotten back to the point where it is three times seven days old. How about a little more heart medicine, Seigneur?"

"Let's have it! And make it a decent drink this time."

The Animator's eyes popped as he watched me take a boastful drink right out of the jug.

"Forgive me for using the dirty word once more, dear Maître,"

I said, handing back the jug and striding along briskly again. "What would happen to me if I fell down dead?"

"Nothing good would happen to you at all," he moaned. "We would have to take you to the Catabolites."

"Well, for heaven's sake, something new again. What on earth are Catabolites?"

"Just thank your lucky stars, Seigneur, that you'll never find out what Catabolites are."

"But I have the firm desire, the inflexible intention, to find out just that."

"Sorry, Seigneur, the Constitution forbids it."

"In the Djebel they concealed nothing from me, not even the most exalted riddles of the universe and the most important moment of my life," I said. But I had touched a sore spot in the Animator's heart.

"Pretty soft for the fellows in the Djebel," he flew into a rage. "A lot of highbrows. They don't even do research; they merely acquire 'aimless learning.' Chronosophy is the smuggest kind of self-complacency. They coast around in cosmic space for the sole purpose of marveling at their own silly marveling and of feeling foreign enough to turn your stomach. And have they really solved any riddles of the universe worth mentioning? The universe is wedded to itself. Even the Bible tells us that Eve was inside Adam in the shape of his rib. We down here in the earth's womb aren't half so pretentious. We have only the best designs. We serve mankind. We don't do aimless research, but research for practical, useful purposes. We practice applied science. It's our business to be practical, practical, practical."

"Still I insist on the Catabolites," I declared dryly.

"The prohibition applies to you too, Seigneur. I can't do anything about it."

We had passed through one of the Daisy Fields. The dead had a strange mucilaginous smell, faintly reminiscent of camomile. Now we turned into the wide road that ran along the outer wall. It was a perfectly smooth, fairly high wall, constructed of a sort of translucent plastic, such as we had known back in my days. I believe that not even Io-Runt, the star dancer, could have developed the necessary agility to scale this wall. Meanwhile the Animator had switched his tactics in order to keep me from setting too fast a pace and putting a strain on his and his men's endurance. The Bath Attendants now marched leisurely at the head of our little party, blocking the road with their flabby, chunky behinds. Next in the procession came he himself, our sightseeing guide, sauntering with relaxed knees. B.H. and I brought up the rear.

This new formation, however, proved to be to my advantage. I slowed down and shortened my steps, so that the interval between the Animator and myself became greater and greater. For to my great joy I had discovered a sort of drainage canal that ran through a grating in the outer wall. I was grateful to my astigmatic eyes for never leaving me in the lurch in a real crisis. In any case it was essential to mark this spot. What I did was nothing more than a plagiarism on ancient myths and fairy tales: I quickly kneeled down at the edge of the field and tied the end of the red yarn that the girl on the Mound of the Wet Nurses had given me to a big clump of blooming daisies. This was the work of a few seconds. Then I rose, concealed the ball of yarn again, and reeled off the red thread as we strolled slowly along. The Animator hadn't noticed a thing. I pretended to be extremely busy with my friend B.H., who incidentally was very much in need of help and encouragement. He could scarcely walk and kept begging, "Let me lie down. . . . It's very pleasant here. . . ."

"I won't let you lie down," I said, punching him in the ribs, "and it's very, very unpleasant here."

"D'you really find it unpleasant?" he babbled. "I don't b'lieve you. . . . Just your stubbornness. . . ."

"You find it unpleasant too, B.H., very unpleasant," I whispered suggestively. "You want to die decently too, instead of being retrovolved. And that isn't stubbornness at all! If I only had some benzedrine or caffeine with me I'd fix you up in a hurry. As it is, you'll have to believe me and trust me."

"By this time all the rest of them are tiny tots," B.H. stammered, tears in his eyes, "my friends Io-Fagòr and Io-Rasa, and the Ancestress and the good old bachelors of our household, and I'm the only one who still has to be an adult."

"And you'll remain an adult, B.H., I give you my word. Come on! Pull yourself together!"

"But I want to be a little baby like the others. It's so won'er—won'erful to be a li'l baby. You don't un'erstand our civilization, F.W., you're still too mobile."

"Thank God that I'm mobile, B.H."

"Are you gentlemen having an argument?" said the Animator, turning one-eighth of his profile toward us. "One of you wants to rest, I suppose. Golden rest, sweet rest, carefree rest, pleasure of pleasures, rest without idleness. It's too bad we still have to keep moving, step by step, freezing in the rain and cold, until we reach shelter."

The Animator's teeth-chattering, hypocritical singsong gave him away. He knew we were getting close to our destination and now he was trying to prolong the distance in order to break the remnants of B.H.'s strength and wear down my resistance. Pleased with my own cunning, I pretended to be utterly exhausted, although I felt stronger and more determined at this moment than ever.

"Keep going, Maître, keep goin' right along," I begged, eliding my consonants as though I had three sheets in the wind, "we're comin', right with you. . . . Le's take it easy. . . . We've got secrets, my frien' and I. . . . Li'l discretion, if you please. . . ."

"Discretion to whom discretion is due," the Animator smiled, lapsing into his twisted phraseology. "Far be it from me to disturb you or to hurry you." And he turned to move on.

Now I grabbed B.H. by the wrists and shook him with all my might. It worked. He began to waken from his stupor.

"Don't you see that I'm battling?" I whispered. "Why don't you help me? Don't make it harder for me, at least!"

The distance between our guards and us had increased. They had just passed a signboard that marked a narrow little side-path leading from the main road back into the fields. At this point the daisies happened to be particularly tall. The Animator seemed to be very sure of us, for he observed strict discretion and never turned around. I talked to B.H. in a louder and louder tone and finally I even sang to him: "Tramp, tramp, tramp, the boys are marching. . . ."

The inscription on the signboard read: "Warning! No one except the Animator on duty is permitted to enter this path!" I don't know what prompted me to the rash decision to double back on our tracks at this point and to give our sauntering guards the slip. In part it was undoubtedly the hope that we might find a hiding place among the extraordinarily tall flowers which reached up to our chests and sometimes even to our chins. Moreover, since only the Animator was permitted to enter this forbidden path, we would get rid of the Bath Attendants. But more than by these logical reasons I was lured by the strong temptation to walk on a forbidden path in the Winter-garden and at its end perhaps to gaze on the most forbidden of all forbidden sights. I motioned to B.H. to keep very still. Then I seized his hand, pulled lustily, and we both began to run. The red thread reeling out from under my coat followed us for a long distance. When only a tiny nub of the ball of yarn was left I tossed it into the daisies. We couldn't see our pursuers any more than they could see us. But instead of stopping and finding a hiding place among the daisies at the side of the path we ran on and on like mad. After a while the path sloped downward. And then it seemed to me that I could hear a con-fused babble of voices like people quarreling. It could have been a moderately spectacular barroom battle at a great distance, or the noise of a bazaar in an Oriental city. But that was true only of the first instant, for almost immediately distinct human voices became audible. There was something wrong about these human voices, however. Although they undoubtedly issued from hoarse adult male throats, yet they screeched in the highest soprano pitch. They were—how shall I express it?—they were dwarflike voices.

* * * *

* * *

*

FINALLY WE PASSED A PLACE WHERE THE DAISIES were withered. Although these last remnants of the dead were completely meaningless it was an unspeakably sad sight. Then we stood—and again I am at a loss to say what we faced as we stood there. It was a kind of a plowed turnip patch that extended far and wide before our eyes, very far and very wide. And out of this plowed field, along with a creeping mist from the furrows, arose this querulous babble of human voices.

Most of my former contemporaries—to whom I was fortunately permitted to return from my precarious situation in the Winter-garden—are familiar with the comic caricature film of Donald, the valiant duck, and they are familiar with his indignant gabbling, in which animal and human sounds are grotesquely mixed. Now, imagine this croaking, quacking, screeching, in-dignant gabbling diminished, reduced in individual volume, but at the same time multiplied into a chorus of five thousand Donalds, and you will have a vague notion of what we heard long before we saw anything.

This soft but sharp, feeble but shrilly screeching eruption of human rage rising from the extensive turnip field made me forget everything else. I no longer thought of my own peril, at least not until I had investigated this phenomenon, and that took a full two minutes. To tell the truth, I had to kneel down in order to discover that I was actually standing at the edge of a kind of a turnip field, although the analogy is imperfect. The concept of a turnip field presented itself because the objects that I was looking at were planted like turnips in regularly spaced rows, each in its neatly cultivated mound of retrogenetic humus. Out of these mounds grew long, nondescript foliage, from the center of which the turnips protruded. They were very large turnips that not only grew under the ground in the approved manner but also projected a considerable distance above the ground in the shade of the green leaves. I had to look very closely for a very long time to convince myself that these enraged, gabbling turnips were tiny aged men who were trying wildly to tear themselves loose from the grip of the soil. They were each about eight to ten inches in length. They waved their arms madly and twisted their torsos in a St. Vitus's dance of agonized exertion. The upper parts of their bodies were well developed and strong, the lower part apparently less perfect. The little faces, on the other hand, were fully modeled like those of Tanagra figurines, unspeakably aged and furrowed with wrinkles and creases. One and another of them had green stalks growing out of their bald pates. All of them had sparse, tousled, white chin whiskers. Their tiny eyes glittered with baleful hatred and their black, horrible, wide-open mouths squawked and gabbled the foulest obscenities that I had ever heard in a single place in a brief time.

"What's that, what's that?" B.H. groaned.

"Possibly our future," I replied.

"No, no," he screamed, "I want to be a baby, but not that."

"Can you prevent it, B.H.? That's the risk you run in retro-volution and there's no insurance against it. Those are the unsuccessful cases, and we don't need the Animator to tell us that. Of course, whether these are the Catabolites, I can't say."

"And all this filth and smut."

"The only way I can explain it," I surmised, "is that the smut that has accumulated in one hundred and eighty years of Astro-mental culture has to come out finally. That's the obverse of the fine manners and elegant behavior."

"Oh, F.W., I don't want to, I don't want to! Why am I so weak?"

I put my arms around my friend. It was like a brotherly vow to do my utmost to save him.

At this moment the angry gabbling of the turnip-men merged into a single cry evoked by our presence. Out of this chorus, however, I distinguished one word more and more clearly from just under my feet. This word was "Seigneur." I quickly stooped down to one of the plants, and the creature I drew out of the ground was none other than the Spokesman of the Io-Fagòr household, the Voltaire-like master of Astromental causerie, who had had the bad luck to become a turnip-man after a few hours of retrovolution instead of an embryo. I held the turnip-man by his waist, sick with disgust. It was anything but a turnip. It was naked, feverish human flesh, small as it was. The big black hole that was a mouth slobbered. Spittle and tears ran down into the tousled beard and dripped on my hand. I recall the following words, screamed out of the hoarse throat: "Yes, it's I, Seigneur, take a look at me, take a smell of me. I've been cheated, I've been cheated all my life. And the idea of the Wintergarden was always the subject of my most beautiful causeries. I want to shout words at you that I never even knew as a philologist—night shit, pus boil, bloody mucus. You're no seigneur, you're a God-stinking edema, a cancer, a tumor. . . . Put me back, back. . . ."

"Give him to me," said the Animator who had arrived unnoticed, took the turnip-man out of my hand, and planted him back in his place, where the Spokesman joined in the terrible gabbling chorus of the thousand other unsuccessful cases. After the custodian had carefully rebuilt the mound of soil around the shrunken causeur, he rose and looked at me.

"You didn't harm me," he said, "but only yourself."

"In what way did I harm myself?" I asked defiantly.

"The more you entangle yourself, the greater your risk. Whoever looks upon the forbidden becomes forbidden himself. I dry my hands in innocence."

"Are those the Catabolites, Animator?"

"No, but since you've gone this far in your irresponsibility, you'll get to see the Catabolites too."

"Why do you let these travesties on the image of God suffer so pitifully?" I screamed, stamping my foot.

"Because a few among them still have a chance," he lisped sharply. "We'll soon see. Then they'll get their slumber bath."

"How is it possible," I raged, "how can the Constitution permit anyone to enter upon the famous voluntary road without informing the volunteers of the horrible possibilities that confront them? The world is wrapped in darkness. And you intensify the darkness. Now I understand Io-Joel's hatred."

"The risks have nothing to do with the Constitution," the Animator replied. "They lie in the individual. We're not at fault. The individual is at fault."

"How can you blame the poor individuals?" I yelled, beside myself. "All they've done is walk into your trap."

"Didn't you read the inscription in your room, Seigneur, the words of a great sage: 'What you are is the reward and punishment for what you are'?"

"I protest! Unsuccessful retrovolution can only be attributed to the carelessness of the functionaries. Otherwise why should one individual turn into an honest daisy and another into a devilish turnip? After all, most individuals are only types."

I knew I was being dishonest when I spoke the final sentence and, of course, I gave the Animator an opportunity to parade his moral indignation, as he had done repeatedly before.

"You're no pious man, Seigneur. You're a nihilist. I, however, serve the immortal soul in my work that knows neither day nor night. Individuals are not types. Individuals are unique and unrepeatable creatures. They are unipersonal, sir. The Wintergarden furnishes irrefutable proof of this fact, for among the tens of thousands of cases that I retrovolved there was not a single repetition. And even these unfortunates here have a chance to eject the evil from their consciousness before they enter the realm of silence."

I was so profoundly moved by the Animator's words that I

closed my eyes and bowed my head in deep spiritual grief. He had called me a nihilist. All my life, as far back as I could think, I had waged war against the nihilism that I carried within me as a child of the nineteenth century. Hadn't I conquered it long ago? Or was my soul still full of error? The devil himself had to appear to prove to me that I was a heretic. My faith in the indestructibility of being was not perfect. I had confounded type and individual. I would certainly share the Spokesman's fate and become a turnip-man. Oh, God, help me and keep me from blaspheming any more. I clung tightly to the hand of my poor friend while the querulous gabbling died away in the distance and we felt the moving sidewalk under our feet again, a rumbling, jolting sidewalk this time, that was undoubtedly intended only for the hired help.

      ❖   ❖   ❖   ❖

        ❖   ❖

           ❖

MY HEART AND MY HAND GET HEAVIER and heavier as I turn to the description of the things we saw in the endless drainage canal along whose high embankment we were now rolling. I curse my fate that transplanted me into the Eleventh Cosmic Capital Year of Virgo, that permitted me to cast a glance into the Minor Intermundium, that led me into the Wintergarden where men deluded themselves in the belief that they had conquered the misery of dying, and that still did not permit me to bring home a lovely wreath wound of pure beauty and radiant hope. Isn't mankind of my century, the twentieth, in greater need of beauty and hope than of the sad truth that all things earthly end in catastrophe and must be rebuilt again and again? They probably picked the wrong reporter when they sent me. No matter how much this thought torments me, there's nothing to be done about it; I am I and no one else, and I have to report what my eyes saw, my ears heard, and my spirit grasped.

I shall not claim that the sight of the Catabolites was worse or even half as bad as the sights that many of my contemporaries attested in the horror camps of Buchenwald or Maidanek. This comparison—utterly wrong, of course—refers only to external similarities, for the Catabolites were by no means victims of torture and murder but, like the turnip-men, merely cases of unsuccessful retrovolution that had fallen by the wayside. I can't even say what the percentage of miscarried cases was, and whether it was great enough to constitute a valid objection to the idea of the Wintergarden. It certainly had no bearing on the subjective side of the idea, the transformation of the process of dying into a joyous experience.

"The risks lie in the individual." The meaning of these words of the Animator was suddenly horribly clear to me. The smooth progress of retrovolution was not dependent upon external circumstances, not upon the retrogenetic humus nor the meticulous care of the Bath Attendants, but upon the candidate himself who lay down voluntarily in the cradle-grave. Astromental mankind had not only supplanted sudden and uncontrolled death by a controlled process, it had also abolished the diseases that formerly led to death. The fatal illnesses, however, that all of us people of the twentieth century knew, that is, know, and experience in our own bodies, are in many instances not undeserved, particularly in individuals who attain a ripe old age. They are the cumulative result of all our sensual sins against our own nature. This body of ours bears the injuries we inflict on it more or less patiently until one day it breaks down. Of course the relation of cause and effect, of sin and disease, was no longer as obvious as it had been in the beginnings of mankind. Astromental people did not gluttonize, they were no drunkards, they used no drugs, their sexual life had been sublimated, and yet even in their world the "unvarying measure of evil" had not disappeared. Their lewdness was only more hidden, their perversions only more concealed. They poisoned their minds with more exquisitively lascivious fantasies and their bodies with more heinous stimulants. They did not fall ill as a result of self-abuse, or rather, they did not wait to fall ill. The effects, however, became apparent in the Wintergarden. They manifested themselves in stoppages in the retrogenetic process. They manifested themselves in the raving, gabbling turnip-men in the plowed field. They manifested themselves in the Catabolites in the drainage canal. Sinful man had to pay with his body even here, where the cleanliest and most complete dissolution of the physical being had been devised.

If the Catabolites had only been refuse, only the corpses of the unfortunates who had suffocated in the early stages of retrogenesis or had succumbed to cerebral or cardiac hemorrhages, I would simply have covered my nose with my handkerchief—which I did anyhow—and turned my back. But the Animator forced me now to gaze on this most forbidden and forbidding spectacle.

* * * * *
* *
*

AND SO I TOO AM NOW FORCED TO LET THE READER gaze on this most forbidden and forbidding spectacle.

The canal along whose levee we moved was neither very deep nor very wide. It resembled one of the small, perfectly straight canals that traverse the length and breadth of the lower sections of Holland. It differed from such canals in the fact that it was not filled with sluggish but none the less flowing water. At the same time it could not be said that the ditch was completely dry. Its marshy bottom was full of pools and puddles which were not produced solely by the eternal drizzle from the lofty cloud ceiling. The Animator didn't need to tell me that the canal was flooded from time to time by opening the locks of certain reservoirs, in order to flush away the Catabolites. In the murky gloom we could even see the place where the ditch ended and where the canal water deposited its repulsive cargo. It was a large lake, extending to the horizon—if the word horizon can be appropriately applied here. Incidentally, the leaden, Stygian character of this lake was not entirely new to me. In my old home on the borders of Slovakia, Hungary, and Austria there were several extensive, shallow lakes that looked a great deal like this one in the bowels of the earth. Only the sinister impression of these lakes in the steppes of eastern Europe was alleviated by a wealth of birds and amphibians. Flamingos and silver herons and Egyptian ibis nested in the reeds, the bitterns boomed and bellowed all day long, and malachite giant frogs took up the chorus at night under the full moon. Here, on the other hand, unbroken silence reigned in the misty, steaming drizzle, although it would be incorrect to speak of complete lifelessness. The most gruesome things down there in that ditch were not the few adult bodies that had not survived even the first stages of retrovolution, nor the more numerous remains of adolescents, nor even the many, many corpses of children and infants with distorted, aged faces. It was not abnormal for a mysterious and tremendous process like that of retrovolution to be interrupted by the sudden death of the unfit. The Animator, who had become extremely laconic—for we couldn't pull any more wool over each other's eyes—then uttered a truth:

"The bolder a human institution, the grimmer the resistance it meets."

The perils to which certain individuals were exposed in the retrogenetic humus were plain to our sight. Among the ordinary people down there who had died an ordinary death during retrogenesis, living creatures were wriggling and squirming. I saw little, reddish human pigs with rooting snouts and hands and feet grown together into cloven hoofs, wallowing listlessly and almost lifelessly in the puddles. In the same puddles I saw human fish, cylindrical trunks, fifteen to eighteen inches long, with glistening scales, and limbs that were almost fins, while their infant heads stared into the gloom with mother-of-pearl goggle-eyes and gasped for air with round salmon mouths. I saw human toads—and this species appeared to be the most numerous—humanized salamanders, or rather, salamanderized homunculi, long-tailed creatures with the heads of human embryos, that slithered over the corpses, tried to climb the walls of the ditch, but always fell back again in mortal weakness. In order to understand these horrid phenomena—I limit myself to three of them—I didn't even require the Animator's explanations. Just as all of nature carries man within it, so man carries all of nature within him. (I had learned that in the important moment when I looked through the gate of the Vyschehrad Home for Incurables and saw the goat-man with hornlike excrescences on his forehead, on all fours, with raised hind-end.) The twenty-six trillion cells that constitute our body are the building blocks for all existing possibilities. They obey the laws of form that are in control at the crucial moment.

I squeezed B.H.'s hand as I spoke but avoided looking at the Animator. "It's perfectly clear to me," I began, "that in the course of retrogenesis one individual or another fails to pass the pig stage or the fish stage and gets stuck there. I also understand that at the same instant the process of cell division gets on the wrong track, and instead of shrinkage new growth in the wrong direction sets in. But I don't understand that the management of the Wintergarden is not in a position to diagnose such cases in time and to prevent such accidents."

"We look at the hearts but not into the hearts," the Animator said briefly.

He insisted on his claim: retrogenesis was not to blame, nor the lofty idea of the Wintergarden by which man had learned to control death. The blame for all these abnormalities rested on the egos that contained them. Among hundreds of thousands of candidates so and so many could never turn into lovely, peaceful daisies.

Ordinary people, average people, were the best bets to become daisies. But everyone who carried an excess of anything within him, whether of vegetative impulses or spiritual disharmonies, ran the risk of turning into a Catabolite before his heart ceased beating. And the human piglets and human fish were not by far the worst possibilities. Personally I was most terribly shocked by the things that I should like to call the independent limbs. Here, for example, I saw a tiny, breathing body that belonged to what we would call a premature, seven-month baby, one of whose arms had not retrovolved. An arm, grew out of one of the shoulder joints, grew in ghastly crescendo, first small and thin, getting larger and larger, stronger and stronger, until it culminated in a powerful man's forearm and a big, heavy, hairy hand. This hand opened and closed and opened again, groped about, sought a hold, dragging along the little body to which it was attached, rested, groped some more, moving slowly from place to place. I had to think of the fairy tale of the man who had struck his mother and whose hand grew out of the grave. What was true of the hand was also true of other extremities of the human body. The whimsical poem about "The knee that wandered lonely through the world" had become reality here, further evidence that the most abstruse notions of the poet's brain are always somehow based on actuality. The most repulsive things of all, however, that I could scarcely bear to look at and that I hesitate to divulge, were hypertrophic male genitals that moved in feeble erections while the infant bodies to which they belonged seemed to be already dead.

"Where," I exclaimed indignantly, "does the Wintergarden get the right to inflict Dantesque, hellish punishments on people who have trustingly submitted to its ministrations?"

"That's a layman's question," the Animator behind us retorted, and he no longer lisped nor indulged in any of his earlier mannerisms but continued in a lower tone. "And for that reason laymen are not permitted to see the Catabolites, because they neither understand nor evaluate correctly what they see. They only hurt themselves. There are no hellish punishments in the Wintergarden. Quite the contrary. By virtue of the debased or one-sided forms which the retrovolved body is forced to assume when psychic defects of the personality hinder the smooth, normal process, the soul is freed of these defects while it is still alive. It is better for the soul to have this disease inflict itself on the body than to take it along into the beyond——"

"We'll not speak of the beyond," I interrupted him brusquely. "The horrid things I am looking at are suffering here."

"Again the layman's wrong thinking. Who's suffering? The salamanders aren't suffering, nor are the pigs and salmons and toads. The hypertrophic limbs don't suffer either, for they have no consciousness whatever, only a certain kinesthetic instinct. Not even the turnip-men, some of whom can still be saved, are really suffering. They are definitely exhibitionists and their copro-lalia gives them pleasure. Besides, it's all over very soon, the water washes down the canal and carries the Catabolites into the Mnemodrome——"

"Mnemodrome? Is this lake here called 'Mnemodrome'?"

"It is, although it's really a lake of Oblivion."

"A sort of Lethe? Did you hear that, B.H.?"

"We call it 'Mnemodrome.' Very few visitors have a chance to see it. Usually only real sufferers."

"Real sufferers? As for example?"

"As for example you, Seigneur, and I."

"Does the Mnemodrome consist of an acid in which organic bodies are dissolved?"

"Far from it. The Mnemodrome consists of Light Water."

"Something new again. What on earth is Light Water?"

"It's the famous water that isn't wet. Haven't you ever heard the chemical term 'heavy water'?"

"Wait a moment. It seems to me I picked up a popular magazine in a dentist's waiting room once upon a time and read an article about heavy water. But it might have been about liquid air."

"Well, Light Water is the exact opposite of that——"

"Is it perhaps baptismal water of Astromental men that causes them to forget? That's nothing new. I keep stumbling on mythological realities."

"That's wrong. Light Water doesn't destroy anything. It is an extractive element. It extracts the swarms of images, the hordes of ghosts from our consciousness. It makes us empty and pure and ready."

"What does that mean? Empty and pure and ready? I fervently distrust such words."

For a moment the Animator relapsed into his lyric tone. "Oh, Seigneur, Light Water gives you the climax of all joys!"

The embankment on which we were rolling had left the side of the Catabolite canal. It had become narrower and the moving sidewalk had become even bumpier and seemed in a bad state of repair. At our right and left grew giant thistles and tall brush covered with alkali dust, reminding me of the shores of the Dead Sea or of the Great Salt Lake. I noticed a number of shovels sticking in the sand, evidence that excavating was necessary here at times. We were all three silent. (The Animator had left the Bath Attendants behind somewhere before rejoining us at the field of the turnip-men.) B.H.'s head was hanging low. Perhaps he couldn't speak any more. I held him tightly. Incalculable danger lay ahead of us. My crystal-clear consciousness of it lent unexpected strength not only to my mind but also to my overwrought body. I considered: should I jump from the running sidewalk and drag my friend with me? It wouldn't have been of any use. After a short sprint the Animator would have recaptured us. Meanwhile the embankment had given way to a rickety wooden pier. This pier extended far out into the lake. The sidewalk stopped moving. I could see the water between the rotten planks of the pier. Mist was rising from it. B.H. and I walked on slowly. The pier had no railing. I had made my plan. Ten more slow, well-counted steps, then I would turn suddenly, hurl my full weight on the little man behind me, and shove him into the waters of the Mnemodrome. Very embarrassing. The last time I hurled my full weight on anybody was when I was seventeen or eighteen years old. Well, it couldn't be helped. One, two, three, four. Just as I took the fifth step the bridge suddenly collapsed and B.H. and I slid gently down a board incline into the water. We didn't fall. There we stood in the fog in water up to our chests. It was really Light Water; it felt like a lukewarm liquid but it moistened neither our clothing nor our bodies. When I pulled my hand out of the water the drops ran down like pellets of mercury without leaving a trace of moisture.

The Animator was standing about fifteen paces from us at the edge of the pier where a section had neatly collapsed on well-placed hinges. If his white smock had not gleamed so brightly he would have been invisible in the mist and gloom. His high-pitched, rhythmic, professorial voice, however, rang clearly through the murky haze.

"Believe me, honorable Ios, this was merely done for your own good. I advise you by all means to relax. No blessing from heaven could make you happier than this immersion. The Light Water will rid you of your cramped reluctance and convulsive resistance. I'll be back directly to receive your thanks, I hope. Otherwise— Or would you like to lead a life such as I have been leading for longer than I can remember, a life without day and night?"

❅ ❅ ❅ ❅
❅ ❅ ❅
❅

WE HAD BEEN FAIRLY LUCKY AFTER ALL in our treacherous slide into the lake, for we stood close together in the Light Water. That made it possible for me to put my arm about my friend again and again. Every time I did it I felt him breathing more deeply, as though life and consciousness were returning to him. It was pitiful to hear him babbling fragmentary sentences, assuring me that he was trying to pull himself together and that he wouldn't give up as the Animator wanted him to do. I really can't say from what source I drew my own confidence and courage. Knowing my own character, I should say they stemmed from my thoroughly unwarranted and incorrigible optimism. It's an almost pathological optimism because it is rooted in the childish, overweening faith that among all humans I am expressly, exclusively, and solely the one to whom nothing ultimately bad could ever happen.

We could move the upper parts of our bodies freely while our legs had gradually settled in the soft, muddy bottom. In order not to waste my strength I gave up the efforts to pull my feet out of it after a few futile attempts. In heavy water, I thought, the body becomes light. In the Dead Sea near Jericho and in the Great Salt Lake a swimmer can't sink. In Light Water bodies must be heavy. There's no sense in speculating. That too is a useless waste of effort. In order to keep B.H. awake I began a conversation.

"I guessed all the time that the Animator was a recalcitrant. All the officials are recalcitrants. Yet he held out more than a hundred years in spite of the fact that he has an Astromental body that isn't immune to the black humus. But my body isn't Astromental and therefore it's immune. As long as you are with me and I hold on to you, B.H., nothing can happen to you."

"Very well, colonel, as you say, sir," he babbled in a dead, drunken tone.

"We only have to work our way up to the bridge. That's all."

After these words of mine it began. What began? There were people all about us. People were crowding around us in the fog, and I couldn't see clearly where they were standing. They were standing on the water; at times they had the flickering character of reflections on the water. But they weren't a bit like phantoms or shadows, they were so plain and so real that I assumed they were standing on a raft or a big flat barge that had brought them near us. But that wasn't possible either, for they were all around us, seeking to attract our attention by waving their hats and by calling to us. I'm sure B.H. had recognized acquaintances among them; his eyes were gleaming. As for me, the first acquaintance I discovered was an old gentleman, the philosopher, Professor H.M., a genial old soul, who had often talked and joked with me when I was a little boy. There he was, big as life, in his ill-fitting sack suit, his long gray hair brushed straight back, with steel-rimmed glasses and a little goatee. The birds that he used to feed were fluttering around him. It was obvious that the entire crowd about us was made up of acquaintances, and not only of acquaintances but also of people who had been very close to me in my most distant past. The sensitive reader will understand, however, and will forgive me for not speaking of the people who had been very close to me but only of a few casual acquaintances whom I happened to notice. The Light Water of the Mnemodrome had extracted this host of perfectly distinct and genuine people from within me, and the Animator had been entirely in error when he spoke of a "horde of ghosts." B.H. undoubtedly was seeing quite different people and presumably ten times as many as I. The strange thing was a certain reversal of the sequence of time. You could have called it a time negative, in the same sense as a photographic negative. The people in the crowd who were standing nearest me and who were most sharply defined down to the buttons of their old-fashioned garments were those who belonged to my childhood and early youth, while those in the more distant and more indistinct ranks were the people who had shared or crossed the path of my life in later years. In the very foreground I even saw a number of men and women of various stations in life who were familiar but whose names I could not recall. I was so accustomed, however, to the sight of even these nameless ones that it seemed to me as though I had never been separated from them for a second in all my life, including my absence in purgatory. In a general way this throng could best be compared to an impressive crowd, jamming the platform of a railroad station to bid farewell to a prominent fellow-citizen who is leaving the country. In a manner of speaking, I myself was the prominent fellow-citizen leaning from the Pullman platform.

It took a long time before I became aware of the situation, for I was much too busy recognizing and recalling people. The others, however, seemed to know very well what it was all about. They waved at me vigorously. There was a half-witted old beggar, of whom I had been very much afraid when I was a child, moving about in a hostile, hateful sort of St. Vitus's dance. Next to him stood a tall, slender gentleman in an elegant fur coat, waving his slouch hat in graceful, rhythmic motions. Why, that was Dr. S., for goodness' sake, our great local poet, the first real poet I had ever known. Our great local poet really and truly looked like a poet, including the long hair, just as a poet was supposed to look at the turn of the century, neoromantic and with a restrained tendency toward decadence. The remarkable thing was that our local poet with his hollow cheeks, his confused eyes, and his drooping mustache was fully aware of the prototype to which he corresponded. Whenever he was invited to recite his poems before a literary club in one of the neighboring small towns he inevitably wrote a stereotyped note to the lady in charge of the affair: "Dear Mrs. Soandso, I am arriving in your charming city on the morning train. I expect to be met at the station by one of the ladies of your club. I may be recognized by the fact that I really look like a poet." For me, however, the boy of yesteryear, he not only looked like a poet, he was one. When I was twelve or thirteen years old I cringed in reverent awe whenever I met our local bard and seer in the streets. At the same tender age I was once privileged to be present in a compartment of a railroad train where several adults were asking him questions about the wonders of poetry, and what sort of a thing a poem really was, and how a good poem could be distinguished from a poor one with perfect precision. The ripe summer landscape of my native land rolled leisurely past the sooty window: distant hills, villages, fields of maturing grain, in endless monotony. In the midst of the yellow grain the July sun presently fell on a forlorn little cemetery so that its gravemarkers and crosses glistened. Our local poet pointed the well-manicured nail of his index finger at this scene and said, "You see, ladies and gentlemen, *that* is a poem." And now he was greeting me in the fog of the Mnemodrome, looking at me earnestly and waving his slouch hat at rhythmic intervals.

Not far from him I recognized the physician. I call him the physician of my childhood although he wasn't at all. He only put his bearded head on my chest in the old-fashioned manner on two or three occasions when I tried to make-believe I was sick so that I wouldn't need to go to school. He did, however, take us boys on long Sunday hikes, through forests and fields, half-naked as Pan, and in his hoarse, cheerful voice taught us to classify plants and to distinguish geological formations. Father Exorcist would certainly have ranked the physician of my childhood among the "sandal-wearing nature-enthusiasts." He would have been wrong in condemning him, however, although the physician of my childhood was a self-professed atheist. Only God, in Whom he didn't believe, knows the love and charity in this man's heart, and the cheeriness that springs from love alone. One evening I met him on the street. He was carrying a knapsack over his shoulder and a stout stick in his hand. "On a hike?" I asked. "Yes, a long one this time," he laughed and shook hands with me as he always did. I didn't know that he was on his way to the hospital, voluntarily and on foot, to submit to a hopeless operation from which he never returned. And now he was standing there in the fog, natural as ever, waving cheerily at me.

These figures I merely drew from the periphery as they caught my eye. But there were hundreds of others waiting, perhaps thousands, waiting for me to take leave of them, and every one of them was so much mine that I could have written many stories about them, filling volume upon volume. They were my people, mine, and they were to be treacherously taken from me by the Light Water. They were my people and I was their king, and in a sudden, blinding flash of conviction I knew that they were to live in my soul as long as this soul lived and that something odious and heinous was about to take place here. But not only figures and faces surrounded me. Scraps of conversation fluttered by like those in a poorly synchronized sound film, noises, and even smells. Incidentally, they were the most banal shreds of gossip imaginable. They contained references to names and things that were all but forgotten. Women's voices named prices of commodities in currencies that went out of existence before 1900. Men's voices waxed indignant about political events and personalities that I couldn't even recall, although the Light Water of the Mnemodrome had extracted these scenes and facts from nowhere but my own inner world. I pricked up my ears when I heard the name of King Edward or of Sarah Bernhardt, or when the querulous voice of an old man deplored the growing brutality of the times since almost a thousand persons had paid high admission prices last Sunday to witness the disgusting spectacle of a football game. Tired cab horses clop-clopped over nocturnal pavements, and hansom wheels rattled over cobblestones. Trams jangled and locomotives whistled; funeral corteges and military bands approached and receded with muffled drums. And there was the smell of heavy coal smoke and of freshly roasted coffee and of rain-spattered dust on unpaved streets and of horse apples and chestnut blossoms; and now it smelled of caramels and chocolate. I was able to localize this smell at once. It belonged to a candy store in front of whose door I had often stood and inhaled the delicious odor. And as though she had stepped out of the door of this odor I saw the young lady in the long, light spring dress and the wide-brimmed Florentine straw hat. She detached herself from the ranks of people waiting for their final dismissal. She seemed to believe she had a right to do that because I had been sweet on her in high school. She waved her tennis racket back and forth and it was frightening how little she had changed. It didn't seem to make a particle of difference to her that she had died of a horrible disease before she was twenty years old and she called to me with capricious impatience, "What are we waiting for? Can't you see I'll be late?"

Just as the young lady uttered these words a great spiritual illumination flashed through me, and I would give a good deal if I could keep it from fading and dissolving under my pen as so many thoughts do that dwell on the brink of the ineffable. How happy I would be if my reader, who never stood up to his chest in the Light Water of the Mnemodrome, could fully grasp the danger to which I was exposed. One thing above all: the retrogenetic humus retrovolved life back to the first-last heartbeat but it did not imperil the personality of the candidate. Or to be more accurate, its effect upon the personality was very much like that of old-fashioned death. The Light Water of the lake, however—I could distinctly feel its sucking and pulling—threatened the completeness of my ego by seeking to separate the content of my life from me. What was I? What are we? I'll try to express it by means of a simile. I was like a photograph. What is a photograph? It is a sensitive surface and a picture imprinted on that surface. The water of the Mnemodrome sought to detach the picture and to leave only the useless, worn-out, empty surface, so that the Animator would have an easy time with me a little later. The faces and figures that surrounded me here in the fog, the near ones and the distant ones, the likes and the dislikes, the attractions and the aversions, the warmths, the tendernesses, the loves—all these I had elaborated in the course of a lifetime into a unified picture. Although this picture was made up of tens of thousands of lines and splotches of color, most of which appeared quite accidental and quite unimportant, yet they formed an indivisible and irreducible entity. Like all other souls I had succeeded in transforming the eternally fugitive into the fugitively eternal. Only man has mastered that art. The present has no dimension and for that reason life becomes life only when it no longer exists. Now I knew with a certainty transcending all religious faith that the colorful life about me, of which I was expected to take leave, was my inalienable dowry, and more than that, it was my most personal life's work which I had to offer to God, the true sacrificial incense that rose to His throne. *Forgetting* was the epitome of all deadly sins. And because I recognized it in more dazzling clarity and in more mortal pain than word-bound thoughts can ever tell, I screamed at my people all about me: "Stay here! Don't move! I won't give you up. I won't give myself up!"

And B.H. who shared my experience also screamed: "I won't give you up!"

As he screamed he clung tightly to me. At that moment I felt a sharp prick in the pit of my stomach. Something pointed had penetrated the skin. I reached under my vest and pulled out the knitted monstrosity of poisonous green that the Wet Nurse on the hill had given me. It still had a knitting needle in it. I unrolled it. It was a strong, narrow strip, useless for any purpose, as far as I could tell, except as a rope. One end was weighted with a stone and had a rusty hook attached to it. Maybe the Wet Nurses weren't as moronic and stupid as they looked. At any rate they saved us. I began to toss the weighted end of the rope at the projecting beams at the end of the pier. It took a lot of time and a lot of effort but finally it caught. B.H. put his arms around my neck. I don't know how I succeeded in pulling the double load out of the water. We dropped panting on the bridge.

"Don't fall asleep," I warned my friend, "don't fall asleep."

The Twenty-Fourth Chapter

WHEREIN, AFTER FURTHER ADVENTURES, WE BUMP INTO THE ANCESTRESS, SURPRISINGLY INTACT, AND FINALLY ESCAPE FROM THE UTERUS MATRIS TERRAE IN THE COWLS OF THE BROTHERS OF THE CHILDLIKE LIFE.

DURING MY ENTIRE LIFE in the twentieth century I had never knocked anybody down. When I was a boy I had been mixed up in rough-and-tumble scraps now and then in the course of which my opponent and I used to roll around on the ground rather aimlessly. In my military career I had fortunately been an artillery man, and my actual service with guns had been brief. I had to set the sights according to the computations of the battery commander and our shells flew out into empty space for we never saw the hostile target. Knocking down a man was something that I read about in the papers, in reports of holdups or of bibulous parties at which the uninhibited and well-paid demigods of the so-called Entertainment Industry used to relax from their artistic efforts. The only place I ever saw men knocking each other down was on the screen in "B" pictures. But I always had the feeling that such rhythmically alternating battles-royal didn't even occur in the most criminal circles and that realism, as is often the case, is accepted as real only because it lacks imagination. And so it was reserved for the Wintergarden of the Astromental world to be the first place where I, a fairly gentle person with a somewhat weak stomach, ever hit anybody on the

head. And with a shovel at that. Let me hasten to confess that I
didn't strike violently or in anger. The purpose was merely to
stun the Animator in order to rob him of his white smock, and
our plan succeeded. I hit him quite cautiously for I was fully
aware of the debility of the retrogenetic functionaries and I
didn't want to commit murder. And yet it was a strange and repulsive feeling when the scoop-end of the shovel landed on the
Animator's deformed skull, an entirely new experience for me.
My friend and I had hidden behind the alkali-white shrubs to
ambush him on his return. Very fortunately B.H. had succeeded
in shaking off the deadly lethargy that overcame Astromental
people in the realm of the Wintergarden. The sight of the Turnip
Manikins and of the Catabolites, and finally the battle for the
people of his own recollections, had sobered him so thoroughly
that he did not relapse into the terrible drunkenness of death
as before. He ran about vigorously and exercised his arms and
legs in order to increase his alertness and to recover the full
use of his powers. Although he didn't speak a word it was a
great satisfaction to realize that he was now at least as passionately anxious as I to escape the blessings of the Wintergarden.

When we peered from our hiding place and saw that the
Animator was not returning alone to inspect our condition but
in company of Bath Attendant Number Two, B.H. also picked
up one of the shovels that lay stacked up at this spot. Although
we hadn't agreed on a concerted plan of action, he swatted the
Bath Attendant just as the Animator collapsed under my gentle
tap. I put Number Two's confectioner's cap on my head at once.
It was quite a job to get the white smocks off the two inert bodies,
and B.H. and I both perspired freely. We had to pull the smocks
over their heads. Luckily the Bath Attendant had brought along
the jug of elixir and it gave me new, fiery strength. Neither the
Animator nor his subordinate was wearing underclothes. They
were naked as Adam on the first morning. It was a gray, spongy
nakedness. When you prodded the flesh of these bodies with
your finger it left a dent. We dragged them up on the pier
and slid them down into the lake over the hinged planks. The

Light Water splashed greedily. They regained consciousness simultaneously and struggled to their feet. I was beginning to fear that they would simply wade ashore since the Lake of Oblivion could have no power over them; for what could they possibly forget? Unexpectedly, however, the waters of the Mnemodrome had far more power over the officials of the Wintergarden than over us. They weren't immune at all. I observed that the Animator could barely move his torso. Of course, it was perfectly absurd on my part, but I felt constrained to speak a few words of apology. After all, it was the first time I had ever hit a man on the head with a hard object and dumped him unceremoniously into the water, Light Water or otherwise.

"I'm very sorry, Maître Animator," I shouted out into the fog. "You're a great scientist, you belong to the highest intelligentsia, and it's therefore doubly embarrassing for me to have used physical violence on you."

The Animator's reply came out of the fog. He was lisping again, but with an effort. "I should have remembered that I wasn't dealing with a civilized person."

"You should indeed, sir. From your point of view I'm certainly no civilized person but a troglodyte. And as a troglodyte I'm too low for the Wintergarden."

"The worst part of it is," came the voice from the fog, "that you're dragging your well-born friend back into the misery of the past."

"Yes, thank God I succeeded in doing that, although it took a great effort. You see, that's why we need the white smocks to get out of your institution unnoticed, if Providence is kind."

"I'm so cold, I'm freezing," you could hear his teeth chatter in the Mnemodrome, and Bath Attendant Number Two also began to moan softly.

"Sorry we can't do anything for you, Maître. But you're one of the head men of the institute, you'll know what to do. If worst comes to worst, you'll find a nice heap of juicy black humus and lie down in it, at last, at last, after a hundred years of recalcitrance."

"And you, Seigneur," the high-pitched, professorial voice rang cuttingly, "you merely squirmed out of the humus out of cowardice, old-fashioned cowardice, because you're afraid of the end. You're a coward and a skunk, and you'd rather stink your existence away in a hole in the ground than choose the end manfully and be master of your fate to the final heartbeat."

"True, Animator, true, every word of it. I love to live, even when my life is as dubious as now. I've no intention of choosing my death voluntarily and of mastering it, even if this mastery is an incredible advance, as many believe. It's very nice to end up as a daisy, white and clean. But the road is too risky when I think of the Catabolites. Death stands *behind* me! I'm not afraid of him, for I've already met him. But I don't want him to stand *before* me."

"Cowardice and not enough moral sense of cleanliness, that's all it is."

"And what about your hundred years of recalcitrance, cher Maître? Isn't that cowardice?" I asked without derision.

"My recalcitrance," he shouted back, "is a sacrifice that you can't even understand. I've taken this existence upon myself because I haven't finished thinking my thoughts. Shall I tell you my thoughts?"

"I'm afraid I haven't time for that—"

"I give you and your friend up as lost, Seigneur. I'm willing to take you back to the stations."

"And what are the conditions, Maître Animator?"

"The only condition is that you help me out of the Mnemo-drome, Seigneur, just as you helped yourself out. After all, if I'm to take you back I'll have to go along."

"I'm surprised, Animator, that Astromental men with their unfortunate gift of clairvoyance haven't developed their powers of dissimulation any better. An overtone in your proposal convinces me that you want to put something over on us."

"The distrust with which you listen to the overtones of my voice is nothing but childish conceit. The Wintergarden doesn't need you."

"In that case, why are you taking so much trouble with me, cher Maître?"

"Every exceptional case arouses the favor of the scientist."

"I'm afraid I'll have to leave you in the soup. You see, I fear that the favor of the scientist would reawaken at once."

"I'll take you safely to the main station, you and your friend. I swear it by Saint Retrogenesis! Now help us out of here!"

"The thing about you that frightens me, Maître, is the most dangerous combination in the world, fanaticism and intellectual obstinacy. I've known people like you for a hundred thousand years and more, from Torquemada down to the racial physicians of the Gestapo with their murderous injections. Besides, I can't help you without getting down into the Light Water myself."

"Toss me the umbilical cord, Seigneur!"

"What umbilical cord are you talking about?"

"The green umbilical cord the Wet Nurses gave you, the God damned cell dividers and knitters!"

I hadn't noticed until this moment that I had wrapped the unfortunate girl's knitted strip (how do I know whether she is subjectively unfortunate?) around my waist like a belt. I turned to my friend with genuine enthusiasm.

"Did you hear that, B.H.? He calls the Wet Nurses' knitting an umbilical cord. Isn't that marvelous? The Eternally Feminine draws us up—and out."

"Well, Seigneur," the Animator cried in a strangely pinched voice, "let's get started. What are we waiting for?"

"I'm surprised, Maître, to find that you're more nervous than I. What can the Light Water do to you? You haven't any memories except shrinking embryos."

"Light Water can't do anything to us," the words came back softly, shivering, hardly more than squeaking.

The next moment proved that it was too late. A rushing and roaring came nearer and nearer. Someone had undoubtedly opened the floodgates, water had filled the drainage canals and was flushing the Catabolites into the Mnemodrome. The surface of the lake began to seethe in the fog and its level rose per-

ceptibly. The Animator and his helper were slowly swept away
from the shore. We heard no further sound from them. Whether
the water that wasn't wet closed over them, I really can't say.

* * * * *
* * *
*

IN THE INTERVAL THAT ELAPSED between the disappearance of the Animator far out in the fog of the Mnemodrome and our meeting with the Ancestress a good many things
happened and most of them were very strenuous. How long
that interval was, is a question that I can't answer, for, as we
know, there was no such thing in the earth's cavity as a division
of time, but only a crawling, wormlike sequence of moments,
enveloping events, conversations, and emotions. We lost our
sense of time down here, not quite, but almost, as we lost our
sense of space in the Gray Neuter. Only the exhaustion of our
bodies gave us an occasional inkling of the length of time that we
had been battling. But this was an unreliable clock, for our
fatigue came in waves and alternated with periods of the most
remarkable energy. It wasn't until we had reached the gray sod
up above and had the stars of the third night over our heads
that we discovered that our sojourn in the hollow realm of the
Wintergarden had lasted about ten hours. My feeling, however,
told me that it was much longer.

At this point I notice that the novelist in me would willingly
yield to the dry travel reporter. That's particularly inappropriate
at a moment when we are dealing with flight and pursuit, a
situation that has always been a perfect paradise for every
epicist. But I have decided to shorten the narrative at this very
point and to skip lightly over the events that followed. Why this
resignation? someone asks. Why waste the opportunity to make
things a little easier for the reader? Why? Because I'm ashamed
of myself. I have treated my reader with the utmost respect.
I have presupposed that he was filled with intellectual passion,

with tremendous curiosity for facts, experiences, and emotions lying outside the sphere of the twentieth century. I shrink, therefore, both morally and stylistically, from making use of the material suspense that presents itself here and to expatiate on the subsequent occurrences to the detriment of the intellectual investigation.

No one will doubt that we lost our way repeatedly and that we jumped on rolling sidewalks that carried us in wrong directions. The fact that we had to pass through several turnip fields was a fearful strain on our nerves. In one of these fields the Turnip Manikins had the physical strength to tear themselves loose from their roots and to fasten their teeth in our legs in vampiric fury. It wasn't easy at all to shake off these ticklike outcomes of retrogenesis. I fear I strangled two or three of them.

We had a number of very narrow escapes. In one instance, for example, we had jumped on a moving sidewalk that carried us in the wrong direction, back into the realm of the greenhouses, where "planting ceremonies" were just taking place. We saw little groups of people standing around the cradle-graves. They consisted in each case of the Animator on duty, several Bath Attendants and Gardeners, and finally the candidate, who had been thoroughly prepared by means of mud baths and wore the ecstatically intoxicated expression that I had seen on B.H.'s features. With tightly closed eyes these candidates seemed to be listening to angels' voices or to be experiencing unspeakable love dreams while the Animator recited something, presumably a poem, and the Gardeners sprinkled the naked, unresisting figures with Light Water. We glided slowly past, trying to make ourselves inconspicuous. Once or twice people called after us. It's a miracle that we weren't stopped and captured. One of the things that helped us was the fact that B.H. was carrying the jug of elixir on top of his head in the manner of the Bath Attendants. While my friend couldn't speak much, he was slowly regaining his strength and his cleverness in spite of our discouraging Odyssey that not only taxed our physical and mental

powers but also sapped our hope and confidence. Without a
doubt the jug on B.H.'s head saved us from the most ticklish
situation in which we were involved. We had left the Hothouses
far behind and were wandering around the Daisy Fields in
search of the outer wall when we suddenly ran into a very long
column of white-smocks coming toward us. It was presumably
a new shift of Enumerators going on duty. I punched B.H. in
the ribs and indicated that we had no recourse but to join the
column. The spongy, eunuchal figures trudged along indifferently.
I was addressed repeatedly and gave indistinct, grudging answers. That was exactly the right thing to do, for all life down
here was indistinct and grudging. And yet I knew that our fate
was hanging by a hair. I had to restrain myself to keep from
shouting with joy when I recognized a section of the Daisy
Fields that we had passed on our earlier tour of inspection. Now
we couldn't miss the outer wall. We dropped behind. I pulled
B.H. from the path into the field. We lay down among the
daisies, crushing many of the flowering dead. When the column
had disappeared and we had risen again, I tripped over something. It was the red thread of the Wet Nurse. The unfortunate
woman had saved us a second time. We followed it to the outer
wall, we squeezed through the grating of the drain, we were outside. We leaned against each other and drew deep breaths.
From this point the differences in elevation were evident. We
were standing on very low ground, while the light reflections
on the panes of the glasshouses seemed to come from mountain
heights. Far above us under the distant cloud ceiling ran many
roads, or rather, bridges. They were nothing but silvery bands
suspended without supports, converging from all directions,
gleaming through dusk and drizzle.

It seemed utterly impossible to reach one of these highways.
(The inexplicable construction of these roads constituted just
about the only bit of "futuristic architecture," as popularly conceived, that I had observed during my entire stay in the Astromental epoch. And this bit of "Utopian architecture" was in the
underworld.) We began to move. That's very easily said. Actually

we tripped and stumbled over a surface that can best be compared with a very hot, very soft leather cushion. It was unsolidified rock and reminded me of the puttylike iron moor on Apostle Peter. I'll say nothing of the laborious difficulties of our wanderings, the most cruel of which was the uncertainty of our objective. I also refrain from describing in detail various moments of terror, as for instance the one when all the great void about us quivered and echoed with doglike voices, barking and shouting the word "Seigneur." We were sure that our escape had been discovered and that a pack of eloquent Cerberuses had been unleashed to track us down. We began to run like mad over the leathery surface, never stopping to think that there was no sense in running if our flight had been discovered. Suddenly the ground was no longer hot. A hangarlike building of reddish material loomed up ahead of us. But I couldn't make out anything clearly because perspiration and the eternal drizzle were trickling into my eyes. The first thing I saw was a sign: "Fresh Spring Water." And beneath the sign water was actually gushing out of an old-fashioned wooden pipe into a deep basin. The drink, which was unexpectedly ice-cold, revived even B.H.

"Why, now I can speak again," he said in an astonished tone.

"And I believe we're on the right road, B.H." I remarked.

The reddish hangarlike building before us appeared to be a combination refreshment station and chapel. Over its Romanesque portal were the words: "Sanctae Illusioni."

"Saint Illusion?" I asked. "Do you know a saint by that name?"

"Why certainly, F.W., she's the patron saint of the Order of the Childlike Life."

"You don't need to answer if it taxes your strength."

"No indeed; it's wonderful to have a free tongue again."

"Was this saint always named 'Illusion'?"

"Certainly not. That's her convent name, F.W."

"And who was she really?"

"A girl by the name of Io-Ha who lost her face in a chemical accident; everything, eyes, nose, lips. But the cheerful sanctity of her soul was so great that she incessantly developed an inexhaustible supply of new faces out of her inner consciousness for everyone who looked at her. And everyone who saw her regarded her as the most beautiful creature in the world."

"I can understand the Brothers of the Childlike Life," I mused out loud. "It's very thoughtful and meaningful of them to dedicate this particular chapel to this saint, here in the realm of retrogenesis and analysis."

Retrovolution of living forms ad ovum is quite an accomplishment, even if you sometimes make a slip and produce Catabolites. But to have a beautiful face when you have no face at all, that's far more, that's the divinity of man. Sancta Illusio, ora pro nobis.

We stepped through the portal into a vaulted hall filled with fresh air and the delicate light of dawn, a most refreshing change from the rainy autumn twilight. My guess had been correct. The building housed a little chapel and a larger room which was undoubtedly an infirmary or at least a haven of rest for the weary. Its purpose was indicated by a number of reclining chairs and couches lining the walls. A motionless figure lay on one of these couches. I couldn't believe my eyes, and so it took quite a little time before I recognized the Ancestress of the Io-Fagòr household. GR³ was wrapped tightly in her dovegray bridal-veil. The black, tight-fitting helmet crowned her lovely little face, and her deep-set eyes surveyed us mockingly. Not the slightest detail of Great-great-grandma's toilette was disarranged even after her long stay in the Stygian realm which, as we know, is notoriously messy. She was in tiptop, A-1 shape from head to foot, exhaled a faint aroma of her mysterious perfume, and seemed fresher and more rested than when we last had seen her. Her Mental, ivory-tinted little hands lay quietly at her sides.

"Well! At last," she said.

"Why at last?" I asked, puzzled.

"You'll want to take off those hideous smocks, gentlemen," the Ancestress suggested, and her courteous command seemed to express the idea that she had recognized us and wasn't taking us for officials of the Wintergarden. B.H. and I dutifully pulled the stolen smocks from each other's bodies although it was possibly a little early to doff our disguise.

"I thought it might be the 'new shift,'" said the Ancestress.

I didn't know what she meant by "new shift" and asked foolishly, "Were you expecting us here, Madame?"

"I wasn't expecting anyone," she said mockingly and added, "You weren't very gallant, Seigneur, when you were so gallant as to let me precede you."

Then it dawned on me. "How could I guess, Madame, that you didn't wish to. . . ."

"My descendants are simply ovettes, and they're scared to death of life."

"But then you would have stayed in the house all alone and you would have been exposed to depressions and fulfillment-disappointments."

"At my age?" she laughed a brittle laugh. "All my disappointments have been fulfilled and all my fulfillments have been disappointed. I'm not afraid of any psychic artillery."

"Did I hear right?" I exclaimed. "You're a recalcitrant too, Madame?"

"Don't be impertinent, sir," she retorted majestically. "I adore the Wintergarden, and I shall visit it when I'm good and ready. But so far I'm not ready."

"Well, we're as young as we feel," I stammered in embarrassment, "that's what we used to say back in my day."

"No, we're as young as we *are*." And at these words her aged, sunken eyes gleamed. It pleased me to find one of the most important experiences of advanced mankind confirmed once more: the experience of heterochronic time. For every individual each year meant a different measure of life. Greater for one, smaller for another.

"Up there, Madame," I said, "you're all alone now, without family, without anyone to care for you."

"We're always alone," she said sternly. "The best that ever came out of me is still living up there."

"You're speaking of Lala, the sweet child. But now she belongs entirely to the victor."

"You missed your chance, Seigneur. Oh, you haven't found out yet where life begins."

"And where does life begin, Madame?"

"Life begins at the point where you stop worrying."

"And that's no small matter," B.H. muttered.

Yes, indeed, it's no small matter. I almost cringed before the personality of this aged Astromental hag. It was incredible that even the brooder heat of this place didn't affect her.

"Have you considered, Madame," I inquired, "that a new world has probably arisen meanwhile, a new historical era, which you might find strange and inconvenient?"

She stared at me. "Strange? But that's just what I'm curious about."

"Curious," B.H. repeated enthusiastically, pleased to contribute something to the conversation.

"I am proud, Madame," I said, "that you will go back with us, if God is good."

"If anyone goes back," she corrected me, "you will go back with me, gentlemen."

She rose lightly and with the gesture of a woman of the world she rearranged her veil drapery.

"Here comes the new shift," she exclaimed, looking at the door.

* * * * *
* * *
*

WHEN I HAD FIRST READ THE NAME OF THE ORDER "Brothers of the Childlike Life" on the wall of our room in the Wintergarden it had filled me not only with surprise but also with some misgivings. Undoubtedly the name was based on the words of Christ: "Except ye become as little children," and so forth. To become a child, however, means to live in the complete present, without a past and a future, a dimension that the adult does not know, the mundane reflection of divine timelessness. This was the deeper meaning of the "Childlike life." At the same time I sensed an overtone in this concept, an overtone traceable to the century to which I belonged and to its skepticism. At that time I had known a certain hypocritical childlike piety that believed itself to be in the full grace of God because it despised the intellect. But Christ didn't say we were to *be* children; he said we were to be *as* children. He demands a new childhood.

It was a most pleasant disappointment. There wasn't a trace of hypocritical childlike piety about the twelve young fellows who came crowding through the door of our shelter, good-humored and noisily cheerful. I used the irreverent expression "young fellows" even though I'm talking about monks who looked very much like our Capuchins. But their manner was so gaily unmonastic that the "young fellows" flowed involuntarily out of my pen. Incidentally, no writer could muster the wisdom and depth to do justice to the manner in which the Church guarded its rights down here in the underworld. The idea of eternal childhood was its reply to the retrovolution of man to the embryonic stage, and therefore it entrusted the problem of the Wintergarden to the Brothers of the Childlike Life. In this manner it showed the right road and showed up the wrong one. And it was nothing short of inspiration that had made Saint Ha, Sancta Illusio, the patron saint of the pit of the Catabolites, the disillusionments personified.

The twelve young monks who now stood around us in a friendly, laughing circle served the religious needs of the east wing of the Wintergarden from which we had just escaped. We had already learned that they were not permitted to administer the dying sacraments but they heard confessions of those who felt the need and they fed and refreshed all comers. I wasn't able to discover how many wings the Wintergarden comprised and how many brothers were simultaneously on duty. I only found out that these had just been relieved by another shift and were preparing to return to the earth's surface. They were to have a well-deserved evening off after their hard work in the unbearable climate of the cavity. They showed neither exhaustion nor fatigue, however, although their brown cowls seemed to be made of very heavy, coarse material. Neither the Ancestress nor we needed to explain why we had sought refuge here. People like us—to scramble a metaphor—were their daily bread, if not the seasoning on the bread.

"Last time we smuggled up fifteen of them," said one of the monks, "in five parties, and we got away perfectly smoothly through a whole chain of Enumerators."

"And yet it was quite a trick last time compared with today," laughed another, "because there are thousands of people crowding into the stations today, running away from the war. There won't be anything to it today."

"A perfect cinch," they chorused.

A radiant youth with bright, blue eyes, undoubtedly the head of the group, took charge. "The main thing is this: never think of the next moment. We shall climb the big stairs together, step by step. But the big stairs don't even exist if you convince yourself that each step is the last."

"I came down the big stairs," said the Ancestress proudly.

"And don't look back," said one of them with an inscrutable smile.

Don't look behind you in Hades. Where had I heard that before? The old, old stories, again and again. But I said, "I simply can't understand why the management is so strict and doesn't permit return travel on the roads."

"That's easy," was the answer. "They don't want any witnesses to talk out of school and to report that things aren't exactly the way the Uranographer announces in his prospectus and his articles."

"No, no, that's not the real reason," the Radiant One shook his head. "The management is ashamed of itself."

"Why is the management ashamed of itself?"

"Because it has made death the handiwork of man, in other words, has made it imperfect."

"If you had your way," the Ancestress grumbled, "we wouldn't even have the Park of the Worker."

A monk, who really looked like a child, clapped his hands. "Now, now, now! Let's not have any silly arguments! Let's rather sing and dance a few prayers and draw out the seconds by inner joyfulness."

"We'll do no such thing," the Radiant One objected. "Our friends have had enough of this bad air and fog and twilight. They want to get back upstairs. We'll get there at a good time, when the war will be over and the danger is reduced."

The eye of the young friar encompassed the Ancestress, B.H., and me with such loving kindness that I began to feel happy. I sensed the boyish friendliness emanating from this man and his companions, a spiritual force that was probably the result of specific exercises. A while ago, when all twelve of them had minimized the dangers that still lay before us I had had some slight misgivings. The all-too-childlike manner in which they tried to talk us out of our fear of the adventure had a tendency to produce the opposite effect on nervous people. Now, however, I had such full confidence in the Radiant One and his co-friars as though they weren't monks at all but the most experienced smugglers. They had brought some cowls out of the next room and began trying them on us. I was surprised to find that the one they chose for me was very light and pliable, despite the coarse material, and that it wasn't even warm. B.H. gave me a satisfied smile.

GR³, however, made a scene.

"What do you think I am?" she cried indignantly. "I, in a cowl with a hood?"

"It's only for a little distance," the Radiant One coaxed.

"No distance is little enough for my vanity. I had only one mission in life and I'll remain true to it."

"What sort of mission, Madame?" I asked curiously.

"To be beautiful," replied the ancient hag, and she was impeccably beautiful even in her anger. And what was even stranger, this avowal of her beauty from the lips of a woman

roughly two hundred years old, didn't sound in the least grotesque but natural and dignified. The monks put their heads
together and finally one of them tried to make her see reason by
the wrongest possible means.

"Look, grandma, the object of the game is to keep anybody
from seeing and identifying you."

"And what about you, reverend gentlemen," she retorted pointedly, "won't you see me and identify me? But even if I were all
alone, I'd sooner lie down in the humus than make myself
ridiculous."

"Probatum est," laughed the head of the friars. "We'll get
along without the disguise. Maybe we'll get along even better."
And the rest of them joined in his hearty laughter.

Somebody pulled the hood up over my head. I sat down on
one of the couches, overcome by a strong feeling that all this had
happened once before. Was this a faux connaissance, perhaps,
or a déjà vue, as the psychologists call it? No! I really had been
on the point once before of fleeing from pitiless pursuers in a
monk's cowl. Marseille, July 1940. The Germans had occupied
two-thirds of France. In a few days, so it was said, they would
occupy the entire country. And I would be lost, for according to
Paragraph Nineteen of the Armistice Agreement, the French
would have to surrender me and everybody like me. I was in a
Dominican monastery. They were discussing the possibility of
putting me and my fellow-victims into cowls and smuggling us
over the Spanish frontier. The only thing that restrained me from
the adventure was the sight of two pseudo-monks who looked
impossible in the garb.

What a delicate feeling for the proprieties the Ancestress has,
I thought to myself at this recollection. The whole business gave
me a very strange feeling, because here was a situation that
repeated itself after endless eons, and, moreover, here was a
harebrained scheme, hatched in the year 1940, that was finally
executed in the Eleventh Cosmic Capital Year of Virgo. I was
still following this line of thought when the Brothers of the
Childlike Life were leading us into the crypt under the altar

consecrated to Saint Illusio and from there, through a narrow door, into a corridor.

"Single file," the Radiant One commanded in a humorous tone. This ancient military command seemed to have been preserved in the discipline of the order.

We went down the passage in Indian-file amid the joking and laughter of the monks who constantly tried to keep us from feeling the terrific tension that held us in its spell. When we had left the corridor, however, and stood facing the enormous circular stairway, I quaked with dizziness. The stairs resembled those in a round tower—only the tower was missing. They grew upward in a gray, metallic spiral, so high that we could only see its lower part. After a few turns it vanished in the dusk and fog of the subterranean, autumnal landscape. I couldn't suppress my dread at the thought of climbing these stairs.

"My God," I sighed, "even in my youth nobody expected anything like this of me. When the Campanile in Venice was reconstructed after its collapse, they put in a nice comfortable elevator. . . ."

The Radiant One patted my shoulder gently. "Nothing to it, my friend. Anybody who wants to get up, has to climb."

I was silent, fearing the sudden heart failure that the Animator had predicted. Insanely enough, I had no objections to dissolving and vanishing, but I was afraid of the failure of my dubious body. Maybe retrogenesis would have been better after all. (Haha, at last you're beginning to appreciate the great accomplishment! That's the way it is with all innovations. Good old conservatism turns out in the end to be nothing but being stuck in a rut.)

"I know this staircase," said the Ancestress, "and I hope no one will imagine that I'm afraid of it."

"Nothing to be afraid of, grandma," said several of the friars, "you'll float right up like an angel, grandma."

"That's enough of that," GR³ exclaimed angrily. "I'm not grandma to you. I'm a great-great-grandmother, and even that isn't quite right, because I've dropped one of the greats."

The friars related that they had sometimes been required to go up and down the big stairs three or four times in succession. In the course of all these speeches and conversations we scarcely noticed that we had already made several turns. Two monks had taken the lovely old crone between them and were carrying her. A friar was walking behind me and another behind B.H., pushing us with strong hands. And so our climb wasn't much more than a pleasure trip. A number of the monks dropped behind. This was done because the Enumerators passed only the twelve monks who were being relieved. A somewhat guttural voice began to sing:

> "Oh dearest women and men,
> We Brothers of Childlike Life
> We know no struggle and strife,
> No turning backward again. . . ."

"We're far more than halfway up," the Radiant One said suddenly.

"But that's impossible," I replied in honest surprise. "We've hardly begun to climb."

"That," laughed the young prior, "is because we've been telling you constantly not to think of the next turn."

It was quite true. The monks developed a physical and psychic rhythm of such power as to force B.H. and me to surrender ourselves completely and joyously to the activity of stair-climbing. All at once my good friend said:

"It's too bad that we're almost there. I wish there were more stairs to climb."

"That's what our clients always say," nodded the Radiant One, bringing up the rear of our little party. And he added, "In a moment we'll be on the main road. I'd like to make the following requests: stick close together; don't talk; and don't turn around."

* * * * *
* * *
*

WE HAD BEEN TOLD THAT THE ROAD in the direction of the Wintergarden would be crowded with people, and it was. The throng was so great that there were traffic jams from time to time and the flood of humanity froze. All these insane people preferred premature retrogenesis to life in a world imperiled by the most modern of wars, not unlike Io-Fagòr and his clan who, to be sure, had hastened ahead of hoi polloi and had thus assured themselves of prompt service on the part of Animators, Gardeners, and Bath Attendants. The newcomers here would no doubt have to wait a long time for their happy-unhappy ends. The white-smocks no longer leaned indifferently against the railings but formed solid cordons with their backs against the stream. The Radiant One winked at me delightedly. The situation was more favorable than ever. We closed in solidly in order to form a compact group of cowls. The monks broke into a choral chant of such strength and vigor that it filled even the void Stygian space. Our solid phalanx advanced against the stream like the sharp prow of a ship, the Ancestress in the center, B.H. and I behind her. The monks formed the perimeter. Although the Ancestress had been carried up the stairs she now gave the impression of hoary old age. I must confess that she now looked old to me, old without any qualification. This appearance of old age, however, was not manifested by weakness, but rather by an aura of quiet fury that enveloped her. Her condition made me more and more uncomfortable from moment to moment.

We had just passed the first cordon of Enumerators. The muscular choir of monks plowed through the white-smocks who turned aside bashfully, unpleasantly affected by the powerful voices of the Brothers of the Childlike Life. One more line of guards was ahead of us and then the game would be won. A moderate distance away we saw the smooth wall of rock called the Station, because the Camerae Caritatis landed there. I am in a position to describe the next occurrence with the greatest accuracy because it seemed to take place in my own soul and to concern me. By some sort of Astromental act everything that went on inside the Ancestress and motivated her insane action was reflected within me to the point of painfulness. I felt the horrid temptation to disobey orders. I felt the woman's defiant stubbornness. I felt her wild arrogance, her unrestrained arrogance, her hatred of the monks, her saviors. And behind all of it I felt her aloofness, her indifference, her what-the-hell-do-I-care attitude that kept her from taking the next few steps and from taking the elevator back up into the world of the living. Was this indifference a true Desiderium Originis?

And so it happened that when we reached the last line of Enumerators GR³ stopped suddenly and turned around gracefully. For an instant our entire group stopped and the chorus was interrupted; three seconds later, however, it began again stronger than ever. I felt a poke in the ribs and stumbled ahead. Although I didn't particularly love the Ancestress, I tried to toss the green rope of the Wet Nurses in her direction. It was the Radiant One who intercepted it. But the Ancestress had been swallowed by the throng that was moving toward the Wintergarden.

A few steps farther on we reached the station of the Brothers of the Childlike Life. Everything went smoothly as peanut oil.

Whether Lala's great-great-grandmother—or, according to her own confession, her great-great-great-grandmother—had reached the end of her Astromental life, that's something I can't say. I shouldn't be a bit surprised, however, if she had changed her mind once more.

The Twenty-Fifth Chapter

WHEREIN I LOSE MY FRIEND, VIEW THE RUINS OF THE DJEBEL, AND WITNESS AN HEROIC ACT OF SELF-SACRIFICE.

THE STATE OF the world as we found it on our return to the surface did not surprise me too greatly. In my own, much more ponderous lifetime I had discovered that the historico-political aspect of a nation could change beyond recognition not only over night but in the course of a single hour. I am thinking particularly of the end of the First World War, the November days of the year 1918, which I spent in the heart of the defeated Central European powers. That war too had been precipitated by a shot fired by a fanatical and irresponsible youth, which had eliminated a prince of very little personal importance. But since at that time the population was greater, the factions more numerous, the conditions more complicated, the motives more chaotic, the weapons more primitive, than so many eons later, it was only natural that that war lasted four years and not a scant twelve hours as the present one of the most remote future. Measured by the "Last War of the Planet," incidentally, which had taken exactly three and three-tenths minutes, this was a rather protracted campaign. We must not forget, however, that this war had been forced upon both parties, Panopolis as well as the Jungle, and that the guilty ones, the silly arms collectors, were nothing but clumsy conspirators who had no efficient military organization. As a transient visitor in this world of the future, I am, of course, in a position to record only the immediate cause but not the deeper motives. Beyond a doubt, however, such deeper motives existed, even if they were nothing more than the polar tension of the contrast between Panopolis and the Jungle. (The reader will recall my repeated confession that I saw all these future happenings as through a refracting prism, that, in other words, their character and meaning were somewhat distorted.) An old proverb says: "Veritas vincit," truth is victorious. Unfortunately this adage is an idealistic overestimate and misjudges life's realities. By the end of the days of mankind, of course, truth will have conquered. Until then, however, the opposite is usually the case: "Victoria verifacit," victory makes truth.

Every historical era reflects the face of the most recent victor. That was true here. It was close to midnight when we arrived on the surface in the general vicinity of the Former Eastside District. The star-sown Astromental sky arched over us. And the world of men beneath it was beginning to assume the face of the Jungle. Thus my last impression of Astromental civilization was that it had ceased to exist and that it was making way for something new, something that so far was very indistinct and inchoate. At the same time, however, the Astromental attainments seemed to be functioning without interruption. The heavenly bulletin board where the celestial lights lined up to form today's "Evening Stars" brought new dispatches every two minutes. To my surprise, however, the tone of these notices was totally different from last night and the night before. The "Evening Stars" lauded the Jungles and their vigorous, unsophisticated inhabitants, who were not corrupted by decadent morals and whose ideal was an active, busy life instead of aimless play and sterile speculation. The sidereal newspaper, moreover, reported on the fate of the surviving conspirators, the arms collectors, whose idiotic hatred was responsible for the great purge. Many of them, it was stated, had already been captured, and in spite of the late hour the juridical commissions were searching the archives of the remotest past for appropriate forms of death punishment formerly used on traitors.

Death sentences? I couldn't believe my eyes. But there in the sky the terrible word gleamed in extensive, demotic script. Only a few hours ago, down in Hades, in the cavity of death, the Animator had severely reprimanded me for uttering the indecent word "death." And now it could be read clearly and distinctly on the night sky, and the people who stared upward didn't faint at all. The change had come much too fast even for me, a hard-boiled victim of world history. Suddenly I understood Io-Fagòr and all those like him, and I respected them from the bottom of my heart because they had preferred to become daisies a few years earlier than necessary rather than be untrue to themselves.

The report on the captured conspirators was followed by a lengthy editorial insisting with a certain degree of anxiety that the Useful Arts which mankind had learned in the course of its earthly career must not be despised and that the beneficent institutions should be retained by reformed human society, even though the latter was based wholly on those magnificent retreats so shamefully miscalled Jungles. This quotation of Io-Joel's words made me laugh.

"Why the dirty laugh?" B.H. asked gloomily.

"I'm laughing because I can imagine the look on the Uranographer's face while he's scribbling this editorial."

"Tomorrow they'll probably kick him out and put in one of their own men."

"What a novel idea, B.H.," I mocked, "tremendously novel."

He pointed silently up at the sky where another report was beginning to line up. It read as follows: "Imminent End of Selenozusia. . . . The Committee for the New World Constitution has just met to debate a proposal for the abolition of Selenozusia. . . . The institution of the Lunar Consecrated Geoarchon, the powerless-powerful ruler, the responsible-irresponsible President without a name, failed so miserably in the face of a relatively trivial danger, that his place will be taken by a Geogeneral, an expert in psychic artillery. . . . The Sentry Booth of the World Major-Domo will soon be replaced by a more dignified official residence. . . ."

"Too bad," I said, "too bad," and I stopped reading because my neck was getting stiff from looking up at the sky.

My impression that Panopolis was beginning to assume the face of the Jungle probably resulted from the fact that we visited chiefly places where the change was most apparent. It might have been different in the residential sections, perhaps even in the Geodrome; in those places the resistance of Astromental culture might not have been so quickly broken. Here, however, in the region of the Former Eastside, the center of which was formed by the corso between the two gateways, here in the district of the prolific families and of the weary and heavy-laden, the celebration of the social reform was in full swing. Although these weary and heavy-laden weren't weary and heavy-laden at all, although they were well fed and well clothed by the sidereal factories of the Worker, it was all the same; in a world without economics and without social distinctions they were the same old weary and heavy-laden, for it's a well-known fact that man lives not on bread alone but also on the gratification of his self-esteem. I need not emphasize that the weary and heavy-laden of the Former Eastside constituted the revolutionary strata of Astromental society and that joy and jubilation reigned in the district between the two ruined gates, not because there was any prospect of life becoming brighter but because the people who had looked down their noses at them would have nothing to say any more. Crowds of Jungle people were already here, men and women, many of them in their peasant smocks with glittering silver buttons, with red tassel caps and little bells on their mustaches. These peasants, however, were very quiet and cautious, even a bit bashful, while the city populace cheered frantically and went out of their way to fraternize. It might even be said that these Astromental proletarians kowtowed to the reserved Jungle people in a strange sort of perverted snobbery. In explanation of this attitude I shall have to add, however, that the men from Mountaintown hadn't come empty-handed; they had brought along many kegs of their brown beer, and the Astromental people, who had never tasted anything like it, were all a little high and irresponsible. A charming historical reversal, by the way: the redskins corrupting the palefaces with firewater. The Mountaintownites for their part had captured a considerable number of travel-puzzles and were having a wonderful time changing their localities like wild. For me it was one of the great mysteries of this war that the Harmonizers continued to perform their duties so faultlessly. But even this wasn't anything novel, for I knew from earlier experience that certain basic functions of life continue to operate in spite of hell, high water, war, and revolution.

Another strange thing was that the people had lighted camp fires and were sitting around them. I repeat, they were sitting, a thing they wouldn't have dared to do twelve hours ago, at least not in public. According to Io-Joel sitting was a reactionary posture. I had taken B.H.'s arm. We were strolling along slowly, enjoying the divinely fresh night air after the incubator heat of the Wintergarden.

"Do you remember Lenin's famous saying," I asked, " 'Revolutions are the locomotives of world history'? Locomotives run forward and backward. This one seems to run backward."

"What of it?" my friend retorted sagely. "It's running."

When all space is curved, why should man alone maintain a straight direction? I was about to ask this question when we passed the entrance that led to King Saul's house. On it was a metal sign with the inscription: "Io-Saul Minionman. Official Jew of the Era." Under it was pasted a paper with two words neatly written on it: "Out Wandering."

"I'd like to bet," I laughed, "that Minionman isn't out wandering but is safely locked up in his curio shop. And he doesn't know whether to curse or bless his darling son for these terrible reforms that are being visited on the world once again, when they've hardly had time to get used to the last ones."

"You may be right," B.H. nodded.

"I know I'm right. King Saul is still busy segregating himself."

"What's going to become of us?" B.H. sighed deeply.

"You're the guide," I said maliciously, suppressing a secret wish directed at the Jungle on Lala's account.

"Let's go to the Park of the Worker," B.H. suggested. "That's the best place for us to recover our strength."

* * * * *
* * *
*

THE PARK OF THE WORKER WAS ALSO FLOODED with tremendous throngs. At a considerable distance we could read a luminous sign hanging in the air: "Unless hostilities on both sides cease by twelve o'clock midnight, the Worker of the Era will go on strike." It sounded like an effective threat. Without a doubt it was much more serious for the conspirators and arms collectors than for the artillery generals of the Jungle, and properly so, as everyone will agree. After all, the Worker was a worker and his sympathies were therefore with the underdogs. At the same time, however, he was careful to guard the principle of neutrality by directing his threat of strike against both parties. The Jungle people, to be sure, lived on the fruits of the earth and were therefore independent of the astral food from the Valley of Springs and Forces, while the Astromentals, lacking all agriculture, were menaced by starvation. The Worker's threat to go on strike had completely served its purpose. After the trans-shadow-disintegrators and the existence-extinguishers of the conspirators had done more or less damage in the Jungles and had dissolved a few thousand people into thin air they ceased firing, if only because the Astromental citizens evinced no sympathy and approval of the coup, as the arms collectors had hoped, but only disgust and anger. Never in the history of the world had a civilization been destroyed more stupidly and more wantonly. The various Constantines, on the other hand, had succeeded in

their purposes long before sundown; wailing and gnashing of
teeth reigned in all sections of Panopolis and there were not
enough first-aid stations to accommodate those wounded by
depression projectiles. The articles of capitulation were signed at
the beginning of the first nightwatch; they were signed by the
unfortunate person who had taken the place of the last Selenozusian. Obviously he signed only with a symbol and no name, for
he had none. The most significant paragraph consisted of a
single, brief sentence: "The boundaries between the Astromental
residential desert and the colorful Oases are hereby abolished."

At one stroke, as we see, everything had changed. The Jungles
had for good reasons been promoted to "colorful Oases," and
from their perspective these Oases for equally good reasons referred to the seat of an almost superhumanly spiritualized civilization as the "Astromental residential desert."

We were informed of these developments by feverishly excited people who were too agitated to notice that I was an alien
in a strange garb. (The monks had taken back their cowls when
they left us.)

So much for the progress of this brief war, if it could be called
a war at all, although it had exacted a great toll of victims. But
we heard something else that sounded incredible and that filled
me with abhorrence. Some of the rebels had been killed, the
greater part had surrendered. But there were still a few heroes
or holdouts or gangsters who had entrenched themselves with
their trans-shadow-disintegrators at inaccessible places where
they could not be reached by psychic artillery. But they did not
direct their destructive pipettes, as might have been expected,
against the so-called Oases. Instead—and it was too monstrous
for reason to grasp—they tried to destroy the greatest and best
thing their own world had produced, the world for which they
claimed to be fighting. In a word, the object of their last destructive frenzy was the Djebel, and the report was that they had
been successful. Someone might think that the motive of these
patriots was to keep the temple of learning from falling into the
hands of the enemy. But no, that wasn't it; I'll swear it wasn't.

The Io-Dos really hated the Djebel more fiercely than the Jungle. The shameful defeat bared their deep hatred. That's the only explanation I can find for this atrocity that made me shudder and grieve.

I count it a high honor to have been taken into the presence of the Worker at this hour. He was so busy he didn't know what to do first, for all the responsibilities of tottering civilization rested on his shoulders. I don't know to whom or to what I owed this distinction; certainly not to the violet wrist-rosette. It had lost its value as completely as the medal on my chest. I seemed to have an unfortunate penchant for decorations from doomed governments. Yet I kept both of them with me.

All the brothers, sons, grandsons, and great-grandsons of the Worker clan appeared to be on duty today, not to speak of the assistants. One of these seven-foot giants cleared a path through the throng for us. Tens of thousands of women and children crowded the playground. The Parks of the Workers throughout the world had all served as places of refuge, for—be it said to the credit of the Jungle—only a few projectiles had struck them. This doesn't mean, however, that I'm conceding any degree of humaneness to Constantine and his ilk. Far from it; I don't want to commit the psychological error of Rousseau, the Encyclopedists, the Saint-Simonists, the parlor Socialists, the Io-Joels, who maintain that the mere fact of not belonging to the ruling class makes one a better man. Constantine and his ilk had every reason to protect the Worker's sidereal machinery in order to take possession of it themselves later on. Every time a lower civilization conquers a higher one, the victor first annexes the superior attainments of the vanquished. At this midnight hour the malachite-green hollow with its countless springs and fountains of forces afforded an overwhelming spectacle. The ground all about vibrated with mysterious activity, and not only the ground but also the ether all the way up to the Intermundia. The stellar rays shooting down into the alabaster bowls and rocketing back again to the heavens were more brilliantly colored than by day; they were definitely more visible though none the less ghostly. It was a perfect downpour, a cloudburst, of beneficent sidereal forces descending upon man and returning to the stars.

Profound silence reigned in the hollow although thousands of Jungle people were assembled here. In deepest reverence they observed the magnificent spectacle, the character and meaning of which they could not grasp.

From afar we heard the golden lion's growl of the Worker at midnight. "Of course you're astonished, you're dumb with surprise. You can sate your hunger by feasting your eyes."

I recognized the cheerful giant's doggerel at once. It hadn't improved after such a day of hard work and devoted effort. But the content of his rhyme was true. If you focused your full attention on the miraculous play of the nutritive rays, you not only felt better but you also experienced a sensation of satiation and warmth. In other words, calories were optically assimilated. I mention this detail because it might point in the direction of completely spiritualized alimentation of an even more future future. My reverie about a human race fed in such an ethereal manner was interrupted by the unique laugh of the Worker who towered above us like a rugged monolith. "Well, Seigneur, you've given me lots of worry; what became of you when you left in a hurry? All day long I've had an obsession that our guest had been wounded by a depression." He stopped with a frown, stamped his foot, and growled, "After midnight my rhythm always gets bad."

"And I need a little morning song for my solar plexus," I said.

The Worker's laugh was like a deep-toned bell. "Then you'll have to wait until morning, Seigneur."

I turned enthusiastically to B.H. "Do you know why I'm so fond of our Worker? He's the only person in the world who can laugh without laughing at anybody."

While we sipped a warm drink the Worker asked us how we had spent the day.

"We escaped from the Wintergarden," I confessed truthfully.

He was honestly shocked. "Well, damn my buttons and strike me pink, you need the hospital now, I think. There's a cozy bed and a square meal too in the Worker's infirmary for each of you."

"Where is the Worker's infirmary?" I inquired curiously.

"It's under our feet and it's very large," he replied, scraping the ground lightly. "My daughters and daughters-in-law are in charge. My granddaughters too make a splendid impression."

"I see, they are all in the nursing profession," I involuntarily completed his rhyme.

"They've nursed most of the wounded back to health," the Worker nodded proudly.

"They have a panacea, a cure-all, I suppose?"

"It's very simple," the Worker laughed, "our women radiate."

"What do your women radiate?"

"Beauty, good common sense, and quiet. Come along with me, you ought to try it."

"No, Mr. Worker," I said. "It sounds very attractive. Many thanks. But that's not what I need. I want something else."

"You'd better think it over," B.H. said reprovingly.

"We're not sick, neither my friend B.H. nor I, although we had a pretty hard time of it in the Uterus Matris Terrae. Still neither of us needs hospitalization. I'll admit that I can't think of anything more pleasant than to be radiated at by radiant young women, especially when they radiate beauty, quiet, and good common sense. But I can't afford it right now. Something else is calling to me incessantly. I should only like to ask the Worker of the Era to do me a little favor. Please, press both of us to your blue-aproned breast, as you did to me once before. That made me feel so wonderful."

"Well, my boy, that's only fair," the Worker jingled happily, "you refuse a woman's tender care, but instead of it you demand the strength, that I, the Worker, am here to lend. Damn it all, even my rhymes are rotten after midnight. Well, come on."

He seized me with his left arm and B.H. with his right, and pressed us both mightily to his chest. From his mountainous insides we heard the golden, growling laugh bubbling like a hidden spring. An unspeakable sense of well-being streamed from his body into mine, as it had done once before. I began to breathe slowly and deeply. With a feeling of complete peace and calm I looked at the tremendous crowd consisting of victors in peasant smocks and vanquished in pastel-colored veil draperies. I felt my fatigue fall from my shoulders like a worn-out garment. Two minutes more of this vitalizing current, I thought, and I'll be ready for anything. At the same time I wasn't equal to this unbounded contentment and began to sob convulsively. I distinctly remember that the same thing happened to my friend.

* * * *
* * *
*

WE WERE STANDING SOMEWHERE on the irongray sod, B.H. and I, all alone, just as at our first meeting. The Park of the Worker lay behind us. We were refreshed and strengthened, by his revitalizing physical contact as well as by the soup and goat cheese that he had served us. Now we had to make up our minds. That is, I didn't have to make up my mind at all. I knew exactly where I was going next.

"Why didn't you accept the Worker's offer?" B.H. said, and I distinctly felt that he had something on his mind, presumably some sort of a grudge.

"I didn't like the sound of the words 'hospital' and 'infirmary,' old man," I replied, "in spite of the Worker's radiant ladies. I would rather sleep outside than in an Astromental hospital bed."

"We probably will have to sleep outside, F.W., for I haven't the heart to return to Io-Fagòr's empty house. And I haven't any residence of my own."

"Haven't we forgotten how to sleep by this time, B.H.? At any rate, I'm wide awake."

"It wasn't I who started to talk about sleeping but you."

"Let's not beat around the bush, B.H. You've got something on your mind. What is it?"

"I have an evil foreboding——"

"An evil foreboding? In regard to what?" B.H. didn't answer.

I had to repeat the question. "An evil foreboding? In regard to yourself?"

"In that case I wouldn't have opened my mouth."

"So it's in regard to me?"

"You're right, F.W.! It's in regard to you."

"Well, now listen, B.H. Didn't I put up a pretty good battle in the Wintergarden? You know, much as I'm concerned about my own welfare, I'm completely impervious to danger. I'm proud to be without imagination."

B.H. sat down on the irongray sod and drew me down beside him, so that I was now sitting for the first time on this earth-encompassing carpet and looking up at the strange, glittering night sky. It was a curious feeling to be sitting on this nerve-grass, dry as paper and unyieldingly tough as hemp.

"Yes, you not only put up a very good battle, F.W.," my reincarnated friend began, "but you distinguished yourself by your energy and ingenuity and saved both of us. I not only am deeply in your debt but I'm ashamed of myself as a native of the era for having failed you."

"As a native of the era you had to fail, but that isn't the right word, because you were ready for retrogenesis from the start."

"And I've been wondering, F.W., whether it wouldn't have been better and more dignified, in spite of all risks, Turnip Manikins, Catabolites, Mnemodrome, and everything else."

"I don't understand you, B.H. Weren't you sick with horror and disgust too?"

"You can't ever understand me, F.W. You didn't get the right slant on the Wintergarden, chiefly on account of your resistance, and your attitude influenced me too."

It was the same old conviction I had found in Io-Fagòr. The conquering of death by means of retrogenesis was the sacred taboo of all who had been Astromentally reared.

"It may be, my friend," I said after a while, "that I wasn't equal to the Wintergarden and that my offended primitivism attracted and unmasked all the evils down there. But you mustn't forget that for me and my time death was a holy ordinance of

God, and man has no business meddling with it. I certainly don't minimize the idea and the practice of your detour around death, but its blasphemous character can't be denied any more than its abstruseness and unnaturalness."

"Now you've just touched on the important point, F.W. Man has always tended to designate bad habits as holy ordinances. One of these bad habits was his passive acceptance of dying. You can't deny that all of human history is a continued, stubborn effort to reduce the authority of God and to transfer more and more of it to the control of man."

"So it is," I replied amicably, "but you should hear the Grand Bishop's opinion on this point."

"I only meant to say——" B.H. began but left it dangling.

"And what about your evil foreboding?" I smiled. "Is it connected with my reactionary recalcitrance?"

"On the contrary," he rejoined briskly, "my evil foreboding is connected with your incredible adaptability, my friend."

"Disappointed in me, B.H.?"

"Disappointed? Heavens, no, F.W. I only had something quite different in mind when I summoned you from an inconceivable distance. I imagined you would come to us as a mild phantom, a shining shadow, that you would share a little of our life with us and look around and observe the world. Instead, you came out of your absence charged with life, with whirlwinds of will and of energy. That's why I'm worried about you. Think of all the things you've had to do. You were umpire in the greatest controversy of all times. You did Comet Calisthenics with the best of them. You were on the most intimate terms with the High Floater. You were appointed as negotiator in the Jungle. As a recalcitrant in the Wintergarden you fought for our lives for ten hours while I hung as a dead weight around your neck. And the big winding stairs topped it all off. Now what's next? It's bound to lead to a bad end."

"Why is it bound to lead to a bad end?"

"Because you're extending yourself too far, F.W., beyond all permissible limits. That's the worst vice imaginable. Virtue stays within modest bounds. That's why concentration, virtue, and health are identical. But vice reaches for everything and tries to egotize everything. And your dissipation breaks all known records. You're trying to combine the most uncombinable antitheses in your little existence. Mark my words, you'll end up in an awful mess. And I'll be the goat who's to blame for the whole business."

"What sort of a mess?"

"Suppose you should fall ill. With these insatiable dissipations of your undisciplined will you're bound to become sick."

"Is that any reason to go to the hospital beforehand and to have the Worker's women radiate at me? Wouldn't that be a dissipation too?"

"Listen to my suggestion, F.W. I'll take you to the nearest caravansary. You'll lie down. I'll stay with you and watch that nothing happens to you."

"You're a good friend, B.H. I know it. But I'll have to turn your suggestion down. I hear a call inside me that keeps calling insistently. Undoubtedly it's a Mental call. You see to what extent I've been assimilated. Someone's calling me from the Djebel."

B.H. was so frightened at the word "Djebel" that he turned pale. It was noticeable even in the bluish star-daylight.

"The Djebel!" he exclaimed. "But that's out of the question."

"Why is it out of the question? On account of the transshadow-disintegrators?"

"My evil foreboding just now was connected with the Djebel. And with us Astromentals foreboding is foreknowing."

"And what does your foreknowing tell you?"

"That you'll meet your end at the Djebel, your relative end, naturally."

"Doesn't my unconscionably long sojourn here have to come to an end some time, B.H.? And I'd sooner choose the Djebel for my end than the Wintergarden."

"You've proved that."

"I've only proved half of my statement. Besides, with due respect to your foreknowledge, it may be just as unfounded as our knowledge frequently is."

I had been on my feet for some time and was gently twisting the travel-puzzle around in my hand. B.H., standing beside me, bowed his large head. He smiled dreamily as he said: "I ought to knock the Mentelobole out of your hand and take it away from you."

"Well, B.H.," I laughed, "what are you waiting for?"

"That wasn't a nice thing to say, F.W.," he said gently. "You know I won't knock it out of your hand. I can't change you any more than you can change me."

"Let's remember the words of GR^3: 'Life begins when you stop worrying.' A silly maxim, by the way. For life really begins when you have something to worry about."

"When you're ready, let's go," said B.H. dryly, taking hold of me so that we would be at the Djebel together in the next instant.

But I retreated two steps. "Wait, B.H. It's possible after all that something might happen to me or to you. So let's say good-by decently in the old-fashioned way. I thank you for drawing my name out of the alphabet. My consciousness has been immeasurably enriched by you. You made me a regal present. Two things I'll know for all eternity: that we two can never disappear out of the world and that it's always possible to meet again. And in spite of various accidents and incidents everything was awfully nice and tremendously interesting."

I shouldn't have to tell the reader that the words "awfully nice" and "tremendously interesting" were a screen behind which I concealed my emotions. B.H., however, the more refined and more sensitive of us, shook my hand silently, looked at me briefly, and quickly lowered his eyes. And I shook the pale pellets into the proper little holes with expert fingers and sent my Keenly Directed Desire toward the Djebel.

When our objective lay before us I thought I had made a mistake. There was no Djebel at all, only a gigantic pile of ruins, huge blocks of crystal and heaps of prismatic fragments over which delicate rainbows of refracted starbeams trembled. The trans-shadow-disintegrators had made rubble and ashes of the most sublime symbolic structure that mankind will ever erect. That's no mere metaphorical phrase, for some portions of the crystalline substance glowed through the night like streams of lava, and colossal masses of scoria plunged down with the thunderous clash of cosmic bass drums and cymbals. Streams of water hissed through the titanic ruin and an unspeakable flickering and fluttering betrayed the concern of the stars that had lost their earthly home. The Chronosophers of all the Lamaseries, Foreignfeelers, Marvelers, Starrovers, and the schoolboys of the Planet Classes had congregated about the vast scene of destruction and were standing in an arc of such size that its ends could not be seen. They did not permit anyone to approach the bottle-green, icelike border area. They made frantic warning signs as we came near. I didn't know what was going on. Were we in the danger zone? A poisonous silence that I shall never forget hung in the air. B.H. suddenly seemed to grasp the situation. He took hold of my hand to pull me away. He began to run madly. I shouted angrily and tore my hand loose. At that instant he stumbled and fell. But the terrible thing was that he didn't fall. He had no time to fall. In the split second between stumbling and falling, the trans-shadow-disintegrator, this ridiculous blowpipe, this damned museum piece out of a dead past, had dissolved him into nothingness. He was not only invisible as I had once been, he didn't even exist any more, he was erased, exterminated, along with every last one of his twenty-six trillion healthy cells. It took me a long time to grasp what had happened. His foreknowledge had not deceived him. The fact that I still possessed my body was an error in calculation. My unpredictable misconduct in tearing myself loose from him had saved me, contrary to all the rules. I regretted it deeply at this moment. I dropped to the ground, stricken with grief. A terrible thought crushed me with its weight: I am alone in the world.

* * * *
* * *
*

I HAD LOST MY FRIEND BUT I WAS NOT ALONE in the
world. A group of young men who had witnessed the disaster
ran toward me and took me in their midst. I recognized them at
once by their muscular, astrally developed bodies. They belonged to the Lamasery of the Astropaths, the gymnasts who
depicted the character of the nearer stars and their constellations
in pantomimic and acrobatic exhibitions. They didn't sympathize
with me, they weren't horrified, they didn't make long speeches,
but immediately began a round dance.

"Pain," said one, "is interruption of movement."

"Healing," responded another, "is resumption of movement."

"Alley-oop, Seigneur," whispered a third right beside me,
"relax, let go, lean."

I scarcely touched the ground as I ran over the surface,
supported by them. At this point I must again obviate a possible
misunderstanding. The flying, or rather floating, trip over the
immense, starlit ruin of the Djebel, on which I now set out with
the help of the young Astropaths, had nothing in common with
the well known "dream-flying" or "dream-floating" that happens
to all of us occasionally at night. I must repeat emphatically
that all such experiences, unusual as they may seem to us people
of the twentieth century, were no dream visions but unquestion-
able realities in the Eleventh Cosmic Capital Year of Virgo. In
other words, I'm not speaking of a dream or even a vision, but of
an actual flight over the ruins of the Djebel, for which the Astro-
gymnasts needed no machines other than their own bodies. The
reader, remembering the account of their activities in the pertinent chapter, will, of course, take my word for it. The youths
carried me as lightly as though I were a downy feather. And I
really wasn't much heavier. The explanation lay in the fact
that the destruction of the Djebel had released the various
degrees of regulated gravitation in its interior and these had now
canceled each other to such an extent that the gravitation
pervading the space above the ruin was extremely low. We flew
along at a moderate altitude. But this altitude and the starlight

were sufficient for me to survey the entire area of the demolished, mighty, artificial mountain. I almost cried aloud with surprise, "Why, the Djebel is an eye!"

My young flight companions appeared to smile. "Didn't you know that? The Djebel is Gaea's eye." And one of them added sadly, "It was Gaea's eye."

No doubt about it. It was Gaea's eye, the destroyed eye of the earth-planet which man had placed here ages ago so that it might look out consciously into cosmic space. From the altitude at which we were floating along in a mild current of air I could plainly distinguish the various parts of the eye. There was first of all the enormous eyeball, suspended and freely movable in a circular earth socket. The forward cleft of this socket was covered with the bottle-green, icelike surface which served as an approach to the actual mountain, the eyeball, and to the numerous gateways that led into its interior. Viewed from above it was obvious that the crystal globe of the eye was not completely demolished; on the contrary, its form was much more distinctly preserved than the perspective from the valley had indicated. I could easily distinguish the cornea, iris, retina, and pupil, as far as these organic structures were indicated by the architecture. Only the uppermost cupola, the highest dome, the pupil, had been completely shattered, and the rooms to which I referred as the "attics of the Starrover" at the time we inspected the Djebel, gaped open to the sky. The design of the pupil consisted of many polygonal facets, a feature of insect rather than human eyes, as far as I know. The eyeball, the main part of the Djebel, could not be seen from below because of the rock formations and crags that surrounded and towered above it and gave it the appearance of a characteristic mountain peak. They took the place of the lids and eyelashes that protect the precious, vulnerable eye. Now they were blasted away and had crashed down into the plain, and the eyeball itself seemed to have sunk far down into its socket.

The magnificent and tragic spectacle beneath our flight showed how man humanizes nature and how nature again and again naturalizes man in endless, cruel alternation. For the events of this day were nothing but the renaturalization of man, his surrender to the blind forces that persisted in him just as they had in the beginnings of mankind. And there was profound logic in the circumstance that the attack on the refined Astromental civilization had not erupted from the Jungle but from the bosom of this arrogant culture itself. This dismal thought brought B.H.'s end so sharply into my consciousness that I groaned.

"I'm to blame for his death. He tried to save me. But I saved myself by preventing him from saving me. So I let him perish alone."

"Movement, movement," the voices about me cried.

"Movement won't do any good," I moaned. "What was the use of escaping from the Wintergarden? He implored me to let him become a baby. It's really a very pleasant method and you don't vanish all at once."

When the Astropaths noticed my useless remorse, they spoke a few words to each other. I felt them descending to the pupil of the Djebel, and a few breaths later we landed on a crystal platform. It was a fairly spacious, circular surface, the highest point of the shattered cupola of the Djebel, the roof of Chronosophy, so to speak. A huge jagged hole, its edges shimmering like jewels, gaped in the middle of the platform. I might call it a shell hole, if I didn't know that a direct hit of a transshadow-disintegrator would scarcely be content to produce such a harmless result. Be that as it may, a cloud of smoke issuing from the hole indicated that the opening led far down into the interior of the Djebel, where fires were undoubtedly raging in the various halls, thinking chambers, and studios of the Lamaseries, perhaps even in the precincts of the Arachnodrome, and that the material of which the mountain was constructed had been transformed into streams of lava by the terrific heat, the violence of the explosions, and the atomic disintegration. It didn't require much imagination to conceive the Lamaseries of the Thaumazonts and Xenospasts as molten infernos and to realize that there was

little hope for anyone trapped there, though he had easily survived the terrors of the most distant Intermundia. But there
were only voluntary victims in the Djebel as I was to discover
later.

The platform where my young comforters had deposited me
was bordered by a balustrade, and along it a line of men in ashgray cowls stood motionless and silent. I diagnosed them without difficulty as old men, as Foreignfeelers, and before long I
was informed that they were the governing board of the Xenospast Lamasery. There was something of great gray birds about
them, silhouetted with hanging heads against the star-soaked
sky. I don't know whether to say that they looked grief-
stricken. Perhaps they were only upset. And it must be upsetting
to be disturbed in the psychic activity inaccurately called
"Foreignfeeling," the climax of metaphysical Starroving. These
old Lamas whose home was among the star nebulae had lost
their earthly home, the shrine of their profound paroxysms,
their Xenospasms. Their telluric base, where they could yield to
their nostalgia for the infinite, had been taken from them. Their
bodies were bent and crippled by astral arthritis. With their
shoulders drawn up like wings they looked like perching eagles.
But their bodies were so gnarled that they resembled the
twisted trunks of clipped willow trees. I didn't count them; there
must have been twenty or more. They were all silent with the
exception of one. This one was undoubtedly the most prominent,
the chairman of the board, a man with a rawboned face and
heavy, half-closed eyelids. He had a soft voice and didn't move
as he spoke. I call him the Indifferent One, although I don't
know whether he really was. At any rate, he didn't betray the
slightest trace of sympathy.

The indifference of the Indifferent One almost looked like
energy because it contrasted so sharply with the agitation of the
Agitated One who was shouting wildly at him and at the other
Xenospasts as he waved his long pointer around in the air. The
Agitated One was the only choleric type I had met among the
restrained and reserved Astromentals. Even in the Gray Neuter

and in the Minor Intermundium he had been unable to curb his anger when his pupils indulged in nonsense. But the present agitation of our dear old elementary teacher was of quite different nature from his customary schoolmaster's ire, his quick, derisive resentment which merely concealed his offended good nature. His present agitation was of a deadly serious character, and its undertone was utter despair. Despite the chilly night beads of perspiration studded his smooth skull, his face was bluish and hollow, his eyes were red, and he ran up and down frantically without showing the distinguished Xenospasts the respect that was due them.

"Haven't I enough pupils," he yelled, "agile, supple lads who could slip through the eye of a needle? There are Io-Rar and Io-Hol, my best ones, my star pupils, Respondents and A-1 Comet Acrobats. There are Io-Scram and ten other advanced pupils, very smart boys, especially good in physical training, and tough fellows besides, whom I would send right straight through the sun globe or any other star without batting an eye. There are—why waste my breath. Am I the only elementary teacher? Aren't there a hundred and seventy-one elementary classes besides my own? And among all those classes you had to pick mine, and among all my pupils you had to pick——"

"We didn't pick anyone," the Indifferent One interrupted the Agitated One. "The boy volunteered to sacrifice himself."

"The boy doesn't even know the meaning of the words 'volunteer' and 'sacrifice.' The boy doesn't know anything except the high spirits that go with his ability, and he's ready for any madcap prank."

The Indifferent One was unmoved. "The voluntary sacrifice will be no less great because it was made thoughtlessly or heedlessly."

"It shouldn't have been accepted," the teacher screamed. "The silly boy should have been put in a corner——"

"But it was accepted," the calm voice murmured, "and the price of the sacrifice is truly great enough."

"The sacrifice will be in vain and the silly boy won't return."

The chorus of the perching gray birds grunted, "Maybe he'll return, maybe he won't return. . . ."

Just then the teacher recognized me, late enough, and rushed toward me. "Help me, Seigneur, for God's sake help me, you know him."

"How can I help you?" I said softly. "I couldn't even help my friend."

"But you know the little fellow."

"I assume you're speaking of the graceful star dancer, the one with the nickname Io-Runt."

The teacher looked at me silently and his eyes filled with tears. With a slow, despairing gesture he pointed to the crater, the smoke from which was getting thicker and thicker. In the tragic silence that followed this gesture the weary voice of the Indifferent One rang dully. "If the little fellow doesn't return, another one will go, and if he doesn't return, then still another one. But one of the little lizards will have to return and bring it up."

The gray eagles on their perches feebly nodded the heads that projected from between hunched shoulders.

"I know that I'm nothing," the teacher wailed, "less than nothing, for I never even got to be a Starrover, and for more than a century I've been jogging back and forth between the dull old planets. But there's one thing that I am with all my heart, and that's an educator. And as an educator I venture to ask the exalted navigators of the star nebulae: Why doesn't the High Floater come up himself and bring it with him? Why does a youthful life have to be sacrificed, a life that may itself be destined for the High Floater's Office?"

To this question, uttered in a tremulous tone, the Imperturbable One replied, "The High Floater will not come up. He has refused to leave his Office. Perhaps he has already fallen down from the vaulted ceiling and is no longer breathing."

Another of the aged Xenospasts broke the heavy veil of his silence and muttered, "Like all great personalities, our High Floater has a bad character."

"He wants to keep the Isochronion for himself," nodded the neighbor of the one who had just spoken.

Now the Indifferent or Imperturbable One said with unwonted emphasis, "But we need the Isochronion and on it we will found a new discipline."

The word Isochronion was just mentioned. It is the last Greek loan-word of my narrative, which unfortunately teems with such foreign words, and for its sake I must interrupt the tale once more. The interruption would be unnecessary if I were quite clear in my own mind about the Isochronion, which was sometimes also called the "Capsula." But I'm not at all clear about it and I have serious doubts whether a person who is bound to the normal consciousness of the twentieth century can ever attain complete clarity about this thing. All I brought back with me was a strong presumption regarding this Isochronion based on concrete experience, an object that was (will be) so important for the world of the future that the gentle Foreign-feelers did not hesitate to send this boy into the molten hell of the Djebel to take it from the living or dead High Floater. In keeping with my established principle, however, I refuse to parade my composite information as sure knowledge and to incorporate it in the plot of my story. On the other hand, I caught a glimpse of the Capsula for a second and heard various intimations about it from the lips of the Xenospasts, so that I feel quite certain that I am on the right track. In appearance the Isochronion was a small, hexagonal metal capsule with a strap on each of its sides. It looked like one of the phylacteries or prayer boxes of the Jews which are fastened to the fore-head by means of straps or ribbons during prayer. What was inside the Isochronion is more than I can say; probably not words of prayers as in the phylacteries. Perhaps it was an inconceivably complicated formula, perhaps a drop of a sidereal essence, perhaps a grain of a drug procured from the world of star nebulae, how should I know? In any case the contact of the Isochronion with a human forehead had a powerful effect on the spirit that dwelled behind that forehead. What kind of effect could it have been? In the Wintergarden, in the realm of cell division and of decay, we became acquainted with autobiological or heterochronic time. It was personal time, the private time of the single organism, detached from the general lapsing of time, the death-encircled time of the ego-island. Linguistically, isochrony meant the opposite of heterochrony. Translated literally, isochrony meant merely simultaneity, in my opinion, the simultaneity of the universe, or more accurately, the simultaneity of all phenomena in the universe. What might be the meaning of the concept "cosmic simultaneity"? It means, if the reader will follow me, nothing at all inconceivable, nothing philosophically abstract. Yesterday the High Floater of the recently concluded era had divulged one of the world secrets to my ears: "The cosmos has the shape of man." Now even if the shape of the cosmos-man, the celestial man, does not correspond in every detail with ours, let us deal with the latter for a couple of minutes. Seen from the perspective of the moving systems of atoms that constitute it, our small body embraces well-nigh infinite time-spaces and space-time. We call one revolution of the earth about the sun a year. Let's call a corresponding revolution in an atom a year also. How many trillions of years lie between an atom in the sole of our foot and one in our scalp? And yet our body is simultaneous, contemporaneous in itself; but only as long as it lives, as long as it has a soul. When the soul departs, the body at once loses its simultaneity. It falls apart into billions of heterochronisms. In fact, death is really nothing but the conversion of isochrony into heterochrony, of the simultaneity of being into dissimultaneity. And at this point— if my hypothesis is correct—I approach the nature of the Isochronion. The universe too, the cosmos-man, the celestial man, had a soul, that is, his parts, though separated by trillions of years, were simultaneous and contemporaneous by virtue of will and consciousness. The Isochronion appeared to be an instrument by means of which the atomary consciousness of the earthman could be attuned to the universal consciousness of the celestial man, or in other words, the earthly, tiny dissimultaneity of our lives could flow into the great simultaneity of the cosmos. For the initiate, therefore, who knew how to use the Isochronion, there was no such thing as a sequence of events but only an endless coexistence, a simultaneity beyond all concept. At every instant his soul contained all associations and all continuities of nature—the fall of a linden leaf thousands of years ago and the explosion of a star millions of years hence. The Isochronion—no matter what it contained, a formula, a drop, a grain, a scent— awakened the limited consciousness of the human to the omni- presence, the omniscience, the omneity of the celestial man.

These concepts indeed contain the final goal of scientific endeavor, and it was quite clear to me why the gray Indifferent One spoke about adding a fourth Chronosophic Lamasery to the three existing ones, presumably the most inclusive and most splendid. I am convinced that my speculations about the Iso- chronion are very near the truth. And still no one is capable of even imagining the utterly new and unknown things that lie beyond his own historical frontiers. We too, in the beginnings of mankind, were not entirely unfamiliar with this synchronization of the individual consciousness with the universal consciousness, this merging of man's heterochrony with cosmic isochrony. We called this phenomenon "inspiration." To be sure, it occurred only like a flash of lightning, as the discharge of psychic voltage, a short circuit of the soul, so to speak, a sudden ecstasy, a heart- breaking transport, a vivid consciousness of unity. It left its faint traces in ideas, in poems, in melodies. But the Chronosophers were not satisfied with fleeting inspiration. It might do for the authors of the Sympaian but not for them. Their aim was a union of ego and cosmos, subject to the will and permanent, a state that abolishes past and future, history and Utopia, memory and foreboding, a state in which man will at last live in the dimensions that he claims to know best and really knows least, the present, the truest reality. As I sit at my desk, despairing of the power of language to transmit ideas, recording these signifi- cant words anent the mighty objectives of Chronosophic science,

I hear myself sigh: "Oh, how much easier my work on this travel report would be if I had the Isochronion!"

For some time I stood lost in thought on the crystalline platform of the demolished Djebel. I only half noticed with a shade of disapproval that the aged Foreignfeelers along the balustrade had turned around and were staring at the sky, where the Uranographer was spelling out another announcement to the effect that the last of the conspirators had been disarmed a few minutes before. I was roused from my reverie by the teacher's heart-rending cry, "There he is. . . ."

When I first saw him the boy was wrapped in clouds of smoke. I thought I could even see little flames which the teacher tried to smother with his own hands. It will always remain a mystery to me why the space-diving suit which the star dancer was wearing and which ordinarily resisted the most intense cosmic heat had not afforded him protection against a terrestrial fire. Only the vitreous helmet was undamaged. The spaceproof material, on the other hand, hung down in charred shreds which the teacher at once began to tear from his favorite pupil's body. There was only one possible explanation: the thoughtless boy, accustomed to acrobatics in the Intermundium and therefore disdaining what seemed to him a slight danger, must have neglected to seal the diving suit hermetically. His lithe body was covered from head to foot with horrible burns. Io-Runt looked proudly at the Foreignfeelers, made an awkward, adolescent bow, tried to speak, and collapsed in a dead faint. From his nerveless, seared, right hand dropped the Isochronion, the metal capsule that contained the future of the human spirit, the price of his sacrifice.

The Twenty-Sixth Chapter

THEY SWATHED THE unconscious, moaning child in wet veils
and laid him in my arms. I don't know why they chose me.
Heavy as he was, I carried him. And I carried him along
at a quick pace while hundreds of people followed. I recall
that there was a considerable number of Jungle peasants in the
throng. The grief-stricken teacher never left my side and kept
urging me to hurry. Maybe they had entrusted Io-Runt to me
on account of the Astromental superstition that I emitted some
kind of primeval force. I was overcome with an indescribable
mixture of pain and embarrassment whenever I looked down at
the round, fever-reddened face and the tightly closed eyes.

We hastened through one of the ruined gateways of the
Former Eastside; we were headed for King Saul's house. Every
child knew that the Official Jew of the Era was a medical practitioner whose ability and knowledge far exceeded the attainments of school medicine. It was only natural that school
medicine or "Body Gardening" (chiefly restricted to prophylactic
practice) had fallen into disrepute in an era of hundred-and-
eighty-year-olds without diseases who chose the voluntary road
to the Wintergarden at the end of their lives. Body Gardening
attracted only subaltern types, like the Bath Attendants in the

622

Wintergarden, and they were not particularly well regarded. In the rare cases of a more serious illness or injury the victim was ordinarily taken to the Worker, or one of the Animators was summoned to the surface, in strictest secrecy, of course. The greatest confidence in this sphere, however, was accorded Saul Minionman and the other Minionmen, along with their sons and grandsons—as long as they were serious, timid, and gentle, in other words, not like Io-Joel. That wasn't surprising, for Minionman had the longest and most continuous experience with human suffering, and beyond that he had focused his attention longer and more continuously than anyone else on suffering and had always lovingly identified himself with it. The teacher, for instance, firmly believed that Minionman had magic powers at his disposal. It was shocking for me to see Chronosophers, who far excelled me in intellect and learning, turn into helpless children in the face of suffering and death.

"Hurry, Seigneur, hurry," he urged. "Io-Saul, he can do everything. He'll repair him in a jiffy."

King Saul had not only taken down the sign "Out Wandering" from his door, he was actually standing there himself, waiting for us with a sad and solemn mien. He had foreseen, no, he had seen everything. For fear of misunderstandings I again run the risk of being a bore and repeat that this kind of seeing had nothing to do with any such clumsy, antiquated contraption as television; the Astromental consciousness had long acquired the ability to tune in and to receive distant scenes and events. In this respect Astromental civilization was probably the forerunner of an even later, even more advanced stage, an Isochronic civilization, for which the boy in my arms was giving his life. But I didn't live to see that stage.

The Jew of the Era was standing between two of his grandsons. They were adolescent boys on the threshold of young manhood. They wore white burnooses, a not quite accurate designation which I have used before to describe the garb of the weary and heavy-laden. Both of them had restless, searching, black eyes and an embarrassed, gentle, somewhat loutish manner. They were Saul-Minionman's medical assistants; he had chosen and trained them for this purpose. His own golden darling, Io-Joel, had never proved useful in this capacity. Minionman's clan, incidentally, was sharply divided into two characteristic groups. The attention of both groups was continually centered on human suffering; the more inoffensive of these was concerned with the cure of curable suffering, the other, the more dangerous, with the restitution of incurably injured justice. Whenever a new Minionman was born his sire knew within a few days whether he belonged to the medically assuasive type or to the juridically querulous, à la Io-Joel.

The crowd that followed us, Astromentals, Jungle people, prolific families, weary and heavy-laden, had grown into the thousands. King Saul's eyes reflected a secret expression of fear and disgust at sight of the throng. He opened the wicket just wide enough for the teacher and me to slip through and then locked it at once. He didn't neglect, however, to replace the misleading little sign "Out Wandering" under his name plate. In the era of the travel-puzzle the concept of wandering was nonsense, of course, unless you were referring to willful, inner absence.

Io-Saul led us into the depths of his house. We had to pass through a long suite of rooms crammed with junk before we reached a chamber which I shall frankly call the operating room. The illumination here was artificial, glaring supersunlight, reminiscent of the brilliance of John Evangelist. The room was empty except for a large vitreous table in the center. Astromental medicine, even Minionman's traditional medicine, knew nothing of appliances, instruments, bottles, vials, tubes, rubber goods, or probes.

The two adolescent assistants laid the unconscious boy on the table after they had first removed his wet veils with incredible tenderness. There he lay, covered from his neck to his feet with horrible second- and third-degree burns. I was cowardly enough to avert my eyes.

For a long time Minionman bent silently over the wounds, then he said, "The terrible thing is that I can't take away the pain."

The planet teacher pleaded earnestly and naïvely, "Take the pain from him and give it to me."

One of the grandsons had brought in a bowl of honeylike balm. Minionman filled the hollows of his hands with the thick fluid and let it trickle gently on the wounds. The balm ran into the wounds in strange, searching driblets as though it were guided by its independent intelligence and will. Unhappily the star dancer regained consciousness in the course of this treatment and began to whimper softly. But King Saul whispered to him in an inimitably persuasive manner. In a little while the boy quieted down and finally he said, "Gee, I thought it was going to be a real special acrobatic stunt and I was going to get a big thrill out of it. . . ."

"What did I tell you?" the teacher exclaimed angrily without at the same time being able to control his sobs. "Nothing but nonsense and pranks and foolhardiness."

Saul Minionman looked at the pedagogue in surprise.

"Have you ever heard of a heroic deed," he asked, "that wasn't done out of foolhardiness?"

Despite the hellish pain the boy tried to apologize. "I'm the smallest and the dumbest one in the class. I simply had to do it. A bigger one couldn't even have slipped through, not even Io-Scram. . . ."

"Don't talk," King Saul warned him.

But after a few panting breaths Io-Runt whispered, "And no one else could have gotten that thing out of the Office. . . ."

After these words he began to scream with unbearable pain. My gaze was fixed convulsively on Minionman. "Will he live?" was the question in my eyes. The answer lay in Io-Saul's look and told everything, but his lips murmured, "The pain will soon pass."

Meanwhile the medical assistants had laid the boy on a light stretcher and had covered him with a cooling sheet that looked like oilcloth. Not a word was said but they knew exactly what Minionman wanted. The boy was struggling to speak again.

"Teacher . . . teacher," he panted.

The teacher kneeled down beside him. He tried hard to swallow his tears and to maintain the pedagogue's unemotional mien. "Here I am. What's on your mind, Io-Runt, my boy?"

"Will I have to write on the blackboard a hundred times . . . 'I must not . . .'?"

"Not a hundred times, but ten thousand times, my dear boy. God will grant my prayer."

"What happens now?" I asked Minionman softly.

"They will take him where he belongs."

"And where does he belong?"

"To his religion, to the union of his fathers."

"I understand. You mean he is to be taken to the Grand Bishop?"

Before King Saul could reply we were interrupted.

Io-Joel Sid stood before us. Of all the momentous conversations that ever took place or will take place in human history, the one that ensued was undoubtedly the shortest. While the dialogue couldn't exactly be described as monosyllabic, it was the next thing to it, for each of the speakers uttered precisely two syllables.

"Content?" asked Saul.

"Partly," said Joel.

The long-drawn, ponderous, yet derisive tone of Io-Saul's "Content?" seemed to contain many, many unspoken sentences: Are you content and satisfied, son, that the overthrow you have been preaching for so long has finally come on us? The part you played in it, I know very well, wasn't particularly inspiring. An agent, an interpreter, a kibitzer. And what about the reforms? Who's been reformed? Your reformation is nothing but a dirty conglomeration. They've been humbled who deserve it, and they've been exalted who don't deserve it. Instead of miserable order we have miserable disorder that will soon freeze into evil rigidity. And tomorrow the new will be the old and you'll have reason to strive for a newer new. Content?

These were the approximate words that I deduced from the

two syllables and from the dreamy, velvety, derisive glance of the father.

Io-Joel, the son, was pale from loss of sleep. His lashless eyes were red, and freckles and blotches stood out on his albinotic skin. He had uttered his curt "Partly" with pedantic indifference and without looking at his father. He failed, however, to conceal from me a number of confessions and concessions which this "Partly" contained: I won't give you the satisfaction, you old Jew, of knowing that I'm licked, even though I'm as sick at my stomach as though I had been hit by a fulfillment-disappointment. I won't give you the satisfaction of knowing that I trembled for your life all day today. Besides, nothing is lost if you're a realist and recognize people for what they are, namely a nasty mob who like nothing better than to see someone else in trouble. And I'm no better than the rest of them. That's why the world will have to be reformed some more even after the present reform. Long live change!

This conversation lasted exactly as long as four drawled syllables. Io-Saul Minionman straightened up and commanded his son with authority and dignity that brooked no contradiction.

"Step behind me and follow me."

The medical assistants picked up the stretcher with the boy. King Saul walked ahead. The teacher and I were at either side of the moaning child. Io-Joel Sid followed. As we squeezed through the rooms crammed full of ancient memories, King Saul drew his cloak over his head and muttered a prayer of which an occasional strophe penetrated my consciousness:

"Our Father, our King!
I precede and I follow the bier of all eras of man.
For eternal is Thy grace that segregates me.

Our Father, our King!
They hate and despise me from Abraham to this day,
They turn aside and look where I am not,
For eternal is Thy grace that segregates me.

Our Father, our King!
And yet I am their physician and my son labors
For their justice from Abraham to this day.
For eternal is Thy grace that segregates me.

Our Father, our King!
Thou wilt end their troubles and give them peace on the day
   of all days.
And then take Thou me too, as the last, into Thy peace.
For eternal is Thy grace that segregates me."

These and other words of a hoary prayer chant struck my
ear as from a great distance while our little procession stepped
outdoors and passed through the small garden where the waxy
flora of this advanced era listened anemically and the giant
moths and dragonflies fluttered above our heads. The night
was still very compact. But the ghostly, bluish starlight was even
more compact. And all the stars in the length and breadth of the
heavens seemed to be working with breathless diligence on a
spider web that was nothing but the growing consciousness of
morning. The crowd in the Former Eastside had doubled. It had
laid a hollow ring of silence around us in which nothing could
be heard but the whimpering moans of the injured child.

The Grand Bishop too was waiting, surrounded by his clergy.
He was waiting outside the church whose illuminated green
windows rose just above the surface. Some of the priests were
carrying candles. It almost looked as though a nocturnal service
had been interrupted, a penitential prayer or a procession. Nevertheless, the prelate was waiting for the dying star dancer in
order that he might have the benefit of the final rites of the
Church.

I am not in a position to render an authentic report on the
relations of the Djebel and the Church. I think it would be quite
safe to say that their relations were not nearly as strained as
those between the Church and science about the middle of the
twentieth century. The dogma of the "Infinitely Mobile Central

Point of All Conceivable Orbits" as well as Ursler's Twenty-seven Paradoxes, only a few of which we had heard, constituted a bridge rather than a gulf between religion and science. Moreover the Church was not exactly what it had formerly been. As Joachim de Floris had predicted as early as the thirteenth century, it had long entered its third, permanent phase, the phase of the Ecclesia spiritualis, the phase of the Holy Spirit, of the spiritual Church. The fact that in recent times monastic orders like the Brothers of the Childlike Life or the Flock of the Poor in Spirit had gained high esteem, could be regarded as a significant indication that the Church was fighting against Mentalism, Intellectualism, and the danger of symbolic dissension within its own walls. The spiritual had developed in the direction of the intellectual, and the intellectual in the direction of the spiritual. Between the two, however, stood the eternally impassable wall that separates belief from research. Even though the Chronosophers were pure mystics, yet their bold voyages into space detracted from the heaven of the bishops, and in some respects they were more dangerous than the old-fashioned Sophists, Io-Sum and Io-Clap, with their arguments about the existence or nonexistence of God. A point in favor of the Chronosophers, on the other hand, was the fact that they rejected the Wintergarden. The Grand Bishop's personal attention to the fatally injured sun dancer was an honor not so much accorded the ruined Djebel as the heroic self-sacrifice of a child. Such acts had become rare indeed in an era of extreme comfort and physical indolence. But maybe the prelate wanted to honor the Djebel after all, because it had been transformed into a heap of ruins by brazen, insane fools.

Wearing his miter and vestments of delicate colors the Grand Bishop strode toward us with upraised hands, followed by several priests. In the middle of his solemn approach, however, he stopped while the following interlude took place. Up to this point I had hardly noticed that the boy's parents, Mentally summoned, had been walking beside the stretcher for some time; a slender young man and a pretty little woman with gold headdresses, who scrupulously obeyed the rules of their civilization and gave no indication of grief even in the face of catastrophe. I really became aware of them only when I began to be irritated by their perfect composure. Such good manners at the bier of their dying child seemed like shocking coldness and heartlessness to me, the man from the ancient world, whose soul was as full of cries of terror and grief as a Greek tragedy. Moreover, they continually leaned over the stretcher in their particularly elegant, transparent veils and talked pitilessly to the little fellow as though trying to persuade him of something. Every time this happened his pain seemed to grow and he moaned louder. The teacher interfered in vain. When the Grand Bishop came in sight the Astromental couple coolly and decisively stopped the medical assistants carrying the stretcher; and all the rest of us, along with the huge throng that followed, were forced to stop too. This was the instant when the entirely unexpected incident occurred, an incident which, in my opinion, was unprecedented on the earth's surface during the whole historical era of the Djebel and the Wintergarden.

Three white-clad figures pushed through the crowd to the cleared space in which we stood; one of them small and slightly deformed, the other two clumsy giants, real colossi on clay feet, like castrated harem guards. No, no, it wasn't our Animator, at least it didn't look like him, nor were the others our Bath Attendants Numbers One and Two. They were two other Bath Attendants and they were dragging along a bathtub full of black soil that they had brought up from the depths of the Wintergarden. Thick, slow perspiration, like beads of wax, stood on their foreheads, for not only physical labor under the real sky but simply the sojourn on the earth's surface was a hardship for officials of the Wintergarden. The teeth of all three of them, but particularly of the Animator, were chattering with cold; the temperature of a normal spring night meant an arctic adventure for them, and they undertook it only for the sake of the good cause. Out here in the open air the Animator apparently found it impossible to utter more than disconnected words. He kept pointing at the bathtub full of retrogenetic humus with an expansive, inviting gesture while he repeated two words over and over again, "Cool, good, cool, good. . . ."

Io-Runt's father, a slender little man himself, straightened up to his full height, such as it was, and spoke with a loud voice that rang through the tense silence. "My poor dear son, you remember the stories you were told when you were still a child, and you know who these men are and what this good cool bath is. It will heal your pain at once. You don't need further explanations. You are oriented."

"Oriented?" the elementary teacher exclaimed in a mocking aside. "He is a genius in orientation. The heavens aren't big enough for him to get lost."

There was a long pause while the boy's attention returned from far, far away. Finally he asked in a faint voice that already seemed wrapped in sleep, "Is it time for me?"

"It's time for all three of us, my darling," said the young woman without permitting a shade of grief to enter her tone.

"Your dear mother is right," the man nodded. "We will lay you gently in the dark bath and your pain will vanish. Then we will conduct you to the place where they will lay us into the dark bath by your side. Thousands upon thousands have done it, many of our relatives and friends. And we three will be together."

"No more pain," the boy wailed.

"Cool, good, cool, good," the Animator panted and pointed invitingly with both hands at the tub which was now standing directly beside the stretcher.

Suddenly the star dancer became uneasy. His eyes searched. "Teacher, teacher. . . ."

"Here I am, my dear bad pupil."

"Teacher, what am I? Am I a Chronosopher? Or am I still too young?"

"I would never have said it before the wicked ears of the

world," the teacher replied firmly. "But now I will say it. In you, my youngest pupil, whom I shall no longer call 'Io-Runt,' in you I see the High Floater of the next——"

"But the Djebel is gone," a sharp voice interrupted him.

The dying boy had seized the teacher's hand and frantically tried to raise himself up. "I don't want to be put where it's cool and where it's good," he cried, "I don't want to. . . ."

"But think of your burning pain," his mother exclaimed, at last breaking into tears as she dropped to her knees.

"I'd rather have the burning pains, much rather. . . ."

The boy gasped and sank back. His poor little breast rose and fell very rapidly. All those who had seen the incident and had understood it were moved to their very depths, so that the weeping of women, sobbing, blowing of noses, coughing, and sharp exclamations could be heard all around.

"Oremus," the Grand Bishop chanted under his canopy as he slowly approached the dying child. A murmuring of prayers and responses came from the priests: "Respice, quaerimus, Domine, famulum tuum parvulum in infirmitate sui corporis. . . ."

I hid my eyes. My throat was constricted by an almost inexpressible knowledge and feeling. In the reacceptance of natural death and pain by the little star dancer a new future had taken the place of the old future. No wonder I became dizzy. It was a little too much for a single observer. But then I felt myself supported and led away by friendly arms.

* * * * *
* * *
*

I WAS SITTING IN THE SEPHIRODROME, the Grand Bishop's library, in the same armchair as the time before. The same ancient quarto volume entitled "Fortalitium Fidei," "Strengthening of Faith," was still lying on the low table. It wasn't the original incunabulum, of course, but still it had attained a respectably hoary old age of several thousand years. A tall, graceful stem-glass before me sparkled with the aromatic, hierarchical wine, the acquaintance of which I had already made. I must have consumed several glasses of it by this time, for despite the sick fatigue in my breast I had a confused, floating sensation of tranquillity that mitigated my sorrow. When I looked up the venerable Grand Bishop was sitting opposite me in his high-backed, thronelike chair. This time he was in mufti, that is, in ordinary black garb, very much like that of his clerical colleagues of a hundred thousand years ago.

I collected my scattered wits and said, "It is very gracious of Your Lordship to grant me an audience at this hour and to extend me your hospitality."

"But it's not an audience that you want, my son. It's something quite different," and a faint smile illumined the prelate's large white face while his blue eyes rested calmly on me.

"Certainly I want much more than an audience," I confessed. "You may be kind enough to recall that you once offered me a refuge in case of need."

"But the refuge was not accepted when the need arose." The Grand Bishop continued to smile although his words were tinged with a mild reproach.

"I admit that I was still too entangled and too curious yesterday. Moreover I've always had a failing for interesting titles. The word 'Wintergarden' exercised a magic attraction on me."

"And now you are no longer entangled and curious?" the Archpriest inquired, and a touch of amusement flickered through his serious question.

Something forced me to bow my head. "No, Your Grace, I am no longer curious. Although your golden wine has comforted me a little, I am very, very sad. I have lost my best friend. And the child up there is dying or already dead."

"In that case even my refuge won't do you any good, my son."

"Frankly, no!"

"What then is the wish in your heart?"

"Was it only yesterday, Señor Gran Obispo, wasn't it much longer ago, that you said to me, 'You have never been dead, Sir'?"

"And you *have* never been dead, Sir."

"Is that absolutely certain, Reverend Father?"

"Considering your description of the state of being dead, which was as vivid as it was wrong, it is absolutely certain."

"But if I'm not dead, I am living. Am I right? Or is there still a third possibility?"

"You are living. There's no doubt that you are living."

"And where am I living, Your Lordship?"

"I ask you the same question, my son. Where do you think you are living?"

"Now and then in the course of my sojourn here I have had sudden flashes of enlightenment on that point. Perhaps I'm living in a model world, a world patterned and reflected ahead of its time, in accordance with some one of the Ursler paradoxes regarding light orbits that create time and space of varying degrees and densities."

"Don't forget with whom you are speaking, my child. And now may I hear your request?"

I slowly drank the last few drops of my wine. "I'm tired of it," I said, the glass still in my hand. "I'm sick of it. I want to leave."

"Hmm. You're tired of it. You want to leave. How do you expect to accomplish that?"

"I came in through some kind of a gate or wicket. We ought to be able to find this wicket or another one like it."

"Wickets are out of my line," the Grand Bishop declared, obviously a little offended.

"It doesn't have to be a wicket or a gate," I hastened to amend. "Any kind of passage will do. I simply can't go on living in two worlds any longer. My poor friend B.H. accused me of extending myself too far, of being so avid for experience that my existence is made up of nothing but antitheses. He says, in the first place, that's immoral, and in the second place, unhealthy."

"Your friend is right on two counts," the Grand Bishop nodded.

"I've lost my way and I haven't anyone but you, Most Reverend Father, to help me out of this confounded situation. I am asking you to help me."

The Grand Bishop appeared to be reconciled; his large pale face was again smiling faintly. "We shall think about it," he said.

"I don't deserve such kindness," I replied with a sigh of relief. "My presence here has had no useful results, even if I am not aware of any conscious guilt."

The Grand Bishop gave me a long, searching look. "Your verbiage is as complicated as ever, Sir."

"That's because I am a great sinner and consequently always on the defensive in every sentence I speak."

"That doesn't make it any better," the Archpriest shook his head sadly. "No matter, we'll think it over. In fact, we've already given orders to think it over."

"You've taken a great load from my mind, Your Lordship. But now it must be time for me to withdraw in order not to disturb you any longer. It can't be long until morning."

"Oh, no, my dear son, no rest for you now," the old man chuckled to himself. "On the contrary. Now you'll have to pay the price of our thinking."

"With pleasure. Whatever I can do is at your disposal."

The Grand Bishop refilled my glass with great deliberation. The crystal hummed like a bell under the impact of the golden wine. I had longed for another drink but had not dared to ask for it.

"The price is not in excess of your capabilities, my child," said the reverend gentleman. "I want to hear the sum of your impressions."

"Fortalitium Fidei." I took the ancient volume in my hand and sniffed at it. The incenselike odor of old books hovered around my head. I leaned far back, closed my eyes, and began to speak.

"First of all, Your Lordship, my former vague belief in hereditary sin, in the fall of man through disobedience, has been greatly strengthened by the experiences of my visit. I was in a position to observe the inexplicable compulsion that tempts man again and again to destroy his hard-won equilibrium. In the present instance it was even more insane and more incredible than ever before. But I'll go further than that. In the Djebel they were kind enough to trust me with the solution of a few mysteries of the universe. I suspect that not only Adam, the earthman, fell from grace, but before him the celestial man, the first image of God. This seems to be a reasonable doctrine without, at the same time, vindicating our forefathers."

The Grand Bishop's fingers drummed nervously on the arm of his chair and his eyes avoided mine. Who ever heard of a musician who liked to have a layman tell him about counterpoint, or of a theologian who enjoyed being frightened by a layman's metaphysical speculations which he recognized as refuted heresies and nothing more the minute he heard them? Confound that fellow Valentinus, was the thought that probably ran through the Grand Bishop's mind. But what he said with a definite trace of annoyance was, "Let's stay on earth, my son! You were very enthusiastic about a world without economics. Are you still of the same opinion?"

"The world without economics is a paradise. But what's the use when man isn't paradisiac? He is the content which he pours into every form. And so all forms are immaterial in the end, since they always enclose the unvarying measure of human insufficiency. I don't know whether the caveman was happier than the denizen of a New York skyscraper around the year 1930, and whether the latter was happier than my host Io-Fagòr in his subterranean house full of fancy light effects, dynamic wallpaper, family recipes prepared by a stellar process, and many other miracles. I only know that a skyscraper or a cottage around 1930 was infinitely more comfortable and more pleasant than the limestone cave of the troglodyte, and that the meanest homestead in Panopolis is incomparably more civilized than a millionaire's villa of my lifetime, not to mention the cloud-shrouded office-sierras and commerce-canyons of Manhattan. Man has succeeded in making great improvements; no one but a stupid ignoramus can deny that. There's only one thing that he has not been able to improve, and that is himself!"

"Very well said," murmured the Grand Bishop, reasonably well satisfied. On the whole he seemed to be embarrassed and worried by my formulations.

"The world without economics," I resumed, "stands higher than the world with economics, or rather, it is more highly developed, in the same way, for example, as an electric hotel kitchen is more highly developed than the open fire at which the savage roasted his hunk of buffalo meat, or as the preparations of the Worker in their turn are more highly developed than the antique electric hotel kitchen. But it doesn't follow at all that the more highly developed food tastes better. In the long run I would get very tired of the tricky Mental soups and creams, and I'm pretty sure that a world congress of gourmets would vote in favor of a roast prepared over an open fire. So it seems to be an ironclad rule of life that every gain is based on a loss and vice versa. I hope that in spite of the victory of the Jungle the world without economics will be maintained. It's a better world, even though man isn't any better in it. But even if man hasn't become any better morally, still he has become esthetically more beautiful. He's not only become more beautiful but also more intuitive, and to make up for it, on the debit side, less emotional and colder. If man was formerly guiltily innocent, he is now innocently guilty, with his vacant, unlined palms."

As I thought of Lala in the village church I fell into a protracted reverie so that I heard only the conclusion of what the Grand Bishop was saying to me.

". . . get back home safely, people will ask you questions. Will your contemporaries believe everything that you will report truthfully to them?"

"Many thanks, Your Lordship," I said gratefully accepting another full glass. "My contemporaries won't be particularly surprised to hear that the Worker and his clan manufacture the simplified and intellectualized consumers' goods for the numerically reduced human race out of the rays of the sun and of

other stars and deliver these articles directly into the houses.
The twentieth century was the early and clumsy cradle of the
later cosmic industry based on the utilization of stellar forces.
The popular scientific journals of my lifetime already spoke
glibly of Alpha, Beta, and Gamma rays. The old-fashioned trans-
shadow-disintegrators hadn't as yet been invented but the scientists were already on the track of the most primitive method of
smashing certain atoms and of releasing the tremendous cosmic
forces within them. Nor will, in my opinion, the institution of
the Djebel meet with insurmountable skepticism. The more
sensitive spirits of all times were aware that man's telluric
consciousness would gradually have to develop into cosmic
consciousness. I personally will be accused of cowardice because
I only visited planets and ascended with the lowest grade in
school, instead of venturing into the higher and highest Intermundia with the Starrovers, Marvelers, and Foreignfeelers. And
finally, as far as the Wintergarden is concerned, in spite of the
lovely Daisy Fields, lots of people will be repelled and horrified
by the Stygian locality and by the whole dirty, messy detour
around dying. Just as I was. But, who knows, there may be others
who will not only find it credible but even practical, and who
will be pleased with the idea of reversing life like a reel of film
and running it backward from the end to the beginning."

"I hope," said the Archpriest with a smile, "that you are not
overrating the willingness of your contemporaries, for I have no
means of judging their reaction. But now tell me, my friend,
what they will definitely *not* believe."

"They will definitely *not* believe," I replied, "that Your Lordship and the Jew of the Era exist."

"Why on earth shouldn't they believe this most modest of all
facts?"

"Simply because this most modest of all facts cannot be believed without belief in the supernatural. Unless you believe in
the first, last, and final revelation of immutable truth through
the Old and New Testament, the assumption that the Church of

Christ and Israel have survived through the decamillennia is not only an old wives' tale but an offensive idea. Only very few of my contemporaries, however, have true faith in the supernatural. The rest of them will say, 'If all primitive religions have been supplanted by enlightened intellectual cognition, then the Church of Christ with its historically limited and conditioned mythologies and dogmas cannot possibly have survived in the face of such enlightenment.'"

"But won't the loyal Jews believe that they stood the test of time?" the Grand Bishop asked with a clouded brow.

"A few devout, orthodox ones perhaps. They'll believe it but they won't want to know it. The modern Jews, however, will be very angry over my report concerning Minionman and his son, because their goal is nationalistic normalization, in other words, absorption."

"You exaggerate, my son. In the beginnings of mankind there were more good Christians than today. And these good Christians will be happy over your account."

"The Protestants and the nationalistic Christian denominations will hardly be pleased to hear that the Catholic Church won the race."

"But the Catholics?"

"The Catholics will be deeply offended because I refer to Your Lordship as 'Grand Bishop' instead of 'Archbishop,' although the former is really correct since your pastoral duties extend over several major dioceses of Panopolis."

"I'm very sorry that you are going to get into difficulties if our thinking should have good results——"

The prelate did not finish his speech because a priest in the garb of a religious order had entered through a secret door. He was a tall, haggard man and he remained standing with his back to the book-covered wall like silence personified. In the first instant I took this shadowy individual for the Father Exorcist. But it wasn't he, although he belonged to the same order, corresponding to the Dominicans of our time.

The Grand Bishop rose. "This," he said by way of introduction, "is the reverend head of our angelogical seminary."

"But—but—" I began to remonstrate, startled because I took the word angelogical for a linguistic designation.

The Bishop noticed my misunderstanding and explained, "Oh, it's a venerable old institute, our seminary for research on angels."

I almost clapped my hands with delight. "That's a field in which I've had some experience," I exclaimed but quickly swallowed the rest of the sentence for this was neither the time nor the place to speak about Melangeloi and other phenomena occurring between this world and what lies outside.

The Grand Bishop took the angelologist by the arm and they retired to a corner where they conversed in low tones. Although I felt that I and no one else was the subject of conversation and that it was my future that was being discussed I didn't prick up my ears. An irresistible desire for another glass of wine—God knows how many I'd had—occupied my full attention. I couldn't restrain myself and I leered at the crystal jug like a thief, with a view to pouring out another glass surreptitiously. The priests had their backs turned to me. I reached stealthily for the jug.

"It's the only accommodation," I heard the angel expert whisper. The word "accommodation" was used in the sense of a means of transportation. Stagecoaches and railroad trains used to be called "accommodations." I held the jug cautiously in my hand.

"I quite agree with you and it's entirely reasonable," the Grand Bishop answered in an undertone. The angelologist took a tiny book out of the pocket of his robe, held it close to his eyes, and began to turn pages. It looked as though he were thumbing the leaves of a timetable. People who turn pages of timetables always have worried expressions. I never looked at a timetable because I carefully avoid everything of a worrisome nature. I always stood by with cold indifference while others thumbed timetables for me, I, a naughty child of the railroad. This time too I was true to my nature. I brought the jug slowly nearer to my glass. And then I was caught in the act. The Grand Bishop turned around.

"What is your exact address, my son?" he asked and pretended he hadn't seen anything.

"Number 610 North Bedford Drive," I replied smartly, blushing from my chin to my ears.

"And is there a church in the vicinity of this address, or a chapel or a shrine? That would be a help, and not only as a landmark," the Grand Bishop said and looked in the other direction, perhaps to give me an opportunity to fill my glass without further embarrassment.

"Why, certainly," I exclaimed, anxious to please, "a pretty little Mexican church called 'The Good Shepherd.' And right across the street from it is a lovely cactus garden."

The Grand Bishop emphatically turned his back to me again. I poured out the wine but took only half a glass. Meanwhile I heard indistinct scraps of sentences:

". . . a genius in orientation. . . ."

". . . put him off at the corner of Bedford Drive and April 1943."

I emptied my wine at a single swallow and gave no heed to the meaning of these shreds of conversation. Moreover, an attendant friar had entered the library by another door, had bowed deeply to the two reverend gentlemen, and had placed a large hourglass on the table, at the same time murmuring the words, "It is finished."

The half glassful of wine was precisely half a glass too much. My head began to spin. An unspeakable sorrow rose in my throat. I knew what was finished and who had finished it. At the same time, however, a word that the Grand Bishop had uttered at the time of our first meeting began to rotate in my brain and torment me. It sometimes happens in the deep of night, in a trough of the sea between waves of sleep, that some word, some action that was accepted uncritically during the day, is glaringly revealed as a lie, as a piece of faithlessness that sinks its poison fangs deeply into our suffering soul. The words of the Grand Bishop now affected me in the same way. Yet I was not suffering on my own account but on account of the boy, the dead boy, who had just finished his part up there. No, I couldn't remain silent, no matter how late it was and no matter how sedately the room spun about me.

The Grand Bishop had dismissed the angel expert with his timetable and had stepped back to his throne without, however, making a move to sit down. I too was therefore required to rise.

"I haven't gotten to the most important point," I stammered.

The Archpriest raised the hourglass from the table and looked at it. Most of the sand had slipped away.

"You have only a very few minutes, my son," he warned, "just as many as lie between imprisonment and release."

"And if I had only a single minute, I can't help it. You told me that the world here and now is more wicked, more sinful, more distant from God, by a hundred thousand years than it was at my time. If that is true, no one can go on living, I can't go on living."

"Did I really say that?" the Grand Bishop asked with a smile.

"You said it."

"Then I told you a half-truth."

"A Grand Bishop does not speak a half-truth."

"Quite right, my child. But it may happen that a Grand Bishop speaks only half of the truth."

"But what is the other half?"

The Bishop's large white face, beaming with pure friendliness, came closer and closer to me.

"The other half of the truth is very simple, my son: we are not only alienated from God through the lapse of time but are also brought nearer to God through the lapse of time. That is because we are moving farther and farther away from the beginning of all things and closer and closer to the end of all things."

And now I had an experience similar to the one on John Evangelist when I had learned in the face of the ninefold brilliance of the sun that the energy of a star could be greater than itself. The room no longer whirled about me, and a spiritual happiness without parallel filled my consciousness with ecstasy.

Today I no longer understand with the same clearness and intensity what I understood at that moment. I understood that we are moving from warmth into cold and at the same time from cold into warmth; from light into darkness and at the same time from darkness into light. This incomprehensible dual movement is the movement of the history of man and the history of mankind. The straight line of time bows before its Creator in a reverential curve in every one of its seconds. And so we are safe, because alienation is nothing but a form of approach.

The Grand Bishop had placed the hourglass on the table. I hardly noticed that he took me by the hand and that we were ascending the toilsome staircase of the ascetics, slowly, laboriously, as I had ascended it once before.

The new day had not dawned yet but it could not be far off; in a few minutes the sun would rise. The heavens were saturated with light but the pale morning star and two other planets were still visible. How well I knew these stars in the cozy little universe that is ours. And now we emerged in the cool morning air. And now my feet were planted for the last time on the irongray sod of the Astromental era of mankind. The next thing I saw was the distant, serried throng surrounding the empty space in front of the church in a wide circle; Astromentals and Jungle people indiscriminately mixed. The red tassel caps flamed like bloodspots among the undulating veils. But what was that? I didn't trust my ears. It was singing, hesitant, childlike, unison singing, a simple chorale, from all sides. The Jungle people were giving the Astromental highbrows their first singing lesson. A good idea. Every loss is a gain. It sounded very thin and schoolboyish. It sounded like singing after a long illness.

And then I caught sight of the dead boy. He was lying on a plain, narrow bier. His head was raised fairly high. His graceful body had been covered with a veil. At his feet the teacher had collapsed and had fallen asleep. At the head-end of the bier a few of the oldest Foreignfeelers stood as a guard of honor, among them the Imperturbable One with the Isochronion bound to his forehead. I recognized it because the capsule gleamed like a mirror in the dawnlight. The parents had left. Undoubtedly they were in the Wintergarden by this time.

I looked at the Grand Bishop inquiringly. He had stopped walking and stood before me, a much larger and more impressive figure than I had thought. With a rhythmic motion he made the sign of a great cross over my head. Then he made a gesture of dismissal. I knew I had nothing else to do but go. A distance of perhaps thirty paces lay between me and the dead boy. As I took the first few steps I was uncertain and afraid that I might spoil everything by a false step or false thought. The following thought, for example, ran through my mind and I didn't know whether I was permitted to think it: he fetched the Isochronion from the depths because he himself is the Isochronion, the simultaneity of the world.

I stopped anxiously. But no one said, "Wrong! Try again!"

On the other hand, it suddenly dawned on me what all the whispering in the Grand Bishop's library had meant and why they had asked for my address. It meant that Io-Runt had been commissioned to put me off or to throw me out at the corner of Bedford Drive and April 1943, for in order to get to the end of our cozy little universe he would have to fly back to the beginning. And Bedford Drive was located somewhere in the first quarter or first third, counting from the beginning.

Very interesting, very interesting, I said to myself, as I strode along more rapidly and more confidently, while the childlike, timid choir of untrained voices wove a veil over me. I could plainly see the face of the dead child. But it wasn't one face, there were two faces. Confounded astigmatism! Where are my glasses? I felt through all the pockets of the dress coat for my glasses, although I knew very well that they had been taken from me. But there really were two boyish faces superimposed one over the other: a gray, dead face on top and a blooming, smiling one underneath, just as a gray membrane half conceals the gay colors of a decalcomania. The gray face became more and more indistinct and the smiling one more and more distinct, the closer I approached. No nonsense now, my boy; or, with the help of God, all the nonsense you please, my entire being chuckled within me. And my entire being was light, bright, airy joy, the very memory of which brings tears to my eyes. Now the smile of the star dancer was very near me. He had hoodwinked them all, for between the half-opened eyelids I saw his roguish glance. And into this glance I strode until I knew nothing more.

* * * * *
* * *
*